VAULT

Unbound Book Eight

NICOLI GONNELLA

MOUNTAINDALE
PRESS

This book is dedicated to my sisters: Krista, Natasha, Rebecca, and Rachel.

CHAPTER ONE

Winter clung hard to the foothills of the Rimefang Mountains. Storms of ice and sleet had blanketed the southern slopes for the past three months, coating ravines and gullies until every step was treacherous. Atop the ice were layers of heavy snow, piled high atop game trails and trade roads in equal measure, blocking the path of all but the most determined travelers.

Or the most desperate.

In the close-packed streets of a nameless town, a small figure struggled through the heavy weather. He was bundled head to toe in fur and wool until he looked more like a Golem than a person. The snow topped the figure by at least a foot in most places—more if you considered his tall, knitted cap—and ice tangled in the scraggly strands of a dark beard that showed behind a thick scarf. Even his eyes were covered by dark lenses, buckled to his head with leather straps, but his thunderous expression could be read in the tilt of his bushy eyebrows.

God damned stupid bullshit legs! Archie dug a heel into the ground but groaned when he barely chipped the thick layer of ice. *Can't walk! Can't even Stoneswim when I can't touch the earth. Fuck!*

Ahead, the warm lights of the only inn for miles shone like a beacon in the gathering gloom, and Archie struggled on. He tunneled through half-worn paths, digging with his leather mittens as the snow kept piling on, threatening to bury him. The flurries were so thick he was forced to rely entirely on his passive Perception Skill instead of his eyes.

Blindsense is level 56!
Cold Resistance is level 2!

Minutes later, he clambered up the steps of the inn, where at least most of the ice and snow had been removed. A solitary lantern hung next to the door, glimmering with sigaldry on its glass panes, and above it was an ice-coated sign.

Deerwick Inn. So this is *Deerwick. Thought I had gotten turned around in the storm.* He stomped his feet, knocking off all but the smallest bits of snow and tried the iron latch. It turned as easy as the thick door swung on its grease hinges, and he was blasted with a wave of sound and glorious heat. *Oh, yes. This will do for now.*

"Close the blighted door!"

Archie ducked in, pulling the latch closed behind him, and was greeted by an absolute wall of people. Humans, Goblins, Hobgoblins, and even a few of those birdfolk stood in tightly packed groups, their shouts and cries filling the space to the rafters. The majority of the crowd, however, was decidedly Dwarven, same as every town south of the Rimefangs. He spotted Goldspinners, Shieldbreakers, even a few Rockjaws wearing their dumb iron masks. All of them bore their clan glyphs proudly on their left shoulders, and in typical Dwarven fashion, it was displayed with as much ornamentation as they could afford.

Middle of a snowstorm, and they're still dressed like they're at a party. Archie had spent far too much time among the Dwarves; they would knife their own mothers if it'd help them flaunt their wealth. Back in Birchstone, it had been almost a game to see how extravagant their feasts and galas could become, all while dealing in rumor and gossip and *politics*. Archie snorted. He'd had enough of *that* to last him a lifetime.

The sound was overwhelming, the smell ripe, but the heat could not be denied. He took off his cap and scarf, releasing a tumble of dark gray curls and an unkempt black beard. The goggles stayed on by necessity. His face was red and numb, from his jaw to the tip of his stupid, bulbous nose, but just a few moments inside the inn had them all tingling painfully. He loved it.

Archie made his way to the counter, careful to keep his hands to himself as he slid through the shifting crowd. Wandering hands in a world of Tempered warriors was a good way to end up dead. The place was packed tight, owing perhaps to the strains of upbeat music at the far end of the room, but if more was going on, Archie couldn't make it out. He had learned early on that his newfound height made simple things he'd taken for granted—like seeing over the heads of folks in a crowd—out of his reach for good. His Blindsense helped, but it would never replace the convenience of his natural sight. Not to him.

Still, he made it to the counter in one piece and, after leveraging himself up onto a stool, flagged down a server.

"Just came outta the cold, love? What'll it be? A bit of warm supper and a room for the night?" She was a matronly Dwarven woman with red hair liberally streaked with white and a bodice cut *entirely* too low. She smirked at Archie's wandering eyes, not bothering to cover up. "Perhaps some company? A handsome Gnome like yourself wouldn't find it too hard on the purse."

The server's words were thickly accented and almost faster than he could follow, but the twinkle in her eye was unmistakable. He smiled wide. "As tempting as that might be…just a meal and a room, if you've the space."

"We do, though it'll be bunking out here with this lot. We're about packed up, what with the storm an' all."

"Out here?" Archie kept his smile, but it was a struggle. He had no interest in sleeping where just anyone could reach him. Focusing his Willpower, Archie ran two fingers across the bartop, gathering sticky ale, cold stew, and the gritty remains of salt. "Are there really no rooms?"

She leaned forward as if to support herself on an arm, but her posture suggested something far different. "We've a couple rooms, but they're for a more…discernin' sort."

Strongarm tactics, eh? Archie reached out and casually let his two fingers trail along the Dwarven woman's hand, leaving a patch of salt sticking to her. Inside of him, a warmth uncoiled like a spool of thread to gather atop her knuckles, glowing an unearthly red-violet. "Come now. Surely you could spare a private room for *me*."

Innocuous Suggestion.

A veil fell over the woman's face, though not one just anyone could perceive. Archie saw it happen, but only because it was his own Skill, and even then, it was barely discernible. He had used Innocuous Suggestion a great many times in the past year, and it was one of his greatest tools. It built up a filter of sorts between the server's Mind and Body, and inside that filter was a single fact: that Archie was an old friend.

"Oh! Oh, it's you. How'd I not notice? Of course I can get you a private room. It'll just cost an extra silver on top. Place is packed, yeah?" she said, straightening her posture. Archie was tempted to press her for a discount, but he was too tired. He had the coin, at least for now. "Just the one night?"

"Yeah. Just the one." Archie adjusted the scarf around his neck—it really was warm in there. "Supper now and breakfast in the morning?"

"Alright," she said, taking his coin and handing him a black iron key. "Room six. Last door on the left. Take a table, and I'll have the boys bring out your supper."

"Right. Thanks." Archie scooted off the stool, falling back below the top of the bar, if barely. It was made for Dwarves, after all, and they weren't *that* much taller than him. Archie slipped through the crowd again, swiftly finding an empty table near the kitchen doors and far from the musicians. It smelled of mildew and vomit, but his back was against a wall, and he had sight lines on the entrance and exit. It could've been worse.

Time rolled on.

His food arrived, the crowd shifted, and the music had become lively enough to bring a few of the drunker patrons to their feet. They danced in the way of Dwarves: rigid lines and exacting footwork accentuated with a heavy stomp at the end of every verse. It was a familiar tune, one Archie had heard countless times back in Birchstone and Redspine Hold. It brought to mind old acquaintances and grudges, and Archie had to clench his fists to keep from tugging his hood up and over his face.

They don't know you, he reminded himself. *You're a hundred miles from anyone who would. Calm down. Don't be suspicious. She's not here.*

She. That woman haunted him and was the real reason Archie was in the middle of bumfuck nowhere. More armor than woman, she'd hunted him across the Rimefangs, into the depths of the mines, and only when he'd slipped through the mountain and into the ice and snow had he lost her. From what Archie had heard since then, she'd raised a hell of a ruckus back in Red Shield Hold, killing and burning their elite guard like nothing. A shiver shook through him, despite the heat. Even the thought of her burning, dead eyes had turned his sweat cold.

The dance ended, but Archie barely noticed. He tipped his mug back, finding some solace in the bottom of his cup, but nearly choked as someone spoke.

"Do you wish to hear what the wind whispers?"

Cheers met the words, even as Archie spat ale into his beard. He looked around, expecting to find a man whispering into his ear, but there was no one. The crowd was seating themselves, all of their faces turned toward the far end of the inn where a huge fireplace filled the wall. A bonfire's worth of flames filled the hearth, outlining the tall but slender frame of a strange-looking man. He had a wide, high forehead that seemed entirely too long and overly large eyes that stared out over the crowd above a faint smile.

Analyze.

Name: Windcaller
Race: Henaari

The rest of the man's information was all question marks, indicating his level or Temper was far above his own. Archie hadn't even seen a Henaari, let alone one dressed so strangely. As opposed to the ornate finery of the Dwarves and the roughspun woolens of the Humans and Hobgoblins, the Windcaller was dressed in hundreds of colorful, thinly cut strips of fabric, the end of which was affixed to a black feather. They trembled and swirled with every motion of the man's body, almost like grass in a summer breeze. Or some endless flock of blackbirds.

"Tell us about the Glimmerghast!"

"No, the March of Fangs!"

"The Demon of Kas!"

Cheers and jeers followed each request, the locals demanding their favorites. Archie hunched his shoulders, careful to keep his eyes moving…but the Henaari drew his gaze like a magnet. The Windcaller did not speak over them or motion them to quiet down. He simply waited in agreeable silence until the audience settled into an uncomfortable lull. Only then did he speak.

"You cheer and ask for legends, happy to hear of horrors. Why is that?" he asked, and again his voice sounded as if he were right beside Archie, instead of a hundred feet distant.

A Human, half in his cups, barked a laugh. "Cuz ain't none of it real!"

As if a pressure valve had been opened, the entire inn laughed with the man. Archie didn't. There was more coming, and he felt it like an icy blade down his spine. An instinct he'd learned to listen to nagged at him, one that had saved his hide many times over. Food forgotten, Archie stared down the Windcaller.

"Hm. Perhaps. Who knows what might have been true in Ages long gone. The march of time is not clean, nor is it simple. The winds howl across the vast dark, where the light of truth has not yet found its way.

Perhaps it is true that the Nym were not real, nor the Geist and their inventions. Perhaps.

"But I do not speak of ancient Ages long since Lost, nor of legends that are indistinguishable from a dream." A complicated instrument of strings and wood was in his hands, and he plucked a note between words. "I speak of the now, for the wings of the Raven are many and carry with them truth. I will share this truth with you, if you wish."

A single note echoed out through the rafters, and the inn was utterly rapt. The Windcaller clearly took that as encouragement, because he started strumming again. His words were not to song, but they contained a musicality that tickled at Archie's ears and tugged at his heart.

"In far-off Nagast, where the fog clings tight, a power has arisen. It flies a flag of blue and red-gold, the signs of a Lord who saved the land from monsters and abominations in equal measure. A Lord crowned by the System itself, anointed with True Authority."

As if on cue, the light of the fire seemed to thin, and shadows sprang from the corners and crevices to gather upon the small stage. As the Henaari spoke, those shadows danced, forming people that fled before monstrosities many times their size…until another landed atop them in flashes of blue and red-gold, as if the fire had been caught within the dark.

"The Lord, called Autarch, liberated the Territory of its threats, both mortal and monster, serving the people as did the Lords of old. All were welcome in Nagast, all were flourishing. But all was not well."

The shadows changed, turning to cheering crowds as the figure burning with an inner fire stood at their peak. Among him were others, a figure with a spear, one with a chain, many with robes and staves, even a man Archie could have sworn was a Dwarf bearing two burning axes. Then, with a change in tempo, walls erupted around them, and the sound of drums intruded. So caught up, Archie didn't even bother trying to figure out where the drums were coming from, and he could only watch as those figures were approached by armies.

"The Hierocracy grew jealous of this Lord's power. Afraid. They sent battalions of Inquisitors and Paladins to take back the Territory." Three large shapes rose above a sudden forest—Manaships—and they disgorged hundreds. Thousands. "The land was beset, their Lord helping another Territory through trials of their own."

Fire spawned among the dark, burning the wall and the people atop it. Many fell as the music sped faster and faster. "Though they fought with all their might, the new people of Nagast could not overcome the Hierocracy. Not when the High Guard arrived."

Rapt or not, *that* drew a gasp of horror from the crowd. Archie didn't know why, but when four figures head and shoulders bigger than the average soldier appeared, he soon grasped the context. Swaths of the defenders were mowed down, the walls were broken, and everything seemed to be teetering on collapse.

"Yet in their moment of direst need, the very heavens themselves split asunder and smote the High Guard. The Lord had returned, and he bore with him a crown of not one but *two* Territories! He rode from the broken sky atop a golden Dragon, washing the field of battle clean in an instant. The Hierocracy, broken and bloody, fled.

"The Autarch of Nagast was triumphant."

Gasps turned to cheers as the hated Hierocracy turned tail. Archie hadn't had much exposure to the weird zealots until recently, but not a single person he'd met had ever much liked them. He had to agree. Down on the stage, the Lord floated above everyone else, a crown now glowing atop his featureless head as people below reached up in adoration.

"Why're you wearing those?" said a small voice. Archie started, his senses completely caught up with the Henaari's performance, and spied a small Dwarven boy standing at his table. He was chewing a finger and staring at his face. "Aren't they hard to see with?"

Archie looked back to the Windcaller, but the man was packing away his instrument, and conversation was starting back up among the crowd. They were whispering mostly, all of them talking about this Autarch guy. Archie clenched his jaw, fighting back the irrational surge of annoyance in him. He wasn't even sure why he was mad. "Aren't you supposed to be turning a spit or something?"

"I'm on break."

Archie rolled his eyes, knowing the expression was hidden by his dark goggles. He stood up, making the decision to go talk with this Windcaller person. "Go have a break somewhere else."

A sound like splintering wood cut through the inn's noise as the thick front door ripped off its hinges. Folks fell before it, and chairs skidded across the floor as men and women rose with weapons in their hands. For his part, Archie could only stare, rooted to the spot like a deer on a busy highway.

No. No no no…

A shadow loomed, black upon the moonlit snow, before it entered. A giant with a full helm, nearly eleven feet tall and covered in dark plate armor that gave no hint to their gender, but Archie knew. The sheer weight of her presence—her Spirit—clung around her like the phantom of a foundry's flames.

It was *her*.

She wore no cloak or fur to ward off the weather, and her shoulders steamed as the snow boiled away before it ever touched her. Weapons hung from her like a portable armory, swords and maces and flails strapped to waist, arm, hip, and back. She was an engine of destruction, and everyone could feel the truth of that in their bones.

"You."

Archie just about jumped out of his skin, thinking that the giant woman had finally found him…but no. With everyone taking to their feet, she would barely be able to spot him. Instead, she had a broadsword pointed at the Windcaller. The Henaari was watching her with a rapt expression on his face, as if he was *happy* to see a bared blade. Or was it her he was happy to see?

"I am seeking a Gnome that smells of salt and stone. He is wanted for crimes against the Hierocracy." The air around her began to darken, and the wood beneath her feet charred. Her broadsword burst into vibrant, golden light. "But first: tell me more about this Autarch."

Archie barely heard the last, because he had already fled. Servers and cooks dropped pots and crockery as he scurried through the kitchen, and a few low-level Skills followed after him, but he burst from the back doors and into the night. The snowstorm still raged, but he didn't care—he would have barged through the gates of hell if it meant he could escape that woman. A little ice and cold wouldn't stop him.

He had almost made it to the treeline when the screaming started.

Archie never looked back, not even when flames lit up the night.

CHAPTER TWO

Words fly upon wind,
Broken song made whole again,
The Fiend is rising.
-Unknown

Small brown birds crowded among winter bare branches, their tiny eyes as bright as their plumage was dull. Diffuse, pallid light spread over everything, blanketing the forest in a hush that even the birds respected. Not a single chirp escaped them, though they shifted on tiny feet as they bore quiet witness to the fall of thick, silent snow.

Felix could feel them there, little sparks of life and blood Mana coiled around threads of air and shadow. With his Manasight, he picked those pieces apart just as he did the thick trunk of green-gold and dusty brown that sat at the heart of the trees beneath them. Around him, more beasts filled the still forest, far more than he would have ever guessed back on Earth. There was the fast-beating heart of the hare two hundred yards away, hiding from the snowy fox that stalked it. Slumbering Glitterhogs rested beneath a low mound, and the family of Mana Voles sat atop a still-living log.

There was also the unmistakable tread of metal feet.

He made quite the target, standing at a bit over six and a half feet tall and layered with lean muscle. He was all but naked, his chest and arms as bare as his feet, and only a thick pair of leather pants maintained his modesty. Black scales covered his arms and legs, but his taloned hands were empty. Muscles bunched beneath pale skin as Felix shifted his stance, tracking the sound of metal even as it slowly circled him.

They're behind you now, chirruped a voice in his head.

I'm aware, Pit.

There were no other sounds than that single set of footfalls, and even those slipped across Felix's ears as if greased. Felix pressed himself, letting sound and taste and touch swirl around him in a zone entirely too wide to deny. Nothing but the steps called out to him…and he distrusted that immensely.

They're going to attack from two sides, Pit said.

I can handle this myself, bud.

Abruptly, snow crunched, and a tree trunk cracked, a staccato report louder than a cannon blast. Metal shrieked through the air, moving so fast it drove the wind before it in a series of hazy ripples. Felix twisted and snapped his hands out, trapping the hafts of twin axes between his dark talons. Silver flame gushed, rolling off his midnight scales without effect as red paint oozed from their edges.

"Really, Harn," Felix said, a touch annoyed. "You were so loud."

The man holding the axes wore a full suit of platemail, including a frog's mouth helmet, and he barked an echoing laugh. "That was the point, kid."

Felix's Perception flared, and his reflexes took over. He rolled to the left, releasing Harn's axes while behind him came the unleashed fury of a dozen suddenly-unmuffled shouts. Steel and ice and lightning coursed through the space Felix had only just occupied, ripping apart the snow and earth in a fountain of debris. Felix danced backward, spotting the Legionnaires from between nearby trees. They flinched when they met his gaze.

Someone's hiding them. Felix's attention caught on something, just beyond the treeline. He grinned. *How rude of them.*

More Skills rained down on him, but Felix flexed his legs, digging his clawed feet into the earth before vanishing entirely.

"He's gone!"

"He's using Stealth!"

"He can't! He said no Skills!"

Felix flashed through the forest, faster than any of them could track. He knew it by the way they spun, all of them attempting to look in a different direction. Yet they moved as if in molasses, whether they were cloaked Henaari, armored Legionnaires, or bulky Yttin warriors. None of them could match Felix's speed.

His unarmed blows were soft but precise, and none escaped until the last fell into an unconscious heap. Nonlethal takedowns had been the smallest of what Felix had learned these past few months, but perhaps the most useful. As the last Legionnaire buckled beneath his hand, Felix scanned the forest, now gone silent again. He still hadn't found the mage who was muffling the soldiers.

"Third Talon down. Who's next?" he asked, waving away notifications of their defeat.

"Me!"

A blackened-green hammerblow dropped from the sky like a meteorite, missing Felix by the barest of margins as he skidded backward through the snow. Beefhammer, all seven feet of Minotaur, stomped forward to claim the space Felix had ceded. His body, more than twice as wide as Felix's, was clouded by a haze of frost that clung to his icy armor.

"Getting faster, Beef," Felix said with a wide smile. His teeth were sharp, and his eyes blazed sapphire. "Not fast enough, though."

"Keratin—!"

Felix didn't let him finish, launching a sharp jab into his armored chest as chitinous spikes thrust from the earth. His scaled fist shattered them and blasted into Beef's icy armor hard enough to toss the Minotaur back several feet. He stomped forward, eager to bring Beef down, but was met instead by a deluge of crystals the size of daggers.

"Gah!" He threw up his forearm, letting the bulk of them shatter against his skin. "Hey!"

"Back away, Felix Nevarre," Hallow demanded in her echoing voice. She stood over four feet tall now, a bundle of vaguely humanoid rocks and crystal with small, blackened green gemstones dotting her face like eyes. "The next will be aimed at your neck."

Felix set himself, ignoring the surge of dull pain from the sigaldry at his feet. Despite their blows and Skills, a glowing array persisted all around them, hidden just below the snow, slowly pulsing in time with the stone disc at his waist.

Beef stood from the ground, dirt and ice cascading from his shoulders, glowering from beneath the red-gold glow of his horned helmet. "Hey, that was fast, man. You said no Skills."

"And I meant it. That'd defeat the purpose of this." Felix lifted his legs, showing the teen Minotaur and Homunculus his scaled and clawed feet. Like his hands, they had been permanently changed into something a bit more…ferocious. "I'm staying in contact with my array."

The lack of shoes was on purpose—his whole attire was—but bare feet were needed to make the entire setup function. Lines of orange, blue, and red-gold glimmered in complex, meaningful patterns that were echoed by the array keystone that hung from his belt. Each time his feet came down, the keystone lit up, and those lines pulled at him, dragging warmth from his bones and replacing it with a bitter chill. It was draining his Mana and Stamina, which in turn was limiting his Skill use. He could have used some of his Skills if he wanted to…but this was training, after all. Felix took a breath, centering himself as he let the *siphon* array work its magic on him.

"So no Skills," Beef repeated.

"None," Felix confirmed before lifting his hand and beckoning them both. "Now, I don't have all day. Again. And don't hold back."

Beef grinned. "You asked for it. Geir? Let's give him hell."

"Aye."

As if from between frozen gusts of wind, Frost Giants emerged, ranging in height from ten to fifteen feet, and they were silent as the moons that currently climbed the horizon. Weapons and armor hammered out of brutal ice and steel glimmered in the diffuse winter light, and their eager breath filled the air with a ragged fog. Felix rolled his shoulders as they stepped forward, each footfall louder than the last as whatever spell had silenced them faded, until the cacophony of crunching snow filled the field.

"C'mon then," Felix laughed. "Fight me!"

Geir and his fellow giants roared, spears and axes and clubs lifted high as ice spiraled outward from them all. Felix burst forward, tearing furrows in the earth as he slipped between Beef and Hallow, and smashed headlong into the Frost Giants' charge. Ice met flesh before shattering into prismatic shards that blasted back toward the giants, even as an axehead descended on Felix's form. Flaring his Agility, he sidestepped the blow, letting it pass mere inches from his left shoulder and delivering a brutal palm strike to the haft. Steel snapped, and the first Frost Giant had only time to widen his eyes before Felix's second strike took him in the jaw.

You Have Defeated Egill, A Risi Warrior!
XP Earned!

Felix flowed through them all, kicking apart their icy workings before they could truly shape into a solid defense and dropping the giants low with a single punch apiece. Breastplates buckled as readily as their knees, which was a good thing, as Felix didn't have the Stamina needed to keep moving that fast for an extended period of time. Already his steps were dragging, his motions were slightly more stilted, and he gritted his teeth as the last of the giants fell.

Still not used to this. Gotta go slower. More precision, less power.

Crystalline daggers pummeled into his side. They broke into pieces against his incredibly tough Body, but it still didn't feel great, and Felix slapped the last few out of the air. "Those are getting sharper."

Hallow was strafing around him, her chunky stone legs plowing through the deep snow as her eyes glowed green. She didn't answer. Instead, she swung an arm, and a dozen more faceted daggers hurled in Felix's direction. He dodged them easily and walked right into the path of a raging Minotaur.

"Relentless Charge!"

Felix knew the Skill well; it propelled Beef from a standstill to a meteoric collision in an instant, and there was very little most people could do against that much mass. Felix, however, was not most people—as Beef appeared, head down and horns angled toward him, Felix burned his Stamina and flared his Agility once more to reach out and seize the teen. Black scaled hands gripped orichalcum coated horns and *heaved.*

"WHoOAAHHHH—!"

Beef had barely a moment to scream as his momentum was used against him. Felix grasped and lifted, spinning as he redirected the force of Beef's charge and sent the Mintoaur flying through the air. Twenty, thirty, forty feet he soared, bashing through tree after tree in a detonation of branch and bark.

"Michael!" Hallow cried out, rushing to him and ignoring Felix entirely. He let her go; she'd be able to administer aid to the kid in the off-chance Felix had actually managed to hurt him.

Felix flexed his hands, checking his arms and torso for wounds he might have missed, but he remained unharmed. His Health regen was basically nil, same as his Stamina, but hurting him was far harder than exhausting him. Still, red paint tagged his arms and sides—small dots from each of Hallow's daggers to mark where he'd been hit. Based on the scoring system Felix had designed, each bit of paint on him was a point in the attacker's favor, representing bringing down his Health by a portion. With twelve thousand points of Health, the chances of them taking him down that way were incredibly low, however, so he had designated two places as instant kills: his head and his heart. If one of them managed to land a strike there, it was over.

If they can get me tired enough, that might even be possible. Felix felt a flutter of nervousness in his belly, and he grinned. *This is* fun.

Without warning, the meadow around him flared with green-gold radiance. From below, wooden walls sprang up, carved and detailed as if by expert craftsmen yet conjured in an instant, until a veritable maze of structures surrounded him. Felix turned slowly, taking in as much as he could as walls cut his lines of sight, and angled roofs rose higher, dimming the already weak winter sunlight.

"Henaari," he breathed. "Clever."

The first volley of arrows smashed into his back, driving him forward a half step before Felix found his footing. Skills laced them, fire and shadow imparting a sizzling snap onto his unprotected skin while red paint daubed his spine. Felix cursed, annoyed at being caught flat-footed, and blurred into motion.

The second volley did not reach him.

Walls shattered before his approach, just as the ice before, and Felix used it to stymie the Dawnwalkers' shots as well as bludgeon those unfortunate to be hiding in his path. Like a speeding train, Felix barreled through the maze of crafted halls, bashing into Henaari spear warriors without pausing to count them all. His Stamina steadily reduced as he ran, each powerful pump of his legs or calculated punch dwindling his finite resources, but keeping track of it all was actively hindering Felix's fight. He got his belly marked with a slash of paint twice before he stopped gauging his Stamina bar and started letting loose.

It took less than ten seconds to hunt each of the Henaari down and incapacitate them.

"You're a damn menace, kid," Harn said, crunching across the scattered wooden debris. His axes burned with a steady flame, silver light licking across the man's armored knuckles. "I'm impressed. Weaving those Pillars really made a difference."

"You've all improved, too." Felix nodded at the enemies groaning into the snow all around them. "I didn't expect to get hit this much."

Harn tilted his head, the motion somewhat alien with his slitted full helm covering his features. "True enough. That's more red on you than I've ever seen." Harn idly twirled his axes. "Makes me proud."

"Me, too—" Felix started to say, before finding Harn *far* closer, *far* faster than he expected.

"Wrath of the Twin Fangs!"

Felix blocked the first hit, but the second scored a line of red across Felix's bicep, painting his skin with more than just pigment as blood splashed outward. Silver flames burned at him, singeing his normal skin, but Felix slapped the weapons away with a scaled hand. They were nothing to his changed flesh, after all.

The two split apart, Felix sliding several paces while Harn skipped back, clearly thrown by Felix's slap. "Oho! Got ya that time!"

"Distracting me with sentiment, now?" Felix laughed. "You're getting tricky in your old age."

"Old? I'm a hatchlin' compared to those old monsters you'll have to face. Just tryin' to keep you on your toes, son." Harn set himself. "Seems like it's working."

Felix frowned but couldn't ignore the truth of Harn's words. He tried to ignore the burning in his bicep, but the way it lingered was unusual for him. He had tons of resistance to pain, but the warm wetness and knowledge of an open wound was…troubling.

Watch out.

A sword the size of a small wardrobe bashed into the ground just behind Felix, scattering snow in a powdery explosion that he neatly dodged.

Pit…

I'm helping!

"You were to hold him in place, Kastos," Darius said, straightening. He hauled back and freed his huge blade from its foot-deep rut before resting it casually on his shoulder. "Not give him a pithy warning."

"Maybe I didn't want you to get the points, hmm?" Harn gave one of his axes a lazy twirl, trailing that silver flame behind it like a comet. "You said we'd get double the points if we took you down without help, right?"

Felix grinned. "If."

Harn laughed, rough and loud. "I'm eager to see these prizes. I heard we raided a few Domains."

Darius scowled, his huge sword gaining a sudden, ethereal glow. "I care little for prizes. I am here to challenge you, Felix. Be prepared."

They came at him like a whirlwind of steel and flame. Their Skills flew in violent bursts upon the forest floor, crescent air blades and silver flame chasing after Felix's darting form. Harn and Darius were both

Adepts—the latter almost ready to advance to Master Tier—and they had might to spare. Trees were sliced apart, shattered, and burned as Felix kept ahead of their strikes. He was relying entirely on his stats and Temper, deflecting blows that came too close to him with his bare hands and the terrain. Try as they might, they could not touch him.

"C'mon!" Felix shouted. He slipped between the savage net of strikes Darius was weaving, batting aside the crescents of white-green air Mana with the flat of his hand. His Stamina was plummeting like a rock, but he had enough for this. "Hit me!"

Darius screamed, his Spirit reflecting the frustrated rage on his face. A song of annoyance danced upon the air. "Wind Drake's Dive!"

All at once, the air tightened and dropped, like a hammer from the sky. Felix had no time to avoid it—in fact, he realized he would have to either take the hit…or oppose it directly. He stood beneath the hammer of air Mana and reared back with a single fist.

The air exploded.

Harn and Darius were thrown back, the snow and dirt hurled into the air, as all around them, the dense trees were hit with razor-sharp, near-invisible shrapnel. When the powder and frozen loam settled, Felix stood alone in the field, clenched fist upraised and his eyes blazing with a sapphire light. Victorious.

"Bonds of Dominion! Tooth and Claw!"

Purple-white chains manifested all around Felix, snaking around his limbs in an instant before drawing taut and exposing his heaving chest to the blades of a length of true chain. He flexed his Will but felt a frisson of alarm as her Skill *pushed* back at him, far harder than he expected. As if in response to the unspoken threat, something unfurled inside of him. A danger that Felix hadn't seen in months.

A fist, clawed and scaled, rose up from within Felix's core space. It sizzled with red-gold flame and sparked with blue-white lightning, yet its form was dominated by a vivid purple glow that seemed to be pulled from the edges of his Hunger itself.

No! Back! He shoved the power away, Willing it to dissipate before it could unleash itself. *Not here!*

As if possessed of its own Mind, the enormous, clenched fist struggled upward against Felix's Will. It pressed toward his channels, seeking egress in a way that scared him far more than some minor binding. Waves of power flowed from the fist like a tsunami, relentless and primal.

Enough!

Felix's Will finally scattered the fist, rendering it into motes of ephemeral light that surged out into his core space. His Will carried onward, bashing against the binding that dared to hold him and blasting it to pieces—but not before he felt a sharp tug against his skin.

Right across his chest.

"Aw, damn it," he hissed through panting breaths. He bent forward, resting his hands on his knees before raising a finger to his chest and dragging it through the paint. "You got me."

"Instant kill!" Evie crowed, dropping from a nearby tree. It was leaning drunkenly, having been completely severed at its base after Darius' deflected attack, and her leap caused it to topple noisily to the forest floor. Brown birds scattered, streaming into the air, but she didn't pay them any mind. "I win!"

Felix rubbed the paint between his fingers, thinking. He wasn't mad just...surprised. "Were you waiting in the tree the whole time?"

"The whole time." Evie stretched, hands pressed to her lower back. "You can't imagine how many knots I've got now. You guys took forever and went all over the place."

"Evie. Of course you'd snake the point," Harn said, taking off his helmet and exposing his scarred and battered face. He was beaming. "Even managed to hold him for a heartbeat. That's some impressive movement, kid."

"It truly was," Darius agreed. "How did you stop him?"

"Binding Skill. Locks folks down real quick while I hit 'em." Evie shrugged. "Though I think it was mostly cuz I have a really long weapon. Harder to avoid, even for freaks of nature like Felix."

Felix rolled his eyes at that and, while they continued to chat, busied himself with the array keystone at his waist. He had no need to keep it running anymore. With a brief coupling of his Willpower and Intent, he cut off his connection to the thing, which in turn sent out a sizzling pulse of red-gold energy across the snow. The array was deactivated, and Felix immediately felt his inner reserves begin to refill.

Where was my warning about Evie? he asked Pit.

She hadn't moved since you started the fight. I thought you knew.

Felix had sensed her up there, but in the back and forth between Harn and Darius, he'd honestly put her out of his mind. He'd been too preoccupied with the literal army he was fending off. *That Skill of hers... Bonds of Dominion. It interacted strangely with me. And...*that. *We need to talk to her.*

You talk to her, Pit chirruped, and his voice started to fade. *I'm sleepy.*

Felix let him go, likely returning to his own core to rest. Instinctively, he checked his Companion's Status Conditions again.

Status Condition: Curse of Flame
Duration: Permanent

Curse of Flame
When this Masterwork weapon deals an injury, the curse born by its blade ensures that said injury is permanent. The curse of flame is to burn forever.

He had to stop himself from grinding his teeth. Too much activity took a lot out of Pit, though he'd gotten a lot better than before. Felix tried his best not to dwell on it, but it was hard. There were downsides to sharing his every thought and emotion with a Companion.

"Alright. What do you want?" he said, distracting himself and clapping his hands to get Evie's attention. Her, Harn, and Darius turned to him, and the same look of discomfort crossed all their faces. "What?"

"It's just weird," Evie said. "Seeing a man's clothes crawl around him like a snake."

Felix glanced down. "Oh." His Garment, reacting to his thoughts and renewed glut of Mana, had reconstituted into a tunic and thick, woolen jacket. "You've all seen that before."

"Just unsettling, is all," Harn said with a shrug. "But you were talking about prizes, eh? What was the reward for hitting him once?"

"Free reign in the Storage Facility," Evie said, an eager gleam in her eyes. "I heard you found some interesting items in that Domain near Shelim."

Felix sighed. "Fair's fair. Go talk to Karys about letting you in. You can take one thing. Just…don't make a mess, Evie. "

The woman raised hand to her chest, a pantomime of shock writ large across her face. "I would never!"

"Get outta here." Felix shooed her away, and she gave him a mocking curtsy in her leather armor before leaping back up into the trees. "Beef?"

"Ungh, yeah yeah. I'm up."

Felix had heard the Minotaur trudging toward them well before he came into view. He looked worn, but he wasn't limping or bleeding—Felix's Voracious Eye confirmed he was fine, just bruised. Hallow was at his side, lumpy hands lifted as if to catch the far larger Unbound.

"Can you rouse the rest of these folks and get them back to the Stronghold?"

Beef stretched his lower back and something popped. "Yeah. I got it. Dang, dude, you hit me hard. How many trees did I go through?"

"Five," Hallow answered.

"Tch, man." Beef turned and started stomping toward the fallen Henaari and Frost Giants.

Felix watched them go with a rueful smile. "Now, unless you two want to follow me to a meeting with Zara, you'd best get back to your normal duties."

Harn shrugged, as if either option didn't bother him much, but Darius didn't move. He sheathed his ridiculous sword behind his back and put his hands on his hips. "We have not trained your Sword Forms in days, Felix. I had thought you would ask that of us, instead of this…game."

"It wasn't a game. I needed to test my training array, and you're the best fighters here." Felix shrugged. "Made sense to me."

"Then, why not use a sword? We could have achieved two objectives at once."

"Man's got a point," Harn agreed.

"I won't always have a sword on hand…and honestly, with my stats, I don't need to focus on technique. Not against anyone here, at least." Felix winced. He didn't like how arrogant that sounded, but Darius and Harn just bobbed their heads in agreement. "Erm. I need to know how to face opponents with superior techniques and of a superior Tier, but the latter are in short supply." Felix gestured to the array keystone at his waist. "This training array is meant to make fighting a lot harder for me. Level the playing field, so I don't dominate with sheer stats. I can't exactly go out and find something in my weight class that wants to have a friendly spar."

Darius considered him a moment longer before nodding. "Hm. I understand." Without another word, the man walked off.

For his part, Harn just chucked Felix on the shoulder. The sound of his steel gauntlet on Felix's shoulder was like he'd punched a rock. "Whenever you want me to come and try to kick your ass, you just holler, yeah?"

"Will do. I've some tweaks to make to the array, plus some alchemical ideas to try. Are you going back to the Forge?"

"I am. My apprentices have been workin' on some side projects, and I need to check them before we try and complete their Quests." Harn sighed happily, looking at the blasted landscape around them. "It was good gettin' out here and doin' some damage. A nice break from bein' Forgemaster and all the…everythin' that requires."

"Yeah. I get it." Felix had a lot on his plate, too. "When I get my next version working, I'll come find you, man."

"See that you do, kid."

Harn followed after Darius, jogging slightly to catch up with the far taller man. Felix watched them go then turned his attention to the trampled forest. He checked his Mana, finding it just about full already.

"Not gonna leave things like this." He focused, plucking at the Skills that revolved within his chest. "Green Shaping."

Mana spun out of his core, a great swath of it that looped through his channels, out of the Mana Gate in his feet, and into the earth itself. The Skill, sounded by his Affinity and shaped by his Intent, sang of green-gold life and life answered. The broken boles and shattered trunks of those trees closest to him bloomed with sudden roots, and the thick tendrils wound around their open wounds like patchwork bandages.

His Manasight traced the fading core of life Mana in each tree and tracked them as he pumped more Mana into them. Felix had been practicing with his shaping Skills a whole lot these past three months, but this wasn't something he'd perfected. It was a bit sloppy and certainly didn't look great, but it worked. Life Mana spread, hitting more and more trees in an ever-widening circle, until all of the trees that his spar had knocked down were replanted and alive.

Green Shaping is level 83!

There. Felix took a steadying breath and let his Mana recover. He'd spent a *lot*, and just because it regenerated fast didn't mean it wasn't tiring to use, especially when the process was so complicated. *Ugly as hell, but it'll do.*

"Let's go see what Zara wants, Pit."

Distantly, he heard a soft, agreeable chirp.

CHAPTER THREE

Felix trudged through the snow, clawed feet now covered by his boots and greaves, not in a particular hurry to get back to his Stronghold. Zara had asked to meet with him that morning—again—and he'd put her off for the last few hours. A few more minutes wouldn't matter.

He stomped toward a certain tree, eager to get out of the snow, but not before retrieving his weaponry. Inside the hollow trunk, he pulled free a crooked bronze sword and a wide-bladed dagger of the same metal: Inheritor's Will and Skyslain's Riposte. They were unassuming weapons, but both were formidable for different reasons and were an essential part of his combat kit. He was only missing the oversized Blade of the Fang, which was currently stowed away in Pit's barding. He placed both weapons against his belt and pushed Mana into his Garment, forcing it to forge leather sheaths for them both.

Much better. Now, to get those cores. He looked askance at the heavy accumulation of snow farther ahead. It was quite deep there, rising as high as mid-thigh in places, and Felix had no desire to wade through it all. Instead, he conjured Cloudsteps beneath his feet with every step, tiny platforms of solidified Mana that hovered an inch above the snow like an elevated pathway. Like many things he'd incorporated these past few months, it combined convenience with an opportunity to train himself—he could have used Rime Shaping, but Cloudstep needed more practice. It also meant he made remarkably little noise as he moved, a detail that wasn't appreciated by the Legionnaires nearby.

"Lord Autarch!"

Three trainees stumbled to their feet, taken aback by Felix's silent approach. Bundled in heavy blue cloaks, they seemed entirely unsure whether to stand at attention, salute, or bow so they attempted all three at once, tangling their winter gear in the process. It was almost comical, but Felix made sure to keep his expression neutral as he rounded the corner of their small dugout. A tiny fire had been stoked against the cold, off-center from three smooth, glowing orbs that sat at the back of the crude dirt windbreak. Felix gestured to the orbs. "How are the cores?"

"Ah, my Lord, they are in good condition and are, ah, glowing very nicely," said one. Lamden, Felix recalled. "The sigaldry snuffed out a short while ago, but until then, they were pulsing at regular intervals. Just as you said they should."

"Excellent." Felix stepped over, dismissing his Cloudsteps and scooping up each core. They were Domain Cores, recovered from within the Foglands, and he'd stuck them on the far end of his training array. All that siphoned Health, Stamina, and Mana had to go *somewhere*, after all. "Yeah. They're just about halfway full. That'll be useful."

"My Lord, if you don't mind me asking, what are these for?" Lamden asked.

"Hm?" Felix looked up from the cores, having hefted them up to his eyes. "Oh they're just batteries. Gonna use them for sigaldry research."

"Ah. Of course, my Lord." Lamden nodded, clearly not understanding what Felix was talking about. "Do you need us further?"

"Nah. Go help Beefhammer with the Claw members, please."

"At once, my Lord." Lamden saluted, followed shortly by the other two, and with a sharp gesture, they trotted off into the snowy forest.

Felix tucked the Domain Cores into his satchel, not being particularly careful with them. They were sturdy things, requiring a good portion of his considerable Strength to damage. That feature plus their ability to absorb and store energy made them extremely useful for enchantments of the more experimental kind.

Much like simple monster cores, Domain Cores were filled with large amounts of Mana and Essence originally, only on a far greater scale. Given that they had to provide an entire Domain with power, that made sense. Removing them from a Domain meant the entire place fell apart—despite the potential for training in Domains, they were also a threat. The three he'd taken these from had been on the verge of breaking through the liminal space that safeguarded all such places. Taking their cores had been necessary to keep his people safe.

Their original stores had been drained already, using the Mana to power Alister's second generation of siege weaponry, but the man's experiments required a great deal of resources. The wood and stone alone kept them on the hunt for high-Tier materials. Utilizing his *siphon* array to drain his Health, Stamina, and Mana then store them all had been Karys' idea, though Felix had been the one to work out most of the sigaldry. The Mana vessel had been simplest—Mana was pure, and everything was made up of it at some level. Health and Stamina, however, were derived from Essence *and* Mana.

That had blown his mind.

Felix had long ago learned everything was vibrations on the Continent. In the whole universe, he supposed. Patterns of sound, each unique and layered atop one another. The Grand Harmony. Among Chanters—Sorcerers, as they were often called—it was common knowledge that all of those patterns became Mana, and Mana composed all. But they were missing a piece of the puzzle, or the information related to Felix had been incomplete, at least. It was Mana *and* Essence that made up all things, with some sort of confluence between the two filling in the gaps.

That meant, according to Karys, that the Health represented his lifeforce, and the Stamina that fueled his every movement was composed of Mana and Essence in various degrees. It was more than a little confusing, but despite the ancient Paragon's patchy memories, he assured Felix that everything was a matter of frequencies and concentrations.

Felix hefted one of the Domain Cores, staring into its partially faceted surface. Within, colors swirled in kaleidoscopic patterns that he knew to be Stamina, somehow. *If it's all just Essence and Mana, that explains why monster cores can fuel enchantments that normally require a steady stream of Mana.* He tossed the core up, catching it in his large, clawed hands. *Cool.*

Cloudstep!

Felix ascended into the naked canopy like mounting a staircase, until he stood above all but the true giants of the forest. The terrain in the Foglands looked almost alien in the heart of winter, but it was not any less beautiful. To the west was the River Eile, too wide and strong to freeze over even as the temperature dropped hard. It was filled with fish and monsters that provided a great deal of food to his growing settlement.

To the east were the Teeth, a range of mountains that separated the Foglands—Nagast—into fairly discrete sections of forests, cliffs, and lush meadows. They were far less lush now, as bare branches and rolling hills dominated every direction, including the north where the land eventually opened up into the icy Hoarfrost, home of the Risi and apparently a blasted wasteland of ice and snow. He'd had to build a wall there, too, though there was little chance of invasion from that direction.

Finally, to the south, his Stronghold dominated.

I suppose I should call it by its name now, he mused, still regarding the distant darkness to the south. It appeared almost like a cloud from so far away, but its true nature was impossible to hide. The Atlantes Anima, his Spirit Tree, was over a thousand feet tall and twice that in canopy width. It loomed above his Stronghold like a guardian, casting a shadow visible even in the waning light of the watery winter sun.

At its base, the River Eile coiled, surrounded by the blue-black walls of a fortress, before careening off the edge in a waterfall so large it was easily visible from several miles away. Clinging to the cliff and the surrounding area, more blue-black fortifications stood out against the gray stone and white snow, and multicolored lights pulsed slowly from atop squared watchtowers.

A Nymean Temple was housed within that cliff, the core of Felix's Stronghold, bearing more secrets than anyone else realized. The Atlantes Anima, grown from the corpse of an enemy and bound to Felix's Authority, had extended its roots far beneath the Temple—so deep, in fact, that it had brought back mysteries. Where its farthest roots cracked the stone, they had found a small, half-collapsed room bearing only an ornate lintel above an empty wall. It was written in some illegible Nymean dialect, but Karys had been able to translate it easily. After some thought and his Tree's insistence, Felix had agreed the word had promise.

Elderthrone.

It certainly was a bold name. Felix hadn't been entirely comfortable choosing it—he certainly didn't have a throne—but Karys had mollified his concerns had. "Perhaps it was once this Temple's name. Or something older, upon which this Temple was built. We Nym were not the first upon the Continent's soil." Karys' words echoed in Felix's perfect memory, repeated with flawless fidelity as if the giant metal man were standing next to him.

"At least everyone else seems to like it," Felix muttered to himself. The word had been on everyone's lips within the hour. He'd even spotted it carved into the shops and signs around town as the people embraced the name. It was better than the alternative that some had proposed. Fiendtown would have been way worse.

He kept casting Cloudsteps as he walked toward his home. He wasn't in a particular hurry, though his meeting with Zara loomed ever closer. He'd put her off more than once during his duties this past week, and—if Felix were being honest—for far longer than that. Months ago, she'd hinted at a gathering, a sit-down chat about things Felix was not ready to engage with. Once he sat down with her, he'd have to put up with Isla, as well as...others.

Isla had been particularly nosy since he'd requested that she look over Pit and his cursed injuries. She could see the Curse of Flame on him—could even trace its influence over Pit's back—but the roots of the curse went deep. So deep, in fact, that they clung to Pit's core space. According to her expert opinion as one of the leading Master Tier healers, there was no way she or anyone else could remove the Curse of Flame without destroying Pit's core space...and potentially his core, too.

Unacceptable, he reiterated to himself. *We just need a new angle.*

Felix pulled his sheepskin coat higher around his neck as a biting wind stung his cheeks. The temperature wasn't uncomfortable, but his reactions to inclement weather were ingrained in him; he'd been raised in Florida, and anything below sixty degrees was *cold. Just like the moment when Harn cut me. It didn't hurt, but it was a distraction.* He bit his lip. *How do I fix that?*

Training. That was the only answer. He needed to fight under the suppression array more often, as he'd come to call it. Felix wasn't talented at combat, but he was tenacious—he'd practice until he could ignore it all.

Status.

Name: Felix Nevarre
Level: 62
Race: Primordial of the Unseen Tide (Greater)*
Omen: Magician
Path: Cardinal Fiend
Born Trait: Keen Mind

Health: 13035/13035
Stamina: 12072/12072
Mana: 10028/10028

STR:3204
PER:2825
VIT:2577
END:2100
INT:2875
WIL:3745
AGL:2466
DEX:2497

BODY - Chthonic Ascent (Adept)
***Resistances*: The Song of Absolution (L), Level 94**

***Combat Skills:* Dodge (C), Level 82; Heavy Armor Mastery (C), Level 15; Blind Fighting (R), Level 78; Wild Threnody (E), Level 85; Hand of Calamity (L), Level 62**

***Physical Enhancements*: Armored Skin (R), Level 88; Relentless Resolution (L), Level 95**

MIND - Fiendforged (Adept)
***Mental Enhancements*: Deception (C), Level 45; Meditation (U), Level 79; Negotiation (U), Level 50; Bastion of Will (E), Level 99; Deep Mind (E), Level 80; Manifestation of the Coronach (E), Level 80; Chthonic Tribute (L), Level 97**

***Information Skills*: Alchemy (C), Level 72; Tracking (C), Level 44; Exploration (U), Level 70; Ephemeral Evocation (E), Level 24; Voracious Eye (E), Level 90; Aria of the Green Wilds (L), Level 88**

SPIRIT - Eldercrowned (Adept)
***Spiritual Enhancements*: Dual Casting (U), Level 78; Manasight (U), Level 79; Manaship Pilot (R), Level 35; Etheric Concordance (L), Level 84; Last Cry Of The Chthonic Host (M), Level 5; Sovereign of Flesh (T), Level 95; Unite the Lost (T), Level 51; Fiendforge (Un), Level 68**

***Spells*: Abyssal Skein (R), Level 77; Cloudstep (R), Level 74;**

Green Shaping (R), level 83; Illusory Double (R), Level 45; Invocation (R), Level 77; Shadow Whip (R), Level 64; Stone Shaping (R), Level 85; Sunken Ward (R), Level 65; Rime Shaping (R), Level 76; Auroral Forge (E), Level 75; Mantle of the Infinite Revolution (E), Level 74; Arrow of Perdition (L), Level 52; Cardinal Flame (L), Level 93; Rain of Cataclysm (L), Level 76; Skein of Fate (L), Level 63; Theurgist of the Rise (L), Level 92; Adamant Discord (T), Level 91

———

Unused Stat Points: 0

<u>Harmonic Stats</u>
Resonance (RES): 1446
Intent (INE): 2443
Affinity (AFI): 2980
Resilience (REI): 1452
Evasion (EVA): 1542
Might (MIG): 1522
Alacrity (ALA): 1962
Felicity (FEL): 2770

His level hadn't budged since the battle against the High Guard, but that didn't stop his progress over the course of three months. Felix had pushed himself, lifting nearly every one of his Skills above Apprentice Tier, and several had passed onto Journeyman or even Adept. The stat rewards from Tiering up had boosted his already enormous reserve of power—another reason for him to perfect his suppression array. Training against people that he outclassed by several thousand stat points made things rather pointless. It was also why he had tested himself against a number of the Domains in the Foglands.

Some Skills, like Hand of Calamity, Arrow of Perdition, or Rain of Cataclysm were impossible to train without hurting someone. It turned out the Foglands had a number of Domains that needed clearing, hence the three Domain Cores in his pack, and Felix had been more than happy to test himself against their denizens. Sadly, his inner council hadn't allowed him to dominate all of the monsters, and Felix had to admit that was the wiser choice—letting the various Talons fight against enemies in a relatively controlled environment was invaluable training.

He'd taken on the Domain boss himself, though. Of the three he'd fully cleared, all of them had put up something of a fight, enough for Felix to stretch his abilities—at least a little.

All in all, the months since Haarwatch had been fruitful. What had stymied him, however, were the Skills that had pushed well into the eighties, or worse, the ones that had crossed over into the nineties. Bastion of Will was now his highest-leveled Skill, at 99, and try as he might, Felix was unable to make a dent toward that final level.

One more level, and I'll have a Master Tier Skill. Felix scratched his jaw as he stood above the trees, the glowing, blue-white platform humming beneath him. Once all nine of his Tempered Skills reached level 100, Felix would be among the rare few Master Tiers on the Continent. It blew his mind a little. He certainly didn't *feel* like a master of anything.

Felix came to a stop, metal boots crackling atop the hardened Mana beneath him. He had been ignoring his core space in order to let Pit rest, but after his battle against the others, he should check on them. The arrangement was new, after all.

Zara can wait a bit longer.

Firming his Will and the Cloudstep beneath him, Felix closed his eyes and fell. Not into the naked forest below, but into the preternatural darkness that lurked inside of his chest.

It swallowed him whole.

CHAPTER FOUR

The first thing he saw were the branches of an opalescent crystal tree, adorned with enough multi-colored leaves to put all of Nagast to shame. The Divine Tree, he'd been calling it, was grown from a Vein of Divinity that he'd stolen from a goddess. He careened toward its bulk, the prismatic shine of its Essence leaves filling the darkness with a near-blinding radiance.

Kinda hard not to imagine I'm falling from my Cloudstep right now. About to hit snow and dirt, face-first. Felix grinned as he flew, despite his thoughts. *Eh. I'd survive it.*

Gathering speed, Felix shot down through the bevy of branches, each one faceted and shimmering with a different color. Leaves scattered around him, turning from perfectly shaped oak, ash, and elm leaves into luminescent vapor—only to reform behind him to the sound of chiming bells.

Between his work on the Stronghold and his Skills, the thing he truly prided himself on that winter was the sheer volume of visualization he'd produced. As he burst from the upper boughs of his Divine Tree, Felix gazed upon the bounty of what he'd wrought—and it was beautiful.

It's a funnel.

Quiet, you. I thought you were sleeping?

Mhmph, Pit mumbled sleepily.

Pit was accurate though, even if he had stolen the term from Felix originally. His entire core space had elevated, forming like a cyclone around his cores and Divine Tree, resembling an inverted pyramid. His Skills shone, each one an orb of swirling colors and dancing patterns that resembled nothing so much as planetary bodies floating in space. They moved, rotating imperceptibly around the circumference of the funnel, each one spinning in a unique dance of its own.

It's a conduit, he reminded himself. *Funnel sounds like I'm baking or assembling a beer bong.*

The Skills themselves were grouped into larger patterns, like planets that had become tidally locked with one another. They were called Skill Arrays, and the strength they provided was not to be ignored. Felix had progressed a great deal with those as well—he had formed his Bastion Array and Shaping Array back before his confrontation with the Creature of Khasma, and he boasted even more now. They floated like glittering jewels around the circumference of his conduit, each one a song Felix could sing if he wished.

Forsaken Array, Vigilant Array. Felix spotted each of them as he named them, checking their positions around his center. *Concordance Array. Three formed in as many months.*

Due to the sheer power the Skill Arrays required to establish their connections, not to mention the need for balance among the Array itself, Felix had taken his time crafting each of them. Karys and Zara had aided him in the beginning, helping him sort combinations in the most efficient ways.

Karys' advice had amounted to "get the rarest Skill you have and attach others that complement it," which would apparently effect the strongest boost to his abilities.

Zara, on the other hand, had pointed out potential matches but warned him off the endeavor entirely. She had claimed it was too dangerous to tie his growth down, even for the boost the Skill Arrays might provide, as they were too inflexible, were he to experience another spontaneous Skill evolution. Such a change would threaten the integrity of his other Skill patterns, perhaps leading to breaking or sundering completely. And that was discounting the possibility of regret—were he not happy with an Array, removing Skills from it was just as dangerous.

She certainly had a point, and Karys had agreed, but Felix had flabbergasted them both with a revelation shortly after the conflict in Haarwatch. He'd ignored their warnings and had adjusted his oldest Skill Array.

Bastion Array

***Primary*: Bastion of Will**
***Secondaries*: Deep Mind, Skein of Fate, Chthonic Tribute**
***Tertiaries*: Deception, Negotiation, Meditation**

Felix had added Deception and Negotiation to it, and removed Voracious Eye, Aria of the Green Wilds, and Relentless Resolution. It had been…incredibly painful, and Felix had danced upon the razor's edge of consciousness the entire time. A combination of his powerful Willpower, stalwart Intent, and soaring Affinity saw him through, if a little worse for wear. The chamber he'd performed the separation in still bore the scars of Felix's insensate spasms. He made sure not to show either of his advisors *that* particular bit of evidence.

Still, the results spoke for themselves, and after tweaking that first Skill Array, the System had retroactively recognized what he was doing and incorporated it into his display. Now all of them were viewable behind a tiny circular icon that faded from view unless he focused on it. It looked like a stylized solar system, white on blue. His other Skill Array was viewable as well, to which he'd added his newest shaping Skill: Hand of Calamity.

Shaping Array
***Primary*: Sovereign of Flesh**
***Secondaries*: Cardinal Flame, Stone Shaping, Green Shaping, Auroral Forge, Rime Shaping, Hand of Calamity.**
***Tertiaries*: Manasight, Theurgist of the Rise, Invocation, Dual Casting, Manaship Pilot**

It was odd, but according to Zara, not the first time the System has made adjustments on the fly. While the Chant operated largely outside of the System's control, their facility with it was still represented by their Harmonic Stats. It hadn't always been so. Regardless, after proving his methods to Karys and Zara, they had abandoned trying to stop him. Felix had proceeded to assemble his three new arrangements.

Forsaken Array
***Primary*: The Song of Absolution**
***Secondaries*: Abyssal Skein, Dodge, Armored Skin, Relentless Resolution**
***Tertiaries*: Illusory Double, Heavy Armor Mastery**

Vigilant Array
***Primary*: Voracious Eye**
***Secondaries*: Aria of the Green Wilds, Exploration, Tracking**
***Tertiary*: Alchemy, Blind Fighting**

Concordance Array
***Primary*: Adamant Discord**
***Secondaries*: Unite the Lost, Etheric Concordance, Ephemeral Evocation, Wild Threnody, Fiendforge**
***Tertiaries*: Last Cry of the Chthonic Host, Manifestation of the Coronach**

Each Array had been named by the System, though Felix had designated the groupings. Using Tempered Skills as Primaries had proven fruitful, especially as all were Epic or higher rarity. That afforded them more spaces for Secondary and Tertiary Skills to join in, supposedly increasing the overall strengthening effect. Aside from that requirement, the composition was one that Felix had ultimately had to feel out. The rhythms and patterns of each Skill had to be meshed carefully with all the others in a way that didn't invalidate their purpose. Harmony was the goal, creating a greater whole while avoiding as much Dissonance as he could.

His Forsaken Array was all about rejecting harm, and each Skill reflected that in some way. Aside from The Song of Absolution, his Dodge, Armored Skin, Relentless Resolution, and Abyssal Skein were the most directly related to that concept. That was why they were Secondaries. Illusory Double and Heavy Armor Mastery had commonalities but less than the rest—though an illusion and suit of armor could certainly help him avoid harm. Felix had been a bit surprised at Heavy Armor Mastery when he'd felt the resonance within it, considering it was his lowest leveled Skill by far and of Common rarity to boot. Still, it had slipped into the Array without issue, and more importantly, it felt *right* in a way Felix couldn't verbalize.

The Vigilant Array was about perception and gathering of knowledge. Voracious Eye stood as Primary there, for obvious reasons, with Aria of the Green Wilds, Exploration, and Tracking as Secondaries. Sensing the natural world around him fed into the concept of the Array, feeding the pattern that had congealed around it. Blind Fighting was a bit of a departure, as was Alchemy, but the former was about preternatural perceptions, and the latter was about using knowledge to learn even more. It all fit together like pieces of a puzzle.

The last and most difficult Skill Array to form had been his Concordance Array. The concept at the heart of it was connection, something Felix had been exploring more and more. Adamant Discord was the Primary, as it was the Skill that allowed Felix to manipulate the connections around himself to push and pull the world.

Unite the Lost, Etheric Concordance, Ephemeral Evocation, Wild Threnody, and Fiendforge were all self-explanatory. Each of them dealt with the unseen threads between people, power, and even memories. The Grand Harmony sang through them all, a unifying song so immense that Felix could only perceive it through the snippets of his Skills. For that same reason, Last Cry of the Chthonic Host and Manifestation of the Coronach were the Tertiary Skills in the Array. The latter was a strange exultation whenever Felix entered the fray, and the former was a piercing song that could bring him back from the edge of death.

Felix still hadn't a clue where all that led, but he could not deny that the Skills had all but jumped into place once he'd brought them into alignment.

A number of his Skills were left untethered to any Array, mostly for lack of resonance with any others. That was a result of his eclectic variety of abilities, he supposed. Cloudstep, Shadow Whip, Sunken Ward, Mantle of the Infinite Revolution, Arrow of Perdition, and Rain of Cataclysm all stood out among the rotating walls of his core space. They were lone, shining beacons in the endless dark, points of contrast from the clusters of Skill Arrays.

More Skills might make my collection complete…or make it more chaotic than ever. It wasn't the first time he'd had that thought, and he doubted it would be his last. Using his Ephemeral Evocation to extract Memories from monsters had been a focus for a bit, though he'd never received anything more useful than animalistic impressions. *I need to fight more intelligent enemies, I think.*

He refocused.

Following the massively thick trunk of the Divine Tree downward, Felix gazed upon his dual cores. They enveloped the trunk itself, stacked atop one another like two rings on the same finger, each one rotating in an opposing direction. Topmost was the red-gold [Cardinal Beast Core] followed by the blue-white [Thunderflame Core], each made of a gelatinous, slow-moving flame that crackled ceaselessly with discharges of light and sound. The flames had thickened recently, and Zara and Karys both agreed that his Mana was beginning to condense further. Soon, they warned, one or both would crystallize, much like his Divine Tree.

A new threshold of power.

For now, those pieces of his cores spat outward as regularly as a beating heart, never stopping and never diminishing the cores' sizes, despite grinding endlessly together. Both of them hovered above the primary feature of Felix's new core space. His Hunger sat at the narrowest part of his conduit. The sparks and sound shot in all directions, many of them upward and outward into the Tree and sides of his conduit, but all of it flowed down eventually into the black hole.

A halo of surging radiance and cacophonous sound spun around his Hunger, swirling at its greatest distance and lensing strangely over the expanse of darkness at its center. Anything Essence or Mana that came close was fuel for its endless appetite.

Hunger hadn't spoken to him since Haarwatch, which made Felix nervous and strangely bereft. It had proven to be an ally, if an altogether strange one. Its last act before going silent was to give up the bulk of power it had consumed in order to fuel the weaving of Felix's Pillars. He was still attempting to repay that sacrifice by consuming monsters and redesigning his core space.

All the Essence he had gathered over the cold winter—and a good chunk of his own personal Mana—was being siphoned into the black hole. In fact, Felix had designed it all to work in that way. Power entered, catching and holding among the branches of his Divine Tree, refined by the Tree's own nature and Felix's Intent, before it spiraled outward among his Skills like barely-seen streamers of cosmic wind. In this way, the Essence was able to linger long enough to be of use to Felix, while eventually ending up at the bottom of his conduit, where his Hunger would devour what remained.

Felix even utilized the Seal he'd grown from the Divine Tree to further refine the shape of his giant funnel. It was copied from the Seal of the Breach they had found across Khasma, where the Creature had been locked away for long Ages. Felix had modified it a touch. Where before his copied Seal spread outward horizontally, now it clung just outside his spinning Skills vertically as well, like a trellis. Stems and budding roots climbed from tip to base, formed into a dense maze of sigaldry and razor-sharp tendrils.

It was reinforcement and threat; if Felix was going to keep on devouring monstrous abominations, he would need all the help he could get.

Compared to the others he had seen, Felix's core space was titanically large. Perhaps he could have corrected this during his long visualization exercises, but there was little reason to do so. Others would struggle to utilize such vast amounts of space, but for Felix, it was almost the bare minimum to contain the forces he had incorporated within himself. A side effect of that, however, was a near-constant need to replenish his Essence stores. That meant devouring monsters, cores, and magic often, so his Hunger didn't deplete him of his strength when he needed it most.

A work in progress.

Below the warped space around his Hunger, the roots of his Divine Tree extended farther still. They were among the only things that could approach that abyss, yet the roots were not unchanged. Still crystalline, still opalescent, the colors were nevertheless muted. Dulled, as if a piece of vitality had been leached away.

His Hunger stripped even the Divine, which was fortunate. The Creature couldn't face it and live, and, if Felix played his cards right, nothing else would be able to, either. He might be gearing up to face the might of the Hierocracy and their grandmasters, but he had experienced enough rare encounters to rightfully fear the true monsters out there.

The roots continued down, combining with cords of light that split through the bottom of his conduit before all of them wove together into nine Pillars, each as thick as his Divine Tree. This was the mark of Felix's advancement. One's foundational Pillars were to be woven before one could attempt Grandmaster Tier, and Felix had them ready well before he reached Master. Their completion had boosted his stats to a large degree, but more importantly, they had increased his capacity for significance by a wide margin.

Significance was a strange thing. Like Essence, there was no meter to gauge how much he contained at any one time, though he could sense the edges of it, to an extent. Also like Essence, Felix was equipped with methods that allowed him to drain others of a portion of their significance. It was a measurement of a person's solidity within the universe, a sort of gravity that grounded people. The greater their power and advancement, the greater the significance they would accumulate. Eventually, he was told, it all crystallized. Who you were would become immutable. Immortal, perhaps.

For his part, Felix was certain he would require far more significance than others to truly reach that point. Whether that was because of his expanded Skill set, his high stats, or even just his Unbound nature didn't really matter. At that point, the only part of him that felt "fixed" were his nine Pillars and the star lattice that sealed their base.

The foundation was surrounded and engulfed in a crystalline lattice that anchored the Pillars to whatever amounted to a floor in his core space. It wasn't as refined as the "air" inside his conduit, where Felix had spent months visualizing exactly what he wanted. The unfocused, almost dirty dark served as a boundary of sorts, where lattices of silver crystal further secured the bases of all nine of his Pillars.

That had been another gift of Felix's Hunger, a deluge of pure power that had pushed the final Pillars over the edge. Each Pillar had been woven from his Tempered Skills, his dual cores, and the thinnest of threads from the consumed slivers of two separate goddesses. They were braided with a complexity that boggled Felix's vision whenever he tried to trace them out, though he wove most of them. The last few, however, had been formed by Pit.

You did a good job, bud, Felix sent but received no reply. He focused for a moment, tapping into the Link that connected them, and heard the tenku snoring away.

Felix left him alone.

All in all, his core space was looking good and operating just as he had visualized it to. The only real question was what that damned fist was all about.

It's powerful, I know that. The first emergence of that conjured fist had resulted in the Creature's final defeat. Except, now it had tried to emerge from his core space entirely. *I don't even see it here. Is it hiding?*

Felix hesitated to attempt another summoning of it—he had no clue what it would do to the environment around him or how to contain its clear power. There were hunters and foragers in the forest below him. Felix would need a large, empty space to truly test it out.

Or I could suck it up and ask Zara about it, he chided himself.

The Naiad Sorcerer had proven herself trustworthy a dozen times over, but her ties to the Chanters made Felix uncomfortable. He'd grown used to Zara after months, but then the revelation that he was expected to fight the Ruin—a civilization-killing abomination that erased *history itself*—had set him back on his heels.

Then, of course, Isla had entered the mix and set everything back further. If the diminutive healer represented how the Cantus Sodalus operated, Felix was not keen on involving them in his business. The woman's continued efforts to meddle around his Stronghold only solidified his distrust…and Zara's refusal to step in made him newly wary of her intentions as well.

So talking to the Chanters about his innermost workings was off the table for now. Karys had plenty of insight, but it was full of holes. He knew the Pillars were good, the Skill Arrays were strong, and the mere presence of crystallized Mana in his core space at all was a sign of great things to come…but the larger significance was lost.

I suppose I can ask him about the fist, at least. Not like he's going to tell anyone.

"Felix? My Lord, are you there?"

Felix blinked back to reality, his core space fading as the world restored itself around him. Green-gold Mana vapor oozed from his Inheritor's Will, buzzing with the voice of his Chancellor. "Speak of the devil. What is it, Karys?"

"It's Kimaris. She has made contact with the Witches of Cold Rock."

"Ooh. That was fast." Felix weighed his options. He had a meeting with Zara, one he'd put off more than a few times already…but Kimaris' mission was important. He nodded. "Be there in a second."

Within his chest, a series of chords rang out as he sounded a Skill. Harmony and Dissonance wound around each other in equal measure, guided by his Affinity and shaped by his Intent as it spooled through his pathways and out of the Mana Gates in his palms. All of it took less than a fraction of a second.

Adamant Discord!

Connections between *here* and *there*, between Felix and Karys, went from ephemeral to hardened steel beams. Felix grasped them, letting lightning course across his fingers, and *pulled*.

He shot off into the sky, a wake of blistering sound trailing behind him.

CHAPTER FIVE

In a short span of months, Elderthrone had grown. Where there was once only the Temple in the cliff and rudimentary houses at its foot, now the town had split into several discrete districts. The first was, of course, the Temple itself. It was named The Eye, ostensibly in honor of their Autarch and his crest, which looked like a blazing blue eye surrounded by tendrils of fire and lightning. In truth, Zara knew that it was named for the view that nearly all denizens of Elderthrone were met with whenever they looked heavenward.

The Spirit Tree's dark canopy—unaffected by winter's cold touch—hung above like a great, unblinking circle that provided them cover from snow and rain while also leaving them beneath a titan's shadow. At its center, the smooth trunk glowed with a radiance that could be clearly seen no matter the time of day. If one were to stare long enough, it would appear as a gleaming rent in the dark sky. "As if a god held them all in its gaze," she had heard more than once. It was silly and more than a little superstitious, but it was an image that could not be denied. Many drew comfort from the effect, but the newer arrivals still shuddered.

The Eye included the Spirit Tree—Atlantes Anima—and the Nymean Temple buried within the cliff itself. A set of grand stairs led from the Upper Hall of the Temple, hugging the towering cliff all the way to its base. The stairs were formed of blue-black stone, shaped into place by the Autarch himself over the course of one fitful night, and they were wide enough to accommodate twenty people shoulder-to-shoulder along its entire length. Wooden statues had since been installed along the outer edge, gifts of the Henaari depicting monsters with such startling skill that it seemed they would come to life at any moment. Each one was a monument to one of the Autarch's defeated enemies, ranging from the banal to the truly terrifying.

It was a strange choice for decoration, but it served to keep many away from the Temple. Perhaps that was why Felix allowed them to remain. He was not one to brag about his accomplishments.

After the drama of the steps, the district referred to as The Foot began. While certainly not a noble name, it was pragmatic and factual. It boasted housing that clung to the base of the cliff, built *into* the stone in many places, and it was highly desired for its proximity to the Temple as well as its relative scarcity. There was only so much space, after all, before one either ran into the river or the forests outside the town walls.

This was where Zara's home was built, and like many of the others, it had also been magically transmuted into the same blue-black stone, chased with glimmering red-gold veins. The material, commonly called Fiendstone now, stretched most of the way up the cliff itself before petering out some fifty strides of the top. It was incredibly durable and, despite the plain design of the buildings, the recent influx of nobles were feverishly trying to acquire even the meanest of dwellings there.

I am thankful that is not my problem to handle. Zara sipped her tea, while behind her the lilting voice of Chanter Isla continued unabated. Zara refrained from massaging the bridge of her nose by clenching her cup. *I have enough on my hands as it is.*

A chill wind stirred the powder between cobblestones, sending eddies down the winding streets of Elderthrone. Just beyond the Foot were two thick walls and wide gates, all made of Fiendstone, as were the barracks at the north and south ends of the town. Tiny fortresses to contain a growing Legion; soon another would be required. The town itself was swelling with people as they trickled in from Haarwatch, not to mention the influx of those who fled Ahkestria. The population was dense with all manner of Races, and for the first time in a decade, Zara found herself in a place where Humans were in the minority.

Henaari, Nagas, Orc, Goblin, Yttin. Even the Risi, System-classified as monsters. So many are gathered here, advancing peacefully, all under his banner. That has to mean something.

All told, Felix's fledgling reign was striking, expansive, and just the thing to impress her superiors—if he ever deigned to show up to their meetings.

"...and we have found a number of reagents once thought extinct. Redneedle and Metier's Heart are abundant in the southern most reaches, while Mograss Cap can be found in nearly any spot hidden from the sun. A veritable treasure trove, one I have used to establish a large healing facility in the Wings." Isla adjusted the sleeves of her elegantly embroidered dress, letting her accomplishments linger in the silence.

"The Wings?" Atop the circular table was a basin of beaten metal, and within it glowed a measure of potent liquid Mana. Suspended atop that liquid was a small head, formed of Mana into a simulacrum of their superior, Mauvim.

"The common living district of Elderthrone," Isla supplied. "It is where my healing could help the greatest numbers."

"And Felix? How has he responded to you establishing such a facility?"

"It...was his idea," Isla admitted, her face twisting slightly. Zara hid her smile behind her teacup. "The boy is no master of Alchemy, but he has remarkable talents. The potions that come from his Laboratory are effective and cheap to produce, allowing my facility to thrive."

"A handy resource for the days to come," Mauvim's little head said, her wrinkled expression as always a bit more exaggerated in the basin. "And where is our intrepid Unbound now?"

Zara feigned inattention, looking to the streets below in futile hope. "What was that?"

"I asked if your charge is planning on missing this meeting, as he has all the rest?" The liquid Mana cast a soft white glow over the entirety of the small chamber. "I am growing impatient."

The raucous sound of thunder crashed above, and Zara caught a bolt a blue-white lightning flash across the Spirit Tree's dark canopy. *Felix...* He did not land at her door, nor on any part of the Foot—instead, the lightning had streaked toward the Temple itself. An unnecessary stop, were he intending to head in their direction.

Zara clenched her sharp teeth for only a moment before schooling her features and Spirit. She turned back to the basin. "He appears to be waylaid once again."

"That is twice now I've been ignored, Zara," Mauvim said in her artificially thin voice. The face in the basin flickered, as if experiencing some interference. "The boy's head swells with his Authority."

Isla nodded sagely. "He is cavalier with the needs of others, I have noticed. He lacks the steadiness Michael exemplifies."

Zara snorted. Beef was a kind boy and quite capable, but Isla was gilding the lily. "That comparison disregards the responsibility already thrust upon Felix's shoulders."

"You forget that Michael is involved in developing better Manaships, crafts that will allow Nevarre's armies far greater maneuverability, not to mention the benefits to trade."

The Naiad opened her mouth, lips drawn back over her fangs. "Isla—"

"Enough," Mauvim said, her tinny voice somehow booming in the small chamber. "I cannot wait. The waters draw near."

"You mean—?" Isla asked, her delicate features brightening.

"Indeed. You must corral your charge, Zara. There are answers to be had, and soon."

Zara bit back the words she wanted to relay and instead bowed low. "Of course, Mauvim."

"Dangerous days lie ahead," she warned. "The Ruin rushes for us, but there are other tribulations coming that we cannot fail to weather."

"The Hierocracy. Does it move?" Zara asked. "We have seen no sign of reprisals for their defeat."

"They are thankfully preoccupied on many fronts." The image flickered twice before resetting. "The waters are before me. I cannot wait. Keep those Unbound safe and on the path. We need them, but they need us to guide them through the growing dark. The Hierophant is not idle, even if they have not gathered another army. Dangers abound. As it was."

"As it ever shall be." The two junior Chanters spoke in near-unison. The basin went dark.

"Damnable rock!" A woman, veiled and wrapped in a dress of dark-blue, struggled up the wide stone steps. All at once, her cane slipped against the polished stone, but a hand thick with callouses caught her by the elbow.

"Let me aid you, Lil—"

"Do not use that name, fool!" the woman hissed, clawing into the man's arm with her too-thin fingers. She dragged herself back to standing, ignoring her companion's wince of pain. "Or do you wish to waste all our effort with a single, mumble-mouthed utterance?"

"Sorry…Ophelia," he said, and it was notable that the oaf did not draw away from her harsh grip. If anything, he stood closer as he glanced behind them. "But you must not strain yourself. You know the healers' warnings."

The woman bit back a retort designed to flay the skin from her companion's bones…and sighed. "You are right, Rodrik." She patted his hand and ignored the foolish smile that spread across his face. "A rarity. Do not revel in it."

"Of course." Rodrick inclined his shaved head and lifted his arm in tandem. His smile did not fade. "After you, my lady."

Ophelia wished to adjust the veil across her face and shoulders, but with one hand trapped in Rodrick's cloddish grip and the other managing her cane, she was forced to ascend. Perhaps she could have stopped, but that neither favored her injured leg nor the crowd that had bunched up behind them. Whispers had started to fly from the moment she'd stumbled, and no doubt in the morning, there would be talk of Ophelia and Rodrick upon the Temple's staircase. Already, she could pick out snippets from the crowd—romantic drivel, mostly. Nothing to be done about it now, but her lips pursed in annoyance and no little nervousness.

I would rather be invisible, but crippled is as close as I can manage. She ignored the savage burn in her legs and torso, made all the worse by the forced march up such ridiculous steps. *I must use what I can.*

She had not escaped death twice to be foiled here, within sight of her goals.

The stone beneath her feet pulsed with each step, so lightly that those without mage training might miss it. She did not. It was the red-gold that veined the dark marble, brightening within a finger-span of each person's footfalls. Ophelia watched it with a derision that grew by the moment. The stone was a magical marvel, the entirety of the blighted town was, and to know in whose hands it laid drew a bitter note from her soul.

The monstrous, wooden statues that lined the edge were better markers for the Autarch's character. Each one leered down at all those that traveled from the Foot, carved with such fidelity that it seemed their eyes burned with true malice. When she saw the horrific visage of a Revenant, she had frozen in true terror. The awful moment had passed, but it was burnt into her Mind, an indelible affirmation of her desire to do what must be done.

Gasps filled the air as those above reached the final landing, and Ophelia banished useless thoughts and hastened their ascent. Rodrick gave a half-hearted protest but followed, as he always did.

"By the light," he huffed. It was a deep bellows exhale, and the man's face was transformed with wonder.

A waterfall thundered to her immediate right, cascading from far above to crash into the river hundreds of spans below. That she had not heard it until they had crested the steps was an impressive feat, considering its size and proximity. More notable still was the wide vista that greeted every person that climbed the Temple's tortuous steps.

An opening in the wall, framed with raw stone, displayed a breathtaking view of the River Eile. Snow fell in the distance, a pale blanketing that was fading with the dimming sun. No wet or chill permeated the space, either from winds or water. Ophelia spotted a series of thin sigils carved all around the opening. She focused and perceived a thin barrier of blue Mana, though the effort cost her quite a bit of Mana.

"It is...sufficient," she allowed.

The Upper Hall itself was perhaps forty strides in width and twice that in length, lined with hexagonal pillars the same bluff color as the non-magical rock of the cliff outside. Between many of the pillars were alcoves filled with colorful mosaics, those nearest depicting men and women in armored robes and bearing stars in their hands. A number of people—artisans, craftsmen—were busy repairing one of the mosaics. It looked to have been damaged by a severe impact and burned, perhaps by fire or lightning.

The space was otherwise filled with messengers and servants carrying various supplies to and fro. Visitors abounded, many of them simply looking around the Hall. A clutch of Gnomes carried baskets of food about, filled with bread and fruits that they handed out carelessly to workers and visitors alike.

Carvings of leaves and vines predominated wherever the wall met the floor or ceiling, and steady golden magelights hovered above. The floor itself was cut into stars, each one fitting into another like a strange puzzle that led the eye across the Hall to a number of doors surmounted by three pointed archways. The largest door was fashioned of a verdant metal and decorated with more robed figures.

Nym. She recognized them and the stars they carried. *He truly made a Nymean Temple his Stronghold.*

She would have been impressed were she not so disgusted. Not of the Nym, though their name was synonymous with deadly danger, but for he who had claimed their legacy.

You are not worth this, butcher.

In the center, so dominant that she could not avoid it, was the trunk of a Spirit Tree. It soared in from above, through an uneven hole in the ceiling, and it took up a large swath of the floor and far wall. It struck her in a way that the rest of the marvels around them did not, and as the mindless supplicants filtered into the Upper Hall, she stood transfixed.

I…can feel its presence. It was like a balm upon the air, a sweetness she couldn't taste with her tongue but her Spirit. An almost irresistible urge to touch its rough bark welled up within her, but sight of its base put that out of her mind immediately. A wide structure made of blue-black Fiendstone clung to the point where Tree and floor met, twenty feet tall and almost completely flat on every side she could perceive. It bore a heavy door on a single side and was guarded by no fewer than six journeyman soldiers.

So many strong soldiers to waste on guard duty. Before it fell, the Guild had feted Journeyman Tiers and gave them positions of power and grandeur. They were worth more respect than standing beside a door. It was yet another example of the fraud mismanaging his resources.

"Ah, I do not see the Autarch," a finely-dressed man near Ophelia's side said. His face was a curious mixture of relief and disappointment. "Must we wait?"

A woman at his side, outfitted to complement the man, sniffed. "What else would you do? Go back down and live in the outer district? That Wing place? Or perhaps with the child-thieves or the ice monsters?"

Ophelia rolled her eyes. She had inserted herself into a group of supplicants treading the Fiend's steps as part of her plan, but their inane prattle had nearly driven her to leap off the side. Thirty in all, they were minor nobility that had relocated from Haarwatch in the hopes that they would find greater favor with the ruler of the Territory than the blunt disregard of Lady Boscal.

Most of them were begging for housing among the Foot, planning to offer tribute of gold and silver or even enchanted items in exchange. Ophelia had heard their pitiful plans on the way up, and she had nothing but contempt for them.

Fools. Felix Nevarre had no kindness in his soul. He was a predator.

She had the scars to prove it.

Ophelia adjusted her veil and the number of amulets and rings that were hidden just below the cover of fabric. Their enchantments buzzed against her skin, but they were supposedly undetectable by others, in addition to disguising her emotions. Rodrick had a similar set on himself. They were provided specifically by her benefactor. Her savior. She would put them to good use.

"Rodrick. Let us find—"

With a blinding crash, lightning struck in the center of the Upper Hall.

Screams filled the Hall for only a second as the supplicants around her cowered against the walls, throwing up whisper thin wardings. Ophelia herself stumbled back, too surprised to muster any defense, but Rodrick stepped in front of her with his arms raised. Dusty-brown earth Mana surged around his palms and feet. "My lady, take cover."

She growled and smacked him on the back. "Stand down, oaf. *Look.*"

The lightning had faded, and in its place stood Felix Nevarre, Autarch of Nagast.

"Oh, sorry about that," he said, smiling in a way that Ophelia hated. That she found it charming only made her more angry. "Forgot people are in here sometimes."

The bastard was wearing some sort of fleece-lined laborer's coat and thick trousers. He would have looked almost normal, were it not for his being half a span taller than he had been before and considerably more broad across the shoulders.

"W-what happened to him? How?" Rodrick stuttered. "His hands…"

Ophelia stared at the Autarch's savage claws. They were black as midnight and belied his true nature. "Monster," she whispered.

The wretched nobles around her watched in fear and awe, unspeaking and unmoving. After a few heartbeats, the man's apologetic grin faded into something more stoic before he simply turned and walked away.

"Go! Before he leaves again!" the waspish woman ordered, slapping at her husband's balding pate.

As if it were the starting bell of a race, the group surged forward, only to meet a sudden wall of jagged ice.

"Step away from the Autarch," intoned a heavy voice. A literal giant, fifteen strides tall if he were a span, had interposed himself between the throng and his liege. He wore a cloak and cowl of purple, and his armor was made of some sort of bone, fashioned into scale mail, as if they were imitating their master.

"Thank you, Veddi." Felix said, and Ophelia watched the man walk away. He spoke over his shoulder. "I don't have time to speak today, but my friend here will guide you to my…liason, Alister Knacht."

Ophelia stepped back at that name, fighting the urge to tug at her veil as a man in blue battle robes stepped from the general crowd. "Yes, well, I *was* on my break, but I suppose duty always calls." He smiled, and Ophelia felt her stomach flop when his gaze crossed hers…before moving on. "I suppose you are here to inquire about housing."

Rodrick put a large hand on her shoulder. "Lil—Ophelia, we need to leave."

She gave him a look that, even through her veil, made the man flinch. "And waste the time and effort climbing those stairs? No. He did not recognize us. Besides, our business is not with my dear cousin."

Ophelia looked beyond the crowd toward the Spirit Tree, where the Autarch disappeared into the fortified building. Its door opened and closed without making a single sound.

"Good. He's gone as well. Come, oaf."

Off to the side, set up against the far wall, three structures had been constructed of wood. They were beautifully decorated and carved with ravens, foxes, and odd crawling…things on it. Ophelia blinked as she approached. Within each structure were three figures in distinctive dress, their appearances matching the sign that hung above them.

Forge, Glyph, and Alchemy. Crafting Hall representatives.

Ophelia approached a Henaari woman wearing a quilted jacket and apron stained with innumerable concoctions. "Hello, I would like to become an Alchemist."

Felix Nevarre was not worthy of his gifts.

Ophelia—no. Lilian Knacht would take them from him.

CHAPTER SIX

As soon as the stone door closed behind him, Felix slumped in relief. Like a bubble bursting, his sense of others vanished into nothing. Wards against sight and sound were layered throughout the wide structure, packed tightly enough that even his potent Perception had difficulty penetrating them. Felix shuddered. The desperate greed, naked ambition, and thrumming fear on those people had clung to him like oily smoke—and still, it had not felt as nearly as unsettling as the ragged awe and sour jealousy they had let sound from their Spirits.

Sometimes I really regret having Harmonic Stats.

He moved. With his Born Trait of perfect recall, Felix had found that the best method to push away a recent experience was to ground himself in the now. He was pretty sure people called it mindfulness back on Earth, but whatever it was, it had proven to be extremely useful when his vivid memories clung too tightly.

Before him, the tiled flooring of the Upper Hall fell away, broken through by the surging growth of the Atlantes Anima. Felix had shaped the gate around the area in order to keep folks out, though it wasn't entirely necessary. Those without the required permissions couldn't get very far, anyway. Still, it helped clear up exactly where people were welcome.

Hello, Atlantes, he sent, sounding the cord that stretched between him and the Tree. *Are you doing well? Need more water? Uh…soil?*

What came back weren't words, just feelings. Much like how Pit had once communicated with him. The rustling of leaves and creaking of branches filtered through his Affinity, noise without sound, felt more than heard. It was enough to get a bead on things.

Good. Glad you're doing well. He patted the ridged bark. *The Fruit has been great. Keep up the good work.*

To his right, a set of stairs extended down into the dark, winding around the trunk in a spiral pattern. They also wound upward, but he wasn't looking to harvest more Spirit Fruit. He went down, taking steps three at a time, until the floor of the Upper Hall vanished above him. There were no magelights floating along the path, mostly because there was no need for them.

Felix's vision in the dark was almost perfect, both because of his high Perception stat as well as his Manasight, which could pick out the ever-present glow of Mana all around them. Moreover, the Tree glowed vibrantly in the dark, more than enough to assist even an Untempered person's descent all the way to the roots.

Felix had no intention of walking so far. The moment he rounded the first curve of the Tree, and the rough stone tunnel it had bored opened up a bit, he hopped off.

He fell like a rock.

For a long, breathless moment, Felix reveled in the drop. His stomach, long used to his flights, did not flip-flop as it once had, but it was still exhilarating to freefall. Riding lightning across the sky was delightful, but this was primal, tickling something at the back of his brain. If only for a moment, he forgot the weird looks from above, the Chanters' plans, and even the near-conjuration of a deadly, magic fist.

Only when the bottom-most floor loomed close did he bother to flare Adamant Discord. Lightning surged upward, a dozen bolts that tethered him to the Temple and slowed his momentum to nothing. Felix landed with a soft *clank*.

"Your control has truly grown," Karys said.

Felix smiled. "Thanks, man. You, too. Normally, you'd have clunked around. Finally getting used to that Body?"

A ten-foot tall suit of armor, fully mechanized and run by a confusing amount of sigaldry, stood before Felix in the luminescent dark. A helmet sat atop its gorget, shading an interior that glowed with twin pinpricks of green-gold light. "It has been a process, but the additions Harn was able to fashion have proven a great boon."

"I was wondering about that," Felix said, cocking his head to the side. The ancient Nymean man had once patched up the old armored

Body with dark iron and scraps, but now the breastplate and right arm were made of smooth, segmented plates that looked familiar. "What did he make those out of?"

"Leviathan bone, from Ahkestria."

"Huh. I thought he couldn't work with that stuff yet. It's durable enough?"

"More than sufficient. It is leagues more effective than the iron scraps I had once used, if not as good as Crescian Bronze."

"What is?"

"Indeed."

"No, really. That was a question." Felix scratched his jaw and started forward. "We can't seem to get any more Crescian Bronze, and we need more sources of metal ore that aren't simple iron or steel. The Domains have been useful to salvage from, but those aren't much better and will dry up eventually. Is the Leviathan bone better than orichalcum or mithril?"

"You would need to speak with Harn more on that." Karys retrieved a rudimentary clipboard from a satchel around his waist and flipped through a few pages. Paper was a new addition to their community, brought to them by a papermaker out of Haarwatch. "He has conducted tests on the various materials he's collected but hasn't given me a definitive list as of yet."

"Hm. Something to talk to him about later." Felix passed by his Chancellor and friend, stepping into a tall archway just beyond. "You have news on Kimaris, you said?"

Karys pivoted smoothly and followed after. "Yes. The Witch reached the Boreal Pass four weeks ago and has been engaged in...diplomatic discussion for that entire time."

Felix laughed. "You mean they're all challenging each other to a physical brawl."

"Correct. The Risi are a martial people, and apparently the people who remained in the Hoarfrost are no stranger to combat. Despite it all, these giants are those who opposed their former chieftain's goal of conquest." Karys looked at Felix, concern creasing the flames of his eyes. "The Witches of Cold Rock remember Grimmar too well. They do not want anything to do with Kimaris or her people."

"That's...unfortunate." Felix frowned, stopping just outside the glimmering silver and gold array that dominated this level of his Stronghold. His Seat and Seal. "Wait. Cold Rock is supposed to be farther north, well beyond the Boreal Pass. Kimaris said she met them in the Pass?"

"She did. That is where our story becomes more worrisome." Karys shook his head. "A Domain break is imminent, and it is located at the northern edge of the Pass."

"The Witches are concerned?"

"They are. Were the creatures within to escape, they would assuredly surge northward, toward the Risi's communities. Kimaris reasons that, with a proper push and some troops, she could quell the Domain and potentially restore her reputation."

Felix rubbed his chin. He'd sent Kimaris and a contingent of her people north in order to secure the northern border. He had modified and improved his Mirk Enclosure, and the work on the core barriers had been vastly improved, but right now, the latter only blocked the walls of Setoria. Nagast was still accessible via the Bitter Sea and the Boreal Pass into the Hoarfrost.

The Bitter Sea was acidic and rife with monstrosities, so Felix wasn't overly worried about that, but the Hoarfrost was another story. Bitterly cold and desolate, the far north was still technically passable, especially since Grimmar had relocated the vast majority of the Frost Giants south.

"How many troops would she need?" he asked.

"Not many. Kimaris claims the fewer the better, as it would prove their prowess more effectively. The Risi respect strength, after all."

"Will they agree to ally with us if we do this?"

"Doubtful. You know them well. They are a prideful people and slow to trust," Karys said.

That's true. It had taken Felix beating the snot out of her best warriors before Kimaris had deigned to ally herself with him, and that was after he'd saved them from enslavement under the Archon. She'd had her back to the wall, figuratively speaking. "If we do this right, it's possible. Or at least we could get an audience with the people at Cold Rock itself."

"That seems far more likely." Karys nodded and started scratching down notes with an oversized quill. "If we could utilize one of the Manaships to provide transit, we could get them there in a week."

Felix waved a hand, dismissive. "Not a problem. Only two are tied up making regular runs to Haarwatch right now, anyway."

"Very well. Who do you wish to send?"

A long silence met Karys' question as Felix regarded the hypnotic swirl of his Seal before him. "A Domain break, huh? Is it strong?"

"Quite. Kimaris claims it has always been a proving ground for their people, ahem, 'whetting the edge of our greatest warriors since time immemorial.'" Karys' voice was as dry as the stone dust in the corners of the room. "It does raise the question as to why they allowed such a resource to grow out of control, however."

"Because all the warriors went south, and most of them died." *To me*, Felix finished silently. He'd killed a *lot* of Frost Giants back when they were trying to crush him into paste. "No one left to prune the garden, so to speak, and now it is about to overrun the walls. Figures that Grimmar would saddle me with more problems. Annoying, even beyond the grave."

"Indeed." Karys waited, quill poised above his clipboard. Impatience rolled off his Spirit like a heat haze. "And who are you sending? The First Talon would be appropriate, I think—"

"I'm thinking I'll go. Alone."

Karys stared, his eye-flames unmoving, for perhaps ten whole seconds. Then, with a metallic sounding exhale, he tucked his clipboard back into his satchel. "I trust that you recognize that such a course is impossible, Felix."

"Why? I could take care of the whole Domain myself."

"I do not doubt your Strength. But you are needed here, Autarch."

"Gah." Felix made a face. "I hate when you use my title."

"It is only to illustrate a point, *my Lord*." Karys didn't often give Felix guff, but now he sounded almost disappointed. "You cannot abandon your Territory to chase after every threat personally."

"Sometimes it's necessary. Like with the other Unbound," Felix said.

"This is not about the other Unbound." Karys hesitated. "Correct?"

Felix sighed. "No. It's not."

"No dreams pointing to the frozen north? Nor visions of ice and snow?"

Felix rolled his eyes. "No."

"Then I would not consider it important enough that you abandon your duties to your people here. According to your own plans, we've not completed half the tasks you set for us."

Felix growled. It was true; a great many things crowded Felix's plate. He was tackling them as fast as he could, but there was only so much he could attend to himself. Felix had to rely on his friends and allies to get it all done. Still, this wasn't just because he was aching for a fight or even the need to test out his Skills. There were higher priorities.

"I need more Essence," he said, quietly. "For Pit."

Karys made a small sound, and a complicated bouquet of emotions rippled across his Spirit. "I see."

Felix didn't need to explain to his Chancellor further. There had been a great many discussions on the topic since the battle.

"Has he shown any further ability to use your Sovereign of Flesh?" Karys asked.

Felix and Pit gained the ability to utilize each other's Skills, which was how Pit had been able to weave Felix's last few Pillars. It was harder than it seemed at first blush, of course. Reliably accessing each other's Skills had turned out to be a crapshoot, at best.

"Only a little." Felix took a long, steadying breath. "But conducting more experiments has been hampered by the fact that I don't have enough Essence to spare. Everything I consume is only able to keep my tank topped off."

"Your Hunger is still so greedy? Can it not sense Pit's situation?"

Felix snorted. "I don't know how smart that thing is. It wants to eat, and it wants me to keep being around to *ensure* that it eats. That's it, far as I can tell."

"So your plan is to consume an entire Domain and use the excess to fuel Pit's recovery?"

"That's the main goal, yeah. But improving relations with our friends to the north is high on the list, too."

Karys' hands fell to his sides, defeated. "I…suppose that is a valuable task that only you can accomplish. I shall arrange the Manaship to fly out in the morning."

"Tonight," Felix corrected. "No point in waiting."

"Very well."

"But first, we need to take care of a couple things I've been putting off," Felix said and started walking across the glimmering lines of his Seat and Seal.

"Such as?"

"Upgrades."

CHAPTER SEVEN

The vast chamber of his Seat and Seal was built like a natural cathedral. A vault of stone rose above them, filling the air with a thick shadow offset by the aurum and argent of the sigaldry below. Seven archways opened up into further chambers just beyond, but only one was lit up.

That led to his Heart of Darkness, the hub for his Shadowgates, while the others were blocked off; the array somehow prevented Felix from even approaching them. The Seat and Seal itself was a series of arrays so complex that they had become something akin to a fractal design. It was insanely elaborate, far more so than even a Mana engine. The only place he'd seen similar amounts of complexity was in the tomb beneath Ahkestria, where a Primordial had been chained up.

Nothing like that here, though. They had checked. Thoroughly. Felix glanced at his wrists. *No chains on me or Pit, either.*

The formation flashed with every step, releasing a series of musical chords as much as light. The looping swirls of gold and silver filled the entirety of the vast chamber, which was many times larger than the Upper Hall. Circles upon circles crossed the black stone floor, interweaving with sigils in tightly packed lines. Interspersed among them were larger glyphs, combinations of multiple sigils in one, that acted as something like focal points for the formation.

Felix knew that much, at least, even if he hadn't much clue otherwise. According to everyone who had seen it, the formation was far more complex than the ones in other Territories, but Felix knew that wasn't true. He had witnessed the Seat and Seal of the Leviathan Depths as well, located beneath Ahkestria, and it had been just as labyrinthine, if not quite so large.

Karys said that the Seals provided to Territorial Lords under the Hierocracy seemed to be intentionally limited, perhaps in an effort to control the power being parceled out. Vess' father, for instance, had a Seat and Seal that were far less complex than Felix's, though Pax'Vrell commanded a Territory larger than Nagast. Considering the System seemed to be predicated upon choice and autonomy, it seemed likely the tyrannical religious mega-state would want to curtail it. No good would come of an empowered, free-thinking vassal.

Felix regarded his wrists again, watching the small scales flex with the motion of his tendons. He wore no chains, but others did. The cudgel others fashioned out of Authority made that clear.

When he'd first gained Authority, it had very little impact on Felix's situation. As he continued on and faced more and more enemies and scenarios where his Authority was required, Felix had discovered that it had a certain potency to it which seemed to increase the power at his disposal. Not in any combat sense, but in access and influence over various System-based constructs. That, and being the Inheritor of the ancient Nymean sword at his waist had proven helpful in a myriad of ways.

It hadn't been enough, however, to stop the High Guard from challenging him for his Territory. He had puzzled at how that could be, but the only solution seemed to be that the High Guard had somehow possessed *more* Authority than Felix did. Considering he controlled two Territories now, that was no mean feat. Zara claimed it to be the Hierophant's work, though she hadn't been able to say how.

Either way, the solution was simple. Gain more Authority, so he couldn't be challenged like that again.

There were options. Felix could invade his neighbors, challenge their leaders, and claim their Seat and Seal for himself. He even had a Quest for it.

The Path of Empire!
Many are the benefits of empire, and many are their enemies. Secure a total of 4 Territories under your banner and gain a reward worthy of the ancient emperors. Beware, for the higher you climb, the greater the winds that will attempt to force you from the Golden Path. Unification may

be your destiny, but violence is your birthright. Gird yourself, Felix Nevarre!
2 of 4 Territories Secured
Reward: XP, Title(s), Advanced Authority, Varies

Aside from the thought making him deeply uncomfortable, it had a host of other problems. Logistics was a big one, moving troops and food and other such supplies. Most other Territorial Lords had claims on their land that were centuries old, and while they couldn't keep large standing armies, they still had access to Hierocratic forces.

The Paladins were the largest of the three orders, with the Inquisitors a close second, and both had branches in every Territory between Nagast and the eastern jungles. Places like the Ghreldan Hills, which had mostly retained their own political and System power, were few and far between. The Hierocracy had dominated a large swath of the Continent. If he moved into any other Territory, Felix would find it an uphill battle to even get within eyesight of the Lord.

His other option was diplomacy. That was why Felix had sent Kimaris north in the first place.

The Hierocracy had not returned to Nagast, not since the Battle of Sunrise Lake, and that fact made Felix nervous every single day. When his people had arrived in Setoria, the remains of the Hierocratic forces had long since fled, leaving behind a stunned populace. Felix had his people offer to allow people to enter Nagast before he closed it off, or to leave if they wished. Many chose the latter and set off across the cold plains beyond.

Felix couldn't blame them.

The barrier they had developed was strong—like, *really* strong—but it wasn't impervious. The concerted effort of several Grandmasters could break it, according to Zara. Their only advantage was how hard it was to reach Grandmaster in the first place. Add in the difficulty of convincing a number of them to act in concert beneath some other command, and it was unlikely the walls would fall.

Still, Felix expected an attack at any moment. They had dispatched valuable combatants against him, and none of them returned. He still held hundreds of the rank and file in Haarwatch, months later. Zara had been sure the retaliation would be swift and sure, but her confidence waned with every passing day.

That mixture of anxiety and an urge to advance had driven Felix into a frenzy of preparation.

"You've decided?" Karys asked from behind, disturbing Felix from his spiraling thoughts. As Chancellor of Nagast, he too strode over the sigaldry of Felix's Seat and Seal without issue.

"I think so, yeah." Felix walked to the center of the formation, and mentally commanded a section of the floor to rise. A glyph depicting a glowing, burning eye dominated the space there, and from the pupil, a hexagonal pillar lifted soundlessly. Above it, a holographic display of his Stronghold flickered into view. "Just doing a final check."

His Authority menus appeared next to his 3D display of Elderthrone, listing all the benefits and features of his home.

The Song of Stronghold!

General Overview

Name: Elderthrone
Stronghold Defensive Strength: 50%
Stronghold Offensive Strength: 52%
Chancellor: Karys Taiv
Master of Glyph: Atar V'as
Master of Forge: Harn Kastos
Master of Treasury: Karys Taiv
Master of Alchemy: Felix Nevarre

Map

Improvements

Fortifications

- **Bulwark - Defensive Fortification, Tier IV**

Effect: +0.05% Defensive Strength Per Unit Installed

- **Square Tower - Defensive Fortification, Tier IV**

Effect: +0.08% Defensive Strength Per Unit Installed
Limit: 1 Tower Unit Per Every 2 Bulwark Units

Living Spaces

- **117 Undesignated Rooms In Stronghold**
- **994 Stone Shaped Dwellings, Tier III**
- **1142 Green Shaped Homes, Tier III**
- **1 Ice Shaped Hall, Tier III**
- **10 Ice Shaped Lodges, Tier III**
- **2 Barracks, Tier IV**

Professional Spaces

- **Forge, Tier IV**
- **Alchemy Lab, Tier VI**
- **Glyphworks, Tier IV**
- **Storage Facility, Tier IV**

Garden, Tier III

- **Flora - Capacity 934/1000**
- **Fauna - Capacity 368/1000**

Spirit Tree - *Atlantes Anima* - Spirit Trees are a rare and powerful organism imbued with elemental Mana dependent on their growth cycle. Due to your strong connection and the circumstances of its origin, the Spirit Tree has taken on a measure of Unbound nature. The Atlantes Anima is attuned to all and none.

- **Spirit Fruit Production: 1/week**
- **Auras: Spirit Cleanse, Swell the Green Wilds**

His little home base had grown by leaps and bounds. Aside from the obvious growth of his citizenry and the walls surrounding them all, Elderthrone had advanced every single Crafting Hall and pushed both its defensive and offensive strength over fifty percent. The two were linked, naturally, with the Glyphworks and Forge making a slew of weapons and armor that enhanced the Legion.

Alister, aside from being named Minor Nobility Liason—a title Felix had made up so he didn't have to talk to all those people—was busy advancing his siege weaponry. His Stinger was responsible for a significant portion of their offensive capabilities, and one of the few upgrades Felix had added in months ago helped the improvements along.

During his battles under the waves, he'd completed an old Quest called The Proving. It had required him to bring five spells to Adept Tier, and upon completing it, Felix had gained a few benefits.

Title: Adept Magus (Rare)
You have shown you can rise above your peers, becoming a true force upon the Continent. Power is yours. Wield it well.
+Increased Authority

...Rewards Increased Due to Advancing 2 Spells of Legendary Rarity
...Rewards Increased Due to Advancing 1 Spell of Transcendent Rarity
Accessing Options...

Please See Your Stronghold Seal To Receive Rewards!

While he'd earned some nebulous increase to his Authority, the System hadn't given him anything else until he'd returned to his Stronghold. Once he had, it had given Felix an option to take a personal benefit or to expend it on his Glyphworks. He chose the latter, naturally. The personal benefit would have granted him a new Skill, but Felix had plenty—too many, some might say—and the means by which he could get more.

On the other hand, the benefit to his Glyphworks had increased the learning rate of all discovered arrays by 25%. That was huge, something Atar and Alister had been overjoyed to see. The aptitude of their apprentices increased seemingly overnight, which had cascaded into more completed crafting Quests and an advancement for the Glyphworks as a whole.

The only other real upgrade to the Stronghold had nothing to do with Felix. The Atlantes Anima simply reached a point in its growth cycle where it unlocked a second Aura. Those, in addition to the Spirit Fruits, had become major benefits for their community.

The Spirit Fruits were exactly what they sounded like, giant fruits that grew on the branches far above. Each one was a marvel, containing immense power that could be used in a variety of ways. Exploring those varieties had helped Felix push his Alchemical Laboratory beyond the other Crafting Halls, all the way to Tier VI. That opened up even greater benefits to production and discovery.

Mostly, the Spirit Fruits were used to create Universal Spirit Draughts that he could align with any Mana type they had access to; meaning it was useful and potent enough to Temper anyone in Elderthrone, no matter their Tier. That reason, coupled with a steady stream of Domain delving and training, was why they boasted so many Apprentice and Journeyman-Tier combatants now.

The Auras were another thing entirely—they were emitted from the Tree itself, a passive effect that touched everyone beneath its immense canopy. The first, Spirit Cleanse, did something similar to Felix's Unite the Lost: it kept everyone's Spirit empty of unwanted foreign influences. That included Marks placed by those who would wish to control or track others.

The second, Swell the Green Wilds, influenced nature rather than people. Crops, herbs, fish, birds, anything that grew or flourished in the wilderness was given a boost to their heartiness and fecundity. This meant their food stores had grown tremendously, which helped support their growing population, and the Stronghold's Garden had flourished as well. It also meant the local pests had also exploded in number, forcing Karys to offer up extermination Quests with frightening regularity.

Small price to pay for the food, I guess. Felix grimaced. *Then again, if I never see that many Venomous Squirrels again, I'll die happy.*

"Felix?" Karys prompted.

He realized he'd been staring at his Authority menus for a while. Stalling. "Sorry. Been putting this off so long that I'm still nervous about making my choice."

Karys hummed something that sounded calming. "Understandable. It is not often one earns a Title that offers a benefit of your choosing for your Stronghold. Even in my time, such a thing was rare."

Felix rolled his shoulders. Months prior, he'd earned the Challenger's Crown I Title during the course of his struggles. It allowed him to do exactly as Karys suggested: a Tier upgrade for a single feature of his "primary Stronghold." The trouble was, the upgrade could be applied to just about anything within Elderthrone. Felix had waffled on choosing what he wanted to upgrade, first thinking about the Alchemical Laboratory or the Storage Facility…but the Crafting Halls had Quests that allowed them to advance, and the Storage Facility would only get bigger as the Stronghold itself ranked up. He'd be allowed to add more Beacons around, which was a useful thing, but was it useful enough to spend such a reward on?

"I'm choosing the Heart of Darkness," he said, finally.

Karys' soft humming stopped. "Truly? I—What is the benefit you seek to gain? They still cannot operate without their pairs, and many are still down. With the Shadowgates as they are—"

"I doubt this peace will last much longer, Karys. I wish it would, but the way everyone is talking, and everything that's already happened… war is coming. Even if we never fight the Hierocracy again, the Chanters say the Ruin will be here. Soon." Felix swallowed, fighting off the flash of panic that overcame him. That was what happened whenever he thought of the Ruin. "We need to be ready."

All of the issues inherent in traveling around with an army without modern roads or a ton of vehicles were solved by his Shadowgates. Logistics was far easier to manage when he could move troops across ten thousand miles in a couple hours. The issue at hand, however, was that most of his Shadowgates were inactive.

Like Karys had said, each portal operated as a pair, one here in his Heart of Darkness and one out there, at the far flung destination. They were unique artifacts, each one built together in some fashion none of them had reproduced. The sigaldry on their surface had stymied all of them, let alone the deeper mysteries contained within. He had no way of knowing what an upgrade to Heart of Darkness would achieve, but its potential was huge compared to making his Forge a little bit better.

Tier Upgrade!
You Have Selected Your Heart Of Darkness!
Are You Sure?
Y/N

Yes.

A ripple of magic expanded outward, sweeping through his Seat and Seal before splashing against the dark stone walls around them. Music followed it, a combination of swelling Harmony and hissing Dissonance, working together in a way that added an incredible depth to the sound. Light and sound coalesced in the sigaldry beneath Felix's feet, racing off in a single direction–directly toward one of the six remaining dark chambers, where it vanished utterly.

Greetings Autarch.
The Third Chamber Is Available.
Do You Wish To Activate?

Yes.

All at once, the dark archway filled with a cascade of molten light. Sigaldry flashed, inscribed patterns filling with the power of his Seat and Seal and serving to further illuminate the chamber beyond. Felix traded a glance with Karys, and they both hastened across the room. Upon entering the Third Chamber, Felix blinked, unsure how to react.

Before them, the chamber extended approximately sixty feet square, with about fifty of it dominated by a sigaldry-lined depression. That was it. Within the depression was an expanse of almost preternaturally still water. It gleamed in the light, kicking back reflections like a deeper, more vibrant version of liquid mercury.

"Is that a swimming pool?" he asked. It certainly looked like one. "No, that's stupid, right? Why would the upgrade provide a swimming pool?"

"No," whispered the gentle giant. His green-gold eyes of flame were bigger than Felix often saw them. "No, this is a Halcyon Hall. And that —" he said, pointing to the water. "Is a piece of the Luminous Void."

CHAPTER EIGHT

"One, what the hell is a Halcyon Hall and B, what is the Luminous Void?" Karys didn't answer immediately, and Felix looked away from the metallic liquid to find his Chancellor gone. "I don't like that he's so quiet now," he muttered to himself. "Karys? Where'd you go?"

"In the Heart of Darkness, my Lord!"

Felix glanced once more at the weird pool before turning around and exiting the Third Chamber. Luckily, it was adjacent to the Second Chamber, arranged around the edge of his Seat and Seal as they were, and it took only a dozen wide steps to make it there. Felix's Heart of Darkness spread out before him, another circular room filled with glowing sigaldry, but mostly dominated by nine huge constructions of incredible artistry. Shadowgates.

Karys was standing behind an inactive one, pointing at the floor. "Look at this!"

He did, noting the swirling, almost knotted array that clustered against the chamber's stone walls. They climbed the dressed stone until about eye level, where they simply stopped. "These are new."

"They are. I imagine they formed right after the upgrade." Karys pointed further down, where nine other lines intersected with the wall in the exact same way. "They're extending from the Shadowgates."

Felix flared his Manasight, tracing the lines of sigaldry at the point where they vanished…and found that they extended *through* the wall itself. His Manasight couldn't penetrate too deeply, thanks to the construction of the Temple, but the array wasn't just anchoring itself in the stone. "It's…going into the Third Chamber?"

"It must be. The Halcyon Halls…they were precursors to the Shadowgates. This sigaldry is linking the Heart of Darkness, the hub itself, to the Third Chamber."

"Precursors? So they do the same thing?"

Karys' shoulders hitched, halfway between a shrug and a flinch. "I am…unsure. I know they were used by the Nym of old for a ritual, but the details were never explained to me. Or perhaps they were and…"

Felix didn't press him. Karys had a number of holes in his memories, thanks to his long sleep, and while he'd been making some progress, Felix doubted it would be fixed any time soon. "A ritual. To do what?"

"To deepen one's connection with one's Territory, I believe."

Felix frowned and walked back to the Third Chamber. The limpid silver pool remained undisturbed. "Let's check. Voracious Eye."

Name: Pool of the Halcyon Oath
Type: Artifact
Lore: Constructed in Ages past, the Pools of the Halcyon Oath were designed to establish a deeper harmony within a Territory. Cast yourself into the Luminous Void and find yourself anew.

"That's…more than a little vague," Felix said after sharing the details with Karys. "But it supports your recollections."

Karys let out a pleased hum. "As validating as that may be, I do share your concerns on the wording of the lore entry. A 'deeper harmony within a Territory' suggests a greater connection with your Authority, and perhaps that is all it means…but the last line. 'Find yourself anew.'" Karys shifted, clearly uneasy. "I find it ominous, Felix."

"Hm. So, I think I have a reason why it's called a Halcyon Hall," Felix said. Karys nodded. "Right. What's the Luminous Void, then?"

"It is an ancient name for a realm of confluence."

"Like the Ethereal Realm?"

"Of a sort. We…the magi had developed a path. A way through the world. This is what the Shadowgates were derived from, where their construction was first inspired. The manipulation and development of these Pools allowed us to unite a vast portion of the Continent."

Felix crouched, inspecting the sigaldry around the rim of the pool—from a safe distance. If the silvery water was a portal or something into the Ethereal Realm, he wanted to stay far away from it. That place had a deadlier and more appropriate name: Desolation. Felix had seen it, or an entrance into it, when he'd traversed the true Void. It had appeared to be a white hole, destroying all that came near even as it spat other things out. Submerging himself into energy like that felt close to suicide.

"A place of confluence...does that mean it combines the Void and Desolation together?" he asked.

"That is my understanding, yes." Karys held up a hand. "If you wish to ask me 'how,' need I remind you that I was but a warrior within my people's empire. Even if my memories were not riddled with holes, this was beyond my purview."

"Fair," Felix said. "Do you know if they used this a lot? Is it safe?"

"To my knowledge, the use of a Halcyon Hall was for Territorial Lords and their most trusted vassals. The creation of the Shadowgate network made it all but unnecessary, so it fell out of favor well before I was born." Karys stepped a few inches closer to the pool, arching his metal neck to stare into its depths. "As for safety...if it were truly safe, I imagine they would not have developed another method."

Felix walked a bit closer, feeling a little like he was approaching the edge of a very tall building. For a guy who had zoomed about in the sky not fifteen minutes prior, it was decidedly strange to feel a powerful surge of vertigo. Felix blinked, but he did not waver. So close, the metallic-looking water seemed both mirror-flat and utterly bottomless, while the sigaldry around its border sparked and shimmered with a gathering purple vapor. Without further warning, a large cloud of purple Mana jumped outward and formed into a small, humanoid creature. Felix stumbled back, a dozen different Skills singing within his chest.

"Greetings, my Lord," it said, bowing directly to Felix. It wore robes draped oddly around its head and shoulders, leaving its too-long torso tightly bound by thick belts. Features that were a mix of a weasel and a Human child regarded him with a deeply serious expression. "You approach the Pool of the Halcyon Oath. To do so is to risk your very life."

Holy shit. Felix closed his open mouth and took in the situation, from the faintly luminous outline of the little guy before him to the continued pulsing of the sigaldry at the pool's edge. "You're a Geist." Relying on a hunch, Felix ran his hand through the space where the Geist stood and found nothing but air. "And an illusion to boot."

The illusory Geist did not react to Felix's hand, but it did straighten. It carried none of the awareness that Paxus had, down in the depths of

Khasma. "The Seat and Seal you bear have allowed you access to the Pool, but to enter before one is ready is to face a certain and devastating death."

"A warning," Karys said. "And a clear one at that. Perhaps leaving is a wise course, my Lord."

"Damn it." Felix shoved a hard breath through his nose. "Kinda shit that I wasted my upgrade on this."

Before Felix could turn away though, the Geist dropped to a single knee. "As Inheritor, you are allowed more detailed information. Please. Ask away."

Felix froze, gaze flicking to Karys' surprised flames. The big man shrugged, helplessly. "What? Ask…? Uh, who are you?"

The Geist's eyes had looked dead before, fixed on a point that Felix couldn't see—now they shifted, and something unspooled within them. It drove a hard shiver down Felix's spine, like watching a snake smile at a joke. "I am knowledge."

"Are you a real Spirit, bonded to this room or something?"

"No. I am a repository of knowledge left by my creators, designed to aid the master of his Temple. How may I be of service?"

Felix frowned. That weird look had almost convinced him it was a real Spirit like Paxus, but maybe it was just a complicated magic AI. "You're composed of Memories," he guessed. The Geist inclined its head in agreement. "What do I call you?" It stared at him, eyes betraying not a single flicker of awareness. "I'm not gonna just call you 'Geist' all the time. I'll call you Knowledge, then. Cool?"

The illusion had no response other than to stand up.

"Right. So! You're an aide. Why am I not allowed to access the Pool of Halcyon Oaths?"

"It is a death sentence to those without the proper preparations," Knowledge said.

"Can you tell me the preparations required?" Felix asked.

"I can. To embrace the pool, one must have woven all nine Pillars, crossed the Third Threshold, and have begun the process of core manifestation."

Felix blinked. He met two of those requirements right off the bat. He'd even crossed the Third Threshold like five months ago. "Pretty sure I'm good, aside from the last one. What's a 'core manifestation?'"

Knowledge remained silent.

"Cool, cool, cool. Can't have people just explain things to me; that'd be too easy," Felix muttered. "Karys? Have you heard of it?"

"I—" Karys paused, and an uptempo melody sprang from his Spirit. "I have not, but its mention has touched upon one of the holes in my memory."

"That's usually not a good thing."

"No, not usually, but this one is strangely clean. As if things had been cut from me…" Karys looked up, his eye-fires gleaming despite the magelights around them. "I cannot know what that might mean, but core manifestation is a natural part of our progression into the higher realms of power."

"Grandmaster stuff?" Felix asked. He chewed at his lip in thought. Felix had taken on a couple Grandmasters at that point, and thanks to clever thinking and the actions of his friends, he'd emerged alive. Not unscathed, but alive.

"It is unclear. I—" Karys' eye-fires burned larger than before. "Felix."

"What?" He looked up to find Karys pointing at Knowledge with a long, black-bone finger. The illusory Geist was staring at Felix with a sudden, upsetting amount of interest. "Oh. That's creepy."

"You are…resonating with this chamber. Might I delve into your Aspects and determine whether you are fit to attempt the Pool?"

"Uh, you think that's a good idea?" Felix asked Karys.

"I cannot sense any malevolence from this amalgamation, but it is a…marvel I was unaware we Nym had developed. Were I in your shoes, no, I would not submit to a delving." The golden giant hesitated, before scratching his golden helmet. "However, you…to err on the side of caution is not your way."

A sharp laugh escaped Felix's mouth. "Right. Okay, Knowledge." Felix had a guess at what core manifestation meant…and he wanted to know if he was right. "Take a whack at it."

"Hold still, my Lord." Knowledge lifted a diminutive hand, and a smoky wreath of Mana sprouted around Felix's head, chest, and legs all at once. "This will only take half a glass."

"Wait, what—?" Felix asked, right as all three smoky circles cinched shut. Silence fell, darkness swarmed, and the world dropped out from beneath him.

CHAPTER NINE

To Felix, it felt like he was diving into his core space. The only difference: he was not in control.

He was suffocated in darkness and a spiraling, fluting concerto. A touch not his own swept over his channels, tracing out every inch of the pathways in his arms, legs, torso, and head. It was a ticklish whisper that burned as it moved, a riot of pain following in its wake. The agony took root in his Body before it speared outward toward his Mind and Spirit, too.

Felix tumbled, his sense of self smothered. It wasn't until a net of searing flame coursed across his chest that he realized they had entered his core space proper. He wanted to scream, but couldn't even take a breath, his throat clogged and lungs plugged up. He saw nothing, but felt the sharp ends of his Divine Tree immolate…before it all stopped.

The magic tangled, the blaze caught within the skeletal branches of his Tree, snagged by the crystalline lattice on the exterior and held fast. The magic surged, again and again. The pain redoubled, but it could not free itself, could barely move at all. Felix could see nothing. Hear nothing. Yet the yawning grasp of a dark blacker than shadow was felt, an eager maw hunting for its meal, as the abyss below reached up and consumed the magic entirely.

Felix landed in a crouch as he came back to himself, senses returned just in time to witness the wreaths of smoke vanish from around his body. The tiled flooring was cold and his hands were feverish, as if he'd placed them within a bonfire not seconds before. Felix pushed to his feet and glared at the illusory Geist.

Knowledge stood, hands at its side, his expression betraying nothing more than a faint…discomfort.

"Felix! Felix, you're back!" Karys gently grasped Felix's shoulders. The armored Nym all but lifted him into a bear hug so tight, Felix felt his bones creak. "Are you hale?"

"I–I'm fine, man. I'm fine." Felix slipped from Karys' grasp, but found his head was aching hard. "What—Knowledge. What did you do to me?"

"I performed a delving." It folded its hands before its long belly. "Your core space and Aspects were contentious. The delving took longer than expected."

Felix looked at Karys. "How long?"

"You've been entombed in that thing's spell for six glasses."

Six hours. Felix couldn't believe it—the experience had lasted all of a few minutes. "Why?"

Knowledge was silent.

Felix snorted, annoyed that he'd been expecting anything else. "Karys? What's been happening in the time I've been under?"

"Nothing much of note, though I did have to fend off Zara's inquiries. Oh, and the Manaship is prepared for travel to the north, as you requested."

"Zara was here?"

"She approached the Inner Sanctum, but I told her you were contemplating a matter of state, and she backed off." Karys held up an object in his thick, golden metal hand. "She left you this."

It was a letter, sealed with blue-green wax and stamped with a symbol of waves. Or perhaps flames. Felix took it. "Feels light. Did she say why she needed me?"

"You missed another meeting with the Chanters."

"Ah. That." Felix tucked the letter into his jacket.

"Yes. You have been avoiding them a great deal, Felix. Zara is a stalwart ally and a powerful asset. If you do not mind me asking, why are you not meeting with them?"

Felix waved away the question. "Not important. I'll go see her after this and apologize."

"Felix—"

"Knowledge," he said, pointedly ignoring Karys' chastising tone. "That little delving hurt a lot. Am I worthy?"

"My delving was incomplete, due to interference within your core space. There is an anomaly at the base of your—"

"I'm aware." Felix gritted his teeth. "So, you're saying I still can't use this thing?"

"You…" Knowledge's words were dragged out in a strange way. Like a chord played too long. "...may."

"Oh shit, really? Does that mean I have this core manifestation thing?" Felix asked.

"Unclear. There is much about you that I cannot quantify properly. Perhaps with time, a lack of interference, and a deeper delving, that would be possible."

Felix narrowed his eyes, and his vision tinged the slightest bit blue and red. If his glowing eyes shocked the weird illusion, it gave no evidence. "So I can use it but, what? I *might* die?"

"Correct. Based upon my assessment, if you choose to embrace the Pool of Halcyon Oaths, there is a 90% chance of your survival."

"That's…not bad?" Felix said, looking to Karys. "90% is an A- back home."

"A what? Felix, if there was only a 1% chance of your death, I would caution you against attempting this thing." Karys' Spirit thrummed with worry and something else. Something muffled. "You would put all of your Territory at risk for this."

Anger. He's mad at me. Felix swallowed, vaguely uncomfortable. Karys was such a gentle, kind soul that hearing anger, however hidden, was like missing a step when climbing a set of stairs. The man was trying to hide it, but Felix could read its rapid, heated tattoo just beneath his Spirit. Before either of them could speak, Knowledge piped up again.

"As a Territorial Lord, you would, of course, have some protection from the process. With that, your chances of survival rise to 95.2%."

Felix chewed at his lip, thinking it over. "And the benefits? What does 'embracing the pool' get me?"

Knowledge lifted his little, furry chin. "To embrace the Pool of Halcyon Oaths is to embrace the totality of your Territory, deepening your connection to your people, the land, and the Grand Harmony that presides over all."

"That was not truly an answer," Karys pointed out. "Deepens connections. Is there a material benefit, or is it simply one of Harmonics?"

Knowledge looked at Karys, and Felix realized it was the first time. The little illusion had so far only ever looked directly at Felix and never with such distaste. "Chancellor Karys Taiv. Former Eidolon Exult. Abdicator of guardianship of the Caryatid Anima. You do not have the Authority to ask such things."

Felix didn't need to listen to Karys' Spirit to know those words had cut at him. "Knowledge. Answer whatever questions Karys has for you. He's to be given the same information you would give to me."

The weird Memory ghost snapped its attention back on the Autarch, returning to its neutral expression. "As you wish, Inheritor."

"Answer the question."

Knowledge spread its hands, but the movement was odd, as if it were a marionette operated by an arthritic old man. "The answer is both and neither. One takes from the Pool precisely what one earns."

"Earns?"

"The Pool is a crucible, meant to forge the worthy with the raw potency of Creation. If one survives the challenge, command of one's Territory will grow. How much is determined by the individual."

"Is this what the Shadowgates were based upon?" Felix asked.

Knowledge paused, as if recollecting something. It was only a moment, then it continued to speak. "The Shadowgates were developed as replacements for the benefits of the Pool of Halcyon Oaths. They are lesser artifacts, a work-around to avoid the risks posed by the Pool."

"You were right. They're connected," Felix said to Karys.

"Ah. That is good to know." The golden giant straightened up. "And the allusion to a crucible and earning one's rewards…that seems to be reflected in the lore entry. Finding oneself anew."

"Yeah." Felix had done that before, during his Omen Path, and wasn't keen on replicating the experience. "So, either risk my life to gain a nebulous benefit or play it safe and never know what's inside. Those are my choices."

"So it would seem."

A slow chirrup interrupted Felix's circling thoughts. Pit, still within his Spirit, gave a sleepy yawn. "What is going on? Why are you afraid?"

"Did that wake you up?" Felix frowned. "I'm contemplating a bath."

"Terrifying," Pit shot back, dry as a raspy croak.

Felix sent a bundle of sense images and his recent Memories. It was a technique they'd been getting better at as their bond deepened. Pit had always been good at it, but Felix had only recently gotten better than garbage at the technique. He left out the painful delving experience. No one should have to go through something like that.

Pit sucked in a sharp breath, sleepiness banished beneath a surge of excitement and worry. "We're doing it, right?"

"It's dangerous."

"But rewarding?"

"Probably. Definitely, if this guy is to be believed."

"Let me out."

"You—are you sure?"

"Don't baby me," Pit said sternly. "I can walk just fine."

With a flash of light, their Convergence ended, and Pit stood beside Felix and Karys in all his glory. He was the size of a sleek racehorse, albeit one that looked to be the merged offspring of a raven and a fox. A large, bushy tail lashed behind him, and four heavy paws clenched at the stone tiles. A birdlike head topped with tufted, feathery ears and two bright, golden eyes regarded the pool before them.

Felix tried and failed to avoid looking at the stumps on his friend's back. His huge, beautiful wings were gone. The stumps were no longer bleeding, but the bone and muscle that gathered at Pit's back were exposed to the air—a gruesome wound frozen in stasis. A great deal of healing from Isla had stopped the damage the damned High Guard had caused, but recovery was slow, thanks to some godawful quality to the attack. Impossible, according to Isla, though she at least had the mercy to say that when she thought Felix wasn't in earshot.

Felix intended to prove her wrong.

Either way, agonizing over this issue wasn't solving his numerous *other* problems. Kimaris still needed assistance, Zara needed to be spoken with, the alchemy apprentices needed to be checked on…the list never stopped.

Pit stepped forward, pushing his face close to the edge of the pool. "Ghost. What is the best thing we can get out of this?"

Knowledge looked to Felix but said nothing. Felix rolled his eyes. "Answer Pit's questions as if they were coming from me."

"As you wish, Inheritor." It turned to Pit fully. "The greatest boon offered by the Pool of Halcyon Oaths is a greater freedom of movement within one's Territory."

"Like the Shadowgates?" Pit asked.

"It is a similar process."

Pit's ears perked up, and an eager joy rolled from his Spirit. "That sounds useful."

"That sounds like teleporting," Felix said. "Or something close enough. That'd be huge. If I had that, how hard would it be to reach the edge of my Territory from here?"

"If you received the deepest level of connection, such a journey would take mere instants."

Hot damn. Felix looked to Karys, unable to help his Spirit reverberating with Pit's excitement.

The old man was already shaking his head. "I am familiar with that look, Felix. Please do not kill yourself in there."

"You know me." Felix stepped closer, fighting off the vertigo that assaulted him again. "How do we do this, Knowledge?"

The Memory construct waved a hand. A section of sigaldry around the pool faded, and Felix's vertigo rapidly diminished but, curiously, did not vanish entirely.

"That is an effect of the pool itself, Inheritor. Step carefully."

Felix shot the construct a glance, but it seemed engrossed in the pool itself. "Pit. You're sure you want to come?"

The tenku snorted and tossed his horse-sized head. "Are you sure you could survive without me?"

Felix grinned. "C'mon, then." His Companion vanished in a flash of light, settling as a solid weight within Felix's Spirit. "Karys, on the off chance this takes a while, make sure Aenea checks on the apprentices' graduation projects. She'll have to grade them herself."

"Very well, my Lord." Karys winced but stepped closer to the pool anyway, enough to lean down to Felix's side. "If you perish here, recall that more than just your life is at stake."

That sobered him, and his confident smile was hard to maintain. "Right. But with this, we could protect the Territory even better. Trust me, Karys." Felix patted his golden pauldron, scales ringing against the metal. "I'm hard to kill."

The first step into the pool was the worst. Dizziness assaulted Felix, almost catapulting him face-first into the goop—but he held fast. He had taken off his boots and gauntlets, even his Garment, at Knowledge's direction. Same with his weapons and Veiling Amulet. No items beyond himself—and Pit—could enter. The liquid felt like nothing when he finally plunged his clawed foot onto a shallow step, and only when his second foot sank deeper did he feel a deep, bone-aching chill. His third step was into nothing, surprising Felix for an instant, before he began to tread the thick water.

"What now?" Felix asked.

Knowledge pointed. Straight down. "You must submerge. Embrace the pool, Inheritor."

Felix could already feel the liquid pull at him. Reflections cast up against his face and shoulders, the placid surface still undisturbed, despite his frantic kicking below. It was a challenge to remain above the surface, despite his Strength. "Hoo boy. Man, does this feel like I jumped the gun a bit. How deep is this pool?"

"As deep as necessary."

"Encouraging." Felix's shoulders went deeper, and Pit trilled in concern. "Here's hoping I get out, yeah?"

"As a Lord, you have a vastly better chance of emerging from this challenge," Knowledge said.

"You said that. My Authority gives me a shield."

"No. Because, to become a Lord within a Nymean Territory, one must be a Grandmaster already, if not a Paragon. The delving was interrupted, but it seems your stats are up to the task, too. That advancement will form the primary bulk of your buffer. Approximately 88% of it."

"He's not a Grandmaster!" Karys shouted. "Pull him free!"

"Oh," Felix said as the liquid rose up over his neck. His jaw. He couldn't move. "Oh, shit."

The pool swallowed him whole.

There was light below the surface.

Silver-chased and fluttering, a pond's reflection on a sunny day, it wrapped around Felix like a blanket. The pool was deep, way too deep, and despite his Perception and Manasight, he could not perceive the bottom. There was only the silver light.

A current wrapped around him, surging downward at a sudden, incredible speed. Felix yelped, bubbles escaping his throat before he could help himself. The liquid tried to press inward, through his lips and teeth, but he held it off.

Sunken Ward!

Within him, the Skill thrummed to life…but it failed before it ever left his core.

I can't use my Skills either, even in here, Pit added with a worried squawk.

A sudden roar filled their ears, a familiar one. It was the sound of a waterfall, except it was so colossal that it consumed every direction Felix looked. The current pulled him along, thrusting the two of them ever deeper, and no matter how he kicked against it, Felix could not escape. So he made a choice.

In it to win it, Pit.

He dove down, swimming with the riptide. His progress flashed by, faster and faster as he went. The roar increased sharply in volume, until it was sight and sound and texture, until he passed through a door the size and shape of the horizon itself.

A cascade of silver water fell from the other side of that threshold, becoming an incomprehensibly vast river that carried him relentlessly forward. Beyond it spread a world of floating mountains, blasted plains, and a sky as dark as a moonless night. There were no stars, only a single moon upon the black. A moon the same argent tone as the pool itself.

Felix knew this place. He feared it.

Felix. This is where the gods saw you.

He remembered that meeting, and others, all too well. The gods were nothing to trifle with, though he'd managed to evade the bulk of their wrath time and again. As the river carried him forward, Felix felt a terror welling inside him he couldn't quell. He knew that moon, remembered it with preternatural perfection, and he was hurtling toward it faster than he'd ever flown with Adamant Discord.

Felix! That's Siva's moon!

The celestial body was ten times the size it would be on a normal night, filling the sky until he could make out a vast collection of details on its surface. Chains of blood and golden light crisscrossed its surface, sunk into craters and wrapped around the curves of its strange form.

No, he realized. *That's not a moon.*

They fell closer, carried still by that powerful current, until he could make out the details that had seemed so incongruous with a true moon. Ridges and valleys, rounded shapes that resembled limbs and wings. How could he have not seen the wings? There were thousands of them, all different in size and shape, yet none of them moved. The golden chains held them fast, bound with hooks and barbs, guaranteeing a terrible price if they so much as twitched.

It's not looking at us, Pit sent.

True to Pit's words, eyes the size of cities interrupted the nightmare mass of flesh and swollen joints. None were focused on Felix nor the river around him. Instead, they were fixed on a distant blue orb. Another, powerful sensation of vertigo hit Felix as he realized they were staring down at the Continent itself. *The whole world.*

It's so…small, Pit sent.

Upon Siva's back was a series of huge bones that rose up at a forty-five degree angle—ribs with gristle and too many tendons. The skin was split, and instead of muscle or blood, there was only a boundless, convoluted knot made entirely of silver wire. It was a maze of impossible proportions, as huge as a country and layered over itself so many times that traversing its circumference would take a lifetime.

The river flowed, pulling Felix nearer the bound goddess and the cluster of silver wire. Even without access to Voracious Eye, he knew those threads.

It's called the Pool of Halcyon Oaths, you absolute numbskull, he berated himself. *Of course Siva would be attached!*

The Goddess of Luck and Fate and Oaths was one of many old gods, now banished from the Continent for whatever reason. Felix hadn't bothered to ask them, and he wasn't going to start now.

Felix? Felix, something is happening. Pit's voice was laced with a rising panic. *Something is wrong.*

Before he could even ask, Felix saw it. Before his eyes, his hands began to melt, sublimating from flesh into spools of diaphanous silver light. His feet, too. There was no pain, just uncompromising certainty as his very proximity to the goddess was ripping them to shreds.

Hold on, Pit! The pieces of Felix that were still him fought against the change, and he could feel its effect slow by the smallest of margins. So small it might have been only in his imagination. The silver light that was once his hands and forearms slipped away, pulled down toward the surface of the goddess.

Felix! Everything is—

Pit! A glimmering ghost of silver ripped free of Felix's chest, already unspooling into a cascade of chaotic threads. *No!*

A piece of him reached out through the endless dark and after his friend. Threads upon threads, Felix could almost feel through them as they tangled with Pit, and he hauled with every ounce of Strength he had.

It's a crucible. A test. A test of what? His Mind whirled, faster than it ever had before. Their struggle slowed, seconds turned to minutes as he flared his Fiendforged Mind for all it was worth. *It's about connections. Bonds.* Felix cast back, but he was alone in the blackened skies and blasted terrain, falling toward an eldritch moon. *I can't sense anything. I can't use my Skills. I*—a detail below caught his eye.

The cords, bound like muscle and sinew, spread across Siva's back.

Inside. It's Authority! My connection to my—

Felix threw his attention inward, his legs and arms unraveling like mistaken knitting. He shoved that detail from his thoughts, utilizing the bulk of his Willpower to do so—ignoring horrors had become something like second nature to him. Instead, he cast about inside, where the millions of connections and Links were tethered. Here, in this place, Felix could feel them like live wires that sparked with electricity.

Everyone. I need you now, he said, pushing his Intent toward the connections. *All of you.*

Felix grasped them all, seizing with a tumult of incredible potency. Still, he forced his broken Body to move and with a mighty kick, launched himself down.

Toward the moon's surface.

C'mon!

Eyes rumbled as they shifted, and he felt a familiar gathering of Will. Felix ignored it, pushing himself harder, even as his legs vanished. He drew closer, the silver lines of the labyrinth below gleaming in the endless dark.

C'mon! We're not dying here!

Will and Intent grasped at connections and the evaporating threads of his own existence, held them fast as he plummeted.

Skein of Fate!

Though it couldn't escape his channels, Skein of Fate was there, humming in Felix's chest even as his torso unspooled around him. Siva *shifted,* and reddened lines of inquiry flashed from the horizon toward him, but his fury severed them before they could find purchase.

A scream of surprise and rage met his audacity.

CHAIN-BREAKER!

No more than a head, a thought, Felix lunged forward. As a net of silver threads descended, glimmering like razor wires, the tendril that was *him* brushed against the world-sized, labyrinthine knot.

IMPOSSIBLE CHILD! BEGONE!

CHAPTER TEN

Felix exploded from the pool. Heavy droplets of silver flung in all directions as his naked form breached the still waters.

"Guh!" he managed between great, gulping breaths. His hand found the first step out, and Felix clung to it. "That was shitty."

Light flashed, and soon Pit's beak clamped around Felix's forearm, helping the man drag himself farther up and out of the pool entirely. The mercury-like liquid sloughed from him, leaving nothing of itself behind, save the ghost of dampness. Felix shivered as he regarded its surface, now returned to glassy tranquility, despite his chaotic emergence.

"Felix! Are you alright?" Karys marched into the room, breath puffing through his metal chest like a bellows. "I came as soon as I sensed your return."

"How long?" Felix asked. His voice was a little hoarse after all that screaming.

"Four glasses."

"Damn." Felix leaned back, still on his knees. Karys handed him his Garment, folded up into a palm-sized square. The enchanted cloth squirmed the moment his Mana touched it and spread over Felix's body in seconds, until he was once again wearing a tunic, jacket, and pants. "Thanks."

"Your gauntlets and greaves are off to the side. How," Karys took a measured breath. "How do you feel?"

"A little wrung out. That wasn't a great experience. Pit? You good?"

The tenku chirruped, but it wasn't nearly as bright as usual. "I'm fine."

No he isn't. Felix kept that thought to himself, guarded in the vault of his Mind. He checked Pit's status, but everything *looked* fine. *That unraveling...that was way too close to what happened in my Omen Path.*

Back then, some facsimile of the gods had unmade Felix, and it had taken every ounce of his Willpower to pull himself back together. He had done so, and it had made him stronger in the end...but now all Felix felt was tired. Seeing Siva had taken its toll, and the memory of her nightmarish form clung to him like hot wax. His thoughts brushed against her image, and Felix flinched, just like he had at first with the Creature in the Breach. This time, Pit flinched as well.

"I hate them," the tenku whispered.

"Me, too." Felix forced his jaw to unclench and his shoulders to relax. "Me, too."

A bell rang out, a deep tolling that resonated across the Inner Sanctum and *through* Felix's chest. He whirled toward its source, where Knowledge stood at the edge of the silvery pool, hands clasped behind itself.

"Lord Autarch Felix Nevarre, Inheritor of the Nymean's Will, Chosen of Veridaan! You have embraced the Pool of Halcyon Oaths and emerged transformed."

Felix stalked toward the illusion. "Chosen of who?"

"Veridaan. Primordial of Oaths, She Who Cannot Be Broken." Knowledge waved a furry claw at the still pool. "All who survive the Halcyon Oath take a piece of her power, binding it to themselves in order to access the Bonds of Fellowship."

Primordial of Oaths? "Siva is the Goddess of Oaths. You're saying there's a Primordial that has power over that same thing?"

Knowledge tilted its weasel-like head, small brows drawn down. "The Goddess of Fortune holds no sway over oaths."

Felix opened his mouth to argue but was interrupted by the almighty wave of sizzling energy that screamed into his Body. Potency surged in his channels, swirling through the center of him like a vast whirlpool as notification windows obscured his vision.

New Title!
Blessed of the Halcyon Oath II (Epic)
You have embraced the waters of connection in the Luminous

Void and emerged whole! You have gained the Skill: Territorial Skimming (Rare)!

New Skill!
Territorial Skimming (Rare), Level 1!
The Cognitive and Ethereal Realms rest within, atop, and behind the Corporeal Realm all at once. It is only your Perceptions that lie to you...or they once did. You can now sense the Dark Passages that thread the Corporeal Realm, tunnels in the surface of the world that tread the line between all three Realms. Skimming allows you alone to traverse the edges of the Corporeal and exit through the points where the barriers between things are thinnest. Stabilization and speed of transit through Dark Passages increase minutely per level.

Before Felix could parse the entirety of his new Title and Skill, another pulse of energy exploded within him, harder and sharper than the last. It ricocheted off his cores like a thousand pieces of deadly hail before piercing directly into his brand new Skill.

Skill: Abyssal Skein Detected!
Title: Chthonic Traveler Detected!
Vein of Divinity Detected!
Due To A Confluence Of Titles, Skills, And Stolen Potency, Your Skill Has Upgraded!

Pain, his constant companion, seared through him. It was a familiar burn, one of evolution and combination that Felix had endured countless times, and it surged as Territorial Skimming transformed.

Territorial Skimming (Rare) Has Become Labyrinthine Wing (Epic)!

Labyrinthine Wing (Epic), Level 1!
An evolution of Territorial Skimming due to the presence of the Void within your core space. Your grasp over the connections to your people has transcended its former limitations, and you have begun to wend your way into the potency of the Halcyon Oath. Stabilization of all Passages has doubled, and

speed of transit has tripled. Both qualities increase minutely per level.

Viable Dark Passage Entry Points Have Been Added To Your Territorial Maps!

"Okay," he said, after a moment. The System energy within him subsided, eaten up by the rapidfire changes to his newest Skill. He flared his Song of Absolution, and even the pain faded to nothing. "Okay, that was intense."

Pit squawked. "Felix! More is coming!"

Power shot through him, not like a wave but a comet. It blazed into his being, trailing a resplendent mantle of triumphant horns and furiously playing cellos that smashed right into his dual cores.

New Title!
Chosen of Unbroken Vows (Legendary)!
You—
ERROR!
[REDACTED] Is Lost!

New Title!
Chosen of Siva (Legendary)!
You—

ERROR!
Title: Chain-Breaker Detected!

Title: Chosen of Siva (L) Has Been Revoked!

YOU ARE NOT ALLOWED, FELIX NEVARRE!

Window after blue window appeared before Felix, each one overlapping the last as error supplanted error, until those last words ripped through it all. They were louder than any bell, stabbing through Felix like a knife from brainstem to gut.

Worse, he could feel that comet of power—that piece of System energy that had wanted to coalesce into a Title—turn away from him. Siva was taking it back.

Title: The Call of Defiance Is Active!
+25% Willpower When Contested By A Foe Of Divine Or Greater Advancement!

Title: Born of Will Is Active!
What Is Beyond You, If You Have The Will?

The threads of their connection came into brilliant focus for him, revealed as heavy cords that slithered between his chest and the pool itself. That connection flared, a goddess leveraging the other side, but it went both ways.

MINE! Felix thrust the totality of his Willpower and Intent against her fragmented one, and piece by piece, felt a shearing across intervening space.

Title: Chain-Breaker Is Active!
No Oath Can Hold You!

Outrage thundered across Felix's Affinity. **CHAIN-BREAKER!**

Skein of Fate!

"More where that came from!" A discordant chaos ballooned outward from his chest, weakening the claws the Siva had dug deep into the comet of potency. "Hunger!"

Darkness swelled, grasping greedy hooks into the brilliant fireball and dragging it down. It vanished into the swirling event horizon. Consumed.

Felix's notification windows shattered to pieces, and all went silent.

"What—" Knowledge's illusory image stuttered with static. Waves of discordant sparks broke up his long, weasel-like body. "Inheritor. Please explain."

Felix wiped a trickle of blood from beneath his nose and stood, again. The goddess' words had driven him to his knees without him noticing. "I was hoping you would do that. Veridaan. Who is that?"

Knowledge's eyes blanked before rattling off the information. "Veridaan. The Primordial of Oaths, a Scion of the Unseen Tide."

"I know that name," Felix said. That's what his Race entry said, after all. "I know it real well. What is a Scion of the Unseen Tide?"

"Unknown. Most information on the Primordials is Lost. Not even memory can withstand the purging flames of Ruin."

Felix grunted. "Figures. But Veridaan wasn't Lost?"

Again, the illusory Geist froze as if accessing some deeper part of himself. "Veridaan remains. She resides within the Halcyon Oath, a—"

"No she doesn't," Felix said. "That was Siva down there. I'd know that damn moon anywhere."

"The Goddess of Fortune is not tied to oaths. She—" Knowledge gained that distant look again, freezing in place like he'd glitched. The sigaldry around the pool flared up, as did a few connecting lines that led into the wall the Third Chamber shared with the Heart of Darkness. When the light died away, Knowledge unfroze with a jolt. "Siva. Goddess of Fortune…and Oaths. She was not contained within the pool's scope when it was last used."

Did he just update himself? Through…the Shadowgates? How's that work? "What does that mean?"

"The Memories which compose my being are only updated when the pool is in use. It has remained in stasis for a great deal of time. Now that you have accessed the Third Chamber, my knowledge shall grow… but the process is a gradual one. Until this moment, I was unaware that her dominion had extended to oaths as well."

That was interesting. "She got more powerful? How does a god get more power? Aren't they the top of the food chain?"

Knowledge was silent.

Instead, a sound like pennies rattling around a metal grate filled the air. Karys was clearing his throat. "The gods were not always as they are, Felix. You know this. They once pressed their thumbs upon the Continent, though their touch has not been felt in a great many Ages. We cannot know how they may have changed since this artifact was last active."

Felix could understand that, even as it made him nervous. The idea of gods getting stronger made his stomach drop, even if they were chained in the sky or whatever.

Knowledge continued, unaware or uncaring for Felix's worries. His voice was dull as if reading a scripted message. "Your connection to the Halcyon Oath is deep, if not as profound as it could be. To do that, one must pass entirely through the crucible and embrace the potency held within. You have earned the right to Territorial Skimming, which allows fast transit between two points within a Territory. Typically twice as fast as Manaship travel." Here he paused, and more sigils flashed across his illusory body. "Your unusual circumstances have afforded you an evolution of Territorial Skimming. With Labyrinthine Wing, you will find your progress to be much improved."

"Fast travel, but limited to only within my own Territories. Got it. It's a Skill," Felix said. "Does that mean the more I use it, the better it gets?"

"The Bonds of Fellowship drive the Halcyon Oath, and it is only through serving the needs of your people that its power will grow."

"Right. Connections." So much of his power recently had boiled down to the links he'd established between himself and others. Felix could stand toe-to-toe with a giant monster, but relying on others let him do so much more. *There's probably a moral in there, somewhere.* "And only I can use this. Can I bring others along?"

"Correct. The amount varies upon the Skill level, rarity of the Skill, and personal strength. However, you may anoint up to nine Exemplars, granting them a reduced version of your Skill. I must warn you, however, that doing so will drain a portion of your significance and invest it within your followers. They, in turn, will gain the ability to bring others with them, as determined by their own strength."

Exemplars, huh? That could be very useful.

Felix could feel it, the edges of his new ability. With a flex of his Will, he brought up his Territory Map. Sure enough, dark marks manifested all across it, even in the areas Felix's people hadn't scouted out yet. *Dark Passages.* He checked his map of Ahkestria and spotted a ton over there, too. None of the Passages jumped across Territorial borders, but he had his Shadowgates for that.

"How fast would I be able to move across all of Nagast?" he asked the illusion.

"Unclear. Due to my interrupted delving, I can only surmise." Knowledge folded his fake hands inside his fake sleeves. "Two or three days."

A lot faster than Manaship, that's for sure. Felix chewed at his lip, his thoughts turning away from the mysterious pool, goddesses, and toward his many other problems. *I'm already late leaving to get to Kimaris. With this, I could get there and back in less time than a Manaship would take on the first leg of the trip.*

For some reason, Felix was eager for a fight. Perhaps it was an effect of surviving Siva's attention down in the pool. He'd fought the gods before, but only pieces of them, and he still ended up hurt each time. If that had been indicative of fighting a goddess at full strength? Felix couldn't handle them in a real fight.

Not yet, at least.

"Knowledge. Can you compile information through the Shadowgates?"

"Disparate scraps slowly mingled into whole cloth. It takes a great deal of time, but it is a function of my array, yes."

"Good. Collect everything you can about the gods and Primordials." Felix gazed into the bright, mirrored surface of the pool. "Lost or not, anything is better than nothing."

"As you wish, Inheritor."

Time to focus on smaller targets. For now.

"I assume, my Lord, that you plan on utilizing your new Skill to reach the Boreal Pass?" Karys interrupted Felix's brooding with his usual polite tone.

"Yeah. With this, I could take care of this Domain break and be back in time to take care of my lordly duties," Felix said. "It's win-win."

"Indeed. I cannot fault your logic, but might I suggest a night's rest? From what I have gleaned, you and your Companion have been through an ordeal. Some recuperation would benefit you both before tackling a dangerous journey."

"I—Well, I can't argue against that. It's already night, isn't it?"

"It is."

Felix sighed. "Pit? What do you think? We'll go handle the Domain break after a nap?"

Pit was staring daggers at the silvery pool, and he blinked his big, golden eyes when Felix spoke. "Hm? Yes. Alright." He warbled somewhere in the back of his throat. It sounded tired. "Sleep…then food?"

"Are you joking?" Felix asked. "Food *then* sleep."

CHAPTER ELEVEN

Late as it was, the evening sped by fast. As dawn stretched its rosy fingers across the valley, Felix and Pit were curled up in his chambers beneath the Temple. The bed was huge, easily large enough to fit both of them comfortably, and while the base was fashioned from stone, it had been padded with a lush mattress and draped in silken sheets. It was the only luxury Felix had actively pursued. The rest of his room was relatively barren, perhaps in spite of the bevy of furs, tapestries, and furniture that numerous people had gifted him. Those had all gone to storage or his friends. Felix didn't spend much time in his room, anyway.

Last time I used this bed was…two weeks ago? I think? He stared up at his ceiling, which was carved from a variegated green stone into a network of interlocking stars and vines. *Greater Serpentinite. Cool rock.*

He hadn't been able to sleep that night. Memories of Siva's vast bulk crowded his thoughts, seeding fissures of horror through even his most mundane contemplations. So, for the last five hours, he had been subjecting himself to a grueling routine. Exposure training. If the gods were horrors beyond comprehension, Felix would just have to get used to it.

His perfect recall pulled up the gargantuan features of Siva once again, and Felix flinched. Not as hard as before, but it hurt. *Again.*

Sometime around hour four there had been a buzzing inside his core space, where his Bastion of Will resided. It was the bulk of his mental defenses and also the highest-leveled Skill he possessed. Distantly, Felix had hoped this would be enough to push it into Master Tier, but no such luck. The buzzing had subsided, and his Bastion went back to dutifully holding ground between his Mind and everything else.

Felix flinched. It was, perhaps, a tiny bit less. Maybe.

The process was boring and had driven him to look into other things through the long night. One had been his Hunger. Felix had been pleased that the dark void inside of him had responded to his call when Siva had tried her shit—it had been basically unresponsive for months. Now it was rumbling pleasantly in his chest, like a cat in a sunbeam.

Hunger. You there? he had asked.

There had been no response.

Felix was simply happy his Hunger had reacted at all. While he hadn't had a problem pushing back at Siva's fragmented Will, he hated to see a System resource vanish from his grasp. Based on how it had arrived in his core space, the Title had likely been extremely potent; who knew what it would have given him? It was, he reasoned, a fair price to pay for a happy Hunger.

The fact that Siva had been able to refuse him the Title in the first place was another thing entirely. Goddess of Fortune and Oaths, she clearly had ties to the power Felix now felt inside of him. She also had ties to his Chain-Breaker Title and Skein of Fate, both of which the goddess did not like at all. *What else is new?*

Skein of Fate let him form and void Oaths, his own and others. There was little in the way of penalties for voiding those Oaths, at least for himself; the first person he'd done it to had basically melted. It earned him the enmity of a goddess and cost him a good deal of energy to use the Skill, but that wasn't as big an obstacle for him as it might be for others. No matter the energy—Essence, Mana, even significance—it was something Felix could find with enough time and Chthonic Tribute. As far as the gods were concerned…well, they never liked him much anyway.

The real question, the one that Felix kept circling back to as he laid in the dark, was whether the Pool of Halcyon Oaths was worth it. He could still sense the thick cable of connection between himself and the pool…and to Siva beyond. Should he sever it with Skein of Fate? He could feel it was possible.

Today will be the test. If Labyrinthine Wing proved useful, Felix would keep it. *And if it's a liability or a trap, then I'll rip it out by the roots.*

Felix's only consolation was in the nature of the Halcyon Oath itself. The cord that clung to him was less a link to the goddess than to oaths themselves, represented by that network of silver threads upon her back. Felix knew that with a bone-deep certainty, though he couldn't explain how. Those threads, if Knowledge was to be believed, did not originate with Siva at all, but instead came from this Veridaan person. A Primordial.

So…what? Siva stole the power from a Primordial?

Were the gods…like him?

Somewhere outside his mountain home, a swell of birdsong filled the air. Felix sat up, halting his painful training. For a moment, he simply reveled in the absence of constant, low-level pain. "Wake up, Pit."

Dawn had come.

There were things to be done.

"Do you ever feel like those murals are watching us?"

Vess was not normally one for superstition, but walking the halls of the Temple was particularly eerie in the small hours of the morning. Admittedly, the corridors she traveled were not used by any save a select few, so they remained unnaturally quiet, even at the height of the day's activities.

"No," said a deep voice. It came from beneath her cowl, where the quilted jerkin folded over her woolen cloak, and it was followed by a golden snout covered in whiskers. Yintarion of the Cerulean Skies wriggled his tiny nose. "They are nothing more than simple art pieces. I smell no enchantments save for durability."

The Dragoon in training considered the twitching snout as it fled back into the recesses of her collar. "You can smell such things?"

"A Dragon's senses are among the most highly attuned in all the Continent. If I could not distinguish between paltry enchantments with only my nose, then I would not be worthy of my heritage."

"But are a Wyrmling's senses so attuned?" Vess asked.

Yin *humphed*, and a wisp of smoke floated out from beneath her collar. "Yes. Well. I once wore the advancement of a true Dragon, and though I am reduced, my knowledge is as vast as the Void itself."

You fool, she cursed herself as wounded pride sang across their bond. She had known it was a mistake the moment the words left her mouth.

Vess had been trained in Diplomacy her entire life, yet speaking with her bonded Companion circumvented her careful phrasing and ignited something impetuous in her Mind. Yin had been reduced when they had bonded, going from a high-Tier Dragon to a simple Wyrmling, and though he did not admit it, he was displeased. "I apologize for underestimating you."

"Hmph."

Vess strode with purpose, despite her wandering thoughts. She was headed to the wide chamber they had designated a sparring room, deep on the fourth level of the Temple. *Elderthrone Temple*, she reminded herself. The name was entirely too new. Felix had outfitted the sparring chamber with a number of training Golems from Haarwatch, and Rory had even gifted them with a special obstacle course to test them well into Adept Tier. It was quite generous and useful to boot, giving their more elite combatants a private place in which to train.

Not everyone was elite, however. It was Felix's stated desire that anyone who wished to advance themselves should be able to do so, and he had made some resources available in both of the barracks in town. There were even similar—but lower strength—obstacle courses and Golems available.

It is an admirable thing, Vess thought. *Care and compassion worthy of a ruler.*

Every morning, Vess would train. She and Yin would practice her Tempered Skills, honing them beneath the tedious banner of repetition. She was officially an Adept Tier warrior, a position that would normally mean she was ready to learn the special evolution of her Dragoon Skills. She had the Skill Books and everything. The problem, of course, was that her Skills had been irrevocably changed. Vessilia Dayne was no longer an apprentice of the Dragoons.

Or, at least, that's how her seniors would see it. One delving and they would realize her core space had been changed utterly from their perfected model. Her Skills no longer aligned with their carefully curated abilities, and thus their plans for advancement were pointless for Vess to contemplate. Instead, she leaned upon her Companion for his sage wisdom and knowledge of how things were done in distant Ages.

According to Yintarion, the Skills she had developed were mostly common among ancient Dragoons, though hers were of far higher rarity than normal. That was a relief, and coupled with Yin's guidance, Vess was certain they would make progress. Already, her Skill levels were pushing into the high seventies, and it was only a matter of time before she made it to Master Tier.

"Yin," she said.

"What is it, child?"

Vess took a breath, bracing herself. "Do you regret bonding with me?"

There was a pause before Yin's entire golden head poked out of her collar. His skull was wedge-shaped with narrow jaws, scaled features, and small crystal horn nubs sticking out of a white mane of fur. The golden tendrils of his mustache twitched, and his big gold-on-gold eyes narrowed. "What are you talking about?"

Vess licked her lips and considered backpedaling, but she had committed to saying her piece. It had eaten at her long enough. "You were mighty before we were Companions, and now…I simply do not wish to be the cause of your remorse."

In the heat of battle, as Yintarion lay dying, Vess had pushed him into a Companion Pact. The Dragon's eagerness to fight and to pay back the debt he felt he owed had done the rest.

"Little Dragoon. Had I resented you or the circumstances of our pact, I would have long ago severed it. Damn the consequences." Yin lifted himself up, revealing his long, serpentine body and small, five-fingered claws.

"I see." Earnest certainty rumbled through their connection, adding a weight to the Wyrmling's words that allayed Vess' fears. "And the fact that you are once again a Wyrmling—?"

"Is a wondrous opportunity I hadn't expected." Yin's body pressed further out, coiling into the air as if floating on invisible currents, before turning so that his little face was only a span from her's. "Who else would be granted the chance to reforge themselves? With the knowledge I have earned in my long years, I know methods and techniques that will establish a more potent foundation than I had previously. Power untold is within my grasp, promising me a fate far greater than the one I had been relegated to before." He wriggled his small body. "Admittedly, the start of the path is more rocky than I expected."

Vess smiled. "You have a plan to recover your advancement?"

"Of course, I do! I am Yintarion of the Cerulean Skies! Nothing is beyond my reach!" Yin did several laps around Vess' head, trumpeting his words into the empty hallways before alighting on her shoulder once more. "I have but to chase down my first Evolution."

"How might I help?" she asked.

"A Dragon does not require aid."

"I imagine not, but I would offer regardless."

Yin raised a ridged eyebrow. "Very well. I merely need special reagents in order to pursue the perfect foundation. Only then might I attempt my first Evolution."

"Reagents? Like what?"

"A great number of precious herbals and metals, mostly. Many of which are available in this strange land, but not all. And certainly not the final, most important piece I need." Yin snorted a blast of luminescent smoke. "The still-beating heart of a Superior Elemental."

Vess' step stuttered. "A Superior Elemental? Those have not been seen in Ages."

"So I have gathered. Even in my youth, such beings were rare, and to be gifted one of their hearts was not a common thing." Yin sighed. "Perfection is quite hard to achieve."

"And what of the eggs?" she asked.

Yintarion frowned. "The eggs need only my flame to keep them in stasis. To take them out of it…it is beyond my knowledge, Vessilia. Even your Autarch could not restore them, with that strange Skill he possesses."

Felix had attempted to utilize Unite the Lost, but had said that the draw of significance was so deep it would beggar even him. Even so, the man had been willing to attempt it, and only Yintarion's objections had stopped him. For all his bluster, Yin did not wish to see someone walk the edge of oblivion for his sake.

"We would need the wisdom of a Dragon matriarch or perhaps the old Dragoons," he continued. "And, from what I have learned, the former are gone and the latter have changed so completely that I would not be surprised if they had burned such knowledge."

A fair assumption, she acknowledged, but Vess refused to let the issue go. "We will simply have to find new avenues to pursue."

"Perhaps." Yin tried for a flat, unaffected response, but grief coiled beneath every syllable of his words. "And perhaps this is simply my punishment. All choices have consequences, little Dragoon."

They rounded a bend in the hall and came into view of the Storage Facility, where a lone figure was struggling with an object bigger than itself. "Evie? What are you doing?"

"Hm? Oh, Vess! Just the person I wanted to, *unf*, see!" Her friend gave her a sharp, conspiratorial grin and nodded at the hand cart by her side. "Think you could give me a hand with this?"

She needn't be asked twice. Vess stooped down and got her arms around a lump of what looked like… "Ice? Why do you have a massive chunk of ice in the Temple halls?"

"Got it from the Storage Facility," Evie said, grunting as they maneuvered the thing into the bed of her small cart. The frame creaked ominously, but it held. "Ah, there we go. Got it as a reward for beating up Felix."

Vess blinked. "You beat up Felix?"

"*You* beat up Felix?" Yintarion echoed her.

"'*Good job, Evie, we're so proud of you*,'" Evie muttered, before squinting at Yin. "You don't think I could do it?"

Yin preened, licking his foreclaw with a long, forked tongue. "Merely surprised. Defeat comes for us all. That it was you is…unexpected."

"What's that mean?"

"Simply that you are undisciplined and impetuous. That you overcame the Autarch is remarkable."

"Hey, I'm—"

Vess lifted a hand, cutting off their fight before it could truly begin. "Evie, we are on our way to training. Do you wish to come with us?"

Her friend gave Yin a long, scathing look. "No. I have better things to do."

"Of course. Training is beneath you," Yin said, his tone light. "Go and have fun with your cold water."

"You know what, yeah. I changed my mind. I could use a good fight," Evie said and bared her teeth. "You up for it, lizard?"

Yin stretched lazily, kneading his claws on Vess' cloak. "Are you?"

"It's here?" Karys asked. His mismatched hands were lifted before him, probing the empty air. "I cannot sense anything at all."

They stood within a grove just east of Elderthrone. Finding the entrance point to a Dark Passage had been easy, but none of them were beneath the canopy of his Spirit Tree, as if the Atlantes' very presence warded them away. On his Territorial Map, the Dark Passages appeared as smudges of shadow, like tunnels across the land, and they were *everywhere*. Where the magical tree stood, however, was a perfect circle devoid of all shadow.

"It's here, and I can," Felix assured his friend. "You can see it on the Territorial Map, too, if you toggle the option."

Karys flicked his fingers, bringing up his own version of the map. "So it is. According to this, the Dark Passage stretches from this grove to the northernmost tip of the Teeth, a distance that would take a week on foot."

"Hopefully far less for me. That's one of the tests of this thing." Felix pointed at the map, tracing his finger from dark smudge to dark smudge. "There's a secondary Passage here, about half a day's march west of the Teeth, and that's where I'll make the final leg. With luck, we'll be at the Boreal Pass in just a few days."

Karys let a soft disapproval sing through his Spirit. With no real face, the man had to rely on conveying emotions through his body language or Spirit; the latter was far easier for a ten-foot suit of armor. "I do not trust them. What of the Whalemaw? Did it not attack Zara when she attempted a similar crossing?"

Felix had thought of that, of course. He patted his hip, where several dinner-plate-sized stones hung from his belt on leather straps. "That's why I have these. It'll keep everything *me* contained. Pit has some, too, as do the Shadows. So long as everyone sticks together, it'll be fine."

"And if it does not?"

"Then I'll have to improvise." Felix shrugged. "But it won't come to that. The last thing I want to do is run into the Whalemaw."

"Tell Zara…tell her that I'm handling a diplomatic errand. I'll be back soon."

"Very well, Felix." Karys bowed, inclining his torso. "Safe travels, and may the winds carry you home."

"Thanks, man." Felix focused, sounding the strange patterns of his new Skill. "Labyrinthine Wing!"

A thick darkness coiled atop his fingers, speckled with traces of silver like glitter along a black fogbank. Or perhaps a tiny field of stars. Instinctively, Felix reached out and, for lack of a better word, split open reality. A yawning portal opened up, filled by the same gaseous black and silver spangles.

"Whoa," Pit crooned. "What a hole."

Felix picked up a watermelon-sized rock and hurled it through the opening. It flew through the dark, vanishing as it passed through the starry veil. It did not, however, land behind the portal. The rock was gone.

"Alright. I've got my sword on me, so if you need to talk, let me know," he said.

"Of course." Karys folded his mismatched hands in front of himself and stood, exuding worry. "I will be here, as always."

"Pit! Shadows! On me!" Felix stepped forward until he was inches from the swirling portal. Behind him, Pit and four members of his personal guard crowded close. "Time to see what this thing is all about."

CHAPTER TWELVE

The starry darkness resolved into something far less nebulous but almost as dim. Felix stood atop a rough summit and beheld a landscape of mountainous peaks. They extended for countless miles in all directions, their bases hidden, drenched in the shadow of a moonless night. Stars glimmered in a cloudless sky, wheeling ever so slightly as the earth turned beneath them.

"Gloomy," Pit said.

Felix didn't argue. It certainly was a far cry from the chill winter morning they had just left. "It feels solid though. Real. Similar to the Shadowgate paths, I think, but…quieter. Huh." He wondered if it was the effect of his Chthonic Traveler Title, or simply moving with a smaller group of people, but the background cacophony of his last journeys was muted here.

"Speaking feels wrong here," Errol said as he pulled his purple cowl up around his ears. The dark metal gauntlets he wore had already started to frost over. "And it is far colder than Nagast."

The Fiend's Shadows spread out around them, five in total. Aside from their leader, Errol, there was Veddi, Devvi, Kress, and Geddin. The first two were Frost Giants equipped with trident and club, both of them somewhere around fourteen feet tall. Short, but they were young and talented with violence. It was how they'd gotten the job. Kress was a Human, Geddin was a Goblin, and both were members of the Arclights before becoming Shadows. Errol himself was a Fist, dedicated to unarmed combat.

Three warriors and two mages. Felix didn't need them, hadn't wanted them, but the Shadows had put up as much fight as Karys. If he hadn't let them come, Felix didn't doubt that Karys would have followed himself.

"This? This is nothing compared to the Hoarfrost," Veddi said. He grinned, showing off slate gray teeth beneath blue lips. "Soon we shall bask in the winter sun."

"Sir? What is the next move?" Errol asked.

Felix peered over the edge of the precipice. It wasn't very wide, perhaps a rough thirty feet across, and the drop was sharp. He could not perceive the ground at all. "First, we find a way across. I had figured this would be simpler."

"I don't see a path," Geddin said. He and Kress were inspecting the mountain behind them. "But the Mana feels stable. I can sense nothing different from the real world."

Kress lifted her arm, where bands of Mana coalesced. "Approximately twenty-two percent ice Mana, fifteen percent earth and air, and the rest is shadow. It's solid, but it feels strange."

Felix pressed his Perception and Affinity to its limits, stretching himself as if reaching across a very wide table. Impressions passed through him, flitting and ephemeral, but definitely there. "Something is moving out there. Voidbeasts, probably. And—" he paused. "Oh, that's interesting."

"Sir!"

Felix stepped forward, almost over the edge. "I almost missed this." He lifted his scaled hands and pressed them against the air, where he felt a soft resistance. Within him, Labyrinthine Wing hummed louder, repeating its pattern over and over again in sharper tones. "Like the Shadowgates, this place takes direction from the one who opens it up. But this place is a lot more…suggestible, I guess is the word."

"Suggestible?" Pit tilted his head, like a dog hearing something they weren't sure about. "What does that mean?"

"Let's find out."

Felix grabbed at the air and sounded several Skills at once. His Shaping Array thrummed, spinning ever faster in his core space, as Stone Shaping, Auroral Forge, Cardinal Flame, and Green Shaping all surged through his core and out of his channels. Mana bloomed in a rainbow of color, pouring from Felix in a liquid...before coalescing into something far more. Stone ripped from the mountains, light and fire condensing within it, as shimmering roots burst forth to surround and encase it all.

C'mon. As with all shaping magic, it took attention to detail and a very large Mana pool to make anything worthwhile, and this was no different. The spells worked with one another, resonating in ways he was still unused to—an effect of the Skill Array—but more than that was affecting them. A structure formed without Felix's direct Intent, flexible roots spreading like a set of ribs and slats as stone and flame reinforced corners and seams. Inside his core space, his Divine Tree was set to creaking, and as if in sympathy, the structure before him swayed in time.

This...this is not what I intended.

All at once, it was done.

Stone Shaping is level 86!
Auroral Forge is level 76!
Green Shaping is level 84!
Dual Casting is level 79!

Congratulations! Due To Extensive Use And Potent Resonance, Your Skill Dual Casting (Uncommon) Has Evolved!

Dual Casting (Uncommon) Has Become Multi-Cast (Epic)! Level Is Maintained!

Multi-Cast (E), Level 79!
You have the Will and the resources to cast several spells at once and have proven it time and again. Now you may cast the same spell multiple times, and each casting will stack, increasing the effects of the Skill as well as the costs. Multiple spells may be stacked in this way—the only limit is your Willpower, Intelligence, and Mana pool.

A vicious twinge stabbed into Felix's chest as the Skill evolved, and Felix was almost driven to his knees before it subsided. Yet, within a few seconds, it did. He checked his core space for a moment, looking at his Shaping Array where Dual Casting once resided. In its place was Multi-Cast, which was quite a bit larger than its predecessor, yet when he inspected its pattern, he breathed a sigh of relief. The Skill Array was intact.

"I saw that. Is the array fine?" Pit asked as Felix's awareness returned. "Evolving the Skill didn't hurt it, did it?"

"It's fine. A little pain, is all." Karys had warned them of such a risk. A Skill Array was based on the patterns of each Skill, and if those Skills changed, well… "I'll test it once we're out of here."

"Hm."

"My Lord Autarch! What—what is this?" Errol asked from across the summit.

Felix glanced up, remembering what he'd been attempting—and pausing as he took in the result. "Holy crap. That isn't what I meant to make."

Before them, floating in the empty air, was a Manaship. Only, it looked nothing like any Manaship Felix had ever seen, and much more like a giant creature. It was huge, perhaps twice the size of any galleon he'd witnessed, and it was made almost entirely of wood. Living wood, if the moss, ferns, and literal flowers were anything to judge by.

A shape not unlike a giant fish hung low beneath three masts that resembled very thick tree trunks, all of which ascended to wrap their branches around a massive, glowing crystal. The crystal itself was blue-white and cast a faint glow that was relatively brilliant in the dark, picking out the feathered details of four midnight-black wings, two to each side, along with a wide, fin-like tail in place of a rudder.

"It looks like the Whalemaw," Pit pointed out. He chirruped in curiosity. "Did you mean for that to happen?"

"Ugh. No. Definitely not." Felix had meant to create a ship, like he heard Zara had done once, in order to ferry them across the dark terrain. Instinctual knowledge from Labyrinthine Wing told him that the Dark Passages were very susceptible to the Mana and Intent of those within them, but this was something else.

"I just wanted a little sloop or a cutter or something. Not…this." Felix stepped to the edge. The ship was floating barely five feet away, and he conjured a Shadow Whip to grab hold of its railing. "It'll work, I suppose. Everyone, get on board."

Without asking any questions, Veddi and Devvi both leaped aboard. They looked at home among the oversized ship, as if the thing were scaled for them, and they barely stumbled as it dipped a few feet when they landed.

"My Lord, what keeps it afloat?" Errol asked him. "That is no magic I am familiar with, and…there isn't a Mana engine within that hull, is there?"

"Nope," Felix said. "Least I don't think so. I sure didn't make one. Go on. If it can hold those two, it can hold you just fine."

The lieutenant swallowed audibly but backed up and took a running leap, clearing the railing easily. The mages followed without any questions.

Pit lowered his head near Felix's. "But how is it floating?"

"Damned if I know," he admitted. "This place is weird."

Piloting the ship proved to be relatively easy. Manaship Pilot still applied, despite a distinct lack of Mana engines, as the craft required a constant stream of Felix's Mana, Willpower, and Intent. Thankfully, none of those were in short supply.

The ship handled well, considering its bulk. Pit insisted on calling it the *Sailwhale*, and Felix refused to acknowledge *that*—but it was true that the thing did move much like a giant whale. The shape of it aside, the living wood undulated, massive wings flapping in steady beats as they wove between the dark peaks in that endless night. Felix could sense creatures moving about, somewhere far, far below, but nothing accosted them in the air. He had almost expected it, considering the amount of light the giant crystal above them was putting out.

Manaship Pilot is level 36!

Soon they reached the end of the Dark Passage. It looked the same as any other part of the interminable landscape, and only Felix's new Skill told him the exit was approaching. *What would happen,* he wondered, *if we kept on going?*

The ship ground against the jagged edge of the final mountain, wood splintering a little. Felix lashed the craft to a few Stone Shaped posts, using several Shadow Whips in place of actual rope. His small crew hopped off, more than eager to be gone, but Felix lingered. He stared at the ship, disbelief still tingeing his thoughts. *I made this.* I *made this.* Aside from the structures and walls around Elderthrone, Felix hadn't attempted much in the way of creation, and nothing so elaborate as what was beneath his feet now. His sigaldry came close, but that was words; this was more.

Can I make this outside of the Dark Passages, too?

"Where's the exit?" Pit asked. "Nothing but rock here."

Felix glanced toward his team. All of them were already on the mountain and spread out, weapons bared as Pit paced across a barren summit. Felix patted the railing of his ship and hopped off, forcing the whole thing to dip fifteen feet or so. He landed with a muted thud on the mountain and ignored the still-surprised looks from his Shadows. He was a lot heavier than he looked.

Labyrinthine Wing!

Once again, Felix's claws ripped open a portal through the Realms. Swirling within was a soft, yellow light and an almost balmy temperature. Felix could smell wet loam, rotting wood, and a musky sort of undertone.

Geddin sneezed. "Smells like the thaw. How long have we been gone?"

"If you do not mind, we shall take the lead, my Lord." Errol said. When Felix shrugged, the man clapped his gauntlets together. "Quickly now. Veddi, Devvi take vanguard."

The five Shadows moved like oiled clockwork, stepping into the portal with a practiced precision, leaving only Pit and Felix behind.

"After you, little man," Felix said. Pit nuzzled him, nipping at his ear with his dark beak before trotting through. Behind him, the ship creaked as Felix's attention strayed away from it. Pieces of it dissolved into liquid and then vapor, boiling away into the eternal night. Felix was filled with the awareness that the ship would be gone in minutes. "Step one, complete."

He walked through the portal—and right into a rushing river.

"Gah! Rime Shaping!"

Ice swarmed upward from the surface of the raging waters, just enough to create a platform for one of his feet. Felix cast about, finding the riverbank only a few feet away, and grasped at the air.

Adamant Discord!

The tiniest lightning bolt surged between him and the shore, hauling him forward to the snow-caked earth and shattering the ice he left behind. He landed just in time to see it all swept away, carried by the deceptively swift current.

"That was unexpected," he muttered.

"You're telling me," Pit said. The poor tenku was sopping wet and shivering a few feet away. In fact, all of his party was, and only the Frost Giants weren't soaked to the bone. "Next time, *you* can be the first one out."

Errol stood, and ice cracked off his armor where the river water had frozen him to the ground. "M-my Lord, pl-please sit. W-we are co-collecting firewood to build a ca-campfire."

Cardinal Flame!

A bonfire manifested between them all, colored red-gold but as good as any natural fire. "Don't bother yourselves. Rest."

"M-my Lord, this is unnecessary. Do not strain—"

"It *is* necessary. You take care of me, and I take care of you. Isn't that how this whole Autarch thing works?"

The giants and mages traded glances, while Errol merely bowed his head. "Thank you, my Lord."

Felix inclined his head. Vess had drilled him in enough lordly niceties to know this much. He looked up at the sky, which was only slightly overcast. He could clearly see the sun, and it was still relatively high in the southern sky. "Judging by the sun, that took us only a few hours. Karys?"

Green-gold steamed from his waist, and the tinny voice of his Chancellor came with it. "My Lord! You have exited the Dark Passage already? How was it? Are you injured?"

"We have. It was wonderfully uneventful. How long has it been since we left?"

"Three glasses. Excellent time!"

Hm. Not nearly as fast as a Shadowgate, but bringing a week-long trip to three hours is huge. "That's great news. We'll be making the second leg soon, just have to uh, recuperate a little."

"And the Dark Passage was safe?"

"I don't know about safe. There were things in there, monsters of some variety, but we avoided them easily enough."

"I suppose that will have to suffice. Perhaps the last portion of your trip will be just as uneventful."

"Let's hope." Felix brought up his Territory Map and checked their location. "I'll reconnect once we land in the Boreal Pass."

"Right. Safe travels, my Lord."

The green-gold glow faded, and Felix focused his attention on his crew. They were looking a lot better now, even Pit, who had started methodically cleaning his legs and chest. "Alright. We'll warm ourselves up here and then we'll head to the next Dark Passage entrance."

Pit lifted his head from preening his feathers. "Where's that?" Felix said nothing, but it was very hard to hide things from his Companion. "Felix. Back in the river?"

Felix grinned. "I'll build a boat. Again."

CHAPTER THIRTEEN

Felix was as good as his word. After everyone had gotten dried off, he'd marched them to the riverbank and conjured a boat out of roots and vines. Well, 'boat' was a generous description. Felix had shaped a wide, uneven barge with a shallow belly and short railings. It was rough and kinda ugly, though a few patches of moss had flourished along its deck.

"Hm. This was definitely easier in the Passage," he'd muttered before gesturing for everyone to board.

The giants proved difficult to accommodate, but no more so than Felix himself, who almost sank the barge when he stepped on it. Normally, Pit would have found that funny, but when his paws got soaked, his first instinct had been to jump into the sky—only to have his back flare in terrible pain.

"You okay?" Felix asked. They were a ways across the river now, battling the swift currents with magic. The Goblin was in the back, pouring some Skill into the rear of the barge while the two giants used their icy weapons as paddles.

"Fine," Pit said. He looked at his Companion's feet and snorted.

"What?" Felix lifted one of his boots, and the Cloudstep beneath them crackled. "This was the easiest solution. I'm too heavy for a bunch of logs."

"Mhm. Surprised it could hold them."

"The giants? They're really light for their size." Felix looked at the two warriors, a chain of new thoughts sparking behind his eyes. "I wonder how many Evolutions they have. You think it's rude to ask? No, right?"

Pit let his friend wander away with thoughts pleasantly occupied and restrained a groan of relief. *Busy is good. He worries too much.*

They moved down the river, and Pit tried to enjoy the calm. The water was a constant murmur bordering on a roar, deep enough that there were no rapids or large rocks to bash their boat against but so strong that it took all of the Shadows' concentration to keep them on course. Pit sat on his hindlegs and all fours, but no position took his mind fully off the pain across his shoulders. It was a burning that never stopped, no matter the potions he lapped up or the salves the healers poured on. Whatever that High Guard had done with his damn sword, it wasn't getting better.

And he blames himself. Pit rubbed a russet paw against where his cheek met his beak. *Silly boy.*

"My Lord? Is that it?" Errol asked.

Felix stopped his pacing. "Oh! Yeah. The entrance is there."

Ahead of them loomed a large island, situated right in the center of the river. A thick, mini forest dominated it, hung heavily with white powder and blue shadows. It was rocky and rough, but there was a low, snowy slope alongside the eastern-most side that they immediately pivoted toward. The current was considerably stronger around the edges of the island, but with a little help from Felix, they were able to beach their barge a few minutes later.

Pit ambled off, for once enjoying the cold snow against his paws—it was a welcome distraction. Behind him, Felix let the barge collapse, the logs and vines rolling free into the river as the crew trudged up the slope.

"Alright. According to my map, the entrance is a ways into those trees there." Felix pointed toward a stand of pale goliaths of bark and green needles. "Stick close and keep an eye out. I don't sense any monsters we should be worried about, but, well."

He didn't need to finish the sentence. They had all experienced just how unpredictable this world could be, and the Shadows perhaps more than most. Protecting someone who got into as much trouble as his boy did was incredibly stressful. *Worth it, though,* he added with a fierce growl. Felix shot him a look, but Pit ignored it.

They walked a time, the giants blazing a trail through the waist-high snowdrifts and everyone else on high alert. Not Felix, though.

"Weird how we had to come to an island to get to the next Passage. Why is the entrance here? Is there a reason?"

"Dunno," Kress admitted. "You said these are spaces between the Realms, yes? Then perhaps it is like crockery."

Felix blinked. "I'm sorry?"

The Human mage flushed. "O-oh um, I mean, like when you drop a plate? The crockery breaks, but it does so in patterns based on how it fell. Maybe…maybe these Passages formed the same way?"

Felix was silent, but Pit let out a contemplative trill. "That's interesting."

"It is. Hm. If that's true, then how did they break in the first place? Did the Realms collide?" Felix wandered ahead, already lost in thought.

The mage stared after him, looking a little uneasy. "Is he…It was just a guess. I haven't the expertise to speak on such topics. I don't think he should consider it so seriously."

Pit laughed, a low warble in his throat. "Then say nothing. Felix thinks it's interesting, so it is."

"Oh." The mage's Spirit blossomed as confidence and a measure of self-satisfied warmth grew within her. "Alright."

Pit chirruped noncommittally, and their procession returned to a companionable silence. They passed a stand of ash trees, and the snow lessened considerably, allowing them to spread out from their single-file line into the forest.

What is that? Pit slowed his stride, sniffing at the air. *That smells…*

It was familiar, but in a way that Pit couldn't place at all. A vague sense of comfort and warmth bounced through his thoughts—memories of himself nestled against his mother, tucked in her fur and feathers as she flew above the Foglands. Now that it was conjured, Pit could almost see it, and each whiff of that intoxicating scent pushed the memories into sharper relief.

"We're here."

Pit drew to a stop, belatedly noticing that all the others had gathered around Felix in a loose semicircle. His Companion raised a glowing hand and slashed open another portal, this one a silver-studded expanse just as the last.

"Ok," Felix said. "Errol?"

"Of course, my Lord. Kress and Devi, enter with both eyes open and secure our landing space."

"Aye, sir," they responded in unison. The Human mage and Risi

Warrior stepped through, vanishing as if they'd sank beneath inky waves.

A handful of minutes later, the giant poked his head back through. "We are good, sir. It is very quiet, but we haven't seen anything come out of the waters."

Errol smiled. "Very well. My Lord? After you."

"Waters, huh?" Felix rubbed his hands together, his eager curiosity contagious. A grin pulled at Pit's expression, too. "I gotta see this."

Inside, it was much the same as the last Dark Passage. The sky was dark and nearly devoid of stars, an oppressive silence hung over the world like a shroud, and their group found themselves on a barren stone island. However, the mountains were replaced by a wide, rushing river that seemed to expand in every direction for miles. In the cloying dark, not even Felix's senses could pick out the shape of its banks.

Once again, Felix had created his flying boat. Unlike the log barge he'd made back in Nagast, the craft all but leaped into shape the moment Felix began, as if it were a mold he simply filled up with magic.

Curious, he mused. Felix ran his hands over the railings as they got underway again. *Is it because of Chthonic Traveler and Labyrinthine Wing that it's so easy to make stuff here?*

Lucky for them that it was so simple. Not ten minutes after taking flight, the little island was swarmed by strange, writhing shapes. *Void-beasts.* He recognized the feel of them, if not their exact type. *Never seen them before.*

Voracious Eye!

Name: Umbraflail
Type: Voidborn
Level: 65
HP: 4309/4309
SP: 3327/3444
MP: 340/0
Lore: Drawn to sources of Mana, these creatures are an evolution of the common Tenebril by reducing the amount of Mana required for them to survive. This means they have begun to subsist on pieces of the Void itself, which has

turned their flesh strange and greatly increased their aggression.
Strength: More Data Required
Weakness: More Data Required

"Oh, neat." Felix relayed the details to his team. "Let's keep away from them. I can...yeah, there's more in the water. We need to get higher."

Manaship Pilot is level 37!

Felix did just that, navigating their unnamed vessel—*Sailwhale!* Pit insisted, again—further away from the river's surface. Below, Felix could sense those Umbraflails moving about, gathering in groups large enough that he could never fully make out the shape of them. Like Tenebrils, they seemed to be mostly made of tentacles, which they used to swim through the waters and push off the numerous ice floes that bobbed in the mighty currents.

Heavy winds buffeted them, strong enough that several times the sharp gusts would produce a shower of multi-colored sparks from the crystal above their heads. Felix wove through them as best he could, guiding the ship among the chill weather with increasing skill. It was likely due to Labyrinthine Wing, but he started to find their path incredibly easy...even as he instinctively knew that, if they fell beneath those dark waters, they would not rise again.

The journey was oddly longer than the last leg. Perhaps that was because of a lack of reference points—it was all water and bobbing icebergs as far as the eye could see. They moved, clearly, but to Felix, it felt like running on a treadmill. However, when the exit drew near, his Skill made him aware of its location like a beacon in the dark.

Another island loomed ahead, this one covered in frost and small, stunted trees. Felix guided the ship down as gently as he could, but he still ended up grinding the bottom of the wooden whale's belly into several splintered trunks. Folks jerked and stumbled, the vessel coming to a rough and ignoble stop.

Pit gave a reproachful chirrup, and Felix grinned. "Sorry about that. We're here."

The Shadows climbed off the ship just behind Felix and his Companion, gathering behind them as he ripped open the exit portal with a glimmering fist. The wind immediately went wild, both around them and from within the portal itself.

"Holy crap, what's going on there?" Felix asked. Just inside the portal the light swirled in a riot of blues, greens, and white as a bone-deep chill rolled like fog into the Passage.

"The Hoarfrost," Veddi said with a long inhale. "That's the Wildfrost. I'd recognize that scent anywhere."

"Home," confirmed Devvi.

"Wildfrost?" Pit asked.

"Big storm that roves the north. Moves like an animal, hunting the weak and uplifting those strong enough to face its wrath." Veddi grinned, his steel-colored teeth gleaming in the arctic light. "A potent sign for your arrival, my Lord."

"Let's hope so. I'll go first, this time." Felix walked up, ignoring lieutenant Errol's protests, and he stepped through the portal.

Snow dominated his view, a lace curtain that immediately blinded him to all but the razor-sharp wind that was so cold it cut through a good portion of his resistance. His Garment rippled, responding to his needs to become a heavy, fur-lined coat and breeches, and Felix took several cautious steps forward.

Honestly, this is kinda nice compared to the bleak river. His legs crunched in knee-high drifts as he made a small circle around the portal. *I don't—Ah. People.*

There were many nearby, two groups, perhaps five hundred yards to the north. His Perception was a bit stymied by the dazzling swirl of wind and snow, so it was his Affinity that caught their presence. Moreover, it snagged on immense quantities of aggression, anger, and pain.

Behind him, the portal flared as his Shadows and Pit pushed through. "Stay together; there's something going on."

Pit shoved his way to Felix's side, ears laid flat against his head as he squinted into the storm. "What is it?"

"I think—" A scream ripped across the sky, louder by far than the howling wind. A fleet of creatures tore through the falling snow, incredibly fast and trailing tails of purple-white Mana. "Shields up! Defensive positions!" Felix ordered.

"The creatures are distracted!" screamed a voice he recognized. It was from one of the group up ahead. "We attack now!"

Kimaris.

"No! They are ours, traitor! Witches! Loose thy power!"

All at once, Felix felt a concussive *whump* as Skills were launched en masse. Through the chaotic storm and the wheeling monsters in the air, he couldn't keep track of the kinds of attacks…only that his people were dead center in the way.

God fucking damn it.

CHAPTER FOURTEEN

The Witches of Cold Rock stood tall in the snow, ten strong and ready for battle. Though their blue skin was lined and their wispy white locks were far from the luster of youth, they had eyes like ice and the bearing of queens. Behind them, fifty Risi stood in leather and fur, with black iron clubs hefted onto their shoulders. The warriors—if one could call them that—were as young and unproven as the Witches were ancient and calculating.

"You are not welcome here, traitor!"

Kimaris took their words like a blow, but she met their gazes, chin held high. "I will say it again: the Chieftain has fallen. Grimmar is dead and his cause abandoned."

A woman with sharp cheekbones sneered. "Then who stands before us? Are you not Kimaris, Witch of the Wilds, Frostborn to the Wastes, kin of Cold Rock? The first to follow Grimmar? The Witch who spoke of the Mother in dulcet tones and stole away our bravest die?"

"I am all of those things, Naberius. But I am more." Kimaris gestured to her people, the warriors who stood at her back. Twenty had come, those that had grown strongest under the Autarch's training, and they were a bulwark of fine armor and weaponry. "*We* are more. Transformed by the might of our new leader, as I have told you time and again."

Naberius smirked. "You come bearing a few levels and new gear and hope to...what? Sway us into following yet another blood-mad tyrant?

No. A thousand times no. The deprivations of Grimmar will never be forgotten, nor forgiven."

"We—"

"You will not be heard! Our warriors have dawdled in this Pass for too long. We will subdue our Domain, then we shall return to Cold Rock. You!" The Witch jabbed a sharp-nailed finger at Kimaris. "You and your pawns will return to the fog wall and never return. You are not welcome in the Hoarfrost."

The blizzard around them raged, howling from the north like a fell beast. Curtains of snow swirled around them, tearing at cloaks and hair, yet Kimaris' eyes never left her former friend. "Let us close the Domain, then. Your charges are barely beyond their first Evolution, their weapons unstained by true battle. To risk them on a Domain break is suicide."

"They are ready to lay down their lives for their people," another Witch spoke up. Berith. "The Domain is an anvil, and we are the cold iron. Battle is but a hammer to shape them for their destinies."

Sudden screams tore through the storm, sharper and frenetic than the howling wind. The young warriors shifted, a few even flinching, as the Witches hissed out rapid-fire Skills of detection.

"Heartsblood Seeker!" Kimaris did the same, casting her senses upward, feeling through the omnipresent chill for spots of warmth. Magic spun behind her eyes, flaring brighter and brighter as she picked out forms in the sky. "Brumalbats. Perhaps two dozen."

"Did the walls fall already?" another Witch asked, clutching a stout stave in her withered hands.

"It is too soon!" Berith hissed. "There are days left before it breaks!"

Kimaris stepped forward, her warriors left behind. "Let me aid you. Together, we can slay the monsters—"

"This is only a small escape. Those of the Hoarfrost will take care of it," Naberius said, venom on her sharp face.

"You lost your people—*our* people—to mere *Humans*," spat Berith from around Naberius' shoulder. "Do not speak to us of martial prowess. Begone!"

The Witches of Cold Rock huddled together, drawing their young charges close as the cries of monsters increased tenfold. Kimaris stifled a curse and went back to her men.

"What should we do?" Battlelord Vidar asked the moment she was close. He was a stocky male by Risi standards, only topping Kimaris by three feet, but he had proven himself in a dozen bloody battles. He had joined Battlelord Ari and Kimaris as one of the Risi's leadership right before they left Elderthrone. "This has gone on too long."

"Tuata na. We are speaking to a wall," another warrior said. Trond, Vidar's second. "They are not willing to move. So they must fall."

"You think we should leave them here to fight a Domain break on their own?" Kimaris scowled up at the bearded warrior. Trond held her gaze for only a moment before he shifted his feet nervously. "They will not survive. I have spent too much time in the Ironskin Domain to know its dangers. I sent word to Karys for aid."

"Aid that will not come, not before they are eradicated," Vidar pointed out. "And us along with them, if we stay here. Let us retreat to the Enclosure. We have extended our hand. Let them reap the consequences."

That would be the simplest play, Kimaris silently agreed. *Let Cold Rock fail before rescuing them…* Yet if a dozen Brumalbats escaped already, then how long did they have until more descended? And if something else, something worse within the heart of the Ironskin Domain emerged? *They would all die.*

The Domain's inner portions were not broached by their people—only Grimmar had ever braved the core and survived. It was one of the reasons Kimaris had chosen to join his faction in the early days. Before the world had gone mad.

"Back!" Trond cried, shoving Kimaris and Vidar to the side. Piercing shrieks exploded from above, ripping apart the ground where they had just stood.

Kimaris rolled to her feet, furs and robes split around her legs, hands already coated in a corona of purple-white vapor. More explosions racked the field, but the majority of them were focused on the Cold Rock warriors. Shapes with jagged wings darted from above, swooping low before unleashing more of those screeching blasts. Not two dozen, but two *hundred*. It was hard to make out details in the chaos, but they had hidden themselves somehow. Each monster was at least as big as herself, with double that in wingspan, and their sonic attacks were deadly.

"Should we help?" Vidar asked.

Kimaris gritted her teeth. Her people were dying—and no matter what that desiccated Witch Berith said, all Risi were her people. "Fall in! We're fighting, whether they like it or not!"

"Aye! You heard her, men! Votan tii nata!" Battlelord Vidar met

Kimaris' eye and nodded as the warriors pivoted smoothly into position. "We await your direction."

Kimaris activated her Heartsblood Seeker, and the heat Mana generated by all living things was unveiled. The chaos of storm and furious combat was simplified, her erstwhile allies demarcated from the flying monstrosities. "Ready your strikes! Aim for the bulk of their forces! On pain of death, do not hit a single Risi!"

"Aktalla! Mid-range! Draw on your ice!" Vidar lifted his hand, now wreathed in crackling ice vapor. "Steady!"

Power gathered around her as Kimaris readied her own power. Curses boiled across her core, grown potent on the glut of experience and Mana she had absorbed these long months. Black joined the purple-white of her Mana, shadows so dark that they buckled the icy element of her Skills, twisting them into newer, deadlier weapons. The Brumalbats struck again, and the bulk of them lifted up, twisting into the air in great loops. *Now. While they're away.* "N—!"

Heartsblood Seeker is level 43!

An abrupt explosion of heat cast the snow and ice around them vibrant, violent relief. Colors skewed, blowing out her Skill's sensitivity until, for a moment, everything was painted in shades of crimson.

"Gah!" Kimaris shouted, eyes half-blinded. The Status Condition floated across her notifications.

Dazzled: Sight Impairment (Minor)

Yet, she was not so blinded that she missed what happened next. The monsters wheeled in the sky, pivoting away from the denizens of Cold Rock and toward the origin of the explosion.

"The creatures are distracted!" Kimaris shouted. "We attack now!"

Her words were loud, perhaps louder than necessary, for Naberius shrieked in response. "No! They are ours, traitor! Witches! Loose your power!"

Icebolts and curses tore through the storm, converging upon the Brumalbats just as the monsters descended upon that strange new arrival. Mana steamed and the blizzard howled, as if echoing the Brumalbats' impending agony, and Kimaris felt a glimmer of triumph thrill her Spirit.

We are worth your attention, Cold Rock! We have not abandoned you!

Skills landed before the monsters reached their target, tearing through one after the other with brutal efficiency. Brumalbats were fodder enemies in the Ironskin Domain, but a hunting party had not faced so many before, not all at once. The sheer mass of them was undaunted by their attacks and unleashed their screams all at once. The snow burst, ripping outward in a concussive blast that peppered the Witch with shards of ice. Kimaris stared, aghast and alarmed, but not at the debris.

A figure stood in the center, dark as midnight and gleaming with blood-red fury.

Autarch.

Lightning blasted in all directions, followed by a thunder so loud it drowned the storm out entirely. Witches and warriors fell back, driven to their knees as incandescent tendrils ripped into the Brumalbats. All of them at once. The monsters screeched and flapped their massive wings, but the hundreds did nothing but careen wildly, hurting one another with their claws.

"SOVEREIGN OF FLESH!"

The words shook something in Kimaris, grabbing hold of a piece of her that she had never known existed. The sky itself darkened, pressed low upon her shoulders as if it were collapsing upon them all. Unholy shrieks filled her ears as clouds and snow and wind roared in sympathetic rage…and then it was gone.

Kimaris stood, barely maintaining her balance, and gazed outward.

"Tuak *na*," Vidar whispered. "They're all gone."

"Not gone," she said, pointing at the cloud of red and black as it swirled above them all. There was no sign of the two hundred Brumalbats, but their pulped bodies had been smeared across the sky—rendered into paste where it wasn't turned to mist. The cyclone pulled down, and all of it vanished into the maw of the only being that terrified her more than Grimmar. More than the Mother of Monsters Herself. "Taken. Consumed."

"Autarch," Trond said, his tone nothing short of reverent.

The word spread like flames on tinder, a whispered affirmation. A *devotion*.

Felix Nevarre. Lord of Nagast and Ahkestria.

The Fiend.

"Well that was exciting," Felix muttered. Those monsters—giant bats made of ice, it looked like—had a good deal of Essence and Mana in them, but not nearly as much as some. "Everyone alright?"

"F-fine, sir," Errol said after a moment. "A few minor nicks from debris. Nothing a Healing Potion won't solve."

The other Shadows grunted or nodded earnestly in agreement, so Felix put them out of his mind. Pit, on the other hand, he patted on the neck. "You good, too?"

"Stop worrying," Pit growled. "Next time, leave some for me."

Felix lifted his hands into the air. "Alright, alright." He looked to the field around them. His burst of power had cleared the area of falling snow for a bit, but it was coming back in force, hanging like a curtain in front of their eyes. Still, he spotted two distinct groups of Frost Giants. "Looks like we showed up at a bad time. That's Kimaris and her team, but…Veddi, Devvi, do you know these folks?"

The giants beside him frowned through the snow. "Witches," Devvi said, followed by Veddi's words. "Cold Rock."

Ah. The aforementioned pissing contest.

Those Witches, ten of them, stomped forward with anger and fear stamped across their Spirits. Youthful warriors followed them, many of whom were limping or supporting one another. A sharp-faced Witch took the lead, back far less bent than the others. She looked close to Kimaris in age, who was even now hustling forward with all twenty of her warriors in tow. "Who dares interfere in a hunt of the Kin on their own lands?"

"Hi there," he said, smiling pleasantly at them all. "I'm here to save your lives."

CHAPTER FIFTEEN

"My Lord!"

Kimaris and her Risi Warriors gave the Witches a wide berth as they approached Felix, refusing to even look at them. They appeared to be in good health. His Voracious Eye picked out a mere handful of wounds on the warriors, while Kimaris was looking pristine in her dark fur cloak and stole.

"Kimaris. Battlelord Vidar." Felix gave them all a smile. "Hope your mission hasn't been too rough, here."

The leader of his Frost Giant faction answered his smile with a dazzling one of her own. "Rough suits the Risi. We are a people of hardships—we do not look away from a difficult task. Even when our efforts are…stymied."

"So I heard." Felix nodded at the torn-up ground and, beyond, the other Risi. "They're giving you trouble?"

"They are, how do you say, stonewalling us," Battlelord Vidar said.

"The Witches of Cold Rock have issued an ultimatum. We are not allowed to cross the Boreal Pass, and no alliance will be had," Kimaris added.

"Is that so," Felix murmured. He walked forward, snow crunching beneath his boots. The Cold Rock Risi watched him with sharp eyes and almost eager Spirits. The Witch from before, Naberius according to his Eye, stepped out to meet him.

"Who are you, Human?" she demanded.

"Felix Nevarre. Autarch of Nagast and Ahkestria. And you're Naberius, Witch of Cold Rock, Heir of the Seidr."

Naberius drew her shoulders back, making the lady giant seem all the taller. "What do you know of Cold Rock. Of the Seidr." Her eyes twitched, just for a moment, toward Kimaris. "What has *she* revealed to you, Human?"

Lotta complicated emotions going on here. Diving into it all with his Affinity was the equivalent of grabbing a hot pan off the stove with his bare hands. Ill-advised, at best. "Nothing. Kimaris keeps your people's secrets, and I don't make a habit of prying. She is here under my orders. To reach an understanding between our peoples."

Mana swirled behind the giant's eyes, a blur of purple, white, and crimson. "You are not strong enough to command even a single Witch, Human. I do not know what trickery you used to kill those Brumalbats, but I can see your mortal Temper. It is lacking."

Felix suppressed the urge to fiddle with the Amulet of Veiling around his neck. It was a Chanter artifact that kept his personal details from being spied on—even gave false details, such as now—and half the time, he forgot he was wearing it. He was tempted to take it off, show the Witches exactly who they were dealing with, but that wasn't necessary. Not yet. "Despite that, Kimaris and all of her remaining people are sworn to me. Perhaps there is a reason, beyond simple strength?"

Another Witch—Berith—jabbed a thick stave in his direction, a scowl twisting her wrinkled skin. "Strength is all, false king! Rule cannot be had without might, otherwise it will collapse beneath the weight of its meanest challenge."

Naberius placed a restraining hand on the older Witch. "'Our peoples.' Those were your words. You would call monsters kin, Human?"

"I would."

No words were exchanged among the Witches, but a ripple traveled between them all. Felix could see the Mana of it, some Skill clearly, as it spread from Naberius to the others. It matched the wave of surprise and outrage that puckered their Spirits. More interesting to him, however, was the dim purl of curiosity. Finally, their silent communion ended.

"You claimed to be here to 'save our lives,'" Naberius said. "I would ask that you explain."

That's almost polite, he mused. "I've been informed that one of your Domains is breaking. I have experience with handling such things, and I would offer my services."

Berith scoffed, as did several others. "Just as Kimaris said. A fool king for a fool girl."

"How?" Naberius asked. "This Domain is powerful and ancient, and it's breaking has been coming for a long while. There is no stopping it, not for an outsider like yourself. At best, you would stem the tide, as you have done here."

A chunk of bloody snow skid across the ground and into the giants' feet. Pit followed after, paws crunching the icy snow. "He did a pretty good job at that, and I wasn't even helping."

"Chimera," another Witch hissed, one so old she looked like a scarecrow in all of her furs.

"Giant," Pit repeated back at them. "See? I can do that, too."

Felix shot his friend a sharp look, but Pit pretended not to see it. "What my Companion is trying to say is that this is not the extent of our abilities. Together, we *can* close your Domain entirely."

"We do not seek that. The Ironskin Domain is a training ground for our people and cannot be lost. Only the Witches possess the Skill and knowledge to preserve its boundaries."

"Okay. That's fair. Then tell me how it's accomplished and, as an act of goodwill, my Companion and I will go and solve the problem."

"Goodwill. From a mortal." Naberius smiled, but the expression was all sharp edges. "Forgive us if we do not trust your word. Even if you swore an Oath, and even if I trusted it, still you would fail. Against the threats within the Ironskin Domain, you will perish."

Felix shoved his irritation down, out of sight. They were being difficult, but what else could he expect? "Then what have you got to lose? Either I stop the Domain from breaking, or I die. For you, that's a win either way."

"He has a point," Berith said. Her withered face was twisted with a dark glee. "With Kimaris and her traitors in tow, it would cull the last of Grimmar's brood."

Felix wasn't a fan of *that* name, and neither was Naberius, apparently. "Still your tongue, Berith. They are *kin*," she snapped.

The older Witch scowled, but stepped back as Naberius continued. "But you have me intrigued, Human. What do you expect to gain from this act of madness? Goodwill alone does not drive mortals or monsters."

"I've never seen the benefit of acting like everyone else does. I'd rather help out a neighbor, if I can."

Felix wasn't sure if it was his argument or the 25% bonus he had for dealing with Giantfolk, but he could see the moment when Naberius decided to agree with him. There was no silent conversation and no ripple of emotion, either. It was like a lightbulb had been switched on somewhere inside her, and her emotions went suddenly still. Neutral, like the ice around them.

"Very well." She snapped her fingers, and the warriors behind them shuffled quickly into a double-file line behind her. "We shall show you the Ironskin Domain, Human. Follow."

They began to march and, after a long look at Kimaris and Pit, Felix did just that.

"The entire thing?" Kimaris' lavender skin had paled as soon as he explained his plan. "I do not know if even your might can withstand the Ironskin Domain's Core, my Lord."

Felix waved away her worries. "I'll be fine. I'll have Pit with me, and besides, the Witches say we can just stabilize the Domain. I won't have to face the Core." *Even if I would prefer that,* he added silently. He was fairly annoyed to miss out on so much Essence, but the realities of inter-Territorial diplomacy couldn't be entirely denied.

Will it be enough? Pit asked. He sounded tired again.

Yes. Felix quashed any doubt in his Mind and Spirit, refusing to let Pit see it. *It'll be enough.*

They were walking along a thin ridge, where the mountains broke up into narrow canyons hundreds of feet deep. The Domain entrance was somewhere ahead, hidden by the switchback path. The blizzard still raged around them, filled with a furious magic that reduced visibility to almost nothing. Even Felix's Perception was blunted as they traversed the treacherous ravines that split the Boreal Pass. The Witches had their newbie warriors using their Mantle of the Long Night to fuel the construction of ice bridges, but they were rickety things designed to fall apart within a few hours, according to Kimaris.

A little surreptitious Rime Shaping fixed that, strengthening them until they were strong enough to hold Felix's weight. *A little getaway path is always nice, too.*

Felix could have gotten there faster with Adamant Discord or even Cloudstep, even accounting for the time he would have had to spend searching for the Domain. He'd assessed every one of the Witches and

Risi Warriors, and none would last long in a fight against him. But right now, he had to make sure he played by their rules.

He was there to stop the Domain break, secure some Essence, and hopefully gain some new allies. Felix forced himself to remember that each time one of the Witches threw him a nasty, contemptuous look. They either could not hide or simply did not care to hide their Spirits, and the sheer, poisonous disdain coming from the elderly Witches was enough to kill a thousand Brumalbats.

They fought some more of those, but far fewer than what Felix had eradicated. Stragglers, really, haunting the depths of the winter storm. Nothing else had escaped from the Domain. Yet.

"We have arrived," Naberius announced.

Ahead, beyond a shelf of stone that acted as a windbreak, a deep fissure marred the mountain. Within that fissure was a shimmering portal.

"Wow," Kress whispered. "It's beautiful."

"The metal-attuned Domain didn't look like this," Geddin agreed. "It was like a hole in the ground with stairs."

"Different Domains manifest in different ways. Has to do with the monsters that began their formation," Felix said. He'd read that from one of the many books he'd snagged from Ahkestria. "I'm gonna go ahead and assume the monsters here love ice."

The entrance looked like it was composed of solid light. Dazzling motes of ice swirled atop its surface, causing a layer of frost to crackle and pop.

"Ironskin Domain. Attuned to stone, metal, and ice," Naberius intoned. Her voice had the cadence of a ritual, and it was clear she wasn't just speaking to Felix, but to all of her warriors as well. "This is our birthright. Our crucible, given to us by the Frostfather when the Mother abandoned us. It is here that our warriors are forged. And it is here that we test the mettle of Felix Nevarre."

Felix frowned. Test him?

"As all chieftains before him, he faces a challenge of great difficulty. He will face the threats of the Domain with naught but himself and his own abilities. We—the Witches of Cold Rock, Heirs of Seidr and the gifts of the Frostfather—we shall test him in the old ways. Felix Nevarre shall emerge worthy…or not at all."

Pit's ears laid back, and a great rumble shook his chest and barding. "They want you to die."

"Maybe." Felix laid a hand onto his friend's neck, where his armor had a thin gap, and scratched. "If I had a level for every time someone has wanted me dead, I'd be a god."

Pit snorted. "You'd be a terrible god."

"What? I'd be great." Felix pressed his forehead against Pit's own, not caring that the metal armor around wanted to freeze onto his bare skin. "There's not enough giants in this pass to take me on."

Pit let loose a trill that was neither acceptance nor relief, but it was the closest Felix would expect. He straightened. "Kimaris. What're they talking about?"

"They will accompany you, my Lord. That much is clear. The other—" She hesitated, staring at the other Witches as all of them shuffled toward the Domain entrance. "To treat you as a warrior looking to claim his right as chieftain is…unprecedented."

"What does that mean in practical terms?"

"I cannot speak on the details of a chieftain's test, but it is a challenge that pits the Domain against the limits of your strength. There are layers within, nine in total, and the farther one walks, the closer one comes to the Domain Core itself and certain death. Yet, the closer to the center one treads, the greater their position when they emerge." Kimaris wetted her lips with the tip of her tongue. "Grimmar was the first to conquer six of the nine layers. It is part of why he was able to unite so many of us and lead the expedition south to—" Kimaris snapped her mouth shut, jaw muscles clenching. She did not look at him.

To Shelim and his friends. Felix fought back a rough, unhealed anger. He had to remind himself that the giants weren't entirely responsible for their own actions, that the Maw had manipulated them—but it took him a moment to calm down. A lot of people had died back then, including Grimmar and almost four hundred Risi.

"Felix Nevarre," Naberius called out, loud enough to hear perfectly over the storm. "Do you wish to walk the path of rule?"

The Witches stood in a semi-circle around the Domain entrance, but three were beside it, watching him. Waiting for him.

Piece of cake, he told himself and started walking over. "Yeah, sure. So long as you promise my people will all remain safe until I get back."

"It is as you say. No harm shall come to them, not from us. But," Naberius held up a large hand about the size of Felix's head. "You alone will enter. Your Chimera will remain."

"What?"

"To walk the path of rule, you must walk without the support of anyone but yourself. The only thing you can truly rely upon. It is—"

This time, Felix held up a hand, stopping them mid-speech. "Screw that. He's with me, and I'm with him. Always."

Pit trilled, matching his aggression. "Yeah. What he said."

"Then you cannot—" Berith started to say, but Felix wasn't listening.

C'mon, Pit. They converged in a flash of light, dazzling the Witches around them. The Witches' screams of alarm and warning were ignored. Felix dashed straight ahead into the Domain.

Ice shattered, and silence descended.

CHAPTER SIXTEEN

Felix had experienced the protections around Domains before, and this one was no different. It appeared as the dark Void, but the floor was glossy and mirrored, providing an uncertain horizon line as circles of radiant sigaldry flickered to life all around him. The sheath around Domains was a liminal space not unlike a Dark Passage or Shadowgate, but unlike those others, this was far more limited.

You Have Entered Into The Domain Of Another.
Beware—!
It App—ERROR!

Entrant(s) Exceed Domain Strictures!
Full Manifestation May Damage Shell Integrity.
Ejecting...

ERROR!
Ejection Failed!
Countermeasures Deployed.

Felix ignored the messages that boomed across his consciousness. He'd seen them before, back when the Domain below Haarwatch was failing. Back then, the presence of him and his allies had strained the integrity of the Domain's bounds, leading to further fracturing of its substance. Just as then, gleaming formations of sigaldry appeared around him: looping, radial structures made of brilliant purple-white Mana vapor. Pressure manifested around his limbs, gravity wrapped about him like a lead cloak, connected to the formations by glittering lines.

He simply walked through them all.

ERROR—!

The countermeasures burst with the shrieking sound of feedback, sigaldry flinging away from Felix like shrapnel. Pressure surged, attempting to hold him in place, to prevent him from entering the Domain at all. Yet Felix's very feet shook the dark until cracks formed across the mirrored floor. Daylight leaked from those fissures, illuminating dust motes wherever they touched and emanating a deep, bone-aching chill.

The exit.

Felix stomped again, and this time, the liminal space could not hold.

Warning!
Entrant(s) Exceed Shell Parameters.
Manifestation Actualized.

Shell Integrity Damaged.
Extant Damage - 75%
Shell Integrity Reduced from 75% to 22%!

Shell Integrity...Stabilized.

The light swallowed up the dark, and Felix dropped as if falling through an icy lake. He landed, legs spread for balance, atop cold stone and snow, while the last remnants of his crossing were blown away by a frigid northern gale.

He was in.

Pit separated from him, landing gracefully and stretching to his full height. "That was uncomfortable. It's not usually so cramped."

"Domain restrictions," Felix said by way of explanation, and Pit nodded sagely.

"Like Haarwatch. The Domains near home didn't feel like that." He rolled a warbling note in his throat, thinking. "Because this one is failing, too?"

"That's what I'm thinking. The other ones were strong enough to handle our entrance...based on what I've heard, this one should be able to handle our strength, too. Haarwatch only really allowed for lower-Tier entrants on top of being busted." Felix knelt down and ran his hands across the cold rock and snow. Stone crumbled slightly, like talc, even without exerting his Strength. "This place seems worse, though."

You Have Survived.
The Challenge Is Incomplete.
Be Wary, Young Primordial.

Oh, there it is. The usual refrain when he entered a Domain. Typically, to exit it, one would face the Domain Core or some guardian beast that was at the center. At least, if he planned to exit on the other end. If he just turned around, Felix could simply pop back out into the mountain pass with his Shadows.

"It called you a Primordial," Pit pointed out.

"It is what it is," Felix said with a shrug. It had bothered him a lot, once, but without the Race change, he wouldn't have been able to withstand half of what he'd been put through. "I'm still me."

Apart from the rocky promontory they stood on, the land was excessively flat all around. A plain of ice and snow extended in all directions, but the sharp winds were not alone among the ice: huge stone and metal spires speared up from the ground, hundreds of them, all at varying angles but none fully straight. Still, they rose so high that clouds of ice enveloped their tops, like a skyborn river of glass. A winter sun struck gleaming highlights off them all, a blinding radiance that forced Felix to reel in his Perception a bit.

He blinked. The cold had a bite to it that was vaguely familiar. It smelled of the vacant space where pollen and rain-turned earth might have been before and, oddly enough, like pine. A memory tumbled on the heels of that scent, when he, his mother, and his sister Gabby had gone north to visit family. It had been an effort to escape the crowds that swarmed their home on school holidays, and instead ended up with them stuck in a blizzard in a small motel sixty miles from anywhere.

There was no warning, as with when he consumed an enemy's Memory. There was only the sudden, total embrace of recollection, fully fledged and detailed in the way only his Born Trait could provide. The feel of cheap sheets, the low-pile carpet that smelled faintly of cigarettes, and even the overstuffed recliners in front of one of those old tvs—the boxy ones, not a sleek flatscreen. His mother, overtired, slept off the long drive north, while he had clicked aimlessly through static and daytime soap operas.

"I'm sick of this," Gabby groaned, and started rummaging through their luggage.

"What are you doing?" he asked. Anything was more interesting than *Days of Our Children* or whatever he had on.

"I'm hungry, and I saw vending machines when we came in."

"Yeah? So? That's like ten rooms away, and in case you haven't noticed, we're snowed in."

Like most motels, the doors led outside, and the unrelenting snow had buried the building. The snow had piled so high that for a few hours they were stuck in the room, with drifts against the doors and darkening the windows. He couldn't even see sunlight through them anymore.

"Whatever." Gabby stood up from the luggage, tugging on what had to be her fifth sweater. This one had a picture of a mermaid holding up a big crystal. "I'm going out."

"You're such a pest. You are not." Gabby didn't stop her march toward the front door, and the recliner squealed under him as he sat up. "You're gonna get snow in the room!"

She stared at him, all challenge and that stupid smirk. "Afraid of a little cold?"

Before he could stop her, she whipped open the door…and was met by a wall of snow that wasn't nearly as solid as she hoped. A wave of white rushed into the room, burying her as she let out the funniest sound he'd ever heard in his life—a goose's honk mixed with a surprised, high-pitched squeal.

He remembered laughing so hard he fell out of his chair.

"It's not funny! Help me!"

The memory left him, gone just as fast as it had arrived. It had been so clear and sharp that Felix took a moment to remember where exactly he stood, though the sight of his own blackened fingers provided a sudden clarity.

Holy crap. That was a doozy. Felix ran his hands over his face. The small scales on his palms were smooth and cold. His Born Trait didn't activate often for memories beyond thirty days prior, a feature he was glad for—he couldn't imagine having that sort of recollection about *everything* all the time. No one needed that.

Felix made it a point not to think about Earth and his family too much. It made him sad, usually, because, at the end of the day, he had left everything behind without a word. His mom, his sister. They probably thought he was dead after that yacht fight.

It's better that way.

"Felix," Pit warned, just as the air fuzzed behind them.

"Ah. Took you long enough," Felix said to the Witches who emerged from outside the Domain. "Only three of you?"

Naberius, nine feet tall and statuesque, glared at him from under sharp white brows. "You should have waited. You have damaged the Domain further."

The other two Witches were far older, stooped and withered, but no less powerful. In the way of monster rankings, they'd each be the equivalent of an Adept-Tier combatant. Certainly stronger than most, but far less of a strain on the Domain that he and Pit. One of them, Sitri, narrowed her pale eyes at him. "How did you do such a thing, Human?"

Felix shrugged. "I thought this place was strong enough that no one's ever beaten it."

"It is," said the third. Fornis.

"And you plan to fix it?"

"We do. We shall."

Felix regarded them all evenly. "Then what's the problem?"

"It is certainly an issue if you break the Domain fully before we can reach the Fifth Layer. That is where we must go to reverse the deterioration of this place." Naberius regarded him down the length of her aquiline nose. "If you can make it."

Felix laughed. "Lady, you—"

Thunder rolled across the landscape, but not from the sky. A stone and metal pillar cracked and collapsed, sending clouds of snow and debris into the air even as its rumbling shook their footing apart.

"Whoa, that's not good," Pit chirruped. He hopped across the rocks, his wide paws barely finding purchase beneath the crumbling earth. "It's falling apart. All of it."

"We need to move, immediately," Naberius insisted. "The sooner we exit the First Layer, the sooner we will put this dissolution behind us."

"Frostfather's mercy," Sitri whispered, lifting an ancient hand to point into the sky.

"Whoa." Above them, those shifting clouds of glass were moving.

Toward them. "Those aren't clouds," Felix said after flaring a Skill. "Those are Brumalbats."

Thousands upon thousands of those man-sized bat monsters surged from the sky, their icy wings ringing like an army of windchimes well before the first shrieking reached their ears. They wound around the other pillars, still too far to attack them but gaining speed by the second.

"Saved some for you, Pit."

The tenku laughed through his closed beak. He tilted his head at the Witches. "You'll want to step back, old ladies."

Naberius sniffed. "We shall aid you."

"Not necessary," Felix said.

Sitri scoffed. "Our aid is all that will save you."

"Then we'll fail, right?" Mana crackled across his hands, looping through his pathways with increased fervor. "You said do this alone, right?"

"A temporary pause," Naberius interjected. "The strictures of our test do not account for this breakdown of order. Our curses will—"

"Nah. We're doing this the right way." Felix said and began to sound the patterns of his Skills.

"Hey!" Pit cut in. He let out a trumpeting cry. "This is *my* turn!"

"I'm not gonna kill them outright, just setting the stage." With his Affinity, Felix flared the song of a Skill he didn't use very often, relishing the sound of it as the Chant amplified its power. His Intent guided it, shaping its eventual release. "Remember the Tomb of Eternal Slumber?"

Pit's golden eyes glinted in the wintry sunlight. "Oh, *yeah.*" He lowered his head and raised his rear, fluffy fox tail lashing the air. "Set 'em up."

Rain of Cataclysm!

Acid Mana fled Felix's channels, billowing outward in a liquid rush as it ascended into the sky. The spell was a big one, meant for a wide area, and that was evident in just how much Mana it used. Virulent green liquid flooded the air, swirling all around their stone promontory until they resembled nothing so much as clouds themselves. The Brumalbats shrieked louder, the first few unleashing sonic blasts that tore holes in his magic.

"Pit!"

"Tempest Fugit!"

Lightning and ice Mana roared from Pit's channels before shooting off directly into Felix's acid clouds. The moment his Skill touched

Felix's, they both could feel their bond sing as their abilities combined and changed. What emerged from the other side of the clouds were dozens upon dozens of frozen spears crackling with bottled lightning and composed entirely of acid.

Ice shattered and thunder boomed as the first Brumalbats fell, but that was only the beginning. Pit shrieked out his Skill again and again, passing it through Felix's clouds and amplifying the effects. Normally, Tempest Fugit was a spear of ice that, upon shattering, unleashed a localized burst of lightning. Now, each spear sizzled through dozens of monsters before the acidic ice wore away and delivered a payload of electrical damage. It was a massacre…but not quite enough. After the first thousand, Pit was flagging, his Mana all but gone.

Allow me, Felix sent through their bond.

The Chant allowed Sorcerers to alter and amplify their Skills without the System. This worked by utilizing their Harmonic stats to access, activate, and shape the Skills inside their own cores. Affinity and Intent were the primary movers and shakers in that operation—though all of his Harmonic stats played a role—and Felix had enough of both that it was a simple issue to change the layout of his acid clouds. His Intent shifted, no longer open and accepting the combination with Pit's Skills, but aimed back toward his Skill's original purpose.

Rain of Cataclysm surged outward, a horizontal, torrential downpour. Acid rain shot through the Brumalbats, eating through wing and claw with ease, until the sky was filled with their dying shrieks and the sound of broken, tinkling glass.

You Have Killed A Brumalbat (x2435)!
XP Earned!

Your Companion Pit Has Gained 2 Levels!
Pit Is Now Level 72!
He Gains:
+20 STR, +18 PER, +8 VIT, +22 END, +14 INT, +20 WIL, +40 AGL, +40 DEX!
+20 AFI, RES, and REI!

Pit let out a cry of triumph as he shimmered with System power, his fur and feathers crackling with retrained might. "That feels much better!"

Felix grinned, but it was halted by two more blue screen notifications that appeared, each bordered by gold.

New Title!
Ironskin Nemesis (Epic)!
By force of arm or magic, you have defeated a truly staggering amount of foes, proving yourself a true threat to the Ironskin Domain! As a result, all denizens of the Domain will see you as a true enemy and will attack on sight. +40 END and VIT!

Challenge Initiated!
Path of Rule!
You have taken the first step upon the Path. The Frostfather applauds you. How far can you climb?

"Huh." Felix looked to the Witches. Their faces were drawn and haggard, and they watched him like he was a wild animal. "You said the name before, but who the hell is the Frostfather?"

CHAPTER SEVENTEEN

"The Frostfather is our god. He of the ice and night, whose power birthed our people," Naberius said.

They were walking across the frigid plains, but most of the snow was hidden under the weight of bat corpses. The enemies kept on coming, even after the initial rush. He devoured their bodies as he listened to the Witches' explanations. To their credit, Naberius managed to hide her shock as clouds of smoky lights poured into Felix's mouth. Her voice barely stuttered.

"Wh-when the first breath of winter arrived on the Continent, the Frostfather was there, shepherding it until it formed our home. The Hoarfrost. From the ice, he made us. The Risi, born to thrive in the lands of cold stone. To rule."

"Wait," Felix said, a wisp of Essence trailing from his mouth. "I thought the Mother had her hands in things. And that mortals pushed the Risi into the north." He remembered that from his first interactions with the Frost Giants…and an instructive discussion with Grimmar. "But you're saying you've always been here?"

Sitri clucked her tongue and her jowls shook. "Born of ice and stone, but with Spirits of fire. The Risi seek conquest. For a great many generations, we lived in the southlands. We claimed them."

"And the Mother is…apocryphal. That one being created all the various monsters upon the Continent is foolishness bordering on blasphemy." Naberius bared her teeth at the middle distance, as if remembering something foul. "It matters little, now. The Cult of the Mother is dead."

Huh. They kept walking, albeit at a fast pace. Felix didn't trust the footing, not with sheets of ice breaking apart hundreds of yards away, but he was also in a hurry. He would have flown if he hadn't acquired an audience. Ahead, the ground had been sheared through when several more spires had fallen during his battle, exposing more and more of the rotting ice and deep, dark water below. Felix half expected every rock they passed under to do the same.

Pit walked beside him, alert and eager. He'd earned two levels in that fight and was still buzzing with the residual energy from all those stat increases. "Don't worry about the Mother," he said. "We killed her anyway."

Silence met Pit's words while confusion, curiosity, and disbelief spun in clouded circles around the Witches. He was happy for the quiet. Felix wasn't going to explain that whole situation, even if they asked.

His thoughts drifted instead to the notifications he had received. The new Title was nice and likely indicated he'd more than surpassed this first layer. That was good, since this was probably the place that needed the most culling. The Brumalbats didn't offer a lot of Essence, but every ocean was made up of individual droplets of water. For now, he'd take all he could.

The second notification was the real issue. It indicated this Frostfather was a literal being and not just some religious thing of the Frost Giants. Felix had no reason to believe some random god was fake, not with how his life had turned out, but it was still disquieting. *Is he another Urge or an actual god? Or just another Primordial?*

The Mother of Monsters had another name, after all. Before he devoured her.

"The goal is to keep moving inward right? Through the layers?" he asked.

"It is. The exit lies ahead, at that glacial ridge there."

"Got it." Felix scanned ahead, noting colony after colony of glittering Brumalbats between them and the miles-distant ridge. "Stick close, then."

It was bloody work, slaughtering their way through the icy plains. Felix and Pit took to it with gusto at first, but it quickly grew tedious. After only a few more battles, the ice bats started avoiding their party entirely, fleeing on sight. Pit and Felix chased a few of them down, but the effort to catch, kill, and consume them swiftly proved futile. The experience and Essence they provided was meager at best, especially in the small numbers they were able to capture at once. Felix considered lingering in the first layer to track them all down, but Naberius told him greater beasts were located at each successive layer. That sounded good enough to him.

Now they stood before a massive glacier that stretched across the entirety of the horizon. It was like a wall, vanishing into swirling clouds of snow to either side.

"Behold. The exit of the first layer and entrance to the second." Naberius gestured to the craggy ice wall before them. It was riddled with crevices and ridges, but there was no cave or tunnel. Just solid ice.

"Okay," Felix said, drawing out the word. "Is this something we have to climb?"

The Witches did not answer, and for once, their Spirits were still. Felix raised an eyebrow. Clearly, this was another test.

Pit looked up. "I think I can manage a climb," he said.

"Don't worry about it. Lemme check it first." Felix scratched his friend's ears, prompting his horse-sized back leg to stomp involuntarily. "Be back in a second."

Cloudstep!

Adamant Discord!

Lightning surged upward, and Felix rode atop of it. He'd made sure to cushion his leap with a Cloudstep, but the sharp sound of splitting ice followed him as he ascended. *Whoops.*

No time to worry about that now.

Felix continued to pull, hauling back with a huge amount of his Strength and hurtling upward at a ridiculous speed. The ice wall before him, however, never abated. He burst through clouds into brilliant sunlight and back into clouds again, yet the expanse of the glacier was endless. It had no top, which meant climbing it was a fool's game.

He shot back down.

"No climbing," he said as he landed, this time far softer than his takeoff. Felix glanced at the Witches. Fornis was peering at him then back up, Sitri had bundled herself in her robes, and Naberius simply watched with a faint smile on her angular face. "What do you think, Pit?"

His Companion was standing closer to the glacier, beak almost pressed against the ice. A crack had split some of the ground and taken a chunk out of the wall, too, and he raised a talon and dragged it slowly against the ice. Chips fell off, and to Felix's Manasight, they smoked with an intense vapor.

"I think we have to break through," Pit said. Without another word, he slashed his talons full force into the ice. A large section broke away, easily twice as big as Pit himself and forcing him to dance backward away from its collapse.

Hurricane Rasp is level 80!

Pit looked back at Felix, a big grin on his face and his golden eyes gleaming. "I got this. Dawn's Advent!"

The tenku swung his paws forward again, and this time they unleashed twin crescents of brilliant golden energy that ripped across the air and into the glacier. Deep, angled cuts sizzled into the ice, billowing with steam. Pit crowed, a bugle so viciously happy that Felix couldn't stop his grin. What followed was a frenzy of burning light, crackling lightning, and furious talon strikes into the glacier's endless facade…until it broke apart entirely.

From beneath the ice, a perfectly formed archway led into a portal of brilliant blues, greens, and whites. Pit cheered. "Hah! *Easy!*"

"Great job, little man." Felix peered through the tunnel, but it flickered strangely when he stepped closer than a few feet. As if it were a candle in the wind, threatening to gutter out. "Oh, I don't think this likes me."

"It is made for the one that breaks it open." Naberius had also drawn close, and they were now looking at Pit in an entirely new way. "You have proven yourself worthy of this path, Pit of Nagast."

Pit perked up, throwing out his chest as his triangular ear tufts wiggled. "Oh?" His bushy fox tail wagged furiously. "Of course I have."

"You must proceed," Sitri urged, motioning toward the lit tunnel with age-spotted hands. "The Frostfather will not wait."

Pit's ears wilted slightly. "Separately? Why can't Felix—"

"The tunnel's for you, man." Felix smiled, though the idea of splitting from his friend when he was hurt was— "I'll make my own way and meet you on the other side."

"Oh. Alright." He fluffed the feathers along his neck and back, casting off pieces of snow and ice. "Here I go, then."

He trotted into the tunnel and in seconds vanished into the light.

"Now you, Human," Fortis said, drawing Felix's attention. She gestured at the ice wall, and when Felix turned back, he found that Pit's tunnel had vanished entirely. "It is time to prove your worth."

Prove my worth, he grumbled to himself. *Right.* The ice wall was cold and extremely hard, but Pit had slashed it open with a few Skills. *Which Skill, though? Hm. Let's just start with a simple strike.*

Felix set his feet and reared back with a simple, clenched fist. No Skills. No magic.

He punched.

A ripple tore across the face of the glacier, wind ripping in its wake as ice was obliterated in a chaos of concentric circles. Ice exploded outward all down the horizon, spitting shards from the explosive fissures that tore open, while dust and snow plumed across the sky.

"Y-you have proven yourself worthy of this path, Felix Nevarre," Naberius whispered.

"Yeah." Felix looked from the destruction he'd wrought to the cavernous tunnel he'd bored with a single punch. It was filled with light. "I figured."

"Eugh," Felix said as soon as he stepped through the portal. His foot crunched on snow and ice, but it was far preferable to the feeling he'd just went through. "It's like my insides took a cold shower."

The Witches followed after, though they showed zero discomfort. "Such is the way of the Hoarfrost," Sitri croaked. "It shall shatter your weakness and leave only strength."

Felix ignored them and instead took in his new surroundings. He was still on an icy plain beneath a winter sky, but it was now later in the day—a perpetual sunset. Those spires of metal and stone were also way more prevalent in the second layer, filling up so much space that the plains were all but hidden beneath their bulk. A few hundred yards ahead, tunnels were cut through the nearest ones, perfectly round as if they had been melted. A herd of huge armored creatures ambled about near their openings, looking like a cross between a multi-horned rhinoceros and a many-legged beetle.

The creatures were rooting around in the snow where large patches had been dyed a dark blue color. *I doubt that's snow cone flavoring.* With a trumpeting roar, one of the monsters charged into a tunnel, bashing full force into the side with its blunt head. The sound of ice splintering filled the air at first, but was swiftly supplanted by the chittering of a hundred familiar voices. *Brumalbats.*

Felix readied himself for another fight, but instead of attacking, the bats scattered in all directions. It was soon apparent why, as the herd of rhino-bugs shot skewers of stone through their swarm. Brumalbats dropped by the dozen while the others fled, and the rhino-bugs gave several triumphant bugles before ripping into their meals.

He didn't miss their razor-sharp fangs or the way their cut-glass eyes caught the crimson sunset and reflected back fire like wolves in the dark.

Voracious Eye!

Name: Obelon
Type: Inferior Elemental
Level: 55
HP: 8700/8700
SP: 13420/13201
MP: 2734/3994
Lore: Born of stone and ice, the Obelon are mighty beasts known for durability and voracious appetites. They can remain stationary for long periods of time, burrowing into the snow to hunt in ambush while disguised as simple rocks. When food is plentiful, they are known for charging their foes and skewering them on their stone horns.
Strength: Tough hide.
Weakness: Poor maneuverability.

They were clearly physically powerful, and their poor speed was made up for by what looked like impressive Strength and Endurance for their level. Monster levels were a little misleading as a gauge, though, since Evolutions played a huge part in their growth cycle. Felix had no clue how advanced these Obelons were, only that his Voracious Eye ranked their overall advancement as a Tier III. Like with people's advancement, the ranking was a feeling more than a System certainty, but he'd never been wrong before. A Tier III was equivalent to a high Journeyman combatant. Easy, in other words.

The Witches seemed to be unconcerned as well, though their Spirits betrayed them. Felix's Affinity detected strains of eagerness above all others, and Naberius was clearly watching him with a steady, unabashed gaze.

Frankly, the moment he categorized their threat, Felix couldn't have given two shits about the monsters ahead or the Witches behind. "Pit?"

I'm here. The answer came through their bond, the Etheric Concordance, words, and sense images. Felix saw a brief vista that looked remarkably similar to his own, but definitely not the same.

Are you okay? Came through the portal without any problems?

I'm fine. These big...turtle bugs haven't even noticed me.

You're...south. I can feel you. Just over that icy ridge. Hold on, I'll be over there in a second—

No! I said I can do this. I— Emotions tumbled through their bond, too knotted to be any one thing. *I'll meet you at the second layer exit, okay?*

Felix clenched his jaw but didn't argue. *Alright, bud. I'm here if you need me.*

I know.

Their connection never faded, but Felix could tell when his Companion shifted his attention away. Toward danger. In the distance, he could hear the sound of thunder.

"Human. Why do you dawdle?"

Barely restraining a snarl, Felix forced himself to let the tension ease out of his shoulders. "The challenge is to just get through the layers, right? Or is there more to it?"

"This is not simply a trial of survival," Naberius said, as if that was enough explanation.

"Fine." This time, he did growl. "Then let's make this quick."

He kicked off the ground, uncaring if he shattered the ice or made the Witches' path harder. He was only focused on the obstacle in his way.

Stone Shaping!

Sliding to a stop right before the rhino-bugs, Felix let his Mana blast forth from him in a wave of dusty-brown. It crossed the final distance to the nearest Obelons and sank into the very rock of their bodies. Two dozen beasts roared in anger and confusion, their many eyes rolling as Felix grasped and *twisted.*

They exploded in a shower of vibrant silver viscera.

You Have Killed An Obelon (x24)!
XP Earned!

Beyond, the herd bellowed and charged him as one.

Rime Shaping!

Stone Shaping!

Dual Skills sounded within him, burrowing into the earth through the Mana Gates at his feet, before erupted in two monoliths of ice and stone.

"You're in my way!" he shouted and slammed his hands together.

You Have Killed An Obelon (x43)!
XP Earned!

All that remained on the field was a shattered column of frosty rock and pools of splattered silver ichor.

Chthonic Tribute!

Then even that was gone.

CHAPTER EIGHTEEN

Bloody Gnaw is level 81!
Hurricane Rasp is level 81!
Cold Resistance is level 40!

Pit darted between the oversized rocklegs, nimbly avoiding the thrusting horns of stone as he slashed through joints and bellies with abandon. Ichor rained down behind him in a silver wake, but Pit didn't pause to relish his victories or even finish off all that opposed him. Some gave chase, but the weakened were finished off by his mere presence—his feathers and fur crackled with the close held might of storms.

Mantle of Tumult is level 78!

You Have Killed An Obelon (x48)!
XP Earned!

Pit felt the experience well up inside him. He was not yet near a quarter full on his current level, but there were so many monsters ahead. Without Felix around, they were all his. The temptation to grind his Skills and advance his level on this layer was high, but that was not the reason he wished to remain separate from his Companion.

I am strong. Wings or no wings. Pit shoved his claws through the belly of another rocklegs, and they fell with a basso screech. *I will prove it.*

Challenge Accepted!
The Path of Rule!
The Frostfather sees your efforts and accepts your drive, challenger! You now walk the Path of Rule, Stormwing Tenku! How high will you climb?

That drew Pit up short, but only for a moment. Mostly, it was kindling to the flame that burned in his breast as he set it against the endless cold. For a moment, he even forgot the ceaseless pain of his wounds, replaced by a wrathful exuberance.

He would *fight*.

Pit was fast, almost as fast as Felix himself, and the size of the second layer seemed smaller than the first. He crossed it quickly, eradicating all the monsters in his path that tried to engage with him. That number was higher than normal, however, thanks to the Title he shared with his Companion, Ironskin Nemesis. All of the monsters treated Pit as if he were a hated rival and went mad whenever he drew their attention. He considered employing his stealth Skill, Gloaming Shroud, but it wasn't necessary.

The rocklegs and smattering of icewings proved to be of little consequence to Pit. His sheer speed made him a nightmare opponent of the slower rocklegs, able to maneuver around them and attack from their blind sides. Repeated uses of his stun Skill, Howl At The Dark, brought the icewings low and often finished the fight for him in many cases, as the huge creatures would smash themselves apart on the rocks below. And all the while, he flung frozen lightning and blinding blades of light at every opportunity.

Howl At The Dark is level 74!
Dawn's Advent (E), Level 79!
Tempest Fugit (L), Level 83!

The cold grew worse the farther Pit ran, until it drove aching pains up through his paws each time they touched the ice. There was nothing to be done about it—Pit simply endured.

Cold Resistance is level 44!

It helped that each enemy he defeated contained an Elemental Core inside them, which Pit devoured with relish. They were bitter and small, but after several dozen, he received a notification.

You Have Digested An Ice Elemental Core (x62)!
You Gain:
+2 VIT
+2 END

The boost wasn't much, in the end. *Maybe when the monsters grow stronger,* he mused as the path opened up before him. The spires had grown dense as a forest now, and he could barely see the sky through it all. *Ah. The exit.*

Ahead, several spires leaned against one another and formed a triangular opening. Unlike the glacier from before, this exit appeared to be completely open—Pit could even see the shimmering curtain of energy inside. Yet, as he drew closer, the wide-open field began to quake.

"What now?" he squawked, hopping back just as the icy earth split apart.

A huge creature ripped itself free of the ground, its body formed of craggy stone and gleaming metal deposits formed loosely into the shape of a Human. Or perhaps a giant, as the thing was easily fifty feet tall. A lump of a head sat atop wide, angular shoulders, and two massive arms hung from its side like malformed clubs. Its feet and torso rolled and shifted against one another as it reared up to stand directly opposed to Pit…and right in the way of the portal.

"You can't stop me," Pit growled.

As if in answer, the monstrous being slammed its hands atop him.

Yet Pit was gone.

Instead, he raced atop the creature's arm, flaring his Agility to its utmost. The monster reacted, grabbing at him with its other hand, but Pit refused to be stopped.

"Tempest Fugit! Dawn's Advent!"

Frozen lightning crashed into the creature's fist, doing little more than stalling its advance. Lightning and ice was clearly less than useful on metal and stone, but blades of light proved far more effective. They cut deep, slicing lines into the creature's palm and even separating a finger. The hand still dropped, grasping at its own elbow and bicep as Pit sped up, but it missed by a dozen strides.

Pit shrieked in triumph, channeling his power through another Skill. The creature jolted at the sound, and its shoulders slumped.

Door Guardian Is Stunned For 3 Seconds!

Howl At The Dark is level 75!
Adept Tier!
You Gain:
+30 DEX
+20 AGL
+15 PER

System energy flooded his veins as he flashed up the Guardian's shoulder and nimbly leaped over its craggy upper back. The creature twitched as the countdown on his stun ran out, but by then, Pit was in position. He straddled the joint between the Guardian's featureless head and its torso and unleashed his fury.

"Dawn's Advent!"

Blade after crescent blade flashed into the breach, light Mana tearing out chunks of stone even as it melted them. Again and again Pit cast the spell, until it blurred beneath his paws, and the stone all around him heated to a cherry red.

New Skill!
Heat Resistance (Uncommon), Level 1!

Heat Resistance is level 2!
...
Heat Resistance is level 15!

The Guardian's hands reached up the moment the stun wore off, but it was too late. Dawn's Advent drilled down, melting stone and steel until Pit spotted a bright purple-white orb through the haze of molten heat. He screeched and, with a final strike, blasted it in two.

The Door Guardian froze, hands inches away from Pit's feathers, before it collapsed with a deafening cacophony.

Pit rode the rubble down, easily able to keep his feet. His sides heaved as he recovered from the sheer amount of Mana he'd expended, but otherwise, he felt good. Strong.

I'm strong. I can fight. He hopped off and walked toward the portal to the third layer. *I am enough.*

He hesitated just outside the shimmering portal and looked back at the rocky remains. The gleam of the white-purple core was there, buried under a few tons of stone. He snorted and turned back toward the fallen Guardian.

I…am hungry.

Felix dusted his jacket off as he landed among the split open fields of ice. "Tch. It tore my sleeve." He funneled a bit more Mana to his Garment, and the split seam sealed itself.

All around him was the rubble of three Door Guardians, their bodies shattered and returned to the craters they had risen from. It had taken him more time than he expected to dispatch the Lesser Elementals, mostly because he underestimated them. A single punch had shattered legs and fists, but it proved less than efficient for their armored torsos. He'd had to shape the stone away and melt them with acid in the end. Though he had to admit, the method had its benefits.

Hand of Calamity is level 63!

"Chthonic Tribute," he whispered and let the stone, metal, and glimmers of icy cores turn to a dark smoke. When it vanished into him, Felix was left with a fissured expanse of ground and three Witches. He cleared his throat. "Let's keep moving."

He ignored their pale faces and shocked Spirits.

Challenge Continued!
Path of Rule II!
You have taken the second step upon the Path. The beasts before you cannot stop your ascent, yet their blood stains you. Weighs upon you. How far can you climb?

"Keep up," he commanded over his shoulder before passing through the portal.

"He conquers them too easily," Fornis hissed. There was little chance of her being heard over the sound of combat, but none of them were willing to raise their voices above a whisper. "Are you positive he is Human?"

"Do you think the System lied to us? Analyze him yourself," Sitri snapped back, her rheumy eyes wide with anger.

Naberius slashed a hand through the air between the two Witches. "Enough, both of you. It is clear that this would-be king is hiding depths from us. It is also clear how Grimmar and our people were defeated when they went south. Against one such as him, I doubt the full might of our coven would stand a chance."

The three of them trailed Felix Nevarre as he took on the Path of Rule. It had been the only surefire way to determine the strength of Kimaris' new leader, one that the Cold Rock Coven would accept without question. Naberius had not expected him to succeed so incredibly, however. In the first layer, he had benefited from his Companion's aid, but then the Frostfather saw fit to separate them.

Naberius had eagerly waited to see how easily he handled the foes in the second layer, only to be shocked as he mowed through them all without rest. The Door Guardians had been the true indicator that something was off. If Felix Nevarre could best three Lesser Elementals within as many heartbeats, then the third layer would pose no challenge to him.

And she was right.

Brumalbats and Obelons existed in the third layer, but far more prevalent were the Ice Drakes that commanded the sky. Not true draconic Types, but Lesser Elementals fashioned by the Frostfather into vicious, winged horrors. Each one was the size of the greatest of giants, with wingspans more than double that, and they had talons and teeth sharp enough to pierce all but the greatest of armor.

They had descended upon Felix Nevarre with the fury of an avalanche, but he had beat them back with magic and pure, brute force. Ice shattered beneath his black fists where it didn't outright betray the will of the Ice Drakes. He could command it, the ice, forcing their bodies apart or ripping their wings from their backs entirely, letting them plummet to the earth. There was no stopping him, not even when the monsters fled.

He followed them into the sky.

Now the man, garbed in nothing more than enchanted cloth, tread over the remains of a thousand foes…and devoured their remains.

What power is this? Naberius had never seen its like, not in a mortal. He was eating his opponents, gaining strength from them as a monster would. *How?*

The man in question gave no answers, even when they mustered enough courage to ask one. He continued on, angry but resolute as they passed over the increasingly rocky terrain. An oppressive weight followed him like a cloak, forcing all three of them to strain themselves to simply remain upright. It was lessened when the man was off fighting, so there was no question as to its origins, only disbelief that such naked aggression could come from a creature so pink and small.

"The exit is ahead," Sitri said.

"Let us wait here," Fornis suggested. "The Door Guardian will come shortly, and I do not wish to be near that Human when the fighting begins."

"Perhaps they will stop him," Sitri, the oldest of the Witches Naberius had brought with her, said. Sitri was typically dour but confident in her own power. It was strange to hear her so uncertain. "If not…"

"If not, then we shall proceed, as we would for any chieftain," Naberius added. "We always abide by the results of the Path of Rule."

A metallic shriek echoed across the landscape as, from the sky, a massive Greater Ice Drake descended. It was easily three times the size of a normal Ice Drake, and, more importantly, it was Evolved.

A true Ice Elemental. Naberius would never tire of seeing them; their sheer power was intoxicating. *Let us see how you do against—*

A bolt of blinding lightning tore up from the earth, and the Greater Ice Drake exploded into ten thousand glittering pieces.

"Frozen winds," Sitri cursed. "What *is* he?"

CHAPTER NINETEEN

Ephemeral Evocation is level 25!
Apprentice Tier!
You Gain:
+10 AFI
+10 FEL
+10 RES

Felix shook himself from the Memory he'd stolen from the last Door Guardian. It wasn't much of anything, though it was beautiful. Hours of simply flying among the frigid clouds, reveling in the wild winds as his transparent ice-wings cut through them. It was a nice experience and even made Felix regret killing the Ice Elemental. A little.

The Lesser and Inferior Elementals offered little in the way of Memories. Not to say they didn't have any, but that they were wan and simplistic. Using Chthonic Tribute en masse as he had been, he'd seen plenty of Memories flash into his core space, but they were all the same: flashes of weather and the occasional bloody violence. Life in a Domain, at least for the weaker creatures, was extremely unvaried.

Not only that, but he'd learned nothing from them. Too weak, maybe. Rime Shaping and Stone Shaping covered most of what they could do, though he had held out hope the Obelons could give him something like Metal Shaping. No such luck.

The fourth layer was smaller than the three previous, as seemed to be the pattern. Felix imagined it as concentric circles, and all of it seemed to converge on the lone mountain that dominated the skyline. Thick clouds and swirling winds blocked the upper reaches of the mountain from sight, even his own enhanced Perception. Still, Felix kept his sights locked on its invisible peak as he ran through rocky foothills, all while killing dozens of Lesser Elementals with each executed Skill. What was up there?

"An eternal blizzard," Naberius told him when he asked. "Winds sharp as honed steel and as cold as the darkness that came before creation. None have ventured into its boundary and survived, let alone reached the peak."

Well. That sounds like a challenge to me.

He'd need the Essence anyway. He was compiling a lot, holding it aside from the regular tithe he fed his Hunger, but more was always good. He had plenty of uses for it.

Hope you're doing okay, bud.

Pit stood shakily atop a pile of bloody meat and fur, half caked with snow that was already turning to crimson ice. Blood poured from between segments of his barding, but he had done it.

He'd survived.

"Breath of the Wild!" Pit said between ragged breaths. Immediately, a wind of light and green-gold motes rose up all around him. His wounds began to close, and the shakes that wracked his horse-sized frame ceased as his Strength and Vitality were temporarily boosted.

Breath of the Wild is level 19!
Cold Resistance is level 49!

The fourth layer Door Guardian had been some sort of giant ape… pig thing, and it was as ugly alive as it was dismembered. All four of its arms had been tipped with metal talons, viciously sharp and far longer than should be allowed. Most of his wounds had come from those claws, and his barding had several deep scratches that would take *forever* to buff out.

Harn…can have…the apprentices do it.

You Have Digested An Inferior Elemental Core (x108)!
You Gain:
+8 VIT
+5 END

You Have Digested A Lesser Elemental Core (x13)
You Gain:
+14 STR
+12 VIT

Ugh. Now *it digests.* Pit scowled at the small boosts he'd received, despite the truly outrageous amounts of foes he'd eaten.

He limped off the corpse, unwilling to root around in the four-hands' remains for an elemental core. He wasn't even sure it had one, and he didn't care now. The portal was right there, and the wind was so cold. Forward was better than stagnation.

The icy surface of the portal slid over him like diving into the bottom of Khasma, except every part of him. Even his Mind shuddered as his thoughts slowed to a trickle. There was only forward. Only the fight. And then it faded, the world turned suddenly warm as a bright noon sun straddled the sky, and Pit gasped.

Spring?

It wasn't, but the impression remained. The terrain was far rockier than the foothills from the previous layer, but the wind didn't cut so deeply, and even the ice underfoot was pleasant rather than a bitter punishment. Pit closed his eyes and enjoyed it, just for a moment.

He could continue in a second.

"Pit!"

Felix barreled out of the snow, appearing as if out of nowhere and catching Pit up in a too-tight hug. Pit's coos of delight were cut short by a sharp, burning pain.

Felix pulled back. "Oh! You're hurt!" He reached to his waist, where a hard-cased pouch sat and pulled free a bulbous crimson potion. "Here. Drink."

Pit did so, happy to see the Health Potion almost as much as he was to see his boy. He drank deep and enjoyed the scritches from his Companion's sharp claws. The potions boosted his flagging regeneration, pushing the worst of his wounds closed, and the lack of pain was a treat more delicious than any elemental core. He relished it.

"I'm glad I found you. The Witches didn't tell me the fifth layer was a sort of safe zone until we got here. Had I known, I would've rushed ahead way faster." Felix was staring up the mountain, frowning. "They're hiding things."

They were much closer to the mountain, and the ice, metal, and stone of the Domain was lifted in miniature peaks that would perhaps be considered mountains in any other place. Here, they were like children playing in the shadow of their father. The storm above flashed, and a deep thunder rolled.

"Witches say it's the end of the Domain up there. I'm more interested in what they're not saying, though."

Pit grunted. "I just want to finish the Path."

"You, too?" Felix nodded when Pit confirmed it, looking as if he'd expected nothing less. "Good. We'll topple this damn peak."

A tired trill fled Pit's throat, and he settled his head against his Companion's once again. They stayed that way for a bit until chanting from down trail pricked their ears.

"What's that?"

"Witches," Felix said. "C'mon. They're down here, doing some ritual thing."

At the bottom of a small crevasse made of stone striated with metal and ice, a strange little stave church had been built. Felix supposed it wasn't really a stave church, but that was the closest analogy he could find. The structure was a single layer with roofs that looked like they'd been copied out of some history book on vikings. Oh, and it was made entirely of cloudy ice.

The door was open.

"I guess we go inside?" Felix said. Pit was following him a few yards back, walking carefully as if he was still injured. Felix fought the urge to obsess, but he'd noticed his friend's Health hadn't healed all the way to full. It was stuck about three quarters of the way there—the only reason for that was a significant injury. *Why's he hiding it?*

"After you," Pit said, tossing his head. "I'll make it there on my own, just fine."

"Alright."

Felix wasn't stupid. He knew his friend was having a rough time; he just didn't know what to do.

He pressed on, pushing through the open ice-door. Beyond the interior of the structure was all one huge chamber. Support struts like narrow icicles stretched between the ceiling and floor, creating the impression that the walls were made of thin sticks, bundled together over and over. In the very center, impossible to miss, were the Witches.

"Frostfather, the Caretakers have come to replenish the gifts you have given unto us." Naberius' voice was just as sharp and high as before, but it had a certain resonant quality. Felix couldn't tell if it was the acoustics of the room or just plain old magic, but he was betting on the latter. "We bring to you sacrifices."

Oh, I don't like the sound of that, Pit sent as he padded up behind Felix.

If they mean us, they're gonna have a bad day. But they're not that stupid, Felix pointed at the giant blue women, who were now pulling oddly shaped objects from their robes. *Look.*

The Witches got busy unwrapping the objects, as they were each covered in a number of animal skins, like weird skin-presents. Felix watched, eager to soak in their process. Upon coming to the fifth layer, the Witches had informed him that this was their task to fix the Domain.

"They each have a designation, like I do, except theirs lets them move through the lower layers like ghosts. Nothing will touch them." 'Caretakers,' they had called themselves, as opposed to challengers. It made sense, if the mechanisms of the Domain needed attention, then why not hire your priesthood to do the dirty work?

"Like *we* do," Pit said.

"What?"

In response, Pit nudged his head forward and a blue window rotated into Felix's view. It was from the Frostfather, as his own had been, and it accepted Pit as a challenger on the Path of Rule.

"Whoa, what?" Felix's Mind whirled. "Is *that* why we were separated?"

The sound of splintering ice filled the building, and they both dropped into battle-ready stances immediately. But, instead of an enemy coming for them, the ground had opened up and was flowing with near-solid ice Mana. The thick, gelatinous liquid power crackled as it formed, shaping into an eight-foot-tall pillar upon which a large, shallow bowl manifested before the entire thing snapped from Mana to true ice. It was an altar.

"Let us do as you have commanded us," Fornis said. "Flesh of prey, given in fear."

"Fangs of predator, taken in battle," Sitri wheezed.

"The breath of life, stolen from the world," Naberius intoned. After each sentence, another item was unwrapped and placed upon the shallow basin of ice. The leg of some hooved creature, dried and festooned with fur. The teeth of a monster, each fang the size of a dagger blade and exuding a vicious poison Mana. Finally, a glass bottle that contained within it a whirlwind. The moment they touched the altar, ice climbed across the offering like crystalline spiderwebs, until they were fully encased.

That's an Inferior Air Elemental. Felix could tell that much before it was entombed in the altar. The magic of whatever was going on here was interfering too much for him to tell what the other things were, even with Voracious Eye.

"Blood calls to blood, the water within us all. We offer that last, to seal our pact." As one, all three of the Witches lifted transparent daggers and drove them into their abdomens.

Felix took several steps forward, shock, concern, and uncertainty warring within him. Blood poured from the Witches' wounds, but none of them had so much as flinched. The crimson stream soaked the ice until the altar basin was brimming full. Only then did their wounds cease flowing, and the ice knives were removed. They were clean.

"Frostfather! Grant us renewal!"

The words of all three in unison shook the chamber. They buzzed through levels of harmonics in Felix's senses as if piercing through something more than frigid air.

The altar began to glow. Purple-white and silvery-gray, it ratcheted up from dim to blinding in a matter of seconds, forcing Felix and Pit both to squint. The structure around them rumbled, just a little at first, as that buzzing noise lifted into higher frequencies. But the rumbling grew louder, the resonance more intense, until it felt like they were standing inside a ringing bell.

Felix bared his teeth, reaching for his Skills, but was surprised by a purple and white notification that appeared in the air above the altar.

Ritual Rejected!
The Frostfather Denies Replenishment Until The Challengers Complete Their Path!
Ascend To The Peak!

"That has—"

"Never happened before."

"Challengers," Naberius said. All three Witches looked to Felix and Pit, varying degrees of shock and dismay swirling openly on their large faces and agitated Spirits.

"Bring it on," Pit growled.

Felix snorted. "What he said."

CHAPTER TWENTY

"The layers below the fifth are safe for us," Naberius said. They walked as they talked, as neither Felix nor Pit were eager to draw their Domain run out any farther than necessary. "But beyond here is where the Path truly grows precipitous."

"Why?" Pit asked a half-instant before Felix could.

"Because the sixth layer is where the majority of your foes are Ice Elementals, instead of their Lesser or Inferior brethren." Sitri's old face pursed, tucking inward like she'd tasted something heinously sour. "Only one has survived to see the sixth layer's end."

"Grimmar," Felix said. He smiled, a weight lifting off his chest. "You had me worried for a second."

Fornis hissed at him, literally hissed—like a cat. "Do not take this lightly, Human! Grimmar was a brute, but a finer warrior I have never seen in all my years."

Felix stopped, forcing all of them to stop as well. "Lady, I kicked his ass after being here for a month. If I can't get farther than him, then there's something seriously wrong with this Domain." He glanced up through the canyon lip above them and into the distant, swirling storm at the peak. "We'll be fine."

The rest of the walk was far quieter.

Eventually, the winding ravines and box canyons opened up into a modestly sized, triangular portal. Modestly sized for giants, anyway. The metal and stone spires that leaned into one another were thirty feet high at their apex, and the opening was filled with swirling, arctic light. As Felix stepped closer, he could feel the deep cold emanating from it, far harsher than the fourth layer had been. Pit sniffed at it and warbled in annoyance.

Felix looked to the Witches and found Naberius approaching. "Will we be split up again when we enter?" he asked.

"No. Multiple Challengers will be sent to the same place from here on out. In a normal chieftain's test, this would be where the Challengers are pitted against each other, as well as the Domain, but..." She gestured between the two of them. "That is not a problem here."

Pit hummed in agreement.

"We, however, cannot traverse the layers beyond this point. It is a place for Challengers only. We shall, however, know how you fare."

Felix eyed the Witches. Sitri looked sour as usual, her cloudy eyes and withered face seemingly built to do little else but scowl. Fortis was more stoic. All of them, including Naberius, were filled with complicated emotions. People, even giant ones, rarely felt just one thing.

Sharp-faced Naberius was the most curious, however. She smiled at him, and it was actually earnest. "I admit to a newfound respect for you, Felix Nevarre. I have witnessed your power again and again during the first four layers, and I believe you *will* best Grimmar's record."

Pit cleared his throat, but the giant lady ignored him. "I warn you, however, not to reach too far. You have already proven yourself to me, and my word holds weight in the Cold Rocks Coven. I need only a potent argument to convince the Kin to allow you to seek the Kingsrock."

"Kingsrock...I remember that name." Felix dug around his memories. "There was a battle there."

"One that sealed Grimmar's position as Chieftain of the Kin, the Cold Children. My people."

Felix's thoughts leaped ahead. "And it's where the Seat and Seal is located, isn't it?"

Naberius gave a tight, barely perceptible jerk of her chin. Her voice lowered as if she were afraid of the others hearing. "It is. As *monsters,* we cannot make use of it, but it is the heart of the Hoarfrost. Claim the Kingsrock and you claim it all. However, and do not think that I am underestimating you, but even you cannot simply approach the the Kingsrock without preparation. Friends." Her smile widened, creasing the sharp planes of her face. "Without an alliance with Cold Rock—without my coven—you will be lost to the storms."

Felix wanted to roll his eyes so hard, it pained him not to—she was pushing her value pretty hard. She claimed she wasn't underestimating him, but Felix hadn't begun to show the Witches what he could do. *You're here for diplomacy*, he reminded himself. "And what would I need to do to claim such an alliance?"

"You need only reach the end of the seventh layer and defeat the Door Guardian. Nothing more. After that, simply declare that you are finished, and the Domain will return you to its entrance."

"And if I go farther? What if I climb that mountain and beat the whole thing?"

Naberius' expression did not change, but her Spirit sang a medley of indignation and stark fear. "You will die. None have ascended the peak. The Frostfather will not allow it. Do not be foolhardy, would-be king."

She walked away, graceful despite her nine-foot frame, and rejoined her fellow Witches. They leaned in close, clearly peppering her with questions, but she ignored them.

"Why change now?" Pit asked, voice pitched for just the two of them.

Felix smirked. "Together, then?"

Without a backward glance, they stepped through the portal.

A blizzard raged on the other side, and it appeared that the noon sun of the fifth layer had truly set beyond the horizon. Apart from a faint, sourceless glow, the Domain around them was drenched in nightfall.

And it was *cold*.

Felix gestured, flooding the Domain with his Mana and pulling a ten-foot wall out from the ground beneath them. Stone, Rime, and Green shaping combined into Fiendstone, and it was more than enough to cut the wind and snow immediately. He kept going, though, until they were encased in a little cube house that fully muted the blizzard's fury.

Auroral Forge!

Cardinal Flame!

Spears of light manifested in Felix's hands, and he stabbed both into the ground beside them before conjuring a floating red-gold flame. The heat of all three of them cut through the cold, and the small interior was pleasantly warm in thirty seconds .

"Oh, that's much better," Pit chirped. "Though I think my Cold Resistance is going to reach Journeyman Tier soon."

Felix raised an eyebrow. "I can put out the flame if you want."

"No! No." Pit cleared his throat. "No. It's fine."

Something bashed into the wall he'd just raised, and they both jerked in surprise. It had moved so fast that Felix hadn't tracked it until it was on top of them already. It hit again and again, a flurry of blows…and the walls didn't budge. Felix pushed his awareness outward, but the creature was already gone. Back off into the storm, he supposed.

"We'll worry about that later," he decided. "Now that we're out of prying eyes, though: do you want to attempt to heal those wings?"

Something shrieked in the distance. Pit hesitated, listening to it fade. "What if it doesn't work again?"

"It will," Felix insisted. "I've more Essence now than I've had since Khasma." *Not nearly as much significance, though.* He kept that to himself. No need to worry Pit more than necessary. "We've practiced this enough times, and I think this might be our last bit of peace until we're out of here. Plus—"

"Okay! Okay." Pit laid down onto his belly, wincing at the cold earth. "Let's do it."

Felix watched his friend for a few seconds before taking a deep breath and sitting himself down as well. "Convergence," he whispered.

In a flash of light, Pit slipped into Felix's Spirit. As they had practiced many times, Felix carefully threaded the bond between them, until he could visualize Pit's core space as if it were directly next to his own. It appeared as a verdant forest, a replica of the Foglands where they had first met. At its center was a tree quite similar to Felix's…and altogether different. Many trees had grown into one another, twining together as if grafted by an artist's hand, until a variety of textures and colors sprang from the trunks into thick, far-reaching branches. Fruit dangled from those branches, glimmering and vibrating—representations of Pit's Skills—while at the center was a nook, a hollow in the spiraling trunks, where a four-sided gemstone floated, crackling with thunder and light. His core.

Felix tightened his grip, Will and Intent as two fists that gently pulled their spaces together. It was *hard*, unreasonably so considering the sheer size of Felix's stats. The first time Pit had made use of their new ability to share Skills, it had been instinctive and reactionary. Every time after that had been like relearning how to walk after shattering their legs, excruciating and full of failures. But practice made perfect. "Pit!"

On cue, Pit reached out with his own Will and Intent, weaving them into Felix's like braiding leather with steel cables. Felix couldn't do the final pull, or else he'd rip the whole working apart. It was up to Pit.

A moment passed then another as the bond between them flexed and swayed. Pit growled, a deep, thunderous cry at the back of his throat and he lunged. Their core spaces jolted, not so much crashing into one another as rippling as they overlapped—and he seized Felix's Sovereign of Flesh.

"Now let it sing," Felix said through clenched teeth. "Guide it!"

Pit flared the borrowed ability, and strains of the Transcendent Skill spread like waves through his forested core space. Through their reinforced connection, Felix fed Essence into his Skill, and those waves began to tower. A wind ripped across Pit's core space, bending branches and flattening the underbrush. The song of it overwhelmed all else–a strident, dominant call.

Pit screeched.

Flesh moved, forced against the curse that sizzled against Pit's back. Fire burned anew, a searing light at the end of two of Pit's Mana Gates—where his wings once were. Felix hurled more of his stored Essence at their connection, feeding all he could to the Skill. Sovereign of Flesh redoubled the pressure, backed by Pit's Intent and Will, and the flames slowly subsided.

We have it, bud!

Felix!

Without warning, their core spaces wrenched apart, riven by a detonation of wildfire that sent Pit reeling out of Felix's Spirit. They were hurled apart in a flash of light, and Pit howled in agony as the blaze atop his shoulders ignited into twin streamers of deep, crimson flame.

Cardinal Flame!

The magic fought against Felix, squirming from his control despite his levels and stats, just as it had every time he'd attempted to grapple it. He managed to catch the bare edge of it, though, wrestling it down until the gout became a trickle, then even that was banked behind the glowering remnants of blood and ash.

"Pit?" His friend was out but still breathing. "Goddamn it."

Behind Pit, the stone walls had charred and blackened, and everything smelled of burnt feathers. Felix hurried over and inspected his Companion's wounds. Blood ran through Pit's fur, and feathers and splintered pieces of bone stuck up in uneven layers, as if there had been growth…and then it had burned from the inside out. Felix toggled Pit's status in his display, bringing up his conditions.

Status Condition: Curse of Flame

It—it's still there. Felix ran his hands through his hair. *Fuck!*

He'd nearly used up all the Essence he'd collected in the Domain, too. All of their efforts, gone in an instant.

"All…all my…I couldn't control it."

"What?" Felix leaned closer to Pit's head. "What're you talking about? Don't blame yourself. I can't do it, either." He'd tried so many times. The curse rejected his command over flesh, a power that he'd once used to rip monsters in half. Healing, it seemed, was far more complicated than destroying. "And it's my fault for thinking it would be different coming from you. This curse…it needs something drastic."

"No." Pit lifted his head, and struggled to a sitting position. "You're not allowed to try it."

"Unite the Lost would fix you!"

"I'm not broken!"

Silence flooded their hut, thick and heavy. Felix sat back in it, unsure how to respond.

"I'm—I'm just…" Pit shook his head, barding jangling around his neck. "I'm hurt, but I can still fight. And you can't know how much significance that Skill will cost you." Pit nosed his beak into Felix's chest. "I lost my wings. I can't risk losing you, too."

"Pit…"

His friend was right. Unite the Lost always cost him exorbitant amounts of significance to use, and if he was drained of too much of it, then Felix would simply…cease. Every other time he'd used the Skill, he'd been flushed with significance stolen from armies of powerful combatants or vast beings with Chthonic Tribute. Since they'd forged his pillars, however, Felix had been busted down to his bare minimum. Just what made him… him.

"Pit, if that's what you want, then okay. I won't risk it." Felix ran his hands over Pit's glossy, feathered head. "I—I don't like seeing you in pain."

"I'm fine," Pit lied. His big golden eyes blinked. "Let's focus on kicking this Domain's butt."

Felix huffed a laugh, and it was only half faked. "Sure. Onward and upward, then."

CHAPTER TWENTY-ONE

"Have they moved?" Naberius asked. She was pacing a tight circle around the Frostfather's Altar like a Hoarhound stalking its prey. "Have they emerged?"

"Not yet," Sitri reported. The wrinkled crone stood closest to the altar, her hands pressed against the cloudy orb of ice that had grown there. Her rheumy eyes, so poor normally, were the best at scrying through ice. "They continue to conjure flames within their shell."

"Why? The Frostfather will not look on this delay kindly."

"Defense is as necessary as offense, Fornis." Sitri stabbed a bony finger at a shape in the ice. To Naberius, it was nothing but a blurry shadow. "The Elementals are stalking them."

"Better to meet them with force," Fornis insisted. "The Human is capable of that much. It will only grow colder the longer they wait—to waste time is foolish."

"It doesn't matter," Naberius interjected. "Look. They are moving."

"Fast, too," Sitri said. "Too fast."

Naberius drew close to the elder Witch. "What is it?"

"They've—they've reached the sixth layer Door Guardian."

"What? Already?" Naberius peered into the ice but it was a clouded mess. "Show me."

Sitri grunted, and her hands paled where they touched the orb. In return, the orb became clearer and clearer to the other two, until they could make out a huge beast. A Greater Savage Therium, a creature born of ice, earth, and steel. It was more powerful by far than the Ice Drakes and the standard Therium. Its six limbs could rend even the greatest Risi Warrior in twain, and its steel claws would not be stopped by any armor fashioned by the Kin.

"Grimmar barely survived this Guardian's attacks," Fornis said. "If the Human was lying, we shall find out now."

"You saw him handle the previous layers. And his Companion was nearly as fast." Naberius shook her head, exasperated at Fornis' rejection of what was in front of them. "I do not doubt he will conquer this challenge."

"The sixth Door Guardian is dead!" Sitri interrupted with a gasp.

"Truly?" Fornis crowded close, as if eager to find the lie. Yet it was clear to all of them: the Greater Savage Therium had been rent in two…and was even now being devoured by the strange Human king. Fornis grumbled and groused, and her words stank of mulish pride. "It…it is true. They have passed into the seventh layer."

If Naberius was being honest, the speed of the battle surprised her as well. Her pride remained intact, however, as she had hitched her cart to the Human king's ascent. She felt more confident in that choice now than ever before. *He must only reach the end of the seventh layer, and we can begin.*

Naberius saw opportunity in the Human king. His power was great and his judgment sound…if all of Kimaris' words were true, the benefits to allying themselves with his Territory were not to be denied. And *she* would reap the greatest benefits for being the one to facilitate their new alliance.

She only had to wait.

"They have…they are in the seventh layer, but it—" Sitri swallowed audibly. The ice had returned to its cloudy interior, at least to the others, but her pale eyes flicked about as if she couldn't keep up. "They're moving too fast. They've killed thirty–no! Forty elementals. They—" Sitri's old voice trembled. "They've reached the seventh Door Guardian."

Fornis hissed.

"And?" Naberius asked, leaning in. She peered into the orb, seeing only flickering shadows.

"And it is defeated. Instantly."

Naberius laughed. She had been *right.* "Incredible. This Human king—"

"He has entered the eighth layer."

"What!?" *No!* That wasn't what she instructed him to do. *He risks everything!* "What of the Elementals?"

Sitri's hands were trembling. "He and the Chimera are moving. The information is unclear, the viewing distorted by a foul sound…but everything is—" She lifted her near-blind eyes to Naberius'. They all but glowed with *awe*. "They are laying waste to all that lies before them."

"Frostfather help us." Fortis pressed a hand over her heart. "They're attempting the ascent."

Naberius ground her teeth so hard she felt blood flood her tongue—she gave it no mind, however. Instead, she and her sisters watched in mute horror as the two Challengers dropped the eighth Door Guardian and crossed into the ninth layer.

The Summit.

The last portal, the one from the eighth to the ninth, was an open triangular archway that was almost a hundred feet high at the apex. Stepping through it felt like swimming in gelatin, cold and thick and entirely unsuited for traveling through. Like the portal didn't want them to continue.

Neither Pit nor Felix cared about that, though.

They jolted as they exited, buffeted by gale-force winds and pelted by jagged ice. Felix conjured a red-gold flame to intercept the razor-sharp hail, and it was more or less effective. Didn't do much for the wind, though.

"There's a staircase!" Pit shouted over the howling storm.

Sure enough, the only thing ahead of them was a set of stairs carved into the side of a mountain and coated liberally with ice and snow. There was no railing, and after twenty feet or so, the right side opened up into a dizzying drop. Felix traced the path, tracking the steps as they wound up the mountain peak until they vanished into the haze of the thickening blizzard.

"Stay close, bud!" Felix shouted, leaning into the wind. "We'll move slow and steady on this one."

"Right…right behind you!"

Felix didn't miss the catch in his friend's voice or the exhaustion that dogged his Spirit. Pit had already been hurting when they'd reunited on the fifth layer, and the attempt to cleanse his curse had only made it worse.

Not to mention the fights getting here. They had moved fast, but not terribly so, considering their Agility. Pit had been adamant in handling any foe that came his way, which slowed down their progress. Felix would have been fine with that, mostly, if not for the fact that every battle only added to the slew of minor injuries Pit bore. Their store of Healing Potions was growing very thin by the time they stepped into the ninth and final layer. *Just gotta step careful. Nothing's been able to really make me go all out yet. We got this.*

Cardinal Flame!

Felix conjured a heavy sheet of red-gold fire, holding it up against the vicious wind. It was enough to melt the oncoming ice and blunt the wind, but it did little to keep away the incredible chill that settled on them. Even through his Song of Absolution, Felix could feel it, and Pit immediately began to shiver. They walked only halfway up the first curve before a System notification popped into view.

Pit's Cold Resistance is level 50!
Journeyman Tier!
He Gains:
+5 END
+5 VIT
+5 WIL

Pit's Cold Resistance is level 51!

"W–we'll th–that is helpful!" Pit chirruped over the howling winds. "Gim–gimme enough time, and I'll be imm–immune!"

Pit's Cold Resistance is level 52!

Felix flared Cardinal Flame, pumping out more Mana into the air around them, but it had little effect when compared to the atmosphere all around them.

"Wh–what're you doing? Kee–keep going!" Pit shouted when his big head bumped into Felix's back. "Gotta keep mo–moving!"

So they did. Their stride ate up distance on the narrow steps, moving perhaps a half-mile around the incredibly huge mountain while the winds tried to tear them free. Unless he wanted to risk Pit falling, running was too dangerous in those conditions, and Felix's Perception was severely blunted by the chaos all around them. He was reduced to taking things a step at a time, his Skills ready to sing out at a moment's notice.

Nothing continued to happen.

Pit's Cold Resistance is level 57!

The walk became interminable. No monsters, just the wind, the icy steps, and the ever-present cold. A faint pressure had begun to press down on them, something Felix recognized from his training against Spiritual pressure. It wasn't something he felt very often, as lesser Spirits were sorta washed out by his own, so he knew immediately that it was relatively potent. Pit felt it, too, but he was likewise barely affected.

It was the cold that was fouling his Companion.

I need a better solution. His fire was only half the solution. *I—hm. Mantle of the Infinite Revolution would heat my immediate surroundings up, but likely too much. I'd worry about burning Pit and melting parts of the staircase. What about this? Sunken Ward!*

Immediately, the worst of the cold vanished, replaced instead by a cool sensation across his skin. Even breathing became easier as the wind that kept trying to crawl down his throat was immediately blocked.

"Whoa! What—Sunken Ward?" Pit exclaimed, and his voice echoed slightly as it transmitted across the spell. "You can use this out of the water?"

"Nothing said I can't. It's about manipulating air Mana around us to keep breathing," Felix said, working out how the spell was helping. "Huh. Temperature and air pressure regulation works against just normal weather, too, not just deep water conditions."

Pit shook himself, shaking loose snow and frost from his fur. "It's still cold but oh, that's much better! Clever!"

Sunken Ward is level 66!

...

Sunken Ward is level 70!

Apparently, the System thought the same, as the Skill jumped five levels. "Let's keep moving. Maybe now we can make some progress."

The words barely left his mouth when a boulder the size of a horse smashed into the stairs ahead of them. Felix shouted wordlessly, Stone and Rime Shaping screaming to life in his channels as he tore apart the projectile, and several creatures swirled through the clouds just beyond them.

Pit let loose a sharp screech as his Howl at the Dark activated, and two of the creatures faltered, their shapes falling out of cover. Felix immediately identified them. "Ice Drakes. Elementals. Strong, too. Pit, can you—"

"Dawn's Advent!"

A flurry of sizzling crescents flew from the tenku's paws, hurtling through space to intercept beast after beast. Pained bellows shook the skies, and the clouds churned with a dozen sets of wings.

Rain of Cata—!

The steps beneath them exploded.

Dodge is level 83!

Felix danced back just in time as a huge portion of the staircase was hurtled out into the empty air, and a blocky creature the size of a city bus crawled from the mountain's side. Metal and stone hands leveraged it upright, and a single eye that shone with an icy light glared at him.

"Oh great," he muttered. "Pit! Focus on the Ice Drakes! I've got these idiots!"

Sovereign of Flesh!

Stone Shaping!

The first Stalagmight, an elemental of metal and earth, ripped itself free of the mountain and was followed by two more. Felix rushed forward, meeting them with scale-covered fists and the song of their undoing. The first swung at him, but he met its huge blow with his own…and shattered its forearm into pieces. Its body softened, seized by Felix's Will as he shaped the stone of its former arm into a pillar that smashed up into its own stupid face.

You Have Killed A Stalagmight!
XP Earned!

The elemental fell, hurled from the path, and Felix took his fury onto the next. He leaped over the broken gap of the staircase, fists blazing with dusty-brown earth Mana—and did not expect a *third* elemental to hurtle from beneath.

"Oh shit!" he managed, just as the Stalagmight grabbed at his feet with one of its huge mitts. It twisted and rolled, not toward the mountain, but out into the empty air beside them. "*Oh shit!*"

"FELIX!"

Pit streaked from the side, more blur than Chimera, as he latched onto the elemental with claws and beak. His weight shifted them back just for a second...before another Stalagmight dropped from above.

They all fell.

You Have Left The Path!

CHAPTER TWENTY-TWO

Adamant Discord!

A tether of lightning lashed back, affixed to the very air itself as Felix fell in a tangle with the Steel Elemental and Chimera. Pit unleashed a heavy barrage of light crescents, each strike carving shallow slices into the elemental's tough exterior as it forced its clumsy, grasping arms away. Felix rotated his body, twisting against the rushing wind until his feet met metal.

Cloudstep!

A platform of crackling Mana appeared just beneath the elemental, stopping its descent just long enough for Felix to flex his powerful legs. He screamed, anger and stress bottled as one, and blasted the monster through his Cloudstep and into the mountainside. The elemental's roar cut off, buried under the sound of screeching metal and falling rocks.

You Have Killed A Steel Elemental!
XP Earned!

Shadow Whip!

From one hand, Felix hurled a coil of shadow, snapping it around his Companion and tangling against itself. "Gotcha!" Felix cried.

In his other hand, the lightning tether glowed fiercely. Felix hauled back on the empty air, grunting at the sheer strain as inertia dragged at his shoulder joint. His Body proved up to the challenge, and moments later, they were both flung upward at breakneck speed.

"The ledge!" Pit shouted out.

"I know!" Felix passed the staircase where they'd fallen, ascending still on the cable-like connection he'd seized from the air. "Time to take a shortcut!"

The mountain flashed by them, a blur of stone as more elementals crowded its surface. Boulders were launched after the duo, but Felix kicked away the few that came close. Ice Drakes swirled in the clouds all around them, their own attacks all but replacing the hail, but Pit met those with superheated light and an unflinching cry.

Yet monsters and weather were not their only obstacles. They'd risen around a thousand feet, the stairway coming in and out of view, when a vicious pressure settled on Felix's shoulders. It shoved him down, or tried to, refuting his claim to the sky.

Felix screamed. The pressure buckled, dimpling the thick cumulonimbus clouds around them as true lightning flashed. Baseball-sized hail came at them sideways, shattering against Felix's newly summoned scales and Pit's barding. The stairway rounded the mountain just above them, and Felix pulled them closer.

You Have Left The Path!
You May Not Return!

What? A sheen of prismatic Mana formed a barrier around the carved stairs, preventing them from landing. *Fine! Adamant Discord!*

Felix blasted upward, hauling harder than ever on his seized connections. Lightning became a bar of blue-white energy as he ascended, faster and faster, hurtling through greater and greater amounts of spiritual pressure. Felix bodied it all, smashing his midnight scales against whatever being wanted him to fail. They shouted, twinned Primordial voices screaming into the storm.

They would not be stopped.

Thick, cloying clouds washed over them, passed them, before they emerged suddenly from the other side. The raging blizzard was gone, left below. Felix stopped, hovering atop a set of Cloudsteps, Pit trembling beside him.

"That's a little intimidating," he admitted.

Spread out before them, flying just above the lightning strewn clouds below, were Ice Drakes. Not one or two or five…but thousands. The immense creatures were strong, but Felix had beaten them handily before. Pit had, too. What they hadn't handled before, however, was the monster that flew behind them. A Superior Elemental, fashioned into the likeness of an Ice Drake but magnified at least three times in all dimensions. Its back was surmounted by ice crystals the size of small trees, while its wedge-shaped head was lit by a purple-white light. Felix's Voracious Eye pinged its power at somewhere around a Tier VI—roughly analogous with a Master at the upper reaches of their Temper.

"Yeah," Pit agreed. His sides were heaving as he breathed, and a few of his minor wounds had opened back up. "Just a little."

Felix could feel his friend's exhaustion, his pain, and the stubborn anger that boiled in Pit's heart. The temptation to make his Companion retreat was strong, but Felix pushed it away. "You ready?"

"I—" Pit growled, but it was laced with a sharp whine. "I can't. I can't fight them all, Felix. I'm too…the climb, the fall, I—" Pit whimpered. "It hurts."

"It's okay." Felix hugged his friend around the neck, tight as he could without opening up his wounds. "I got you, bud."

Convergence!

Pit initiated the retreat, vanishing in a flash of light and settling like a lead weight in Felix's Spirit. For a moment, Felix simply stood there, contemplating the approaching horde. He had perhaps thirty seconds before the distance Ice Drakes reached him. More than enough time to center himself. To breathe.

The Superior Ice Drake shrieked, sending a violent shockwave across the clouds. Felix leaned into it, ignoring the way it threatened to shatter his ear drums. He was focused. The horde drew closer.

Time to end it.

He shifted his weight and the Cloudstep beneath him groaned as he leaned forward. "Adamant Discord."

Conjured platforms exploded as he took off, the very clouds around him blown through in an ever-widening circle. Felix rode lightning, skin shining with light and fire. The closest Ice Drakes opened their jaws and unleashed a torrent of freezing, unshaped Mana. Felix met it with all the fury and power at his disposal.

Rime Shaping!

Felix took hold of the unshaped ice Mana before him, splitting it in half as he sped through the breach. Each portion he shaped into blunt projectiles, hurled sideways at the line of Ice Drakes, even as he ripped his fist through the first.

You Have Killed An Ice Drake!
XP Earned!

More were on him instantly, but Felix did not hesitate. He tore them apart, their frosty bodies no match for his command over their own element. A few escaped his control, though, attacking from awkward angles as a dozen became a hundred. That was when he got clever.

Cardinal Flame!

Auroral Forge!

Auroral Forge is level 77!
Multi-Cast is level 80!

Explosions of red-gold flame and blades of whirling golden light spun from his channels like the counter-melody to frost's concerto. Wings were sheared through, bellies ruptured, and ice-flesh melted into arctic rain. Kill notifications streamed across Felix's consciousness, acknowledged and dismissed by instinct, as his dark claws wrought savage destruction on the horde around him.

Chthonic Tribute!

Dead elementals burst into color-streaked smoke, devoured as Felix fought. He was lightning, and his strikes were thunder, filling the murky sky with cast off reflections. The elementals couldn't harm him, not with Sovereign of Flesh, and he would not tire before it was over.

Another roar ripped through the pile of bodies, almost scattering the Essence Felix was consuming. "Your turn, huh?" Felix asked, just before the Superior Ice Drake slammed into him.

"Not today!" he shouted and caught the monster's descending jaws between his scaled hands. Bat-like wings pumped, driving them down into the clouds as its thick, stout neck flexed against Felix's grasp. "God, your breath stinks."

Potent ice Mana rushed up its gullet, easily visible to Felix as an ascending radiance. He twisted aside, slamming the beast's jaws shut just as its glacial breath hit. "Nope! Keep that to yourself!"

The Superior Ice Drake screeched, icicles bursting from the sides of its mouth. Felix released its snout at the same time he drove his spiked knee into its chin. The elemental's head snapped back, the pathetic remains of its breath attack spent into the clouds around them, along with several of its sword-length teeth.

It collected itself swiftly as they plummeted, still falling through the flashing clouds, and reoriented on Felix. This time, it was far faster, its broken maw open to swallow Felix whole.

He was happy to oblige.

Felix dove into its open mouth, cutting off the power of his Adamant Discord as he rode the slick length of the elemental's throat. Instead, he conjured spell after spell, the same one repeated with Multi-Cast, until he shone with red-gold flames.

Multi-Cast is level 81!

Cardinal Flame surrounded him, melting the ice enough that his fists broke through the elemental's constricting muscles with ease. The creature spun, hurling itself in circles to dislodge him, but Felix couldn't be stopped now. Its insides were confusing, but he punched his way through until he hit a layer of ice that refused to give way. Felix grunted, peering inside before grinning.

"Got you." Cardinal Flame shifted, moving from his whole body to pull inward toward the Mana Gate at the bottom of his skull. "You wanna imitate a dragon? I'll do you one better!"

Blinding, red-gold flame roared from Felix's mouth. He grasped it as it emerged, shaping it from a blooming gush to a welder's flame. The spell compacted again and again, strengthening each time he sounded Cardinal Flame, rapidly devouring his Mana pool but increasing its potency with every instant.

Multi-Cast is level 82!
Cardinal Flame is level 94!

Fissures ran through the elemental, but Felix stayed focused on the slowly melting ice before him. The monster shrieked in pain and panic. Then he was through, the ice opened up just enough. Felix slammed his claws down, piercing the gleaming purple-white core of the elemental.

Chthonic Tribute!

Everything fell apart.

Felix dropped, summoning multiple Cloudsteps beneath himself to arrest his fall. The first dozen shattered beneath his weight, but he slowed enough to stop as the entirety of the Superior Ice Elemental was rendered into Essence, Mana, and a decent stream of significance.

Hell yeah. Way better than the measly dollops I was getting from the other enemies. Felix watched the skies, half hoping for another to come for him.

Clouds swirled around him, completely obscuring anything beyond a dozen yards. *You hear that, Pit? Gimme a couple hundred more like that, and I'll have more than enough to use Unite the Lost.*

Better...better get moving, then.

Felix snorted. *Yeah yeah. I'm on—*

Thunder boomed above him at the same time Felix's senses screamed in panic. He threw up his arms, just in time to bear the brunt of a metal fist the size of a sedan.

"UNF!"

The Cloudstep beneath him exploded into pieces as he was driven straight through it, rocketed downward through the clouds by the unmitigated force behind that punch. Felix ripped out of the clouds and crashed into the ground, cratering the ice and stone beneath him.

From above, a gargantuan figure dropped. Felix's eyes widened, and he grasped a potential connection up and to the left before zipping away. Lightning flashed, and he barely dodged the school bus-sized feet that stomped hard into the earth. Clouds of snow and stone dust rose up, obfuscating the creature as it slowly stood up from its crouch.

Damn. Felix realized he hovered above a wide, icy plain, marked only by a few upthrust rock formations. A plateau. *It's the summit. And this*—his Voracious Eye flashed—*the Final Guardian.*

It was a Superior Steel Elemental, Tier VI just as the Superior Ice Drake had been. It was formed entirely of metal and shaped into a blocky representation of a humanoid. Two arms, two legs, a stout torso topped by a thick neck and square head. It was huge, too, somewhere around fifty feet tall. Frost clung to it in spots, the snow marking the strange definition to the elemental's musculature.

Damn. Dude's got twelve-pack abs. Felix was fit and crazy strong, but the elemental looked like it lived at a gym, and it was always core day.

A booming laugh ripped across the air. Not from the elemental, who Felix doubted could even open its sculpted mouth. Instead, it was from the clouds above and was accompanied by a sudden, intense spiritual pressure and even worse cold.

"That's not creepy," he muttered. The cold ratcheted up further, until even Felix was uncomfortable. Felix had no shaping magic to affect the creature. Metal was beyond his control, so he couldn't affect it like the Ice Drakes. He pulled at his Mana, sounding Cardinal Flame once more...only to find his flames would not manifest. The cold choked them out entirely.

The elemental stomped out of the fading dust cloud, gaining speed with each step. It lifted an arm, clearly telegraphing its attack, something that Harn had told Felix time and again to never do in a fight. That is, unless your opponent had no chance of stopping it anyway.

"Fuck it," Felix growled. "You wanna brawl? I'm game."

Adamant Discord!

He shot forward like lightning itself, fist pulled back the same as the elemental. Within his fist a corrosive green power gathered, splashing outward in a thick, undulated wake.

Hand of Calamity!

Wild Threnody!

They met, fist to gargantuan fist, and it was as if a mountain had split in two. A sonic boom tore through the air, followed closely by a wave of pure, potent acid and the sparks of metal on metal. The elemental staggered back, hand mangled and wrist bent.

Felix followed. There would be no wasted time or testing this enemy.

Hand of Calamity!

Wild Threnody!

He sounded his acid shaping Skill over and over, stacking the patterns until they hummed with such ferocity it hurt his ears. Felix lashed out, landing on the elemental's forearm and bringing all of his might to bear. With a nightmarish screech of metal, the creature's arm bent inward.

More.

Again he hit, this time a savage kick at the elemental's other arm, knocking it away and snapping off two of its fingers.

More!

Felix wreathed himself in acid, letting the waves of thick Mana envelop him entirely before hurling himself straight into the monster's chest. The elemental lifted its arms, but its bent appendage left an opening, and Felix rammed into—through—the creature's steel carapace.

Directly into its core.

Chthonic Tribute!

Just as the Ice Drake before it, the core dissolved, pouring into Felix's open maw before the rest of the elemental followed. The Essence and Mana were nice, but again the significance was finally more than a whisper-thin rivulet.

Multi-Cast is level 83!
Hand Of Calamity is level 67!
Wild Threnody is level 86!

You Have Killed A Superior Steel Elemental!
XP Earned!

Final Guardian Defeated!
You have ascended the Path of Rule and fought to the very summit of the Ironskin Domain! Congratulations, Challenger! You have proven worthy of rule!

New Title!
Ironskin Champion IX (Epic)!
You have successfully conquered the ninth layer of the Ironskin Domain, proving your worth to the Frostfather! +20 END, VIT, DEX

"What?" Felix frowned at the notifications. "That's it? A single measly Title?"

The sky rumbled again, but there was no booming laughter. A steely silence hung all around as the blizzard went unnaturally still. Even the wind had stopped blowing.

"I know you're there!" Felix shouted into the sky. "I need more than this! We—" Felix snapped his mouth shut. "Fine. If you wanna hide, then so be it."

He squared himself off, letting midnight scales crawl up his face and over his mouth, until he was covered in a second jaw of razor-sharp fangs, a nightmarish half-mask.

"I'll come to you."

Adamant Discord!

CHAPTER TWENTY-THREE

Felix ripped through the cloud layer atop a bolt of lightning and found chaos.

The storm that had quietened raged anew, and gale force winds ripped at him while snow and hail tried to blind him. He cast his senses out, Perception and Affinity both, and found that the storm was not the same as when he'd fought the Ice Drakes. The sky itself was dark, purpled by the bruised underbelly of clouds the size of cities.

A shadow gathered there, just beyond the storm. Within it.

"You dare challenge me, monster?"

The voice was literal thunder, flashing with strange lightning that leaped from cloud to cloud. The sound cracked as sheets of ice formed on the winds, smashing into him with abandon. Felix struck them, obliterated them with fists swollen by Sovereign of Flesh, and all ten feet of him hovered in the depths of fury.

"Yeah."

Thunder roared, and in a flash, pillars of stone and metal hurled toward him from above. Felix reared back, more than fast enough to meet their assault, but found he didn't need to.

"Dawn's Advent!"

Crescents of brilliant light sizzled through the blizzard, snapping the pillars in two and deflecting them entirely. At the same time, Pit materialized next to Felix…and immediately began to fall.

"Cloudstep! Cloudstep! Cloudstep!" Felix shouted, and platforms of

Mana manifested below his tumbling Companion. "Bud. You gotta warn me next time!"

Pit warbled at him. "Focus on that!"

Above them, the clouds shifted and swirled, forming into a miles-wide bearded face. Its eyes flashed with lightning, and its mouth was filled with a shadow so deep it could have been the Void. Specks emerged from that dark mouth, but they soon resolved themselves into huge, car-sized pillars.

"Fall!" the thunder commanded.

"NO!" Pit screeched.

Cloudstep!

Felix conjured step after step as they ran upward, against the wind and into the downpour of elemental pillars.

"Dawn's Advent!" Pit cried. The crescents slashed into the frozen projectiles hard enough to slice them into pieces, and Pit ran through the lesser debris.

Felix, meanwhile, found the Mana too potent to take control of completely and resorted to his fallback option.

He punched them apart.

Pillar after pillar. Ice, stone, or steel. He met them all with his enlarged fists and diamond-hard scales. Ice splintered, stone shattered, and steel was sent flying as the impact deformed it into meaningless scrap.

Yet the deluge did not stop, and their ascent, while rapid, was nowhere near the gargantuan cloud-face. "Pit! We need to get closer! I need to—!"

Emerging sideways from the clouds, a building-sized boulder of stone and steel hurtled into them. Felix jabbed his fist forward into it, pouring all he had into Stone Shaping at the same time. They connected, and the boulder deformed before his titanic Strength and potent Skill, but it drove him back hard. He split his attention, Multi-Casting a dozen more Cloudsteps behind him to stop his fall, shattering one after the other as the boulder drove him back and down. He stopped it eventually, leaving Felix hip-deep in the splitting rock, trapped between its weight and his reinforced platforms.

Which was when he spotted the *other* boulder. Headed straight for Pit.

"Pit!"

His Companion spun just in time to take the full brunt of the projectile to his chest, before stone and tenku plummeted below.

"PIT!"

Laughter shook the heavens, and the cloud face split into a triumphant sneer. "One Challenger remains!"

"Chthonic Tribute!" Felix drove the force of his rage into the boulder around him, absorbing all of it into his channels with a mighty inhale, as well as the Cloudsteps beneath him. "Adamant Discord!"

Felix blasted downward, riding the powerful connection between him and Pit, until he could see the building-sized pillar…and the Chimera that strode atop of it.

Pit ran, shards of ice formed around his body as a deep darkness filled the spaces between them. The ice congealed, forming into a brutal set of armor twice the size of his normal body, until he resembled nothing so much as a nightmare of cold shadow. He got the end just as Felix landed beside him, and opened his ice-jaws wide, screeching a call like thunder itself.

The sky answered in kind.

Pit Has Digested His Opponent's Mana!
Pit Has Gained A Skill!

Dark Glacial Guard (Epic), Level 1!
Compel both shadow and ice to do your bidding! Forge armor made from dark ice around you to protect your Health from harm, directing all damage to your Mana pool.

Felix laughed, looking at his friend as they rode the boulder down. "Hell yeah, dude! Let's kick this guy's ass!"

"Yes!"

Shadow Whip!

Adamant Discord!

Felix shot back up, heart fluttering with a wild glee, and pulled hard on his shadowy tendril with his free hand. From below, Pit shrieked and catapulted forward, held tight by the Shadow Whip. At the apex, Felix let go and Pit soared upward, twisting between falling chunks of ice and stone before his armored claws sank into them. Pillars cascaded down onto them, and Pit leaped between them as he ascended, running almost vertically up their plunging sides.

Felix followed behind, tanking hits from the endless debris as he smashed his free fist into stone, ice, and steel. Sheer Strength,

Endurance, Vitality, and the raw power of his Adamant Discord tore them to pieces.

Dark Glacial Guard is level 2!

...

Dark Glacial Guard is level 22!

Each bit of debris that hit his Companion chipped a piece of dark ice from around him, yet it only bolstered the Skill. Luckily, Pit's regeneration was very good.

They did not stop. The rain of elements continued while the spiritual pressure mounted, heavier than ever before. The voice in the clouds roared in frustration, but another shadow flitted behind it, a thing of dark wings, keen eyes, and an eager, joyful laugh.

Endless Raven…

The Urge was gone in an instant, and perhaps Felix could have convinced himself that it had never been there, save for the scream of rage that echoed through the storm.

"BEGONE, GODLING! THIS IS MY DOMAIN!"

A wave of concussive force ripped outward with the Frostfather's shout, blasting back clouds and pillars alike. Felix and Pit fell back, hurled along with them. He caught them both atop more conjured Cloudsteps.

A cacophony of stone and metal and splintering ice filled the air, chased by the thunder of unnatural lightning. The clouds and debris, once blasted back, rushed forward toward a single point, until it all glowed so fiercely Felix had to avert his eyes.

The Raven's laugh faded.

Felix looked back up and beheld the truth. They stood above the clouds, or perhaps beyond them, level with what appeared to be its highest peak.

"Holy crap," Pit chirruped softly.

Exploration is level 72!

The Frostfather *was* the peak. A body of stone and steel and ice, a living glacier attached to the top of the hulking mountain like a gargoyle lurking on a ledge. It bore the roughest sort of head, no more than a series of triangular lumps atop monstrously large shoulders, while innumerable arms were folded across its craggy body. Eyes the size of semitrailers bore into them with the purple-white light of ice Mana, swirled with silver and dusty-brown.

Voracious Eye!

Name: Frostfather
Type: Supreme Elemental (Ice/Stone/Metal)

The rest was all question marks, but the ineffable sense of its advancement was clear. A Tier VIII monster.

A High Grandmaster. Felix shifted his stance, unsure what might come next. *This is gonna be rough.*

From a series of enormous caverns, a voice like thunder and landslides cracked the air. "You dare to assault me in my own Domain, monster? In the kingdom I have wrought? I have given you accolades enough to ensure your rule over my Cold Children. That should be enough!"

The mountain cracked, and those arms of corded steel and stone lifted, their hands grasping onto the empty sky. "But no. Not for you, creature. You and your *Chimera*. I should never have allowed either of you on the Path of Rule. You do not appreciate its weight."

Spiritual pressure poured onto Felix, a hammer atop his head and shoulders that would either break him or send him plummeting below. Pit whimpered.

"Your children…You're not a god," Felix said. If he had been, Felix would have found opposing the Supreme Elemental's Will to be far easier, thanks to his Call of Defiance Title. Instead, it was taking all he had to push up against the spiritual pressure. Beneath Felix's feet, his Cloudstep splintered, forcing him to divert his Will to casting another. The pressure redoubled. "And even if you were, I don't particularly like them."

"And yet you will bow to me, little king," the Frostfather growled. Those monumental arms moved outward, surrounding them above and below as the pressure fell upon them like a rockslide, and the air itself froze. Felix's thighs burned with the strain of remaining standing, and Pit's icy armor burst to pieces.

Dark Glacial Guard is level 24!

"I'm–not–a–king!" Felix pushed himself to the limit and hurled the pressure away, blasting it into pieces. The Frostfather's eyes of gleaming steel widened. “I’m the Autarch, Frosty. And I didn’t come all this way just for accolades.”

He needed more than Essence, more than Mana. He needed significance.

A High Grandmaster monster should have plenty. Hold on, Pit. Felix let his Skill hum to life, and the never-ending abyss within him roared. *Chthonic Trib—!*

The very air around Felix froze, turned kaleidoscopic as it crystallized into chains around Felix’s limbs and neck. The Frostfather loomed, its spiritual pressure bore down with greater urgency as an utter, absolute cold crashed into them.

Rime Shaping!

Felix tried to seize and shatter the bands of ice across his body, but it was like emptying a sinking ship with a bucket. Every piece of ice he overpowered was replaced by more elsewhere.

“Cease your struggle! Succumb!” The Frostfather moved, faster than Felix would have ever expected. An explosion ripped through the air, so loud it broke some of his icy bonds—the mountain itself disintegrated around the Supreme Elemental as dozens of truck-sized fists surged forward.

There was no escape.

FELIX.

RELEASE.

Within him, Felix’s Hunger roared, and something familiar unfurled in his chest. A danger he had been suppressing all this time, one that clawed at his channels like a caged animal. Felix let it go.

Power rippled through Felix’s core space, power that shook him to experience. As if all of him were bundled together, woven into a greater whole…and then was shoved through every single Mana Gate he possessed.

Felix howled.

A dark fist, clawed and scaled as his own, manifested in the air around him. It was more than three times the size of the Frostfather’s hands, and it sizzled with red-gold flame and blue-white lightning, wreathed in both even as it was dominated by a vivid, dark purple glow. He’d been afraid to unleash such a thing against his allies, but here, he had no such compunctions.

He struck.

The phantom fist moved faster than Felix ever had, all but teleporting into the oncoming offensive and *obliterating* the Supreme

Elemental's hands. Stone and steel and ice fell to dust, and the Frostfather raged.

"Impossible! You are too weak for Core Manifestation!" The mountain rumbled, and the Frostfather stood on enormous, rough-hewn legs. "Kneel! Accept your weakness!"

"You first! Dawn's Advent!" Crescents of brilliant light crashed into the Frostfather's bulk, comically small but potent. Explosions rained down on the Supreme Elemental as Pit surged forward, leaping through the air to land atop the mountain itself.

"Chimera!" Thunder crashed, and more hands appeared to smash against the Frostfather's craggy form. Pit dodged the blows, speeding across his surface as surefooted as any goat. "A mistake of Creation! You—!"

"FROSTFATHER!" Felix roared. His knees shook, and blood ran from his nose and eyes, but he streamed power from every inch of his body. "Don't touch Pit!"

The dark fist unfurled, and an eye was revealed in the palm of its hand—an eye that screamed with a riotous noise that shook everything. Dissonance and Harmony both, chords of power. The Frostfather fell back, very nearly knocked from his mountain as he was blasted by waves of cataclysmic light and sound.

Stone, steel, and ice was rendered into dust, split and sloughed into the abyss below as it revealed a gleaming, jagged core. Pit leaped atop it, claws of his Dark Glacial Guard stabbing at its surface as Felix fell to his knees.

The fist flickered out.

Felix opened his fanged jaws, and blood poured from between them. He coughed, and something warm and wet tore loose in his chest. "Ch–Chthonic Trib—!"

"I surrender!" the Frostfather bellowed. Fear hung thick in its Spirit, and the brutal cold retreated. "I surrender, creature!"

Felix blinked, and even Pit stopped his assault. There was silence… then a harsh, cawing laughter.

CHAPTER TWENTY-FOUR

Jesus, what am I doing? Felix fell back on his heels, letting the spinning pattern of Chthonic Tribute die down to a low hum. "Pit. Back off."

His friend gave Felix a curious tilt of his head but said nothing as he withdrew his ice-shaped claws from the Frostfather's core. The only problem was he was now trapped down on the Supreme Elemental's surface.

Right. Cloudst—Gnh! Felix tried and failed to muster his Mana for another Cloudstep. His channels had been torn to shreds by that last attack, and forcing his power through them now was like pouring alcohol on an open wound. He hissed at the pain; it was sharp enough that it stabbed straight through his Song of Absolution, and that was to say nothing of the looseness he felt around his lungs.

"Felix?"

"Stay there, bud." Felix marshaled his Sovereign of Flesh, letting the Essence he'd stolen fuel his Health regeneration as he let fade the secondary set of monstrous jaws. A powerful itch overcame him as things shifted inside, crawling back into place within the shadows of his guts. It sucked, but with some effort, he stayed standing. "Frostfather. I accept your surrender."

You Have Defeated The Frostfather, Supreme Elemental Of Frost!
XP Earned!

Your Companion Pit Has Gained 2 Levels!
Pit Is Now Level 74!
He Gains:
+20 STR, +18 PER, +8 VIT, +22 END, +14 INT, +20 WIL, +40 AGL, +40 DEX!
+20 AFI, RES, and REI!

You Have Gained 1 Level!
You Are Now Level 63!
+20 to STR! +22 to PER! +22 to VIT! +26 to END! +24 to INT! +28 to WIL! +26 to AGL! +29 to DEX!
+20 All Harmonic Stats!
You Have 15 Unused Stat Points!

New Title!
Conqueror of Ironskin Domain (Legendary)!
You have achieved what no one else has in the history of this Domain: defeated the Frostfather in combat. Your connection with ice, stone, and metal Mana has deepened, and your dexterity with all three elements has increased!

Rime Shaping is level 85!
Stone Shaping is level 95!

You Have Digested Your Opponent's Mana!
You Have Gained A Skill!

New Skill!
Ferric Shaping (Epic), Level 1!
You have parsed the secrets of stone to find the refined ore within. The patterns of metal have revealed themselves to you, and the base metal iron is yours to shape.

Felix staggered back as System energy flooded his core space, only distantly aware of Pit doing the same. Notifications jumped out at him. Felix read through them all, smiling grimly as he read the last. *Another shaping Skill. Probably from that Superior Steel Elemental. How many more are there?*

"You…have defeated me, creature." the mountain below rumbled. "Are those rewards sufficient?"

"Pretty good," Felix admitted. He grunted as a spike of pain shot through him; he was pretty sure a bone just reset. "And stop calling me 'creature.' My name's Felix."

Purple-white eyes flashed curiously. "Why did you seek my destruction…Felix?"

Because I'm stupid and worried and in a damn hurry. "I'm in need of something, and I hoped I could find it here. I didn't. Defeating you might have pushed me toward where I needed to be, but I don't want to kill you. I don't want to kill anybody, if I can help it." He sat, keeping the pain from his face as he dangled his legs off the edge of his Cloudstep. "Sorry about that."

The Frostfather's Spirit, held all around them like the atmosphere itself, was hard to miss. Likewise, the odd twist in its music was very noticeable. *Shock,* Felix could tell.

"I did not expect apologies. Not from a Primordial."

Felix huffed a small laugh. "Oh. Right. Well, I'm a lot less crazy than the usual variety."

"Smaller, too," Pit added.

"Indeed. You are unlike your kin in many ways…Felix. But not entirely dissimilar."

The mountain shook, and Felix tensed despite the pain, only to realize the Supreme Elemental was sitting back down himself. Pit wobbled but stayed standing. The Frostfather's feet of stone and metal and ice vanished beneath his craggy exterior, until there was no delineation between him and the mountain itself.

"Not dissimilar. I'm going to assume that's a compliment," Felix said.

"Mhm," the Frostfather rumbled. "Those that I knew were wise beyond measure, before the gods laid their curse upon them. Awfully perceptive, as well. Your words cut me to the quick, just as theirs once did. I am no god."

Felix folded his arms. "The Risi would argue otherwise."

"Do not be confused, Primordial. My hand was instrumental in creating the Cold Children, but the confluence of the Grand Harmony and Dissonance cannot be touched by one such as I. Not alone."

A great, tempestuous wind began, so powerful that Felix once again surged to his feet. Only to find that the Frostfather was…sniffing. "Ah." There was a sadness in that word, so much that the sky began to purple with rain clouds. "Scion of the Unseen Tide. I knew your mother well."

"My mother?" Felix wrestled down a spike of alarm and confusion. "What are you talking about?"

"Your predecessor. Your maker." The mountain rumbled. "She who became the Unending Maw."

Felix frowned. "You knew her. It. The Maw. How? Why?"

"I am old, Felix. Very, very old. Yet, compared to her, I was a child. She helped me create the Cold Children. She is their mother, too."

Shit. Grimmar was right. "The mother of monsters," he said.

"An apt name. The curse affected her least of all, but all of her kind suffered. We suffered."

"Who's 'we?'"

"The Elementals. Have you seen any outside my realm, Felix?"

"Some," he admitted. "Sprites."

"The least of us. All that remains upon the Continent in any real sense. We were vanquished in Ages past—a casualty of the war."

"The war. Between the Nym and the gods?"

The Frostfather chuckled, a sound like a rockslide. "Far before that, Felix. The war that began it all. The War for Creation."

The War for Creation. That phrase had meaning. Weight. Felix almost felt like he could hear the significance in it. Before he could compile his thoughts, the Frostfather continued.

"Before the old gods rose, before the mortal Races, *we* were the rulers of the Continent. Masters of its elements and peoples. Then we were struck down by *them*, and our lineage diluted. Weakened. Turned to Naiads and Nixies and Sylphs. The Primordials did not help us. They were too busy fighting their own battles to do more than mourn our fall." Those eyes, like burning spotlights now, flashed at Felix. "But you…you are powerful. Potent. Free of the flesh curse that felled your kind. How?"

"I'm special," Felix said. "Tell me more about this war. It was the gods versus the Primordials?"

"Eventually. Your Race…Greater Primordial." The Frostfather sighed, that sadness replaced by a slow anger. "I remember some, but I did not fight in the war. I was merely an Inferior Elemental then, a limited Mind, but I recall the stories. The Greater Primordials were the generals of the war, driving their lesser brethren into glorious battle. Thousands against the might of the new gods."

"They led them? A whole army?" Felix asked. He imagined Elderthrone but filled with nightmarish Primordials.

"No. There were others. The kings of all. The gods before the gods and precursors to the Ancient Scions. The Cardinal Beasts."

Felix's breath caught in his chest. *Cardinal…?* Like Cardinal Fiend, or Cardinal Flame. *Like my goddamn Named core?*

The Frostfather rumbled yet again, and this time it was with curiosity. "Surprise laces your Spirit. When did you become the Maw?"

Felix grimaced. He didn't like *that* phrasing. "Less than a year ago."

"Less than—too soon. Your power is still mostly nascent. It will take an Age to mature fully."

An Age?! Felix doubted he'd live that long, not with the enemies he'd been accruing. "I don't have that kind of time."

"I can imagine not. The gods stir. Even I can feel it here, in this cage I built for myself. I will grant you three boons, Scion. As tradition demands." A new hand, this one open and flat, rose from the mountain upon an arm of corded stone and steel. It stopped briefly near Pit, who hopped aboard before it was lifted the rest of the way to Felix's platform. "My power is limited, but I am ancient. I can offer you knowledge above all else."

Felix placed a hand on his friend as he returned to his side, his icy armor banished for now. "Alright. How does that work? Do I just ask some questions?"

A single finger lifted, easily twice as tall as Felix's ten-foot battleform, before curling onto the palm. "Yes, but I shall provide the first. You are awakening, Scion. You summoned a manifestation of your core into the world, a feat that should remain beyond your advancement…and yet you did not die at its unveiling. I knew the Maw as well as any Elemental could, and her Hunger knew no bounds. You desire Essence, Mana, and significance, yes?"

"Yes." Not for the reasons the Frostfather was suggesting, but Felix couldn't deny those words. "As much as I can."

"I can sense within you all nine Pillars of your mortal advancement. You stand upon a threshold of power, and with more to consume, you will become truly fearsome, it is true. But you are a Scion of the Unseen Tide." Stones tumbled from around the Frostfather's core, still open and gleaming in the wintry air. "You must learn what that means. Seek that which unites and divides. The breaking and the binding. If you find that, Scion, you will find a Path to power greater than any I could offer."

That which unites and divides. Unite the Lost did the former, and Skein of Fate could break Oaths as well as make them, but Felix had a feeling the mountain wasn't talking about his Skills.

"That is the greatest knowledge I could give you, Scion. You may ask twice more." The Frostfather held up two more fingers.

Felix considered his options. He could ask more about the Path the mountain was on about, but doubted he'd get more than he already had, especially since he lacked the right information to do anything but restate the Frostfather's own words.

Could make *him tell us,* Pit suggested.

Maybe. But we already pushed him to the edge. Felix patted his friend on the neck, along the metal scales of his barding. *Other than consuming his core and hoping to grab a Memory from him, I don't think there's much else we'll get from that line of thinking.*

Well…

Pit, little pig. We're not eating the god of the Frost Giants.

Hmph. Fine.

Felix had almost lost sight of their diplomatic goals in his fight, and he wasn't planning on doing so again. An idea bloomed.

"Alright. My first request is that you fix the boundaries of your Domain," Felix said. "The Risi still need this place to train their people."

"Done. Gladly." A wave of shimmering Mana rippled outward, down the mountain and into the distance. The background vibrations around Felix shifted, ever so slightly, and a second finger curled down. "My lesser children have been growing too strong without the Risi to prune them back. Your rampage has solved that, Scion. You and your Companion.

"What of the last boon?"

Felix traded a look with Pit. The tenku looked tired, hitting the end of his considerable Stamina as he panted. Pit nodded. "My Companion is hurt. He is under a curse, and it prevents him from healing his wings. Can you remove the curse?"

The Frostfather was silent for a long, tense moment, then motes of ice and stone separated from his remaining finger. They hovered around Pit, rotating around him like tiny satellites. After several minutes, the ice and stone retracted, and the Frostfather grumbled. "I cannot. The curse appears to be wound through him and his core space. To remove it would kill him."

Pit shrank back, tufted ears held low, while Felix fought off a wave of helpless rage. *Fuck. Same as what Isla said.* "Then what can I do?"

"I am not a creature of healing. I could, perhaps, replace his wings with ones of ice and steel." The stone and ice shifted but did not draw closer to Pit again. "But there is a storm within you, Chimera, one that will not suffer my presence. I can offer one thing."

"What?" Felix looked at the mountain, torn between hope and frustration so big he didn't know what to do with it. "What can you offer?"

"There is a treasure, an artifact created in Ages lost that can heal anything, Body, Mind, and Spirit. Even this curse." A shimmering ring of chaotic elements appeared above the Frostfather's finger. Flame, ice, lightning, shadow—too many Mana types to count flitted through its structure, all of them whirling around like a miniature hurricane. "The Mote of Frenzy."

Felix reached out, but his hands passed through the whirling display. An illusion. "Where is it?"

"It was last in the hands of my brother, a Supreme Elemental of Fire and Stone. Powerful, but not invincible. He was defeated at the hands of the Dwarves, captured and taken. Killed him, perhaps." The mountain shook again, and house-sized chunks of stone and steel rained down from the Frostfather's shoulders. The purple skies turned pink and orange. A sunset of rage. "If anyone has the Mote, it is them.

"The Dwarves do not let go of what they claim."

CHAPTER TWENTY-FIVE

"Don't tug at those," Harn snapped. His hammer never faltered, ringing against some red-hot piece of steel. "You'll open up your wounds again."

Evie dropped her hand from the cloth bundled around her left shoulder. *Stupid Adept Perception. Can't get anything by him.* "It itches. And I wouldn't be openin' my wounds if you let me have a Healing Potion!"

Harn stopped and pointed his hammer at her. "And you wouldn't be hurt if you didn't go an' challenge that Dragon. This is your punishment, kid."

Burnin' bloody ash. "He's a Wyrmling."

"And you still lost."

"I bloodied him a little," she muttered. Harn simply looked at her from under his heavy brows, and Evie leaned back in her chair, folding her arms with a grunt.

"Hmph." Harn tossed his steel back in the forge behind him. They stood in the center of the Forge Hall, while all around them bustled two dozen apprentices of varying ages and Races. Harn's setup was above and beyond all the rest—as it should be, him being the Forgemaster and all. Work tables surrounded him, tools hung from special racks, and a bevy of bowls and jars and barrels lined his sides, all filled with powders and oils. The huge forge rumbled, some inscription on it flaring as the metal heated up.

Evie pulled in short, shallow breaths and stifled the mad urge to itch.

Not because he said to, just because the stitches were a little tight—she didn't want to pull them. They still felt weird. Evie hadn't had a natural healing wound since before she Revealed her Omen. Healing Potions might be rare, but tonics and salves were sold at the corner of every street in every big city, and Mags had always made sure they were healed up.

Damn lizard cut me deep. Their fight hadn't gone the way Evie had hoped, not once that Wyrmling summoned a host of magic water snakes. *He's too damn small to be so strong.*

After the fight had ended, Vess had taken her to the healers, which was where Harn had run into them. He'd hauled her off and growled down anyone that tried to stop him. Evie had been getting an earful in the days since. She shifted in her stone chair, looking for a position that wasn't back-twistingly uncomfortable. "You couldn't get nicer seating?"

"Blame Felix," Harn grunted. The steel beneath his hammer, fresh out of the forge, was cherry red and quickly morphing into a chunky hook. "He designed the place. Or the Stronghold did. Hrm. Not actually sure on that."

"How's that work?" She settled on a half-leaning position, which put her opposite shoulder against the back of the rocky chair. The itching continued, but the stitching didn't feel so snug. "Rock just up and decide to be tile and tables? And how's it make an anvil like that?"

Harn smirked and patted the horn of his anvil. It was a strange thing, all made of crystal and shot through with golden sparks. "Made this myself, with some help from the boys. Mana crystal from Ahkestria makes a mean anvil."

Evie rolled her eyes. The sheer joy in Harn's voice pleased her, though, despite how annoying he was being about her fight. "You seem happy. Must be some anvil."

"Yes, he certainly does love it," said Palin as she swept into view. She had a bundle of flowers in a wide harvesting basket propped against her hip, and she gave Harn a peck on the cheek. "Hello, dear."

"Hrm." The man's face was as stoic as ever, but Evie was getting good with her Affinity. His Spirit soared with Palin around.

"Evie, why are you still bandaged?" Palin asked. She cocked an eyebrow at Harn. "Why hasn't she been healed?"

"She's healin' just as she should," Harn said. "All actions have consequences, eh?"

"Harn—"

"Palin, it's fine." Evie stood up, not eager to be in the middle of some couple's fight. "It's healin' up nice."

"Hm." The woman's expression was a match for Harn's; stubborn as iron. "If you say so, Evie. But if you need anything, even if it's time away from this lug, come down to the Giant's Flagon."

Evie grinned. Palin had started up a new tavern near the Bitterward, where the Frost Giants had made their little community. Business was booming, she'd heard. Giants had quite the appetite, after all. "Appreciate it. Might take you up on it soon, if Harn doesn't start workin' on my armor."

Steam billowed up with a screaming hiss as Harn quenched his work. "I told you, kid. I'm workin' on the Masterwork weapons. I'm close to figuring them out." He lifted what looked like a sharp hook out of the quenching tub and set it on his workbench. "Just need to make a few tools."

Palin and Evie shared a look. Harn had been fussing with those Masterwork weapons since Felix had taken them from the corpses of the High Guard. A sword and a spear, each one heavily enchanted and nasty sharp. They were stored below his benches, Evie knew, locked in some enchanted mini vault that came with the Crafting Hall. Even still, she imagined she could feel their power radiating upward. Like a half-heard scream.

"Been workin' on that for a long time," Evie said.

"Hrm." Harn fastened another piece of metal to the hooked one, driving a thick pin into some sort of hinge. "Be easier if I had a proper Forgeflame. Haven't found the right spark for that yet, otherwise this mighta been solved already. I'm only a bit into Adept, but I can see the path, rocky as it is. Just gotta walk it."

Palin set her basket down on the edge of a workbench. "Harn. Can't you set it aside and help Evie out?"

"They got spells worked into 'em, Palin. Spells that can level a battlefield." Harn's hand gripped the air, as if he were grasping the weapons now. "If I can peel back the protections, we could copy them. Put them on our own weapons. Then what happened in Haarwatch wouldn't happen again. Couldn't."

The last words came as a growl from the squat warrior, and Evie remembered him in the weeks after the battle. They'd lost a lot of people, folks Harn personally trained.

Palin slid her hand over Harn's fist and held it. "Let's keep Evie safe, then."

Stupid, fucking Affinity, she thought, blinking away a new burning in her eyes. *Makin' me feel things.* She flexed her shoulder slightly, happy to focus on something else.

Harn cleared his throat. "Fine. I'll get started on it, I just need some extra bits." He grabbed a piece of chalk off his bench and scrawled a number of things onto a piece of slate before pushing it toward Evie. All without ever taking his hand from Palin's. "Go find these and bring 'em back. I'll get started on shaping the ice you gave me."

Evie looked at the slate. "I don't know what any of this is."

Harn rolled his eyes. "You, big man! Help her find these materials."

A large apprentice shuffled over, though his head seemed ready to shrink into his shoulders. *Great.* Evie grabbed the slate. "Ugh. Fine. C'mon."

As she walked away, Evie spotted Palin lean over and gave Harn a kiss. "You big softie."

Harn grumbled, and Evie squeezed her Affinity shut. She didn't need to know about *those* feelings.

"And this, uh, this is here, I think."

Evie looked at the big man leading her around. He was very wide, like most smithing apprentices—didn't get far at the craft if you lacked Strength. Aside from that, though, she didn't think he was very good at his job. "You sure you know what we need…what was it? Rodrick?"

The big man mumbled something she didn't catch, reaching up for another handle. They stood in front of a huge bay of cabinets, all of them stone, and each one was labeled with a series of sigils she couldn't read. Based on how sweaty the man was, Evie was half convinced Rodrick couldn't read them, either.

"Rodrick! I can handle this," said another man, a Half-Orc Evie faintly recognized. He was wearing a thick white tunic and leather breeches beneath a thick smithing apron, and a number of tools hung from a wide belt.

"The Forgemaster asked me to," Rodrick said. His voice sounded kinda familiar, too, but at this point, Evie couldn't remember who she'd already met in Elderthrone. "I can't just, uh, just walk away."

"I know. And I won't tell him if you don't." The Half-Orc smiled. "If he asks, you helped her out, alright?"

The sheer relief from the big man was palpable, and not even to her

Affinity. The way his shoulders sagged and hand relaxed spoke volumes. "Thanks, Loquis."

Rodrick nodded nervously at Evie and scuttled off.

The Half-Orc looked at her sheepishly. "Sorry about that. Rodrick's only been here a few days and doesn't know the layout. Dunno why Commander Kastos would have picked him to help."

Evie shrugged it off. "He's…distracted." She refused to look back at the central forge or let up on the chokehold she had over her Affinity. Who knew what he and Palin were doing at that point. She handed Loquis the slate. "Here. These are what I need."

"Oh. *Oh.* These are rare. Alright." The slender man looked around for a second before gesturing sharply. "Come with me."

He led them to another set of stone cabinets, and these rotated around some center column. Loquis started pushing at them, spinning one set out of the way. "Here it is." He set a finger against the sigaldry on the cabinet and a small, blue-white spark leaped out. The cabinet popped open, and he rooted around inside.

Lightning magic. Evie snapped her fingers. *That's right.* "You're that Arclight," she said.

"I'm sorry?"

"You're that Arclight I chose to come with us to Ahkestria." Evie raised an eyebrow. "You're a Claw member. Why're you doin' grunt work in the Forge?"

The Half-Orc blushed for some reason. "I didn't think you'd—um, well, all of us in the Legion were required to take up a craft."

"What? By who?"

"The Autarch. I say required, but it was more of a recommendation." Loquis shrugged his shoulders. "But when the Fiend suggests something, you listen."

"I guess." Evie wrinkled her nose, imagining herself brewing some smelly potions or carving out those dumb glyphs. "Don't really see the point, is all."

"Oh it's not so bad," he said, reaching back into the cabinet. He pulled out several chunks of rock, all a silvery green color, and placed them in his satchel before closing the door with a click. He rotated the storage chests again, this time selecting a sigil that looked like a sunburst. "I could have gone with sigaldry, most of my fellow Arclights did. But I find working with metals to be more…I dunno. Soothing."

"Soothin'?" Evie let her eyes roam the chamber. The apprentices nearest them were manning bellows and banging hot metal with hammers and weird rods. It was loud and hot and sweaty. "I'd rather be fightin'."

"You're quite good at that, so I understand." Loquis put two clear, crystal rods into his satchel, but it was getting pretty full. "I'm not really made for it."

Evie laughed. "What're you talkin' about? I remember more than you just zappin' me with that lightning. You were in the thick of it the whole time. Takes more than blind luck to survive that many scrapes."

"I—" Loquis blushed again. "Thank you. That means a lot, coming from you."

She shrugged. "Just tellin' the truth. You and that Pava girl and… what's-his-name. That Dwarf."

"Asaad?"

"Yeah, him. I remember all of you doin' great in the fire temple."

The Half-Orc beamed. "Really? They'll be glad to hear it."

Deception is level 34!

Evie didn't remember them in any of those battles—she barely remembered their names, though the Half-Orc had always stuck out. Still, it was a harmless lie.

And he does look cute when he blushes. For a mage.

CHAPTER TWENTY-SIX

In a quiet, snow-coated glade, a portal split the air.

Birds scattered, and small creatures skipped across footprints that had barely filled in, while the rent sucked up the air around it like a gasping man. It widened, loosing a fluting note that soon trembled with vibrato—until it stopped. There was only silence and the night-dark hole, and both of them breathed in the stillness of the forest.

From star-drenched darkness, two booted feet crunched into the same footprints they had once left. Veddi and Devvi stepped out, brandishing their weapons, while Errol followed close behind. Errol made a sharp gesture. "Fan out, secure the glade."

The giants did so, as did Kress and Geddin, moving through the deep snow with sure steps and serious Spirits. The Fiend's Shadows were fast and thorough, returning a bare half minute later. "Sir, the glade is clear," Veddi reported.

"Lord Autarch. The way is safe," Errol said softly into the breach. It rippled, and Felix emerged, Pit at his side.

"Thank you, Errol," he said.

"Our pleasure, Lord Autarch," Errol said, saluting.

Why'd you let them do all that? Pit asked. *I could feel the glade was empty through the portal.*

Why do you think? Felix asked.

Pit tilted his head as the Shadows rearranged themselves around the two of them. *To make them feel useful?*

Sorta. And because we can't do everything, even if we want to. Felix glanced at the portal as it closed with a soft, exhaling pop. *We don't have to fight every fight.*

His Companion let out a contemplative trill. Felix ruffled the feathers of his cheek, where his barding didn't cover, before grasping the hilt of his hooked blade. "Karys. We've returned."

Green-gold lights spun up, hovering around it like fog. "I am pleased to hear of your return. It has been less than nine glasses since your departure. I assume the issue with the Risi has been resolved?"

"More or less." His return from the Domain had been met with wide-eyed stares and thunderous applause. The Witches had sided with Felix before he could display his Title for beating the Frostfather—they still hadn't seen it, but apparently the Witches had been watching up until the point he challenged the Supreme Elemental, after which their connection had broken. Beating the Summit of the Ironskin Domain was unprecedented, and seeing how Felix had returned unharmed, Naberius was quick to champion him as a contender for rule. He still wasn't entirely sure how that would resolve itself, but Felix had plans to make, and none of them were in the north. Not yet, anyway. "Kimaris is headed back to Cold Rock now to secure our foothold."

"Foothold? I thought we only sought an alliance with the Risi?"

"I was more effective than I anticipated," Felix said, his voice as dry as he could manage in the wet snowdrifts. He quickly outlined the possibility of a healing artifact for Pit, something he'd already shared with the Shadows. "I'll be back to the Temple shortly, and we'll need to gather our people together to discuss a new trip."

"The location of this miraculous artifact was revealed to you?"

"It was. I'll tell you more in person."

"Very well, my Lord. Is there anything else we can do to prepare?"

Felix took a short inhale before letting it all go. "Please inform Zara that I'll be heading to speak with her shortly, if you would."

"Of course."

The connection faded, and his blade dimmed. Felix stood in the empty glade, thinking. The Mote of Frenzy hadn't left his Mind since he'd learned of it—not the entire trip across two Dark Passages and certainly not now. The Frostfather's only other words before they had parted concerned the Mote, words that Felix could not forget.

The Mote of Frenzy is chaos unchained. To grasp it is to wrestle with the dark underpinnings of what is and what could be. It must be mastered, or else it will consume all that attempt to use its power. Be wary, Scion.

It was hope. Felix clung to it, and even Pit was cheered by the pronouncement.

"I got this." Pit nudged his shoulder with his head. "You just get us into the vault."

Felix cracked a grin. "Yeah. Let's get to planning. Shadows. Go back to Elderthrone. Tell Battlelord Ari the good news."

"Aye, my Lord," Veddi said with his own wide smile. "All of the Bitterward will hear of your victory! Blessed by the Frostfather Himself!"

The lot of them sped outward, mages and warriors racing through the ancient woods and into a gathering gloom. It was partly due to his Spirit Tree and partly due to the waning winter sunlight. *Sunset soon.*

"Convergence?" he asked Pit. His friend looked tired but not nearly as tired as before their trip.

"Hm."

His Companion vanished in a flash of light, landing in his Spirit before Felix ascended into the still, gray sky.

Have you considered your last Pillar, Felix?

Flying across the sky on sheer momentum, Felix was caught off guard by the tenku's words. He flared Adamant Discord again, pulling on another connection to the Stronghold far ahead of them. *A little. I just—*

Haven't bothered because of me. Because of how much Essence and significance it would take to weave a tenth Pillar.

Felix sighed. *Right.*

In the aftermath of the battle with the High Guard, Felix had earned a Title that allowed him to weave another Pillar on top of his sturdy nine.

Champion's Convocation (Legendary)!
For weaving all nine Pillars before level 100 and before reaching Master Tier, you may weave further still! A tenth Pillar awaits you, if you've the courage to face it!

Now that he wasn't stockpiling Essence and significance to spend on Pit's wounds, Felix supposed he could spare more time for its construction. There was only one problem. *I just don't know what Skill to use.*

Pit warbled. *What do you mean?*

Felix arced high into the sky, breaching the cloud cover and bursting up into the far darker night that awaited the lands below. He relished the sensation, the utter freedom of movement his Skill afforded him… and felt Pit do the same. For an instant, they were both flying again.

He dropped.

I fiddled with the idea of it. Used Karys to help me, even. Everytime I started the process, I had a wall thrown in front of me, and not just because of you. Felix let the wind of his descent rustle his hair and clothes as he swiped through a backlog of notifications, before finding the right one and displaying it for the both of them. *See?*

WARNING!
You Must Temper Another Skill In Order To Form A Tenth Pillar!
Process Halted!

Well, that's stupid.

I agree! Felix laughed and flared his favorite Skill. Once again, the connection between him and his Stronghold transformed from ephemeral to unbendable steel, and he hauled back on it, launching himself forward at breakneck speeds. Lightning sizzled from the connection, a byproduct of the process, and thunder boomed in his wake.

Karys had advised Felix not to try before he'd given it a great deal of thought, and Felix had taken the opportunity to shove the issue into the back of his head. *I'll think on it. There's a best path forward, and I'll take it as we march toward the Dwarves. Deal?*

Deal, Pit trilled happily at him.

Etheric Concordance is level 85!

Felix flew on, not quite so fast that he broke the sound barrier again, but certainly not slowly. Elderthrone expanded in his vision, the town appearing to almost grow faster than it had in recent months, as more and more people moved in. The refugees from Ahkestria, Haarwatch, and Setoria were everywhere—Felix could spot them, many of them still looking too thin but healthier despite it all. Bustling crowds filled the residential areas and the markets but were especially thick around the two Legion Barracks.

The path toward power was enticing to everyone, and Felix made sure none were turned away.

Oh? Down below, just before the proper walls of town, a figure in white and silver stood at the edge of the River Eile. Shapes swirled in the water before her, scaled and longer than most buses. *What's she doing?*

He flipped and redirected his momentum with a quick and sharp burst of sizzling lightning—in seconds, he had landed atop the banks of the river. "Hello Vess."

"Felix. Welcome back." The heiress smiled at him, flashing her dimpled cheek as her soft brown hair fell from behind an ear. Her teeth were remarkably white against her darker skin. "Or have you not left yet? The details on your trip were not explained to me."

"No, I'm back. It went faster than planned."

"I imagine it went well. Unless you have come to whisk me away to battle again?" The words were said with another smile, and though her spear remained leveled at the waters, it seemed all of her attention had shifted to him. Had he noticed the gold in her brown eyes before? Or was it just more prominent now?

"Better than expected." He stepped up to her, conscious of how close she was to the water. Of how close he was to her. "What's going on here?"

"Lunch," rumbled a new voice. Yintarion slithered from the bushes downstream of them, his long, serpentine body so similar to the shapes Felix had spotted beneath the waters. "Autarch."

"Yintarion."

"The Naga are returning," he said, his golden eyes flashing. He licked his lips, revealing a black forked tongue. "They have caught something."

Sure enough, moments later, two snake-like Naga emerged from the depths of the river with a huge fish in their jaws. Water sprayed into the air, drenching the banks, but Felix turned it all to pellets of ice with a flex of his Will and Mana. It rattled off Vess' armor harmlessly, and she laughed.

"My Lord," said a third Naga, and this one was an evolved form known as a War Naga. In fact, he recognized her immediately. "I did not know you would be here and have not brought a meal for you as well. My apologies. My men can—"

"No no, Lavix. That's fine." Felix waved the War Naga down, stopping her from diving right back into the river. "I've already eaten. I think."

You have not. And neither have I. Gimme.

You'll get your fill in the Temple. I have a lot of food in there.

But…big fish.

Patience, lil pig. "*Ahem.* Why are you fishing for Yintarion?"

"Because he requests it of us. And though we were once enemies by circumstance, that was the Fathom. The Dragons carry our respect, and Yintarion of the Cerulean Skies, he that brought us to battle against your enemies my Lord…We will gather fish for him."

"And it is appreciated, Lavix. I need the energy," said the Wyrmling between bites. The huge fish, easily the size of a dinghy and covered in thick scales and deadly looking spines, had been slapped onto the icy riverbank like a wet sack of cement. "For my Evolution."

"His meals need to contain a certain amount of nutrients, as well as meet some other strange requirements that I do not fully understand." Vess watched her Companion take huge bites, devouring the fish with fascination. "Where does he put it all?"

"I've wondered the same thing about Pit many, many times."

Yintarion swallowed a chunk of fish the size of Felix's head and growled at them. "We Dragons consume our prey and press their power into our cores, building up a thick base for our evolutions. It is part of how all monsters advance, though all are a touch different."

I put it in my belly.

"You, Autarch, must operate in a similar way, no?" Yintarion took another bite and slurped it down. "With your Primordial Hunger?"

"Something like that." Felix didn't actually know what his Hunger *did* with all the stuff he ate, just that he was able to use a lot of it for his own growth until it was fully digested by the big abyss inside him. "Lavix, how are your people doing? Have they encountered any further troubles in the river?"

"No, my Lord. With the aid of your consort, we have been thriving."

"My consort?" Felix felt a horrified flush wrack his skin from toes to hairline. "Oh. No. Sorry, Vess isn't—uh, not like that. I don't have a consort."

"We are not wedded, Lavix," Vess said. That smile was gone, but humor danced in her eyes.

"Wed? Ah, lifemates. I apologize for my assumption." The heavy-featured War Naga bowed, muscular, humanoid arms crossed over her barrel torso and long serpentine tail. "Your customs are strange to us. That is why many of my kind wished to remain in Haestus. Such close proximity to so many of the land Races is quite overwhelming."

After the lot of them had been overtaken by the Creature in Khasma, Felix had gone out of his way to reestablish their Oath to him. The Deepking had been more than ready to accept a far more deadly punishment, but Felix had zero interest in that. He couldn't blame the guy for falling prey to the insidious influence of a piece of Divinity grafted onto a damn Dragon. *If I can forgive Yintarion, I can forgive the Nagafolk.* He'd said as much to them all, but a rare few were willing to stay in Nagast.

"Don't worry about it, Lavix. How are your hatchlings?" he asked, quickly changing the subject.

"They are developing well, my Lord. The hunting is good in these waters, and the prey is rich in Mana. It will allow my people to grow strong."

"I'm glad. Remember to reach out to us if you need to—all of my people know to treat the Nagafolk with respect."

"Of course." Lavix bowed again. "For now we shall leave you. Our own hunts await."

"Farewell, Lavix," Vess said.

With barely a whisper of a splash, all of them vanished beneath the surface of the wide river. Soon after, they vanished even to Felix's senses. There was only the soft lapping of the waves and the sloppy chomps from a hungry, golden Wyrmling.

Vess stepped away from the bank and released her spear. It floated behind her on a cushion of air Mana. "Felix. Would you walk with me awhile?"

Yintarion gulped down something pale and wet. "Yes, take that Chimera of yours away from my meal. I can practically hear him salivating."

Am not.

"Hmph," the Wyrmling shot back before diving into his meal again.

"Be kind, Yin," Vess admonished her Companion. He ignored her, and she rolled her eyes. "He will take a while with that fish, and I'm late for another meeting of my own back in town. But—" she hesitated and tucked a lock of hair behind her ear. "I have been meaning to speak with you."

Ooh.

Shut up, Pit. He fought off the urge to wipe his palms (when had they gotten sweaty?) and gestured back into the forest. "Sure. Let's uh, sure. After you."

Vess smiled at him and walked away. Felix followed.

CHAPTER TWENTY-SEVEN

The pervasive quiet in the woods was broken only by the percussive crunch of snow beneath their boots. Felix and Vess walked, not speaking, between frost-coated ridges and winding, old-growth trees wide as houses. The nervousness he felt had vanished, dwindled beneath the thick silence and replaced by a familiar wonder.

Songbirds chirruped in the branches above, hopping about in tiny flurries of brown and off-white. A long-tailed cat skulked between trunks, claws muffled by heavy fur as it stalked a trio of wide rodents. Even the river had its say, hidden now by a tall hill, yet still a soft, sibilant murmur that underlied the greater silence. Felix let himself sink into the orchestra of strange noise, unlike the Grand Harmony or chaotic Dissonance, yet composed of both. *The Green Wilds*, he supposed. A tapestry of a thousand—a million—different things, all combined. *Interconnected chaos.*

"It is beautiful here."

The sound of Vess' voice jarred him from his reverie, but Felix only smiled. "It is."

"I forget, sometimes, that this is the same fog-drenched wilderness we struggled through last year. I think it even smells better than before."

"Doesn't surprise me. Atar has been looking into the original illusion array the Geist made, and it was powerful. It affected all the senses, even the Harmonic ones." Felix sniffed, taking in the empty cold scent of winter, the sharp spice of nearby trees, and the furtive musk of some passing beast. "I can't imagine how hard it was to move through all that."

"Mm," Vess glanced at him. "Harn and Magda were of great help, but I remember so much fear in those days."

"About the same for me. No illusion for me, but that didn't make this place any less terrifying." Felix laughed. "I can barely believe I made it through, back then."

"Snatched from your home, sent into a deadly environment filled with monsters—it is a wonder you remained sane, let alone rose to the challenge. You are a remarkable man, Felix."

"I try." He regretted the words as soon as he said them—had that been too cocky? He certainly didn't think of himself as remarkable. "Being Unbound has a great deal to do with it, I think."

She nudged him with her elbow. "You give yourself too little credit. Always have. Beef arrived the same time as you did, faced terrible challenges, and he lags several Tiers behind you, even now."

"Beef is a kid—"

"Thirteen years is five years older than I was when my combat training began."

"He–wha? Really?" Felix frowned. "You were training to fight at eight years old?"

"Officially. The Dragoons take those as young as four to begin their instruction. My father did not wish that for me, not so early, as I had the myriad lessons of statecraft to learn." Vess stepped carefully around a protruding root, as graceful as a dancer. "But I snuck out into the training yards every night, from the moment I was strong enough to hold a practice spear."

Felix whistled. "Damn. That's intense. And it kinda proves my point: on Earth, we don't fight. Not like that, anyway. Most people don't know how to throw a punch, let alone a spear. Beef didn't, and neither did I." Flashes of memory rose up in him, of his early days in the Foglands and numerous failures at fighting. He shoved them away. "Both of us just got lucky, and part of that is in being Unbound."

"It is a boon, I cannot argue against that…but you, Felix, are kind and compassionate." She flung her arms outward, as if to encompass the forest and beyond. "None of this would have happened if you did not care enough to stand up. You established a *kingdom*, Felix. You cleansed a curse on an entire Race, faced down ancient terrors, Grandmasters, Primordials, and the gods themselves."

Her hands dropped, clanking as they slapped against her armored hips. "Perhaps some of that was due to luck, and perhaps someone else, in your same position, could have accomplished the same. But would they have chosen to do so, Felix? I have met too many warriors so impressed by the swing of their own blades that they never question what lies before them…nor what comes after. Perhaps, Felix Nevarre, your strength lies in being *you*."

Felix hadn't a clue what to say to that. Fighting monsters and gods was one thing, but taking a compliment? His brain stalled out, and could only manage two words. "Thank you."

Vess tucked locks of her hair behind her ear once again. It had fallen out while she had spoken, and her cheeks flushed. "You are very welcome."

The deep lowing of some creature shook the evening air with a raspy, basso gasp. Ahead of them, the path wound around a hill to reveal the river once again…and a huge moose the size of an extra jumbo elephant. Moss covered its back, brown and faded with the season, with thin tendrils stretched between a set of crystalline antlers bigger than the fish Yintarion was eating.

"Moss-Back Stag," Felix whispered. The creature was a couple hundred yards out into the water, but its ears twitched toward Felix despite his volume. It lowed again.

"Beautiful," Vess murmured. "Reminds me of when we first saw them."

"Right before we fought the Archon, yeah." Felix grinned at the memory. "Haven't seen them much since."

"I've read they are pack creatures, but this one seems to be alone." She clucked her tongue. "It has been attacked."

Once Vess pointed it out, Felix could easily spot half-healed wounds on the giant moose's back and legs. What he'd taken as cloudiness on its antlers was likely blood, dried and caked onto the tines. The creatures were peaceful, if territorial, and they had a lot of Health for their level, not to mention excessive Strength. This particular specimen was a Tier III beast, but those categories weren't always as strict as folks liked to pretend. He had no doubt that a Journeyman Tier who decided to fight a Moss-Back Stag would find themselves overwhelmed in short order.

"Could be a hunter overestimated their abilities or underestimated the Stag's," Vess said.

"Or there's a strong predator in the area. I'll tell the Dawnguard about it, either way." Felix added it to his growing list. "It's isolated here. Let's leave it be."

They kept going, following the thin game trail through the forest. When they'd gained an appreciable distance from the creature, and the quiet started to stretch too long, a voice chirped up in his head. *This is* boring.

I thought you were tired?

I can be both. Oh! Ask about Yin's evolution. I wanna know.

Felix suppressed a groan, but he had to admit his own curiosity. "Vess, how is your bond with Yintarion?

"He mentioned his first evolution. Is that happening soon?" Pit's first evolution had taken months to occur, but every monster was different. Copse Grubs, for instance, would evolve into Emberflies only after eating the tree they were born inside. The Moss-Back Stag was once smaller before it evolved into its gargantuan size, requiring a ton of food and some sort of mineral they got from the mountains. When Vess shook her head, that only made him more curious. "What does he need?"

"Apart from sufficiently powerful prey, he needs them to reside within the four elemental Mana types. Creatures of earth, air, fire, and water. Light is also important, though finding creatures that are imbued with it is a tough task. According to Yin, that fish only reached the bare minimum of his requirements, and only for water." She pulled a scroll from a tube at her waist and unrolled it. "This is what he needs, apart from the food. He suggested that much of it was available here, in the Foglands."

Felix took the scroll and gave it a quick scan. "Hm. The Tier III ore is easily obtained now that we control that metal-attuned Domain near the Teeth, and Tier IV wood and stone are stocked up in the Storage Facility. He needs to eat all of that?"

"Apparently. The interplay of the elements is very important to the process, according to Yin. The five Mana types are to be layered together in some fashion unique to Dragons, and that," she said, pointing at the list. "Will allow him to leave behind his Wyrmling form." Vess gave a helpless shrug. "He is eager to return to his former might."

"I would be, too," Felix said, looking at where she pointed. He knew the Wyrmling didn't have much in the way of Health, Stamina, or Mana. A single, half-hearted strike from Felix could break him, and even Pit outmatched their ancient ally. "Oh. The 'heart of a Supreme Elemental.' I, uh, I assume that means its core?"

"Yes, but 'willingly given.' I am unsure how that is done, but Yin seems less worried about that part than finding one in the first place. I have heard of Elementals, the Inferior and Lesser kind are rare but found around the Continent. A Supreme Elemental, however, is not something I have encountered in life or books."

Felix scratched his chin. "I have, but…well, it's complicated. I don't think we can get his core without starting a whole war with the Frost Giants."

Vess blinked at him. "His?"

"The Frostfather, god of the Risi, is a Supreme Elemental. Just found that out today," Felix said. "And he surrendered to me, so going back and killing him now seems…yeah, I'm not doing it. I won't say no to having a Dragon in our back pocket, but not like that."

"Like I said, Felix." Vess beamed at him, and that dimple came back. "Honor and compassion."

"Ahem," he cleared his throat, partially to distract from the flush he felt on his cheeks. "Even uh, even if we had a core, I assume he's not jumping straight from Wyrmling to Dusk Dragon, right?"

Vess laughed. "He wishes, but no. The path is a winding one, and Yin is eager to forge a solid foundation before evolving."

Makes sense. Just like us. "How's the training been? Have things started to make more sense with your Dragoon…ness?"

"Yes and no. Yin has devoted much of his time to teaching me the ways of my new Skills, and my proficiency with them has increased by leaps and bounds. He suggests methods that my trainers never had, techniques that I struggle with, but I am beginning to see their value. It is…rewarding."

Felix watched Vess speak, saw the glint in her eyes and the hundred-watt smile that she couldn't suppress. "You look happy."

She laughed. "I am. We have survived a great deal, and I am moving toward my destiny. How could I not find joy in that?"

"So the plan is to hunt for what Yintarion needs?"

"In a sense. I—I'll be needing to return to Pax'Vrell."

Felix stopped walking. "What? Why? Now?"

Vess' smile dimmed. "Not right this minute. When the thaw comes, I'll begin the journey back. I need to speak to my father…and the Dragoons. They have knowledge there, archives that might document what really happened all those centuries ago when the Dragoons betrayed the Dusk Dragons. Knowledge that could save the eggs."

The eggs that you can't save. Just like Pit. Felix shoved away the thought, but it loomed close, as it had for months. "If the Dragoons betrayed the Dusk Dragons, wouldn't they have destroyed the evidence?" he asked.

"That is…likely. But I must know. If they can be saved, if the ancient history of my order can be salvaged, then we can become stronger than ever before. Not just me and Yintarion, but all of the Dragoons. Strong enough to shatter the shackles the Hierophant has placed on my home for centuries." Vess snatched her spear from the air, brandishing it as if she wanted to start right at that moment. "It would mean an ally for you, an entire Territory, free."

"Well, I can't argue against that," he said.

Argue against it! Pit urged.

"I can come with you," Felix suggested. "Back you up."

"That is sweet of you, but I must stand before the Dragoons alone."

"You'll have Yintarion with you. What's one or two more?"

Or an army? Pit added.

"He—Well, I suppose you are right." She released her spear, letting it float on her Skill's near-invisible cushions of air. "And I suppose I am poor at asking for help. The last time I did so, I followed Isla's advice and nearly restructured my core space. I was emotional then, afraid of stepping off the Path that has been prepared for me. Yet if I had continued, I would not have bonded with Yin nor discovered the truth."

Felix stopped her and put a hand over hers. Her skin was hotter than he expected, and soft. "There's nothing wrong with being scared. I'm scared all the time." Vess' face was a lot closer than he expected, too, and her eyes were very dark, save for that ring of gold that glittered in the last of the evening light.

"And now?" she asked. Her fingers laced with his. "Are you scared now?"

Felix swallowed. "Absolutely."

"You—"

A sword the size of a door slammed into the earth mere feet from them, followed by the exceedingly fast descent of its large wielder. "Lady Dayne! I need you to disc—" He finished standing up and looked at Felix in surprise. "Autarch. I was not told of your return."

"Hi Darius. I, uh, just got back."

Darius looked at him, at Vess, and at where their hands were clasped. They both let go; Felix to grip his dagger and Vess to fiddle with her hair. The boulder of a man didn't even blink, but his face settled into something very explicitly impassive. "I am glad to see you here. We have training to catch up on. Are you free tomorrow at dawn?"

"Erm. Could be. Probably." Felix bobbed his head and drummed his fingers on the hilts of his weapons. "I'll talk to Karys. It'd be good. Sword training is always ah, good."

You're saying 'good' too much! Pit sent.

"Excellent." The large warrior turned to Vess and bowed at the waist. "Lady Dayne, I'm in need of your ear, if you've the time."

"I—Of course, Darius," she said. To his surprise, she took up Felix's hand again. "Thank you for the walk…and the conversation, Felix."

"Yeah, totally."

Something soft and sad flitted across the woman's gaze, something Felix felt the bare edges of despite the way he stifled his Affinity around her. Disappointment? Or was it something worse?

Say something.

She stepped away, but Felix held onto her hand. Gently.

"Felix?"

"I uh, owe you dinner. How about I make that up to you? Tomorrow?"

The words came out in a rush, but he barely stumbled over them. They hung between them, almost physical for how heavy they felt. Felix met her gaze, and in that moment, he was certain he had met gods less intimidating.

She smiled, and the last crimson bits of sunset filtered down through snow-laden boughs.

"Absolutely."

CHAPTER TWENTY-EIGHT

Vess watched Felix zip into the sky, and despite the lightning that enveloped him, she could still make out his form quite clearly.

"Working on your Perception, Lady Dayne?" Darius asked.

Vess coughed and turned away from the sky. "What is it you need, Darius?"

Her father's Chosen Hand was following the fading trail of Felix's ascent. "Are you certain of your path?"

Vess blushed. "That is none of your business, Hand. Felix and I—"

"Are not what interests me." Darius chuckled and glanced down at her. The man was just as tall as Felix had become. "He…I think I understand the Autarch now. Your father might have some words for you, but not I. Not anymore. No, what concerns me is that Dragon. I don't trust it."

The Hand's words for Felix set Vess off-balance, but she was quick to plant her feet again. "Him. We have spoken of this already. Yin is not a *thing*, Darius."

Darius snorted. "*He* is a monster the Dragoons swore to eliminate utterly. An order that you and I both trained for all our lives. We've seen how dangerous draconic Types can be, how clever and bloodthirsty. And you've bonded with it." He held up a hand, forestalling Vess' angry response. "Him. I need to know that you are well. The changes…have you had any issues with your core space? Your Skills?"

Vess took a calming breath before replying. "My core space is stable, and my Skills are strengthened greatly. Nothing has changed since last we spoke on the subject, save that I am greater now than even two months prior."

"I…am happy to hear that," he said, and his Spirit rang with the sound of earnest forbearance. "I can see that you've grown more powerful, Lady Dayne. That much is obvious to even those who do not know you as well as I do. You have told me the Dragon's perspective on the Betrayal, how the Dragoons moved against them and not the other way around. I cannot accept that, yet."

Darius was right: they had both been trained by the Dragoons since a young age. She couldn't expect him to buck the tradition of centuries based on her testimony alone. *Yet, if I cannot convince him of things, how can I convince the order? Or my father?*

"But…I can trust you. I have been trusting you. I only ask that you hold whatever the Dragon says at arm's length before embracing it—I could not bear something happening to you."

"Darius…"

"With regard to the Autarch," he said, clearing his throat as his Spirit went utterly opaque to her senses. "If you desire to pursue him, you will need to tell your father. He deserves to know, considering the implications, and from your own lips."

Vess pursed her lips. "I plan to visit home again. Soon."

The big man grunted. He'd been spending too much time with Harn. "Good. For now, I need not tell you to proceed cautiously."

"I know. I plan to find out what that was. We were lied to, Darius. All of us. My mother, too. I want to know why, and that requires me to return home." She felt a hurricane in her chest, swirling without relief. "We will have the truth, and we will grow stronger for it."

Darius blinked at her. "You'd bring a Dragon into Pax'Vrell?"

"He is proof."

"He is the enemy, Lady Dayne. Wyrmling or not, you can expect an uproar." He regarded her with hard eyes. "I simply hope you are ready for such a fight."

In the distance, Vess could feel Yin basking in the glow of the last rays of sunlight, his meal utterly demolished. She smiled, but it was a thin, grim line.

"We will be."

You did it! Pit cheered. *Finally.*

Felix still felt the embarrassment that had crawled up his spine and across his cheeks, despite the rush of success that propelled him across the skies. He felt lighter than he had in a while.

I didn't need audience commentary, Pit.

I was helping!

Felix grunted, a smile curling his lips as he redirected his Skill and plummeted toward the ground once again. This time, he fell hundreds of feet in several long seconds, directly into Zara's courtyard.

Lightning splashed outward, harmless but bright, as he pressed last second against his connections to the stone itself. He landed gently and straightened himself, unconsciously adjusting his tunic and jacket. A few people gasped at his arrival, but for the most part, the bustling activity continued uninterrupted. The sight of servants still made him a little uneasy, but a glut of folks had migrated to Haarwatch explicitly to take up jobs like maid, ferrier, and butler or whatever. Just in case, though, Felix made sure everyone was getting paid fairly. Vess had suggested a few stations in his burgeoning government that had made overseeing all the minutiae a bit easier. He still had barely any idea what he was doing, running a whole Territory, but delegation had become his best friend.

Thankfully, not too many folks had need of servants outside the cliff district—*the Foot,* he reminded himself, laughing under his breath. Silly name. *Who would want to live in a place called the* Foot*?*

A lot of people, obviously, based on how many homes he'd had to shape into the cliff face. Felix's original intent was to make cool stone houses that stacked vertically and sat into the lower-Tier stone of the cliff. But with the influx of petty nobles and monied folks from Haarwatch and even Setoria, it had quickly become a hot spot for the "important."

Bleh, elitist idiots. Plenty of housing across Elderthrone, and they all want to fight over two dozen I made here.

Felix hustled through the courtyard, playing with the letter that Zara had left him. He'd opened it on the journey south, and it contained only a single line.

Felix,

Please see me immediately. We must discuss your future.

~Zara

Ominous and non-specific. About what I've come to expect from Chanters. He shoved the letter back into his inside jacket pocket.

He smiled at the various people he saw around the estate. They knew him by this point, and more than a few gave back cheerful greetings. A few riffs of surprise spread out from some, those unfamiliar with the Autarch landing in the courtyard unannounced. *Probably hired recently.* He looked up at the looming edifice of carved stone, noting all the fine details he'd never put into it. *Haven't been here in a bit.*

Just inside the front doors, a woman in a black dress with crimson skin and golden eyes stood with her arms folded before her. "Good evening, Lord Autarch. How might we be of service?"

"Oh, hey Melle, I need to talk to Zara."

"As you wish, Lord Autarch. Follow me." The Hobgoblin handmaiden led him to a side room outfitted with plush chairs and an empty fireplace. "Please, be seated in the parlor while I fetch Lady Zara." She curtsied and disappeared deeper into the house.

This is eerily familiar, he thought, looking around the parlor. The chairs, the mantle, the tiling on the floor…all of it was the same as Zara's mansion back in Haarwatch. She even had bookshelves installed around the fireplace, thick with tomes he recognized from her shop. Felix ran his hands across them, feeling their molded spines, the faint ridges of gold leaf on the sigaldry. He was contemplating taking one and reading it in one of the overstuffed chairs when he heard the quick clop of booted heels down stone stairs.

"Felix. I was wondering when I might see you again." Zara smiled at him, warm and welcoming despite her shark-like teeth. A brightly colored kingfisher sat on her shoulder, watching him as she gestured with an ocher-toned hand. "Please, sit. Do you need anything to eat?"

A flash of bright, white light filled the parlor, and Pit bounded across the floor as a russet-furred puppy. "Yes, please!"

Zara laughed. "Keru can lead you to the kitchens, Pit. We have plenty of roast Glitterhog to spare."

Pit let out a high-pitched howl and bounded after the kingfisher as it flew off Zara's shoulder and around the corner. The sound of flapping wings and scrabbling claws on tile soon faded.

"Karys tells me you went north. I had not expected you back so quickly, but your Chancellor told me not to worry." Zara sat opposite Felix, folding her long fingers across her lap. "I must admit, I was… vexed at your disappearance."

"Yeah. Sorry about that. The issue was urgent, but I've gotten a new ability that allows for much faster travel within my own Territories." He quickly explained what he knew of Labyrinthine Wing.

Zara leaned back in her chair once he was done, a tension fleeing her body that he hadn't noticed until it was gone. "That clears up a great deal of my confusion. This new ability allowed you to travel to the northern border in half a day?"

"Way less than that. Most of my time was spent resolving a border dispute with the Risi, not traveling."

"To move so quickly, even along Dark Passages…is there a limit to how many you can bring?" she asked.

"It's limited by my 'personal strength' and the rarity and level of the Skill itself. So far, I've had zero issues bringing five others with me, and the Passages were way more structured than what you've described."

"It would be exceedingly useful for your Legion and Claw to be able to move across your Territories so swiftly. Nine Exemplars…a heady power." Zara frowned. "I would advise only giving it to those you trust a great deal."

"Mhm." Felix had thought the same and had already made a bit of a list. "I'll be handling that shortly, in fact."

"How are the Risi, then?" she asked.

"Fractious, apparently. The Coven of Cold Rock was there, along with a bunch of novice Risi Warriors. Thankfully I left an impression, and Kimaris went with her people to work out the terms of our new alliance." Felix was fairly certain Naberius wanted more than just an alliance, but he'd handle that when he had the time. "But that's for another day. Now I…well, I'm here to talk."

Zara spread her hands, palm up. "Are we not talking now?"

"You know what I mean." He fiddled with the hilt of his dagger, which buzzed pleasantly beneath his fingers. "I've been avoiding you."

"So I have gathered." Her ice blue eyes flashed. "Why?"

"A lot of reasons. Partly because Isla left a sour taste in my mouth, partly because Pit's condition has taken all my attention, and none of you could help." Felix gritted his teeth and swallowed the mingled hope and anger Pit's curse brought up in him. "And mostly because I don't know what your people want with me."

Zara leaned forward in her chair. "I have apologized for Isla's behavior, Felix. I know that is not much, nor nearly enough, but I do trust that she was attempting to do what was best, given the circumstances."

"I—" Felix wanted to rant about that, to rage against how Isla had nearly destroyed Vess' core space in her misguided attempts—but he held back. It wouldn't solve anything, and Vess had come to terms with her power. "I don't know that I believe that, Zara. Isla seems to be playing a game where I don't know the rules or the stakes. I know you Chanters want the Unbound to fight the Ruin.

"But I don't know what that means! I don't know what the Ruin is, what it can do, or how to stop a force of nature *that can erase history itself?*"

Books fell off the shelves around him as the force of his voice shook the air, turning the Mana around them into a tempest. Furious, he grasped that Mana with Cardinal Flame and hurled it into the fireplace, where it ignited the unblemished wood. Zara flinched.

"I want to trust you, Zara. But this order of yours…" Felix grasped at the air before letting his hands fall down to his sides. "It hides too much."

Zara stood up. "Then, in this moment, I will be as open and as honest as I can, Felix."

"Really? No lies? No omissions?"

"I will tell you, as it was once explained to me," she said, and her voice was sonorous. It echoed in the parlor as if it were ten times the size. "The Cantus Sodalus is the last remnant of the great Sorcerers of the Fallen Halls. Once called the Empyrean Halls, before the Ruin."

"Wait." Felix held up a hand. "The Empyrean Halls was a Nymean thing. You're saying the—you're saying your order is—"

"A relic of the Nymean Empire," she finished. "Yes."

"What's the point of it?" he asked. "What's your order's mission statement?"

"To protect the Grand Harmony, those who can hear it…and to prepare the world for the coming of Ruin."

A flurry of feathers and flapping wings heralded Zara's kingfisher friend, Keru. He tore from the hall to land in a crash on the mantle. "Lady Zara! The basin is lit!"

Felix frowned as Zara's entire body tensed. "It seems they have arrived a bit sooner than I anticipated. If you had been here sooner, or if you would have met with us—no. I should have explained all this long ago. Felix." She licked her lips nervously. "The Cantus Sodalus wishes for entry into Nagast."

"What? From where?"

"From the Bitter Sea."

"The one made of *acid*?"

CHAPTER TWENTY-NINE

"Oh, that makes more sense," Felix said, some time later. The gray sand beneath his feet was just as pale and gritty as he remembered, as were the green vinegar waves that crashed nearby. "They're in a Manaship."

A fair distance out, barely a speck on the horizon, was a Manaship flying a series of colorful flags. Zara said they were traditional indicators of peace, prosperity, and deference—common flags to fly when entering another nation's sovereign land.

"Did you think they traveled the Bitter Sea on an ancient sailing ship?" Zara asked.

"We don't have Manaships on Earth. Well, we have planes, but that's—my point is, the water isn't made of acid where I come from. Just salty." Felix scanned the beach and the horizon, feeling strangely vulnerable. "I'm used to folks sailing on the water, not over it."

"Ah. So that was why you were so comfortable with our trip through the Leviathan Depths." Zara nodded to herself. "Aside from the Yttin, your warriors were terrified of sinking."

"Huh. I recall their fear, but I just figured they were just scared of what was in the water." Felix's eyes never stopped moving, his Perception flared as much as he could manage. "I am. Especially here. These waters are even more dangerous than the Depths."

"The Dread, I believe you called it?" Zara frowned at the green swells, nose wrinkling slightly at the astringent breeze that carried off of it. "A Bloodbeast."

"Mhm." Felix hadn't seen the Dread in almost a year, not since it had almost killed him. Not since it had Marked him for the Maw and changed everything. "Tell me more about the Cantus Sodalus."

Zara regarded him a long moment before speaking. "As you wish. I told you of our purpose, and perhaps I could regale you with the struggles of our storied past. The conflicts resolved between nations and Territories, the monsters bested and cities saved. I do not think you are so interested in those, however."

Felix smirked. "I mean, that sounds cool and all, but no. Not at the moment. Tell me about the summoning. How did it work?"

"The summoning is an ancient ritual, perfected by the Nym but rarely used. It takes a great deal of power to enact, and a greater amount of concentration. The Hierophant performed the ritual atop her Shining Palace, at the apex of En'Cridhe. The Star of Heaven in the old tongue, believed to be built by the Nym." Zara showed her sharp teeth, still staring at the green waters. "The official history claims it was the Pathless himself who lifted the alabaster towers. Mortals, it seems, are almost as good at erasing history as the Ruin itself."

"Star of Heaven. Sounds like the Nym, that's for sure."

"It is obvious, isn't it? Regardless, the Hierophant controls the Shining Palace—it is the Seat of her Authority, after all. So the summoning ritual was performed there, and you Unbound were intended to be brought directly to En'Cridhe. Would have been, had we not interfered."

"How?" Felix asked.

Zara's veiled Spirit rippled, a faint, vague emotion that Felix suspected hid a great deal more. "Some of our own sacrificed themselves to take the place of the lesser clergymen. They disrupted the ritual at the last moment, turning the summoning toward chaos. Dissonance."

"And had us all flung across the Continent," Felix finished for her. "Why not alter the ritual so that we were summoned to a place you chose?"

Zara clenched her jaw, eyes still distant. "The wardings around the Shining Palace are too great. The time, Skill, and power required to alter the ritual was not available to us—we learned of the Hierophant's plan too late. Considering the state of the Foglands at the time, it is a wonder that I found you at all."

"You have the Maw to thank for that," he muttered. Felix had wondered more than a few times where he might have landed and what might have become of him, had the Maw not apparently tipped the scales in its favor. "Okay. So the ritual was disrupted, all the Unbound got summoned but scattered, and you Chanters went out searching for us. Now you found me, Isla found Beef...what about the rest?"

"That is what I hope we can discover together." She nodded at the oncoming ship, now a slightly larger speck on the horizon. "Others are still searching, and only Mauvim knows all the details. Part of the reason she wished to come here. To meet you."

"Mauvim. You've spoken of her before. What's she like?"

"She is the oldest of us, but the founders of our order were dust long before she was born. She is wise, but not the kind to take fools lightly." Felix could all but feel Zara's side-eye, but he ignored it and she moved on. "There are others among the order who hold influence, but she is the one to convince. If you have Mauvim on your side, then we can move with greater assurance."

"On my side?" Felix asked. "I thought we were all supposed to be on the same side?"

"We are as all people, from the lowest valleys to the highest peaks. The Cantus Sodalus is united in our cause, but not in how to serve that cause." Zara sighed. "This shouldn't be news to you. You've met Isla."

A bark of surprised laughter escaped Felix. "I mean, I wasn't gonna say it, but yeah. I was aware of some tension." He paused, considering his words carefully. "I don't like her or her methods, Zara. She's wormed her way around Beef, and she tried the same with Vess. If the rest of your people are like that, I don't want anything to do with them."

Zara didn't say anything for a bit, and Felix let her collect her thoughts. The thought of Isla messing with Vess' core space still ignited a sharp heat in him—it swam up his chest and floated around his head, burning to leap out of his mouth. He held it back and simply waited.

After a time, Zara spoke. "Vess' circumstances are strange and certainly outside the bounds of what I have experienced before. A Link to you, a bounty of Primordial energy passed through it, so much that it changed her? Not only that, but it was a *positive* change. Before you, Felix, the touch of a Primordial was death or rebirth into something horrible. I cannot say I would not have tried to help Vess in the same way…but I will admit that my methods would have been different."

She grimaced and met Felix's eyes. Blue to blue. "Isla seeks to master what she cannot understand, to yoke it to her Will. It is what makes her such a remarkable healer; she persists until she can conquer injury and disease. For you Unbound and those caught in your orbit, she must come to realize that is not the way. I will make her realize it."

A weight fell from Felix's Spirit, and it was heavier than he had suspected. He smiled just a touch. "Thank you, Zara."

The Naiad inclined her head. "A dangerous path looms before us all; I would not have us walk it alone."

The Manaship was closer now. It had to have been moving very fast, based on its progress and the very faint wake that creased the Bitter Sea beneath it. Felix could tell the craft was flying high, but not nearly as high as it should have been. He focused his eyes, letting them brush up against the protections of his Territory. Mist instantly appeared all around him, thick enough to trouble even his Perception. It only worsened as one rose higher, where the setting sun made it bloom with diffused light. *They're flying low for better visibility*, he realized. He contemplated exempting them from the Mirk Enclosure but decided against it. *Time for that after. They'll be here soon.*

He didn't have a lot of time.

"Zara."

"Yes?"

"What do you know of Core Manifestation?" he asked.

"Where did you hear that term?" The Chanter shifted her weight, and her left hand twitched. "It wasn't Isla, was it?"

"What? No. You can relax. I know about it because I've *done it.* I only know the name from the Frostfather, though—oh I didn't say, but he's a Supreme Elemental that rules a Domain to the north—" At her look of overwhelmed confusion, he waved off the rest of his words. "Point is, you're not spoiling my advancement by telling me more. I'm at the edge of it."

Zara's face was a mask of wonder. "Surely it is too early, Felix."

"Tell that to the mountain I beat up."

"I should not be surprised, not anymore. Isla spoke of Beef achieving it already, but I was skeptical. Now you…Perhaps I was hasty in dismissing her claim."

"Wait, Beef did this? When?"

"In the depths, I'm told. Shortly after reforging his core space."

And he didn't tell me? "Does he know what he did? Did Isla explain it to him?"

"She said she has not, and Beef seems to think it was an extension of his evolved Chitin Construction Skill." Zara pointed at Felix. "You cannot tell him, either, Felix. It will—"

"Interfere with his advancement. Yeah, I know. Have a little faith, Zara. I've been helping him train for a while now, and I think it's gone very well so far."

"Much to Isla's chagrin, I imagine," she said with a sharp smile.

"Oh yeah. She hates it." Felix was proud of that. *It's the little things.*

Zara eyed the oncoming ship, now able to make out their set of triple sails far easier. "Regarding Core Manifestation…it is a feature of your advancement, but only *after* one weaves their Tapestry. To my knowledge, Felix, you are only on the cusp of that stage. Unless something has changed?"

"No, you're right. I'm…well, I need to resolve one last thing before beginning whatever the Tapestry Stage is." He rubbed at his chest, recalling with visceral detail the amount of pain he'd experienced in the Ironskin Domain. "Unleashing that hand was like ripping my insides out."

"You are lucky to be alive. Unveiling a Core Manifestation so early would have ripped anyone else apart."

"I had that feeling, yeah." Felix frowned at his scaled hand against his soft green shirt. "Tell me about the Tapestry Stage. You're there already, right?"

"I am. It is incomplete, for now, but I know the path forward. You've already advanced through the Weaving Stage with incredible speed and potency. That firm foundation will serve you well, as you consider the whole."

"The whole?"

"It's called the Tapestry Stage because you must pull back and take in the whole of your core space…and draw out a Revelation. You," Zara cut herself off, laughing. "You have a hint for yours already. This…hand you summoned."

Felix wrinkled his nose. "My Tapestry Revelation is a big hand? That's a little underwhelming."

"Describe it, if you please."

He did, noting the color, the apparent construction, and even the feel of it as it manifested. She seemed intrigued by all of it, especially the eye within the palm.

"It didn't really look like an eye, I guess, but that's the best way I can describe it," Felix said. "It just…shattered the Frostfather."

"Incredible. I cannot draw your conclusions for you, Felix, but focus on what you know of this clawed hand. The experience of it, and how it relates to your core space. Your Revelation need not be momentous, just significant, for that is what fuels it. You must gather greater and greater significance to complete the Tapestry Stage and unify the whole of your core space."

"Unify." Felix rubbed at his chest absently. "Alright. I'll think on it. Oh!" He snapped his fingers. "I used the hand before. It was what I defeated the Creature with, back when I ate it in Khasma."

Zara's eyebrows climbed nearly to her hairline. "Two manifestations? One internal and one external, and still you live. I urge you to show more caution, Felix. That hand will kill you if you continue to use it before you are ready. Without your Revelation, you sacrificed parts of your Aspects to draw that power out. That is why you felt so terrible afterward. Too many times, and your core space will fragment, and your Skills will sunder. All of them, all at once."

"That's…not good."

"I know you've experienced a sundering before, but things are different at your stage of power. Before, you could break a few Skills and survive with some pain. Your core space is fundamentally *you* now. Break it, and you break the very nature of who you have become, and it will never return."

Well. Shit.

Felix sat with that knowledge for a bit, turning it over in his head. A companionable silence stretched between them, interrupted only by the crash of the vinegar surf and the faint cry of distant birds.

Eventually, Zara gestured around the beach, empty except for the two of them. Even Pit had remained in Zara's house to gorge himself on Glitterhog. "Are you sure you do not wish for a more royal entourage? We are not far from Elderthrone; you could have the Legion and your Shadows in place in short order."

"I don't need a retinue. If they're going to meet me, they're gonna meet *me*." Felix squinted. "Wait. Are they riding even lower than before?"

The Manaship was closing in on the shore fast…but, for some reason, it was almost touching the waves below it, creating a huge wake behind it. Things stirred in the waters, leaping at the craft, but spherical barriers flashed where monstrous fish dashed themselves fruitlessly against it.

"They are." Zara sounded just as concerned as Felix felt. "What is—"

A piercing shriek split the sound of wave and wind, followed by a massive, hooked tendril that slammed into the ship.

"Goddamn it!" Felix's hands burst alight with lightning.

The Dread had come to play.

CHAPTER THIRTY

"The shields! Bolster the shields!" Yorun, Makewright and Captain of the *Cipher's Venture* commanded, control rod in hand. The wind was against them now, and his ship was losing power—soon they might all fall into the acid below, but not if he had anything to say about it! "Samul! Godwik! Mainsail-haul!"

His Wooden Golems pivoted smoothly, oiled joints bouncing smoothly with the turbulence as they carried out his orders.

"This is unnatural," Tzfell said amid the chaos. She stood between trotting Golems, scurrying Gnomes, and flinching, fledgling Chanters, calmly regarding the tentacle above. Her bald head gleamed, even in the dull winter light, shimmering with geometric patterns etched into her skin. As a Dwarf, the tentacle was easily three times her height in length. It flexed against the barrier generated by the Manaship's engines, barbed hooks and suckers grappling and almost digging into the magic. "It is hanging on, despite our speed, and I cannot Analyze it."

"Neither can I," admitted the statuesque Emelda. Her beautiful face was pinched, but only comparatively. They both looked to be carved of stone. "This may require more effort than we expected."

Yorun scrambled across the tilting deck, hands digging into the deck as he tried to reach their group. "Sorcerers! Can you not cast this thing away? It's destroying my ship!"

"It is *our* ship, Captain Yorun, until you've completed your service,"

Tzfell said, her demeanor as calm as if she were discussing things over tea. "Do remember our deal."

"I remember! But I'm not much use dead!" he snapped back. *And this ship ain't useful to me if it's crushed!*

"Move your Golems and your fellow Gnomes to safety, captain. We shall deal with this," Emelda stated. She was sweating, but her expression was just as eerily calm as the other. Both of them raised their hands as the shields *quivered.* "Quickly, now."

Yorun threw up his hands in defeat and grasped the control rod hanging from his belt. It gleamed once again as he shoved his Will through its matrices. Spellforms flashed into being, spinning outward on near-invisible lines, straight into the cores of his creations. "Corsairs to stern! Drop lines and take shelter!"

The moment the words left his mouth, the entire ship—*his* ship—jerked to a stop and threw him into a tumbling roll. Yorun cursed and tried to right himself, but it was drowned out by the sound of shattering glass as the ship's barrier collapsed. From above, the nasty beast's tentacle fell…right atop a huddled group of younglings.

"Look out!" he shouted, and his control rod flared.

Two Corsairs leaped across the deck, their wooden and tin limbs outstretched, and tackled the younglings out of the way as the hooked appendage ravaged the deck. One Corsair Golem rolled to safety, arms cradling one of his apprentices and a youthful-seeming Chanter, while the other was split in half at the waist…but not before its arms scooped around two more of his apprentices.

Yorun gasped, relief flooding his very bones. "Youngling! Get my apprentices down below!"

The Chanter in training nodded furiously, her curled locks bouncing, before she and the remaining Corsair hurried away with his apprentices between them.

Yorun got to his feet, his core chugging along inside his chest as his Skills tried to marshal—only to stutter to a stop as he saw the wreck ahead. "My ship!"

The first tentacle had smashed into the deck, too, but its sheer mass had torn open a huge hole in the planks, made worse now by its frenzied thrashing. Splinters filled the air and wet, gurgling screams emanated from somewhere over the railing…where an acrid smoke and sizzle caught Yorun's attention.

"We've landed in the water! Sorcerers! We need lift!" he shouted.

Blood and screams met his words as more tentacles emerged

from the sizzling brine to slap their jagged lengths against wood and sail and line. Golems were smashed, slicking the decks with viscous oils to mingle with pools of dull blood. Magic burned in the air, flashes of light, shadow, flame, and ice impacting the monster's mottled limbs. Claws of force and spears of air stabbed at its rubbery flesh, only resulting in more tentacles rising from the sea.

"It is…eating our Skills!" a Sorcerer cried out. The main deck was swarmed with the robed men and women, all of them singing. "Nothing we do is making a mark!"

From the rear of the battle, Yorun saw the truth of it. Spell after spell struck the writhing, lashing tentacles and were turned into wisps of vapor or cascading liquid. The Mana from the broken spellforms didn't simply dissipate, either—they were sucked up by the monster's hungry limbs.

What are *you?* Yorun gasped, unable to catch his breath as everything he'd spent his fortune on unraveled around him.

The ship rocked, tilted to its side as the creature roared again. Yorun fell again, his small limbs no match for the blood-streaked deck. He fetched hard against the railing, driving a wheezing exhale from his lungs as he dangled precariously over the churning acid waves below. His eyes widened in horror, pain forgotten, as the misbegotten shape of the creature was partly revealed. "AHH!"

Dozens upon dozens of eyes stared up at him through a veil of sickly green, the smallest the size of his head and the largest bigger than the tallest of his Golems. They *burned* with a lamp flame orange, and whispers surged in Yorun's Mind.

DESCEND.

VIOLATOR.

DESCEND.

Something grappled him, caging his limbs among his vestments like a swaddled babe, and Yorun thrashed.

"Be still!"

The voice shook him, literally vibrating his chest and head like the tolling of a gargantuan bell, and Yorun went slack. He gazed up and back at the withered form of the Sorcerers' leader as she held him tight against her bosom. Mauvim.

"What is—?" he began.

"The Dread is compelling us all. You must not listen." Her voice was leather on steel, and it carried a force of pure command that he recognized from his time in the Neeran Fleet. She was bent and walked with a knotted cane, but the force of her Will was palpable.

She set Yorun down, and his legs felt like jelly. He locked his knees and clenched the rail but refused to look over the side again. "What do we do? The creature is too strong."

"We persevere," she said, before snapping her fingers. A sound like a ballista bolt rang out, and the very air rippled. "Emelda! Tzfell! Attend." She turned those fingers toward the water, where more tentacles lifted in response. In challenge. "It is a Bloodbeast, and it is not yet done."

Faster than the Gnome could track, more hooked tentacles whipped up and over the guardrail, slashing into the sails and rigging before descending in a hurricane of wet devastation. It was met by the crooked stance of an unbowed Sorcerer…and a song.

A cage of solid light and gleaming white metal surrounded the tentacles, arresting their momentum mid-swing. Thunder crashed, a song of triumph weaving through the roar of waves and beast—Yorun staggered back, his Spirit overwhelmed.

"Sing the shields!"

A renewed effort spread, and the strange, unnatural magic of the Chanters supplanted their terrifying reality. A visible shield striated with light formed around them, slicing through countless vile, mottled appendages like butcher knives through cattle. Ichor rained down, eating away at his precious ship before the Sorcerers could burn away the Bloodbeast's segmented flesh.

A horrid bellow shook the ship, and waves of acid erupted up the sides of their newborn shields as the creature reared back. Yorun clenched his jaw, fighting against his rising gorge–a fight others clearly lost all around him. The creature was twice the size of his ship, its body long and covered in pebbled skin, rust-red scales, and putrid, yellowed flesh. Hands and arms stretched out, Human-seeming save for their terrible length and disgusting number. Dozens of them lined the bottom of the Dread, outnumbered only by the barbed tentacles that festooned the sides of it as it rose on thrashing fins. Spines rose from its back and orb-like head, glowing with a virulent green that traced across its form like uninterrupted flame.

"Sing!" Mauvim ordered.

The Dread screeched, a sound made of a thousand voices. Orange and green Mana burst in all directions, smashing into the reinforced shields with enough power to pitch Yorun's entire ship backward. They rode the swell, held in place only by the clutching grasp of the tentacles on their starboard side.

Yorun fell, clutching at his ears. Chanters fell to the deck, eyes and ears bleeding, screaming. Tentacles, hundreds of them, rose from every conceivable direction, filling the fog-ridden air until they all but blocked out the sun.

It has us! We're doomed!

"GET DOWN!"

The Dread twisted, wheeling its unveiled maw toward the shore. It screeched, maw wide open, as a bolt of blue-white lightning blasted into its face.

Lightning and fire spun outward bashing into their shields until all Yorun could see was chaos. When it resolved, there was a figure—a Human—floating above the waves. He was clad in only dark green trousers, thick silver bangles around his ankles and wrists, and…his skin wasn't skin at all. *Not Human.* Yorun pushed himself up. *That's…that's the Autarch. The man from the stories, himself.*

The Dread was not done, but it clearly did not want anything to do with the Autarch. It lurched to the side, an orb of condensed acid blasted out of its hideous maw. An orb that was half the size of the ship. It screamed through the air, burning the sky itself as Yorun stood transfixed by sudden, certain death.

The Autarch raised a single hand. "Hand of Calamity," he muttered…and the world *sang*.

The orb burst, scattering in a great arc around the Autarch before it halted entirely. The man curled his claws, and the streamers of acid shot backward. Right into the Dread's huge, unblinking eyes.

It screeched, the acid boring sizzling holes in its hide, and the Dread dropped back into the water.

VIOLATORS!

"Who are you talking about?" The Fiend asked.

VIOLATORS WILL BE DESTROYED!

The Autarch went stiff before he looked back at the ship. At Yorun, whose stomach dropped and threatened to rip out of him entirely beneath that gaze. The Autarch turned away, facing the Dread again. "They are welcome here. Stand down."

Yorun had a moment of stunned disbelief—surely this behemoth would not simply *go away*? And yet…it did. The waves parted, and the Bloodbeast sank below, until its lamp flame eyes were swallowed by the deeper dark of the Bitter Sea.

We…live?

"Well, that was rough," said the floating Autarch. He levitated before Yorun's ship, his mouth wide in a smile and his arms open. Inviting. "Hi. I'm Felix Nevarre. Welcome to Nagast, members of the Cantus Sodalus."

Whatever the Sorcerers replied with was lost to Yorun, because he could not take his attention away from the Autarch. He knew why the stories called him the Fiend, now. *His eyes.* Yorun swallowed and found his throat painfully dry. *His eyes burn. Like flames.*

Like the Dread's.

CHAPTER THIRTY-ONE

The Chanters didn't say much after Felix showed up. The stooped old lady had only bowed a little before she swooped off, clattering across the heaving deck on a knobbly cane, calling out for the injured to be gathered together. The entire ship soon transformed from a clutch of silent survivors into people with purpose. Now, bloodied Chanters dabbed at dried blood on their faces, while several Gnomes in green-gold tabards were treated for broken limbs and puncture wounds from wooden shrapnel. Among them all Wooden Golems loped, agile hands armed with tools as they began to repair the busted Manaship.

"Lord Autarch the ah—the engines are shot," said a Gnome dressed in more gold than green. *Yorun*, according to his Voracious Eye, after a brief amount of resistance. Felix looked closer at the man, noting the chain around his neck and slight bump just under his tabard. *A Veiling Amulet. Chanter made. Interesting.* "I—we cannot fly. The Sorcerers they, ah, they suggested you might be able to help?"

"Oh. Yeah, I can help." Felix was a little miffed to be their errand boy, but he couldn't just leave them to sink into the Bitter Sea. He also couldn't fault them for taking stock of the wounded, even if they did ignore him. *What did you expect? Applause? Worship?* He snorted to himself. *You stopped them from getting killed by the Dread.* He didn't need validation or thanks.

It wouldn't have hurt, though.

A short time later, Felix flew ahead of their broken Manaship. It was incapable of flight, but it still floated, and the Chanters' shields kept it from getting burned away in the highly acidic water. So, while Felix flew, he hauled the *Cipher's Venture* behind him. Tethers of shadow clung to the bowsprit and prow, wrapped around wood and steel as surely as any steel towing cable, while a steady wave rolled beneath its hull, propelling it forward.

Shadow Whip is level 68!
Hand of Calamity is level 70!

The shore was a decent distance away—Felix had been forced to hurl himself almost two miles out to reach their ship—so he took the time to think on a few things. Namely the Dread itself.

It listened to me, which is new. Felix hadn't faced the Dread in real life since his arrival on the Continent nearly a year ago, but even when he revisited their meeting in his Memories, there was never any conversation. The Dread, he had thought, was a monster capable of murder and only murder. *But that isn't right. The Maw used it to Mark me when I arrived, which means it's either a puppet or it can take orders. There's no one around to puppet it anymore, so I guess that means it's smart enough to chat.*

That understanding was further fueled by what he'd noticed as the Dread had left, and Felix fired off his Voracious Eye.

Name: The Dread
Type: Bloodbeast
Level: 1344
HP: 4342877/4343091
SP: 3216712/3216846
MP: 1134928/1134928
Lore: The Dread is the last living Bloodbeast intentionally forged by the Primordial known as the Unending Maw. It feeds upon all those that enter its waters, driven by dark instincts and its very blood, and nothing will stop it once it begins its assault. Of all Bloodbeasts, there is only one greater still living.
Strength: Incredible reach, Strength, and the ability to consume the Mana around itself.
Weakness: It has relatively low Agility, and there are limits to how much Mana it can consume at once.
Link: Tier X

A Tier X Link. He couldn't afford to check his core space right then, to confirm that the Link was with *him*, but Felix didn't doubt it. *It listened to me…of course it did.*

The Maw was dead, eaten up by Felix himself, but its Hunger lived on. The reason the Dread was a Bloodbeast was because of the Maw, because of what it had done to him–originally a Geist warrior, they had been thoroughly transformed by the Maw's power, turned into a monster. A slave.

My slave, now. His skin crawled at the thought. *I'm not standing for that.*

Yet when he panned the waters around him for the beast, there was nothing. The Dread had vanished, and Felix hadn't the time to hunt it down. *Soon*, he promised himself.

It only took fifteen minutes to pull the ship to shore. Once the gray sands were visible, he sped up, pushing more and more of his Mana into the acidic water. The potency faded the closer they drew to shore, thankfully, but that also meant Felix's control was equally diluted—he didn't have a water shaping Skill yet. So he just ramped it up.

Hand of Calamity is level 71!

Shouts of alarm rang out on the decks of *Cipher's Venture*, but they were fine. A huge wave swelled beneath the hull, lifting them up at an angle and sweeping them toward the shoreline. Felix surged ahead, crackling with lightning as he let his Shadow Whips slacken, and he spun up one last Skill.

His magic sank through the water into the sand below. A ramp of hardened sandstone lifted, casting green brine in all directions moments before the *Cipher's Venture* sailed up its rising length. The Chanters shouted *again*, and this time their shields popped like a bubble. Several of them tumbled onto their butts, but it was fine. Felix stopped feeding the wave, pulling his power back until it was no more than a white-capped swell of mostly water.

The sandstone flattened and widened, retaining just enough of a groove to guide the Manaship's hull into his impromptu dry dock. Felix dropped back, hauling tight on his Shadow Whips and spinning the entire ship sideways into the raised platform. It wobbled, wood and metal creaking in the magically hardened slip, before it settled in with a deep, crashing boom.

"You're all set!" Felix shouted as he dismissed his Shadow Whips. Folks aboard the ship climbed back to their feet, some bruised but mostly just embarrassed—all of them staring at him. The Chanters' Spirits gave off nothing, but the Gnomes were torn between appreciation and annoyance. Yorun, at least, gave him a shaky thumbs up from the helm.

Was that petty? Felix hovered for a moment, crackling with static electricity. *Yeah.*

He'd earned a little bit of pettiness, sometimes.

Felix flew on, down toward where he'd left Zara. In her place, though, was a shield of swirling blue water Mana. It was clear his remnant wave had crashed right into the Chanter, gouging deep pits out of the sand to either side of her.

Oops.

The shield collapsed, splashing around Zara's feet to reveal the woman standing unharmed....while beside her was a far more disheveled-looking Isla.

Felix landed next to them, the wet sand squishing around his boots. "Oh, hey. When did you get here?"

"Just in time for your little show, apparently." Isla shook her half-sodden dress, and Felix didn't miss the dirt on her cheek or the brambles caught in her normally immaculate hair. "Is that the craft with our people aboard it? Did you truly just haul them to shore like a—like a fisherman to market?"

"Your skirt is smoking," Felix pointed out.

The Chanter cursed, and even that was musical. A series of green-gold tendrils flowed upward from her feet, wrapping around her blue gown. The smoking was smothered immediately, but the hem of her fine dress was ruined. "Yet more indignity. This cost me a great deal to import from Tevin."

"In the Ghreldan Hills?" Zara looked as if she just put something together. "So that is where you've been getting your finery."

"The trade through your Beacons is quite nice," Isla admitted. *Begrudgingly,* Felix thought. "I have long been without luxury, holed up in that sand pit of a city, and while Nagast is no cultured metropolitan...it has its charms."

"Uh. Huh," Felix said.

"What?" she asked, narrowing her eyes through a curtain of tangled locks.

"I just don't know how to respond to a compliment from you." He turned toward the ship just as a gangplank was extended out of the side. "It's a nice change."

Isla spluttered something unintelligible, but Felix didn't really care. The gangplank crashed into the Stone Shaped dry dock along a long, flat plane that ramped downward toward the rapidly drying sand. Thirteen figures disembarked, each of them moving with a slow, processional gait while a swell of song took to the air.

Woodwinds and strings sang a concerto of peace, humility, and appreciation as the Chanters descended. None of them wore anything close to a uniform, either in color or fabric or design, but there was something distinct about each one that Felix flagged as different from other people. He narrowed his eyes, unsure of what he was seeing.

A few more followed right after the Chanters, three boys and three girls of varying Races, each garbed in simple robes of undyed wool and flax that absolutely looked like a uniform. A shitty one, but still. They had something of that strangeness about them that he had noticed in the Chanters, but it was fleeting at best. Perhaps it was just harder to spot, due to surprise. *Apprentices, obviously…but how old are they?* He doubted any of them were older than fifteen, and the youngest looked to be a literal child of seven or eight.

Behind them came a contingent of Gnomes, all of them garbed green and gold tabards, wide leather belts, and a bevy of odd tools. A panel sewed into the front of their tabard depicted three interlocking gears overlaid by a hammer. Yorun led them, along with a handful of Wooden Golems that marched in single file down the ramp. Felix spotted a control rod in Yorun's hands, a fine one made of crystal, wood, and mithril. It hummed almost as loud as the Chanter's marching song, buzzing like he was standing under a set of power lines.

God, they're milking this entrance. Did they forget I just saved them? At his side, Zara and Isla fidgeted as the slow procession made its way toward them all. They were nervous. Surprisingly, Felix felt extremely steady about it all. Which was good, considering what he needed to do.

The Chanters stepped onto the sand, and where they tread, it turned to verdant grasses and wildflowers. Spring bloomed in winter, each step forming a path that led them through the acid-strewn sand toward Felix.

Well, okay, that's pretty cool. Felix chewed his cheek, thinking. *Could I do that? It'd just take some Green Shaping, I think.*

The Chanters reached them after a solid five minutes, the squishy ground grown into a verdant causeway. The growth slowed down as their processional song faded, becoming a murmuring melody that lilted among the cold sea air. The men and women in the lead parted, making way for the elderly woman with the cane. Felix had noticed her before but had refrained from using his Eye on any of the Chanters—since folks with an Affinity could feel that sort of intrusion, it was just polite. He assumed it was Mauvim, though. She was nearly bent double atop her knobby cane, and the skin of her face and neck was fighting a losing battle with gravity and elasticity.

"Zara," she said, her voice sharp and without any waver. "I am pleased to see you in the flesh, once more."

The Naiad curtsied. "And I you, Mauvim."

They embraced.

"Isla," Mauvim paused, squinting at the slighter woman's face as Zara stepped back again. "You have something in your hair." Isla's face turned a very interesting shade of pink before she started to pull at her locks. Mauvim said nothing, only turned to face Felix. "Lord Autarch Felix Nevarre."

Mauvim bowed, her crooked body somehow making it look effortless. The others copied her bow, if not as deep. She looked around as she straightened. "A fine place, this beach. And a finer protector."

Zara shifted. "You speak of the Dread."

"A Bloodbeast," Mauvim said. "Those are exceedingly rare, and for good reason."

A dark-skinned Chanter, younger-looking than Zara spoke up. Her voice was stern. "They are to be killed on sight, for their very touch warps flesh and rots the blood."

Yorun gasped, and more than one set of eyes turned on him in surprise. The guy didn't care though. In fact, he was pissed. "It touched so many of us! My people—!"

"Are fine. I apologize for making you worry, captain," Mauvim interrupted. "*This* Bloodbeast is cleansed, somehow. Untainted by the flesh curse." She stared at Felix. Through him, almost. "Remarkable."

Felix had nothing to say to that, so he ignored it. "Why exactly are you here?"

A faint ripple spread through the group, but Mauvim met his steady gaze. "To teach…and to beg for asylum."

"Asylum?" Isla asked. She cast her gaze across everyone, across the battered ship. "Where did you sail from?"

"Neer, atop the Klaven Cliffs. We only narrowly evaded the Hierocratic blockade," a Dwarven Chanter said. She was bald with very interesting tattoos across her scalp and face. They interlocked like geometric knotwork and glimmered like metal. "This ship and our Makewright friends here were all that we could pull from the flames."

"The Hierophant has moved on the Neerans? What has changed?" Zara asked.

Mauvim lifted a hand, palm down. "All shall be answered, but this is not something to be discussed in the open. Our plan was to fly to your Stronghold, Lord Autarch, but your defenses are too strong. Even discounting your Dread, we can barely see in this fog. I would like to see your Territory before it grows too dark. We have a great deal to discuss, young man."

Felix snorted. "That we do. But you'll not be entering my lands without an Oath."

This time, the ripple of emotion was *very* obvious. The dark-skinned Chanter scowled at him. "You would bind us, boy?"

"You expected to just fly into my Territory unchallenged?" Felix stared down the woman, and he felt his eyes burn. The growing dark around them was illuminated by blue-white and red-gold. "Let me be very clear. The only reason you are allowed here now is because I trust Zara. The Cantus Sodalus remains unproven." He swept his gaze across every one of them. "Give your Oath, or I'll put you back out to sea myself."

"Alone, Autarch?" The dark-skinned Chanter asked, and a percussive rhythm gathered behind her voice. "Against us all?"

Felix let his Voracious Eye spool up, identifying her. "If it means keeping my people safe, Emelda, then yeah. Alone."

A loud crack shattered the rising tension, forcing Felix and Emelda's gazes to break. Felix glanced at Mauvim and her lifted fingers. "Enough. Emelda, all of you, stand down. This is not the way. We seek shelter and asylum, and we seek to prevent the end of all things. Only here may we find succor, where the armies of the Hierophant have been beaten back not once, but twice." She took a deep breath, as if all the talking had taxed her. "We will take your Oath, Lord Autarch Nevarre. I only ask that it does not take away our power of choice."

Felix frowned. "Of course not. Unless that choice is to betray me and my people. I'm not in the business of making people my slaves." Thoughts of the Dread flickered through him, but Felix shoved that aside. *Later.* "I only ask that you not disclose the secrets of my people or Territories, not to take up arms against my people or Territories, or otherwise act against any Territory that I hold Authority over. On pain of loss of your Temper, your levels, and your stats."

Skein of Fate is level 64!

The Oath congealed around his hands, a spiraling loop of silver thread invisible to all others. A faint pressure laid atop of it, a distant hand attempting to pull it away from him—but Felix shouldered it aside as his Call of Defiance Title activated. *Get outta here, Siva.*

He swore he heard the air around him hiss.

Skein of Fate is level 65!

Without hesitation, Mauvim dropped to a single knee before Felix. "I give my Oath to you, Lord Autarch."

One by one, all of the Chanters did the same, some taking a bit longer than others. The Gnomes knelt as well, as did the Wooden Golems, funnily enough.

Skein of Fate is level 66!
...
Skein of Fate is level 68!

"Zara," he said, feeling the Oath latch around each and every one of their visitors. Yet before Felix could get another word out, the Chanter dropped to a single knee.

"I, too, give my Oath to you, Lord Autarch," the Naiad said. The Oath bound around her Spirit as well.

That leaves… Isla stood not far off, hair still in disarray but her expression regal enough for a queen. She pursed her lips.

"Oh, very well."

CHAPTER THIRTY-TWO

Evie stood atop the waterfall, looking back over what had once been a riverbank before Felix had gotten his hands on it. Now a castle soared upward in the early morning light, all of it built of that dark stone of his. There was a crenelated wall, at least thirty strides high, and inside that was a large, hexagonal building, three stories tall and fitted with small arrow-slit windows. The whole thing was built around the Spirit Tree, which sprouted from the very center.

I should be used to this big plant by now, but… She looked up and up, all the way to the dark canopy of leaves, emerald despite the icy winds. Hanging fruit glowed up there, small as pinprick stars and just as bright. "How long has this castle-thing been here?" Evie asked.

"A few weeks," Vess said. She was not nearly as distracted by the castle's appearance as some others. Instead, her attention was held by the gaggle of new folks. "Felix said they arrived last night, seeking asylum."

Chanters. Evie liked Zara well enough, but Isla gave her the creeps, especially after she heard what went on down underwater. "I thought they were supposed to help *us*."

"The reason for their flight is what concerns me," Yintarion said from Vess' shoulder. The blighted lizard was always there. Lurking.

"The Autarch said they mentioned Neer, which is far to the south of us, and one of the few local powers that have kept the Hierocracy at bay. Now the Klaven Cliffs have fallen too, or will soon." Vess drummed her fingers on her enameled breastplate. "I feel equally under and over-dressed."

"What, you wanna get all gussied up for them?" Evie nodded at Vess' back, where her spear floated in a weave of air. "And give up your weapon in a pit of vipers? Nah. That seems stupid."

"They swore an Oath, Evie. We have nothing to fear from them."

"Mhm. Oaths are well and good, but why did Felix have to force them into one? Says a lot about how trustworthy *he* finds 'em."

"That is a good point. The urchin speaks with uncommon wisdom." Yintarion slithered out of her collar, floating on his back. Evie frowned at the lizard. He flicked his forked tongue at her. "Uncommon for her, at least."

"Ooh, I'm going to step on your tail, you limp noodle!"

"Evie! Yin! Enough." Vess glared at both of them. "We have a meeting to attend." She strode off, heading for the gates of the big Fiendstone castle.

Yintarion stared after his Companion for a beat or two then followed.

"Let's go inside, I guess," Evie muttered to herself.

"Why am I nervous?" Felix asked.

Pit stopped nibbling on his forepaw. "Dunno. Why?"

"I faced them on the beach, made them swear an Oath. Even Isla. This should be anticlimactic. Right?"

"Right," Pit said, beak working on his other leg now.

"Right," Felix echoed, chewing at his lip.

They both stood within a sparsely furnished antechamber, just on the other side of a delicately crafted wooden door. The Henaari and Risi had a hand in building the small fortress, each of them contributing something to its construction. The door was Henaari-make, fabricated by their incredible Skills to show a sun rising over a set of fog-shrouded mountains. Centered in the door was a depiction of his Spirit Tree. Above him, a branching sculpture of ice hovered, and it radiated a cool blue light that mingled well with the smaller yellow-gold magelights. Similar sculptures were all over his little fortress, providing a bounty of illumination to every chamber, hall, and corridor.

His part of the construction had only taken a few days, owing to his considerable store of Mana, but Felix had remained too busy to see much of the finished product. He ran his hands over the door's carvings, frankly astounded at the level of detail in the Henaari's work. At the base of the Spirit Tree, where it met the waterfall, there was even a tiny little castle.

The Bastion of Atlantes. It was a good name, in Felix's opinion. It took inspiration from his own Bastion of Will, and of course the Spirit Tree it encircled. The walls provided extra security for the powerful entity in addition to being a cool place for a castle. The gaping hole in the roof of his Temple was now protected from above and below, which had become a considerable security risk, now that more people were around.

No one had dared to sneak into the rooms far below, but a few had thought to climb the Spirit Tree. Their intentions were innocent enough —new residents, eager to see the Spirit Fruit with their own eyes. It was soon clear that the Atlantes Anima could defend itself. The would-be sight-seers had later claimed that it felt like a deep, abiding terror had struck them, forcing their breath to quicken and their hands to shake. It only increased as they climbed, until all they could do was curl up on the stone-wrought steps and weep for it to be over.

When the Henaari caught wind of that story, it had spread across Elderthrone within the day.

Not a single soul had attempted to ascend the trunk since. Felix figured the Bastion would help deter that even further.

Felix and Karys had designed the Bastion to be a more public place to speak to and hear out his people's grievances. It had only started out as an audience chamber, like in old medieval castles, but had grown as they'd considered more and more uses for the space. Karys had patterned a lot of it on the fortresses he had been stationed in his youth, back when the old man had fought in the war. As such, most of the rooms were labeled in interesting ways; the Outer Chords for the defensive walls, and the Inner Harmonies for what Felix knew as the inner bailey. Felix let the man name them as he wished, even if he wasn't comfortable with how fancy they sounded.

He pressed his ear to the intricately carved door but heard nothing beyond it. Felix was so used to his Perception's reach that it was a little unnerving, like going suddenly deaf. A lot of sensory wards wrapped the Bastion, but nowhere quite as completely as the room just beyond the door. He had wanted whatever meetings that happened to be private, after all. Unless he wanted to eat several layers of wards, what happened inside the Hall of Songs was beyond his senses.

He stood, waiting. Something was wrong, and the delay between their arrival and Felix learning all the details was maddening. Worse, if things continued going the way they were, Felix would likely have to reschedule his dinner with Vess. He'd already flaked on training with Darius, though that didn't sting his conscience so much.

At his waist, his Inheritor's Will buzzed to life. "My Lord? Are you ready?"

Felix squared his shoulders. "As I'll ever be, Karys." Behind him, Pit stood up, his armor clanking slightly. "Showtime, bud."

The doors before him opened, and at the same time, Karys' voice reached his ears. "All rise! All rise for the Autarch of Nagast, King of Ahkestria and the Leviathan Depths, Returned God of Thunderflame, the Blue-Eyed Fiend, Felix Nevarre."

You had to say the god bit, Karys? Really? Felix strode out into the Hall of Songs, focusing on the architecture to stifle his nerves. Like his antechamber, the Hall of Songs had a piece of elaborate ice hanging from the ceiling, though this one was many times bigger. A vaulted ceiling patterned with stars was supported by large pillars, and the floor was polished until it had an almost mirror-shine. The Hall of Songs was the largest room in all the fortress, and that was to accommodate the huge circular table at its center.

It had been built according to Karys' old memories of the prior Hall of Songs. Apparently, a round table was pretty common, but unlike in the old King Arthur stories, Felix's seat was lifted up on a dais so that there was little confusion about who was in charge. It was shaped into the likeness of some sort of beast with clawed arms and a profile that looked suspiciously like Pit.

I like your chair, Pit sent. *It looks…regal.*

Everyone else was standing before high-backed wooden chairs festooned with carvings of vines and flowers. All thirteen of the full-fledged Chanters were there, plus Zara and Isla, though their apprentices were squirreled away in Zara's place in the Foot. There was even a space for Yorun, that Gnome captain. As visitors, they took the traditional spot directly opposite Felix's seat, while his left and right were filled with representatives of his peoples.

The Hall of Songs, Karys had said, *is a chorus. All must have a voice.*

Vess, Evie, Atar, Alister, Harn, Beef and Hallow were there—the latter two sitting in the same chair—along with Battlelord Ari, the Farwalker, A'zek, Lavix, and of course, Karys. His Chancellor didn't have a chair at the table but stood behind and to the right of the dais. Felix mounted the steps to his seat—throne, really—as Karys kept talking. "Accompanied by his Companion, Pit of Nagast, Guardian Beast!"

Pit preened at the introduction as he sat on the left of the throne. Felix took his own place, but remained standing. "Visitors, friends, vassals of Nagast. Thank you for meeting with me this evening. Please, sit." He sat down, and everyone else followed suit. Out of the corner of his eye, he spotted Vess giving him a proud smile. They had rehearsed that bit. "I would like to extend a formal welcome to the Chanters of Cantus Sodalus who, as of last night, have been granted asylum to stay in Nagast."

Mauvim bowed her head, though it only barely reached above the table. "We are pleased to be here, Lord Autarch. The journey from the Klaven Cliffs was long."

"That brings us to our first order of business, actually," Felix said. He leaned forward, elbows on the clawed arms of his throne. "What happened in Neer?"

Mauvim kept his gaze as if she expected this line of questioning. "Four months ago, the Hierocracy placed a blockade around the Neeran Territory. According to official reports we acquired, this was a trade issue between the Neeran Queen and Hierophant. We suspect that was not the truth, but there was no movement from either party to end the stalemate, even as commerce within the city began to dry up. We still had fish from the sea and plentiful meat from the Domain beneath the cliffs. But tensions were running high, especially among the slums and the rest of the city." The old woman placed a gnarled hand before her, all knuckles and skin. "If I may use a Skill?"

"Sure," Felix said. Mauvim was very strong, according to his Eye, but he doubted she'd try anything now. Even so, he felt his Hunger clench in anticipation. "Go ahead."

Light bloomed from Mauvim's palm, a riot of purple and green-gold that wove into a blurry image. The image sharpened, refined itself, until it was like Felix was looking through a window at a city perched high atop a set of cliffs. Elegant towers of gray-green stone rose high into the sky, while an expansive slum hung from the cliffs, tacked on by rope and chains to the fractured edge. Waves crashed far below, where dark waters churned to lavender foam.

What a hole, Pit sent. *People live there?*

Apparently.

"Fishing the Darkwine Sea is dangerous, but it was the only method the Untempered poor had to secure their own food. Without the

Queen's largess of bread and ale each evening, a resentment began to build in the slums. The Tempered could raid the Domain, bringing back a great deal of food for their families, but it was not enough to go around. Or, perhaps they were simply unwilling to share.

"Tensions rose between everyone upon the Klaven Cliffs until it all boiled over. Fighting broke out in the streets, Untempered against Tempered, leaving only a few dead…but it was enough. Riots ran rampant, surging from the slums to the palace gates." As they watched, the skies darkened and sleek-looking ships appeared around the city of Neer.

A bombardment began, blasting through wards and the unprotected slums, igniting flames that ate their way through the distant vista. "As things reached their highest point, the Hierocracy attacked. There was no warning, no attempt at negotiation. Neer was put under siege, and it is clear the Hierophant intends to claim it as her own."

"Why?" Vess asked. "Disrupting trade is bad enough for the region, for the Hiercracy itself, if my understanding is correct. Neer forms a hub that many lesser Territories buy and sell through. Taking it over I understand, but this isn't an occupation or even a vile suppression." Vess jabbed an armored finger at the burning illusion. In it, small white-armored figures in red cloaks had begun to flood the streets. "This is eradication."

"Well put, Heiress of Pax'Vrell. You do your father proud," Mauvim said. "It is exactly as you say. We do not understand the Hierophant's design here and were forced to flee before we could investigate further. All those practicing worship of the old gods were being put to the sword, and in Neer, that is a great many people. We saved who we could, but aside from the Gnomish Makewrights, we were able to do precious little." She shook her head, and for a moment, she let her Spirit unveil. Sorrow and misery clung to her words like a dirge. "We were not enough."

"You did what you could, Lady Chanter," Yorun said, his voice gruff with emotion. "But, ah, maybe I can offer some more insight." He cleared his throat, clearly nervous to be speaking. "The slums and a good portion of Neer proper were in an uproar already, you had that right. But it wasn't just because of a lack of food."

Yorun licked his lips as sweat beaded on his forehead. His Spirit rang with fear. "It was cuz of you, Lord Autarch."

CHAPTER THIRTY-THREE

"I'm sorry, what?" Felix wished something more refined had immediately popped out of his mouth, but Vess' etiquette training only went so far. "I've never even been to Neer."

Yorun was almost shaking in his seat. "Please forgive me, my Lord. I spoke out of turn—"

"Whoa, hey. Calm down, man. I'm not gonna kill you for telling me information," Felix said. He winced internally as he realized that some lords might actually do that. "Just…explain it for me. Please."

The Gnome's Spirit slowed its frenetic tempo, but only barely. "Alright. Well, those of us Makewrights—that's us." He pointed at his tabard with the golden gears overlaid by a green hammer. "We fix things. Armored carts, Manaships, Golems, you name it we got our hands in it, and it makes us useful to the nobles. Even had a commission from the Neeran Queen we were workin' on…before."

His expression folded like a flimsy chair. "Anyway, we were rubbin' shoulders with the nobles, but all of us come from the slums. The only thing anyone could talk about for ages was the System alert we all saw. 'A New Territorial Lord Has Risen!' No one had ever heard of you, but we all assumed you were some noble. At least 'til a Henaari rolled into town."

The Farwalker, representative of the Henaari, tilted his hooded head, his features hidden in shadow. "Oh?"

"Yeah. A Windcaller, dressed in those feathered shirts, come to tell stories in the city. Yet instead of going to the nobles that would pay her a hundred crowns a night, she came to the Darkwine Perch, right at the edge of the slums. It was packed that first night, as everyone and their mother was out trying to take the edge off their hunger. A good story does wonders, you know?" Yorun cleared his throat again and licked his lips. "She sang a lot. So many stories from far-off lands and ancient Ages…but then her tune changed. That was when she sang of a king, born of nothing, who rose to throw off the Hierophant's law. Who defied the heavens themselves to claim a Territory that had once been Lost. And—and she gave us a name. Felix Nevarre. Autarch."

Felix swallowed, but his throat had gone thoroughly dry. "Your people are spreading rumors about me, Farwalker?"

"No, not my tribe…but then, the Windcallers do not listen to Farwalkers or Synod." The hooded Henaari produced a feather from inside his voluminous robes. It was black, but it caught the light as if greedy for it. "They speak light into the dark. They serve Her."

From somewhere far above, a bird cried out, loud as distant thunder. Pit shrieked right back, and the sound broke into fragments that tumbled into breathy laughter.

Beef spun in his seat, looking up into the well-lit rafters. "Uh, I'm not the only one who heard like, evil laughter right?"

"No. I heard it, too," Evie said. She poked the Farwalker. "Your bird is loud."

"She has Her moments."

Felix lifted a hand, cutting off the chatter. "Yorun. Are you saying people were upset because someone told a story?"

Yorun scratched at his arm, clearly uncomfortable. "Well, it wasn't just that. We all know the Henaari don't lie, and Windcallers can't. It's why most cities don't like 'em around; they find things out, tell them far and wide, and no amount of gold or power makes 'em shut their yaps. So when she said you did what you did…it got folks to thinkin'."

"Dangerous," Isla murmured. Zara shot her a sharp look.

"The youngest caught on quickest. They started askin' questions. Questions none of the old folks could answer. 'Why are the nobles in power? Why does the Queen rule in a palace, while we balance on chains over the sea? Why can't we all be Tempered?' What could we say? That's just how it is? That's what we had to endure, so—so it's fine? All the right words didn't sound so good anymore.

"The questions kept comin' after the Windcaller vanished. Grew louder when fish grew too scarce to feed everyone. And then it just…

someone got in a fight. Dunno who, but a Tempered noble killed someone." Yorun's eyes were haunted. "The fightin' started, with harpoons and pikes against armored guards. Hundreds died, mostly Untempered, but so did a few nobles and guildfolk. By the time the Hierocracy broke down our gates, Avet's Mark was lit in the Azure Square, and half the city was on fire."

"Rebellion," Zara said softly.

"And further proof of heresy, according to the Inquisition," Mauvim added. "I do not know who scrawled the Mark, but it was not those among the slums."

"A Mark requires a Master to make," Felix said. "But I thought those were placed on creatures and people?"

Mauvim's lined face twisted, her jowls shaking slightly. "It was placed upon a Neeran Queensguard, and its influence transformed him into a walking inferno before he perished. An entire district ended in flames. *Someone* wanted the city to fall."

"An Inquisitor?" Beef suggested. "They got flame powers right?"

"Avet's Mark is from the god of change himself, able to be placed only by a chorister of the dark god. Like myself," Zara explained. "It is not something the Hierocracy could fabricate. This was confirmed?"

"We only learned of the Mark after the fact, but our limited scrying has confirmed the resonance of the Mark," Tzfell, the Dwarven Chanter, said. "I confirmed it myself."

"Sounds like the gods are mixing in again," Felix said. "Or at least their followers. Zara, you said no one receives messages from them anymore, right?"

"Correct…but nothing is certain anymore. Your own struggles have proven that. If the gods were well and truly gone, you would not have faced them multiple times in the last year alone." Zara shook her head. "Change and revolution are cornerstones of Avet's sphere of influence, but he has always been one to influence events with far more subtlety."

"'Of all the gods, only two bore no moon. Only two, of the light and the flame. Pathless and Avet, order and chaos,'" Vess said, and the words had the sound of a religious tract.

Huh. Interesting, Felix thought. *They* don't *have moons, do they?*

"What I know of Avet comports with Zara's accounting. Despite your experiences with the gods, Felix, I cannot believe they would sow destruction so willingly and without cause," Vess said.

"Didn't Noctis just try and eat you?" Evie said.

"That was no goddess, whatever its claims," Vess insisted. "It was mad and twisted by its long incarceration—"

"It was a true sliver of the goddess Noctis," Yintarion said, crawling out from under her collar. Several Chanters looked at him with wide eyes, a few losing control of their Spirits long enough to let loose a strain of deep, haunting curiosity. The Wyrmling sniffed in their general direction but focused on Vess. "I would know, little Dragoon."

Mauvim tapped her knobby cane into the ground, cutting through the light chatter that had begun. "Whether the Mark was falsified or not, the answer is still the same: Neer has fallen, and the Hierophant is making moves to take other Territories as well. We have received word of several other attacks to the south and the east, where the Hierocracy butts up against the vast jungles of the Interior."

Despite the gravity of her words, a smile creased her face. "Only here has the Hierophant's forces been defeated. Not only that, but according to the intelligence we've gathered, Nagast is now considered 'off-limits.'"

Karys roused at that, and Felix felt the same restless curiosity. "Why?" he asked. "Because we bloodied their nose? I expected retaliation for that, honestly. It's what happened last time: we drove the Inquisition out, and the High Guard followed."

"We do not know why," Emelda said. "Only that every one of our sources have confirmed that the order was delivered to all of the Hierei at once in a beam of sunlight."

"Hierei?"

"The highest-ranked Priests of the Pathless, second only to the Hierophant herself," Zara answered.

"Okay. So, the Hierophant sent out a group message to leave us alone?" Felix was a bit baffled by that. "That's…good, I guess."

"It is," Emelda agreed. "But the Hierophant has no recorded Skill allowing her to do such a thing. This, we believe, is the Pathless' doing."

"Hah," Pit trilled. "I bet he's scared of me."

"The Coward in White," Felix muttered. "What's their angle?"

"For this? We do not know. It is likely you have proven too difficult to crack, and he is waiting for a better time. They will come, that is certain. The Pathless is a jealous god. He wishes to be the *only* god and for the others to remain banished beyond this Realm. This we know." Mauvim's voice was hard. "He has found a similar mind in the Hierophant."

Felix tented his fingers, thinking through the information he'd received. "Alright. So we have the Pathless ordering us a no-fly zone and the Hierophant starting wars all over. That brings me to my next question for you Chanters: the Unbound. You're obviously trying to find us, but what's the plan when we're all together?"

Beef peered over everyone's head toward Mauvim, clearly eager to hear the answer as much as Felix.

"As I am sure Zara has told you, our role in your summoning is sadly reactionary. The Hierophant made the move; we merely diverted your arrival as our only recourse." Mauvim looked between Beef and Felix. "Yes, the step we have been attempting for over a year is to gather you all together. Mainly to keep you from the Hierophant's clutches, but also to best guide your immense potential.

"She has already claimed one of you, and based on the reports we have of that one's power, we cannot afford to let her take even one other. The Hierophant's plan is unknown to us, but her aspirations are not: like her god, she wishes Authority over all the Continent, for all Territories to fly her banner. She dreams of unification, but it is a unity of blood.

"We had intended to provide a safe haven for you Unbound to grow, and it is a profound twist of fate that we have instead come to you for the same. Still, we will provide the guidance we promised, training you all in the Grand Harmony. For it is the power of Creation that will be able to best the Ruin."

Atar frowned before speaking for the first time. "Chanting. That's just boosting our Skills with Affinity and Intent. How is a slightly better Sparkbolt going to defeat a being that erases history?"

"If that is what you think the Chant is, then you are not paying attention," Mauvim said. Her hard eyes bore in Zara's direction. "Or your teaching has been lax."

"So you're saying you can teach us, Beef and me, enough that we can match the Ruin?" Felix asked.

"Alone? No. There is little one person can do against the Ruin. It is a force that even the gods respect. But nine Unbound united? Working together, we will shake the heavens."

The way she said that resonated in the Hall of Songs. Felix couldn't help it; he got goosebumps.

"That sounds good," Pit chirped.

"It's also incredibly unspecific," Felix pointed out, ignoring his chills. "What does that mean?"

"We do not know. The Nym's records are gone; we operate only under limited information. The Path of Arrival is a fragmented record, with only the summon ritual itself surviving unscathed."

Felix had heard that term before, but it took him a few seconds to place it. His Adept Mind whirled through his memories like walking through a vast palace. He snapped his fingers. "I might have a solution for that, but I'll need to organize a trip to find out."

Karys leaned over him, eye-fires narrowing. "Where, my Lord?"

"Khasma. To see Paxus."

"Ah. Of course. Do you expect him to be well enough to answer questions?"

"I mean, I hope so. It's been months," Felix said.

"Where exactly do you intend to go?" Mauvim interrupted. She was stone-faced again, but it was obvious she wasn't thrilled about something.

"Short trip into the Ghreldan Hills. Shouldn't take longer than a few days," Felix said, waggling his fingers. "A week, tops."

"You are far too important to risk on such a mundane journey. Allow my people to undertake it for you."

"No. I have people for this," Felix said. "Lavix, would a few of your people be willing to escort a few Claw members into Khasma?"

The War Naga hissed—it was an agreeable sound that Felix had gotten used to, but some of the Chanters pulled away. "Of course, my Lord. My people would relish the opportunity to see Haestus again, even only in passing."

"I appreciate it." Felix looked back at Mauvim, and if anything, her stone face had turned into granite. "Now. The last and maybe most important point to address: have you found any of the other Unbound?"

The old lady clenched her jaw a few times before answering. It was absolutely clear she did not like how Felix was controlling the conversation. "We have members of our order searching the Continent for all of them, save yourself and Beefhammer. However, we are certain of only one other, and she is under the thumb of our enemy."

"Imara," Felix said. "The one the Hierophant caught already."

"Yes. But Corrupted or not, she gives us hope," Mauvim said. "She has remained in one location for many months because she is hunting another Unbound. A Gnome that goes by the name of Archibald."

"Where?" Felix asked.

"As of our last missive, the Rimefang foothills. Heavy snow has locked this Imara in place as she scours the mountains for the Gnome

Unbound. It is the primary reason we still believe Archibald is still there…havoc descends whenever the Corrupted draws near him, leaving a trail of destruction all across the Dwarven Holds."

"Why are you calling Imara 'the Corrupted?'" Felix asked.

"Because she is dangerous," Emelda stated. "For she has been bent to the Hierophant's will."

Felix recalled touching upon the connection between him and Imara. It had been strong, but it had also been very, very strange compared to all the rest. Dangerous. *Might be something to that,* he decided. "Why don't we take Imara down first, find this Archibald, then bring them both back?"

"The power the Corrupted holds is incredible, Autarch Nevarre. Entire Dwarven armies have proven ineffective against her, and she has breached many of their greatest defenses. Alone. It is uncertain what Tier she has reached, but she is not to be underestimated." This came from Tzfell, and it was the first time the Dwarven Chanter had been anything except calm. She sounded terrified. "I do not think you are a match for her."

"As well, a contingent of Priests and Inquisitors are on their way to support her," Emelda added. "Archibald is alone and on the run. If we cannot find the Gnome soon, it may be too late. The Hierophant will have him."

"And if that happens, then we may as well open our arms to the Ruin now," Mauvim said. "For we will be well and truly Lost."

CHAPTER THIRTY-FOUR

The night was cold, but for once, the flurries had ceased. The mountain air was pristine, lent an incredible clarity that still roared across the foothills, sharp as glass. Within a wide pit dug into the snow, a fire burned, crackling across the winter-wet logs and releasing a plume of pale smoke. A hulking figure hunched next to the fire, over it almost, which cast a wild shadow across the banks. Spikes and blades protruded from every plane of her, swords and maces and flails strapped to her back and hip and thigh. Before her, atop the smoke and flame, was a bubbling, steaming pot.

Imara, Chosen of the Pathless, was cooking dinner.

"Hrm." She turned the gray-tinged slop with a dull iron spoon, noting the lumpy texture as the grain slowly boiled down. She sniffed. It smelled of…nothing. She lifted a spoonful of it anyway. She did not need to eat very often, but when she did, it required a massive amount to sate her growth. Better, then, to eat frequently. It was more efficient.

She ate the slop, chewing through the parts that weren't quite ready. It was hot, bland, and mealy…but it would do. *Food is but fuel for the light within.* Those words rose from the depths of her Mind, spoken with her own voice like a law she would never disobey. There was little point; to refuse fuel meant to extinguish her light, and that she would never allow. No matter how many tried to snuff it out.

The food tasted of…ash. All things did, whether it was the meanest gruel or a king's banquet. She tried to remember what it should have tasted like, but that was beyond her—since her awakening upon the streets of Amaranth, it was like a fog had coated her sensations. Only when the Hierophant had blessed her had that fog vanished, evaporating under the light of the sun.

Still chewing, Imara lifted her other hand. Her gauntlet was pristine, made of a dark metal she could not name and crafted with such precision that it fit her like a second skin. By contrast, the small boot she held was of shoddy workmanship. It was crusted with mud and snow, and it had been repaired several times before it had been discarded.

Watchtower's Gaze.

Gold surged through her, igniting her channels with a willful radiance that gathered behind her eyes. The world unfolded before her, a puzzle she had mastered, until it revealed the secrets it had lying in wait. She could count the stitches on the boot leather, note the scratches against rock and root on the roughened sole, and detect the faint, frozen scent of animal scat along a heel. Inside, where the fetid stench was strongest, was the impression of a small foot.

The accursed Gnome. Why would he leave this behind?

The boot had been discarded in the crook of a tree, well above the snow line and at the very edge of the foothills. It was as if the squirrely Gnome had lost it in his haste to be away from her—yet there were no footprints beyond the tree, nor sign of struggle. She was fully out of the Rimefang Mountains now, at the edge of the Hoarfrost, and at eleven feet high, the snow was still waist deep on her. For the smaller wretches, that meant it was well over thrice their full height. The Gnome could have burrowed, as he had in the past, which would eliminate the appearance of footprints atop the snow…but there was no sign of that, either.

It was a trick. It always was. Imara simply did not know how, yet.

She had been chasing her quarry for weeks now. Months? Time… blurred. Collapsed. *The outside world could not be trusted*, she had been told. *Trust lies within.* Within, however, contained no sensation of cold or dark, just unceasing light. She was not tired, yet she sat. She was not hungry, yet she ate with motions fueled by Will alone. The light was all she required…but the Hierophant had given her a Need.

Find the Unbound, Imara. Find him and bind him to the light.

Imara focused her Watchtower's Gaze, inspecting the tree trunk once again. It was only a few yards away from her dugout, still half-buried in snow, untouched except where she removed the boot. The bark was scuffed and scratched, marked by beasts and monsters that she could feel hiding from her now…but other than the boot, there was nothing else. Her quarry could disappear in a way she did not understand, but it had frustrated her time and again. Clearly a Skill, it allowed him to stay ahead of Imara's relentless pursuit despite the disparity in their power. Despite her mandate from the heavens themselves.

She narrowed her eyes. *Something is coming.*

Seconds later, a roar shook the night as a beast easily twice her size exploded into her camp. It charged her, a streak of fur, fat, and fury, forcing her to meet it head-on. Imara swung her mace, catching it across the jaw and hurling it backward with a titan's Strength. The monster crashed back into the snow, dazed.

The light told her what it was: a Forest Troll. Twice her height, three times her width, and packed with enough fat and fur to ensure it could withstand the brutal winters of the mountains. It was all but invisible in the snow, too—all but its face. Wrinkled and gray and covered in twisted, malformed horns, it was a gruesome beast. A mouth filled with crooked yellow tusks opened as it stood up, heaving a hoarse cry from between bloodied lips.

Imara set herself, replacing her now-bent mace with a curved falchion. "Come, beast. Meet your end."

It charged again. A massive arm swept toward Imara, an attack that clearly relied entirely on the monster's brute Strength and overwhelming mass. There was no finesse, no technique or magic that brewed along its veins. Imara caught it cold, the force contained, as her falchion rose in a blindingly fast slash. The blade cut cleanly into its shoulder joint, severing it in an explosion of ichor that hissed as it half-drenched her fire.

The Troll screamed with fear, and Imara clucked her tongue. "My food." The pot was covered in dark ichor, and the fire was a smoking mess. "You have ruined it."

The Troll's bellow increased in pitch and a portion of its bulk shriveled as, before her eyes, its arm regrew. It was simply gone one moment and then there, bursting forth from its severed shoulder like a mother giving hideous birth. Imara blinked as it spread a fur-less claw at her, tipped with gleaming metal talons.

"Disgusting. Blessed with Strength but devoid of Purity." She pulled a second blade, this one a heavy, triangular dagger lit with golden sigils. "Your death will serve Order and the light—"

The Troll stood up, its wrinkled face fully in the light of the twin moons above, and she cut off her words. Upon its forehead was a sigil etched in blood and salt, and it caught the moonlight like water.

Not a trick, she realized. *A trap.*

It grinned at her, bestial eyes too *knowing* for its nature, and a second Forest Troll emerged from the snowfield to her left. A third from the copse of trees on her right. All of them bore the same sigil, and it seemed to glow more fiercely as they surrounded her.

"Very well." She brandished her blades. "Let it end."

They attacked.

It was not a dance of equal skill. It was an assault too fast for most to follow, let alone survive. Claws of steel met Masterwork plate, drawing sparks in the dark, while falchion and dagger met fur and fat. Ichor spilled, spun around them as wounds were opened and healed in the blink of an eye. Fingers, hands, legs; severed and crushed and sliced. Regrown. She was faster than the Trolls, stronger, but their regeneration outpaced hers by miles.

The light spoke of their levels, their Health and Stamina, but none of that mattered. She did not care, nor did she require the information. Imara would best them because she must.

The fight dragged on, sprawling across the snowfields and into the treeline. Trunks exploded, knocked down by the force of their strikes or severed by sword and claw. She remained unhurt, her armor and Temper too great for the Trolls to affect…but they would not die, either. She fetched up against a frozen ridge and threw her blades to the ground. The Trolls circled, now looking far thinner as their heinous wounds regenerated. They regarded her with caution. Worry.

"I am a fool," she said, breath misting. "Order deems that all things take their place. Yours is not to die by force of arms."

The Trolls hissed, tusks dripping with spittle.

Imara lifted her gauntleted hands and walked forward. "The light is required." The Trolls surged forward, all of them at once, and Imara let loose her inner light.

Their shrieks were wretched, but she did not care. The song of the light was too loud, too brilliant to notice anything else. Daylight returned, blotting out the stars themselves as a star rose from within her—the roar of her holy power ripped outward, engulfing all of them.

Darkness followed.

The biting wind howled across a charred and blasted terrain, empty of trees and stone and snow for thirty feet in all directions. Empty of all things save Imara herself. She looked up into the stars, now returned, and took a deep breath. "Thank you, my Lord."

There was a moment, a brief instant of pressure against her Spirit. Words flowed from within, from the guidance of light. *Stay the Path, my Chosen.*

Imara shuddered, her massive frame wracked by a suggestion of incredible, untenable power. Power that would be hers, if only she completed her Need. She knelt, pressing her bare forehead to the charcoal earth. "I swear it."

The light had faded completely now, however, and there was no guidance. No presence or pressure. Imara stood and retrieved her blades, preserved by their enchantments, before stomping through the steam and smoke. Back to her campsite. There, she found a blasted fire pit and the half-melted remains of her spoon and pot. There was no salvaging it, nor the slop inside. She would simply have to eat another time.

Find him. Mark him.

She was wasting time. Her quarry had enslaved those Trolls to distract her, and he could disappear in a way she still did not understand, but he always resurfaced. A path worn by the Trolls' movements was clear, and she didn't need to sleep.

Imara set out, blurring across the terrain. *The light will find you, Unbound.*

Behind her, in the cold wind and toppled forest, there remained only darkness.

And ash.

CHAPTER THIRTY-FIVE

"First Form!" Darius commanded. "Owl!"

Felix rushed forward, hooked blade leading the way. The movements of First Form, also known as Owl Form, were inspired by the quiet and observant nature of that bird. They emphasized slow, deliberate strikes and precise footwork.

It was a sadistic choice for the obstacle course ahead.

Blades as long as spears swung for him, rotating on sigil-driven gears and pulleys that moved with the speed of an oncoming train. Felix stepped forward, lunging as a horizontal edge sliced just below his armpit. He twisted, pushing another foot carefully into place as more swung for his neck. The whisper of cold metal slid across his skin but left no mark. For a man with Felix's Agility, the course should be child's play; no matter how fast the gears spun, they would not have caught even his shadow. Yet had he moved at full speed, it would have defeated the purpose of attempting it at all.

"To fight with a sword is to converse in the language of violence," Darius said. He was visible just outside the twisting maze. "Each engagement is a dialogue. Your footwork and your sword are your words. You must choose them carefully."

He kept moving. Step after careful step, repeating the pattern he'd hewn into his memory.

The footwork wasn't a problem—his Body responded to his

thoughts almost before he had them—so it was simply timing. Waiting for the right moment to strike.

With a final precise lunge, Felix cleared the whirling blades. He stepped onto a wide platform, a thin staging area right before the next section. He took a steadying breath and checked the stone disc at his waist. It pulsed in time with the suppression array he had laid below the course before starting, and a dull pain tore at his Mind, Body, and Spirit.

Darius scoffed. "Hesitation, Felix? I thought you had mastered the course and your suppression array?"

"Never together," Felix told him. "I'm acclimating."

"You know your enemies will not grant you such grace. Onward! Second Form! Falcon!"

Felix stepped into the next section, which was a forest of thin metal wires that hung from above. The moment he entered, however, an array activated and drove Mana up and through the complicated machinery. Each wire, anchored upon a pivoting socket, began to oscillate at greater and greater speeds.

Razor-sharp whips. Felix dodged the first few as they sped up. *Always fun.*

He dove into the fray, sword flashing out in rapid parries and pinpoint strikes as his feet blurred. A falcon was a fierce predator imbued with great speed and accuracy, and the Form emphasized rapid footwork and lightning-fast strikes. The razor whips flailed in almost random directions, devoid of any true pattern save chaos itself.

Falcon was suited for its challenge, and Felix had to loosen his own restrictions on his Agility and Dexterity in order to match it. His crooked sword never stopped moving, deflecting every lash while slipping across the flexible wires to prevent getting entangled. Whips sliced and stung at him, cutting his Garment but never once touching his skin as he zipped through their wild embrace.

He was through it all in the span of fifteen seconds, exiting with a blast of trailing wind onto a fifty-foot diameter platform carved with relatively basic sigaldry. Felix knew it well: a warding circle, meant to keep Skills within the boundaries of the platform.

"Some conversations are short and brutal," Darius said, and Felix heard him throw a lever somewhere just out of sight. Hatches opened all around the edges of the platform, and a ratcheting sound resolved itself into twenty different plinths that rose through the hatches. Upon them were Golems made of translucent glass and shimmering bands of red-gold orichalcum. Each bore a long spear of metal. "Some are more drawn out. You must know which one you are engaging in and choose the Form that suits it."

As one, the Superior Glass Golems activated. The sigaldry through their translucent bodies lit up with gold and silver, flooding their limbs with a simulacra of life and propelling them toward *him*.

"Third Form! Eagle!"

Felix flowed into the Form, Inheritor's Will sweeping outward to deflect three spears at once, and for the first time, he was forced to unsheathe his Skyslain's Riposte as well. The dagger leaped to his hand with a burst of blue-white lightning, and it lengthened mid-swing, taking out the legs of two more Golems.

Same as on Earth, the eagle was known for its keen eyesight and powerful talons. The Third Form emphasized strong, sweeping movements and powerful strikes. It was a Form to take on multiple opponents at once, but it required a great deal of Endurance and Strength to properly display.

The Superior Glass Golems moved with a fluid grace that far surpassed their lesser brethren, and their strikes were enough to blast holes in the reinforced flooring as Felix dodged them. Felix had fought them several times now and was always surprised at how *good* they moved for what were basically magic robots. They were armored, too, far more heavily than others, owing to the excess of orichalcum on their frames. Damaging them was a tall order for most, and Felix was still pulling his punches.

Well, mostly.

He caught spears within the hook of his sword, spinning them into one another before hitting their feet with his Riposte. The Golems toppled, bodies and weapons crashing against the metal platform like a gong, and Felix kept moving. He didn't crush their chests or shatter their limbs. The point of this section of the course was to prove his technique with Third Form, not to destroy the expensive robots. That alone was a challenge. Felix was used to going all-out in every fight, so these bouts were about control over fury.

Eagle's sweeping movements were truly ideal for so many foes. He took them down again and again. He avoided preternaturally fast thrusts and slashes, parrying to open up their guards before knocking their weapons from their hands entirely. The moment he did that, the Golems stuttered to a stop, as if he'd pulled their plug.

"One whole minute." Felix came to a stop in the center of the platform, panting. "That was harder this time."

"Harder? You—you vanquished twenty *Superior* Glass Golems!" A familiar Gnome climbed up onto the platform, staring at the downed and frozen Golems. It was Yorun, and he was trailed by two other Gnomes in similar Makewright garb. Other members of his Arclight Legion moved in the background, fiddling with bits of sigaldry. "They responded better than anything I've ever controlled, and you didn't stop for a second."

"I believe he means that it was harder to control himself," Darius interjected smoothly. He landed atop the platform in a flurry of wind, his half-cape fluttering behind him. "Breaking something is one thing, but mastering them is another entirely. Thank you, Yorun, for helping us run the course. You can imagine how difficult it is finding someone with the right Skills out here."

Yorun tugged at his ear and cleared his throat. "Well. My pleasure. Happy to help the Autarch any way I can."

"You did a good job," Felix said with a smile.

Darius hustled all the mages off the course shortly after that, while the Golems were reactivated and put back down into the holding area just below the training platforms. Felix disengaged the suppression array. Glimmering lines of sigaldry faded away, and a weight lifted from his Aspects as the stone disc at his hip darkened. It always felt good, like scratching an itch he'd been ignoring for an hour. As useful as the training was proving, it wasn't pleasant.

They were in the depths of his Stronghold now, in a wide chamber dedicated to this sort of thing, though the course had been installed separately. The entire training facility, as Felix referred to it, was an unused room in his mountain fastness—too big for personal use and too private for just anyone to have access. Even getting the mages down there to run the course was a hassle, considering they had to pass through the multiple checkpoints from the Temple far above.

Karys took security pretty seriously.

Thankfully, the training course was easier to run for folks with less demanding needs. His friends, many of whom had rooms just down the hall, often made use of it. The settings were variable, able to accommodate their advancement to an extent by swapping out a few materials, even a set of lesser Golems. The Golems—including the Superior Glass Golems—were a surprise gift from Cal, something she called "a meager thanks" for his efforts to defend them. Rory had said as much when he'd offered to stay on and teach the Legionnaires, bringing the training courses with him.

Felix truly appreciated it—while the others found challenge against Steel and standard Glass Golems, he did not. The Superior version was still ultimately weaker than Felix, but at least they made him sweat so long as he suppressed his Aspects, regeneration, and held back his raw stats. Control over brute strength; it was a test of his patience, but he felt more confident than ever with his Sword Forms.

Plus, his friends had a *really* hard time fighting them, and that had been fun to watch.

Now they were more prone to using the expansive sparring ring Felix had built. He'd modeled it after the one in a warehouse in Haarwatch, where he'd first been trained, shaping its boundary walls out of rock and filling the interior with a thick coating of sand.

It was this that Darius angled his head toward, as the mages filed out of the room. "Let us test your Sword Forms, Felix. I sense improvement in you, but I find a spar speaks volumes."

At his waist, Felix's sword buzzed. "My Lord? The Nagafolk have assembled."

"Oh good," Felix said. "Tell them I'll be there in a minute."

"Very good, my Lord." The sword dimmed.

"Seeing them off first, followed by your own departure?" Darius asked.

"Yeah. You sure you don't want to lead them? It's an important task."

"With you taking Commander Kastos with you, I'll be needed here. Your armies have grown substantially, and if we plan to be ready for the dangers the Hierocracy poses, we have a great deal to do."

"That's fair. Thank you, by the way," Felix said. "For everything."

"As Lady Dayne is committed to your cause, I could not in good conscience leave your people as…ragtag as they were. Discipline and technique are my bread and butter, and that is what I have imparted. It may hurt my pride a bit, but you are the reason they have progressed so much, Felix. Without your influence and example, your Legion would still remain bickering factions…or worse, farmers and laborers."

"Not really sure that's *worse*, dude."

"You know what I mean."

Felix grinned. "I do. You're saying I'm the greatest boss you've ever had."

Darius snorted. "You are certainly the strangest. I hope you intend to keep practicing during your journey."

"I plan on it. I'll have Harn there, and he's promised to put me through my paces," Felix said. "Vess and Evie, too."

"Commander Kastos is a remarkably adept man, though I do find his technique to be...wild. More in line with your normal style, in fact. Be sure that he is pressing you on your fundamentals. They are important." He hesitated, touching the tip of his tongue to his teeth. "I know that you will, but I would also ask that you take care of Vessilia, Felix. Do not let her come to harm...and do not break her heart."

Felix blinked at the man. The words had all the pieces of a threat, but they lacked any heat. Instead, they were a cold promise. "I don't intend to."

Darius only bowed, fully at the waist. "That is all I can ask."

CHAPTER THIRTY-SIX

"...and do not break her heart."

"Stupid perfect recall," Felix muttered, jogging up a staircase three steps at a time. As if he wasn't nervous about his dinner date already, now he had Darius' intimidating face seared into his memories. "And what changed his mind so much?"

Much as he appreciated the man's aptitude and training, they didn't really see eye to eye on...well, anything. The guy had become nicer back when they'd gone into Ahkestria, but other than training up his Legionnaires, Felix hadn't had many words with the Hand. Now...this.

As if he wasn't nervous about dinner with Vess already.

Felix was still scratching his head over it when he reached the gold and silver junction of his Seat and Seal. The room was dark as ever, with all of the light emanating from the insanely complicated lines of his array. Felix spotted his chancellor immediately. "Karys. Was it any trouble getting them down here?"

"No. The Nagafolk handled the stairs remarkably well, but we may wish to install a lift of some sort. Moving larger citizens as well as supplies might be challenging in the future."

"That's fair. This place isn't really designed for visitors." Yet, if Felix planned on using the Shadowgates more often, that needed to change.

"It is a Stronghold. Making it easier to access is a perversion of its purpose."

"Well, when you put it like that, I guess I'll cancel the order to put a big open doorway out front." Felix walked into the Second Chamber, trailed only slightly by his chancellor. "I had the welcome mat picked out and everything."

A low murmur of conversation cut off the moment Felix walked into the Second Chamber and ran his Eye quickly over the lot. Between the nine Shadowgates were several wagons of supplies—food, water, potions and the like—all lined up in a neat row before one of the better appointed gates. Among it all were twenty-five Nagafolk led by Lavix and twenty-five members of the Fiend's Claw. All of the latter saluted sharply, while the former prostrated their serpentine bodies upon the smooth, inlaid floor.

"Please, at ease, everyone." They did, and Felix clapped his hands, mustering up a measure of enthusiasm he didn't entirely feel. "Alright! How're we feeling? Everyone ready to go?"

"We are, my Lord," said a swordsman at the front. He had shaved his tiny trash stache, but Felix recognized him easily. The cocky warrior's hands rested easily on the twin swords at his hip, confidence belied only by his shuffling feet.

"Glad to hear it, Kylar." He nodded at all of the former Haarguard—Kikri, Davum, Nevia, and Vyne—now Claw members. They were the ones that had helped him through the Foglands to face the Archon, and he was glad to see they had volunteered for this trip. "The journey might be a bit strange, but you'll get the hang of the Shadowgates before long. You have the warding stones?" Sharp nods rippled across the space, the Nagafolk adding their sinuous bobs as well. "Keep them close, and stay in formation. While you're in there, the Void is closer than we like."

He walked forward, stepping right up to the Shadowgate linked to Haestus Temple. Like all of them, it was made of various precious and semi-precious stones, carved into a perfect circular shape before liberally decorated with dramatic sculpture. Fields of wild, malachite grasses and deep, swirling pools of cool, multi-colored kyanite. Pale, pinkish feldspar hills rose up above, framing the opaque shadows within the circular gate itself. It was one of four Shadowgates they had repaired in the months since their discovery, but the only one they had made use of; the others remained deactivated out of security. At least in Haestus, they had an entire colony of Naga to keep out threats.

"These pools…I recognized their shape," Lavix said. She had slid forward and ran a thick-fingered hand across the multi-colored stone.

"The artistry recalls the finest portions of our home. The gods made this, did they not?"

Felix cleared his throat a touch uncomfortably. "You mean the Nym? Yeah, pretty sure they built all this."

"You do us a great honor to allow us to traverse these halls, my Lord." She bowed her humanoid torso at the waist. "Thank you."

"Don't worry about it. You're doing me a favor in turn. All of you are." Felix pitched his voice to address the entire fifty-person party. "You know the task, and you know the questions. You know how to signal when you need to return?"

Lavix nodded, as did Vyne, the defender warrior. He was wearing a water-warded satchel around his broad frame, no doubt containing the scrolls of inquiries they had for Paxus. They had all been given the rundown on how to use the Shadowgate itself to signal back to Karys—it was a feature of the gates they had found only a bit ago, and it made using them even more convenient. Vyne saluted again. "Yes, my Lord. We shall see it done and return quickly."

"Good. Be safe out there." With a flex of his Will and a smidgen of significance, the Shadowgate activated. The darkness at the center of the gate thickened and spun, becoming a curtain of liquid ink.

"Form up!" Kylar shouted, and the Claw and Nagafolk shuffled into place. "Activate ward!"

A high-pitched note sang from the backs of a few of them, where basalt slabs hung from custom packs. A circle inscribed itself into the air before vanishing slowly.

"Forward march!"

Felix watched them all disappear into the Shadowgate, a gnawing worry in his gut. He couldn't describe it or name it, but it was there.

"The worry of a leader," Karys said.

"What?"

"I know that face, that feeling you are experiencing. I remember it from all of the times I sent soldiers on missions. These few, however, are not entering a battlefield. Take comfort in that, if you can."

"I—" Felix scratched his jaw. "Thanks, Karys."

"Of course. The caravan is just about ready for you as well, my Lord."

"Ah. Right." Felix took a moment longer, peering into the inky void of the gate. It would remain open until they received a signal from the other gate that folks made it through, but that could take an hour or two. Through his Adamant Discord and Skein of Fate, he could feel the people within moving away, a rumble in the bottom of his gut…but it was fading, fast.

With an effort, he walked away, and Karys followed dutifully after him.

Pit lounged against a thick tree bole and burped. Before him, a bevy of food had been laid out on a wide stump, ranging from plump fruits and vegetables to slabs of cooked and seasoned meat. Wild monster meat, of course. It was far better tasting than those strange bird-lizard things so many people ate. All of it had been given to them by a clutch of Henaari hunters. An offering, they called it, and Pit had been more than happy to partake. Now, though, he idly swatted a pair of wrinkled red things across the newly cut stump.

"What's wrong, tenku? You're not one to curb your appetite."

Pit glanced at his…well, "friend" was a stretch. A'zek was a fellow Chimera, though his subtype was more cat-lizard compared to Pit's fox-bird. A harnoq. A'zek was busy sharpening his claws against an iron-hard tree, and each drag produced sparks that danced across the snowy field.

"Just not too hungry, I guess."

"Hm." A'zek dropped back to all fours and padded closer. Despite the thick snow, the harnoq didn't so much as dent it with his steps. "Unusual. Is this regarding your injuries? Or the trip you are about to embark upon?"

"No. Yes." Pit shrugged, wincing at the pain that shot across his back. If he sat still long enough, he could forget about it entirely. "Have you ever heard us called Wardens of the Stars, A'zek? I think it's important, but I don't know how."

"Ah. I am familiar with the term." The great cat sat just on the other side of the wide stump and sniffed delicately at a piece of thick, blue-tinted meat. "A Nymean title, if I recall. To do with our cores."

Pit sat up, forepaws sinking into the snow. "Yes! That's it. What does it mean?"

"That I do not know." A'zek released a cloud of Mana vapor from his mouth, and a three-pointed star gleamed. An illusion. "My core is the same. After my first Evolution, it congealed into this, and my core space grew more detailed."

"Just like mine, except mine is four-pointed. What about your second Evolution? What changed then?"

"More detail again, but the core itself remained the same. Instead, my changes were my Mind and Body." A'zek stretched, putting his dark, spotted fur on display. Like Pit, his hide was a mixture of two kinds: fur and scales. His feet and hindquarters retained a lizard-like appearance, while his head and majority of his body resembled a panther. The main exception was his tail, which lashed behind him like a whip tipped with a cruel-looking barb. "But I have not progressed further than my second Evolution. My Path has stalled, my advancement too tied to my Companion. You are on the road toward learning more than I could ever know about our people."

Pit warbled dejectedly. "Doesn't feel like it. I only just figured out what a Guardian Beast is, and then only just."

"The Path of the Guardian Beast is about choosing our goals. You know this. You chose yours in the desert. No longer the shield to your Companion, but the blade at his side. You chose magic and speed over brute size and strength, just as I chose speed and greater gifts of Intelligence to better aid my own Companion."

"Fat lot of good it's doing me now," Pit grumbled.

"That is enough of that," the harnoq snapped. Pit flinched, and A'zek's voice softened. "Without wings, you question your place. How can you attack without advancing? How can you defend without moving into the path of violence? These are things you must answer yourself, with or without the Curse of Flame."

Pit opened his beak to say something, anything to refute that, but found himself without words. He *did* miss his wings, though he was sure not to tell Felix that. If he had them during their confrontation with the Frostfather, Pit could have been far more effective. Gained more cores. More levels.

"Wings or no, you will soon soar into new lands, Pit. Answers will come, if you are but stalwart enough to bear them." A'zek nudged Pit's downcast head with his own. "You are a Chimera. A noble tenku. A Guardian Beast. Remember that when you face down these new threats…and know that, while we are few and scattered, the Chimera are resilient. If you can find more of us, they might be able to tell you more of the Path ahead."

Pit trilled, new thoughts tumbling through his head. Ideas. "Thanks, A'zek." In the depths of his core, he felt a pull from the direction of the

Stronghold. *Felix.* He stood up and shook snow from his fur and feathers. "Please watch over Elderthrone while I'm gone."

"I swear it. None shall threaten our home." The giant cat gazed at the spread still remaining on the stump. "You are leaving this?"

"What? Of course not." Pit chomped down onto an overripe melon. "It's a long trip."

CHAPTER THIRTY-SEVEN

Atar hunched forward, peering closely at the sigil he was inscribing on a length of stone. His hand ached, cramping up despite his Adept Tier Body—the amount of inscription he had done in the last week was enough to make a lesser mage's hand fall off completely. It wasn't enough, though, not when Atar's gaze flicked back toward the gleaming metallic tome that sat to his side. A ridiculously complicated spellform stared back at him, bolstered with power and illusion so that it rotated on the page. It was a Master-Tier spellform, the building blocks of a Skill, and if Atar could master it, he could add it to his own power.

His stylus snapped in the middle of the next sigil.

"Burning **ash**!" He slammed the broken stylus down, and it was consumed in a burst of white flame. A content humming began in the back of his Mind, growing louder with every heartbeat.

yes. burn the offending object! sigaldry is for children and invalids. were you to embrace me, atar, i would propel us to heights never before dreamed—

A sharp slap hit the back of Atar's neck, shocking both mage and the chatty Urge within.

"Quiet, Flame," Alister said. He set down a tray of fine, cream-colored porcelain and a steaming hot kettle on the workbench and fixed Atar with a sharp glare. "Or I'll sic Felix on you."

The cloying warmth in Atar's head vanished so fast that Atar had to shove his hands down to keep from falling over. He groaned in relief as much as pain from the slap. "Did you have to put all your Strength into it?"

"Hardly. Your Endurance is just shoddy, Professor."

Atar remained bent over his burnt work, staring now at the ruined expanse of sigaldry.

"Atar, you're going to break your neck if you don't fix your posture," Alister chided him as he helped prop up the fire mage. "Are you transcribing the book again? And on Tier III stone this time? How long have you been at it?"

"Tier II kept catching on fire," Atar muttered. His pure white hair fell over his eyes, and he impatiently swiped it away. He needed a haircut, but hadn't the time for…what day was it? "It's taken a while. But it's ruined now." He growled the rest and shoved the fouled sigaldry into one of the material reclamation buckets. Luckily, the stone hadn't snapped, so his apprentices would shave the stone down before they could use it again. "I thought you were dealing with the nobles today?"

Alister pulled a face. "I was. The influx of Chanters was noticed, and a number of 'concerned citizens' demanded an explanation on why 'dangerous elements' were allowed into the Territory." He snorted. "Or at least to know why the Sorcerers were allowed to live in the Foot, when *their* petitions were weeks old."

"Petty fools."

"Mhm." Alister leaned over, peering at the Masterwork tome they had taken from the High Guard. "Have you made any progress at deciphering this?"

"Almost none. The spells all lean toward augmentation and life Mana more than other elements, and that proves to be a barrier almost as strong as their Master-Tier construction. Felix insists that the vibrational patterns are mutable and, well…" Atar lifted his hand, and a small bird appeared, made entirely of white flame edged with crimson.

"That's one of the spells!"

"No, just a shaping. This is effectively the same as my Sovereign Stars. The Flame within me has given me a great deal of control over my chosen element, but that hasn't allowed me to replicate the effects of the tome's spells." Not to mention, his static bird lacked the strange awareness the spell specified. It was a puppet, nothing more.

but it is our puppet. with it, we could do so much…

Alister handed him a cup of steaming tea. "I would call that progress, love. I certainly couldn't shape my force Mana into a bird."

"The flexibility is promising," Atar agreed. "Flame has taken to the shape, in fact."

Now the odd Urge inside him had taken to looking like a bird within his core, sitting atop a perch inside its black cage. It had fully replaced his old core, once bound entirely to another Urge…but Atar retained a great deal of control over the fiery occupant. It didn't truly feel like an Urge, but something different. Something new.

Atar had come to terms with his new tenant. It was useful, at least.

"Has it tried to push you a lot recently?" Alister asked, brows down as he stared at Atar's chest. As if he could see into the fire mage's core.

"No. It has been riled by the tome's magic, but otherwise it simply…seethes."

"Less manipulative than the Highest Flame, at least?"

Atar laughed. "Yeah. Though it tries."

"Mhm. It is quite chatty. I am curious how much of its claims are true, though. How exactly could it give you more power?"

by unleashing the bonds of flesh and ascending, foolish boy. urge or godling, we could be mighty beyond reckoning!

Atar rolled his eyes. "It prattles on about other Urges but rarely gives specifics. I've given up attempting to tease sense from the thing. I'd rather talk about you. How're the jealous nobles treating you?"

"Had a couple incidents, but nothing to be concerned about. Usually just flashing my Adept Tier Skills is enough to stifle the whining and grandstanding. Some are fine. There's hard workers and talent even among the silver spoons…but it's few and far between." Those who were actually willing to contribute to Elderthrone were afforded greater benefits in the growing town. Apart from just handling the complaints of minor nobility, Alister had graduated into something of a community planner, dipping his hands into relations with the Henaari, the Nagafolk, even the giants.

"Most end up getting sent back down the Temple steps. I try to give them advice on how to establish themselves here, but many don't listen. Still. They've housing in the residential districts. For free, too, since Felix insists on not charging for housing." Alister shook his head. "I don't really understand that, but he's the boss, and it mollifies a lot of the less well-off nobles. If that's the only benefit, I'll be grateful."

"Could be worse, you could be handling the Alchemy Lab," Atar said.

"Why? Did something happen?"

"Just a minor explosion. Acid and oil-based, I'm told. Nearly burned down three of the apprentice stations."

Alister grimaced. "How many did Aenea flay for that?"

"Seems like an honest mistake. Careless beginners attempting things they shouldn't. Not everyone can be as well-trained as our Glyphworks apprentices."

The Crafting Halls worked hand-in-hand on many projects, but Atar couldn't deny there was some competition between them. Harn was constantly pushing to create arms and armor out of materials too strong for Atar to inscribe, and he was fiddling with arrays to enhance their offensive and defensive capabilities without needing the various salves and potions Aenea and Felix produced. The Quests available to him as Glyphmaster—and the other crafting leaders—allowed him to push the capabilities of his apprentices and the Hall itself to the limit; typically increasing production speed, reducing resource losses, and duplicating the effect of inscriptions. The list went on, and Atar had worked hard to unlock as much as he could…and still there was farther to go.

Just as Atar was about to make another attempt at the Masterwork tome, Alister leaned in close. "You sure you don't want to go with Felix?"

"To the bitter north? And then to the Dwaves? I'll pass. If I want to freeze my ass off, I'll just jump in the river here. Save some time."

"But what of Flame?"

"What of it?"

"Challenge and pressure could press you to greater control. Perhaps its voice would not be so loud, were you to strengthen your Will. Traveling with Felix is a sure way to gain levels; just look at all of us that went to Ahkestria."

yes we could grow! dominate this wintry land!

Shut it. "Many who started that journey did not return, Alister. Too many of us." Atar's Mind conjured memories of his mages, barely known but under his command. Dead. Pierced by spider fangs or the horrid growth of vile spores. He repressed a shudder. "No. I'm quite fine with my experiments here, where I can be useful. The Flame is under control here. I can figure out my Path without putting myself into mortal danger every other day."

"Hm."

"If you value it so much, why don't you go instead?" Atar regretted saying it the moment it left his lips.

"And leave you behind? Who would remind you to eat and sleep? Who would wrangle these damned apprentices? Face it, Professor, you would be lost without me."

Atar huffed a laugh. "Don't I know it."

The others could have their glory and levels. Atar had what he wanted.

"You can't be serious, Michael."

Beef gritted his teeth at that name, but he kept packing his large leather rucksack. It was basically a backpack, but he was in a fantasy world. He'd use the fantasy terms, thank you very much. "Of course I am. Hallow is already out there, all three of her."

"Recall her. You cannot go. I forbid it."

Beef turned toward the Chanter for the first time since she had barged into his rooms. She was standing with her arms crossed, dressed to the nines and wearing that sparkly tiara. Barely as tall as his waist, she didn't compare to his muscled bulk…yet a piece of him quailed at the thought of facing her down. "Isla. It's another person from Earth. We gotta save them."

He put his eyes down, grabbed his backpack, and made to leave. Golden-green vines grew across the doorframe an instant before he reached it, blocking his path. "Hey!"

"The rescue operation is work for the adults, Michael. It's bad enough that Felix is putting himself into the enemy's reach…You cannot risk yourself."

"You mean *you* can't risk it." Beef knew she was claiming credit for his growth and progress, that it earned her some sort of notoriety among the Chanters. He saw her bragging about it. "I can help."

"You cannot believe that. Your progress lags behind as you fiddle with your necromantic Skills or those ships, instead of honing your Body."

"Those ships are important! You said so yourself!"

"They are, but that does not make what I said untrue. You need to be stronger. Here, with me and the Cantus Sodalus. We can push you to greater heights than some trek into the frozen tundra."

"Hey, I did a lot for saving Ahkestria! And I fought those dumb High Guards, too—"

"And almost died, child! Think! Do not let dreams of heroism cloud your rationality, Michael!"

Something inside of him boiled over—a piece of the rage he kept simmering at all times. It galvanized him, propelled his feet forward until he loomed over the diminutive Chanter, his bovine nose nearly touching her own. "My name. Is. Beefhammer."

Isla opened her mouth, but Beef was done.

He charged at the net of vines, his horns shredding them as he blasted through. He was gone.

"C'mon, old man! We're gonna be late," Evie said from the porch. Behind her were several Frost Giants, all of them with large, reinforced crates on their backs.

Harn grunted. "I'm comin', ya harpy."

He was in the house he'd built—not in the Stronghold, or at the Foot with any pain in the ass nobles, but in the Scale where the merchants all lived and worked. Harn looked over his house one last time, from the comfortable chairs to the archway leading to his personal smithy. Knick-knacks and rugs covered the space, transforming his sparse decorations into something far softer. Homey.

Palin stood at the far end, framed by the sunlight drifting through glass-fitted windows, running her soft hands against one another. "Do you have to go?"

"I'll be back soon as I'm able. Make sure the apprentices know to keep away from the Leviathan Bone. Except Rafny or Elle. They can make free use of it."

"Harn—"

"Oh, tell Aenea that the latest alchemical bath was her best yet. It improved the helmets a great deal. All the details are in my notes, so you can rattle those off to her if she asks."

"Harn, I don't want you to go."

Harn grunted and looked up. Her eyes were red-rimmed, and her hands clutched at her elbows like the things were about to fly apart. Instead, the list of tasks in his head tumbled away, dissolved into smoke under that stare. "Kid needs me, Lin. They all do."

"*I* need you."

As an adventurer, Harn had gotten used to a great number of

things. Stabbings. Burnings. Blunt force trauma. He wasn't so used to this, though. "Lin."

"Look, I know you need to go. I know that. I just—I only saw a piece of the danger you faced, heading into Ahkestria. I know you can handle yourself. I know how powerful the Autarch is—"

"Just call him Felix—"

"The *Autarch*, Harn. He's stronger than a hundred people like me, more powerful than you, too. He is dangerous, and he draws danger to him like a lodestone." She swallowed. "And because you're a good man, you'll get caught up in that, too. You have a good job here. An important one, running the smithy. Stay and help that way."

Harn sat with that a moment. She wasn't wrong. The kid regularly brought a heaping mess on his own head just by existing. He walked up to her, took her in his hands. She gripped him tight. "My uncle always said I was born to the anvil…but there's times when you gotta put away the hammer and take up the axe."

"Sounds too smart for his own good," Palin said with a sniffle. She let go of him, and Harn stepped back.

"Smart? Nah. Dumb as they come, my uncle, but he knew the world. I know it, too." He walked to the door and stepped out onto the porch. Evie was down a bit, standing with her giants and pointedly not looking at him. "I'll be back, Lin. Count on it. Count on me."

"I will," she said. "I do."

CHAPTER THIRTY-EIGHT

Seeing the Nagafolk off didn't take long, and Felix was thankful for that. He had entirely too much to do and too little time to do it in. Lists of supplies, people to wrangle, and Pit had gone off somewhere without telling him. The last wasn't a big deal—Pit was entitled to his alone time—but when he was setting out on a trip like the one they'd planned… well, even little things started to feel overwhelming.

He and Karys stood atop his Stronghold, near his Bastion of Atlantes and the swooping trunk of the Spirit Tree itself. The winter wind was bracing, and it helped calm his rampaging thoughts. "Karys, have the people I requested been assembled?"

"Yes, all have been briefed on your journey, though the details were held back for the majority, as you requested."

Felix grunted. He didn't like hiding things, and he wouldn't for long, but the only way to stay ahead of events was to keep everyone guessing. Even in his own Territory. "The Chanters?"

"Zara was informed. I left it up to her to speak with the others, as you desired."

Felix didn't love the idea of leaving the Chanters behind; he didn't trust them well enough yet. "I'll be leaning on you to watch over the Cantus while I'm gone, Karys."

"Do you truly think they are a threat to Nagast?"

"I don't know. I want to trust them. If even half of them are as powerful as Zara, they'll prove incredibly useful to the Territory. I just don't know how much Isla's attitude is simply her…and how much is a reflection of the Cantus Sodalus."

Felix trusted Zara to have his back in a fight, but pitting her against her own order? His confidence could only stretch so far. It was why he'd allowed Zara to inform her order of his departure. Depending on how the rest of them reacted, Felix was certain he was going to learn a great deal.

"Evie and Harn are gathering the Frost Giants, while Vess leads the contingent of Claw members to the northern gates," Karys reported.

"Mm." The real question was how to get everyone out of town without being noticed. "I suppose I'll find the first group and use Abyssal Skein to move them to the grove. The Henaari hunters aren't—" A noise filled the air that was a combination of music and laughter. Felix pivoted, peering into the depths of his town. "What's going on down there?"

Karys tilted his big, metal head. "You claimed you needed a distraction. I arranged for one."

The laughter and music grew, and far below, Felix spied a procession of Henaari musicians that wound across the residential Wing district. Behind them, clapping and dancing to their jaunty tune, was a growing crowd of folk. Children skipped ahead, trailing brightly dyed ribbons in their hands as bouquets of blossoms bloomed atop lamp posts and cornices.

Farther up, where the Wing met the markets of the Scale district, a profusion of stalls were piled high with delectable food and sweet treats. They were manned by folks in cloaks emblazoned with his personal glyph, and the moment the crowd reached the market, it spread everywhere, rushing to visit vendors and dance in the swept Fiendstone square.

"Huh." More musicians and singers came from other directions, from all districts, until the market square overflowed into another and another.

"I asked a few of your Shadows to stir up the crowd, get them ready to celebrate, but it seems that was largely unnecessary." Karys closed his eye-fires, clearly listening. "Their joy spreads so quickly."

"No kidding." Petals flowed around the squares, carried by song and scent and a sense of released tension. Illusory glimmers sparkled above them, hung like bunting from the air itself, and they rained down like fallen stars—much to the delight of the children. Food and wine flowed freely, Felix seeing not a single cent exchanged, as shadow-play performers began to tell tall tales. "They wouldn't notice if I marched out of town with every giant singing a dirge."

"If anyone asks, the Lord Autarch will be sequestered within his Temple, doing Lord things," Karys said with a laugh.

"You're a cool dude, Karys. Have I ever told you that?"

"I don't believe those exact words have ever graced my ears, my Lord. But I appreciate them, regardless."

Felix couldn't help his own Spirit rising in the presence of so much enjoyment. His heart bubbled in syncopation. Down below, a young family danced with abandon, treats clutched in their hands. "You did good here. Send my thanks to the Farwalker, too."

"No need, my Lord. " The Farwalker wheeled out in his chair, easily navigating over the rocky terrain.

"Oh," Felix said with a blink. It wasn't often people snuck up on him. "I'll tell you in person, then. Thank you for this."

"There is a reason why most celebrate often in the colder months, especially as the storms of spring approach." The Farwalker wheeled a bit closer, his hood still covering his features in an impenetrable shadow. "A bit of levity to withstand the dire."

Karys rumbled agreement, a metallic sound from deep in his chest. "Governance is a convoluted creature."

"Tell me about it," Felix said. "But I doubt you rolled yourself all the way up here just to say that, Farwalker. What's on your mind?"

The Henaari spread his calloused hands. "Since you are leaving yet again, I hoped that we three could chat for a time."

"About your tenth Pillar," Karys added.

Felix glanced between the both of them. "Teaming up on me, huh?"

"Just working with an ally to work at this particular knot. I am out of my depth. My memories regarding Pillars are clear enough…but a tenth is a rarity I am unsure how to approach. Just as I told you. The Farwalker has provided me with sound counsel a number of times now, so when he approached me about the matter, I saw no harm in discussing it."

"Oh, really." Felix frowned at the Henaari. "What do you think, then?"

"The Henaari do not have records of such a thing, but I know of the realms beyond Master Tier. Pillars. The Tapestry and Revelation.

All of it bound tight with the weight of significance, firmly rooted in the world. It is a heady combination that no few seek…and most cannot hope to reach so far. If they do, they often flounder at the finish line, their foundations too weak to contain the might they seek to bear."

"Not a problem with you, of course," Karys said. "Your foundation is truly outrageous as it is now. The issue comes from introducing a tenth Pillar into things."

"Yes. You must find balance, above all else."

"Balance." If anything, Felix just frowned harder at the two of them. "Explain."

The Farwalker pushed back his hood, revealing a gaunt face that could be anywhere between sixty and two hundred. "The nine Skills that encompass the bulk of your Pillars are evenly distributed across Body, Mind, and Spirit. To choose a tenth Skill that is only of one Aspect would be to introduce imbalance to your foundation. It is our advice that you must choose a Skill that encompasses all three Aspects at once."

"Which Skill matters a great deal. We surmise it will have a… cascading effect on the rest of your foundation. Especially once you incorporate this Core Manifestation as well. The resulting implosion of your core space would render you worse than dead. You would be… nothing." Karys shuddered, setting a loose panel to rattling. "Lost."

That gave Felix pause. "Is that what happens when the Ruin comes? They're...imploded?"

Karys flinched. "Another jagged edge in my memory. You know as well as anyone that the Ruin cannot be recalled. The feelings, however…they linger."

Felix mulled that over. *I'll need to re-categorize all of my Skills. I know Sovereign of Flesh straddles two Aspects, but I haven't fully investigated the rest.* His hands twitched, eager to be on the road so he could start poking at his options. "I appreciate the advice. It makes a good amount of sense, with what I know of the System. Do you know anything about Core Manifestations?"

The Farwalker shook his head. "Precious little. So few of the Henaari have reached Master Tier, let alone anything beyond that. I know that it is a thing that should set the heavens to trembling, and that it represents the heart of who you are. You are bringing forth a Skill built of all of your accumulated choices and designs. Or so the shadow-plays claim. In a more real sense, I suspect that whatever you accomplish with your Pillars will directly affect its creation. I would give your Skills a great deal of thought."

"How'd you find out about my tenth Pillar?" Felix asked the Henaari. He said nothing, only shrugged, but Felix could guess. "The Raven?"

"Perhaps not the most powerful of Urges, but She has ears in the most unexpected places."

"And spreads rumors wherever she can, apparently."

"Not rumors. Truth. It is Her Role. And you do not guard your tongue as much as you think, Felix."

"That's fair. I didn't forget about that Windcaller, though. I dislike being used to start revolutions, Farwalker. People *died* because of the Raven, in Neer and in who knows how many other places."

"Stories inspire. They ignite. But they cannot catch on green wood, Felix. It was the world that piled the kindling high and set us all in a pot to stew…it is not the Raven's fault, nor yours, that it boiled over."

"She's turned up the heat, at least."

"As have you, Autarch. Did you think your ascension would have no consequences? Did you think none would be hurt as this world turns to face the obliteration that comes for us?" The Farwalker toyed with his cloak, fashioned of dark feathers. "It has been hidden from all, but that will not last. The Endless Raven would see it rectified."

"She plans to spread the word on the Ruin?" Felix asked, surprised.

"She does. Do you object?"

"No. They should know what they're dealing with. People in charge like to contain information to stop people panicking, but…this feels too big to be a secret."

"When people know, it will spark fear. That is certain. Fear of the unknown and rage at those who hid it all. But it must be faced, and if we die, then we die knowing the truth."

"When the Ruin comes," Karys said with an echoing, somber tone. "We will all face it together."

"It is a test the world must weather." The Farwalker gave a seated bow. "Your place, it seems, is to lead us."

"I never asked for that," Felix said. He knew it sounded whiny, but there it was. The truth. "I didn't ask for any of this."

Karys laid a dark bone hand on Felix's shoulder, but the Farwalker merely replaced his hood. His features vanished into shadow once again. "None of us ask for our fates. The System touts choice, but we only choose the turnings; we aren't the ones who built the Paths. You're different. You've ***become*** different. You can forge new paths, new trails for us to follow."

He tapped Felix's chest, just above his core. "Primordial. Unbound. King. Fiend. The choices before you are different and vastly more important than our own.

"Choose well."

CHAPTER THIRTY-NINE

Thanks in part to an impromptu festival, everyone made it out of Elderthrone with little effort. Vess was more than a little surprised at that—the guards they had posted at the walls weren't ones to slack off, after all. Yet every one of them had been distracted by one thing or another.

Did Karys set this up? she wondered. Vess had spotted Henaari, giants, and Yttin among the distractors, leading their fellows along the wall or giving them food and drink. She might have been alarmed, were it not for the excitement and joy that radiated from Elderthrone. *Remarkably effective.*

Yes. The metal man is quite adept, Yintarion sent along their bond. He was still curled away between her collar and her fur-lined cloak—even his mental voice was muffled and drowsy. *Please, little Dragoon. Keep your thoughts quiet. Dragons require their rest.*

Of course, Yin. Her Companion had eaten yet another deep river fish early that morning, and it seemed his digestion was getting the better of him. *Rest well.*

Mhm.

The caravan came to a stop a short distance into the forest, settling between a pair of hills that kept them hidden from the walls. Just in case. They were fifty strong, all of them Claw members, and they moved with a preternatural stillness that Vess still found odd to witness. Their efficiency and professionalism was leagues beyond anything they had displayed before, back when they had first set out for Ahkestria. Admittedly, only the best were allowed to accompany them on this mission, considering its importance and danger, but it just went to show how much Darius and Harn had put into their training.

Vess stood at the front, with Harn, Beef, Hallow, and Evie to either side. "Are we waiting for Felix?"

"Aye. And Pit." Harn was in full battlegear, though his armor looked a bit different. Darker. "At ease!"

The Claw relaxed around them, their tight formations softening slightly as small conversations sprouted up among the soldiers. Whether they were Human or Goblin, Henaari or Yttin, they all wore a set of armor with similar elements: dark plate etched with scales, nondescript cloaks, and dark helms of a strange design. All of it had the faint haze of enchantment to her Elemental Eye, but she hadn't the expertise to even begin to identify what sorts. Analyze picked out the details of their make, but only on a surface level. "Leviathan bone. You have made good use of it, Harn."

"Hm. It's a damn good material. Stronger than steel, able to hold an edge like nothing short of orichalcum, and it takes enchantment like a dream." He tapped his own chest. "Upgraded my own set with it, in fact. Was worried my Born Trait wouldn't interact with it properly, but turns out those bones are more metal than not."

"I hate to be rude, but what is your Born Trait?"

"Ain't rude, kid. Resilient Steel." Harn's frog-mouth helm peeled backward as if folding into itself, leaving his head completely bare and exposing his self-satisfied grin. "Despite the name, it lets me have a limited influence over any kinda metal I can touch. It's a Mana and Stamina hog, though."

"I thought the armor itself was enchanted?"

"It is. That just expands my control into something a bit more like a shapin' Skill. Lets me control a bit more, at the cost of even more Mana and Stamina." He pulled one of his twin axes from his belt, and it, too, was made of dark Leviathan bone. The bearded axe head rippled, gaining a spike along the back before returning to its normal look. "Useful in a pinch."

"Hey that's like me," Beef said, his deep voice breaking slightly in his excitement. He hurriedly lifted up a sharp war pick and conjured a spiked maul around its length. "Mine's a Skill, though."

"Chitin, right?" Harn asked.

"Yeah. Wait, no. Keratin now, according to the Skill evolution."

Beef went to scratch his head, but was stymied by his orichalcum helm. "I uh, don't know the difference. One's bugs. The other is…fingernails?"

"Gross," Evie said.

"Wait, no. Imagine I said something cooler," Beef pleaded. "It's like…horns! And claws!"

"Too late, Beefy. Now please put your Fingernail Smasher away, it's upsetting the soldiers."

Vess turned more toward Harn, ignoring Beef and Evie. "Is the bone easier or harder to control?"

"Harder, and the cost is a good deal more than my high steel set." He shrugged, sliding his axe back into his belt. "Worth it."

Considering how unstoppable the man had proven in the past, Vess was inclined to agree. "Is that why you were so drawn to smithing?"

Harn grinned. "Part of it, yeah. Mostly it was just…makin' things is nice, when all you do is destroy."

"You a philosopher now, old man?" Evie asked, turning away from the Minotaur and rubbing her hands together from the depths of her thick fur cloak. Beef was behind her, clutching his weapon to his chest like an overprotective mother. "I hate waiting. I don't care how good my resistance gets, this cold is in my bones."

"You have an ice core, Evie."

"And you have a buncha wind, doesn't mean you can't hate how it messes up your hair."

Vess laughed and held up her hands in surrender. "Point made."

"Good. Ugh. Why're we out here, when we could be Shadowgatin' across the Continent? I'll take some Void beasts over all this snow."

"There is no gate that opens near the Rimefang Mountains…at least not one we can open from this side," Vess explained. "We hope to rectify that on the return trip, so long as we can find the paired gate and restore it." A couple of the remaining Shadowgates showed a series of mountains in their designs, but they couldn't be certain if any were correct.

Vess had once seen an ancient map of her own Territory, etched into metal older than their current Age, and it showed lakes and mountains where none now existed. The Shadowgates were many times older than that map—there was no telling how the Continent had changed. "That is partly why we brought so many of the Claw with us. They can scout far more efficiently while we travel."

"And what're they plannin' on doin'?" Evie asked, nodding at the grip of men and women in heavy woolen travel clothes and fur cloaks a touch finer than anyone else's.

Vess didn't have a clue. The Chanters had joined them moments after their group had left Elderthrone. Ten of them, including Zara and Isla, hadn't spoken to them at all. Instead, they were simply…waiting.

Harn shrugged. "I don't really like the idea of them comin' along, but they're strong. That'll be a help."

"You trust 'em?" Evie asked. When Harn didn't answer except to grunt, she looked to Beef. "What about you, big guy? Isla's your minder, right? You trust her?"

Beef's jaw clenched, but he didn't answer, either. Instead, the small rock Homunculus at his side did. "Mich—*Beef* does not feel comfortable with them at this time."

"You neither, huh?"

"Evie. Enough," Vess interrupted. "If we are to travel together, then it will be better if we can all get along."

"Oh c'mon, Vess! You can't tell me—"

Elemental Eye is level 79!

Invisible to most, the sound-ward around the Chanters burst apart, releasing a series of alarmed shouts from within. The Chanters stumbled back, clearly surprised to find a dark figure at their center, a man whose eyes gleamed like motes of fire.

"Ah, Felix. Just the man we've been waiting for," Zara said. She was one of the few who had not moved; just her and the elderly Mauvim.

"Hey, Zara."

"How did you breach our ward?" one of the Chanters asked. An Elven man named Laur. "I was holding that and did not feel you at all."

Felix just shrugged, and Vess fought off a smirk. Darius might have been training him with swordplay, but he was a student of Harn's, through and through. He turned to Mauvim. "Why are you all here? I gave some pretty specific instructions to Zara earlier today."

The stooped woman leaned on her cane and peered up at Felix's face. "You demanded that we stay put, while you leave on a dangerous mission into lands unknown. We cannot condone that, Lord Autarch. You are too important."

Felix raised an eyebrow. "Are you forbidding me from going to rescue another Unbound?"

The old woman squinted. "We wouldn't presume to do so, Lord

Autarch. We must offer the choice of our protection, however. It is our duty. The danger presented by the Continent is desperate enough, not to mention the threat of the Corrupted."

"My choice is to go without any of you."

Mauvim bowed. "I will respect that choice, just as I hope you will respect mine to send these Chanters on a journey of their own. They, too, have business within the Rimefang Mountains."

Clever. Mauvim was circumventing Felix's approval while still allowing him to save face. She wasn't a fan of the tactic, but there was little Felix could do against it.

Yin roused at her neck, stretching his little claws. *Mng. What is?*

The Chanters are outmaneuvering Felix.

Hmph. Useless.

Vess looked down to see Yin's lizard-like face peek out of her cloak. *What is?*

All of it. What is cleverness before the might of a Dragon?

A massive surge of pressure dropped onto them like a hammer from the heavens. Vess gasped in surprise and she wasn't alone—her friends and the Claw members stumbled, though all retained their feet. The situation was far different for the Chanters, however.

Every single one of them had been brought to their knees.

Felix stood over Mauvim, his eyes truly burning now. Licks of red-gold and crackling blue-white snapped outward as branches snapped from nearby trees, and the snow itself was pummeled into a perfect circle. The limits of that circle stopped just shy of Vess and the others. *His Spirit*...They weren't even feeling the full brunt of it, just the overflow.

The Spirit of a Dragon, Yin said, approvingly.

"I tried being nice about it, but I don't have the patience for politics, Mauvim." The words came out as more of a growl than words. "I told you my choice. I thought that was sacred to you?"

"We...simply...wished to help."

"Hmph. You want to help? Fine." A silver cord swam out from Felix's palm, coiling around and around as the loops formed a complicated knot. "I'll bring two Chanters. I'll choose who, and they will follow every order I give them while on this journey. Agreed?"

The pressure let up, and two Chanters rushed forward to help Mauvim to her feet. She waved them both off and stood under her own power, cane bending alarmingly. She eyed the Oath in Felix' hand. "That would give you a great deal of power over my people."

"It does. If it helps, I swear not to endanger their lives without their consent." The silver knot changed, thickening. "I can't have distrust among those with me."

"Very well." Mauvim took his hand, and the silver knot suddenly tightened between the two of them. Neither of them so much as twitched. "I imagine you will wish Zara and Isla to accompany you—"

"No," Felix interrupted. "I need an expert in wards and an expert with Dwarves and their culture, and both need to be good in a fight."

"I am a dab hand with wards, but no expert," Zara said. "I would suggest Laur in my stead."

Vess raised her brows. *Did they plan this?*

"Excellent," Felix nodded at the Elven Chanter, who looked more than a little poleaxed.

"And I am quite versed in Dwarven culture," said the tattooed Tzfell. She gestured to her Dwarven features. "As you might suppose."

Vess might have imagined it, but Zara twitched her chin, and Felix clapped his hands. "Perfect. Will you take the same Oath?"

They both agreed to it and soon were hunched over as the Oath settled into their Spirits. Beneath Vess' hood, Yin just laughed.

Perhaps cleverness has its place, too.

CHAPTER FORTY

The company marched through the Fogland forests, making short work of the distance with their Tempered Bodies. Zara was happy to note that all of those going with Felix were at least Journeyman Tier, and their Aspects were powerfully bolstered by the Territory's signature Essence Draughts. Distilled from the Spirit Fruit of the Atlantes Anima, they were powerful and nearly universal—hence the ease with which every Claw member plowed through waist-high snow drifts while carrying packs weighing at least half their body weight. Though small, it was a mighty force.

They reached a small grove in short order. It was heavily wooded, nestled so deeply into the wilds that Zara could sense dozens of weaker beasts flee their approach, and almost perfectly in the middle of nowhere. She cast her senses outward, mundane and Harmonic, yet she found no telltale sign of the Dark Passage Felix was meant to access.

Strange. Usually, these things left a mark upon the Continent, typically due to a great deal of usage over the Ages. The Passages in the Verdant Pass, for instance, had small stone pillars that were once decorative indicators. Here, there was…nothing.

The company came to a disciplined halt, with the Chanters trailing some distance behind. Zara walked apart from them, mostly to avoid Mauvim's curious questions. There would be time for that later. *Though, perhaps not too much later.* Ahead, Felix detached himself from the rest at the forefront and made a beeline for her. The unassuming Lord was wearing his usual garb: a thin tunic, dark trousers, boots, and greaves. His only nod to the bitter cold was the thick black jacket made of some unfamiliar fabric.

"If you wish to disdain the cold, then I suggest going all the way," Zara said by way of greeting. "The giants will likely find it more impressive were you to reject the jacket."

Felix plucked at the lapels of his jacket and laughed. "I'll keep that in mind." With a free hand disguised in the folds of his jacket, he formed a series of handsigns. <Keep an eye on them.>

"Please do, it is sound advice," she continued, while her hands fluttered. <Do you trust them so little?>

"As you said, first impressions are important." Felix turned to Mauvim, who had advanced the moment Zara had started talking to the Lord. She was accompanied by the rest of the Chanters, their faces studiously blank. "Zara will be your liaison between my Territory and the Chanters. All questions and projects are to go through her first, and Karys will be the final arbiter in my absence."

"Yes. A wise choice," Mauvim said. The way a few of Zara's fellows' faces twitched was a sure sign that Mauvim's words surprised them. Did they expect her to fight a losing battle? "Zara is one of my most trusted friends. I will gladly defer to her judgment in these matters."

No. Mauvim was canny as they came, and while Felix had won a small battle here, he was far from victory in the war.

Felix merely inclined his head—his etiquette training with Vess was clearly paying off—and gestured to his soldiers. "Commander Kastos, I'll open the rift now."

"Aye. Claw! Fall in!"

The order was needless, as the soldiers had not moved from their resting positions. All of them looked forward, eager to see the Autarch in action. Zara was, too.

Mauvim crunched through the snow, stopping only when she was next to Zara. Her sharp gaze was glued to Felix as he returned to the head of his company. "He moves with surety. You said he gave up the Crown of Ahkestria?"

"He did."

"Hm."

A ripple tore through the grove. It was a thing of wind, certainly, as snow and air was sucked into a widening black rift approximately twenty strides in diameter…but it was also a song of strange provenance that flowed over every one of the Chanters present. Zara rocked back, unable to help herself as the wave hit her Harmonic senses.

"This feels nothing like a Dark Passage," Isla muttered.

"It is chaos…contained," Laur said.

"Some might call that order," Zara pointed out.

"And they would be wrong. This is not the order of Harmony, but it borrows from it." Mauvim tilted her head, her eyes closed as she listened. "It bears the roil of Dissonance far stronger than anything I've felt in years."

Excited murmurs swept through the Claw as Felix stepped away from the star-filled rift. They were far less affected by the vagaries of the Grand Harmony, but their burgeoning talents could pick out the change. It was an air of uncertain danger, and the Claw were eager to face it.

"Forward march!" Harn commanded, taking the lead, and the first Talon quickly slipped into the breach behind him.

"Is this a new Skill?" another asked. Zara thought it was Aidel, but she sounded so much like her sister Dalene that it was a toss up.

"Or an old one, come again?"

That *was Dalene.* Zara knew the woman had an obsession with ancient Skills. All of the Chanters had a taste for history, but a few among them pushed it further than the rest. All of the Chanters were holding hushed conversations, while she and her twin sister were scribbling furiously onto vellum pads.

The rest of the company vanished into the rift, the blackness swallowing every single one of them without issue. Zara studied it, curious as to how it was so different from the Passages she had opened in the past. A fascinated Laur and stoic Tzfell followed the Claw, poking at the rift itself before taking the plunge. They vanished as all the rest, swallowed by an impenetrable darkness. Pit, Evie, Vess, Beef and his Hallow creatures were among the last to slip through, leaving Felix alone to stand before a field of stars.

A piece of night splayed across the earth.

"Be safe, Felix," Zara said. "Stay away from the Corrupted one, and return swiftly."

"You know me," he said with an impish grin. She was struck by how little he resembled that scared and confused young boy she had met in Haarwatch only a year prior. "I'll return within the month, another Unbound in tow."

He slipped through the rift, and it folded into itself with a prolonged, whispering chord.

"A Skill is for certain," Isla said after a moment. "The System is compensating for him. To walk the Dark Passages as we do takes true skill."

Zara, knowing it for a Skill, silently agreed. Apart from the disruptive song of its creation, she had been unable to pierce the rift's construction with her senses. Now that it had gone, she couldn't find a trace of the rift, let alone muster the strength to open it back up. The Passage itself was too faint, too inaccessible to them. Without the System to aid him, it was unlikely Felix would have been able to traverse such a Passage.

Mauvim heaved a sigh. "That boy might reject crowns, but he walks like a king. I simply hope he learns where we stand before that power goes to his head."

She turned and began trudging back toward Elderthrone, the rest of the Chanters swiftly following suit. Zara stayed, and soon a brightly colored kingfisher flew down to alight on her shoulder. He said nothing, merely watched the Chanters walk away. "Where have you been, Keru?"

"Observing," he said. "They do not like him very much."

"Mhm." The fresh air was a balm for her thoughts, already a welter of plans and ideas. She and Felix had discussed a great many things the night previous, and the possibilities whirled through her Mind.

"How much of that was *your* hand, Zara?" Isla had remained as well, and she stomped over, staring daggers at the much taller Chanter.

"I haven't a clue what you're on about, Isla."

Isla snorted her disbelief. "I must say, this Mask is far craftier than Ana or Wrydda. Or did you just take your god's mission to heart? Change is not needed here. We hold ourselves apart. We are meant to guide the Unbound, not *serve* them."

"As always, your point is muddled by your own ambitions." She looked down her nose at the blonde woman, thankful for her Mask's height. Looming was quite effective at times. "We serve the Continent, and the Unbound are the key to saving even a small piece of it from Ruin. Do not forget that."

"I never have and never will. But I wonder if you forget what we risk as that boy places us further and further under his thumb. I'll not be a puppet to a trumped-up Lordling, Unbound or not." Isla spun on her heel, skirts in her hands, and stomped after the others.

Zara watched her leave, waiting until she and the rest were well out of sight before allowing herself a beleaguered exhale. She recalled her words, spoken often to Felix the night before. *This is no small task you set before me, Felix.*

I know, he had said. *And if I didn't think you could do it, I wouldn't have suggested it at all. But the Cantus Sodalus needs to work with us, and the first step to that is communication.*

He was right, she knew, but convincing the other Cantus members would be a grand undertaking. They harbored a wealth of knowledge and capabilities, but all of that was considered quite private. Persecuted as they were across the Continent, a Chanter was almost required to hold their secrets close. Visceral examples were made of those who could not. Theirs was a power that worked outside of the System, a power that the Hierocracy and its allies could not control.

The Chanters were like the power they wielded, just as Felix was: unfettered. It was an inevitable consequence of touching the Grand Harmony. Choice was paramount, and the surest way to maintain autonomy was to hold a tight lid on the secrets of one's power. Foes could not easily combat that which they could not anticipate.

Felix had already convinced them to bend the knee. Only time would tell if the Cantus Sodalus was willing to truly work with him and the other Unbound he was soon to gather beneath his banner.

She stroked Keru's breast, and the little kingfisher cooed in appreciation. "There is much to do," she said.

"Better get started, eh?"

"Just so."

CHAPTER FORTY-ONE

"Well…that's new," Evie said.

Before them was the same floating conglomeration of wood, stone, and crystal as he'd created before, just as large and strange as the first time. Living wood shaped into the form of a huge, four-winged whale covered in moss, flowers, and crystals. Masts shaped like tree trunks rose up into the featureless dark of the Passage, their branches uniformly wrapped around a thick, glowing crystal so that it resembled nothing so much as a magical blimp.

"We call it the Sailwhale," Pit chirruped.

"No, we don't." Felix rolled his eyes, stepping clear of the soldiers as they marched aboard. "Stop telling people that."

Somehow, despite his beak, Pit made a raspberry noise before trotting up the gangplank.

"Kids, right?" Evie gave Felix a sympathetic pat marred only by her Cheshire grin. "C'mon, Beef. Let's go find a place aboard."

The Minotaur regarded the ship with hesitation. "Is there space for Hallow's Bodies?"

"Yeah. Have the Multipede go below decks. There's a hatch near the center of the ship. Her other Bodies can go wherever. Just keep the Skink away from the rigging, please. Those wings are sharp." Felix watched them join the procession, Evie leaping ahead of everyone else while Beef and his Risen waited patiently at the rear.

"A strange creature, that lizard," Yintarion said, floating just to

Felix's left. His own serpentine body undulated through the Manacurrents that coiled across the dark landscape. It wasn't quite air or shadow, but a mixture of both. "Its wings are quite remarkable."

"It's a nasty fighter," Felix agreed. Back when Beef had been looking for more Risen, he'd been the one to point him toward the colony of Skinks that was located between the Stronghold and the Bitter Sea. The teen had found a whole lot of them, including a Skink Matriarch that was twice the normal size. He had ended up defeating it and using Hallow Raise on its corpse. "I had to survive them in my early days on the Continent. They're agile and can spit acid, too."

"Hm. A pity that your subordinate took the only one worth killing—it would have made a fine snack, considering its prior attunement to air Mana."

"You can tell that?"

"You cannot? Its Body might be flooded with necromantic Mana now, but its essence is still stamped by its original nature. That is how that Hallow creature is able to access their original Skills, like the acid spit you mentioned."

Huh. "I didn't know that," Felix admitted.

"Happy to be of service," Yintarion said. "Come, little Dragoon. I wish to rest upon something softer than your armored shoulders."

Vess followed, mouth quirked with a grin as she leaped past Felix and onto the deck of the Sailwhale.

Oh great, now I'm doing it, too.

They were on their way within minutes. Folks settled in with little issue, the majority of the Claw retreating below decks to rest during the short journey. Everyone had been briefed on what to expect in the two Dark Passages they had to traverse, as well as the short jaunt in the middle. They had taken in the strange environment with considerable ease, though notes of fear tumbled through their collective Spirits. Felix could sympathize—the dark mountains, black on black skies, and endless clouds were intimidating.

How would the Claw feel, had they been able to sense the creatures that lurked below?

"I think it's the light," Pit said.

Felix looked down at his side, where the horse-sized tenku was curled up, his bushy tail wrapped just over his hooked beak. "What about the light?"

"It's why they're not afraid. The crystal makes me feel…safe."

The big crystal above them *was* a bright source of blue-white light, and it cast a wide corona around them as they traversed the expansive dark. Felix supposed the light would be calming in such a situation, though he checked his Status Conditions to see if it had any real effect. It didn't.

"It feels like you," Pit added.

Felix looked up again. "Huh."

He stood at the helm, a large, spoked wheel that seemed ripped right from Felix's old storybooks. He wasn't entirely sure of the mechanisms within the ship or if there ever were any—Felix hadn't designed any when he had shaped the vessel—but when he turned, the wings flapped, and the tail-like rudder shifted. The midnight feathers fluttered with each adjustment, undulating more akin to swimming than flying…but it was effective.

While most of the Claw were below decks, there was a small contingent stationed around the railings, posted there as lookouts and guards. Harn was big on vigilance, and Felix appreciated it. He couldn't flare his Perception all the time, and piloting the ship took a bunch of his concentration. A few lingering gazes from them was a small price to pay.

Thankfully, those gazes weren't so bad anymore. Familiarity went a long way toward making them comfortable with him, it seemed, but perhaps it was also a matter of power. All of the soldiers with him were at least Journeyman, and a few were well into that Tier already. It was widely known that Felix was an Adept Tier, though the particulars were fairly muddled. The divide between Journeyman and Adept was great…but maybe the Claw had learned some confidence along with their discipline.

Either way, Felix was happy about it. Familiar faces abounded, people Felix recalled traveling alongside him through the Scorched Expanse. Some were older acquaintances, one of whom was standing nearby, staring with naked terror over the edge of the ship.

"You alright, Mervin?" Felix asked.

The man started but managed a sloppy salute. "Of course, sir. My Lord, I mean."

"Felix is fine."

"Yes, my Lord." He hesitated, opening his mouth twice before blurting out his words. "It is good to see you again. Thank you for including me in this journey."

"Everyone here earned their place." Felix smiled. "And it's good to see you, too."

Mervin gave a nervous grin. "You remember me?"

"Course I do. You helped me find Haarwatch." Felix adjusted the wheel, tipping the ship ever so slightly. "Plus, you covered for me, back with the Inquisition."

"That all feels like a lifetime ago."

Felix agreed with that. "Sorry, by the way. For how we met."

"For—you saved my life from those Skinks. You've nothing to apologize for." Mervin shuddered. "I still can't believe Lord Hammer has one as his helper."

"Oh, that. No, I meant leaving you behind at the gates. With the Inquisition."

"After you, ah, blasted one of them with lightning?"

Felix laughed. "Yes. Again, sorry. It was…a bad day."

"For me as well." Mervin's Spirit lifted, pulling away from the terror that had been boiling just under the surface. "But…I survived. Same can't be said for everyone else."

"We've been lucky," Felix agreed. "I noticed you were staring over the rail."

"Ah. Yes. The dark is just…unnerving. My father used to say only evil dwelled in the shadows. Saw plenty of monsters on the homestead, and few of them ever came around in the daytime. I–well, it's foolish, I suppose."

"It's not foolish. But I've been stalked by things in the daytime as much as the night." Felix adjusted the wheel again. "Light or dark—too much of either is blinding."

"I can't argue against that, sir. Only—the Pathless was a beacon to us farmfolk. After what they've done…"

"Hard to feel too excited about a god that sends goons to kill you."

"Yeah."

Felix didn't press the kid. He had a lot of problems with the Pathless, but it wasn't the time. He let things lapse into silence, but Mervin was all but squirming.

"My Lord, I am concerned. I have a Perception Skill, and it keeps telling me that something is down there. I swear I saw something move in the clouds."

"That?" Felix could feel them, creatures trailing after the ship just as they had on his last journey. "Don't worry about them. I think they're chickens."

"Chickens, sir?"

Felix restrained a sigh. *It's not his fault that chickens don't exist here.* "Cowards. They're afraid to come after us."

Mervin looked askance at the black beyond the ship's light. "If you say so, sir."

The ship pulled slightly to the left, and Felix adjusted the wheel, applying his Willpower and Intent to his strange vessel. "What Harmonic stats have you unlocked, Mervin?"

"O-oh, uh, I have Resilience and Might unlocked. They have proven invaluable. I'm told they aid with recovery as well as feats of Strength—"

A Half-Orc in robes hustled forward before giving a sharp salute to Felix. "Pardon me, my Lord. Might I borrow Mervin?"

Felix flared his Eye, letting his senses roll across the ship's deck. "Sure. Is something wrong, Loquis?"

"No, nothing. Lady Aren is," he cleared his throat, as if the words were hard to say. "Bored. She wanted to spar with a few of us. If you don't mind, my Lord."

"I see." Felix didn't feel anything amiss, so he waggled his free hand at them. "Fine with me. Just tell Evie to leave enough of you to keep watch. Otherwise, Commander Kastos will have you all running laps for the rest of the trip."

"Aye, sir." For some reason, the Half-Orc blushed before saluting and pulling Mervin along with him. They fled to the foremast, where Felix could see Evie had gathered up a gaggle of folks, all of them with their weapons bared. She was limbering up, her chain secured around her waist.

Let her have some fun. She knows not to get carried away. Felix checked on everyone else. Beef and Hallow were below decks. Harn, too, while Vess was sitting quietly at the prow of his ship, dangling her feet over the black. The glimmer of metal around her neck was Yintarion, like a golden stole. Apparently, the ship didn't have any beds, so Vess was his next best option.

Stop stalling, he told himself. He was avoiding his Skills list, avoiding having to make a tough decision. *Status Screen. Skills only.*

The System responded, pulling up all of his Skills, just as he'd seen a thousand times. There were…a lot, and a long time ago, he'd organized them into general Body, Mind, and Spirit categories. Beneath that were things like *Resistances* or *Mental Enhancements* that further divided what the Skills accomplished. But, as time went on, he'd noticed the list was less and less useful—the designations seemed almost arbitrary, but the System had obeyed back then.

What would it do now?

System. Organize my Skills by what Aspects they affect.

The blue window vanished, and after a moment, Felix thought the whole thing had just glitched out. He'd seen *that* before, too. But no, because there was a droning noise just at the edge of his hearing. It grew, growing more tumultuous with volume, as if it were a landslide of percussion instruments bearing down on him. Notes and chords twanged and plucked, squeaked and hummed, pulsing across his senses without sense or pattern.

Until it stopped.

BODY - Chthonic Ascent (Adept)
MIND - Fiendforged (Adept)
SPIRIT - Eldercrowned (Adept)

The blue window reappeared, showing only his three Aspects, along with their Tempered names. The Skills were gone.

"What is this?" Felix reached out and pressed against the first Aspect. His Body.

<u>**BODY - Chthonic Ascent (Adept)**</u>

Dodge (C), Level 83
Heavy Armor Mastery (C), Level 15
Armored Skin (R), Level 88
Blind Fighting (R), Level 78
Illusory Double (R), Level 45
Mantle of the Infinite Revolution (E), Level 74
Labyrinthine Wing (E), Level 1
Wild Threnody (E), Level 86
Chthonic Tribute (L), Level 97
Etheric Concordance (L), Level 84
Hand of Calamity (L), Level 71
Relentless Resolution (L), Level 95
The Song of Absolution (L), Level 94
Last Cry Of The Chthonic Host (M), Level 5

Adamant Discord (T), Level 91
Sovereign of Flesh (T), Level 95
Fiendforge (Un), Level 68

NOTE: Some Skills Listed Fall Under More Than One Aspect. Do You Wish To Display Them?

Felix grinned. *Yes.*

CHAPTER FORTY-TWO

Felix massaged the back of his neck as he leaned away from the System screen, sitting now on the deck of his ship. His Aspects were aching, strained in ways that made his core space feel more than a little shaky. It wasn't so much that his physical form was exhausted, but the metaphysical piece of him that was Tempered. His Body, Mind, and Spirit felt raw, like he'd spent days standing before constant, hurricane-force winds. Though the System had prompted him to display Skills that fell under more than one Aspect, it didn't like actually populating that list. He'd had to prod it over and over again, restarting that cacophony he could hear through his Affinity.

Dissonance rattled through him with each shake-up, the System bucking slightly against his requests before sending things he could only describe as probes back at him. Lancing thrusts of dissonant noise, stabbing at his Body, his Mind, and his Spirit. Sometimes singularly, sometimes all at once, but it was ceaseless. As if the System was warning Felix away from what he was doing.

Yet no glaring "warning" messages popped up before him. There were no glitching menus or alerts. As far as Felix could tell, this was a normal function of the System—and it would happen to anyone that tried to squeeze more information from the System than they were offered.

Regardless, it was finally done. His Skills were sorted.

"Show me my Single-Aspected Skills," he commanded.

BODY - Chthonic Ascent (Adept)

Dodge (C), Level 83
Heavy Armor Mastery (C), Level 15
Armored Skin (R), Level 88

"Wow, that's not a lot." These were the standard displays, and they had been the easiest to coax out of the System. This time, Felix had filtered it so that each Skill listed was only under a single Aspect. "Especially compared to the earlier list."

MIND - Fiendforged (Adept)

Alchemy (C), Level 72
Deception (C), Level 45
Negotiation (U), Level 50
Tracking (C), Level 44
Voracious Eye (E), Level 90

"A bit longer, but still way less than I expected. What about the next one?"

SPIRIT - Eldercrowned (Adept)

Cloudstep (R), Level 74
Green Shaping (R), level 84
Manaship Pilot (R), Level 37
Rime Shaping (R), Level 85
Shadow Whip (R), Level 68
Stone Shaping (R), Level 95
Sunken Ward (R), Level 70
Auroral Forge (E), Level 77
Ferric Shaping (E), Level 1
Arrow of Perdition (L), Level 52
Cardinal Flame (L), Level 94
Rain of Cataclysm (L), Level 76

"Okay, that's more like it." Felix considered the three blue screens open before him as he nudged the helm with his knee. "Spirit has a ton more singularly Aspected Skills than anything else. Is that because of their rarity?" He was seeing a pattern so far, with lower rarity Skills having less Aspects associated with them. But would that play out with his other lists?

"Show me my Dual-Aspected Skills."

BODY/MIND

Blind Fighting (R), Level 78
Relentless Resolution (L), Level 95

MIND/SPIRIT

Exploration (U), Level 72
Manasight (U), Level 79
Meditation (U), Level 79
Invocation (R), Level 77
Bastion of Will (E), Level 99
Deep Mind (E), Level 80
Ephemeral Evocation (E), Level 25
Manifestation of the Coronach (E), Level 80
Multi-Cast (E), Level 83
Theurgist of the Rise (L), Level 92

SPIRIT/BODY

Illusory Double (R), Level 45
Mantle of the Infinite Revolution (E), Level 74
Labyrinthine Wing (E), Level 1
Hand of Calamity (L), Level 71
Last Cry Of The Chthonic Host (M), Level 5
Sovereign of Flesh (T), Level 95

His Body and Mind combination still had the least number of Skills. They were an odd pairing, but the two Skills listed were obvious in hindsight. Blind Fighting was all about utilizing his physical self while mentally anticipating his opponents, while Relentless Resolution was like having his thoughts translated directly into action. Mind to Body.

Mind and Spirit was the largest list, containing almost exactly what Felix would have expected. Still, seeing Exploration there was a surprise.

He would have figured that to be entirely of the Mind, but there seemed to be some extra element there. The Spirit of discovery, maybe.

The last was Spirit and Body, which featured an eclectic collection of Skills. Notable was Illusory Body, mostly for the fact that Felix would have sworn it was entirely of the Spirit, and Labyrinthine Wing, for the same reason. That he could extend his Perceptions into his Illusory Double made him think it would have been a Mind and Spirit Skill, but apparently not. The others made perfect sense, though, especially Sovereign of Flesh.

His guess that low rarity was in proportion with the number of Aspects was wrong. Clearly, he had a number of Dual-Aspected Skills that were as low as Uncommon and as high as Transcendent, the highest rarity he'd discovered so far.

So what's the connection? Is there one? There was one last category to check. "Show me my Tri-Aspected Skills."

The window popped up, but it fought him. Pressure piled atop his Body, Mind, and Spirit like he was lifting something stupidly heavy—it was hard to think. Hard to *breathe*.

A noise like a thousand wind chimes sounded, and the pressure vanished.

BODY/MIND/SPIRIT

Abyssal Skein (R), Level 77
Wild Threnody (E), Level 86
Aria of the Green Wilds (L), Level 88
Chthonic Tribute (L), Level 97
Etheric Concordance (L), Level 84
Skein of Fate (L), Level 68
The Song of Absolution (L), Level 94
Adamant Discord (T), Level 91
Unite the Lost (T), Level 51
Fiendforge (Un), Level 68

"Okay," he said between heavy breaths. Pit was up and staring at him in concern, but Felix waved him off. "I'm okay. Can you steer for a second?"

"Of course."

Felix laid back, fully spreading his six and a half foot frame onto the living wood. The blue screen hovered above his eyes, unable to be ignored.

Most of these are high rarity, but not all. Abyssal Skein is the lowest at Rare. Adamant Discord and Unite the Lost are the highest rarity, not counting Fiendforge. That Skill was a Unique one, a rarity that was outside the normal ranking. Few people ever developed Unique Skills, but they varied in how powerful or even how useful they were. *So, rarity isn't a deciding factor. Maybe it's simply power.*

Maybe. Or maybe reach? Pit suggested with one of his paws on the wheel.

Felix grunted. *Reach?*

Yeah, like. Pit hesitated, bobbing his bird-like head. *Like how Song of Absolution is all of your resistances put together and more. Or how Wild Threnody is all of your Mana Skills translated into physical combat. I've been reading more, and some of Zara's books talked about scope, which is just a fancy word for reach, I think.*

What'd the book say about it?

Pit warbled in his throat, trying to recall. *Something about each Skill having an innate scope. Uh, the way the thing is thinging makes it do one thing versus another thing.*

Felix snorted.

What? It makes a lot of sense to me. Pit lifted his head, pointing his beak into the air. *I guess readers like me are just too smart.*

You're the smartest, Felix agreed as he sat up. *I should read this book, though.*

Pit trilled in joy. *Yes! Reading is fun. It's in my left saddlebag, near the Fang's hilt.*

Felix stood up—he was tall now, but certainly not tall enough to reach Pit's haunches from the floor. Yet, before he could shift his Blade of the Fang, sat so carefully in Pit's barding and saddle, screams filled the too-silent air. "Jesus, what now?"

At the prow of the ship, right where Evie and the Claw had been sparring, a dozen shapes had detached from the black distance. Squirming, seven-foot-long serpents descended, their lengths covered in multiple wings, claws, and too many heads to count. They hissed before falling on the soldiers.

Void beasts. His Eye flared. *Hydragoras.*

Felix took only a single step forward before stopping himself, much the same as the Void beasts. Chains of purple light seized over half of them, halting their advance as if they were suddenly turned to stone.

The rest were hit by a flurry of slashing swords, brutal bashings, and lightning bolts. White fire rained down on the Claw members, breathed by several monster heads at once, but a Yttin with a large shield tanked the hit.

More Hydragora emerged into the blue-white radiance of his ship, their cries fierce and somehow desperate. Evie and the Claw met them without hesitation.

That Half-Orc, Loquis, hurled lightning around with abandon, his spells striking true every time before arcing across nearby enemies. Mervin was out there too, wielding a sword with impressive technique.

Huh. Is that Crane Form? Darius hadn't bothered teaching him that one, but Felix had seen it used a few times.

Even Beef emerged from below decks, Hallow at his side in two of her three Bodies—Homunculus and Razorwing Matriarch. Chitinous spikes, crystalline darts, and the high pitched buzzing of deadly wings filled the air.

"Good," Felix said, settling back on his heels. "They can handle that while I finish this up. Pit? Can you keep piloting the ship?"

"I got it."

"Awesome. I'll just be a few more minutes."

Felix pulled up his Tri-Aspected Skills again. With another twinge of sonic masochism, he pruned the list, removing any Skills that he had Tempered with in the past. That left him with six options.

BODY/MIND/SPIRIT

Abyssal Skein (R), Level 77
Wild Threnody (E), Level 86
Aria of the Green Wilds (L), Level 88
Skein of Fate (L), Level 68
Unite the Lost (T), Level 51
Fiendforge (Un), Level 68

But which one is the best choice?

Abyssal Skein was powerful, focused on eliminating his presence in the world by suffusing himself with…*something* from the Void. It was his only real Void Skill, for whatever that was worth. Wild Threnody concerned itself with the Songs of War, which amounted to channeling his Mana Skills through his weapons—whether it was blade, bone, or fist—and had a certain amplifying effect to them. Aria of the Green Wilds was a strange one, opposite to Wild Threnody really in that the Green Wilds were a counterbalance to the Songs of War.

In the past, Felix had found it mostly useful as an information gathering tool, allowing him to work with natural reagents in his Alchemical Lab that might have otherwise stymied him. It was definitely strong. He had a strong connection to the Atlantes Anima because of the Skill, and Felix couldn't disregard the fact that he had a damn tree growing in the center of his core space. That was not a coincidence.

Skein of Fate and Unite the Lost were...problematic. One was a Skill evolution he'd earned after defying a goddess, and the other was tied to his Primordial Race and cost him an arm and a leg each time he used it. What would happen if he chose either one?

They were unpredictable choices, and all choices had consequences.

The last, Fiendforge, was a Unique Skill and had been essential in aiding his friends and allies' development. His own, as well, though it was mostly only ever used as a sort of stabilizing agent. It would be a safe choice, he imagined, providing an extra layer of solidity to his foundations...but little power.

Abyssal Skein seems good, but I don't really like the idea of putting more of the Void inside of my core space. Wild Threnody is all about offense. I mean, I can always use more combat power, but that doesn't feel right. Felix stared at the blue window before him, tapping a finger to his lips. *Is there something I'm missing?*

The idea nagged at him that perhaps the right choice was a Skill he didn't have yet. It was a tantalizing thought, but all it did now was return him to an earlier problem: even if he *did* learn a new Skill, whether stolen from a Memory or an evolution of a current one, how could he ensure it was Tri-Aspected?

Short answer was: he couldn't.

Not yet, anyway.

Karys and the Farwalker had said to seek balance, and he wasn't going to ignore that advice.

The ship gave a sudden, sickening lurch. Men and women cried out, several Claw members stumbling in their battle with the Void beasts. Felix closed the blue window before him and looked just in time to see a mountain looming in their path.

"Pit!"

"I have it!" The tenku spun the wheel, pressing his huge body against it as if to shove the entire ship out of the way. The tactic would have been ridiculous if it weren't for the huge amount of focus his

Companion put into the move—Felix could practically hear his Intent and Willpower strain as the entire ship careened forward.

They banked hard, the midnight wings straining and the rudder-tail slapping hard against the charcoal stone. The ship jolted, twisted out of true as the deck tilted nearly ninety degrees, and people screamed.

Green Shaping!

Pieces of the Sailwhale burst outward, the living wood grown into flexible vines under Felix's control. People had fallen overboard, and they were too far away to reach with something like Shadow Whip…so he snagged them with the vines.

Pit cranked on the wheel again, his paws and beak moving furiously as his Willpower and Intent thrummed through the vessel's frame. The ship leveled out, even as they fishtailed across the dark expanse.

Pit Has Gained A Skill!
Manaship Pilot (R), Level 1!

Manaship Pilot is level 2!
…
Manaship Pilot is level 7!

Claw members rushed to the railing, several of them starting to haul on the vines as their fallen friends climbed back up. Felix turned to Pit. "You okay, dude?"

"Yeah!" Pit said, halfway between a trill and a screech. "Did you see how I dodged that mountain? I got a new Skill, too!"

"I saw," Felix said, giving him a distracted thumbs up. "Try to keep the Claw inside the ship though, please."

"Oh. Right."

"Why the heck were you headed toward a mountain?" Felix asked.

Pit looked guilty. "Something hit the hull. Something big. I didn't see it, but I couldn't keep this thing on track."

Something big, Felix mused. The monsters, Void beasts all, were being driven back. Lightning sizzled among them, baking their dark hides and bursting the glowing Mana sacs beneath their numerous jaws. None of the Claw had fallen, least of all Evie, Beef, or Vess who had just joined the fray; but the Void beasts had taken a few bites from them.

The ship lurched once again. People fell down, stumbling to their knees or worse, as the entire vessel was brought to a sudden halt.

"See?" Pit screeched. "I told you!"

Felix looked over the stern, and just over the flapping wooden fin of the Sailwhale were a series of thick, pustule-laden tentacles clinging hard to the ship's hull. They emerged from the clouds near the mountain, and four sets of eyes burned with white light.

"Absolutely not," he muttered, throwing himself directly off the ship.

"Felix!"

He ignored Pit, letting gravity take him as he descended at speed. From below, he could see more. The tentacles were far bigger than he had assumed, mottled like a Tenebril, and many, many more were questing up from beneath the clouds.

The creatures were hungry, he could feel that. It was like an echo of the black hole inside of him. Felix almost felt sorry for the creature, big and scary as it was; Void beasts followed their nature. They were scary and gross, but he doubted they were evil.

Still. We're on a tight schedule.

Felix unveiled his Spirit for the second time that day…only this time, he didn't hold back.

A pressure descended upon the Dark Passage, and as it did, the clouds, the mountain, and the darkness itself jolted. Spasmed. By Will alone, Felix arrested his fall just above the clouds, and he glared down into eyes that were bigger than his entire body.

"**Let go**."

The creature convulsed. Without a sound, it detached its tentacles and retreated. Even the mostly dead swarm fled the upper decks, flying after their larger counterpart.

Felix watched for a few moments, Perception and Affinity flared… but none of them returned.

"Hmph."

He flew back up to the ship.

CHAPTER FORTY-THREE

When Felix came back to the ship, he found a crowd of onlookers: Arclights with spells dancing on their fingers, Blades and Bones with weapons drawn, and numerous Yttin and Henaari bearing spears and tridents—ready and willing to mete out death but finding only Felix and the empty dark.

They burst into applause.

Felix stifled his embarrassment as he flexed his Willpower and Alacrity, the two stats that allowed one to fly in the Void. They were a little less useful in the Dark Passage, perhaps due to the sheath between them and the true Void, but Felix had more than enough to make up for the difference. He landed on the stern, the Claw members making space for him, and gestured for them to quiet down. "Anyone hurt? No? Good. You did well. The beasts were fought off, but we're not through yet. Keep your eyes open."

The Claw all saluted, fist to chest. Felix had never wondered what "pride" might sound like, but it was fun to learn. A series of swelling violins and cellos, picked and enhanced by breathy, staccato notes swirled around his soldiers.

It was strong and barely dented when Vess started shouting. "Everyone return to their posts!"

They did, hustling back down the steps from the helm, quite a few returning below decks. Felix spotted mages using their Mana Gauge

Skill to test the air, while others hauled the corpses of the Void beasts for study.

"That Void beast was massive. Is it gone?" Vess looked over the railing, more than a little disappointed.

"It is. Hey you," Felix snagged a Goblin Legionnaire before she could move too far away. "Haiza. Go to Commander Harn. Remind him about using Willpower to maintain your footing here. Tell him I can't catch everyone when they fall overboard."

"Sir?"

"He'll know what I mean. If he has any questions, send him to me."

"Yes, sir!"

She ran off, right past Chanter Tzfell and Chanter Laur. The Dwarven woman watched her with pursed lips. "You know all their names?"

Felix smiled. "I have a good memory. How can I help you two?"

"We had thought to aid you, but it seems well in hand," Laur said. He was dressed in a bottle green jacket that only reached his waist, with a flowing tunic of cream-colored silk and matching trousers. His long, auburn hair was loose, only collected around his temples by a band of woven leather. "A shame, as I was eager to see how my wards would deal with such creatures. They were Void-born, yes?"

"They are."

"I thought these Passages were safer than the standard?"

"They're *different,*" Felix said. "I don't know how much safer they are. Who said that?"

"It is remarkable what can be gleaned by an understanding ear," Tzfell said. "We sought to help, but to do so, we need understanding. None told us what these Dark Passages are, how you are able to access them, or where we are going."

Laur nodded along. "What is to prevent greater threats from intruding through the dimensional sheath?"

Felix opened his mouth to argue, but he closed it again with a grimace. "You're right. But that is for a reason. Trust that we are safe for now, and I'll explain the rest shortly."

The Elf looked ready to say more, but Tzfell placed a restraining hand on his forearm. "Of course, Lord Autarch. We shall be in our rooms until then."

Felix and Vess watched them leave, lithe Elf beside stout Dwarf, neither of them lacking in a certain grace. It pricked at his senses, the way they moved, something he'd noticed before but still couldn't pin down.

Vess thumbed a small monster core at her waist, carved with a series of relatively simple sigils. A sound ward popped up, humming inaudibly around them. "Why do you distrust them so?"

He looked amusedly at the sound ward, but Vess gave him a flat stare. "I am simply following your lead."

"Fair. Less distrust, more...I've yet to see what they're bringing to the table." Felix's easy smile flattened into a grim line. "I've escaped being a pawn for Primordials and gods. I'm not interested in being one for the Chanters."

"Well said."

Felix blinked. "Really?"

"Are you so surprised? We have traveled together for a long time now, Felix. I trust your judgment. And I look forward to hearing your plan." She stepped away, footsteps light upon the deck, air boosting her movement. Her footwork, as always, was deceptive—she was there one step and gone the next.

I agree. Flawless judgment. Pit sent, still standing at the helm. More mountains loomed some distance ahead. *Now, how do you slow this thing down?*

"Erm, maybe I'll take over from here."

They reached the exit a few minutes later, and this time, Felix made sure to conjure a raft *before* anyone exited the Dark Passage. The waters were just as frigid as before, and a small snow flurry had settled in during their absence, but it was simple enough to get his company onto the Rime Shaped raft before moving toward the island at the river's center.

Felix had Pit's book in his hand, though he hadn't managed to crack the spine by the time they had fetched up against the rocky coastline of the island. He was busy thinking, comparing and contrasting his options for advancement. There was no easy answer, and as the Claw disembarked and began to blaze a trail into the island's interior, he tucked the book into a thick leather pouch his Garment fashioned at Will, clasping around the tome so it would remain secure from the wet and the cold.

He really loved his clothes.

Pit was ahead, sniffing through the snow before bounding into drifts twice his size, clearly having the time of his life. Harn led the company, marching toward a spot Felix had marked out on his map. Evie and Beef were chuckling at some shared joke, with more than a few of the nearest Claw members cracking smiles. Vess walked with some others, Blades mostly, illustrating jabs with her spear while Yintarion nodded wisely from her shoulder.

Felix tried to enjoy it, but it was hard, knowing what might be coming.

This next leg should be simple, then the Hoarfrost. Plans tumbled through Felix's Mind, chasing after one another as he considered option after option. He didn't have all the details, was in fact missing several large ones…but it would do. He hoped.

He hadn't expected the attack in the Dark Passage, not really. The creatures had avoided him the first time he'd traveled to the north, but something about them had drawn the beasts. Likely the Mana from so many people. There was far more here in the Foglands than there was in the Void, and even if the Dark Passages had some, it was thin.

Not for the first time, Felix appreciated just how much Mana existed in the Corporeal Realms. He'd grown used to it after nearly a year, but the idea that physical reality was just stacks of vibrating Mana was wild to him. It was thick in the air, like they were swimming through an invisible sea. Manasight caught it all, glimmering and blinding if he focused on it too much. A thousand swirls of vapor, liquid, and solid Mana, all of it vibrated at infinitely variable speeds. As long as Manasight was activated, it was like drowning in a kaleidoscope.

As he'd grown with the Skill, the sensations were less intense. Or, at least easier to navigate. The air tasted of silver and smelled of cold violence banked beneath frigid water. Why? Felix was never really sure, though he sometimes had hints. Manasight was much more than sight—it was synesthesia, a combination of multiple senses that he had found intensely confusing in his early days. He was pretty sure it tapped into the Grand Harmony somehow. Only by letting the sensations flow over him could he make out reality behind the chaos—like those fuzzy illusions they used to put on posters when he was a kid. Focus just beyond the bedlam, and he could see reality in a new way. He—

Tzfell passed in front of him, slipping through the waist-high snow as if through a silken curtain.

Manasight is level 80!

The Mana, he realized. When normal people moved through air

Mana it created eddies and gusts. The Chanter, on the other hand, was slipping through it *and* the snow without a ripple. He looked for Laur, who was doing much the same. *I can't believe I didn't see this before.*

Tzfell stopped and glanced back at him, a small smile on her tattooed face. "He is sharp-eyed, this one. You can see?"

Felix nodded. "I can. How are you doing that?"

"We live in balance, Autarch Nevarre. Harmony. We move as the Realms move." She paused. "You…fight the world."

"What?"

Her lips thinned, and he swore her tattoos shifted. "You see, but you move as if you cannot hear." Tzfell looked up, way up, until she met his eyes. Her irises caught the dim winter light like faceted gems. "You walk in Dissonance."

The Dwarf kept moving, but Felix drifted to a stop. Thinking.

The second Dark Passage was a touch longer than the first, but Pit insisted on piloting the ship again. Felix had agreed, not only to help his Companion build up the Skill, but also for the extra eyes and ears in the case of another attack. A significantly larger number of guards were stationed on deck, and all of them were on high alert. No Void beasts had visited them yet, but they were ready.

Within the captain's quarters, located just under the helm and behind a thick crystalline door, the team was having a meeting. The interior was mostly bare, just as many of the chambers on board—Felix's subconscious was not big on furnishings, it seemed. There was, however, a table in the center of the room. It was large and circular, clearly a scaled-down recreation of the table in the Hall of Songs. Vess and Yin, Evie, Harn, Beef, and the two Chanters were arrayed around it, staring at one another beneath the steady, blue-white light of a crystal chandelier.

Felix drummed his hands on the table. "So. Now that we're well underway, let's discuss the plan."

"What plan? We're just going to the Dwarves and back," Evie said. "Right?"

"Bit more to it than that," Harn grunted. "Gotta get to the Rimefangs in the first place."

Felix pointed at the grizzled warrior. "Right. We're heading north to the Boreal Pass and from there into the Hoarfrost proper. Once I claim the Hoarfrost, I'll be able to use Labyrinthine Wing to traverse the *stupidly* large distance to the Rimefangs. Without it, we'll be traveling for months…by then, we'll very likely have lost the Unbound Gnome completely."

His friends nodded along with his words, their Spirits at ease. The exception were the two newcomers; both Chanters were small storms of turbulence.

"You're simply…taking control?" Laur asked, clearly skeptical.

"That's the plan, yeah," Felix said. "Why?"

"The Hoarfrost is massive, taking up a large portion of the Continent's northernmost edge. No one in living memory has been able to take it from the giants or the monstrosities that live among them."

"My people have tried to take it by force many, many times." Tzfell added. "They have never once succeeded, not for longer than a season, across the breadth of an entire Age."

"Listen, we brought back an ocean to a desert. I think we can take some ice from a few giants," Beef said. When Felix gave him a surprised look, the kid smiled and gave him a thumbs up.

Heh. "I have a plan."

"And what is it?" Laur asked.

"We enter the Hoarfrost and take it."

"That's…not a plan," Tzfell said.

"Sure it is," Harn said. "Two steps. Easy as droppin' an axe."

"We already beat up the ice king," Pit added.

"Grimmar, was it?" Tzfell asked, fingers drumming on the table. "Would the Frost Giants not want revenge?"

"That's not what I—"

Felix stopped Pit with a gesture, instead shrugging at the Chanters. "Maybe. Maybe not. We'll handle that when we get there."

Laur fiddled nervously with his lace cuffs. "With so few? Why wouldn't you bring an army?"

"Too many people. Gets real noisy," Evie said. "Plus, who would watch over our home?"

That was the first time Felix remembered hearing Evie refer to Elderthrone like that. It was heartwarming. "The Witches of Cold Rock Coven will support us when we get there. We've hashed out a deal. The other Covens will likely be opposed, unless they've won them to their side, but we only need one Coven to vouch for us to approach Kingsrock."

"Why's everything called 'rock this' or 'rock that'?" Beef asked.

"Ain't much else up there," Harn said.

"Cheery."

"And this Kingsrock is what, exactly? Another settlement?" Laur asked.

"It is their holiest of places," Tzfell answered eagerly. The geometric tattoos around her left eye twitched. This time, Felix was positive they moved across her skin. "Finding it is an achievement my people only managed once in all our years, and it did not end well for them. None can approach it without dire consequences. Do you plan to fight a war by yourself, Lord Autarch?"

Felix smiled. "If things go to plan, I won't have to."

CHAPTER FORTY-FOUR

A small, hiltless blade appeared in Felix's hand. It was crooked, pitted, and dull along the long edge, but he marveled at the ability regardless. Shaping things out of raw Mana was still a trip. With a flick of his wrist, he threw it down into a post of wood he'd shaped up from the deck. The blade went right through the post and out into the dark.

Hm. No problem doing damage, even with a shitty knife. Felix imagined the same would happen were he to throw a butter knife at someone. A keen edge didn't really matter when you had over three thousand points of Strength. He conjured another crappy blade and aimed it at a second target, another shaped post. This one, however, was wrapped with a Leviathan bone breastplate he'd borrowed.

He threw it a bit softer, and the crude iron shard blasted itself apart.

Okay. Material definitely matters. So far, Felix had only been able to conjure iron objects, and his efforts with multiple tiny daggers had advanced the Skill to level 8 in a short span of time. *What about quantity?*

He focused, marshaling a large portion of his Mana before feeding it through the buzzing pattern of Ferric Shaping. The Skill sang, louder and more chaotic than before, as five crooked blades appeared in Felix's hand.

Ferric Shaping is level 9!

Oh, nice. In quick succession, he threw all five iron shards into the Leviathan bone breastplate. Putting all his Strength behind them, he was able to blast a hole the size of a grapefruit in the center of the armor.

Ferric Shaping is level 10!

Okay. Materials matter less when faced by overwhelming force. Got it. That particular fact was one Felix was aware of generally, but he hadn't ever seen it put to the test. At a certain point, Temper and stats overwhelmed most other things…unless they found a material that could hold up. Leviathan bone was the strongest material they had found, outside the metal the Archon had produced. *My bet is that Merodach had a sort of metal shaping Skill, too. Just a lot more advanced.*

Felix's hope was that, with enough practice, he could push Ferric Shaping to the same heights. Better weapons and armor, formed from his huge store of Mana instead of being mined or stolen from Domains? It would be an awesome benefit to his people.

He summoned another blade, this time copying a sword he knew very well. A bent and twisted copy of his Inheritor's Will congealed in Felix's grasp, blunt and even vaguely rusted somehow. At his hip, a twinned, buzzing chorus sounded—it came distinctly from his two Crescian Bronze weapons. The real Inheritor's Will was the loudest, and Felix's Affinity translated the buzzing into an expression of clear disdain. He blinked, looking between his crude facsimile and the real deal. "Are you mad?"

Buzz.

Felix swallowed. "Whoa. Mad because I made this like you?"

Another cacophony of buzzing answered him, and Felix scratched his head. He knew Crescian Bronze had a Will—it was what made forging it so crazy hard—but his two blades had never reacted to other weapons before. Felix banished the crude blade, and the buzzing faded…and when he summoned another, this one looking like a simple knife, the buzzing was not nearly as loud. Nevertheless, each use of Ferric Shaping after that was accompanied by a certain melody of derision.

Ferric Shaping is level 11!

"Look, I know they aren't good, but I'm trying." Felix patted the hooked blade and the smaller Riposte beside it. Strangely, both weapons seemed…was content the right word?

Before their ship hit the end of their journey through the Dark Passage, he tried a few more experiments. His swords displayed zero reaction when Felix shaped shields or basic pieces of armor from the Skill, which was kinda funny. Apparently, they only disliked *competition*, and the armor, no matter the crude craftsmanship, was beneath their notice.

And the armor was crude. Blocky and too heavy, it looked more like beat-up slabs of metal than anything intended for battle. They had little appeal, and their weight made them impossible for others to use. The first proper breastplate he managed to shape weighed somewhere around a thousand pounds. Few could carry it, let alone fight in it. Felix was going to have to push himself to a far higher Tier to get anything good out of the new Shaping Skill.

Ferric Shaping is level 15!

When the Sailwhale reached the exit of the Dark Passage, Felix was still mulling over his plans. Pushing Ferric Shaping to a higher level was necessary so that he could include it in his Shaping Array, not to mention the other benefits…but he was just killing time. His tenth Pillar remained un-woven, his Skill unchosen.

All choices have consequences, he reminded himself. *But I gotta make a choice eventually.*

He just had to ensure it was the right one.

———

Felix was the first to emerge from the Dark Passage, splitting the starry rift to reveal a clear and crisp field of snow. Large hills rolled across the terrain, but the storm that had plagued the area previously was gone, leaving only bright mid-morning sunshine to sparkle across the ice. The trip hadn't taken very long for those outside of the Passage, though it had felt like hours to the rest of them. As the rest of his company poured out of the rift, Felix checked quickly with Karys, who confirmed that the Passage had performed just as it had the day before.

"It appears to be incredibly stable, my Lord."

"Thanks, Karys. We'll talk soon."

"Of course. I hope to see your list of Territories soon expand."

Felix spotted six blue-skinned giants hustling over a nearby hill. "Me, too." Their connection cut off, and Felix raised a hand toward the approaching Risi Warriors. The lot of them bore spears and axes made of blue ice, but none were particularly aggressive. And they looked really young. Like *really* young, few of them taller than ten feet tall. "Hello there. I assume you're the welcome wagon?"

The giant in the lead pulled up a dozen yards away from Felix before ducking his head. "Lord Autarch?"

"That's me."

Relief sang through his Spirit. "I am Warrior Orvar. We were told to wait here for you and escort you to Cold Rock when you'd returned. This is everyone?"

"It is."

"I see." The young warrior's face was guarded, but his Spirit was like a window into his thoughts. Disbelief mingled with disappointment rippled through him and the other warriors, followed swiftly by a faint ember of something darker. "Follow me, please."

The Risi Warriors turned and trotted back up the nearest hill, and Felix followed. "C'mon, folks."

"We're not going to walk to this Cold Rock, are we?" Laur asked. For all that he moved through the snow easily, he was clearly unused to physical exertion. "It is leagues away, no?'

"Hm. I like it. A little exercise would do this crew good," Harn said.

They crested the hill with little trouble, and Felix spotted a small, ice-shaped hut formed against the craggy sides of the pass. Fetched up against it, though, were a fleet of sleek sleds that had been made by a much more talented hand. Traces of gossamer frost were fitted around enormous, white-furred Hoarhounds that pawed at the ground as if eager to be off.

"Ooo, Hoarhounds," Pit cooed. "They're bigger than me. Lots bigger than the few we have in Elderthrone. Why is that?"

"No clue," Felix admitted. "Maybe you can ask them when we get to Cold Rock."

Pit nodded. "I will."

Orvar and his men were busy getting the sleds ready, but they gestured broadly to the crafts. "Lord Autarch. Please take a seat, and we will take you into Cold Rock."

"This is more like it," Laur said, hustling forward to climb aboard the lead sled.

Felix gestured for everyone else to follow. The vehicles had been made to accommodate giants, so his company was able to fit into all six sleds without difficulty. Even Hallow's Multipede was able to curl up in the bottom of the rearmost one. Before long, everyone was settled in, and the giants climbed into the driver seats. They clicked their tongues before flicking the reins lightly.

The Hoarhounds shot off, hauling the sleds behind them as fast as any car. A few surprised shouts came from his Claw as the frigid winds blasted into them all, but none of them fell out. The ride was smooth.

Felix, seated in the first sled with the Chanters and his close friends, raised his voice over the rush. "Orvar, where is my representative, Kimaris?"

"She has been welcomed into Cold Rock already. The Coven is meeting with her and feting her warriors." His Spirit tilted closer to that dark ember Felix had noticed before, tinged this time by a healthy dollop of jealousy. "She is safe behind our walls."

"And would she not be safe outside of them?" Vess asked.

Orvar spared her a glance. "More than monsters hunt the Hoarfrost, my Lady."

The trip across the Boreal Pass was swift, but it afforded Felix plenty of time to read. The book from Pit was interesting but not particularly long; the information within, however, was dense. Around two hours lapsed during their snowy sojourn, and Felix read over the tome twice in that time. Understanding it, however, would take far longer.

The book, titled *Quintessential Skills*, was written by Pagewright Tern, the same person who had put together Felix's other favorite book, a treatise on ethics and use of power…a treatise that was, apparently, banned by most nations. *Quintessential Skills* detailed the basic function of Skills as interpreted by Tern's studies. He viewed Skills as the System quantifying a reciprocal relationship between cause and effect. For instance, a person who devoted a significant amount of time to learning swordplay would earn Long Sword Mastery.

The *cause* was practice use of the sword, and the *effect* was earning the Skill. In turn, the Skill would confer basic information to the user as they leveled it, which was termed as a "System knowledge packet." Felix agreed with that; he recalled learning new Skills through trial and error and improving a lot at the early levels. Tern went on to detail how those knowledge packets had a decreasing rate of return as the Skill grew in level, and it was then up to the user to learn more actively to push the Skill to higher Tiers. Repetition, stress, and intentional study all contributed to leveling, at that point.

All of that jived with what Felix knew of Skills. Tern himself admitted that this was the most commonly held belief in all the Continent. It was the following section that was the most interesting.

"Above all else, each Skill contains within it a seed of influence. Whether one calls it scope or reach or purview matters little, so I shall call it scope. The scope of a Skill acts much as a Domain does around a monster core: it creates a tiny realm that defines what the Skill can accomplish and how. This is distinct from the pattern of the Skill, though we know each Skill has a unique resonance to them. The pattern is the vehicle by which the Skill enacts its scope. Scope is a reflection of something deeper than the sum of its parts—it represents the potential of truth, translated by the potent System into a discrete unit. A Skill."

If Felix was understanding it correctly, Skills had more to them than he'd first assumed. *So, if a Skill has the right scope, it will broach all three Aspects and achieve something greater. With the right power and scope combined, you get higher-rarity Skills and evolved abilities. Huh. Okay. How do I go about ensuring I can put together a proper Skill?*

The book didn't cover that, sadly. Felix had plenty of experience with combining, evolving, and even stealing Skills, but it was always a crapshoot. He couldn't rely on luck to get him through the coming challenges—even after they'd saved this Unbound, they had to get the Mote of Frenzy from the Dwarves somehow. Then there were the other Unbound to find and whisk away. Other challenges, on and on, until the day the Ruin arrived.

How many more days before that happens? No one had known for certain. Mauvim believed it would be soon, and the Hierophant clearly agreed, considering she summoned the Unbound in the first place.

Don't worry about it, he told himself. *You just have to get strong enough to stop a world-ender. Easy peasy.*

"We have arrived, Lord Autarch!" Orvar shouted.

Through the frigid spray, Felix beheld an ice fortress shining in the midday sun as if it were made of diamonds. It clung to the top of an upthrust rocky butte, the ice spread into crevices and cracks until the stone was all but coated in transparent blue frost.

"Gorgeous," Evie said. She rubbed at a spot just below her chest, where her core was located. "All made of ice, huh."

Ahead of them was a wide-open field, flat in all directions around the fortress. The sleds zipped forward, Hoarhounds guiding them carefully across the terrain as trench after trench were revealed to them.

They were nearly invisible in the glare of the sun, which would have given them a bad day had they blundered into one. Each huge trench was filled with razor-sharp ice spikes, and more than a few were soaked in dark blood.

We move forward. One step at a time.

The sleds navigated an almost invisible path between the chaos, and soon they approached the walls. "Open the gate!" Orvar shouted at the guards, and a deep rumbling sounded from somewhere above. "Open the gate!"

The giants at the gate hustled as much as any huge creature was able to hustle, and the large door lifted up as their sleds approached it without slowing down. Someone gasped as they passed through, their drivers' heads just barely clearing the gap, but Felix was watching something else. The warriors atop the walls were as young as their escort, younger maybe, judging by the plethora of unlined and unbearded faces he saw. Moreover, they looked exhausted, and a few sported bandages around red-soaked wounds. They had been fighting recently.

Perhaps that's why some of the traps had blood on them. Felix turned in his seat, gazing back out over the field. He could spot a couple larger smears on the pristine snow, but most detail was lost in the glare of the sun. Then the gates dropped behind the last of their procession, and his view was cut off entirely.

"Welcome, Lord Autarch, to Cold Rock." Orvar said.

CHAPTER FORTY-FIVE

The interior of the fortress was far homier than Felix anticipated. He expected martial defenses and an abundance of ice; what he found was similar to almost any town he'd encountered up to this point. It had shops, taverns, a smithy, even a kennel for the massive Hoarhounds.

Also a lot of ice.

The walls were made of it, a blue so cloudy it bordered on white. Purple-white Mana vapor was thick in the midday sunlight, gleaming almost as bright as the snow piled high in the corners of the streets. Children with brooms, dressed in leather and fur, worked hard to keep the snow contained. Felix assumed they were children, at least, based on their slender limbs and basic proportions—basically Humans, save their blue skin and six-foot height. They were the first to notice the strangers in their midst, and their chubby faces spread in excited grins.

"Ta lana! Kas ta lana!" one of them cried out.

As his company exited the large sleds, the hustle and bustle of the town ground to a halt. Older women grabbed their children, pulling them back as they regarded Felix's team with fear. Rotund shopkeepers emerged, axes and hammers in hand, while mothers and youthful female citizens lifted four-foot long knives made entirely of ice.

"Tu roun! Morvena ais koma!" Orvar shouted into the tense silence. "Set aside your wrath! They have been invited by the Coven!"

As if the words were a magic spell, weapons disappeared, and the people returned to their chores and duties without a single word. Only the children seemed unaffected, their curiosity singing as brightly as their boredom.

"That's about the welcome I expected," Evie muttered. Harn was next to her, hands caressing the hilts of his axes as he scanned the area.

Beef let out a huge, whooshing breath. "What the heck was that about?"

"The Risi do not suffer intruders," Tzfell said, and her sedate voice was troubled. "Laur. Where were your shields?"

"Summoning a ward is just as dangerous as drawing a weapon," the Elf said, hand to his chest. "Did you wish to escalate things further?"

"Calm down, everyone," Felix said. "And keep your weapons and spells to yourselves. The last thing I want is a massacre."

"And if they give us no choice?" Tzfell asked.

Felix frowned down at the Dwarf. "Then I will handle it. Understand?" She bobbed her head but said nothing else. He looked to Orvar. "Where do I find the Coven?"

"Their instructions were to wait just inside the gates," the young warrior said. "An escort would come to relieve us."

"And so it has."

Down the wide thoroughfare came a handful of familiar Risi Warriors, led by the youthful figure of Kimaris. Her white hair snapped in the arctic breeze like a flag, billowing almost as much as the purple and black gown and cloak she wore.

Felix smiled. "Kimaris. Battlelord Vidar."

The lot of them—Witch and Warrior—stopped a dozen feet before his company and dropped to a single knee in unison. Fists went to heart and earth. "Lord Autarch! Hail the king!"

Felix maintained his smile. Barely. He gestured for them all to rise to their feet. "You're leading us to the Coven?"

"I am," Kimaris said. She pointed further up the street, where the road wound up a steep cliff toward a structure made entirely of icy columns. "The Coven awaits within the Frostfather's Embrace."

Looks like the little hut they had in the Domain, Pit sent.

You're right. To Kimaris, he said, "Alright. Let's get moving, then. I don't want to waste time."

"As you wish, my Lord." Kimaris made a shooing motion at Orvar, her manicured nails gleaming in the sun. "Go on, boy. We'll take them from here."

Orvar grimaced, and that dark spark inside him flared up just a bit more. It was anger and rage and several other emotions packed together so tightly that it was hard for Felix to pick them all out. He seemed poised to say something—do something—but the young warrior only ducked his head and left with his men, hustling up the same central road.

"There is a lot of anger in him," Vess said in a low voice.

"In all of 'em," Harn pointed out. "This place is boilin'."

"Where's he going?" Evie asked.

"To report on your arrival, I don't doubt," Kimaris said before turning her wide grin on Felix. "Thank you for returning so soon, Lord Autarch."

Felix could feel the strange miasma of discontent all around them, now that his friends pointed it out. It was so omnipresent that it felt almost environmental. "Is there a problem?"

"What is a problem, but an opportunity to change things to our advantage?"

"So that's a yes."

Kimaris' beautiful face creased with a faint grimace. "The majority of the Coven supports your claim on the title of Chieftain, but there is a vocal minority that does not. We have been trying to sway them but, well." She cleared her throat. "My people are almost as stubborn as the Dwarves."

At his side, Tzfell snorted derisively.

Kimaris' nostrils flared, but she ignored the Chanter. "Lord Autarch? If you will follow me."

"Keep an eye out, folks." Felix inclined his head and motioned for everyone to get moving. He stepped up until he walked just behind Kimaris' billowing cloak, while his sworn Risi Warriors surrounded him like a guard of honor.

Harn marshaled the Claw behind them, and soon everyone was marching in formation up the winding road. Evie took up the rear for some reason, but Felix didn't question it. She knew what she was doing. Felix marched at the head, of course, with the Chanters and the rest of his friends close to hand. Pit had tried insisting that Felix ride him, but caution had won over the need for pomp—with his friend's open wounds, Felix feared exacerbating them with his legs. Pit had glumly agreed.

The journey through Cold Rock was illuminating for a number of reasons. For one, Felix had never really seen any Frost Giants, aside from the Risi Warriors and Witches. Frankly, he'd thought that was the extent of their society. Now, though, he saw giant merchants, butchers, hunters, blacksmiths, and even tanners. The last one was pretty gross, if only because of the gnarly tanning pits that Felix could smell from hundreds of yards away. Sometimes high Perception wasn't so great.

More amusing was the gaggle of children trying—and failing—to stealthily tail their group. They kept running into one another and giggling, which drew a smile from more than a few of the Claw.

The second and far more important realization Felix had was how much Grimmar had damaged Cold Rock. While there were people around, all of them were very old or young, with a rare few actually looking something like an adult like Orvar. Grimmar had taken the best and strongest with him when he invaded the Foglands, following the siren song of the Maw…and Felix had just about killed them all.

Not all of them, he reminded himself. Kimaris and the others in Nagast had been saved, reverted back to their natural forms after the Archon had turned them into monstrous Arcids and mindless Reforged. *But also not nearly enough.*

He'd killed a lot of giants…creatures the System designated as monsters. A Type, not a Race. The people of Cold Rock made it clear that the System was wrong.

Why is it like this? Inside his chest, his Hunger rumbled. *Wasn't asking you.*

Hungry.

Felix blinked. His Hunger had been quite silent recently. *You'll get food soon, promise.*

Yes. Food Is Coming.

That's what I said. Felix rolled his eyes. His Hunger was a lot like Pit in many ways—one-track mind. *Hold tight.*

"Quite civilized for monsters," Tzfell said, following his gaze. Beside her, Laur sniffed.

"I've seen very little reason for them to be classified as monsters." Felix pointed at a Risi woman hanging a bundle of clothes over a low fire, a large baby bound to her back. The woman was singing, and the baby was fast asleep. "I've seen scenes like this in just about any town."

"The designation of Type is not something for us to question, Lord Autarch. Monster or mortal, it is the System that decides such things. For the System is but an arm of the music that shapes us all," Laur said, as if explaining something fundamental. "You could say it is the will of the Grand Harmony."

Felix curled his lip. "The System is not infallible."

"I never said—it is the choices we make that determine our lives—"

"And if you were born a Type instead of a Race? What choice was it that decided that?"

"Well—monsters rarely have the ability to form a potent Mind. Few would ever notice. They are animals."

Felix scowled so hard at the Elf that he took several steps back. He pointed again, this time to the Risi children that were following their procession. "Do they look like animals?"

"I—I only meant to say—"

"That Types are monsters. No. I got that." Felix took a breath, calming himself. "The Inquisition calls their enemies monsters, too, you know. Choristers, Sorcerers, whatever."

"I'm aware."

"Then you know why they do that, right?" Felix's memories flashed back to the sewers beneath Haarwatch, where worshipers of the old gods died in droves while the Inquisition filled them with fire. "It's way easier to kill a monster than a person."

Felix greatly doubted anyone that claimed to know the will of a greater entity, whether that was the System or the gods. It didn't help that he didn't really trust the System, and he *definitely* didn't trust the gods.

Soon, the pathway opened up to the church-like structure at the very top. It loomed high to Felix, though it seemed a bit more normal when compared to the general dimensions of the Risi. Like the chapel in the Ironskin Domain, the building was made of icy staves curved into a swooping shape that came to a high peak and left a large portion of the flooring wide open. Twenty-foot-tall windows covered nearly every wall, all of them made of perfectly transparent panes, yet none of it looked delicate or weak. If he focused on it, the Mana that filled the walls shone like the sun itself, so thick was it layered into the ice.

Kimaris led them through the large double doors and directly into a familiar chamber. The interior had no walls and occupied the entirety of the structure. Aside from a tall altar with a glass-like orb at least five feet across, the only real decorations were chairs made of stone, all of them arranged in rigid lines before the orb. Just beyond it was another set of chairs—thrones, almost—facing the others.

All of them were filled with Witches.

A youthful guard tapped their spear against the ground, and the sound rang out like a bell. All of the Witches that didn't notice the doors open pivoted in their seats to see the newcomers approach. "Announcing Kimaris, Witch of the Waters!"

Kimaris' shoulders twitched at the title for some reason, but the Risi woman smoothly entered the arrangement of chairs, Felix and his company trailing behind her. "Witches of Cold Rock Coven, allow me to introduce my liege: Autarch of Nagast, King of Ahkestria and the Leviathan Depths, Returned God of Thunderflame, the Blue-Eyed Fiend, Felix Nevarre."

Inwardly, Felix groaned. *Ugh I need to remind people to stop using the Returned God one.* Outwardly, he kept his face stoic and stepped forward until he was just ahead of Kimaris and her warriors. Pit kept pace at his side, a warm presence in impressive armor, while his friends moved slightly so they were arrayed just behind him. "Well met, Cold Rock Coven. I am happy you agreed to meet with me."

"Well met, Autarch Nevarre. I am Vepar, leader of this Coven. It is rare someone so…Titled would deign to speak with us." The woman speaking was in the center of the front row, a seat Felix would have assumed was reserved for the leader, even had she not said so. The seats were elevated, putting the already huge giants well above his party. Naberius, Sitri, and Berith flanked her but said nothing. "Your kind typically only come for our heads."

"I assure you, I am here in peace. I only wish to claim what is mine, as the Ironskin Champion." An unsettled murmur spread through the Witches, but Felix waited.

"Show us," the woman demanded. Her eyebrows were thick and aggressively angled, though her Spirit was more or less calm. "How far did you walk down the Path of Rule?"

Felix lifted his hand and summoned a blue screen with his Title before motioning it outward. He ignored the various youthful guards and sent it only to the attending Witches.

Ironskin Champion IX (Epic)!
You have successfully conquered the ninth layer of the Ironskin Domain, proving your worth to the Frostfather! +20 END, VIT, DEX

Gasps filled the ice church, and whispered words followed.

"The Frostfather—!"

"*Ninth* layer!"

"—farther than any other—"

"Silence!" Vepar demanded, her eyebrows as fierce as her voice. She regarded Felix from her elevated position. "Your completion of the Path of Rule is noteworthy, Lord Nevarre. It is clear you are mighty, for a Human. For this reason, I am willing to enter into a peaceful treaty with your kingdom. But we cannot support your approaching Kingsrock."

"Mother Vepar, you cannot be serious! Not only did he complete the Path of Rule, as you have admitted, but he fixed our Domain!" Kimaris looked out to all the Witches, encompassing them in her words. "The source of our training and sustenance. Without the Domain, Cold Rock would be finished, and that is at the feet of this man."

"We would not be so beholden to the Domain, had your beloved Grimmar not ripped our warriors and hunters away, Kimaris," Berith snapped.

Vepar raised a hand. "Enough. I will be the first to admit that he has done a great service for our people. And he has progressed farther than any Risi Chieftain in living memory…but he is not of the Kin." Nods of agreement started spreading around the chamber as the Witches caught onto her meaning. Vepar regarded Felix with cold eyes. "You cannot approach the Kingsrock."

Felix shrugged before summoning another Title and sending it out. To everyone.

Conqueror of Ironskin Domain (Legendary)!
You have achieved what no one else has in the history of this Domain: defeated the Frostfather in combat. Your connection with ice, stone, and metal Mana has deepened, and your dexterity with all three elements has increased!

No whispers met this revelation, only shocked, breathless silence.

Vepar cleared her throat. "But, who are we to gainsay the will of the Frostfather?"

Felix almost laughed. Those words had cost the old Witch something to say, judging by her pained expression. He only inclined his head.

His people had read the Title but seemed unconcerned. The other Witches all watched, their Spirits as flabbergasted as their faces.

"Ahem. If you wish to approach the Kingsrock, then you shall need an army. Normally you would have a clan of advanced warriors to aid your approach, but we are at a distinct disadvantage. Our warriors have been greatly depleted due to *this one's* interference." Vepar gestured at Kimaris, who flinched. "We cannot spare any of our people, Lord Autarch."

"That's fine," Felix said. "I'm good with what I have here."

Vepar leaned forward, her age-spotted hand clutching the arm of her throne. "The approach to the Kingsrock is filled with great danger. Not only from the terrain and the beasts below, but from *us*."

Felix frowned. "Explain."

Naberius spoke up. "If I may, Mother."

"You may."

"All clans are alerted when the Kingsrock is approached, and even the weakest will mobilize. The approach is an opportunity to test ourselves against one another, but also to claim the riches within the trapped fields around the Kingsrock. To be chosen as our new Chieftain, you must reach the Kingsrock and defeat all contenders that have walked the Path of Rule."

"I thought people either made it or died?"

"Many live, having achieved only the first few layers. They are still highly regarded, but they are not fit for the role of Chieftain," Vepar said. "If they defeat you, however, they will take your Title for their own."

"They can *do* that?" Pit asked. Several nearby Witches jolted in surprise at his voice.

"They can, Honored Tenku," Naberius said. "It is our way."

"We can deal with the issues as they come up, I'm sure," Felix said. He was more than confident in himself, and his people had proven themselves time and again. "Just point us in the right direction, and we'll be out of your hair."

"Indeed. We must open the way to the Kingsrock…it is not a place that can be reached by normal means. Allow us a day to prepare, Lord Autarch." Vepar drummed her skeletal fingers on her chair's arm. "So long as we are not opposed, the initial steps will proceed smoothly."

"Feldspear has been raiding our hunters these last few months. Your fixing of the Domain means a great deal for that reason, above all else," Naberius said.

"Feldspear?" Felix asked.

"Feldspear is our sister Coven to the north. They did not support Grimmar as much as we did. *I* did," Kimaris explained, a flush of anger in her cheeks and regret in her Spirit. "They held back their tithe of warriors."

"Meaning they might pose the greatest challenge to us before we can arrange for the approach. After that is another story entirely." Vepar gestured for the other Witches to gather. "We must—"

Food Is Here.

“What?” Felix asked, hand to his chest. Vepar looked to him.

“What is going on?” Vepar asked, her impressive brows drawn. One of the young guards ran up to her and started whispering. “What do you mean? If it’s an attack, then the horns would sound!”

A basso note shook across the earth and sky, shaking chips of ice down from the ceiling and jostling their insides. Felix felt the sound in his *teeth.* Gasps rang out around the chamber as the Witches began summoning their aides.

Yum.

CHAPTER FORTY-SIX

"There's an attack?" Felix asked. All around him was chaos as warriors hustled to and fro, beckoned and dismissed by the various Witches. How the hell did his Hunger know?

"It appears so," Kimaris said, and hissed when the horn ripped through the air again. "Two blasts means they've come with a significant force."

The orb in the center of the room burst to life, its murky insides suddenly animated as the elderly Sitri laid her hands upon it. "It is a mighty host. It seems our sisters in Feldspear no longer wish to wait."

"Of course not!" Vepar exclaimed. Her pale blue skin was patchy with bright purple spots across the wrinkles. "And they've come with all their might, which easily outstrips us, thanks to you, Kimaris! Sitri, how many?

"I count…two hundred Risi Warriors…sixty Hoarhounds…fifty Berserkers—"

A screech emanated from the sky, far fainter than the horns, but it sent a cold thrill through Felix. He knew that sound. "Brumalbats." He rushed to the windows overlooking the gates, blurring past dozens of Witches. They were specks in the sky, even to his vision, but they were advancing toward Cold Rock at speed. "I count over a hundred."

"Ooh. They taste good," Pit said. A few Witches looked at him askance. "What? They only burn a little. Like that leafy thing. Felix, what's that leafy thing called?"

"Mint?"

Pit trilled, happy to remember the word. "Mint! Yes. Their cores taste like mint." He clacked his beak. "I would like some more."

Felix tapped his lips while the Witches scrambled, issuing orders to knots of warriors. The tread of giant feet was a counter rhythm to the distant beat of Feldspear's drums. He could see them, just beyond the lip of Cold Rock's walls. Armored Risi Warriors lifted weapons into the air and shouted things in their language that drove their fellows to cheer. Hoarhounds snapped their jaws, eager to be released, big as horses and a thousand times meaner.

At the lead, a smaller selection of giants stood separate. They wore no armor, their blue skin totally bare save for the crimson-dyed furs wrapped around their shoulders and waists, and they were unarmed except for their huge fists. Felix's Eye tagged them as the Berserkers, which made sense. He focused on their entry, ignoring everything but their name and lore.

Name: Risi Berserker
Lore: An Evolved form of the Risi Warrior, Berserkers have learned to draw strength from the beasts around them and have chosen a Path of Cold Rage. They can draw upon their anger to power their magic, supplementing their natural born gifts of ice and granting them a short-term boost in Strength, Endurance, and Vitality.

They charged as one.

The unarmed giants hit the spike pits well before the larger force, and they proved ineffective. Crimson ice flashed around them, matched to their strange pelts, and formed a set of brutal armor. They leaped over the pits, ramming through the ice spikes without slowing. Arrows and rocky projectiles flew from atop the walls, impacting the raging Berserkers with even less effect. Seconds later, they hit the walls of the fortress town. Ice tumbled off of it as crimson light splashed into the defenses. They held, for the moment.

Mother Vepar was deep in conversation with Sitri and some other ancient-looking giants while the charismatic Naberius moved around the room, directing the flow of Witches and Warriors. "Mobilize everyone we can! Witches! To the walls! If Cold Rock falls, we will not survive the night!"

Below, the gate trembled.

Their orders grew increasingly shrill as ice cracked and fell off Cold Rock's walls. White-haired Frost Giants scurried out of the stave church, magic coiling about their hands and feet in equal measure.

They're panicking, Felix realized. Ideas blossomed and wilted in rapid succession in his Mind. His Perception fed him countless bits of information, all of it chaotic and piecemeal, but there was something there. A Path forward, he knew it—his Perception snagged on something. *Oh. Interesting.*

Kimaris, at nine feet tall, easily watched out of the same window as Felix. "They won't last. They're too green. Vidar, can we bolster the defenders?"

The Battlelord shook his head slowly. "We can, but even we don't match up against the Berserkers, not at those numbers."

"We have to try," Trond, his second-in-command, said. His Oathbound Frost Giants all watched with despairing expressions.

Harn drew close, his voice low. "Felix. What do you wanna do?"

Eat Them.

Felix ignored that. "We haven't finalized any agreement, but Cold Rock is an ally. There's only one thing we can do." He bared his teeth. "Show Feldspear who they're messing with."

"Aye. Claw! Attend!" Harn stomped toward their company of fifty soldiers, axes leaping to his hands. "Autarch says we're headed to the wall. Swords, Bones, and Fists with me. Arclights, Dawnwalkers, and Yttin Divers go with Captains Aren and Dayne. Do us proud."

"Aye!" Feet stomped and bone plate clattered as the Fiend's Claw saluted in confirmation before rapidly splitting up. Harn and his people headed out the doors immediately, leaving at a sprint, while the rest congregated around Evie and Vess.

"My Lord—" Kimaris started.

Felix cut her off, speaking to the warriors behind her. "The Claw will take the brunt of the attack, but I'll need you and your Warriors to back them up. Are you up for that, Battlelord?"

"Tu falla, Autarch. We serve."

The giants saluted Felix, much as his Claw had, and followed them out on fast feet.

"And what of me?" Kimaris asked, her voice sharp. "Am I to remain here, held separate from my warriors?"

Beef raised a hand, three forms of Hallow peeking around his wide Body. "Uh, I'd like to help too."

"You're both with me." Felix let his Perception swell, taking in as much of the battlefield as he could, sifting it all through his potent Mind. "We have a different task."

Evie and Vess led their team onto the promontory just outside the fancy ice house, where the mages and ranged fighters started preparing their Skills. Arrows began to glow in quivers, hands were wreathed in elemental Mana, and a few of the Yttin even started praying. Something about a "beast."

Weird, but if it helps, Evie thought with a shrug. The ice bats were coming into normal view now, almost reaching the walls of Cold Rock, and her heart thudded in her chest.

"Flyin' monsters." Evie rubbed her hands, an eager grin stretching her lips. "Haven't fought any sky creatures in a while. Eh, Vess?"

"It is a nice change of pace," the prim warrior agreed.

She knew Lady Dayne better than most; they were best friends, after all. Vess was just as excited about the fight as Evie was. Spears formed around her, conjured from metal and air and angled toward the oncoming threat. The Dragoon even brought out that pack of discs she'd gotten from the snakes. Evie hadn't seen how effective they were, but she was really curious.

"Hm. Low-Tier creatures," Yintarion said, still lounging beneath Vess' collar. "Not worth the effort to eat."

Lazy lizard. Evie rolled her eyes. "Don't let us interrupt your nap time."

A small snort of smoke emerged from Vess' shoulder. "You're lucky you're not worth the effort, either."

"Oh you little—"

"Enough. Focus on the Brumalbats. Take them down now, argue later."

"No no, they're mine," Pit protested from behind them. He trotted forward into the sunlight, barding gleaming. "I called them already!"

Evie shrugged. "We're just followin' orders. Felix didn't say nothin' about you in the fight."

Golden eyes glared at her so hard, Evie was afraid she would catch on fire. "Felix isn't the boss of me."

"You will fight with us, Beast?" one of the Yttins asked. Evie blinked. He was addressing Pit.

Pit puffed out his chest, the metal scales of his barding glinting further. "Of course. I'll rip them apart."

The Yttin Divers, ten in total, separated from the group and all bowed to the Chimera. "Lead us to the End."

"Uh, that's—do they mean the end of the battle?" Loquis asked her. He regarded the armored warriors with more than a little unease.

"Sure. Maybe. Don't worry about it, Lightnin' Boy." The sound of screeches grew louder, and magic flickered across the blue sky. "Bat's are closin' in. Form up! The town ain't too big! We can reach them from this ridge!"

Mages and Henaari hustled forward, lining the promontory edge before the ice house. To the side, Vess bowed to Pit. "I'd be proud to have you fight with us."

Pit cooed. "Thank you. I can help."

"I know you can." Vess gestured to the Divers around him. "Please take the Yttin to the forefront, where your harpoons and Skills can have clearer shots."

The lead Yttin saluted. "As you wish, Captain."

Evie was barely listening. Leading was more boring than fighting, and her targets were coming into range now. She uncoiled her chain and felt the cold hands of her magic spreading outward around her like a cloak. She shivered.

Today was a good day.

The gates were bowing inward by the time Harn and his people got to them. He motioned furiously for the guards at the nearby winches. "Open the gates!"

"Raktu las! No! Crazy Human!" spat one of them. The rest just looked terrified, of him and of the attacking army.

"Open the gates, young Warrior," said a deeper voice behind him. Harn turned to find the looming form of Battlelord Vidar standing with his own warriors. The giant inclined his head toward Harn. "We will fight for Cold Rock today."

The angry giant clenched his jaw several times before huffing a steaming breath. He kicked free the wedge holding the winch wheel in place, and dark metal chains started moving. At the same time, the gates themselves rocked as a crimson glint smashed into it from the other side.

"Hold formation," Harn ordered.

The gates burst apart, and a twenty-foot-tall, red-armored giant marched through. Shouts rang out, and ice-forged claws slashed out of the ground, while spears and throwing axes rained down from the young guards. The huge Berserker shrugged it all off, laughing viciously as he pushed into the town…and met Harn.

"Little Human with metal skin," the Risi leaned forward, a sneer distorting his bearded face. His armor was made of red-tinted ice, and a mantle of similar colored fur framed him against the now-broken gates. More of his warriors were moving inward, but they slowed, eager grins on their faces. "Is this a treat for us, Cold Rock? Do you give us tribute to earn our mercy?"

"Blind gods, but you're ugly," Harn said.

"What?"

"Stupid, too."

The Berserker bellowed and dropped an ice-coated fist atop Harn. The stone around them cratered, deep fissures splitting in all directions before shards of rock were spat upward by the force of the blow. But there was no blood.

The giant goggled. "How—?"

Harn still stood, one arm upraised and holding the Berserker's icy fist. He regarded it from beneath his visor. "That's it? Wrath of the Twin Fangs!"

The giant stumbled back, his arm now fountaining a dark blue ichor onto the ground as he screamed. Harn clucked his tongue. "Too easy." He pointed his sizzling axe forward, just as the other Berserkers started rushing the gate. "Forward, all Talons!

"Kill 'em all."

CHAPTER FORTY-SEVEN

Harsh screeches scratched at Loquis' ears, and it was all he could do to shout orders over the din. The Brumalbats swarmed the blue sky, their ice-wreathed wings glittering like diamonds in the sunlight. They were huge, easily the size of a man, with twice the wingspan. A few weapons were hurled from the town below, but the simple black iron spears clattered harmlessly off their hides as the beasts swooped down. Women and children ran through the streets and into their homes, but they weren't fast enough.

"Aim for any that swoop too low to the town! Keep them from the people!" he said.

Arrows and magic ripped from the Claw members, their Skills singing brightly in Loquis' Affinity. Compared to the ineffectual spears, the effect was astounding. Perhaps forty of the giant bats were mortally wounded, with half as many somewhat wounded.

You Have Killed A Brumalbat!
XP Earned!

Loquis lowered his hand, staring at the horde. He wasn't sure if his lightning spells had actually killed them or just hurt a bit, what with the amount of attacks darkening the sky. They'd need another volley to be sure of the creatures' resistances.

Before a second attack could be mustered, three dozen bats peeled off from the main horde and immediately wheeled toward their position. Loquis shouted a warning, and the mages to his left and right unleashed a torrent of lightning Mana. A number twitched and faltered, but only a single severely wounded bat actually perished.

He cursed. "They're resistant to lightning damage! Hit them with anything else!"

The Talon switched to their alternates, mowing down bat after bat with flame, shadow, force, and life magic. Everyone avoided ice and lightning if they could–everyone except Pit. Loquis was certain that the Chimera did not play by the same rules as the rest of them, as his massive ice spears that burst into tiny lightning storms killed all they touched.

For his part, the Half-Orc's only non-lightning spells were short range. Thankfully, he had a crossbow at his waist. Loquis pulled it up and squeezed the trigger…but the damn thing jammed. Before he could drop the weapon, a surviving Brumalbat dove, fangs opened wide for his throat. Loquis flinched, calling up a force ward—

Blood, hot and wet, splattered against his face. Loquis jumped back, moments too late, to find the Brumalbat split in two before him. *Did I—?*

A chain covered in sharp blades retracted from the corpse, flinging half of it into the open air. "Whew, nasty little things, huh?" Evie said.

"You saved me," he managed through the ichor on his lips.

"You uh, you got some gunk on ya," Evie said, motioning to his face. "Next time, hit 'em with force or fire spells."

"Right." Loquis gritted his teeth against the embarrassment. He'd underestimated the Brumalbat's speed, otherwise he'd have readied his shorter range Skills. "I've got a few."

"I know. Hit their wings. They don't like it." She turned away, flicking her chain free of the smoking guts at her feet.

"Wait. Let me help," Loquis said. He leaned down and ran his hand across the least deadly part of her chain, holding in a grunt of pain when a blade nicked his finger. Magic followed in the wake of his hand, a sizzling orange that made her chain links glow.

"Ooh, what's that?"

Loquis stood back up, pinching his injured finger to stem the blood flow. "Incendiary Charge. Short-term buff; it'll add extra fire damage to your attacks, and a low, low chance to set things on fire."

"Huh." She jerked her arm, and the chain snapped out into the open air, where it caught the face of another diving monster. The creature screamed in pain and careened into the cliffside below. Evie laughed and punched his shoulder. "I like it."

Loquis hid his pain—again—but couldn't hide his beaming smile. "Come back when you need it re-applied. I'll be–uh, here. I mean, of course I will be."

Evie just laughed again and leaped into the sky. The Half-Orc mage watched her as she defied the laws of the world and flung herself about with the whirling of her glowing chain. It snapped out, wrapping around a Brumalbat from face to rear, allowing the agile warrior to spin around the still-flying monstrosity. Her chain ground into it, metal Mana flaring to chew through its icy flesh as she reached the zenith of her rotation and let go.

She rocketed out into the greater swarm.

"Wow."

"Tempest Fugit!"

Pit braced his legs as another twenty spears of ice burst from his Mana Gates and tore into the cloud of Inferior Elementals. Each one skewered a bat before exploding and releasing bursts of lightning that arced between the others. The lightning wasn't doing as much as it would on others, but Pit knew how these ice monsters worked. He wasn't concerned—not about doing enough damage, at least.

What did chafe at him was his landbound position. He kept firing Tempest Fugit because that was his best long-range Skill, but it left him feeling like one of those magic ballistas Alister made. The Yttin were next to him, hurling their harpoons in graceful arcs before yanking hard on the braided silk ropes attached to their ends. Those ropes were coiled around thick, girdle-like belts, allowing their powerful back appendages to get involved in the retrieval process. More than once, a resisting Brumalbat was dragged close, allowing Pit to finish them off and eat their core.

Evie was out there, practically flying as she slaughtered her way across the sky. Vess was, too, and she *was* flying, standing atop a floating spear as she commanded her weapons like a general did their troops. A maelstrom of bronze discs and silver spears surrounded her, creating a zone of death that the Brumalbats feared to enter.

It was impressive and frustrating. Down on the ground, Pit's vantage was limited, meaning he couldn't fire on the enemy. He was eager to eat as many cores as he could, but not if that meant he hurt his friends.

A trio of Brumalbats dove through the Dawnwalker's volley of arrows and let loose a flurry of bladed ice shards from their wings. Right behind it came a terrible screech, a sonic attack that didn't hurt so much as needle their concentration. The Henaari flinched, and that was enough.

Dark Glacial Guard!

Pit was there between the ice shards and the Dawnwalkers, his lean body coated in floating panels of shadowed ice. The attack bounced harmlessly off of him, and he retaliated.

Dawn's Advent!

A crescent of golden energy ripped into the banking bats, slicing them from skull to sternum. Diver harpoons speared their chests, snagging the corpses at the last second.

You Have Killed A Brumalbat (x3)!
XP Earned!

"Raven guide you, Honored Tenku," one of the Dawnwalkers said.

"Mhm." Pit made a vague gesture with his paw. "Same."

The Henaari shifted away, angling themselves so that they had better shots at the monsters attacking the city below. Their bows had incredible range, so they were well-suited to the task. Pit just watched as his chances at affecting the battle dwindled.

"Reinforcements are on the way. Where are they all coming from?"

Pit looked farther out, to where the Yttin Diver was gesturing, and saw nearly a hundred more Brumalbats arrive. They emerged from the depthless blue sky as if conjured, but they certainly smelled real. "Something funny is going on," he said. "Stay here. I'm gonna find out."

"As you will, Beast."

He needed to get higher, and there was one thing Pit hadn't tried yet. Though Felix was far away, his Companion's core space was close, and he could feel the Skills within shine like torches just around the corner. *I'm gonna take this, Felix. Hope you don't need it.*

Cloudstep!

A platform long enough to hold his entire body flickered into existence twenty feet above the cliff's edge, and Pit leaped atop of it. The structure held—for all of a second. It shattered into purple and blue vapor, and Pit tumbled down. Someone above shouted in panic, but Pit hadn't the time to worry about them.

Cloudstep!

This one was angled, and Pit flexed his legs just as he landed and pushed backward. The platform still shattered, but he was able to redirect himself. Pit leaped into the cliff, hindquarters first, before pressing off with every ounce of Strength he possessed. The rock cratered, and Pit shot outward at considerable speed for a good distance.

Just enough to land atop an attacking Brumalbat.

"Excuse me!" he shouted, digging Dark Glacial Guard claws and his own into the monster's back as he jumped off. Gouts of ichor flowed in his wake, and the monster careened into the earth. Pit, however, was not so easily stopped.

Another Cloudstep flashed ahead, and he pressed a paw to it before summoning another. And another. Each one shattered in less than a heartbeat, but if nothing else, Pit was fast.

He ascended. Higher and higher, heading straight for the oncoming storm of monsters. Nearly a hundred, they were an avalanche of elementals, all teeth and claws and burning evil eyes. They screeched at him, their sonic attacks distorting the very air. The sound cracked his conjured armor, peeling off chunks of ice and shadow with every reverberation, but Pit didn't stop.

Dark Glacial Guard is level 25!
Apprentice Tier!
You Gain:
+12 END
+12 STR
+12 VIT

Pit marshaled his core and the magic that swirled within. Ice and lightning swelled, the patterns singing from the branches of his twisted tree until they pulsed through every channel Pit possessed. Without his wings, Pit was down by two Mana Gates, but he could manage this much.

"Tempest Fugit!"

Felix stopped in his tracks, nearly causing Beef and Hallow to run into him.

"What's going on?" The big teen asked. "Did you find them?"

"No," Felix said. "This is something else."

Etheric Concordance sang in his chest. Pit's emotions had been running hot for a while, but it was a battle. The little guy was always overeager about fighting, especially if food was involved. Now, however, his Companion's emotions reached a fevered pitch, and Felix jerked his head back toward Cold Rock.

There, in the daylit sky, was a cascade of shimmering ice. Distant, gruesome pops and faint screams came from the horde...before all of it was inundated by bolts of lightning. It spread and, for an instant, connected every single Brumalbat in a web of light.

Connection... A twinge burned from his chest, and he followed it to his Adamant Discord, as if it were alerting him of a new link. Felix chased that sensation, catching the sound of it through the air and his Companion bond in equal measure. "I feel it," he said aloud.

"Feel what?" Beef whispered.

Felix pointed to a nearby hill, one of many outside the flat approach to Cold Rock. It appeared to be the same as any other, save for the now-bright link that rose like a beacon before it guttered out. "There. The Witches are controlling the horde from there."

"Mother of monsters," Kimaris muttered. "How can you tell that?"

"I couldn't, not 'til now. I felt them at the start of the fight, but they've been moving around somehow, probably with an illusion or a ward or something." It was one of two reasons why he hadn't reached them already and ended things. He'd sent his Illusory Double out to scout the area, but it hadn't been able to find the Witches either, and he'd recalled it. "They either have someone very strong there, or they're just really good at tricks."

"The Feldspear Coven is not known for subtlety," Kimaris said. "We must prepare for a hard fight."

Felix nodded and gestured for his allies to hunker down. They were moving under his Abyssal Skein, so he wasn't too worried about being discovered, but the capabilities of a Coven were unknown to him, and they'd already surprised him once.

Illusory Double.

Once again, shadows pooled beneath Felix before growing up at his side. It swiftly formed into a dark version of Felix, the shadow detailed enough to mimic his fur-lined cloak and even the swords at his waist. It was all black on black, though, the only color coming from its eyes. Those shone like distant stars dotted by a gleaming flame. Felix finally understood why everyone thought his gaze could be so unnerving.

At the start, Felix had been concerned that his Double wouldn't be included with his Abyssal Skein, but that Skill had quickly traversed the connection Felix had with the construct. As before, the darkness of the Void sank into the Double, and it faded by several shades.

Go.

The Double loped up the snowy hillock, feet making zero noise as it ghosted atop the snow. A piece of Felix's Mind moved with it, his Perception riding shotgun in its head, which let him see and feel what his Double experienced.

Illusory Double is level 46!

He found their gathering just over the ridge, holed up within a field of ice chunks and rocky outcroppings. There were twenty-six of the nine-foot Risi, and each was positioned around a glowing red circle of sigaldry, their arms raised as an ephemeral power rippled between them. A series of mounds were interspersed among the rocks and ice chunks, appearing random at first before his Perception threaded through the thin snow coating.

Interesting.

In the center of the grotto was the red circle. Objects were placed in the circle, things that ranged from sinister to innocuous: two bloody vertebrae from something very big, a series of burning coals, two sets of fangs, one of ice and one of metal, a chunk of dark ice, and several small mounds of colored powder, each one a different hue. A giant-sized skull sat in the center, stripped of skin and covered in far too many horns, one of which looked as if it had grown into the poor creature's eye socket. Sigils glowed balefully from every inch of its surface.

The Witches were speaking.

"A foul beast of ice and shadow has decimated our beasts!" one hissed.

"At least the Warriors have penetrated the gate," another said.

"They have been pushed back! Warriors in bone have arrived and have stopped the Berserkers in their tracks!"

"They aren't even of the Kin! Why are they here?"

"Unknown magic sours the air, sisters. What is happening?"

"We all felt it. Do not let yourself fear. The battle is not yet lost." A

Witch that was half-a-head taller than the others turned her bright purple eyes on her fellows. "Bring in the Destroyer."

Felix's Double blinked its bright eyes. *Well that can't be good.*

"They're controlling the Brumalbats through some ritual," he said through his main Body. Whatever sigaldry the giants were using was unfamiliar to Felix, but that much was clear. "And they're getting desperate. Something about bringing in a 'Destroyer.'"

"An Inferior Elemental horde, now a Destroyer. Only a full Coven could do that." she gasped. "That means all of Feldspear Coven is on the field now...if you take the Coven, they can do nothing."

"Are they all as strong as the Witches in Cold Rock?" Beef asked. "Because they felt tough."

"They claim to be stronger, but Mother Vepar has never been successfully challenged in six decades. By any of the tribes."

Felix banished his Double, worried that it would be found. "C'mon, before I lose them again. My plan should work just fine, but don't take any chances."

"Got it," Beef said. "Hallow?"

"My Bodies are already moving."

Felix cracked his neck, the sound swallowed by Abyssal Skein. "Then let's go meet the neighbors."

The Witches were in the midst of chanting when Felix landed among them all.

"Hi there." For a shocked moment, no one did anything, but their Spirits raged. Felix lifted his hands. "Let's not do anything we'll regret later, okay?"

Fully half of the Witches acted at once, hurling a literal blizzard of ice magic at him. Felix lifted his hand, Rime Shaping the blast...only to find Kimaris' magic joining his own. The blizzard was spun aside, coating nearby boulders in six inches of ice.

"Face me, Feldspear!" she cried, engaging with as many Witches as she could. Spells rained down, but Felix couldn't worry about her. He had other goals.

Ten hidden Berserkers burst from those low, snowy mounds, exactly where he'd tagged them earlier, but Felix ignored their frenzied approach. A Multipede exploded from the heavy snow behind them, smashing into the Berserkers like a freight train. The Sharpwing Matriarch bisected one of the giants, her wings too much for its crystallized rage, and the Homunculus peppered them with shortsword-sized Crystalline Darts. Last was Beef, who splattered the enemy with every swing of his maul. The earth shook as the giants were taken down in seconds.

Half of the Coven scattered, turning chaotically to face Kimaris and Felix, while the rest seemed rooted to the spot around the red ritual circle. Kimaris fell to her knees, overcome by sheer numbers, and Felix zipped to her side. A maelstrom of magic descended on him, but Felix didn't care to figure out what it was gonna do. He opened his mouth.

Chthonic Tribute.

The storm of power hit him and was devoured. Silence overcame the grotto, the Witches gaping like fish out of water. Felix ran his tongue against his teeth, grimacing. "Gah, that tasted bad. Why did that taste bad?"

"You ate their curses as well as their elemental attacks," Kimaris said through gritted teeth. She smiled at the shocked Witches, a grisly, bloody thing. "It was all they had."

"Oh, good." Felix turned back to the Witches and the circle. "Then we can end this."

Six Witches were down, felled by Kimaris' power, and the Berserkers had been demolished. Beef stepped up alongside them, Hallow's Bodies fanning outward to surround the enemy. As they moved, shards of ice rose from the ground, gleaming with ice Mana as protective wards wrapped around the remaining Witches. The purple-eyed leader stared daggers at Felix.

"Oh, I used to have one of those," he said, pointing at the ice shard. "Look. I don't need to kill you. I'll give you one—"

"Tu ratha, *Human*!" she spat. "Whatever Cold Rock paid you, it was not enough! You will merely be the first to die." She lifted her hands, and whatever ritual they were enacting surged. "Come, Destroyer!"

"Oh, come on, I'm just trying to talk!"

As if conjured from nothing, a monster surged across the tundra, a blur of steel and fur. To Felix, it moved like it was underwater, but he knew it was too fast for everyone but Beef. *A Superior Savage Therium*, he realized. He'd run into them in the Ironskin Domain, but those had been a lot smaller. *Strong, big reach, and decently fast. I'm not gonna risk this fight spilling onto my friends.*

End it fast.

Felix flared Sovereign of Flesh.

The Therium's Will proved as durable as its Body, which is to say not at all. Flesh sundered from bone and blood as Felix imposed his power on the beast, and the Superior Savage Therium unraveled.

It was gross.

Felix shaped the viscera away from his people while flaring Rime Shaping. The ice shield flashed like opalescent lightning before each one of the shards cracked in half, and the shield failed. He let the majority of the beast's guts splash against the Witches, coating their fine robes and white hair.

Rime Shaping is level 86!

"Like I was saying: one chance." Felix bared his normal, human teeth, and every one of the Witches flinched. "Stop. Or be stopped."

CHAPTER FORTY-EIGHT

Evie landed in a roll, springing up to her feet as her spiked chain retracted into her hand. Behind, the last of the Brumalbats fell in gruesome pieces, their icy wings and dark ichor splattering the cliffs below. A Yttin harpoon speared the center of the nearest corpses and snapped back, snagging the majority of its guts. They splatted messily beside her.

"Gross."

Pit landed beside her, his dark armor making him look far larger and more intimidating…were it not for his eagerly wagging tail. His icy maw was already greased by foul liquids. "No no, they taste good. You should try it."

"I'm thinkin' I'll pass."

Pit shrugged. "Your loss." He chomped down, squirting ichor to either side as he happily munched away.

Evie grimaced and averted her eyes, for once not interested in the snacks she'd secreted away in her armor. In the distance, a bolt of lightning shot up into the sky, arcing back toward Cold Rock. "Felix is coming back," she said.

"That looks bigger than normal," Vess pointed out. "He's carrying something…?"

"Oh. It's done," Pit said behind a mouthful of bat meat. "That took a while."

"What is?" Mother Vepar asked. "What did your leader do?"

"Look."

They followed the jut of Pit's beak, where the lightning landed just inside the walls. Felix, his fur cloak fluttering all around him, had landed gracefully in the center of the courtyard. Seconds later, a cage of ice crashed next to him, kicking up a geyser of snow straight into the air. A blinding cloud spread everywhere before it reversed course, sucked back inward into Felix's open maw. Inside the cage, tumbled onto their knees and backs, were dozens of Frost Giant Witches bound in blue-black manacles threaded with red-gold veins. None of them looked happy in the slightest.

Mother Vepar gasped. "He…captured them? That is not done. Their powers—our powers—cannot be held or restricted without an elision collar. I don't suppose you have those with you?"

"We do not," Vess said.

"Then it is pointless. Dangerous. They cannot be trusted, and we cannot hold them," Mother Vepar said. "The moment they are free, they will turn on us."

"I hesitate to agree, but the Witch is right," Tzfell said. "The Risi know only violence and the rule of might, but even that is trumped by an opportunity to weasel out of their given word." She pointedly ignored the wrathful glare of Mother Vepar and looked back down at Felix. "They cannot be bargained with, no matter the level of one's Diplomacy Skill."

The Witches said something, but it was hard to hear over the constant wind. Felix responded, and the Witches flinched back as if he'd lunged at them. They didn't say anything else. Felix, however, raised his head toward the Feldspear giants still fighting just beyond the gates. His voice rang out in peals of thunder. "It is over. Your Coven has surrendered. Lay down your weapons and silence your Skills, or die."

The Feldspear forces, dwindled by half, breathed heavy, ragged steam into the air. Berserkers drenched in as much blood as ice, fondled their spiked fists with dire expressions, and the normal ranks weren't much better.

Evie stared at them and was surprised to find she had no rage left to burn. She only felt a pain in her lungs, as if she was being squeezed. *C'mon. Listen to him. Surrender.*

The giants made no move to drop their weapons, and Felix lifted a hand. Evie turned away, unable to watch the slaughter to come. *Idiots!*

"Beef!" Felix called.

Evie cracked her eyes. "What?"

Something very big and very wet crashed into the field beyond the gate. Someone nearby—a mage, probably—made a retching sound.

"I find Felix's brand of Diplomacy to be quite effective," Vess said after a moment. "Do you not agree, Chanter Tzfell?"

Pit let loose a screeching cry, and blood flung from his icy jaws.

Mervin stood among the giants, staring at a corpse.

Moments ago, he'd been fighting the giants with everything he had; dodging huge weapons and conjured ice. He had just taken down two Risi Warriors before a Berserker had cornered him. Those crimson bastards were strong and fast, and Mervin had been forced to take one too many blows to his arm and shoulder.

Every bit of him was sore, but Mervin had plenty of fight left in him.

Then there was lightning, and the Autarch called for the enemy's surrender. No one responded, and Mervin figured he had a long afternoon ahead of him…but then a crash sounded above him, followed by a bullish lowing.

A corpse as large as any Berserker had splattered onto the field, bursting like an overripe balloon. Mervin had tried to leap out of the way of the gunk, but it spread everywhere and drove the desperate battle to a sudden standstill. Now here he stood…and the Berserkers backed away, blue faces now several shades paler.

Mervin furrowed his brows. The immense thing was shredded and didn't even have a head, but that only seemed to worsen the terror in the giants. He can hear it, dancing along their overlarge Spirits.

Lightning flashed above, and the furry body of Lord Hammer was suddenly atop the gates of Cold Rock, hands filled with a fang-filled skull as big as the Minotaur's chest. He lifted it as high as he could before spearing the thing onto a black iron spike atop the gate tower.

"We killed your Destroyer!" Lord Hammer shouted, his voice loud but uncontrolled. It rattled Mervin's eardrums painfully. "You wanna fight? You're next."

Lord Hammer's words might have driven a nail into Mervin's skull, but the effect on the giants was far more profound. All of them, Warrior, Berserker, and even Hoarhounds dropped to their knees and haunches. Weapons clattered into the hard-packed snow, and crimson ice crumbled from arms and chests.

"Thank the light," Mervin gasped.
The battle was done.

After dragging their cage up to the ice fortress, Felix had only lingered long enough to remind the Feldspear Coven of their new Oath. They'd nodded, faces grim but resolute, and Felix had left Mother Vepar and her Witches to handle the battle's aftermath.

Mostly.

Harn remained behind with half a Talon to guard the surviving Risi Warriors and Berserkers, which Felix had put up in a small enclosure he'd shaped from Fiendstone. The rest of the Claw were recovering in housing reserved for Cold Rock's Warriors, most of which now stood empty. None of his people had been injured, thankfully, but quite a few had spent their Mana and Stamina on the attack, and Felix required them all to be ready to move at a moment's notice. They were not staying in Cold Rock long.

The Witches granted Felix and his retinue the use of their own private grounds, located at the back of the ice church and built into the sturdy stone. Some hours after the battle's end, Felix lounged there beside a crackling fire, seated upon a chair three times too large and staring into a comically oversized hearth. The fire barely filled up a third of it, but it banished the majority of the air's chill.

Pit lounged by the flames, a book spread between his paws and a pair of small glasses perched atop his beak. According to his Companion, it was another book on tactics for fighting aerial enemies. He hadn't talked much about the fight against the Brumalbats, but he seemed equal parts annoyed and excited about how it had gone. Felix didn't push. He was feeling some very similar emotions, if for very different reasons—but the last thing he wanted to do was talk about them.

Instead, he sat in his huge chair and regarded a number of items spread out beside him. They were the objects taken from the ritual circle, collected into sacks and jars by Felix himself: bones, teeth, burning coals, a chunk of ice, and four colored powders. His Eye tagged the last as metal ore mixed with bone dust of several elementals. He had learned from Kimaris that the Brumalbats and the Superior Savage Therium were being beckoned by these reagents, and that the circle of sigaldry was a sort of agreement with the Frostfather.

Both creatures were elementals, after all. Felix was annoyed that the

Frostfather had sent his monsters after him, but Kimaris was quick to point out that no Witch *spoke* to their god…it was transactional. Items were laid out to create the connection, and the power of a Witches' circle powered the conjuration. What Feldspear had done was create a double circle, committing every single one of their mages to bringing forth that army of elementals.

Connections again. Felix ran his hands over a glass jar containing a pile of still-burning coals. They hadn't dimmed in the slightest since he'd collected them. *It keeps coming back to that.*

Felix let Adamant Discord sing within him, and faint blue lines appeared to sprout from everything around him. He focused, narrowing his vision to the reagents, and studied the hazy lines they bore. The coals were the faintest, a braided cord leading off to the south for several yards before fading; its connection to the hearth fireplace was far stronger. Like called to like.

The two sets of fangs, one ice and one metal, had more connections, but they were diffuse and in all directions. According to his Eye, they were the teeth of a Brumalbat and a Savage Therium, so that made sense. Same with the bloody vertebrae, though it shared a sharp connection with the metal fangs; likely, they were taken from the same beast. The four powders and chunk of dark ice had the strongest link back southward, toward the Domain where Felix had faced down the Frostfather.

Ice and stone are the strongest link, clearly to attract their god's interest. The organic parts are for specifying the particular creature they wish to summon. And the coals… Felix wasn't sure about their purpose, and he returned to his memories of the ritual circle.

In his Mind's eye, he traced out the shape and pattern of the Witches' sigaldry. It was stranger than what he was used to; thicker and less nuanced than his own style, but filled with strange slashes and dashes, like claw marks. It was like reading English translated into Russian, then back into English. Legible, but hard to parse.

The coals seem to be another anchor for the summons. Representing their… hearts? No. Cores. Felix sat back, rubbing his chin. *Hm. Interesting. It also is linked to the skull at the center. So a two-way anchor, maybe.*

The skull itself, ominously called the Skull Of The Forsaken, was a potent device. Though it had been situated at the center of the ritual circle, it didn't have anything to do with the conjuration of monsters. The same thick sigaldry lined the Skull, but Felix was able to identify the root of what it did: scatter an echo of the user in multiple directions. It was a distraction, and it ran off blood.

Eat It.

I'm not going to eat it.

Skull Strong. I Hunger.

Felix felt a bit guilty. His Hunger had been salivating at the Witches from the moment they'd found them, and it had been grumbling ever since he'd let them live. Felix never thought he'd see a living black hole sulk, but there it was. Something to cross off the bucket list.

I promise you'll get something better soon. The way to Kingsrock is not going to be pretty, I can almost guarantee that.

Promise? The pause after that word felt like it was weighing something. **Deal.**

You Have Received A Quest!

Wait, what?

Delicious Devour I
Your Primordial Hunger has requested a reward for all of its hard work. Prey must be Tier V or higher if a monster, Master or greater if a mortal, or the equivalent in magical potency. Rewards dependent upon prey devoured.
Reward(s): Doubled Significance, Varies

Accept?
Y/N

Felix lowered the skull into his lap. *You can help me increase my store of significance?*

A deep rumble shook him from within. **Yes. Some.**

He accepted it without hesitation. A Quest that would net him double the significance for doing something he was going to do anyway? And judging by the little "I" at the end of the Quest title, it was likely this was a chain of Quests. *I'll be sure to feed you very very soon, Hunger.*

A low rumbling shook him from the inside out. **Good.**

Felix still had some time before they were due to set out with the Coven, and he considered going out hunting. He doubted, however, that he could simply stumble on something better than Master Tier in the wild Hoarfrost. He looked at the Skull in his hands again. It might be useful…but his Hunger wanted him to eat it.

"Well, let me try it out first." He lifted his finger and, with a sharp tug, slashed it open with his own claw. A small drop of ruby blood welled up before his regeneration closed the cut, and Felix quickly smeared it across the Skull of the Forsaken's brow. Immediately, a connection between him and the Skull manifested—a thick, braided line of dark crimson, flecked with gold and blue.

He pressed his Intent into that connection, and shouts erupted from outside his rooms. They were muffled by stone and glass, but Felix jolted to his feet.

Pit peered out a window. "You're sitting in the middle of the blacksmith's forge, Felix." He paused. "And on top of someone's meal at the bar. Oh wait, now you're walking."

Felix dashed to the window and saw just that: down below, a copy of him marched forward before leaning as if to look through an imaginary window. Startled giants were everywhere, most of them running from his sudden appearance. A few of the blacksmith apprentices swung crude iron clubs at his illusory form, but the blows passed right through him. Felix immediately cut the connection between him and the Skull, and the illusions immediately disappeared.

Someone knocked on his door.

"Hey, sorry about that. It was just an illusion, though—" he started, but cut himself off when he saw the two Chanters standing there. "Oh. What can I help you with?"

Laur craned his neck, as if to see behind Felix. "Did something happen? We heard shouting, and now I can almost smell the expenditure of Mana."

Felix gave a polite smile. "I wouldn't be worried about it. What do you want?"

Tzfell looked as stoic as ever and ignored her associate. "Might we come in, Lord Autarch? I believe we have some things to discuss before our journey resumes."

"Things?"

"Regarding the Kingsrock and the dangers that lie ahead."

"I'm quite aware of both, Tzfell," Felix said, beginning to shut the door. "And I'm really busy tonight—"

"Kingsrock is a Nymean ruin."

Felix stopped, the door half-closed on the two Chanters. "Dammit. Come in."

CHAPTER FORTY-NINE

Felix shut the door. "Explain."

The Chanters stood in the center of the room, eyes roaming over the jars and sacks, the fire, and Pit, who sat unperturbed on the woven rug. Laur, in particular, stared pointedly at the Skull of the Forsaken.

Tzfell folded her arms below her bust. "The Kingsrock was once a Nymean stronghold. The oral histories the Dwarves tell of the Hoarfrost try to diminish that fact, and the written records of it have been wiped by the Ruin, but the clues are all there. The path to approach is even called the Starfield Step."

"Why wouldn't you have mentioned this before?"

Tzfell lifted her hands placatingly. "I did not mention it previously simply due to the mixed company we find ourselves in—or did you wish this knowledge to be bandied about among your entire company? It would have soon traveled into the ears of the Frost Giants, and they need no more reasons to covet the Kingsrock."

"That's fair, I guess." Felix gestured, yanking on a bright connection with Adamant Discord at the same time. A pair of giant-sized chairs slid across the stone tiles as tiny branches of lightning burst from his fingertips. "Take a seat."

"Thank you," Tzfell said, eyeing the chairs. "I had not realized you had such fine control with that ability."

Felix scooted aside the jars and sacks with his hands before sitting down himself. "That's because most things don't respond well to getting hit by lightning, even if it's just a little." He pointed to the minor char marks on the frame of the chairs the Chanters perched atop. "The act of drawing on the connection creates a sort of…friction. Thankfully, the Risi over-built these."

"Fascinating," Laur said, studying the blackened markings. "Connection to…you? What sort of connection could you possibly have to a Risi-wrought furnishing?"

"The longer I've been here, the more certain I am that we're all connected," Felix said. "Some are whisper-thin threads, and others are thick as chains, but they're all there. For instance," he pointed to Tzfell, and the bald Dwarf raised an eyebrow. "Tzfell bears a number of threads to the Frost Giants. They're weak but definitely there."

"Tzfell?" Laur shifted toward her, clearly surprised. "You've dealt with the giants?"

"Many Dwarves have. I met my fair share in battle a century before you were born, Laur."

"You said you came from the Rimefangs originally," Felix said.

"I do. The clans of the Rimefangs have long fought against the monsters of the Hoarfrost, the Frost Giants primary among them. There is not much here, only snow and stone, and anything else the Risi Kin need, they turn to raiding to acquire. The Rimefang holds have been their target for an Age, delivering death to a great many border villages in their eagerness for our resources. That, I imagine, is what you are detecting, Lord Autarch."

Felix sat back, tracing the many ephemeral threads that spun out from the Dwarven Chanter. Laur had some, too, but they were almost invisible aside from the ones to Felix and Tzfell. When a person interacted with another it established a fragile connection in his sight, so thin as to be invisible. With Tzfell, hers were delicate but distinct and spread around her like a cloak. His Mind caught on an idea, and he flared his Manasight. He'd never tried that while looking at the threads, but they were made of Mana as much as anything. He wrinkled his nose. They tasted of stale violence and sour yellow disdain.

Manasight is level 81!

…

Manasight is level 85!

"You hate them," Felix said at last.

"That…is fair to say. I can remain civil, however, if that is your concern."

"It's part of it, yeah. If things go as planned, these people are going to be under my Authority soon, and the last thing I want is elevated tensions. If you can hold your grudges in check while we're here, then we'll be fine."

"I can manage that, Lord Autarch." Tzfell's tattoos shifted atop her skin, altering the geometric pattern slightly. "But there is a portion of our history I must explain."

"Okay. Tell me."

"I mentioned that the Dwarves once made the approach toward Kingsrock, and I also mentioned that it cost them a great deal. A Prince of the Undermount led a war party into the Hoarfrost with the intent to conquer it, and they slayed all who came against them. Risi Warriors and Berserkers fell to their mithril blades, while the teeth and claws of elemental beasts could not penetrate their enchanted deep-stone armor. When they came to the Starfield Step, their approach was heralded by lights in the sky and chaos in the tundra. Somehow, the Kin were ready for them, and the Dwarven war party faced their collective might.

The Prince managed to beat them back, but the deadly traps within the Starfield Step harmed his people the most. Hundreds were lost in the chaos. At the end of it, the Prince was left with two score warriors, but he was able to climb the Kingsrock."

"Climb?" Felix asked. "Is it literally just a rock? I thought you said it was a Nymean stronghold?"

"The accounts of its appearance are muddled. This was a long time ago, centuries before I was born, and the Dwarves do not keep written archives." Tzfell clenched her jaw. "The Ruin stole into the records regardless, altering memories just enough to turn things askew."

"Okay. So, then what? This Prince made it into the stronghold?"

"He did. Inside he found 'great treasures' that once belonged to the Nym, but the specifics are not told outside the halls of the Undermount. For a time, the Prince tangled with the Authority of the Kingsrock, but he could not make it submit to him, even though he stood upon its Seal. After an uncertain amount of time, he lost even that. The Prince was driven out by a gathering of Frost Giants and their monstrous allies. His retreat was bloody and cost him half of his surviving warriors, but it cost the giants as well—it was the beginning of a long enmity between us."

"So these treasures are why you believe it to be a Nymean ruin?" Felix asked.

"Yes."

"That's pretty thin," he said. "What happened to the treasures?"

"That is unclear. The Prince was said to arrive home with a king's fortune, but the nature of it is unknown to those outside the royal family. His exodus was such that I imagine a great deal was left behind within the Kingsrock."

"Hm."

"I wished to come here and tell you this because I believe we should remain as upfront as possible with one another. The Cantus Sodalus needs the Unbound, the entire Continent does, and I would have your trust, if I can."

"I appreciate that attitude. Trust is hard to make and simple to break, but this is a good step."

Tzfell bowed in her seat, followed closely by Laur. "I only ask that you trust us enough to help you. The powers we bear are not inconsiderable. Laur is, of course, gifted with wards and shielding spells, and I am adept at conjuration and battle magic. Our true value, however, comes from the knowledge of our long years of life, and it is that we wish to offer to you, Lord Autarch."

Felix was curious about their specialties, and he made a mental note to ask more about that later. "How so?"

"To delve into that, I wish you to know that your Conqueror of the Ironskin Domain Title has shocked both of us. While Zara has informed us of your battle against Divine agents and slivers, I will admit to certain doubts. Truly, a Divine being, no matter how limited, would be able to overcome a mortal—Unbound or not."

Felix just smiled and spread his hands, palm up.

"Yet your Title makes your accomplishment clear. You battled the Risi's god and defeated him…that alone is a deed worthy of legend. I wish only to know…how?"

"I punched him."

"I'm sorry?"

"*Really* hard."

Someone knocked on the door. Felix frowned, but the Chanters weren't distracted.

"You killed a myth with your bare fists?" Laur scoffed. "You expect us to believe that?"

"I don't care if you believe it, that's what happened," Felix said. His Perception flooded the corridor outside of his room, and he stood up. "I appreciate your honesty, and the information you've given me will be very useful. But understand that I carry secrets that aren't just mine."

He opened the door just as Vess raised her fist to knock on it again. She was dressed in a beautiful, ankle-length gown embroidered with swirling patterns along the hem and up the long slit at the side. It flared over her hips and cinched at the waist and left her strong arms bare. She smiled, a deep dimple forming in her dusky cheek, and her golden brown eyes crinkled at the edges as she gave him a once-over. "Did you forget, Nevarre?"

Felix stared a moment longer before clearing his throat. "Of course not. Why would—they were just leaving, actually." He turned to the Chanters and thanked his luck that they were already striding to the doorway.

"We appreciate your time, Lord Autarch. Know that we are available to offer our input on any…extraordinary events that you encounter." Tzfell bowed to him and gave a lesser one to Vess. "Lady Dayne."

Laur followed on the Dwarf's heels, pausing only to give Vess' hand a chaste kiss. "Milady."

"Chanter Laur."

He turned his sharp features to Felix one last time. "That Skull you recovered is quite interesting, Lord Autarch. I would love to look into it with you, if you have the time."

"I'll think about it."

"Very well." He retreated down the hall, his long legs easily overtaking the shorter Chanter.

Vess watched them go. "What did they want?"

"Information, but at least they offered something in return." Felix took a deep breath and released it, pushing the Chanters' visit away from his thoughts. "I thought you were going to be here a bit sooner?"

"Yes, I apologize for being late. Someone materialized an illusion of themselves in my dressing room."

Felix's eyes widened, and panic swarmed his chest so bad that Pit looked up from his book. "Uh…"

Vess squinted at him, but after a moment huffed a small breath. "Good. Your emotions are as shocked as your expression. I will take that to mean it was unintentional…and that you saw nothing."

"Saw—? Were you changing?"

"You will never know." Vess' cheeks were flushed as she walked away from the door. "To dinner, Lord Nevarre?"

Felix scrambled after her.

CHAPTER FIFTY

Harn brought his hammer down. Sparks flew like a brilliant waterfall of purple-blue motes before they vanished, eaten up by the relentless cold. Outside the forge he'd commandeered, night had fallen. The winds were brutal, but Harn welcomed them—tonight, his work required more than simple heat.

He lifted his hammer. The haft was of rich, golden-green wood and the wide head was fashioned from a chunk of purple-white crystal. Mana crystal, in fact, part of a set of tools Harn had fashioned for his personal use. None among Elderthrone could manufacture Mana crystal, of course, that required a level of power beyond a Master…but Ahkestria had a remarkable selection of raw materials. He'd arranged for their construction in the Leviathan Depths, and it had cost him more crowns than he'd seen in his life.

Worth it, he thought with a grin. Harn set the hammer down beside the huge black iron anvil and inspected his work.

Mana Folding is level 64!

The layers are solid. Steady. He rapped his knuckles against the breastplate. It rang like a bell, and a spark of bright purple flashed from the point of contact. Smithing, far as Harn was concerned, was less about following rules as it was following the shape of things. The armor in his hands was once a hunk of ice, but by listening to the material and his instincts, Harn was able to make something *more.*

The shape had come out just as he envisioned it at the outset, which wasn't always the case. He was better at Smithing now, his Skill pushed well into Adept, but problems always had a chance to arise. Those problems and imperfections were amplified by the materials; something too advanced, too strong, and he'd struggle with making even the simplest of tools. His lengthy experience with Leviathan bone had prepared him well for the strange material he'd been handed.

Harn set the breastplate down. "Evie. You know it's rude to lurk."

An annoyed grunt came from the rafters above. The forge was built to the specifications of giants, and the ceiling was at least forty paces high. "How long have you known I was here?"

Harn picked up his crystal hammer and put it away with his others. "Since you snuck in through the window."

"Noctis' tits." She dropped to the ground, falling like a leaf from a tree and landing without a whisper. "Thought I was gettin' better."

"You are. But so am I," Harn said with a grin. He nudged the breastplate on the anvil toward her. "Here. That's for you."

"It's done?"

"Aye. Was tricky working with ice, but when it came down to it, that stuff hammers out like steel. Just needs cold instead of heat."

Evie lifted the chest piece of her new armor and gazed at it in wonder. "It's beautiful."

Harn grunted. "Better be. Had to burn six Mana Potions on that; the ice kept soaking up my Skill faster than I could provide it."

"Really? Is that normal?"

"Not for base iron or steel, but higher-grade materials are thirsty. Leviathan bone requires me to drink four per span of material, or else my folding can fail, and High Steel needs three. And those are reduced numbers, thanks to my Skill levels."

Evie clutched the cold material to her chest, a small gasp her only admission to how blasted cold it was. "Is it strong?"

"The Mana Folding I did strengthened the material, and it was already tough as High Steel. With my hammers," Harn said, nodding to his unrolled pack of tools. "I was able to push it well beyond. Can't do more to it, not just cause I've hit my limit on Mana Potions for the day. More, and it'd stress out the matrices in the ice. But it's better'n my armor, that's for sure."

Evie grinned. "Excellent. Next battle, I'll wade hip deep in bodies."

"Don't get carried away. It's strong, but it ain't perfect. Orichalcum and mithril are different beasts entirely, and if you run into weapons made of it, you dodge. No direct hits. It'll score and break, and if it's made anywhere near as good as mine, mithril will cut you in half."

"How often can I expect that, though?"

"Not a lot, I admit. But we have a way of runnin' into too many dangers all at once. Just keep its limitations in mind."

"Fair enough." Evie looked around. "Where's the rest of it?"

"Over there, in the smith's chest." Harn gestured to a wide box where completed pieces were set out. Arm, leg, shoulder, all the bits were covered in the strong, flexible material. He'd even forged a helmet. "They'll link up if you feed 'em a bit of Mana. A trick I learned makin' strapless armor for the Legion."

Evie slipped the pieces over her body, locking them into place with a deft hand. "It's cold."

"Surprised?"

"I shouldn't be." Evie rotated her shoulders, checking her range of motion. The pauldrons moved perfectly. She twisted her torso, grinning all the while. "Snug as sin. You got better."

"Best believe it, kid. Check the details." Harn swiped his hand, sending a blue screen rotating into her view.

Name: Frostguard Armor
Type: Armor (Set) (Enchanted)
Lore: Forged by Adept Smith Harn Kastos, this set of armor was made specifically for Evie Aren. Mana Folding has been used to imbue every bit of this icy set with power, greatly increasing its durability. When equipped by someone with an ice-attuned core, the armor grants them additional synergy.
Of A Piece II - Forged to fit seamlessly together without straps or buckles of any kind, it enhances the Dexterity of the wearer by +10.
Rime-Hardened III - Increased durability due to increased density of ice Mana.
Iceborn Synergy - Enhances the potency of ice-based Skills.

Evie whistled. "That's pretty."

"It ain't enough, but it'll keep you safe, and that's as much as I can manage for now."

Evie punched him in the shoulder, and her ice-covered fists rang against his bone plate. "Big softie."

Harn grunted. "Wear the helmet. I know you don't like 'em, but it'll be stronger with the full set."

"And hide this gorgeous mug?" Evie hung the helmet from the belt that had been worked into the armor. "I'll keep that in mind."

Harn studied her, making sure it all fit properly. Nothing jumped out at him, and her motion tests were flawless. "You look good. Big. Adult, even."

"I can buckle my shoes and everythin'." Evie looked down at her new, icy boots. "When I need to."

"Mags would be proud," he said.

Evie froze only a heartbeat before she hugged the burly warrior, and Harn only put up with that for so long. "Alright, alright. Get off. You're givin' me frostbite."

Evie stepped back, eyes brighter than usual. "Didn't wanna hang on too tight, anyway. Not sure how Palin does it. Like grabbing a block of steel."

"Speakin' of, grab that material there. We got work to do before we head out."

"What? I thought we were restin' before Felix had to run at some rock."

"They are. Me and you got things to do." Harn eased the slab onto the giant-sized anvil. "That armor of yours is high-grade, too complicated and time consumin' to recreate tonight. But I'm not lettin' this ice go to waste, either."

"What d'you need me for?" Evie asked.

Harn grinned, and his scars made it monstrous. "Mana battery."

"Ugh."

The place Felix had found didn't really have a name. It was a tavern of sorts, one of the few in Cold Rock, but the food was excellent, according to Kimaris. When the two of them entered, the place was filled with patrons, each of them bent over huge tables with mugs the size of small barrels. The whole place was carved out of the rock, looking more like a cave than a building, but there was a firepit in the center where some sort of meat was sizzling, and several glowing shards of ice along the ceiling provided further illumination. There was no music, but the chatter was lively and very loud. Felix even spotted a few of his own oathbound giants in the crowd, mingling with the younger Risi.

"I heard the food is great," Felix said, by way of apology. He adjusted his fine black jacket and examined the embroidery along the sleeves again. It was of blue flames, but he Willed the stitching away. It felt a bit too fancy for the place. "Sorry for the noise."

Vess was beside him, as beautiful as ever. Her gown, a green and blue affair, was far nicer than the leather and furs all around them, yet she looked as if she belonged. "I like it fine. It's lively."

A young girl made her way to the two of them, wiping her hands on a once-clean apron. She looked to be no more than fifteen, all skinny arms and legs, but was taller than Felix by at least a foot. "Sol talla, Humans! Welcome to Etta's! I'm her daughter, Sata. Haven't had any Humans here before, but you came with the Frostkiller, yes?"

"Frostkiller?" Felix asked.

"Yes, the one that skewered that Therium's skull? Everyone's been talking about him all evening! A Minotaur! They're a Lost Race, you know?"

Felix smiled. "We arrived with him, yeah."

The girl's face lit up. "Amazing! You hungry? Thirsty? We got places at the bar and a few tables over by the firepit. Us giants don't much like the heat."

Felix spared a glance for Vess, but she merely watched him. He cleared his throat. "Do you have anything a bit quieter?"

The girl glanced between the two of them, and her blue skin flushed darker. "I see. Follow me."

They did, pacing behind the youthful server as she led them past the rowdiest of patrons and into a smaller hall beyond the bar. Smaller was relative, of course. The corridor was tall and wide, just short at only thirty feet. Black-iron doors were set into the stone here, only a few, and the girl led them to the one on the very end.

"Here you are. Quietest place I know," Sata said, opening the door and revealing a long chamber set with chairs, table, its own firepit, and a long open area set with fur pelts. Felix and Vess walked in, and the girl smoothed her apron. "I'll get you some grub and wine. Ma said she's only got the hard stuff left, but if you came with the Frostkiller, then I know you're tough enough." With a wink, she left.

"A delightful child," Vess said. "And so tall. What must she think of us?"

"It is odd, isn't it? Standing in these spaces meant for them?" Felix gestured to the oversized table and chairs. They made him feel like a toddler at the dinner table. "I imagine they see us and can't quite wrap their heads around living so small."

"A likely thing," Vess agreed. She paused, considering the table with him. "Should we sit?"

"Ah, give me a second."

Stone Shaping!

Beyond the firepit, a table and chairs rose from beneath the fur rugs, shoving them aside. They were blocky and plain, but properly sized for them. "That's better. After you."

"A ruler and a gentleman." Vess sat at the table, arranging her skirts across her long legs. She wiggled, slightly. "A little hard, but at least my feet touch the ground."

Felix frowned, concentrating. Finesse with his shaping Skills was hard for him, but he'd been practicing with his metal work. He focused on the seats of the chair, letting the pattern of the Skill flow through him. It wanted to move stone, form it, carve it, to allow the earth to take shape. Carefully, Felix shaved off a piece of the seat beneath Vess, curving it slightly.

Stone Shaping is level 96!

Vess jolted in her seat before looking down. "Oh, that's much better!"

Felix goggled at the notification. *A level from just that? Why?*

"Hello? Felix? Is something wrong?"

"Hm? No. No, it's fine. I just gained a Skill level for that modification, and I'm not sure why. Stone Shaping was already level 95, and it's been torture pushing any thing beyond level 90." He scratched his head. "Last time it went up, I was fighting a Greater Elemental."

"Well, I would imagine it's a matter of understanding. Most do not face as many life-threatening situations as you do, some not even in their entire lives. Yet they still manage to level their abilities. My own growth has been accelerated by your troubles, but even still I have needed to grasp a greater understanding of my Skills to truly push them."

"Right. Yeah, Harn and Cal mentioned that before," Felix said. *Months ago.* "They said that anything after hitting Apprentice Tier would be a lot harder to advance. I've definitely seen the 'greater understanding leads to gains' theory in action before, but mostly it hasn't really mattered."

"Your Unbound nature, perhaps?"

"Maybe."

"Undoubtedly, your insistence on resisting forces far beyond your Tier and level has contributed to your swift rise." She held out two hands, balancing them like scales. "Risk. Reward. I do not know much of Master Tier, but I cannot imagine it is a simple thing to Temper into, Felix. Perhaps you shall require greater understanding, going forward?"

Felix sighed. "I was afraid of that."

Vess smiled, and her cheek dimpled in that way Felix found very distracting. "You will figure it out. Later, we can discuss some techniques I was taught as a child."

"Techniques? Like your visualization one?"

"Just so. Coming from a place beyond the Continent, I cannot begin to understand what you have not been taught, so we can go over the basics. Hopefully, they will be of some use."

"If they're anything like your visualization technique, then I'm down for it. That saved my butt down in the water."

Vess' smile deepened, and it was like her smile got brighter somehow. "That makes me happy, Felix. Now," she straightened, leaning away from the table to adjust her hair. "Let us talk of other things. It is so rare to have you alone, uninterrupted, and without prying ears. I plan to take advantage of it."

Felix battled a flush in his cheeks and lost. He leaned back, fiddling with his cuffs. "Advantage?"

"Felix, please. I am of the nobility," Vess said, her own cheeks coloring prettily. "And among us, there are things one must know when cour—getting to know one another. Only, this might be…rude."

"I trust you," he said.

Vess huffed a relieved breath. "And I, you. I do not wish to make you uncomfortable. If you wish to stop my questioning, that is absolutely fine. In fact, I can stop now if you are feeling—"

"Vess. Please," Felix said. "What's the question?"

"Tell me of Earth," she said. "And your family."

CHAPTER FIFTY-ONE

"Ah." Felix wasn't quite prepared for that one. "Well, home is…was Fort Lauderdale. That's in Florida. Which is in the United States—I'm not sure how much context I should give."

Vess waved a hand. "Was it nice? Florida?"

"It was too hot, too humid, and too sunny. 'Nice' is a bit of a stretch…but it could be beautiful."

"Hot and sunny sounds quite pleasant at the moment."

Felix chuckled. "You know, it's weird. My resistances are so high that I can ignore the temperature, but I still feel it. I might actually like the heat back home, now."

Vess leaned in. "And your family? What were they like?"

"Around. My mom's always been the stable center of our little family. Took care of all of us before and after my dad passed. Got me through school, my sister, too. She fought for us, tooth and nail. My sister was still living with her when I last saw them." Felix dragged his finger across the smooth stone table, a sourness bubbling up from within his chest. He clenched his fist and shoved it back down. "I miss them."

Vess reached out and placed her hand on Felix's. "I would love to meet them, one day. If they are anything like you, they are worth knowing."

Felix grinned. "Well, Gabby isn't all *that* great."

The black iron door swung open and Sata returned, this time with a young boy helper, both of them belaboring under trays piled with steaming food. It wasn't fancy, but it smelled delicious, and it was a *lot.* Felix had to quickly shape an extension onto the table to fit it all.

"Oh you…brought your own table?" Sata said after placing her trays down. "Well good thing. This suits your folk more."

The boy, even taller and more gangly than her, set a carafe hewn of literal ice between them all. "Where'd it come from? I didn't see it lugged down here."

Felix waggled his fingers, and a set of plates and cutlery manifested before himself and Vess. "Magic."

Ferric Shaping is level 16!

…

Ferric Shaping is level 22!

The boy's eyes widened. Sata patted him on the chest. "Let's not bother the nice Humans, Nall. Have a nice meal, Frostkiller's friends."

The two young giants left, Nall staring at them the whole while. They shut the black door with an echoing crash.

"I like that about you, Felix."

"Hmm?" He had lifted his plate and was inspecting the uneven surface with a critical eye. The knives and forks were even worse. "The plate thing? I was showing off a little. I should've made them outta stone. I'm better with it."

Vess laughed. "No. Not the plate thing. You really do not mind, do you?"

"Don't mind what?"

"That the giants seem to have given Beef the credit for today's battle."

"Oh. That." He set his plate down. "No, this is the best-case scenario. It was the point, after all."

Vess lifted an eyebrow. "The point? You planned for Beef to take responsibility?"

"Yeah. I'm not always gonna be around, especially if I keep expanding my Authority. Eventually, I'll need others to step up and help me out, and it'd be easier if the Territories respect them. I gave him the remains of the Greater Savage Therium and told him to make it a spectacle. He did good. He grows a little reputation with the giants, and I get a little anonymity for a bit longer. It's win/win. Plus, the boost is good for his ego. I think he's been stewing about not being more of a help last time we fought the Hierocracy."

"You…that is wise." Vess picked up her slightly warped fork and stabbed it into the steaming roast next to them. "Before long, you will no longer need my lessons on diplomacy."

"Don't worry. I promise I've got plenty of dumbass left in the tank."

She snort-laughed, then put her hand over her mouth in embarrassment. "You certainly have a way with words."

"Usually they just get me hit in the face," Felix admitted. He cut into the roasted haunch next to him, and a burst of spicy aromas filled the room. "Oh, this does look good."

Talk faded as they dug into their meal. There were six separate dishes on display, each portioned for far bigger stomachs, but the pair of them were hungry. It had been a while since he'd eaten anything, and there was only so long someone could go before that caught up to them.

The food was tasty as well as plentiful, cut from some beast Felix hadn't encountered before, and it was heavily seasoned. The giants may not have liked the heat, but that didn't apply to their food. The roast haunch wasn't even the worst of it; that title was reserved for a pair of punch bowls filled to the brim with sauce, grain, vegetables, and more meat. It was sort of like a curry, if someone decided to make it with hellfire.

It was delicious.

The last few bites of it went down, just as hot as the rest, but they vanished before Felix could swallow. *Hey!*

Too Weak, his Hunger rumbled.

That's because it wasn't meant for you, jerk. Felix frowned at the empty bowl before gazing hopefully over the rest of the platters. They were all of them empty—a few were even wiped clean. *Damn.*

"I'm surprised you left the plate and cutlery behind," Vess laughed. "I assume your Hunger is unsatisfied. You didn't get to eat the entire army, after all."

"It is a bit riled up, yeah. Then again, discounting the last few months, it usually is. I should be used to it by now." Felix sighed and leaned back. He straightened quickly when the thick stone chair gave a baleful groan. He quickly reinforced it with more rock. "You'd think I'd be used to that, too."

"I was regularly kept off-balance when I was a child as a form of training. I find it helpful to keep myself centered as often as possible and flow with new events." Vess took a sip from the chilled wine. "Learning to anticipate constant change is an uncomfortable habit, but it is worthwhile."

"Really? Was that from all the combat training you've talked about?"

"No, actually. My father's methods for teaching governance were quite grueling."

Felix grunted, unable to hide his surprise. "You started learning to fight when you were nine, what about the other stuff? Diplomacy and oration and all that."

"From the cradle." She smiled faintly at Felix's wince. "Evie reacted the same way, and I appreciate the sympathy, but I do not regret it. Unlike many on the Continent, my childhood was happy."

"Sorry. Mine was a lot more…I want to say carefree."

"Ah. Yes, that is something that was drilled into me quite young. My father was fond of telling me that 'the burdens of Authority are great and take a lifetime to master.'"

"He sounds like a good guy."

"He is one of the best. I am eager for you to meet him, one day. He would be able to drain the rest of your 'dumbass' away, I would think."

Felix laughed, and Vess was right behind him. "Your dad taught you about ruling, but what about your mom?"

"Mother was more interested in combat. She was a lot like yours. Strong."

"My mom's tough, true. Back when I was little, after my dad was gone, I saw her take on our landlord when he got handsy." Felix smiled as the memory rose up clearer than ever in his Mind. "Never saw her use a spear, but she had a mean right hook."

Vess laughed. "Very similar, then. My mother was our protector. The core of our House. Our Territory, even."

"What happened to her?" Felix asked.

"She fought something beyond her," Vess said, voice stiff. "A cautionary tale, some said. The Pathless priests once did a sermon on it…after my father heard of it, they never did again."

"She was a Dragoon, right? And a Chanter. Must have been some threat."

"She was, and I don't know. The details of her death have been withheld from me my entire life. To protect me, my father claimed. I was unaware of her history with the Grand Harmony until Zara told us, but it helps explain a great deal about my mother's power. She was well known for tackling tasks far too large for one of her Tier. More than once I woke at night, listening to my father trying to argue her down from some hunt." Vess pushed crumbs across her plate with her bent fork. "She rarely listened."

Felix grimaced. He held his Affinity close when he was around Vess, but he didn't need magical senses to tell she was still hurt by whatever happened with her mother. He cleared his throat. "Did you have a chance to explore Cold Rock a little?"

"A touch. After the battle was over, I spent some time checking on the wounded. There weren't many, thankfully, and I got to wander through their market a bit more. You?"

"Not so much. I've been prepping for tonight. After this, I'll be meeting with the Coven to discuss the approach to Kingsrock."

"It is called the Starfield Step, yes?"

Felix glanced at the shut iron door. "Yeah. The Chanters think its Nymean."

Vess leaned closer. "Trapped?"

"Undoubtedly."

"That should prove interesting."

Felix agreed. "It's possible we'll encounter monsters and enemies on the approach, but that'll just make things interesting." And if he was lucky, some of those monsters would end up being Tier V and up. His Hunger rumbled in agreement. "The real trick will be the Kingsrock itself."

"Are you to…climb it?"

"They've been pretty vague on that part. Feels very much like a 'get there and figure it out' sorta situation."

"It is beneficial that you are good at improvisation, then."

"Good seems like a stretch."

"You will survive, at least."

"Fingers crossed," he said. "Remind me to tell you about the time I survived getting lost in the Everglades. And that was before I had all these cool powers."

"A harrowing experience, I assume."

"Embarrassing mostly, if I ignore the part with all the crocodiles."

Vess tilted her head. "You do miss it."

Felix smiled, but it was a soft thing. The edges of that experience in the Everglades were softened by time and his hardships on the Continent. Compared to what he'd been through recently, it was almost a fond memory. "Yeah, I guess I do."

"Do you believe Zara? That you could be sent home?"

"I do believe her, but I doubt it's so simple. The fact that the

Chanters don't know enough about the Summoning Ritual makes me doubt it…but I can't lie: the idea is enticing."

"If you were given the choice, right now, would you leave? Go home to your people, your family, and leave the struggle behind?"

"I—I don't know." If he could run back to Earth, would the trouble just follow him? Crazy as it seemed, he was pretty sure his planet existed in the same universe…and who knew what the Ruin might do. He'd had visions of the consequences of running away from it before, back during his Omen Path. It had come to Earth. "I miss a lot of things back home, but we've made something here. Leaving Nagast behind, all of you… nah. The fight's here. I'm not running from it."

In recent months, Felix had mostly run toward his problems, and frankly, that was far better suited to him. He couldn't leave the Continent to face Ruin without trying to help.

Vess reached out and gripped his hand. "I am happy you are here, Felix." She smiled, cheek dimpling.

"I believe you."

"Can you not feel it?" she asked. "Your Affinity is far stronger than mine."

"Oh, uh. I don't…use that around you," he said. "It feels like cheating? Like I'm reading your mind without permission. Not really fair, considering I don't stop myself with others."

"That is sweet, Felix, but unnecessary. If you need my permission, then you have it." She tucked a strand of hair back behind her ear with her free hand, and her other one never left his palm. "Read away."

Felix tentatively relaxed the stranglehold he had on his Affinity around Vess…and found a startling deep well of a great many things. Sparks of amusement and curiosity sang around her, while a halo of lingering melancholy slowly faded from her thoughts. A deep thrum of joy was there, filling the gaps of her Spirit. Happiness.

To be near *him*.

The next thing he knew, Felix was kissing her. She tasted of spices and strong berry wine, and her hand tightened on his.

Hmm.

Felix blinked and pulled back, confused.

Another voice sounded off, a gleeful sort of chirrup. *What happened? Did he kiss her?*

Yes.

Oh, finally! *I gotta tell Evie. She owes me three monster cores.*

Wha–did you—Shut up. Felix shut out the sound of his Hunger and

Pit. Not so much muting them as closing a door in their faces. He could still hear them, but muffled.

"Did I do something wrong?" Vess asked, searching his expression. "You seem angry."

"Not at you," Felix said. "I've just got too many passengers on this road trip."

"Ah. Yin is a bit intrusive at times, too." Vess grinned at him, the dimple in her cheek pressing deep. "He promised to ward our bond this evening, however. For privacy."

Felix tried but couldn't keep the smile off his face. "That–ahem–that's nice of him."

"Mhm."

"Maybe he can teach me that trick sometime. Actually, as a Dragon, he probably knows a lot of magic. I never got a proper chance to talk to him about shaping—"

"Perhaps we can talk about Dragons another time."

"What? Oh. *Oh*—"

She kissed him, and for a while, Felix didn't care much about magic.

CHAPTER FIFTY-TWO

The sound of skis over frozen tundra was almost as loud as the wind that whipped down from the distant mountains, interrupted only by the heavy pants of the scarred Hoarhounds yoked to each of their sleds. Night had well and truly fallen, but the dark was a fleeting thing, due to the waxing moons above; the snow-reflected light was enough to cut the shadows into a false twilight.

Felix sat at the front of their company, first among a fleet of thirty such transports, only a small portion bearing his own people. Despite the Cold Rock Coven's statements to the contrary, a sizable number of their Witches and Warriors rode behind him on their journey toward the Kingsrock.

"How much farther?" Evie asked. Her breath was white steam under the moonlight, but her armor gleamed brighter. Felix had been surprised when he saw it and the other Claw members, each of whom now bore weapons of the same material. Harn had been busy.

"It is close," Kimaris answered.

"Hope so. Been sitting in this sleigh for hours," Beef muttered. He shivered. His Cold Resistance wasn't particularly impressive. "Aren't we supposed to be there by dawn?"

"Yeah. The approach opens at dawn," Felix said. "I figure we have another half hour before the sun comes up."

They had left a few hours after nightfall settled on the Hoarfrost. The Witches conjured up the huge sleds, each one three times the size of the ones that brought Felix to Cold Rock. Enough supplies were stacked onto a single sled to feed an army for weeks, and nine of the other transports were filled with Witches and Warriors meant to reinforce Felix's troops. Mother Vepar herself was there, riding just one sled back, her eyes fixed on the horizon.

Kimaris and Naberius told him this was a vote of confidence in Felix's approach, since the path to the Kingsrock brought a great many dangers, and the Coven was trusting him to keep them safe.

Felix was betting it had more to do with the *other* Coven he dragged along.

Five more sleds were filled with the enemy Witches, their hands no longer bound and their mouths uncovered. Ten others contained the Warriors and Berserkers that had survived the confrontation with Felix's Claw. All of them were presences in his Mind, each bearing a knot of silver strung to somewhere deep in Felix's chest.

"I do not trust them," Naberius said, following Felix's gaze. "Do you truly think they'll keep to this oath they made?"

"I'm sure of it," Felix said. He'd given them the choice to serve and fight for him or to be imprisoned in Cold Rock's newly formed Fiendstone jail. The Warriors had been quick to agree, and the Witches hadn't been far behind. The Risi, he had found, were quite proud—they knew they were beaten, and Felix could sense little to no resentment over that fact. That didn't stop him from making them swear fealty to his Seat and Seal, though. He wasn't *that* stupid.

"Felix has a way with words," Vess said from his other side. Felix shot her a look, his Mind cast back to a few hours prior. She grinned at him, and he had to fight down a blush. "And Oaths have power, if you know the way of it."

Naberius frowned. "We have heard of this magic, but it is not something of the Kin. I cannot help but distrust such things."

"I am sworn to the same Oath as the Feldspear Coven. All those the Autarch saved from enslavement are," Kimaris pointed out. "It is binding, yes, but it does not weigh on us. I have found that living in his city has granted us greater freedoms than I ever had while living in Cold Rock."

"To me, it sounds as if you've given up one master for another...but I shouldn't be surprised," Naberius scoffed. "You were always quick to choose subservience when it benefitted you. For yourself and others, no matter the consequences."

"Grimmar was chosen at Kingsrock, just as all Chieftains. Our choice was valid, Naberius. The Mother spoke to him! How could we ignore that?"

"And now the Mother of Monsters is gone, is she not? Or do you hear her whispers, still?"

"I—"

"The important thing is that Feldspear is here to help. I asked, and they agreed," Felix interrupted. Both Witches tore their heated gazes from each other and focused on him. He had no intention of refereeing another pissing match among the Coven. "They will provide support once we are within the Starfield Step."

"We shall see. Were they the ones who shared that name with you?" Naberius asked. "The details of the Kingsrock are hidden for a reason."

"No." Felix didn't bother to elaborate. "What's that?"

They crested a slope in the erratic terrain and there, to the east where the sky was beginning to lighten, was a set of thick spires. Felix squinted, his Perception flaring, and made out the shape of nine stones set vertically in the tundra. They were arranged in a loose circle, like the gap-toothed smile of some half-buried beast.

"That is the approach." Naberius' Spirit sang with anxiety and steely determination. "We must make it there before the sun rises. Warriors! Faster!"

The drivers lashed their reins, and the Hoarhounds put on a burst of speed. Felix wobbled back, sliding on the icy interior, and everyone else gave little lurches in their seats as the thirty sleds sped down the slope and up another.

The sky brightened even further.

"Faster! Put everything you have in it!"

The standing stones were ahead, weathered by relentless wind and cold, but they looked at least fifty feet tall. A hundred feet away, but they loomed like dour sentinels. Felix thought he could make out carvings on them, but the rising sun cast them all into sharp relief. Rays of light struck them and reflected off of shimmering inclusions in the rock.

The sleds whipped forward.

The dawn broke, and the standing stones were suddenly wreathed in light. Colorful ribbons burst around them, cascading across the sky as a song followed after. It rose to a sudden crescendo, a surprise orchestra of flutes, strings, and a deep, percussive rhythm.

Thump.

Thump.

Thump.

They breached the space between the stones just as the song reached its climax...and the world itself *twisted.* Felix jolted as vertigo claimed him, and he gripped the edge of the sled so hard he felt it crack. Thankfully, the sensation was short, and the Hoarhounds coasted to a stop.

"We made it," Kimaris said in clear relief.

"Where exactly did we make it to?" Evie asked. She looked up, and Felix followed her gaze.

Whoa. The sky was filled with swirling, almost liquid clouds made of gold. As he watched, thick threads of purple, blue, and greens zipped across it like strange lightning.

Mother Vepar's sled stopped close by, and she lifted her arms just as she raised her voice, pitched as if to address everyone present. "Welcome, Autarch Nevarre, to the Starfield Step."

Below the strange skies was a chaotic landscape of shifting ice. Glaciers the size of buildings shifted in all directions with little warning, smashing into one another hard enough to scatter debris like razor-sharp hail. It should have sounded like bombs going off, but everything was eerily silent.

Their thirty sleds all sat atop a strange flat area bounded by thin, vertical rocks–miniature replicas of the standing stones they had just passed through. They were unremarkable, save for the green moss that grew along the side facing them—Felix was pretty sure it was the only wild greenery he'd seen since entering the Hoarfrost.

Though we're not exactly in the Hoarfrost anymore, are we?

Feels like the black mountains, Pit sent from another sled away. His beak was raised to the sky and sniffed at the air. *But different. It's...zestier here.*

Zestier?

Pit nodded. *The air tastes spicy. Like it's waiting for something.*

I'll keep that in mind, he sent back. "Are the stones keeping sound out?"

"They are. The magic of this place is deep and unknown, but these places are the only safe spots within the Starfield Step." Mother Vepar pointed just beyond the mossy rocks, where a path led down into the churning fields. "That is where our challenge begins. And *that* is where we must go."

Beyond it all, rising at the center, was a lonely mountain. A corona of shimmering light surrounded it; threads of purple, blue, and green danced atop its peak like the aurora borealis.

The Kingsrock.

"We must make it to the base of the Kingsrock and anoint you in the old ways," Mother Vepar said.

"What does that entail?" Felix asked.

"We must beseech our ancestors to obtain the blessing of the Kingsrock, then anoint you with the fallen stars. I cannot tell you more than that; just know that it will take time, and we must move quickly. You can clearly see that the Starfield Step is dangerous, but not only because of its volatile terrain. It is trapped. The remains of the unquiet dead litter this field, and they do not take visitors lightly."

"Unquiet dead. Like necromancy?" Felix asked.

Mother Vepar's mouth thinned to a grim line. "Yes. There are… things within the ice that use such magic. You do not know woe until you have stared into the face of your fallen brethren, now set on ending you. That terror has felled more warriors than the crushing ice."

"How fun. Beef, Hallow. Do you feel anything?"

The Minotaur sniffed the air. "No. I can't feel anything beyond those rocks. Like nothing exists out there."

"The wards are too strong," Hallow agreed. Her Homunculus form tilted its roughly humanoid head at the boundary stones. "Not even Harmonic senses are getting through."

Felix realized she was right. He felt nothing beyond the barrier, though he could see the chaos quite clearly. "Chanters? What are those mossy stones protecting us from?"

"Sound, as was said," Laur said. He stood by the boundary stone and was staring at them intently. In the distance, another pair of glaciers slammed into one another before completely collapsing onto a third. "Those impacts are undoubtedly loud enough to deafen, even at Adept Tier. Perhaps at Master Tier, too, depending on your Body's composition. These wards are *complicated,* though—I am unsure what could breach them, if anything."

"Alright. Mother Vepar, you mentioned traps. Do you have them mapped out?"

"No. They move with the ice, just as the creatures within."

If Felix knew anything about Nymean ruins, it was that their traps didn't mess around. That would have to be the first priority as they moved forward. "What's the method the Kin use to get through here, then?"

Mother Vepar scoffed, but it was Naberius who spoke up. "You must decide that. You are a prospective High Chieftain and must prove yourself worthy."

"Another Path of Rule?" Felix asked.

"It is our way."

Great. Felix skimmed his Perception across the silent chaos beyond their landing ground…but just as the others said, it was like they didn't exist. Thankfully, his eyes still worked, and Felix spotted an obvious trail leading down from their staging ground into the Starfield Step proper. "Alright. The smart move would be to send scouts ahead, but I don't know that any of us would do well getting caught between those glaciers." He looked up, into the liquid gold sky. "We could fly, maybe."

The Witches exchanged looks, and Kimaris winced. None of them spoke.

Felix sighed. "Or not. Vess? Can you make sense of this?"

The Dragoon was staring off into the distance. "Going on the ground is a fool's game. The ice is moving erratically, we have no clue what sort of traps lie in wait, and there's an unknown necromantic threat. The sky appears to be safer, but we cannot count on it."

Yin clambered up her shoulder, smoke trailing from his little snout. "If the Witches speak truly, then we cannot dally here much longer. This Starfield Step requires our full strength. To do less would be to invite disaster."

"The lizard's right. Gotta bust through. Worrying and bein' cautious is for folks that got time to waste," Evie said.

A sharp, clarion call pierced the Starfield Step, somehow bypassing the excessive wardings to shiver down each and every one of their spines. It was followed by over a dozen bolts of liquid color from the molten sky, each landing in a different place miles away.

"What the hell was that?" Beef asked.

"The other tribes," Mother Vepar said, her wrinkled cheeks quivering. "They are here."

"Wait. How? We just got here, and it took us hours to reach those standing stones," Felix said.

"The tribes were alerted the moment we rode the dawn's light, but this is not our world. Time does not work the same here as in the Hoarfrost, and those who built the Kingsrock were not bound by the laws of monster or mortal." Mother Vepar gestured sharply to her Warriors, all of whom had clambered back aboard their sleds. "They could be here any moment. We must move."

"Damn it. Get it!" Felix commanded, and everyone rushed back to their places. "Harn!"

"Aye?"

"Split focus, full defense."

"Aye, sir. Talons to arms! Long and short-range Skills to bear! Focus on port and starboard sides!"

Felix turned to the others on his sled. "Tzfell, Evie, Pit and Vess: I need you for aerial support!"

"As you wish, Autarch."

"Of course, Felix."

"Stab and slash upwards, got it."

"What're we killing?" Pit asked. "Did anyone say?"

"No clue. Just blast anything that gets above us." Felix climbed up next to the Risi drivers as they nudged the hounds toward the boundary stones. "I'll handle the path ahead. Go!"

The Risi snapped their reins, and the Hoarhounds took off like a shot.

CHAPTER FIFTY-THREE

The moment they pierced the boundary ward, it was like a mountain falling on his ears. Glaciers hurled into the sky, thrown vertical as well as horizontal by some insane force, only to collide with one another in cataclysmic impacts. Those savage detonations tore at his ears and shoved at his chest like a mattress filled with pure lead.

"Laur! Shields!" he cried out.

"Already done!" the Elf shouted. Immediately, the terrible decibels were muffled—not extinguished entirely, but Felix no longer saw anyone clutching their skulls.

Good enough.

The hounds straightened and sped down the trail, a bare plane of white amid the glaciers, thin but serviceable. Felix's Perception and Affinity spread out, uninhibited now, pinged off of the unmitigated mayhem all around them. He flared them as his Mind tried to catalog everything going on, but it was a *lot*. He couldn't—

Felix's head snapped up. *Rime Shaping!*

A handful of jagged, house-sized boulders fell from above, debris from a distant collision, and Felix's Will met it mid-flight. They resisted for only a moment before he took them apart entirely.

Rime Shaping is level 87!

All that fell atop them was a torrent of loose snowflakes.

"Keep going! Full speed!" he commanded.

"Uta na!" one of the Warriors called, and the Hoarhounds' pelts crackled with purple vapor. They put on another burst of speed.

"You cannot waste yourself on the entire team!" Naberius shouted at him. She clutched at the rim of the sled, and there was fear in her eyes. "The Step responds to power, and if you display too much, it will respond in kind! Focus on us! Ensure that we make it through, and we Witches can claim the Kingsrock for you!"

"No!" Felix speared his Will through another falling slab of ice, boring a tunnel through its depths just in time for their sleds to race through. "Everyone makes it through!"

Thankfully, the glaciers didn't only explode toward them, and the path opened up as things split apart before them. The trail widened to hundreds of feet, with deep snow drifts to either side, like the world's freshest ski slope. Craggy cliffs of dark stone were revealed just beyond the snow, hemming them in. Felix took the moment to gaze beyond their group.

Pandemonium reigned in the Starfield Steps. The molden sky was filled with flashing lights, while colored threads gathered like strange lightning, striking downward at various places in every direction. The other tribes were moving, and quickly.

"What happens if the other tribes get to the Kingsrock first?" Felix asked Kimaris.

She opened her mouth, but Naberius cut in. "Then the claiming grows far more deadly."

"What does that mean?"

"There is no time. It will be hard enough if we get there first. Do not tempt fate!"

Felix flicked his gaze to Kimaris, but the woman only nodded mutely. "Faster, then. Warriors! Can we get more speed out of the hounds?"

"Ta, for a bit," one said beneath his horned helm.

"How long?" Felix asked.

The other Warrior driver gritted his teeth as the hounds shouldered through a six-foot drift of powder. "A handful of heartbeats. It's for bursts of speed only."

The path was open now, with most shifting glaciers further away from their progress. The snow was dragging at the heavy sleds, but they seemed to be moving at the same pace as the other tribes. "Hold it in reserve. Be ready when I shout, alright?"

"Ta falla!"

Felix looked back over the twenty-nine other sleds, all of them racing in a neat row. His soldiers had their hands on weapons, and their eyes fixed on the environment, and that included Kimaris' giants. The other giants and Witches, Cold Rock and Feldspear Covens, sat back. The Warriors and Berserkers all had eager expressions, but the Witches were pale. It was hard to get a bead on their Spirits among the tumult, but it was clear they weren't nearly as happy to be there as their subordinates.

Felix!

He spun around, guided by Pit's sudden warning, but was only just in time to see his sled rip across a glowing line of sigaldry. *Nymean work,* he noted, even as the details of it were lost to terrain and distance. He caught enough to guess at it…and that guess was confirmed as the cliffs to either side burst asunder.

"Monsters! All sides and comin' in fast!" Harn called out.

Living boulders chased with streaks of shimmering metal clattered out of the rubble, their angular insect legs blurring as they sped up. Felix knew them—or a version of them, at least.

Voracious Eye!

Name: Greater Gold Obelons
Type: Greater Elemental (Stone/Metal)

Like their lesser versions, these were shaped like immense, horned beetles crossed with rhinoceroses. The difference now were the veins of bright gold across their bodies…and their incredible size. Each one was twice the size of their sleds, and they were *fast.* They moved to match their speed with all the gusto of a rampaging herd of tanks.

"Greater Elementals! Stone and metal types!" Felix called out. "Tier IV!"

"Aye! Tough bastards, then!" Harn's axes ignited with silver flame. "Bring 'em down!"

From both sides of the convoy, a barrage of Skills was unleashed. Fire and lightning snapped outward, blasting against rocky hides, while ice and shadow impacted heads and legs. Despite the sheer amount of Skills, few Obelons fell.

What was worse, projectiles manifested around the Greater Elementals, rotating atop their backs like tiny asteroid belts before hurtling toward the sleds. The wards rippled but held under the first volley, but the creatures did not relent. As their group raced across the snow, the Obelons pummeled them with tire-sized boulders at utterly ridiculous speeds. The shields began to flash, ripples becoming a rainbow of hues.

"You need to end them!" Laur said, a shrill note in his voice. "They will overload the wards if this continues!"

"Brace!" someone else yelled, just before an elemental careened into their sleds. The thing's horns dipped low, as if to skewer them, but a blazing silver axe met it, and they were the first to fall. Insectoid legs snapped, and the elemental tumbled off into its own herd.

"Hide's too tough to penetrate! Aim for the joints and eyes!" Harn commanded.

"A good observation," Tzfell said, stepping up to the armored commander. "But tell your men to aim their Skills at my target."

Harn grunted. "Call the shot, lady."

"Magnetic Strike!" A series of geometric shapes burst from the Dwarven Chanter. Each one was made of lines and sound, all a distinct color and pitch, and they flew toward the nearest Obelon like an arrow. They hit, and suddenly the shapes seared themselves into the creature's rocky hide, gleaming with a dull silver against the gray and gold. "Fire now," she ordered.

The Claw released their attacks at the same elemental. Unerringly, the Skills zipped toward the etched metal patterns on the Obelon's back and legs, and each one landed with an unnatural *whomp-snap*. In moments, the creature fell, its legs snapped under its sundered shell. The Claw cheered.

"Eyes on the prize! Next target!" Harn said.

"Looks fun!" Beef pointed at the opposite side of the convoy, where the Obelons sent their full barrage of stones at their shields. "Keratin Conception!"

Insectoid legs of dark chitin exploded up from the snow, skewering the beasts like pikes, only to shatter as more piled atop them. The herd faltered, stymied for a moment by the Minotaur's strike, and he capitalized on it. "Hallow!"

"On my way," she said, voice echoing as always.

The Sharpwing Matriarch flew outward, releasing a high-pitched drone as it wove among the Greater Golden Obelons. Wings sharper than most blades sliced through the elementals' rocky limbs, severing legs and scoring deep wounds along gold-veined sides. A few of the creatures tried to retaliate, but they found themselves pelted with foot-long darts of hardened crystal. Hallow's Homunculus stood atop Beef's shoulders, arms firing round after round of darts. Eyes and mouths caught the worst of it, until the snow was littered with dark ichor.

"The way narrows!" one of the drivers called out.

Felix's attention snapped back to the team and the path ahead. The wide-open terrain was swiftly vanishing, and with it the Obelon threat… but in its place was a twisting, descending box canyon that was coated in slick, glistening ice.

Shit. "Hold onto something!" he shouted, just as their sled hit the downward slope.

The Hoarhounds howled, their fear too strong to be ignored, and the drivers frantically hauled back on their reins. It was pointless, though, as first one then all of their sleds were sent rushing down the slickened path. The walls of the canyon itself closed in, almost meeting in some places, and the sky's golden light was muted to a dim twilight. Explosions shook them, the glaciers still shifting in erratic, unpredictable ways.

Rime Shaping!

Felix cast the Skill again and again, pressing more of his Mana into the spell with every cast. He grasped at the ice as it whipped past, scoring it and hardening its texture into something the hounds and sleds could find purchase on. After a full twenty seconds of that, it even started to work.

Multi-Cast is level 84!

If only the walls of the box canyon had stayed in place. Another heaving section of the earth dropped into an unimaginably deep crevasse, tearing apart an entire side of the path and leaving it hanging over an empty abyss.

"Shit! Rime Shaping!" Felix said, mustering whatever else he could. "Stone Shaping!"

He pulled stone and ice together into an upswept lip, improvising the angle to hopefully keep them from falling to their deaths. Long experience mixing those two Skills made the job easier than he feared, and considerable time mindlessly watching the winter Olympics did the rest.

What amounted to a half-pipe of hardened ice and stone manifested atop the far edge just as Felix's sled hit it. The hounds whimpered, their footing gone as their skis ground against rock, striking sparks into the abyss…before sled after sled hugged the corner and sped onward.

Rime Shaping is level 88!
Stone Shaping is level 97!

"Woohoo!" Evie cheered. "Let's do that again!"

"I vote no," a Half-Orc beside her whimpered.

Fire bloomed against the top of the shields, flaring the wards into a prismatic cascade as the elemental magic spread outward.

"Oh, what now?" Felix groaned. Beside him, Laur grunted in clear pain, and Felix spotted blood dripping from the Elf's nose.

"Flying monsters," Vess reported, jerking her chin upward.

Twenty char-black creatures descended from above, each one shaped like a hellish bird with wings made of fire. Plumes of flame spewed from cruel, hooked beaks.

Voracious Eye!

Name: Greater Cinderwing
Type: Greater Elemental (Fire/Air)

"Greater Cinderwings! Greater Elementals of fire and air!" Felix reported. "More Tier IVs!"

"*More* Greater Elementals?" Tzfell exclaimed. "How many can this blasted place produce?"

"We have them!" Vess announced, conjuring ten gleaming Spears around her shoulders. Evie gripped her chain, and Pit angled himself to get a better view. "Will your ward allow us to pass through?"

Laur nodded rapidly. "Yes! Just be quick! Your Skills cost me nothing, but your Bodies will deplete my Mana fast!"

Vess and Evie shot upward, the former leaping impossible heights while the latter snagged her chain atop a passing Spear. They hit the descending elementals full-on, Evie flung over Vess' head just as the Cinderwing's breathed another cone of flames. They were met with cold steel and savage winds.

"Tempest Fugit!" Pit shrieked. Twenty spears of ice manifested and shot outward within the same eyeblink, each one finding a target among the Greater Elementals. The ice shot was especially effective, but the burst of lightning within each one served as a nice chaser. The Cinderwings died in droves.

Still, washes of fire hit, rocking their sleds as the path once again straightened out. Each Cinderwing that died exploded, blasting their wards and weakening them. Felix couldn't focus on it, but he knew anyway; Laur wouldn't shut up about it.

Ice and stone blasted from the cliffs around them, raining down from the fiery explosions. The sleds were hit, and several got tilted onto single skis. Risi Warriors hurled themselves aside, throwing the sleds back onto both solid footing, and Felix eyed the Witches at his side. "Not gonna help?"

Mother Vepar clutched at her fur mantle, face pale beneath the wrinkles. "We cannot! This is a test for your people! Our aid cannot come until the Kingsrock!"

"How convenient! Damnit!"

The world moved again, this time splitting the path ahead into jagged and unpredictable crevasses. The hounds didn't slow, fast enough and smart enough to judge where they could go and where they couldn't—until a literal chasm snapped open ahead.

Rime Shaping!

Mana flowed from Felix's channels and crackled into a thirty-foot wide bridge that spanned the sudden gorge. His sled shot across it, catching air as it hit the slight arch, and the others followed right behind.

"Watch out!"

Felix wasn't sure who said it, but he flagged the problem immediately: another shift in the tundra sent a rift across the ground…and sent the far end of the chasm toppling into the abyss. His bridge cracked and broke apart, with more than half of his people still atop of it.

"No! Cloudstep!" Crackling platforms of pure Mana formed beneath his convoy, catching those that tumbled off and angling them toward safety. The platforms shuddered, but held. Felix screamed at the weight, and the distance continued to open up between him and the slowed portion of his team. "Stop the sled!"

"We cannot! More ravines ahead!"

Felix cursed. "Pass the word! Now's a good time for that speed boost!"

"Ra falla dag!"

The Hoarhounds ahead of Felix shimmered with purple vapor before it sank into their haunches. The entire vehicle lurched forward as their pace doubled, and the same call went down the line.

Cloudstep!

Cloudstep!

Cloudstep!

The ground was falling apart and too unstable to shape anything from the earth, so all he could do was rely upon his old Skill. Felix poured all he had into it, thousands of Mana, and still the sheer tonnage of hound, giant, soldier and sled was like daggers into his chest and brain. Pain lanced up his arms and shoulders, as if he were holding the Cloudstep platforms on his very back as the tundra disintegrated beneath their skis.

C'mon! Hold it!

Platforms crackled and splintered, but they held. Their convoy dropped and bashed across the unconnected Cloudsteps, jostled by each lunging leap…until the last of them reached solid ground, more than a hundred yards behind Felix's position.

"Jesus Christ," he gasped. His knees felt like water. "They made it."

Cloudstep is level 75!
…
Cloudstep is level 81!

Adept Tier!
You Gain:
+10 DEX
+10 AGL
+10 INT

The path wound through another series of hard-banked turns, and Felix had to grip the sled to keep from toppling out. His insides surged with a bolt of System energy, which then expanded into a frenetic burst of something *more.*

SYNERGY DETECTED!
The Skill Cloudstep (Rare) Has Synergy With Sunken Ward (Rare)!
Do You Wish To Evolve Them?

Warning!
Evolution May Result In Death And Cannot Be Stopped Once Begun.
All Choices Have Consequences.

Continue?

Y/N

Now?! Felix groaned, but he mentally jabbed the affirmative. He wouldn't pass up the opportunity. *Why'd this have to happen now?*

Evolution In Process...

Music cascaded across his core space, followed closely by the ache of newly stretched limbs and spasming muscles. He braced against the Warrior beside him and dimly heard the man grunt in pain, but it was a distant thing. The evolution didn't take as much out of him as some others, but it was fearsome. A gruesome burn compared to having his arms melted off.

He barely noticed when they passed over another brilliant seal of sigaldry.

"That's a Dwarven trap!" Tzfell warned. "Metal and sharp…look out!"

A few rogue Obelons that had followed them across the wide crevasses were suddenly shattered by a hundred blades that slid out from nowhere. Sigaldry flashed all around them, blinding the whimpering hounds as more stout blades cut upward into the sky itself. The Cinder-wings swooped out of the way just as Evie and Vess landed among their craft again.

"That trap isn't done!" Vess warned. "Look!"

Felix couldn't; his vision was covered by a notification.

New Skill!
Storm Shaping (Epic), Level 1!
The flow of air, water, and lightning have been baked into your very bones, and you have delved deep within them to find the kernel of their truth. Breathe deep, Ascendent, and know that you shape the tempest itself.

He swiped it away.

"Down!" Beef shouted.

A huge, silver-green blade, fifty feet long and hewn out of pure, gleaming metal dropped atop of them at an angle. Everyone threw themselves to the side, but Felix stood tall and bared his teeth.

He took it straight to the chest.

CHAPTER FIFTY-FOUR

The blade bent and groaned as it impacted his Adept Tier Body, but his scales were seconds too late to appear. It sank into his chest, and blood poured from between his fingers. Felix's Health dropped by a whopping sixty percent.

Armored Skin is level 89!
...
Armored Skin is level 92!

The Song of Absolution is level 95!

"Felix!" Vess screamed.

Felix! Pit leaped forward, shoving his horse-sized body against the wounded man. Felix gripped hard onto Pit's barding, feeling the metal warp slightly in his unsteady hands. *You're bleeding!*

Armored Skin is level 93!
The Song of Absolution is level 96!

I'm...good.

Vess moved toward his side, too, but more blades swung at them from the Dwarven traps. Thankfully, none were as heavy as the one that still stuck into Felix, and she mustered her Spears to deflect them away.

The warding around them had vanished, rent asunder as the powerful trap closed around them, and the cataclysmic tumult of the Starfield Steps inundated them all. The Hoarhounds yelped, feet floundering amid the slashing blades, while giants and Claw alike fell back into their seats.

"We need those wards!" she shouted over the din.

Laur had fallen to the ground but was already chugging down a brilliant purple Mana Potion. "Gimme a moment!"

Felix stood, Pit at his back, silver-green metal bent and twisted around his bloody torso, and screamed. "Chthonic Tribute!"

The blade burst into streams of light before vanishing into Felix's open mouth just as the last sled made it across the final chasm. Felix bent over, weathering the agony with the sheer force of his Will, as Sovereign of Flesh patched up his wounds.

Mm. Give.

No. I need it to heal. For armor, Felix said.

Give More.

"The Kingsrock! It is ahead!" Kimaris shouted in joy.

Felix lifted his head; he could just see it over the shifting walls of ice and stone. The tumult of the Starfield Steps made judging distances hard, but they'd be there soon. The path was narrowing again as more glaciers shifted rapidly inward, and the sound beat at them all like a mace to their eardrums. "Laur!"

"Working! On! It!" the Chanter howled, his Mana fleeing from his grasp like a storm of liquid light. A chorus overlaid it, baritone and sonorous, and it rippled as it crossed over Felix's body. The cataclysmic sounds dulled once again. "There! It won't last long!"

Manasight is level 86!

"Sigaldry," he hissed. It gleamed further ahead, the same shape as the Dwarven traps, but it was layered over elegant Nymean script. Felix pushed his Perception outward, but was unsurprised by what he found. The path was too tight. They couldn't maneuver around it, likely as intended. He was too far away to know what they'd do—they were too complicated, and the layering made them look a jumbled mess. "Another trap ahead!" he announced, and his voice boomed over their convoy. "Brace!"

The wards won't hold!

I know, Pit. He took a breath, banishing the lingering agony from his Mind. *Keep me standing, please.* "Open the front of the ward!"

"I can't! The whole thing would collapse!" Laur protested.

"Then just exclude me! Just my face! Can you do that?"

The Chanter gritted his teeth, his sharp features gaunt. "Yes, but you'll—"

"Just do it!"

Pit rumbled against his back. *What're you doing?*

Keeping a promise.

The wards wobbled, a bubble bent inward from the top third of the front, until it passed its ephemeral plane across Felix's head and neck. The brutal noise of the Step assaulted him immediately, bursting blood vessels in his ears and nose that his Sovereign of Flesh raced to repair over and over again. The sleds sped onward, hounds flickering with purple vapor as they activated another speed boost. The shifting glaciers flashed by, a blur of blues, purples, and greens. Felix raised his hands, spreading them as far as he could as if he were gripping the world.

"Chthonic Tribute!"

The air howled, pulled into Felix's maw along with ice and Stone and the remnant fire of fleeing elementals. The path ahead withered, crumbling at the edges as pieces of it were yanked into his Tribute, but the glaciers still closed in as solid blocks that would not budge. They *persisted*, fighting against his Will and Intent with a mulish obstinance, as if the landscape itself fought back. Power gathered just beyond his senses, rising in answer to his own, maybe.

Was that why the Witches couldn't help him? He cast that thought aside. There was no room for it.

He focused, narrowing his attention until all of his concentration was laid upon Chthonic Tribute. The Skill whirred with greater ferocity, the pattern in his core trembling with the music of its activation. More was torn away, wind and ice consumed, but not enough.

Felix gritted his teeth, scales crawling up and over his ears to shield them from the savage noise. A second set of fangs grew over his lower face, bright white and razor sharp, but he paid none of it any mind.

He cast himself into his core space.

Down, past his Divine Tree, through the center of the lattice-work funnel and his roaring Skills. Into the darkness that sat at the root of his core space, just above the pillars that were his foundation. His Hunger bellowed, Mana and Essence ripping into its ever spinning accretion disc, and Felix advanced closer, until he felt his senses strip away as well.

Sight and hearing went first, then touch and balance. Taste was last, oddly enough, but then curiosity was gone, too. Anything that wasn't his need to consume was fed into the black hole.

Somehow he stopped, balancing atop the event horizon where his Hunger was so incredibly powerful that he was certain a single wobble would send him plummeting into an endless abyss. Never to return. But all of that was subconscious, a fleeting impression from someone else. For Felix, everything extraneous was stripped away. Absorbed.

Thought of himself vanished, of his people, of the strange golden sky and the Risi tribes that raced against them.

MORE.

The world beyond shook, a quake he felt even in his numbed state, and swaths of Mana and Essence poured into his core space like rivers of molten light. Purple and white and green and orange, all of it congealed into a brilliant torrent of power—all of it fed into his center.

YES.

There was no finesse, no technique. There was only Hunger.

"What the hell is he doing?" Beef asked. "What is—this is insane!"

Vess agreed. Ahead of them, the terrain itself actively dissolved into streamers of vapor and viscous liquid, all of them pouring directly into their front. Into Felix. It was too bright to look at, and her Elemental Eye had gained four levels just trying to glimpse into the chaos. Felix himself shone like the sun, and their only saving grace was Pit's bulk that shielded them from the worst of his blaze.

Beside her, Naberius' lavender skin was almost a match for the vanishing snow. "How—this is impossible. I thought we had his measure, I thought—What is he?"

"You'll get used to it," Evie said, just as a glacier exploded into the sky. "Look out!"

The mass of rock and ice tumbled toward them, inexorable in speed and cataclysmic in scale. Despite their wards, their struggles through the Starfield Step, she knew there was no fighting such a thing. It would crush them all. Vess flexed her legs, shoving herself forward toward Pit, intent to grab both of them—

And faltered. The glacier hadn't fallen onto them…it had been pulled.

Into Felix's open maw.

What is—She felt sympathy for the Witches. Felix had never used his power in such a way before. The glacier was ripped asunder, rendered down into Mana and Essence…and consumed completely.

"Imagine!" Evie shouted, a laugh of relief on her lips. "You kissed that mouth!"

Before Vess could even manage a blushing retort, their sleds burst through a sudden hole in the convulsing terrain. Their target shone ahead of them, caught up in a field of golden light that put Felix's display to shame. "Kingsrock! Dead ahead!"

It was half a league away, if that, and the landscape had flattened out into another snow-filled field. Spikes of stone and ice erupted at irregular, surprise intervals, but they could not withstand Felix's Skill. The path was clear. *We will make it!*

"Giants!" Hallow warned them, pointing a stubby stone digit toward another path that emptied out onto the field. A huge worm-like creature—easily matching the Depthwurms they had once faced—raced across the snow, its hide plated with thick armor and coated in jagged, icy spines that stuck up from its sides and back. A contingent of giants rode its back, perhaps fifty all told, each armed with incredibly long black spears.

"Petram Coven! They've tamed a Razorspine?" Kimaris watched the oncoming giants with fear and awe etched across her Spirit.

"We must move faster!" Naberius hissed.

"Maybe some help?" Vess asked, her Spears manifesting at her side again. "I can carry your Witches onto its back. We can—"

"No!" Mother Vepar shouted, her voice shrill with panic. "We cannot fight a Razorspine like this! We must make it to the Kingsrock first, or all is lost!"

The Razorspine roared, displaying snapping mandibles the size of one of their sleds, and its many eyes gleamed with crimson light. It surged toward them, closing the distance as the trapped spikes shattered harmlessly against it. Black iron spears flung at them, rebounding off of Laur's wards, but they shivered with prismatic distortions.

"I cannot hold this much longer," he said.

"Looks like they're not interested in attacking," Beef said. "Look, they're moving ahead."

"Meaning they'll get to the glowy rock first, dummy," Evie said. "That's not good."

"Oh. Right." Beef swallowed. "Shit."

"We must take that creature down." Tzfell said, casting a look at the

Witches. A sneer chased itself across her face. "With or without their help."

Vess looked to Felix, but he was still there, locked in place and absorbing every trap that tried to activate around them. Snow and stone was pulled into him like a strange cyclone…and an idea flashed into her Mind. "Evie! Beef! Go and board that Razorspine! Slow it down and watch for my signal!"

She appreciated how neither of them questioned her, but simply leaped to action. Evie threw her chain, increasing its weight and decreasing her own at the same time; it dragged her aloft at incredible speeds. Beef followed after, hanging from the hindquarters of his Sharpwing Matriarch.

"What do we do?" Kimaris asked, and Hallow's other two forms looked on.

Is this how Felix feels before one of his wild gambits? she wondered. It was exhilarating and terrifying. "We need to change direction."

Evie hadn't a clue what Vess planned, but she trusted her more than most. She landed atop the craggy hide of the Razorspine, her chain-throw leap proving only effective enough to catch the tail end of the armored bug. She swung her weapon down at the thing, but it only drew sparks off its hide.

Course it couldn't be that easy.

A field of undulating ice spines rose before her, but she kicked off the thing's rough segments with enough force that the wind whistled in her ears. Each time, she landed on another ice spine, leap-frogging across the huge creature's back, looking for giants. She was glad the Step's concussive noises had died down, but it was still plenty loud—loud enough that her approach was well covered.

Ten giants were nestled well at the top of the Razorspine's back, settled atop a strange platform made of ice. They each bore spears of black iron, and a ice-shaped crate held several more in reserve. Evie crept forward, tracking their gazes back to her convoy. The Razorspine had left it behind, but the Hoarhounds had sped up again. Now, they were slowly gaining on the worm, and the giants looked unnerved.

She had to slow the thing down, somehow. That meant getting to whoever was controlling this thing, and that wasn't the Warriors ahead of her. Most of them didn't even have beards, just a few wisps and a dream.

"Kas nu tuanta. What is that?" one asked.

"Looks like a glow shard, but shaped like a…child?"

"Tu ralla. Then what's it doing? The traps aren't working against it, and those are just Hoarhounds!"

"I don't know, ask the Witches!"

Aha. They're the ones pullin' the reins. She crept ahead, looking to bypass them entirely. Unfortunately, one of them was actually paying attention.

"Atan! A Human!"

"What? Kill it!"

Spears were flung at Evie, but she was already moving. They didn't even come close. She spun, unfurling her chain again, and caught two more spears in midair, deflecting them off the Razorspine entirely. "I don't wanna fight you!"

"Too bad!" one roared, before lunging at her with another long spear. She twisted away, leaping twenty paces all at once. More giants followed, weapons thrusting after her, but the Warriors weren't skilled enough. "You're fast for a Human, but they're all weak! You'll slow down eventually!"

"You'd think that," she said. "But you've already made a huge mistake, kids."

"Distractions!" Another crowed and pulled a triangular-shaped club out of another ice-shaped barrel.

Evie shrugged. "Maybe. But really…you should look up."

They did. Evie wasn't really sure what the Frost Giants expected, but it certainly wasn't a half ton of Minotaur dropped onto their heads. He landed among them, maul slamming into a Warrior's shoulders with stone-breaking force. The Risi collapsed with a scream, and Beef straightened. "Dang, that was a good line, Evie!"

"Where've you been? Takin' in the sights?"

"This thing is fast! Hallow had to compensate for how heavy I am!" He caught a triangular club with a single, ham hock fist. "Ooh, cool weapon!"

"Ugh!" Evie slipped through a fifteen-foot giant's guard, leaving the bull to his work. The Risi Warrior grabbed at her, intending to crush, but she caught him in the throat with a spiked ice gauntlet that manifested around her fist.

Rimefang's Wrath is level 69!

She followed up with a lashing chain, slicing a deep wound across another giant's exposed thigh. They both collapsed, still breathing but hurt deeply.

"Hey! Leave some for me!" Beef shouted and swung his stupidly huge maul. The giant weapon caught Risi Warriors in the gut, sending them flying off the platform. "Whoops! Keratin Conception!"

Jointed, insectoid limbs snagged the giants from the air, wrapping tight around them before binding to the ice platform itself. Beef let out a sigh of relief.

"What're you doin'?" Evie asked.

"I'm capturing them," the big idiot said. He gestured and more conjured limbs wrapped around the two she'd just downed. "It's what Felix would want."

Evie groaned. *Stupid*— then she groaned again. Because he was right. "Alright, fine! Lock 'em down! I'm going for the Witches!"

"Aye aye!" he said with a cheerful salute.

Just beyond the ice platform was another long section of monster and spines. Evie zipped through that, flaring her Agility for all it was worth. Vess had asked her to slow the Razorspine down, and she had wasted too much time already.

She found the Coven of Witches hunkered down just behind the flared ridges around the Razorspine's head. Flashy magic writing was hovering in the air between them, and several of the Witches were chanting something. All around them, however, were gleaming, purple wards, and the moment Evie appeared, they started lobbing projectiles and curses at her. Evie dodged them all, the projectiles clanging off the worm's hide, and the curses sizzling into nothing just over her shoulders.

"Hey! Slow this thing down!" she demanded.

Another spell hurtled for her, and Evie had to chain leap to get out of the way in time. The thing skipped off the worm's back before exploding in a shower of radiant sparks.

"I'll take that as a no, then!" Evie flung dagger after dagger at the wards, but each was turned aside, and even her chain couldn't penetrate their defenses. Still, each Witch she distracted seemed to slow down the big bug. Evie risked a glance at the convoy. They were gaining now, but —*What is she doing?*

Down below, she saw Vess standing near the brilliant shape of Felix. She pointed, and the convoy of sleds cut across the slowing Razorspine's path…and that vortex of craziness that Felix was emitting ripped into the glacial walls.

The stone and ice groaned, huge cracks ripping apart sections of its face. The Razorspine let out a wail, and the Witches stopped attacking Evie, focusing on their glowy magic.

Oh! She realized before whipping her chain forward. She shot over the hunkered down Witches and landed on the nasty bug's blunt head. The thing was awful and damn slick, but she wedged her feet between two ridged scales before looping her spiked chain around its twitching mandibles. It was *just* long enough to return to her hand.

"Ugh! Hey, ugly!" she called out. "Slow down!"

She hauled back with all of her Strength. The Razorspine screamed, its mouth pieces flexing about and almost ripping the chain out of her hands.

"Yyero's rotten ass!" she cursed. "Beef! Help me!"

The Minotaur landed beside her only heartbeats later, his expression confused. "The Witches didn't even notice me."

"They're too busy–unf! Keeping this thing under control!" Evie jerked her chin toward the ends of her chain. "Help me out, here! Grab these ends and pull to the side!"

"Got it!" he said, putting his furry mitts over the bladed links. "Gah, they're sharp."

"Don't touch that part!" Evie looked down, and her eyes widened. "Pull right! Now!"

Beef did so, his pile of muscles proving useful for once. His biceps and deltoids flexed, veins popping beneath his thin fur coat, and he shouted. "C'mon!"

The Razorspine twisted, something bursting behind them in a conflagration of purple light, and it's face sheared into the glacial cliff... just as the whole thing vanished.

"Jump!" Evie screamed, and tackled Beef off of the side...just as the Razorspine twisted and smashed into the sudden crevasse at cataclysmic speeds.

The thing's head turned to instant, gooey paste.

You Have Killed A Razorspine!
XP Earned!

Burning ash, she marveled as they fell. *That alone almost put me up another level.*

The ground rose up, and she lightened herself just as the Sharpwing Matriarch caught them both. Beef made a guttural *hnggh* noise, his shoulders wrenched backward in Hallow's claws, but it was only for a second before all of them collapsed back into the foremost sled.

Evie landed with an easy grace, and Beef…well, he hit the ice like a wet slab of leather.

"Hot damn, we're good!" Beef roared, his voice muffled against the sled's floor.

Evie laughed through big, ragged breaths. "When you're right, you're right!"

Ahead of them, the path opened onto a gleaming, polished platform made of what looked like a huge, monolithic slab of metal. Their skis hit it and slid across it like water, the sound of the Step utterly silenced. A huge tower—or mountain, maybe—loomed ahead, normal rock topped by soaring towers and a corona of gleaming lights. Kimaris and that fancy one started cheering, soon followed by the other giants and their wrinkly leader.

"Kingsrock!"

"We've done it!"

We? she thought, more than a little punch drunk from the fall. *Didn't see them on that bug.*

The sled though…it didn't stop. Theirs, at least—the others began to slow, hounds panting, but theirs seemed to be *gaining* speed. She blinked, looking at Vess, but she was staring at Felix. Evie winced and shielded her eyes, unable to see their illustrious leader through the gleam of his Skill. It was consuming the air so fast that they were being hauled along behind it, like some sorta Mana engine.

"Hey. Why aren't we slowing down?" she asked. "Felix! Stop doing…whatever that is!"

He didn't answer. He didn't stop.

And the Kingsrock was coming up *fast.*

CHAPTER FIFTY-FIVE

"We made it!" Pit cried out. His Companion was right up against him but the roar of the winds almost drowned out his voice. "Felix! Let go!"

"He cannot hear us!" Vess reached out and hissed in pain as the light around Felix intensified. "I cannot reach him!"

"I got it! *Convergence!*"

Pit vanished and reappeared within Felix's Spirit, which in the weird, not-quite-real worlds within worlds of core spaces, was only a short distance from Felix's own core. He dove deep, past the Tree and the spinning rings.

Felix!

There was no answer, even in the man's own core space. Rivers of Mana and Essence poured in all around him, spiraling down from above like a dive-bombing waterfall. Pit flew among it, Willing himself farther and farther into the maelstrom. It was there, in the dark, that the Chimera saw his friend.

Felix! Wake up!

Pit soared down, faster and faster. The streams hurtled alongside him, hauled into Felix's center so swiftly that their luminescence ran eye-searingly bright and agonizingly hot. Pit dodged, banking left and right between them all, but the streams were converging at the black center of his Companion's core space.

Right where Felix stood.

The streams weren't hitting him. In fact, there was nothing around his friend, except the yawning darkness of his Hunger. The streamers of power fed into the flat disc of it, spinning as if down an enormous, titanic drain, and Felix was balanced at the very edge of its brightest current. He stared vacantly into nothing, as if he couldn't hear Pit at all.

Bad Hunger! Let him go! Pit demanded. It howled in response, a riot of Dissonance and Harmony, so close to that noise from the grinding cores above that it was indistinguishable. *You already ate enough!*

Still.

Hungry.

I don't care! There's no more food if there's no more Felix! So cut it out!

There was no answer, only a continuation of its feeding frenzy. Felix tottered closer to the darknesses' center.

Fine.

Pit's ears popped as everything went utterly silent. The streams of Mana and Essence vanished, their power scattered into the wider expanse of Felix's core space. The sound of chaotic music abated, a caesura of aching absence. Pit didn't hesitate. He flew right into Hunger's reach, pivoting by dint of Will and Alacrity just enough to snap his hooked beak onto Felix's rugged coat.

I got you!

Chthonic Tribute is level 98!

Felix blinked awake, suddenly aware of a great many things—and unhappy with almost all of them.

"Pull!" someone yelled. "Toss anything you can!"

"I'm trying! He's yanking us along too fast!"

He didn't know what they meant, and he didn't care—Felix was far too preoccupied with the mountain they were bearing down on. He reached for power and found something new.

Storm Shaping!

Winds ripped from between his hands, carried with the force of a hurricane. Thunder roared, snapping between his arms, and their sled bucked under the sudden force. It rattled, twisted, skipped out to the side. The Hoarhounds yelped, their traces snapping as the wind threw them out of the way, and their ice sled bashed into the Kingsrock like a battering ram. It snapped in half.

Storm Shaping is level 2!

...

Storm Shaping is level 11!

"Oouf!"

"Hrrk!"

Felix rode the spinning sled to a stop, his two hands securing the Risi drivers in their seats, too. Everyone else, however, was thrown onto the golden ground as the bed split in two. Felix tensed before releasing a pent-up breath as his Eye cataloged their Health. They were all fine, though the Chanters weren't happy.

"Holy cow," Beef said, landing some distance away. He was one of the few who had gotten away. The Sharpwing Matriarch had attached to his back and flown him completely off the sled, and Hallow's Multipede had Naberius and Kimaris on her back.

"What was that?" Naberius asked. In the distance, the other sleds approached, moving far slower.

"Storm Shaping," Felix said. For the first time, he noticed the Spears, chain, and chitinous appendages lodged around the sled's skis. "How long were you trying to stop?"

"Not long," Evie said with a groan. "Had only a few ticks between enterin' and stoppin'." She kicked the ground. "Not like we could pierce this gleamin' gold, anyway."

"You were moving us quite fast," Vess added. Her eyes roamed across Felix's body. Searching. "Felix? Are you alright?" She put her hands on his shoulders, as if she needed to steady him, but he felt more than fine.

"I'm good. Just got a little carried away."

"A little?" she asked.

"More than a little. I—" Felix felt at his chest, where thick scales coated him beneath his mended Garment. With a chill, he knew that his Hunger could have chosen *not* to release him. He could have been stuck there. "It feels stronger. My Hunger. The pull of it was incredible when I just...let go."

Vess laid her hand over his. "Let go of what?"

Of everything, he wanted to say, but he could feel the curious gaze of Tzfell and Laur boring into the back of his skull. Instead, he mustered a smile. "My good sense, I guess. Sorry for making you worry."

Vess rubbed her fingers over the back of his hand. "I am simply relieved that you are fine."

Pit reappeared in a flash of light next to Felix. "Don't worry, guys. I gave that dummy a talking to."

Vess curled her fingers around Felix's. "Dummy?"

Felix blinked. "My Hunger?"

Pit nodded, looking fierce. "She didn't know she was hurting you. I explained it. Easy peasy."

"She?" Felix and Vess asked at the same time.

"We have attained the Kingsrock! Moreover, we are the first to have reached it!" Mother Vepar raised arms into the sky and released a spray of ice crystals. They caught the light like sparkling flares. A cheer went up, Warriors, Witches, and Claw members joining in as the sleds had come into range. Everyone, even the Feldspear Witches, were relieved to have arrived in one piece. "Yet this is not the end! Warriors! Form a perimeter! We must secure our place against all comers."

"More of this 'we' talk," Evie muttered. "Haven't seen them do much but sit tight."

"Think they're planning something?" Beef asked.

"That would be stupid, kid. They ain't stupid," Harn said. "They're supportin' Felix now, and his success is their success."

"I agree. They are not fools," Vess said. "It is the other tribes I am worried about, as well as the remainder of this strange ceremony."

"Lord Autarch," Mother Vepar continued. "Normally something like this would require more pomp and pageantry, but the other tribes will be upon us soon. I would ask that you present yourself to the Kingsrock, as all our Chieftains have done."

Felix glanced at the sheer wall of stone, only a couple feet from his position. "Present myself?"

"Place your hand on the Kingsrock," Mother Vepar clarified. "And we shall do what we must."

That's…ominous. But Felix hadn't come all this way *not* to claim the Kingsrock. He took two firm steps and put his clawed hand atop the craggy stone.

It felt warm, as if it had been baking in the summer sun, and was not nearly as rough as it appeared. Felix smiled. It was actually really nice, at least until something rippled beneath his palm. Unnerved, he pulled his hand back, just as a deep bell tolled, not so much echoing through the air as vibrating through everything. Felix clenched his teeth against it, and several of the abused ice sleds broke to splinters.

From the ground rose a series of familiar boundary stones, these uncoated by moss. Glyphs surged with light, illuminating looping swirls of script that were far too complex for Felix to immediately parse.

Ribbons of light manifested in the air, stronger than ever before. A phenomenon similar to the aurora borealis back home wrapped around the monolithic majesty of the Kingsrock, adding to the effects of the strange sky. The monolithic structure was normal stone at ground level, almost seeming like a mountain ripped straight from the earth—but hundreds of feet up, it transitioned seamlessly into fluted towers and delicate walkways. Felix couldn't make out much more than that, though, and even the ground level was oddly distorted.

"Felix?"

"Yeah, Beef?" Felix said, still trying to peer past the light above.

"We got a problem." Felix tore his attention away and saw Beef hefting his maul. The Minotaur was nervously regarding the golden ground. "My core is going *nuts*. There's something coming."

A hundred feet away, fists the size of water barrels punched through the metal earth, tearing screeching holes that geysered with liquid light. Blackened-green Mana followed, thick and syrupy, clinging hard to the desiccated bones of enormous Giantfolk corpses.

You Have Received A Timed Quest!

Survive Against The Unquiet Dead!
Duration: Ten Minutes
The Challenger and their Retinue may fight—up to 100 members, not including the Challenger. If a member of the Challenger's Retinue dies, time is lost. If the Challenger dies, they fail. If all of the Retinue perish, the Challenger fails. Their Title will be unmoored; any that defeat them will take it.
Reward: Title, Authority

Prepare Yourself, Challenger.

"You gotta be kidding me," Felix groaned.

Mother Vepar and her Witches and Warriors stood close to hand. "This is your greatest challenge, Lord Autarch. Survive, and you shall be worthy of the title of Chieftain!"

He ran his Voracious Eye across the amassing undead. The giants were listed as Berserkers, Stonehands, and Frostcallers. No Witches or

Warriors, but higher evolutions of the Risi people, specializing in endurance, in enormous strength, and in deadly ice magic, respectively.

They were Tier III and Tier IV creatures. Powerful even in small amounts, but over four hundred clawed their way out of the earth, and they weren't alone. Smaller corpses flooded out of the large rents, stout creatures bearing axes and halberds and swords in their thick mitts. All of them wore heavy, brutal-seeming armor.

"Those are Dwarven warriors," Tzfell said. Her tattooed face was pale. "Ironclads. Adept Tier. And that," she lifted a shaking finger and pointed at a single Dwarven corpse adorned in some sort of silver-green armor. It held a hammer and a really thick shield. "Noctis wept. That is a Forge Knight."

"Forge Knight?" Felix asked. His Eye roved over them, and he grunted in understanding before the words left the Chanter's mouth.

"A Forge Knight would have been a leader among the Prince's personal guards. They are legendary warriors. Master Tier."

Mm.

"The Dwarven Prince. You think these are corpses from that war?" Felix asked, ignoring his Hunger for the moment.

"They must be."

"There are at least three hundred of the lesser Dwarves," Laur pointed out. "That many Adepts…Not even counting the Master Tier, I have never faced so many powerful foes."

"Good thing I'm not asking you to," Felix said. "I got this. Alone."

"Hey!"

"With Pit," Felix amended. His Companion trilled happily. "Everyone stay back."

"Oh good. I could use a nap," Evie said.

"You sure?" Beef asked. "Those are a lot of monsters. And undead are kinda my thing."

"I'll see if I can save some corpses for you," Felix said to the teen. "How many more Bodies can you handle, Hallow?"

The Homunculus on Beef's shoulder tilted her head. "A few more, depending on their strength. Beef has grown quite strong. Soon, we shall be legion once more."

"Aw, thanks!"

Are You Prepared, Challenger?
Y/N

Felix considered the blue box prompt, mentally checking over everything on his person. Pit summoned his dark ice armor over his barding, suddenly looking twice his normal size and three times as ferocious. He hovered his finger over the *yes* option.

"Here they come," Harn muttered.

Felix looked up to find, not the undead, but dozens of other Risi tribes pouring across the golden plains toward them. They rode upon strange beasts and ice sleds, wrapped in wardings and sizzling curses and bristled with black iron weapons. There was even another Razorspine, bearing a separate tribe upon its back. In less than thirty seconds, they had surrounded their small party.

"Are we…fighting?" that Half-Orc mage asked.

"Naw, they're waiting, looks like," Evie said.

It certainly seemed that way to Felix. Witches and Warriors glared at them all, but their Spirits surged with hate when they saw non-giants in their midst. *This could go sideways real fast.*

The Feldspear Witches marched up to Felix. Their leader, a woman with bright purple eyes, looked like she wanted to fight him, but her words belied her expression. "Do not worry about the other tribes. And do not fret over the undead, either. The Feldspear Coven will aid you, Lord Autarch."

"No. The Cold Rock Coven will. You are not required," Mother Vepar said. She and her Coven had scrambled after their rivals, and the two groups stared daggers at one another. "With us, Lord Autarch, you are assured victory—"

"No." Felix said. "Both of you stay out of it."

"You cannot—"

Felix held up a hand, and the Covens went silent. *I could get used to that.* "You want me to prove I can do this? Then I will." He nodded at the other tribes, who were gathering into loose knots of bristling warriors. "You keep an eye on them."

"They would not interfere now. Not with a System challenge."

"Good. Then your job is easy." He walked forward, away from the giants and his company. Pit trotted behind.

Are You Prepared, Challenger?
Y/N

Yes.

Do You Have A Retinue?
If So, Designate How Many.

Yeah. Just one.

Warning!
A Large Retinue Is Recommended.
Do You Wish To Proceed?

Felix rolled his eyes. "If people could stop arguing with me for five minutes, that'd be great. Yes."

That bell tolled again, shaking through his chest and bones. The undead perked up and, as one, turned and faced Felix and Pit.

"Alright, bud." Felix cracked his neck. "Showtime."

CHAPTER FIFTY-SIX

"I'll take the little ones," Pit said. "You take the big ones."

Felix grinned as the undead trundled forward. They were faster than he expected for corpses, but not fast enough. "Are those your tactics books talking?"

Pit nodded, giant eyes serious. "'Divide and conquer.'"

"Right. Go."

They split, Pit strafing around the knot of undead. "Tempest Fugit!"

A swarm of ice spears zipped toward the smaller enemies, impaling several before bursting into jagged shards and lightning. Some fell, like marionettes with their strings cut, but most kept moving toward the Chimera.

Pit changed tactics.

"Dawn's Advent!"

Crescents of radiant light followed after the spears, slicing through frozen bone and corroded metal like paper. Pit juked left and then right, releasing curved light blades at every pivot. Swathes of undead fell, pieces hurled in opposite directions while the ice on them boiled into steam.

The Ironclads weren't intimidated in the least. They swarmed, sacrificing dozens in the attempt to get in range of their lumbering swords and axes. Soon, they were too close for his long-range magics, battering at his dark armor with Adept Tier Strength. Pit lashed out with his claws, trying to maintain some distance, but there were too many, and the Dwarven corpses did not fear his might. A few of them latched on, their skeletal hands digging between the plates of ice and shadow, then a few more.

They were trying to bury him.

Pit shrieked, and many of the undead stumbled back, clutching at their broken skulls.

Howl at the Dark is level 76!

It wasn't much space, but it was enough to twist his body. Pit popped his hip, and a weight slipped free of a dark scabbard. A giant, eight-foot tooth hurled into the air, flipping end over end. Pit caught it in his beak and brought the Blade of the Fang to bear. He swung. It was carved with esoteric symbols, honed to a razor's edge, and the undead before him were split tip to taint.

"Tak taht!" he said around the Blade's hilt. The dead said nothing, only lunged at him again.

Pit pounced, Blade first, and twisted in midair. He punched through the horde with ease, sending their corpses flying.

You Have Learned A New Skill!
Long Blade Mastery (Common), level 1!
Wield the blade to defeat your enemies and protect what is yours!

Long Blade Mastery is level 2!

Pit crowed and flipped the Blade up into the air, catching two Ironclads across the skull with his Hurricane Rasp before it came back down. He caught it easily and slashed.

Long Blade Mastery is level 3!

Oh, this is fun!

Felix darted toward the giants, and the ground groaned in protest with every footfall. With the speed at which he moved, that meant his audience heard a ringing, discordant note that followed Felix into battle. A dirge, but not for him.

A few struggling Ironclads crossed his path, and Felix paid them no mind. He kept moving, and their Adept Tier Bodies were turned to shrapnel.

Moving fast was a strange sensation; the world wanted to blur around him, but his Perception and Intelligence compensated. The result was a strange slow motion. Most of the undead, those rated around Journeyman and Adept, moved as if they were underwater. A few of the larger giants were quicker, though, plodding ahead at a decent clip.

He hit them first.

Red ice met his scaled fist, and a Berserker's arm imploded from the sheer force. Felix drove through the corpse—now double-dead—and spun into a high kick. His silver boot took off another giant's decrepit head as he soared upward and over three others.

Shadow Whip!

Four tendrils of pliable darkness sprang from his fingers, their root-like ends grasping onto an undead foe.

Adamant Discord!

With his other hand, he connected himself back to the golden earth and hauled inward with both arms at once. Lightning flashed and thunder boomed, though it was nothing compared to the sound of Felix's landing. The earth rang like a sundered gong, and red-ice warriors were simply torn to pieces.

Shadow Whip is level 69!

...

Shadow Whip is level 72!

More came, undaunted by his attacks. Felix wasn't sure how much Mind remained behind their dull eyes, but their Spirits were flush with a cold determination. They would not stop until he was dead or they were.

Hooks and blades made of red ice slashed for him, borne on arms longer than Felix's entire body. He met them with his hooked blade, and Inheritor's Will sang as it neatly severed even the most brutal-looking implement. The Berserkers died by the dozen, chests split and limbs scattered, but they were only the first wave.

Next came the Stonehands, another evolution of the Kin, where

Warriors bound themselves to elemental earth somehow. However it worked, it meant their bodies were powerful—thick with muscle, fat, and a shimmering dusty-brown vapor that trailed their every movement. Stone armor manifested around their arms and shoulders, similar to the Berserker's abilities, and each blow Felix avoided dented the metal earth.

With large amounts of enemies, Felix had learned that his best bet was to bombard them with spells from a distance…but he was trying to impress. His Perception danced across the gathered tribes, noting their tense expressions and eager glances toward the Kingsrock. He aimed to add the Hoarfrost to his Territories, and that would be far easier if the populace respected him.

Time?

9:34 remaining…

Felix growled. He rushed in, well within their reach but also inside their guard. The Stonehands summoned boulders to drop on him, but Felix met them with a vicious headbutt—the boulders splintered, pieces scattered like grapeshot in all directions. The shrapnel blew holes through undead chests and legs, dropping more of them than anything else he'd done yet.

That had to change.

A single swipe of his hooked blade split one Stonehand in half, and a pivoting follow-through ended another three. Their pieces fell, freeze-dried dust that spread in his wake. Felix moved, faster and faster, sword never stopping as he flowed through Third Form. Each sweep of his weapon ended with dismembered undead, and every shift of his stance was to engage yet another group.

On and on they came, a relentless tide. Frostcallers appeared, more svelte than a normal giant and accompanied by a chill mist. Their cadaverous hands worked the air into bars of ice, intending to trap him as the Stonehands and Berserkers rallied. His arms were lashed by rime and stone as their bodies piled atop him. A mass grave, come alive.

I don't have time for this! He had put on enough of a show. *Chthonic Tribute!*

His Hunger surged, a glee contained within its roar as Felix's Will caught against whatever was animating his opponents. *Something* fought back, bucked against his Mind, but it was not enough.

The undead atop him burst into dark, blackened-green vapor. All of it was consumed.

Felix stood among the glimmering gold, the last vestiges of undead Mana and Essence on his lips. They weren't all dead. Pit still fought against the Ironclads and a few Risi stragglers. Still, Felix glanced at the tribes, gauging their reactions. None were looking at the Kingsrock so eagerly anymore—instead, they were focused on him alone.

Mm. I Hunger.

You're worse than Pit. I damn near ate the entire Starfield Step, and now this. What more do you want?

One More.

Manasight is level 87!
Blind Fighting is level 79!

He pivoted just as he felt the change; a wayward rush of air Mana, and the descending pressure of a titan's Strength. A hammer came for him, a smear of silver-green, and Felix caught it against his swiftly-unsheathed Riposte. Only a dagger, the Crescian Bronze and his Strength were more than enough to surmount the undead and its mithril. For that was what the silver-green metal was, according to his Voracious Eye.

The Forge Knight was wearing a full set of it.

"Aren't you all kitted out," Felix muttered. The hammer was actually putting pressure against his dagger; it wasn't the worst thing to absorb a blow, but it was close. "What say we call this fight off? I know a Minotaur who'd be happy to meet you."

Steam poured from between its slatted visor, stained by the blackened green light of its eyes.

Felix took that as a *no* and kicked it in the chest. The undead slid backward, hard enough to bash *through* a straggling Risi Berserker. The giant fell into dusted chunks—the Forge Knight emerged, unscathed.

Interesting. Pit! You good?

I'm fine! Pit was a whirlwind of destruction, but the Ironclads he fought were tenacious and numerous. Still, he kept his remaining hundred distracted, lessening their numbers by the second. *Ask the Quest for more enemies! I'm running out!*

Just try to keep a few intact for Beef. Felix smiled, a weight dropping from his shoulders as he met the bright eyes of the Forge Knight. "This one's for me."

The Forge Knight charged.

It was far faster than any of the others. Its heater shield swung, bashing for his legs while its hammer came down from on high. Height, however, was relative, and the Dwarf was barely four and a half feet tall. Felix jumped, hopping over the strike and flaring Adamant Discord. Lightning surged, and he yanked on his connection to the air twenty feet distant. His direction changed just in time, as the Forge Knight stopped and reversed its own blow with incredible speed.

Then the guy *threw it.*

The hammer hurtled between them, a comet lit by blackened-green flames, directly at Felix's face. He hauled on another connection and dropped flat to the earth. His silver-green hammer shot by, blazing through the space Felix had just occupied and missing him by literal inches.

"Whoa." Felix stood up. "No wonder you thought you could take on an army of giants."

The Forge Knight inclined its helmet.

Felix blinked in surprise. "Did you just—"

Manasight is level 88!
Blind Fighting is level 80!

The hammer came back, utterly silent despite its gnarly speed. Felix twisted, dodging the weapon by the smallest of margins. The Forge Knight caught it nimbly by the haft before resetting itself. Felix laughed.

That was cool.

Mother Vepar stared in disbelief at the carnage unfolding before her. "Are they…toying with them?"

The girl child shrugged, her mouth half-full of bread and some sort of roast beast. "It's a time limit. Figure he's just waitin' out the glass, right?"

"He ate them. Warriors of old, claimed by the Kingsrock for this glorious test, and now they are gone."

"Dead's dead," the girl child said, propping her chin up on her fist. "Or undead, I guess. What's it matter if he cuts 'em up or eats 'em?"

"That is not—They are our honored fallen. To treat them this way is—"

Naberius laid a hand on her shoulder, her sharp face gleeful. "Look, Mother. Look at the other tribes."

Vepar did look, and she found dozens of the Kin staring at the battle with growing unease. "They are unsettled."

"And furious, yes." Naberius could not repress her own grin. "But afraid. Even they cannot contend with *that*."

Spells flashed among the horde, and the undead fell to pieces. Again and again. The Human's pet was a terror, somehow wielding a Kin-sized weapon to wreak havoc upon the field. The Autarch himself… well, he proved exactly how he earned his Titles.

"They will regret leaving Cold Rock to the whims of Feldspear," the younger Witch promised.

Mother Vepar, however, could not keep her eyes off the Human. *And what shall we regret, when this all ends?*

She truly did not know.

CHAPTER FIFTY-SEVEN

7:21 remaining...

Felix bobbed and weaved around the Forge Knight's swings. The weapon wasn't huge, but it was hefty, and the arm behind it was tireless—and talented. Every move from the Dwarven warrior was precise, each hammer blow carrying the momentum of the previous one, and its shield was just another weapon in its hands. The undead displayed some interesting Skills, too, and used them with the talents of a tactician. Felix felt like he was fighting Harn, in many ways.

As far as he could tell, the thing had that hammer toss and recall ability, another one that lent greater oomph to its strikes, a dash-like charge movement ability, and a Skill to heat metal. All metal, it turned out, as the undead warrior had tried to sear Felix's feet in his own boots. Unfortunately for the Forge Knight, Felix could handle a little cooking, and he'd put the red-hot boot into its mithril-armored gut.

Rounding out its offensive abilities, the Forge Knight could repair small rents in its own armor as well as emit a battle cry that made it stronger and faster. Those were quite interesting, especially if other Forge Knights could add onto the effect. He could imagine a battalion of Forge Knights, all of them boosted and self-healing beneath nigh-impenetrable mithril armor. It was a nightmare scenario for his Claw, were they forced against such an enemy. Felix filed away the information, adding to the pile of details he'd been collecting.

C'mon. What else have you got?

Felix was determined to learn as much as he could during the fight. It was part of why he hadn't pressed to end the Timed Quest. Tzfell said the Forge Knights were elite warriors, and it was likely that the order or whatever still existed among the Dwarves. The undead warrior was smart, but it stuck to the same script, keeping its distance while it circled Felix, shield up and hammer low.

The moment Felix showed a sign of an opening, the Knight would activate its charge and rush to take advantage of it, swinging its hammer into his legs or bashing him with the shield. Hammer throw. Heat metal. Retreat, repair armor if necessary. The creature wasn't a construct, but either the Dwarves weren't very creative fighters, or the process of becoming an undead puppet wasn't great for ingenuity. Felix was betting on the latter.

The Forge Knight rushed him.

He sighed. "Fine."

Adamant Discord!

He caught the Dwarf in brilliant cords of lightning and swiftly yanked on their sudden connection. At the same time, Felix stepped aside, letting the smaller warrior zip past him at crazy speeds. It made it about thirty feet before it floundered, smashing into the golden ground with the screeching squeal of metal on metal.

The Risi tribes looked on, only a few feet away from the Forge Knight's half-buried form. Most watched intently, the Warriors and Berserkers breathing heavy with intense eyes. Others though, their gazes flicked between the Knight and Felix. Their Spirits were deep wells of descending notes, slowly circling around something they refused to acknowledge.

Not impressed? Felix shook his head. Maybe he should have led with a big area of effect spell after all.

An Ironclad tumbled past him, pieces of its armor ripping apart from a massive rent in its breastplate. Dust poured out of it, followed closely by blackened green smoke that vented from every part of its broken body. *Pit's having a good time.*

The tenku was ripping through his opponents, a whirling dervish of fur, feathers, and razor-sharp Fang. He was getting pretty damn good with that old sword, too.

Pit's Long Blade Mastery is level 25!

...

Pit's Long Blade Mastery is level 39!

Apprentice Tier!
Pit Gains:
+5 STR
+5 END
+5 DEX

Pit's Dark Glacial Guard is level 26!
...
Pit's Dark Glacial Guard is level 42!

Pit's Mantle of Tumult is level 79!
...
Pit's Mantle of Tumult is level 80!

Pit's Howl at the Dark is level 77!
...
Pit's Howl at the Dark is level 79!

The Blade of the Fang swung with every flex of Pit's neck, but he shifted his grip several times while Felix watched. He ran with it held to the side, cutting down the far slower undead, and he spun it into a reverse grip when he threw himself backward, slamming foes into the ground. The Fang cut through them like a butcher's blade. The last of the corpses crowded close to him, but he pulled on his Mantle of Tumult. The shroud of wind and lightning synergized well with his Dark Glacial Guard, making him look like a storm come to life.

Pit met his eyes and knowledge without words spread between them. The fight was just about over. Dust and smoke filled the air, and the few that remained would be dealt with soon. Felix nodded and regarded the Forge Knight from thirty feet away. The undead was crawling out of its hole, pieces of its armor sealing shut like liquid as other parts heated up.

It uses its heat metal and repair Skills together. Huh. Neat. "Okay, man. Time to end this. I appreciate you letting me learn." Felix wasn't sure why he'd said that, but it felt right. As did the slight bow he gave the Knight.

Just like before, the Forge Knight inclined its head before resetting itself, shield up and hammer out.

Felix did the same, bending his knees and lifting his Inheritor's Will up into a guard position. His Riposte was back in its sheath. He wouldn't need it. "Let's go. Full power."

In a blink, the Dwarven warrior was there, shield thrust where Felix's gut once was—it found only empty air. Instead, the Forge Knight made a desperate turn, deflecting Felix's claws. Sparks leapt from the mithril shield, and its hammer rose in an upswing.

Felix caught it, grunting at the force of the strike. "Damn. You are strong. I know a guy who'd love to give you a new job." He forced it down, heaving it until the hammer lodged itself into the golden earth.

The Knight pulled at the haft in vain, but was unable to free it. Instead, the ground began to heat up and soften—but Felix shaped ice over the buried hammer, and the undead's Skill failed. It swung its glimmering gaze on him, blackened green smoke escaping the slats of its helm, and swung at him with his shield.

Mine.

"I know." Felix slapped its arm away. He reached out and laid his enormous, clawed hand over the Knight's helm, ignoring the Dwarf's powerful blows to his arms. "Sorry, Beef."

Chthonic Tribute!

The Knight screamed, a sound that raised the hairs on Felix's neck and made his teeth hurt. His armor stretched, dissolving as it broke apart…releasing a geyser of dark smoke and blackened green light. It swarmed into Felix, carrying enough power with it that his gut twisted. His Hunger roared.

The scream stopped.

You Have Killed Mavir Galion, Dwarven Forge Knight!
XP Earned!

"Good fight, Mavir Galion," he muttered to the fallen Forge Knight. All that remained of the Dwarven warrior was his heater shield and hammer. He hadn't meant to eat the guy's armor—that could have been useful—but there had been no separation between them. The Dwarf had been his armor, and his armor was him. "I'll make sure you're put to good use."

It was the best he could do.

Felix waited a moment, but there was no System notification. He frowned. *Hey. I thought you were supposed to double my gains?*

Not Done.

I see. Felix could feel his Hunger's jaws worrying at the Essence of the Forge Knight. As a Master Tier, he supposed it would be some time before it was digested fully. Which meant he couldn't complete the Delicious Devour Quest yet.

His most recent Quest, however, flashed across his vision just as Pit landed beside him.

6:44 remaining…
All Unquiet Dead Are Silenced.

Quest Completed!

Survive Against The Unquiet Dead!
Duration: Ten Minutes
The Challenger and their Retinue may fight—up to 100 members, not including the Challenger. If a member of the Challenger's Retinue dies, time is lost. If the Challenger dies, they fail. If all of the Retinue perish, the Challenger fails. Their Title will be unmoored; any that defeat them will take it.
Reward: Title, Authority

New Title!
Champion of the Long Night (Legendary)!
You have proven yourself before the Seat and Seal of Khalheim! You have earned the right to approach the Gate of Gloaming! As Champion, you have proven yourself in battle and must be commended! +10 levels for a single Skill of your choice below Adept Tier!

Your Authority Has Increased!

Due To Completing In Record Time, Your Rewards Are Increased!
Due To Dispatching A Master Tier Opponent, Your Rewards Are Increased!

New Skill!
War Cry (Rare), Level 1!
Used to—

ERROR
Due To Synergy Between Your Primordial Nature And Affinity For Dissonance, This Skill Has Evolved!

Quiet Cacophony (Epic), Level 1!
The Forge Knights of old knew a wild cry meant to bolster their allies, but this is its opposite. Soft, precise, and offensive. Debilitate your enemies with the subtle sounds of Dissonance! Let loose the Chthonic Depths! Inflicts instances of Disorientation, Disquiet, and Disgust. Greater levels increase control over effects, including intensity and duration.

"You got a…whisper Skill?" Pit asked around the haft of the Fang.

"I guess?" Felix closed the notifications, though the Title he'd received lingered in his Mind. "Might be useful, though."

Pit spat out the Fang. "I *guess*."

Felix leaned over, picking up the huge sword and placing it back into the sheath on Pit's barding. "This sword fits you. You should use it from now on."

"Did you see me? I was all whirlin' and slicin'."

"Can't believe we haven't given you a sword before. You're a natural, dude."

"Right?"

A deep, gong-like noise rose from beneath them, and the broken ground began sealing itself up. Felix grabbed the hammer and shield, pulling the former from the ice he'd buried it in with a firm yank. He jerked his chin toward the corpses still piled on the ground. "Go get those, please."

"Sure."

Pit trotted off, his long legs eating up the distance, and Felix regarded the silent tribes around him. They watched, hands on weapons, shoulders tense, but it was their Spirits that told the true story.

Maybe it's too soon for respect, he thought with disappointment. He hefted the hammer to his shoulder, and several of the Kin flinched. *Fear will have to do. For now.*

A second bell tolled, and this time, it was impossible to ignore. A searing notification appeared fifty feet above Felix, visible to everyone, a sapphire blue box decorated with scrolling gold and silver. The words shouted into all of their Minds, not spoken, but known regardless.

Behold!
The Champion of the Long Night!
Approach, Champion!
Approach the Gate of Gloaming!

It was like a seal had been broken. Cheers and whooping cries filled the air as the Claw and the giants of both Cold Rock and Feldspear joined in. Evie wolf-whistled at him, and a few over-enthusiastic mages sent fire and lightning crackling into the sky.

"This one has proven himself!" Naberius cried out, turning to address the still silent tribes.

"He is to be our new High Chieftain!" Kimaris added.

Despite all they just witnessed, cries of refusal echoed among the tribes. Felix picked out many of their words, and Grimmar featured heavily. Those were the loudest among the Risi and the most bitter.

Naberius gestured to the Kingsrock. "The Frostfather has spoken! He is Champion!"

Several Berserkers moved to approach, violence carried in their twitching muscles, but Witches held them back. One in particular with green and purple swirls upon her skin stepped forward. Floated, really, because while her long gown brushed the gleaming ground, her feet did not. "He is not of the Kin, Witch of Cold Rock. Worse, he is Human. No mortal may rule us. *They* can attest to that."

She gestured to the piles of Ironclads that Pit was scooting across the ground. The Chimera paused, looking at all the attention he was receiving, and puffed out his chest.

"The Dwarves tried to take our birthright from us, and their blood has stained these grounds ever since. Our ancestors denied them, as we have continued to do for countless centuries. We have all witnessed the strength of this mortal. It is...incredible." The Witch swallowed. It was the only betrayal of her nerves, for her Spirit was rock steady to Felix's Affinity. "But it does not matter. We will not bow down to a Human, not even if we must sacrifice our lives."

"He bears the Titles of the Frostfather," Mother Vepar countered. She pushed ahead of Naberious and Kimaris, addressing not just the floating Witch but all the tribes present. "The Path of Rule has been walked! He reached the Kingsrock first! You saw him defeat the unquiet dead with the help of only one other. Among them was a greater foe than any here could face, and he didn't simply survive. He ended the

Quest in less than half the time! He has proven himself worthy three times over!"

It wasn't enough. Felix knew it before more Witches joined the floating one. Words were bantered, back and forth, all while tensions drew higher and higher. Axes were hefted, magics glimmered just out of sight, and before long, the Risi would wage war against itself—and they would lose. He and his company would be forced to spill the blood of an entire people on these grounds.

Felix refused.

"What would prove to you that I am worthy of leading you?" he asked. Yelled, really. It was loud enough that it punched through the argument, echoing across the terrain like thunder. The arguing ground to a halt.

"You wish to claim a place as our leader?" The floating Witch asked. She clearly held some rank among the Kin, because no one tried to talk over her. "You cannot. You are an outsider. A *Human*. The Kin cannot place you above ourselves, not after what the mortal Races have done to us. But," she said, dragging the word across her lips like a bared blade. "If you truly have the Frostfather's favor, then let us see it. Claim the Kingsrock, well and truly. Claim it as the first High Chieftain once did, Ages past."

Excited murmurs rippled through the assembled tribes, and more than one Witch nodded in agreement. Felix frowned and motioned his giants closer. "What are they talking about?"

"A legend," Naberius hissed. She bared her teeth at the floating Witch, and if she had hackles, Felix was sure they would be lifted. "A myth."

"It is our oldest story," Mother Vepar told him. "The first of us came upon the Kingsrock and were proven worthy. From atop it, we ruled for an entire Age, before treachery and deceit sent us falling to the earth. It was then that we spread into the southern lands, where we spent many centuries."

"And when we returned, the Kingsrock was no more than stone," Kimaris added. "No Kin has been able to get the Kingsrock to respond. Reaching this place, conquering the challenge of undead has been our test since our history began. No Champion has ever opened the Gates of Gloaming."

Authority, Felix realized. He looked to the Kingsrock, to the soaring towers far, far above it. Ribbons of glacial light still wreathed it, reminiscent of Laur's wardings. Even if he flew up to it, Felix had doubts he'd get through that way. Still, he set that aside as Plan B.

"Fine," he said to the tribes. "Give me a second."

The floating Witch smiled wide and gestured imperiously toward the Kingsrock. "As you wish, mortal."

Felix walked to the giant monolithic structure, motioning for his friends to stay back. Pit was still rolling those corpses, and Harn was with his soldiers, but Vess and Beef slowed their steps, clearly having planned to come help. Evie, however, was reclining against a bundle of supplies that had spilled onto the ground.

She gave him an encouraging thumbs up. "Go get 'em, champion."

The Kingsrock was mostly cylindrical, though it had variations to the structure, as it appeared to be entirely natural. Appeared so, at least. With Skills like Stone Shaping, Felix was positive he'd never know natural formations from magically manipulated ones ever again. Still, something about the Kingsrock's imperfections seemed genuine; a rough surface here, a crack there.

Right where the rounded shape of the stone bowed inward, he found a faint impression of large stars carved into it. Nymean stars, progressing from two-points all the way to twenty-seven points. They rose up and over in an arch, as if framing a giant eighty-foot-tall doorway. Yet the forty-foot space between them was simply a blank wall of solid stone.

His hip buzzed.

Felix grasped his Inheritor's Will and unsheathed it in one smooth motion. A bronze light unfurled from it while two glyphs shimmered urgently upon the flat of the blade, near the hilt. He knew those glyphs well, though they hadn't been used very often.

Etheric Division - The first of several arrays. The blade may cut through spellforms and Mana formations at the Inheritor's request, but it is gated by the advancement of the Inheritor.

Etheric Unification - Nymean power resonates with the Blade, drawing other sources of Nymean sorcery toward itself.

The weapon twitched in his hand, the tip lining itself up with the empty plane of stone. It wanted him to move.

Felix listened, letting the sword guide him into a strange series of positions. It was only after the third one that he realized they were stances, similar to the three Forms he'd learned from Darius, but alien, too. The blade jerked, buzzing higher and faster, and Felix struggled to catch up. He scrambled, flaring his stats to meet the weapon's demands, until it gave a keening wail, and Felix thrust forward a final time.

The Inheritor's Will sank into the stone up to the hilt.

Ancient inscriptions rippled across the Kingsrock, spreading from his sword to encompass the entirety of his vision. The area immediately before him illuminated with a bronze light, turning flat stone into a carved relief in seconds. Towering mountains before a setting sun, heaving ice, swirling clouds, and raging beasts that looked very similar to a Razorspine. At the center, where his sword was embedded, a deep incision split the stone, forming two massive doors.

Felix pulled his Inheritor's Will free, and the entirety of the Starfield Steps shook. A note of pure, unadulterated Harmony sang from his blade's edge, and the glyphs atop it were like miniature suns in his hands.

Holy crap, Pit sent. Felix agreed.

"Ta falla! Outta the way!"

A burly Frost Giant surged through the crowd and charged at Felix. He swung his huge axe, but Felix dodged it with ease—the man's focus was on the doors. "I'm High Chieftain! Not you!"

The guy was fast, Felix had to admit that. He ran to the newly-formed doors at incredible speed…and crashed into them *hard.* The giant bounced back, wards flashing with rainbow light as he was tossed unceremoniously to the ground.

The crowd erupted with bellows, and more giants began to charge.

Felix shook his head and took a single step toward the doors. He put his hand against them and lightly shoved.

They swung open, light as a feather.

Authority Recognized, Inheritor!
Be Welcome, Autarch of Nagast!
Be Welcome, King of Ahkestria and the Leviathan Depths!
Be Welcome, Champion of the Long Night!

Pit crowed. "How's that for proof, Witches?"

CHAPTER FIFTY-EIGHT

"Do you think it is safe?" Vess asked.

"I really doubt it." Felix peered into the dark hall beyond the Gloaming Gate. It bored straight into the Kingsrock, and the thick shadows were unmarred by the inscriptions now illuminating the outside of the gate. "If this was made by Nymeans, then I won't be surprised by more traps."

"You were welcomed. Your Authority should keep any defenses at bay, no?"

Felix shrugged. "Probably."

A small shape jerked at Vess' shoulder, and the motion was followed by a series of rapid snorts before Yin poked his small head out of Vess' cowl. He squinted into the light. "This is the Kingsrock?"

"Good morning, Yin. Yes, it is."

"I approve of the decoration," he said, jerking his bearded chin toward the golden ground. "The boy got us here?"

"He did." Vess looked at Felix, who was smiling at them both. She felt a slight flutter in her stomach, entirely unconnected to her core space. His eyes were so blue when he smiled, like something inside of him was glowing. "It was quite impressive."

Yintarion squinted at her then sniffed. "I smell elementals. You fought some while I slept?"

"I did. I would have woken you, but—"

"No, I required the rest. Digestion is important and taxing."

Yintarion crawled out of Vess' cowl completely, perching atop her silver and white pauldron. He stretched, similar to the house cats her cousins owned. "What kind?"

"Fire and air. Earth and metal," Felix answered, now crouching near the entryway and running his hands along hexagonal tiles. They were inlaid with silver and gold, depicting interesting, swirling designs. "Greater Elementals."

"Oho." Yin turned on her, his golden eyes intense. "I need them."

"I will see what we can do. The enemies were left back in the Starfield Steps, outside this area." She didn't relish the idea of hunting those treacherous glaciers, not alone, but if Yintarion needed them to advance his Evolution, she would not balk. "I will see what we can do after we secure this place."

"Ah. Yes. The Kingsrock. What of the giants? Ah." Yin angled his neck around Vess' head, peering at the prone form of one giant as well as several others huddled close. They watched Felix with angry eyes but had not made a move since he had opened the gate. "Do they remain an issue?"

"No," Felix said. He glanced back at the giants and the gathered tribes beyond them. "Not if they got the hint."

Kimaris, Battlelord Vidar, and all the giants sworn to Felix had approached, setting themselves between the tribes and the Gloaming Gate. On their heels were the Feldspear Coven and the Cold Rock Coven, jostling for positioning as before. The floating Witch, the one who had addressed Felix previously, simply watched from a distance. Vess couldn't quite make out her Spirit, but her expression was pinched as several other Witches spoke rapidly in her ear.

Impressive demonstration or not, Vess doubted their words had anything to do with acquiescing to Felix's Authority.

"My Lord," Kimaris said by way of greeting. "I think we should proceed within, before relations…escalate."

"Probably smart." Felix straightened from his inspection and ran a hand through the air just inside the gate. "I think it's safe. There's a lot of Mana moving around in there, way more than normal. Keep your heads on a swivel. Harn? Have the company bring up the rear."

"Aye."

The Claw marched closer, hands near their weapons but nothing drawn. They came up behind the allied giants, adding a second barrier between Felix and the gathered tribes. Vess lost sight of the floating Witch and her attendants completely.

"Vess. Evie. Beef. Walk with me."

She followed Felix, the others—with the Chanters trailing behind—just after.

Felix stepped into the corridor. It was warm inside and smelled of damp minerals, not sulfur but almost salty. The ornate tiles beneath his boots didn't fall apart or light up with sigils, and the towering walls were carved into thin, rectangular panels that framed sweeping pastoral vistas. Someone with a great deal of talent had faithfully recreated the barren expanse of snowy tundra and the looming northern mountains, and in much the same way as the Shadowgates and other Nymean ruins, colors were denoted by different types of ore and stone. The ceiling was too high to see normally, hazed by a veil of shadow and some sort of thick Mana. That was what Felix had been really concerned with during his investigation…but it remained suspended, doing who knew what, but at least not actively harming him.

"The way seems clear. Everyone—" Felix drew a quick breath in surprise as he turned around. All of his friends and allies had fallen to their faces, their necks corded and limbs jerking spasmodically as they tried and failed to regain their feet.

"We–can't move!" Evie gasped.

Vess was on her side, right arm splayed outward and quivering. She lost the battle and slammed chest-first to the tiles. "Nnf, Yin? Can you—?"

"I cannot. I, too, am pinned." The golden Wyrmling hissed like a cornered cat. "I dislike this greatly!"

"It hurts!" Beef moaned.

Shit. Pit? He saw his Companion standing without any issue, though his ears were laid back as he surveyed the scene.

"I'm fine. What's happening?"

"I don't know."

"Felix! The–the Stronghold is denying us!" Tzfell said from the ground. Even she had been pressed down to her belly. "Spiritual pr-pressure is being used against us! Access the Authority! Allow us in!"

"I can't." He mentally jabbed for his Authority Screens, but only those for Ahkestria and Nagast appeared. He had increased his Authority in the Hoarfrost, but he hadn't claimed the Seat and Seal yet. "There's nothing to access!"

Several of the giants started gagging, as if the pressure were cutting off their airflow. Felix growled. He would have to drag them all out, or else his friends and allies would be killed by System-based bureaucracy.

Death by red tape. Shit. I—His Inheritor's Will buzzed once again. Felix grasped the hilt and, just as before, Felix could almost understand it. He drew out the hooked blade, lifting it until the hilt was level with his eyes. "What do I do?"

The blade quivered, pulling his arm upward. Felix allowed it, letting the Crescian Bronze guide him as he raised the weapon into the sky. It felt light as a feather until the glyphs began to blaze. The weight of it crashed onto him like a mountain, forcing Felix to put both hands onto its hilt to keep it aloft. It tilted, asking without words, for him to act.

Felix slashed downward, and the very air was sliced in two.

The air howled as it whirled forward, dust kicked up and into swirling cyclones that bifurcated the corridor. Inheritor's Will glowed, the first glyph then the second. Etheric Division split the Mana all around them, disrupting the Spiritual pressure before the second glyph ignited. Etheric Unification. That strange hazy darkness fell, pulled into the Inheritor's Will with all the strength of high tide, until nothing was left.

All was quiet in the aftermath, and Felix was sweating buckets, as if he'd just fought the hardest fight of his life. His arms screamed at him, muscles protesting as he lifted his hooked blade once more. The thing had grown incredibly heavy, so much so that he feared his sheath would not hold it, but it slammed home without issue.

Within his chest, Felix's Hunger grumbled, like Pit denied a treat. *You just ate. Don't be greedy.*

Yeah. Don't be greedy, Pit echoed.

Felix decided not to point out that particular bit of hypocrisy. Instead, he helped Beef up, Vess and Evie having already regained their feet. "You should all be fine now."

"What'd you do?" the kid asked.

"I cut through the red tape."

There were no other defenses within the interior of the Kingsrock, or at least none that assaulted their party. After entering the Gloaming Gate—and letting it close behind them—Felix and his hundred-strong group progressed through the tiled corridor and into a very large, domed chamber at what seemed to be the center of the structure.

No light brightened the space; no windows, magelights, or even torches were mounted on the walls. Thankfully the Witches summoned hand-sized shards of ice that glowed with a steady, icy-blue illumination. It wasn't much, but it helped most of them parse the increasingly vast layout of the Kingsrock.

Felix didn't need any of it, and he walked ahead, Pit at his side. The domed chamber had a beautiful floor of inlaid stone, depicting a very large four-pointed star set into the dark material. Several corridors led off of it, including three sets of stairs that ascended the sides of the dome before entering some sort of loft area. The place was so large, every step from their company sent faintly musical echoes up into the dome.

"Nymean built," Laur said from nearby. "That cannot be denied. You were right, Tzfell."

"Mhm." The Dwarven Chanter held a small flame above her palm and pressed it close to the floor. The tattoos on her face twitched. "I am happy I was. This place is in immaculate condition. It should prove a treasure trove of details on the Lost Nym."

"Don't go poking about just yet," Felix warned. "That likely wasn't the only trap."

"Wise words, Autarch. We should make finding the Seat and Seal our highest priority. It should be the most warded location in the structure. Can you find the strongest wards, Laur?"

"That is all I can find. Wards and more are sung into the stone itself, so densely that I cannot parse them from the interplay of Harmonies. This place is a masterpiece of architecture and magic." Laur tried something, but the magic sizzled above his palm. "There is a song here I cannot penetrate. The Seat is hidden from me. We might be standing on it, for all I know."

Felix glanced down at the inlaid flooring and flared his Manasight. The place was awash in vapor, pools of liquid power, and even solid bars of crystallized Mana. All of it was interwoven into the stone, the metal, the wood of the balustrades on the staircases. Laur was right; the place had been built by someone far beyond Felix's level of shaping skill.

Kimaris walked up to him, a shard of light above her shoulder, and spoke with an awed hush. "It is more than I could have imagined. It—look, my Lord. The stairs."

Felix immediately spotted what she meant—he had seen similar designs in other Nymean structures, but none quite so stark. The center of each staircase was designed for a very small person to use, such as a Gnome or Geist. On either side were the more standardized steps used by Humans, Orcs, Elves, and others. But far larger treads surrounded them both, ones that were clearly built for giants.

"Is this truly where the High Chieftain resided?" she asked.

"I really hope so," Felix answered. Because otherwise, he had wasted his time finding the place. "Do your legends tell where to go from here?"

"Only that the High Chieftain ruled from on high, over all he could survey."

Felix looked up the nearest staircase. "Right. That makes sense. We're going up, people!"

They followed the stairs, ascending to the loft a single story above. There the rooms were just as grand, built for dimensions far exceeding Felix's. Doorways and halls proved no issue to the giantfolk that followed him, and more than once, he heard a soft exclamation of delight at the novelty.

Most of the chambers were empty of furnishings and finery, as if everything that wasn't bolted down had been taken long ago. There wasn't even any dust, though Felix was sure no one had stolen it. Something about the abundant enchantments around them kept surfaces clean and tidy, and even the snow and dirt from their boots dissolved in their wake.

The halls soon grew too numerous to count. Archways led from room to room, their denuded nature offering little to differentiate between them. Where they saw stairs, they ascended them. Dead ends abounded, however, forcing them to double back often, even retreating back down staircases before hunting for another. Their steps were a sharp staccato scale, ascending. Descending. Moving yet monotonous.

Frustration grew among their company, and even Felix was getting annoyed. Every path felt like it would lead them to the top, but inevitably there was another level above even that. Eventually, the rooms began to have new details, mostly sculpture, but that was a whole other problem entirely.

They varied from reliefs like the entryway to busts and even depictions of complete creatures. However, Felix was disgusted to find most defaced in some way. The reliefs were gouged and scratched, empty holes denoting where precious gems once resided. The busts were cracked and sagging, the full creatures missing limbs and eyes and teeth, the metal or stone melted by some terrible flame until they were unrecognizable.

Someone had ransacked the place.

"This is blasphemy," Sitri said in a thin, wavering voice. "The relics of our people. This was a majestic Therium. Now it is scrap."

"This place was sealed. Who could have done this?" Vess asked. Her outrage danced across Felix's skin.

"Dwarves," Naberius said, and the word dropped with disdain. A faint note sounded, far off. Angry glances were shot toward Tzfell, but the Chanter ignored them.

"A bold claim," Laur said. Tzfell said nothing.

"Not so bold as her kind. Only the Dwarves have dared to steal our heritage. Only the Dwarves have waged war on us for an Age!"

"A war started by the giants," Tzfell finally said, voice rising. A faint hum threaded through her words, as if her magic was only syllables away. "You have raided our towns for far longer!"

"Thieves and invaders!"

"Savage monsters!"

"Enough," Felix said, leveling a glare at everyone. It wasn't enough. The swell of music crescendoed, a burgeoning riot that tugged at his heart. Insistent. Cajoling.

Naberius and some other Witches reached toward Tzfell, magics curling across their fingers. Tzfell hummed, her shoulders blooming with loops of strange geometries. The song shouted, it roared.

The melody was violence.

Felix shuddered at the touch of it. Refused it. He drew his hooked blade. It blazed, bronze light burning like the sun in his grasp before dimming, leaving only a sharp, dissonant screech. The keening sound startled them all, Chanter and giant both, and the song that had pressed at them vanished into nonsensical chords.

"This isn't helping anything," he spat through bared teeth. "Listen! The Kingsrock is manipulating us."

"The Dwarves—!"

"It's a trap! Can't you hear it? God!" Felix shook, shoulders bucking as if throwing off a thick, stifling blanket. "You can tear each other apart later! On your own terms." There was a tugging from his sword, and Felix trailed off, focusing on the blade. "Huh."

"What is it?" Vess asked, voice hoarse. He didn't recall her shouting.

"The sword wants us to go this way."

Evie held the bridge of her nose while leaning against Beef for support. "It ain't been wrong yet, right?"

Pit followed the path of the twitching blade. He let out a confused trill. "That's a wall."

"Not for long," Beef declared—before charging into it head-first.

CHAPTER FIFTY-NINE

Beef was done with all the fighting. It had crawled up his spine, an old familiar feeling from back home—from his parents. It had taken all of his Willpower not to lash out at the nearest giant. When Felix mentioned the wall, Beef didn't have to think. He needed out.

The wall, however, was much less than he expected.

"AH!" Beef shot through the illusion and directly onto a wide balcony that, unfortunately, had no railing at all. Almost a thousand pounds of muscle didn't stop on a dime, and Beef hurtled out into the empty air.

Light flashed, the aurora around the Kingsrock surging across his fur, sparking from his orichalcum-coated horns. Another roof, another storm overtook him. For a moment between screams, golden twilight became rain-soaked night, and the ribbons of light became lightning in a Texas sky.

He fell.

"AHHH Ker–Keratin Conception!"

Mana fled from him, burning across his channels to eject itself from the bottom of his hooves directly into the tower. Chitinous limbs, segmented and strong, snapped around his middle.

"Heurk!"

The appendages groaned, pieces snapping off to fall around him like rain. Beef followed their descent. His head whirled. They were way higher than he had thought, and the wind whipped at him like a violent knife. Thin towers spread in all directions, with tiny, far away bridges between them…but below, he could see the golden ground around the Kingsrock. It was a tiny circle, a frisbee disc among heaving glaciers, dotted with a swarm of blue and white specks. Giants, the size of ants.

Beef threw up.

"Eugh," he moaned. "Hope that doesn't hit anybody."

"Mich—Beef! Are you hurt?"

He pivoted, looking back up at the balcony he'd charged off of, and found Hallow's three Bodies peering at him with concern. He gave a shaky thumbs up.

"I will be right down!"

The Sharpwing Matriarch buzzed out, curving around until the undead lizard latched onto Beef's pauldrons. Taking several breaths to brace himself, Beef dismissed his chitinous conjuration and immediately fell again…before the Matriarch's wings counteracted gravity, and they ascended back into the sky. In moments, they were on the balcony again, though Beef's knees were quivering so hard he almost dropped to all fours. Almost.

Hallow fussed over him, using the rocky Homunculus to check him over. There were scratches on his knuckles where he must have hit the tower on the way down, and a few straps on his armor were split. Hallow tsked at each new detail. "Are you sure you are unharmed?"

"No." Beef sucked in a jagged lungful of air, but it wasn't enough. His stomach couldn't stop cramping, and his feet—hooves—shook. "No."

"Beef?" Felix emerged from the solid wall, sword first and his blue eyes blazing. The illusion rippled around him like water, but the Autarch paid little attention to it. Instead he focused on Beef and then on the balcony itself, which rose into a set of stairs on their right. "What happened?"

Beef forced the words out through his jumping chest. What was wrong with him? "Fell. Almost."

"You're good, though?" Beef gave him a shaky nod. "Damn. They don't even have railings out here." Felix stood casually on the edge of the incredible drop. He didn't look worried in the slightest…but then, Beef had witnessed the guy literally fly on the back of a lightning bolt. He wasn't sure Felix ever got scared.

Hallow rested a stone hand on his own. "Beef. Your heart rate is—"

"I'm good," he said, talking over Hallow's echoing voice. Her last Body had pushed through the false wall after Felix, and both the enormous Multipede and smaller Sharpwing watched him with concern in their blackened-green eyes. He stood up. "Just didn't expect an illusion. That's what it is, right?"

"It is," Tzfell said, striding through. She and that Elven dude ran their hands in weird gestures across the fake wall, and it rippled. "A high-Tier Skill forged this illusion. Well beyond Master."

"It is tied so well into the architecture that I would never have seen it," Laur admitted. "This must be Nymean made, or perhaps Dwarven craft."

"Not Giantfolk, Sorcerer?" Naberius asked sharply. "You are too new to the frost. You cannot guess what might we bear, hidden from the likes of you."

"For all your talent with curses and elemental ice, this is beyond your people," Tzfell said. Her words were calm, but her intent was sharp as bared steel. Beef hunched at the animosity he heard in their Spirits, big shoulders drawn inward. He shook.

"Stop." Felix was there, sword in one hand. He lifted his other one and brandished a snap-crackle of lightning between his claws. "I told you. You're being manipulated by a spell."

"What?" Mother Vepar asked. Her old face always looked like she'd eaten half a lemon, but now it twisted up even more. "I am in full control of myself."

"Explain," the Dwarven Chanter said.

"If you would listen, I wouldn't have to," Felix said. "It's a trap, just a lot more subtle than the first one. There's a construct pulling at our aggression, our fears, and I can't get it to stop. All of you need to control your emotions, now, before someone does something they regret."

"I would not regret taking a Dwarf down a peg," Naberius said.

Felix squared up against her, small compared to the giant's nine-foot height. "I would *make* you regret it."

The Witch's Spirit spun, a clash of noise that drove Beef's molars against each other. He braced for violence, grabbed his hammer haft… but she backed down. The music faded.

Felix gave a sharp nod to everyone present. "Good. Get the rest to follow. I know the way."

He led them up the steps, just to the right of the balcony. It was wide enough for the giants to walk two abreast, but they proceeded single file due to the whipping winds. The aurora was much more pronounced there, weaving among the towers like actual ribbons. They reminded Felix of his core space, of how he envisioned his Tempered Skills. There was some sort of magic going on with them outside of decoration, but he couldn't tell what.

The Kingsrock was hiding things.

Inheritor's Will led them across their first bridge, over a hundred feet long. Just like the balcony, it was without any guardrails to speak of, and a single misstep would send them plummeting to the earth. Felix wasn't worried for himself, but many in his group lacked the Skills to survive such a fall. They moved carefully.

Across the bridge was another spiraling staircase that led down into a tower, once again through a false wall. The interior there was much the same, filled with emptied out chambers and defaced artworks that looked too heavy to be moved. All the while, that foreign music beat at them, driving their emotions wild.

It was easier to ignore now that they recognized it—Felix hadn't ever felt a thing, but he could certainly hear it working. He had already tried to activate either glyph on his hooked sword, but they hadn't helped. Etheric Division had cut through the lingering spellforms he'd spotted… but the sound returned after only the briefest of pauses.

Etheric Unification simply refused to work at all. That led him to believe that it *wasn't* Nymean magic, but something left by a former occupant. The giants? Or the Dwarves? It was impossible to tell, and he wasn't about to ask anyone and open that can of worms again.

They finally pressed across another thin bridge, higher than the last, and had to endure the increasingly violent winds. Rope was passed out to tie themselves together in pairs, but Felix didn't trust that alone. Pit was there, balanced atop the bridge. Without his wings…Felix grasped at the air, forcing his Mana out of himself in great streams, and took control of a piece of it.

Storm Shaping is level 12!

Felix didn't so much stop the wind as he bent it around them all, until he formed an invisible tunnel along the top of the bridge. The air howled, split above and below it, but they were untouched. "Move. Quickly."

Storm Shaping is level 23!

Multi-Cast is level 85!

By the time his entire party was across the long bridge, Felix's channels stung. The low level of his shaping Skill meant more Mana was required to achieve just about anything, but it also meant the cap on the amount of Mana he could put into the Skill was low. Felix suspected he would have had trouble shielding just himself, had he not also had the Multi-Cast Skill. By stacking casts of Storm Shaping, he built up enough of a bulwark, just at the steep cost of thousands of Mana.

Well, steep for most. Felix checked his Status. His Mana was already rebounding and would be full in a few more seconds.

Beyond the bridge was another gate. It was similar in size to the Gloaming Gate and covered in similar carvings. Local nature was depicted here, but also a stylized crown, shaped like nine stars bound together by a curving band. Rays of light exuded from the crown, a starburst pattern centered on where the gate was meant to split in two.

As Felix walked up, Witches and Chanters alike stepped back from it.

"We have tried to open it, but it refuses our touch," Mother Vepar said. She placed a calloused hand against it, and a shimmer of glacial light sparked off. Her hand was tossed back, and she winced.

"There is a complex warding here," Laur said. "I could perhaps disassemble it given enough time…but I think that is wasted effort." He nodded to Felix's hand, where the Inheritor's Will swirled with the same glacial light.

"Hm. Probably." Felix looked around. The tower they stood on was where the aurora seemed to linger the most, each ribbon of light undulating away before returning. As before, it reminded Felix sharply of his core space, and how each Tempered Skill was connected to his dual cores. For that reason alone, he was positive they were in the right spot.

He brushed the engraved crown with his fingers. The gate opened on smooth, soundless hinges.

"Was that a crown?" Pit asked. "Are you getting another one?"

Felix narrowed his eyes down the short corridor, which split ahead to the left and right. "This place has been picked clean. If there's a crown here, I'll eat your barding."

"No! I like this armor."

Inheritor's Will pulled Felix forward, one slight nudge at a time. It chose turn after turn, up another flight of stairs and through passages that were choked with dust. That caught everyone's attention, as right where the Kingsrock cleansing enchantments failed was also where it began to smell of an ancient and decrepit fire. Char marred the walls, baked black into the stone, ashes mixed freely among the dust. The ransacking had been absolute in that place.

Tempers flared again, but it was a weak thing. The manipulating enchantment had also failed, and soon a solemn sadness replaced it. They walked in silence, until finally they were directed to a narrow alcove somewhere deep in the tower. The moment Felix walked up to it, the sword went limp in his hand.

"This is it, I guess," he said, sheathing the blade.

"Looks cozy," Evie said.

"I dunno if I'll even fit in there," Beef added.

Felix kneeled down in the alcove, running his Perception across the floor. It was clear that, at some point, a heavy object had occupied the space. Judging by the boot-shaped indent in the floor, it had two very wide feet—feet bigger than his torso. *A Golem, maybe?* He wasn't sure, but it had likely been taken by whoever stripped the place.

The wall at the back was where the real details were located. It was marked very faintly with stars, and those hung below a blackened placard. Felix reached up and scrubbed at it, flaking off Ages of dust, char, and debris. Words were revealed, carved deep into the stone, and they were in an ancient language that Felix suspected was Nymean. The language bypassed his conscious thought, their meaning rolling through him without hesitation or confusion.

"Enter If You've The Will, Claim It If You've The Right," he read. The same words he'd found in Elderthrone.

Authority Acknowledged.

The alcove transformed. The walls folded into themselves, masonry pulling out and down to combine with the floor, while the ceiling stretched high into a vaulted expanse. A two-hundred-foot span of polished stone flooring stretched ahead of them, contained within circular walls that appeared to take up the majority of the tower's circumference.

Hexagonal pillars clung to the edges, lifting triangular pediments filled with detailed sculptures, all of which framed a far larger mural featuring a snow-capped mountain surmounted by a field of stars. Directly beneath that was an absolutely monumental throne carved from what looked like ice, stone, and metal.

"Well. Throne room found, I guess," Felix said.

"And it is sized for a giant," Naberius said. She stared at the throne like a lioness sizing up an antelope. "As we knew it must be!"

Without waiting, the Witch strode forward and onto the polished stone, intending perhaps to grab the big chair with her own mitts. Felix wasn't sure, because the moment her foot came down, a brilliant series of silver-gold lines erupted into being. Naberius shouted and was thrown backward, as if she had been swatted by an enormous hand. She landed hard among her people, a furious scowl already on her face.

"Learning to exercise patience would do you well," Tzfell said primly. "It seems we have also found the Seat and Seal."

"Apparently. Everyone stay put," Felix said. He stepped forward. A sharp tingle ran through his heels, but otherwise, he was unharmed. *Whew. That would have been embarrassing, otherwise.*

He strode toward the throne, which was situated at the exact center of the complicated array. It was just as fascinating and nonsensical as the working beneath Elderthrone. The farther from the entrance he stepped, the more mind-bending the silver and gold inscriptions became. It folded around itself like a fractal knot.

Felix still had no clue how the things worked, but he knew he needed to stand in the very center, where the pattern was empty. A veil of shimmering light now separated the throne from the rest, the exact same as the aurora that hung around the Kingsrock itself. He approached it on sure feet but slowed as the huge chair loomed close. Felix took a steadying breath. "Here goes nothing."

He stepped through. That bell tolled again, the floor shook, and the sky outside the windows filled with swirling colors. Immediately, the power of the place surged against his skin, covering him until it found his Mana Gates. There it paused, gathering to pinpricks of blinding radiance, and Felix had to blink away the afterimages.

Authority Recognized, Inheritor!
For Conquering The Ironskin Domain
For Displaying Mercy For The Frostfather
For Overcoming The Starfield Steps
For Overcoming The Unquiet Dead
You May Lay Claim To The Lost Territory Of Khalheim!
Do You Wish To Establish Your Authority?
Y/N

"Khalheim," Felix said. The tolling continued, a single note that pulled at his center. "Does that include all of the Hoarfrost?"

He didn't expect an answer, but one bloomed in his Mind regardless, unveiled to him like a dream. A series of vistas, viewed as if from the head of an onrushing gale as it ran the length and breadth of the Territory. Snowy tundra gave way to bleak, forbidding mountains to the north and south, while the west became impassable glaciers that fizzed in an acidic sea, and the east turned to a vast forest of dark conifers and prowling shapes.

The vision ended, and Felix's attention returned to his Body with a snap. He shivered. "I'll take that as a yes."

Do You Wish To Establish Your Authority?
Y/N

Felix braced himself and reached out to mentally toggle *Yes.*

"Aye," said a dour, gravel-throated voice.

Felix jerked to the side, finding another figure standing beside the giant's throne. They were wearing heavy armor that looked worth a small kingdom—gilded with geometric designs and decorated with jewels—but their face was bare. It was a Dwarf with a massive beard combed and twisted into three, gold-capped braids.

And he was entirely transparent.

"I aim to claim this crown, and no monster will stop me."

CHAPTER SIXTY

It's a Memory, Felix realized. He'd seen more than his fair share...just never out in the real world. *What is—is the Seal projecting this?*

He ran his hand through the ghostly Dwarf, and it felt much the same as when Knowledge had appeared in his Stronghold. This time, however, the illusion spread, until it described a sphere approximately thirty feet across. Other Dwarves showed up, many of them dressed in armor like the Forge Knight. Many looked battered, and every bared weapon was streaked with uncleansed gore. The floor was dull, as less than a quarter of the Seal was lit up.

"System! Did you hear me! I claim this throne! For the Undermount! For House Galion!" The Dwarven prince struck at the throne then clutched his gauntleted hand in pain. "Damned ancient ruins. It is like it cannot hear me at all!"

"My Lord," one of the Forge Knights spoke up, and somehow Felix recognized him. Was it the way he stood, or the hammer and heater shield on his arm? "Cousin. We cannot hold the gates any longer. You've tried to pull Authority from these stones for months!"

The Prince whirled on the Forge Knight, the same one Felix had fought down below. "You overstep yourself, *cousin*."

The Forge Knight ripped off his own helmet, revealing a square-jawed face endowed with a mussed and sweaty beard. "I followed you on this foolhardy mission, Bavan. I stayed silent when you insisted we press into the Frost Giant's stone-cursed Domain. You have had my hammer and my shield since the start…but I cannot stand by now. The monsters are at the gates, and we cannot stay here."

"This is my birthright, Mavir! The records—!"

"Damn the records! We will die here!" Mavir stepped up to his cousin, until their armored chests almost touched. "We must flee!"

Something shook the room, but it was beyond what the Memory showed. Regardless, every Dwarf in the room shifted nervously as a deep basso pounding sounded. The Seal sparked once more before fading again.

Prince Galion growled, and he grasped his cousin's collar. Mavir let him but did not shift his confrontational gaze. "Fine, cousin! We shall flee from our birthright, tail between our legs!" He shoved the Forge Knight away. "And you shall lead the way!"

The Memory dissolved without warning. Felix looked around, but there was only the shining Seal and the throne at his side.

"What the hell was that?" Beef shouted over the gleaming Seal. He was pressed up against the boundary like a kid at the penguin enclosure. "Were those ghosts? Why do you talk to so many ghosts?"

"Memories," Yintarion said, hovering above the crowd. "Set in stone."

Felix placed his hand onto the throne, and an electric jolt ran up his arm and down his spine. The words repeated, but he didn't need them. *Yes*, he replied. *I claim this place.*

The world flexed, it shattered and reformed, and along the way, an orchestral triumph rang through all the halls of the Kingsrock. It crescendoed, reaching a peak that was beyond hearing, beyond even Felix's Affinity, before it swooped back down. The Seat and Seal ignited in curtains of silvered-gold.

Authority Recognized!
Unbound Detected!
Greater Primordial Detected!
WARNING!
Authority Cannot—

Inheritor Status Recognized!
Inheritor Status Supersedes All Bloodlines!
Authority Granted, Champion!

Felix's chest was on fire, the System power like a scouring pad ripped through his center and channels. He breathed, pulling the agony close, and fed it all to his Hunger.

This Territory Has Been Lost!
What Is Your Choice?
Forsake Or Unite?

Unite!

Power fled his core, ripping through tender channels and into the throne before him. Mana, Essence, and almost all of the significance he'd accrued. The world flexed once more. People screamed.

It was done.

Khalheim!
The Shield Unbroken!
Lost No More!

All Hail The Inheritor, Colossus of Khalheim, Felix Nevarre!

Felix's ears were ringing as the notifications piled on top of him, and he only briefly realized he'd taken a seat in the massive throne. It was cold beneath him, bitterly so, but it was sized perfectly to him now. He blinked. *When had that changed?*

He jolted upright, looking at the notification that still stared him in the face. *That didn't—did it?* He grasped his hooked blade and poured his attention through it. "Karys! Karys, are you there?"

The Inheritor's Will buzzed once before glowing with green-gold light. "Felix? What has happened? You sound panicked."

"Did you see the notification?"

"For claiming Khalheim? Yes, I did. I received word of your ascension to the throne via our shared Authority Screen." Karys' voice was warm. "I'm quite proud, my boy."

"Uh, thanks," Felix said. He straightened up. "But what I meant was, did you get a System announcement? Like when I took over Nagast?"

"No. Nothing of the sort. I imagine just your Chancellors were made aware of your new Territory."

Felix leaned back, relief flooding every inch of his body. He hadn't just broadcasted his location to the entire Continent. Again. "Good."

Yet, the thought lingered. As the takeover of Neer proved, all Territories were under threat by the Hierocracy. Khalheim was only different in that the Pathless had no reason to seize the north. According to Karys and Zara, everyone considered the Hoarfrost as a monster-filled wilderness with no resources to easily harvest. Felix imagined that, if his enemies found out he ruled the north, that would change.

They need to prepare— Before he could complete that thought, another deluge of System alerts appeared in a series of descending chimes.

Quest Updated!
The Path of Empire: 3 of 4 Territories Secured!

The Path of Empire!
Many are the benefits of empire, and many are their enemies. Secure a total of 4 Territories under your banner and gain a reward worthy of the ancient emperors. Beware, for the higher you climb, the greater the winds that will attempt to force you from the Golden Path. Unification may be your destiny, but violence is your birthright. Gird yourself, Felix Nevarre!
3 of 4 Territories Secured
Reward: XP, Title(s), Advanced Authority, Varies

Oh. Excellent. Felix hadn't originally been sure if the Hoarfrost would qualify as a Territory for that Quest, but he'd grown more confident the longer he'd spent up there. It was vast and mostly wilderness, but it was vital and had plenty of people who called it home. *Just one more for… something good, I hope.*

He wasn't sure what would happen when he claimed the last Territory, but he had no doubt it'd be interesting at least.

Hidden Quest Completed!
Throne of Khalheim!
You have persevered against incredible odds and arrived here, at the heart of the north. The Seat and Seal of Khalheim have judged you worthy, Felix Nevarre, and from you shall the new line of Authority extend!
Rewards:
+Mithril Chest
+Title
+5 Levels

Now that's more like it. He'd hoped for something like that. Eagerly, he tabbed through the next two notifications.

New Title!
Colossus of Khalheim (Legendary)!
The people of the Unbroken Shield have always been warriors of terrifying capabilities and immense stature. When the Nym united the warring bands of the Hoarfrost and established the Kingsrock, the greatest of these warriors took on the mantle of leadership and the onus of defending the north from all threats. The first was called the Colossus, and that name has resounded through the Ages, heir after heir…to you.
+100 END, STR, VIT
+Increased Authority Within Khalheim
+Complete Access To The Stronghold Of Kingsrock

You Have Gained 5 Levels!
You Are Now Level 68!
+100 to STR! +110 to PER! +110 to VIT! +130 to END! +120 to INT! +140 to WIL! +130 to AGL! +145 to DEX!
+100 All Harmonic Stats!
You Have 90 Unused Stat Points!

An influx of System power raged through him. Even though he'd expected it, Felix could only choke out a gasp before falling out of his throne. His hands clenched, fingers tearing through stone like soft clay. His head swam, lost amid a sea of surging inputs from overtaxed senses. He felt the Kingsrock around him like living flesh, like his own skin. Giants outside traipsed upon him, feet tickling like insects—so small. Insignificant before the bones of the earth itself.

The Kingsrock pierced the world. Or rather, it was the upthrust arm of something far greater, and Felix glimpsed it. For a moment, a veil parted, and he saw…a green majesty, a chaos of design without end, a fractal unfolding of all things over and over. An egg, broken and spilling yolk, but gleaming with the light of stars and singing the song of Ages. It was—connected. A web of colors he couldn't name, bound to a vibrating field that was everlasting and always changing. An appellation swam up to him, from nameless depths: The Continent.

He could feel—*No.*

It was gone.

A vacuum replaced it, clutching at him as sensation fled. Replaced by a surge of incandescent sound that sang an ode to all things, lost and found. That bell sounded again, but it was not from the system...but from him. It was the roar of his Hunger and the eager creaking of a Divine Tree. But above all else, it was the clashing noise of his cores grinding into one another, the product of Harmony and Dissonance filling him to the brim. It spilled outward, into the throne room and onto the Seat and Seal.

Gold and silver light were drenched, until the color of the vast array transmuted like reverse alchemy. No longer aurum and argent, it burned like fire and lightning, blue-white and red-gold.

People cried out, giants and Claw falling back and shielding their eyes. A nova of radiance subsumed the chamber, connecting Felix and the Seal. An umbilical of potency lifted him back to his feet before setting him down into the throne itself.

A shockwave rippled out, igniting sconces with merry flame and blasting open wide windows. A song faded, not ending but merely sinking below the surface of his skin, into veins of blood and channels of Mana.

Silence descended.

"Felix?" Pit crept forward, the only one remaining on his feet. "Are you—"

Vibrant mist poured from Felix's mouth, his eyes bulging as a familiar Skill moved within him. That ghostly Dwarf returned, but this time, he was surrounded by Forge Knights bearing a stout banner of gold on black. The mist spread, until the ghosts looked real as flesh... and fire sprouted among the walls.

"Put it out!" Mother Vepar hissed, still crouched at the far end of the room. "Before we're consumed!"

"Stop! It is not real," Vess said, halting the giants in their tracks. Even the Claw had moved to act upon seeing the visceral scene before them. "None of them stir the air. It is a Memory."

"Another one?" Harn growled. "I'm about sick of enemies I can't hit."

The radius of this Memory expanded far more than the last. It filled the throne room, revealing those same armored Dwarves carrying ragged banners, some featuring a burning hammer and others a shield bearing a single nine-tined crown. The Dwarves were breaking artwork, melting it to slag with their Skills whenever things were too heavy. Fires raged, much as Mother Vepar noticed, burning up the walls and across the Seal. The Dwarves ran, carrying all that they could—and froze, just before they left.

Time stopped.

Rewound.

The fire vanished, the artwork restored itself, and fine tapestries were made whole once again. The Dwarves zipped along, played at high speed until they were a blur. Then they were gone. The golden sky rippled, liquid churning with threads of light over and over again… before it all turned blue once more. Cold wind howled through open windows, and Felix saw the sun and moons arc across the cloudless sky, so fast that they formed solid lines that curved across horizons.

"Empty Ages," Tzfell whispered. "How long ago does this go?"

Eventually, the vacant years came to an end. The Memory jerked to a stop and showed the room around them—the entire top of the tower, in fact—was unfinished. Dwarves were there again, not wearing armor but curious robes and smocks that gleamed with stitched enchantments. Gnomes and Goblins and Geist moved about, too, along with a great many other Races, inscribing things into the stones that were being laid onto the walls by enormous Frost Giants.

"What—what is this?" Naberius whispered.

"The beginning," Kimaris said. "Before…before everything." She gasped. "Is that—?"

A number of tall figures strode about, some in full robes, others stripped to the waist. The former were directing a number of activities, from the inscriptionists to the artisans putting a mural together. The latter were hauling stone alongside the Risi and Dwarves, all of them sweating as they moved massive, multi-ton blocks into place.

The Memory froze there, a tableau that set Spirits soaring across the throne room. It dissolved, condensing once more to thick mist before rushing back. Not to the Seal, but to Felix.

He ate all of it.

Mana, Essence, and Significance swelled within him to a point well beyond where he was previously. All he spent and more returned, just as when he'd raised his Spirit Tree and restored Naevis.

What Is Lost Can Be Regained.

Felix gasped as the flood of power finished with him. The last words of the System hung like a divine proclamation above his head, and he stared at them for several long seconds. They soon faded, replaced by Skill notifications.

Ephemeral Evocation is level 26!
...
Ephemeral Evocation is level 43!

"Noctis' tits," Evie whispered.

As if to punctuate her words, a massive Mithril Chest slammed down next to Felix. A crippling spiritual pressure followed it, pushing those below Adept back out of the throne room entirely. Incredibly, Beef struggled back in, fighting against the pressure. His eyes glittered, and glee surged along every inch of his Spirit as he shouted.

"I. Wanna. See. The. Loot!"

Felix kicked the lid open, and the pressure vanished. In its place was a terrifying pull. All of the Mana around them surged forward, collecting around the Chest like a storm cloud. Lightning flashed, multi-colored and blinding.

Beef gasped. "What's in it?"

Felix blinked against the light and peered down.

CHAPTER SIXTY-ONE

The objects within the Chest sang with power, exciting the storm of Mana that gathered above it. He could have just eaten the accumulated power, but it would only return. Some items simply had that effect on ambient Mana. So he ignored it, squinted through the chaos, and spied three items nestled atop a padded interior.

He lifted the metallic piece first, marveling at how it shifted in size the moment he removed it from the Chest. It looked to be the size of a coin inside, but it was a touch larger than his palm, and far more beautiful than it originally appeared. The variegated colors of the metal were beautiful, describing a strange pattern atop bronze-like material. The middle of it was decorated with a nine-pointed star, indicative of the Nym, and the rest was made up of three interwoven bars. The bars were broken off on both sides, segmented, but the piece overall was slightly curved.

It looks like a badge or something. Felix marshaled his Voracious Eye, but another notification interrupted him.

Hidden Quest Discovered!
Restore The Crown!
The Crown of Elysium has been lost since its bearers were faced with Ruin. Pieces of it have been scattered across the Continent, hidden away so that the forces arrayed against the Golden Empire could not destroy them, too. By taking the

Throne of Khalheim, claiming the Territory of Nagast, and resurrecting Ahkestria and the Leviathan Depths, you have proven yourself worthy of bearing the First Fragment. Unite them, Ascendant, and return that which was Lost.
Rewards:
+Authority
+Title
+Varies

"Another crown?" Felix held the object up, marveling again at its strange design before activating his Voracious Eye.

Name: First Fragment (1 of 3)
Type: Artifact
Lore: A piece of the Crown of Elysium, made of Crescian Bronze, and last worn by She Who Was A Thousand, also known as the Herald of the Dawn and the final Empress of the Nym.

Felix swallowed hard. *The Herald's crown...* The scope of what he was doing hit Felix like a truck, and too many emotions tried to cram themselves into his chest all at once. Wonder was most of it, though, and Felix had a hard time tearing his eyes away, as if it had its own sort of gravitational pull. It was like his Hunger in that regard, but where his Hunger was a yawning emptiness, the Fragment was incredibly *solid.* As if, were he to drop it, the shard of metal would punch through the entirety of the Kingsrock. There was a weight to the crown, something far beyond its mass. *It's so old and seen so much. I can't imagine the amount of significance that's gathered in this thing.*

Like the hooked blade at his hip, the piece of crown had once been worn by the Herald. He had no idea what Elysium was, though he'd heard of something called the Elysian Accords from Paxus. Hopefully, the team he'd sent to Khasma would succeed at their task; it would make getting information from the bodiless Nym far more convenient.

Is that it, though? Just a name and the person who wore it? Surely, such a crazy artifact would have more details, like a list of enchantments. Felix pressed harder, trying to squeeze out anything else from the hunk of metal. He failed, however. After a dozen attempts, all he gained was a massive headache and a few levels for his Voracious Eye.

Voracious Eye is level 94!

He reached into the Mithril Chest for the next item. Like the First Fragment, this was also shrunk by the Chest's strange magic, appearing to be only the size of a teacup. When removed, however, it expanded until it was two feet tall and many times heavier. Felix tensed, worried he might drop the object, if only because it looked so fragile.

"Wow," he whispered. It was a large sculpture of an armored worm, much like the Razorspines they had encountered, and it appeared to be carved from a single chunk of ice. Tough ice, too, as it felt more like stone than frozen water. The details were incredible, with every scale and spike rendered with exacting precision. It looked almost like it would come to life in his hands.

Voracious Eye!

Name: Boreal Guardian
Type: Artifact
Lore: Territory and their Lords were once one, and this Guardian is that bond made manifest. Just as Risi Witches summon beasts to their aid, this artifact will summon a powerful Tier VI protector from within Khalheim's hidden realm. It will only obey the commands of the Colossus of Khalheim or their Chancellor, and it cannot leave the confines of the Territory.

Felix let out a long, appreciative whistle. Tier VI was the monster equivalent of a Master Tier. "That could be useful."

The last item appeared to be the size of a hatchet in the Chest, but it was by far the largest of the three. Felix grunted as it expanded rapidly to its natural dimensions, but it was more to do with its unexpected length than anything else. A massive, Frost Giant-sized hammer, made of what looked like ice, metal, and stone in shades of gray, green, blue, and white. The haft itself was over nine feet long, joined smoothly with the hammer head as if the thing had been made all of a single piece. The head gleamed, a brutal shaping of ice wrapped with bands of metal and stone. Sigils were inscribed across those bands, Nymean ones, along with a large glyph at the very top. It almost looked like a stylized wall being split in half.

The Mithril Chest vanished, and the crackling cloud of Mana began to disperse. Felix didn't pay it any attention.

Voracious Eye!

Name: Bedlam
Type: Weapon (Bludgeoning)
Lore: Designed for the mighty warriors of Khalheim. Once, such weapons were commonplace among the defenders of the Unbroken Shield. Now, this greathammer is all that remains. Forged by a true Shaper and enchanted by Glyph-witches, it was once meant for a high-ranking officer and, as such, was designed to allow them to lead their forces into battle. Carry it well, warrior.
Disruption VIII - When swung, there is a 45% chance of disrupting a spell or Skill within melee range.
Bludgeon Defense XII - While wielding Bedlam in both hands, you are 70% immune to all forms of blunt force damage.

"Look at you. King on his throne," Evie said. The others had crossed the Seal and approached Felix as well, though the giants remained in the back. They were watching him, though. Very cautiously.

"It's surprisingly comfortable," Felix admitted. He set the hammer down carefully, but still it boomed as the head hit the ground.

"The Chest contained just these? A statue, a hammer, and…a piece of jewelry?" Vess peered at the treasures he'd received, no doubt using her own version of Analyze. "I can only see the very basics of the hammer and statue, but that metalwork is beyond my Skill."

"That is something remarkable, little Dragoon." Yintarion slid out into the open air, undulating toward the First Fragment in Felix's hand. His eyes gleamed, and he smiled. "Congratulations, Autarch. It appears you are on your way."

"To what?" Felix asked.

"I suppose that depends on you," the Wyrmling said. "That crown has not been seen in a great many Ages. Even when I dwelt among the Dragoons, it was a lost treasure sought after by countless would-be kings. That it has come to you is no coincidence."

"Mm." Felix had been hurtling headlong toward leadership for a while now, but this felt different. More important, somehow. "Well, let's not celebrate yet. Apparently, there are three pieces to this crown."

"It's a crown?" Beef leaned over, squinting at the bent piece of metal. "Congrats?"

"Can I see?" Harn asked. Felix handed it over to him, and the warrior-smith grunted as it touched him. "That's quality workmanship. There's layers to the forging here that I didn't think were possible. Mind if I study this?"

"No, go ahead. The more we know, the better. My Voracious Eye can't pull much except some lore from it, and even that's kinda useless."

"Anything interestin', at least?" Evie asked. She had crouched beside the Razorspine sculpture and was eyeing it. "Aside from some pretty carvings?"

"That is a summoning artifact," Tzfell said. She and Laur had lingered over the dimmed Seal, obviously studying its loops and patterns, but now they strode toward Felix with purpose. "A powerful one, unless I miss my guess."

"Tier VI, yeah," Felix confirmed. "It's limited, though. Can't use it outside of this Territory."

"For such power, I would hope so," Laur said with a shudder. "I cannot imagine a thing like that unleashed upon a city."

"I can." Evie, who was still crouched next to the artifact, except now she ran her hands almost lovingly over the worm sculpture. "Just think of all the redcloaks we could take out with this."

The Elven Chanter opened his mouth, perhaps to protest, but then closed it. He inclined his head toward the girl. "That is true."

"What about this thing? That's cool," Beef said from the side. He was hovering near Bedlam, the greathammer.

"It is cool," Felix agreed. He pushed the haft of the hammer toward the Minotaur, grinding the head against the polished floor. "But I've got enough weapons."

"Wha—for me?"

"Don't think he means it for Evie, kid," Harn said, not even looking up from the Fragment.

Beef curled his furry mitts around the hammer, eyes wide as saucers, and only grunted a little when he took the whole weight. "What the crap! This is heavy!"

"Too heavy for you?" Felix asked.

"No! No. I got this." The hammer went up onto his wide shoulders in an attempt at a casual carry. Beef grimaced, but he stayed upright. "It's totally great."

"We'll train with it. Get you used to the new weight in no time." Harn looked around. "We stayin' here a while?"

Felix nodded. "I'll need some time to get everything sorted, but I wanna be gone by noon tomorrow."

"Alright. Time enough to do some huntin' out in those glaciers."

"A grand idea, smith," Yintarion said. "I am in need of a few specimens."

"Yin. I told you I would hunt for you soon."

"Yes yes, I know, Dragoon. But the man is looking to train. Let us kill two armies with one avalanche, yes?"

Beef scowled, still caressing his new weapon. "Two armies…? You mean like 'two birds with one stone'?"

"Why would I kill a bird?"

Felix snorted and stood, patting Harn on the back as he passed him. "Before you lead them on a hunt, let's set up camp here first. I know there are rooms through there," he gestured toward a far off door. "Enough for everyone here and then some."

"Aye. I'll get on it."

"Vess?"

"Yes?"

"Walk with me?"

The dark-eyed spearmaiden's lips turned upward at the corners. Not a smile, but she was pleased. "Of course."

Yintarion stayed behind, hovering around Harn's shoulders as the rest of the Claw were moved across the throne room. Vess was watching Felix, stealing small glances at him whenever he wasn't looking. She started saying something once or twice, stopped, then settled on, "What is your plan?"

"Housekeeping, mostly." He nodded ahead, where the giants had slowly entered the chamber. The Witches were cautiously exploring the semi-charred room, running hands over broken murals and split columns.

"How can I help?" she asked.

"I dunno. I just, uh, wanted you around?"

Vess blushed, but her smile deepened, pressing a dimple into her cheek. Felix grinned.

The Risi Warriors spotted him moments later. "Colossus," the first of them said, before they all dropped to a knee.

Of the Witches, Kimaris noticed first, and she, too, took a knee. Her Battlelord and Warriors did the same, followed closely by the Feldspear

Witches. Mother Vepar and the Cold Rock Coven were the last, but they knelt as well.

"Colossus," Kimaris said. "What would you have of us?"

"Nothing too taxing." Felix idly scratched his jaw. "Don't think you're gonna like it, though."

He told them. He was right.

CHAPTER SIXTY-TWO

"Would my lord wish for a menu? Or perhaps just a wine list?"

"No, no, I'm still waiting," Atar said. "He'll be here, any moment. My apologies for the trouble."

"For the esteemed Glyphmaster, it is no trouble at all." The server gave a wide smile and retreated back into the hustle of the restaurant. He no doubt had other, actual customers to attend.

The restaurant was a fine establishment called Savina's, and it was practically buzzing with custom. The interior was packed and the street dining just as full, despite the chill winds that stole down the wide thoroughfare. One could attribute it to the people of Elderthrone and their indomitable Spirits no matter the weather…or to the heat arrays that Atar's apprentices had installed across most of the town's streets.

The cast iron table Atar lounged in was chilly but not frozen, and a number of patrons around him had unbuttoned their jackets and loosened ties. Snow fell in frequent flurries, but none of it accumulated or even reached them. Yellow heat Mana pulsed in regular intervals along the major arteries crossing the Foot and Scale districts, making for a pleasant experience on even the coldest of days. Atar planned to have the Wings done within the next week. Hopefully.

Atar toyed with the empty goblet in front of him, tilting it in circles as his Mind ran new thoughts to the ground. New Quests had fallen into his lap, ever since the Glyphworks was upgraded, and the sheer variety of them had buried him over the past two days. It was all he could do to make the time for this dinner, in fact. Yet here he was, sitting. Waiting.

where could your alister be? perhaps he is in trouble. in dire danger.

Be quiet, Atar commanded. Flame settled back, a bird in its cage. The mini Urge never seemed particularly put out when Atar shot down its constant rants. Just patient. It unnerved Atar more than he liked to admit. *Alister is fine.*

His beau had been overworked as much as Atar had, these last few days, if for different reasons.

"Ah!" Atar said, finally spying his date. He flagged down his server. "I'd appreciate that wine list, now."

"Of course. Here is the menu as well." The man proffered two thick pieces of cardstock to the mage and bowed himself out just as Alister closed in.

"So sorry I'm late," he said, twisting between cast iron seating and other patrons. He approached Atar with a wide grin and a distinct hitch to his gait. "Gods, it's good to see you outside of that stuffy lab."

They embraced, pressing close for a brief moment before Atar held the man out as if to inspect him. "You're limping. What happened?"

"This? Nothing particularly interesting, just foolish." Alister sat down carefully at the table, wincing as he did so. "The steps up to the Eye were icier than I expected. I slipped. I may have finally advanced into Adept, but my Body isn't so stalwart as some."

"Tch. The apprentices are supposed to take turns clearing those steps!"

"It's fine, Atar. I'm fine. Better me than someone more frail." Alister shifted in the hard seat, clearly uncomfortable. "The ice is being cleared now, anyway. Let's just enjoy our dinner."

"Very well," Atar said, but a piece of him was already reviewing the duty roster.

yes. find them and end them. insubordination cannot be condoned.

I said *quiet, Flame.*

look at him, atar. he aches. if you grew your power, if you let me join you, then we could ensure nothing bad ever happened to him. we could boil the seas and burn the very moons...

Atar shoved his talkative Urge back and lifted the wine list, handing it over to his date. "Since you're walking wounded, I'll let you do the honors."

"How magnanimous," Alister drawled. He glanced at the list. "This wouldn't have anything to do with the menu being in Levantian?"

"Of course not." Atar picked a piece of dust from his doublet. "I am simply being exceptionally thoughtful."

"Mhm. I'm still surprised you haven't learned that language yet, considering how many of the Pagewrights use it. All nobility is forced to learn it from youth, if for nothing other than proving how refined we are."

"It has been…something I haven't had the time to master," Atar admitted. He tucked a lock of white hair behind his ear. "Self-study outside of the Glyphworks has been entirely too rare."

"Don't I know it. I barely see you anymore." Alister reached across the table, threading his fingers into Atar's. "This is nice, though."

Atar grinned.

"My lords, compliments of the chef." The server had returned, this time carrying a small green bottle capped with crimson and gold wax. A number of small sigils were inscribed into the top, and they glimmered with power.

Alister took the bottle and his eyes widened. "This is a Nowabrev."

Atar raised an eyebrow. "Isn't that very expensive?"

"More than expensive. This bottle would be enough to retire to Levantier permanently." Alister tried to hand the bottle back. "We cannot take this."

The server smiled, and Atar felt the man's Spirit pulse in genuine joy and pride. He did not take the wine. "Ah, but we insist. It is one of our few Adept Tier wines, thankfully saved from the fall of our previous establishment in Haarwatch. And, while the walls were destroyed, my life and the lives of all who work here at Savina's were saved by the Autarch and those who fought by his side."

The server bowed, fully at the waist, and Atar realized that all of the servers were doing the same, all around the restaurant. Patrons watched, too, necks craning and eyes drinking in the spectacle.

Their server stood after a long moment. "Your entire meal is on the house."

"That is…quite kind," Alister managed.

They ordered food, Alister picking for the both of them, and the server left…but they remained the center of attention. Even the folks passing on the street would linger, if only a little. As members of

Elderthrone's elite, both mages were relatively well-known in addition to being an uncommon sight outside of the Eye and Crafting Halls. Atar hunched his shoulders, his chest burning under curious gazes and emotions that he only barely managed to ignore. Alister had a rougher time of it, however.

"Blind gods, but I dislike this Affinity," Alister said. The bottle of wine sat unopened between them. "How do you manage it?"

"You have to squeeze it off, like contracting a muscle," Atar explained. He thumbed an inscribed keystone at his waist, and a sound ward flashed around them before fading from view. Now, at least their words were private. "It takes practice, though. I still am not able to shut out anything particularly intense or too near."

Alister chewed on the inside of his cheek. "Perhaps we should speak to the Chanters. Get some proper training, as Zara has been suggesting. I hear she is trying to set up a sort of school here, to help those of us that have unlocked our Harmonic stats."

He'd heard about that. Zara and the Chanters had been engaged in heavy talks since Felix's departure. Zara had kept them in the loop, especially in regards to Felix's plan, but the Cantus Sodalus was intense. They were inordinately interested in anyone that had developed Harmonic stats thanks to Felix's presence, hence the school idea. "Training would be ideal. But when? It's only been four days since Felix left, and the amount of work in all Crafting Halls has more than doubled."

Alister sighed. "That is true. The nobles are a constant pain, but now that regular Manaships are moving between Haarwatch and Elderthrone, I'm being driven to distraction."

"Darius was just about the only person happy with the recent influx of people. I believe more than half has joined the Legion, and you can tell. The barracks have been alight for days now," Atar said.

"If only all of them were here to join the Legion. Instead, the other half are all crafters and skilled laborers. I just received word that several guilds are vying to set up in town." Alister waved his hand at Atar's confused look. "Don't get me wrong, I am happy. It means Elderthrone is thriving and will continue to do so...but it also means contracts, charters, and the minutiae of *taxes.*"

"Can't Karys help? He knows more about bureaucracy than a thousand clerks. He could probably whip up all of that in an afternoon."

"Karys has offered, and we plan to meet soon, but he's been preoccupied with that expedition to Khasma. We still haven't heard back from them, and it has the man worried. Besides, he's had his hands full dealing with the Stronghold ranking up, too."

Right. Atar had been inscribing a new array in the Glyphworks when his display had been inundated with notifications. Apparently, Felix had done something amazing and impossible again, and while they did not know all the details, there had been sweeping changes. At the very least, it had unlocked many upgrades to their Crafting Halls and several new features for the Stronghold at large.

"Rank IV," he said. "The upgrades to the Beacons are interesting, considering our expanding reach. The Autarch's Emporium will prove a good tax on the wealthy in this town, I think."

"You're not wrong. The Protector's Guild has an auction house in some of the larger cities, and it was always lauded as the guild's primary source of income. Giving access to a centralized marketplace through the Beacons is a remarkable feature that will only provide benefits in the years to come."

When Felix had upgraded the Stronghold, the Beacons that he could summon now had access to a unique space that people could travel *into*, like a Shadowgate. Normally, the Beacons only transported goods, not people, but this also did not send folks to the Storage Facility. Instead, they were brought into a wide chamber that resembled nothing so much as an amphitheater and had access to what was best described as a storefront and auction house. Goods could be put up for sale by anyone, though only appointed officials could manage it all. Few knew of its existence yet, but that would change soon, Atar imagined.

"It's interesting that not all Beacons have access to the Emporium. Just the one here, in Ahkestria, and this new one he put up." Alister laughed. "I can't believe he's taken the Hoarfrost. Do you know how long people have feared that place? Their raids are the stuff of nightmares for children on the northern borders."

"He turned my home into an ocean. I no longer have the capacity to be shocked by Felix's accomplishments," Atar said.

"Oh really? Then it wasn't you that I heard shouting about the upgrades in the Glyphworks?"

Atar blushed. "I—he increased the fidelity of all inscriptions! And glyph creation! What, am I expected to *not* shout?"

Alister only laughed.

Their food arrived a short time later, fresh, hot, and absolutely crawling with magic. Atar could feel the expertly cooked meal as if it had its own presence. And oh, the taste. He had missed good restaurants since Haarwatch had been destroyed and was quite pleased that he'd insisted on coming to Savina's.

They ate at first in companionable silence, the two mages exchanging words only between courses. They spoke of small things, happy achievements, and new ideas. Sigaldry was, of course, their shared love and was never far from their minds—but they also discussed their home, newly built in the Foot and exceedingly empty. Now that proper crafters had settled into town, the options for decorating their home had expanded, and both were eager to explore the new selections.

"I'm unsure. I prefer darker tones in a home, especially a library."

"That's because you grew up in this fog-drenched wilderness," Atar said with a sniff. "No offense intended, but the warm tones of my home will be far more effective at brightening up our library."

"I prefer fog-drenched to sunbaked, dear. Why not—"

Glass shattered all around them as a terrifying explosion ripped through a neighboring building. Atar was on his feet and running before he realized it, and Alister was right behind him.

"Get back!" he commanded, shouting with his Adept Tier lungs to be heard over the screams. People were panicking, but they obeyed and opened up a pathway for the mages to squeeze through the clouds of dust.

On the other side, he beheld giant gouts of flame tearing through the half-collapsed husk of a building. It had only been next door, Atar realized. If it had been any closer, than he and Alister would've—

"Pillars of the Domineering Sentinel!" Alister hissed. Blue force Mana surged from the man's feet and into the street before erupting within the tilted structure. Pillars of blue light pushed upward, placed just so beneath the charred but still-extant beams. The groaning ceased. "That should hold it, for a bit at least."

A window burst, weakened glass shattering before erupting in a geyser of flames. From within, people screamed.

"Atar!"

"I heard it!" He lifted his hands and grasped Flame within his chest. *The fires. Take them. Don't hurt anyone inside!*

a paltry task. i shall end the conflagration and grow with its—

Just do it!

All at once, the raging flames extinguished, turning to threads of molten light that coiled inward toward Atar's palms. Terrible, inexorable heat surged through his channels, lighting up his gray skin as if his blood had turned to fire…before fading as it all reached his core. Flame spread its wings and wove the threads into its form, growing the tiniest bit bigger.

Within the burned shop, there was only blue-lit smoke and the coughing of survivors. Atar dove into the rubble. "Hold on! I'm coming in!"

Inside, it was a maze of fallen beams, charred wood, and crumbling plaster. He had to step carefully over places where the broken glass had fused to the floor, creating slick footing…and again when he encountered two bodies. Or what was left of them.

"Hello? Where are you?" he called into the shop. The only response was a deep, unsettling groaning from wood and stone.

The smoke was awful, but Atar fished a fresh keystone and stylus from his pouch. He quickly inscribed sigils for *air*, *current*, adding hastily deduced parameters before capping it all with the glyph for *purification*. He pushed his fiery Mana into it, forcing it along the air-attuned array he'd created, until a small but steady breeze whistled into existence. The smoke moved, pushed away from him as if he were the center of a spinning vortex—because he was.

Debris was kicked into the air, but without the smoke, it was far easier to see where he was going. Atar found the first survivor in the back, behind a heavy counter that must have shielded her and the two little ones from the blast.

"Are you alright? Can you stand?" he asked.

The Dwarven woman blinked at him owlishly. Perhaps she couldn't hear him, but when Atar moved to help her up, she stood without issue. Two children, no older than five years old, were clutched to her chest. They all had blood running down their ears, but they were breathing. Atar just about fell over in relief.

"Let's get you outside."

"You absolute fool!"

Lilian's words were soft, but her tone was harder than mithril. Dabney, the great brute, hung his head beside her as they hustled away from the merchant's district.

He was wringing his hands, casting frequent glances behind them. Smoke still poured into the sky, visible in the magelights that swarmed the district. "I didn't think it'd fail. I—"

"No! You don't think!" Lilian smacked the man with her cane, and her veil nearly fell from her face. She hurriedly adjusted it back before yanking on her idiotic accomplice with the other. "That has always been your problem. Remember! **I** do the thinking here."

"Yes, Ophelia."

Good. At least he can remember that much. Lilian rubbed her temples as they walked, slowing their pace so they didn't look so suspicious. They were far enough away from the explosion that few would link two simple, poorly-dressed crafters to it all. *Light, where did this go wrong?*

The two of them had been heading out with the intent to test their newest alchemical solution when they had chanced upon her cousin and that two-faced slime, Atar. She'd been eager to stop and listen in on their conversation—the situation in Elderthrone was changing, fast. She had been in the Alchemical Lab when Aenea had gotten visibly excited about some sort of upgrades, and it had only taken a few well-placed compliments to get the woman to explain. Somehow, Felix had upgraded the rank of the Stronghold, which meant all sorts of opportunities.

What she really wanted to know was if Felix was returning and when. No one had noticed him leaving at first, but that secret had gotten out relatively fast. Lilian's true work was far from complete, but the longer Felix remained away, the better.

Then the two mages had erected a sound ward, and despite her various tools, it proved too strong to breach. She had ordered Dabney to keep marching to the forest, as they had originally planned.

That, of course, was when the thick brute's containment vessel had *broken*. The entire thing started glowing a brilliant, cherry red, and they'd been forced to toss the reagents as far as they could…right onto the roof of a nearby shop.

"Those poor people," Dabney moaned. "Do you think anyone…?"

Lilian didn't answer that. Even if they had, it couldn't matter. "It was a clothier for used woolens. A commoner's shop. No one of any import was there."

If anyone had been, of course, then it was Felix's fault. Why were commoners out in a wealthy merchant's district, next to one of the finest restaurants, at that time of night? They should have been abed, resting for the important work they provided in the mines and forests. All of this "free time" and "fair income" that Felix had mandated was ruining an entire generation of workers. Spoiling them, and for what? His government was balanced atop of a few unqualified fools. There was no nobility to support it, to create true value for it all.

It would fall, whether Lilian acted or not. *How* was another matter entirely.

"At least we know they are effective," Lilian muttered. "The entire roof was blown off that shop."

"Yeah, but the Fiendstone wasn't scratched," Dabney pointed out. "I saw it as we ran. The rest burned."

Lilian cursed. "Stop looking back. It makes you look guilty."

"I am guilty. That shop, it—"

"Enough." If that wretched material was unmarred by their concoction…it meant problems for their plan. "Still. This is good to know. We must increase the Tier of the batch. That will be easier to do, now that the Crafting Halls have upgraded."

"Dunno. That Dwarf won't let me touch a forge. Says I'm clumsy. I had to cobble the mechanism together while she slept."

"Don't use that as an excuse. Your sloppiness nearly cost us our lives and potentially exposed our plan. We will need to be much more cautious after this." Lilian increased her pace, the tapping of her cane now a rapid tattoo. "Come. We should return, before we are missed."

CHAPTER SIXTY-THREE

Felix sat on the edge of a balcony and marveled at the sky.

Liquid gold filled the vault of it, from horizon to horizon, like a lava lamp or one of those weird squishy toys you could buy at the gas station. It looked like oil and smoke, swirling clouds of it all backlit by some enormous, never-ceasing sun. More immediately overhead, the sky was festooned with rolling ribbons of glacial-colored light, auroras that spread from the Kingsrock like banners.

The wards that kept people from ascending the Kingsrock had dimmed, but only by Felix's command. Separated into this strange, liminal space, there wasn't a single threat that worried him outside of the massive structure. Not even the tribes of Frost Giants that had opposed his claiming—after all, he'd let them all in.

His followers hadn't much liked that.

Two whole days had passed since he'd claimed the Seat and Seal of Khalheim. Felix hadn't been expecting to stay so long, but it had been necessary for several reasons. Putting aside the issues with the Risi, Felix had to assess the condition of his newest Stronghold. It was Rank II, the same as Elderthrone when he'd revived it. Many of its features had decayed over the Ages, in addition to whatever the Dwarves had done, but it had several special features that were unique to it.

First was the underground forest beneath the golden earth. It sat at the very roots of the Kingsrock, flourishing in massive subterranean caves, and it absolutely teemed with life. Since the claiming, the

Kingsrock was like a piece of Felix's body, and he could feel the creatures moving about down there without even focusing on it. If he did, Felix could investigate every square inch of those caverns. Powerful creatures resided in those trees, not as strong as the Greater Elementals out in the Starfield Step, but they would prove excellent for food and training fodder, if the Risi treated them properly.

The second feature was part of the first: a wide, underground river sprouted within the forested caverns, filled with fish, monsters, and the coldest water Felix had ever experienced. Even atop the highest tower, he shivered as his thoughts returned to the moment he'd pressed his newly gained awareness into that water. It was only his Mind, but it had felt like his entire body was numb, burning, and turning into solid ice all at once. The river seemed to come from the Corporeal Realm through boundary stones, and it returned the same way. The stretch of it beneath the Kingsrock was like a minor diversion of its natural course, and it fed the beasts of the forest well, acting as an important part of its complex ecosystem.

Third was the elaborate formation that kept the Kingsrock within the Starfield Step. Felix had learned, upon gaining Authority over Khalheim, that the strange rock palace was not originally beneath the golden skies and shifting glaciers. The Starfield Step was in fact a liminal space, much like a Domain or the Dark Passages, suspended between Realms like a soap bubble clinging to the side of a wet dish. The boundary stones played a part in that, acting as the delineation between the Starfield Step and the Corporeal Realm. There was a mechanism to shift the Kingsrock back into the Hoarfrost, and it was fully functional. If Felix wanted, they could instantly appear within the snow fields of the northern tundra…but there was no reason to do that, really.

The very last thing Felix had found while scouring the Stronghold was a small shrine of sorts, built into a hidden chamber adjoining the throne room. Being hidden, it had escaped the ravages of the Dwarven invaders, and it was good that it had. The room wasn't huge by giant standards, and its angled walls were shaped into a nine-pointed star and decorated with carvings of vines, leaves, and a myriad of small beasts. In an alcove at the rearmost wall, a cold obelisk stood, made of mingled metal and stone and coated with ice. It resembled Beef's new greathammer, in fact, though it was inscribed with several giantfolk glyphs.

Frostfather, they said.

The moment Felix touched it, a spark had welled up within the obelisk, and a voice boomed into the space. "You have claimed Khalheim, I see."

"I have." Felix had looked around the star-shaped room. "How are you talking to me through this thing?"

"Anointed ice carries a piece of elemental power, and I am the Frostfather."

"Meaning your power connects through the ice, like a receiver."

"I...suppose." The mountain-sized Supreme Elemental had rumbled a sense of approval through the obelisk. "Your power is great, Colossus. If you allow me, I can imbue my own potency into the Kingsrock, as I did in ancient Ages. Together, we will lift my children from the depths they have sunk into."

"How exactly does that help me?"

A notification had appeared before Felix. "My power will be made manifest throughout the Kingsrock, and it will bind the Kin to you all the tighter. All in Khalheim that swear fealty to your Seat and Seal will receive one of two Titles: Might of the Colossus or Magic of the Colossus."

Felix had whistled when he read the descriptions. "These are impressive Titles."

"My presence will also influence the potency of the creatures in the caverns below the Kingsrock. A portal into my Ironskin Domain will open, and I shall continue to offer Quests to my children as I have for Ages, allowing them to grow stronger, faster."

"That's...quite a bit, but I know there's no such thing as a free lunch. How does all this help you?"

"I will be happy to aid my children, but more than that...I am old, Felix Nevarre. I have seen civilizations vanish into the cold expanse of time, and it leaves me hollow. The Nym might be gone, but the Kin still live. The Unbroken Shield rises once more. There is hope, thanks to you."

Felix hadn't explained to the Frostfather that *he* was technically Nymean; explaining his Primordial and Nymean natures was too involved to just casually toss out there. Still, the benefits on offer were potent, and Felix had no reason not to trust the Supreme Elemental. He had agreed, and the obelisk had crackled with icy Mana before spreading outward through the star-shaped room, until the entirety of the floor and walls was coated in a thin line of spiraling frost.

Sitting atop of the balcony and overlooking his new Stronghold, Felix was happy he had said yes. He could feel the Frostfather's influence, now, but it certainly wasn't overwhelming. Just as he had promised, his potency was mostly gathered in the caverns below the Stronghold, and Felix's new senses could even pick out the strains of ice, stone, and metal Mana that had begun influencing the beasts below. It would, in time, prove to be an excellent resource for the giants. Perhaps some proper elementals would spawn within the caverns, even outside the Frostfather's shifted Domain.

Just outside the immediate area, the Starfield Step shifted and crashed silently. During the time it had taken Felix to comb through the Kingsrock and its functions, his team had gone hunting elementals for practice and profit. Beef had spent much of it training with his new hammer, Bedlam, and though it was still a touch too heavy for him, he was making progress. The Claw was there, too, drilling their forms and large-scale combat coordination under the watchful eye of Harn. They had hunted the outskirts, luring monsters from the Step without risking too much of the shifting terrain.

Felix had considered stopping the heaving glaciers—it was within his abilities as Colossus—but doing so would trigger the Kingsrock's return to the Hoarfrost. The dangers of the Starfield Step were part and parcel of the defensive Realm-shift, after all. He didn't have any interest in removing Kingsrock from its protections—in fact, he was counting on them—so his friends had been forced to make do with the dangerous terrain.

That hadn't stopped Vess, Yintarion, and Evie, however. Those three had pressed deeply into the Step, this time far more agile than a team of sleds and a few hundred Risi. Yintarion had loudly requested to eat several of the Greater Elementals in the Step, and Vess was nothing if not accommodating to her Companion, quickly hunting down a Greater Cinderwing and Greater Gold Obelons. Early on the first day, the Wyrmling had tucked into his impressively sized meal. Last Felix had heard, he was still in a food coma.

Vess and Evie had continued, training their Skills and pushing themselves as much as possible as they navigated the hazardous terrain. Pit had even joined them, much to Felix's dismay, pressing himself just as much as they had. He took it upon himself to keep them safe from the various swarms and unexpected traps they encountered, which allowed him to train his Perception and Agility as he raced collapsing glaciers and exploding pathways.

It was treacherous in the extreme, but Felix couldn't deny the joy it gave his Companion. Besides, he could trust Vess and Evie to keep an eye on Pit, just as the Chimera was watching out for them.

Someone far below him shouted angrily. It was met by more voices, a back and forth that sounded less like an argument than a debate. Felix cocked his head, listening. It was the giants, of course. Things were getting more heated down there.

Felix double checked his notifications and screens. He had only just gotten off another call with Karys, and so much had changed back home that he felt like he might be missing something. Apparently, claiming a new Territory with a shared border had some additional effect on his Authority back home. Elderthrone had grown, becoming a Rank IV Stronghold and gaining a number of fascinating upgrades.

The Crafting Halls had all gained a boost as the Stronghold produced new, higher-quality tools from nothing and installed them. This increased their ability to work with higher-Tier materials, not to mention the flat bonuses to production and 10% chance of each finished piece jumping up an entire Tier in quality. It was huge, and Karys had been rightly excited to talk over the details.

His Storage Facility had grown, increasing its capacity by a huge amount and even combining with his Stronghold's Garden feature. This allowed them to grow and store more easily accessible foodstuffs, things they could easily pass onto their populace and his other Territories. An increase in stable storage was also implemented, increasing their capacity to hold and preserve magical items like alchemical potions, array slabs, and draughts, without losing any potency.

Of course, he couldn't ignore the upgrades to his Beacons, which were used to access his Storage Facility. Now he could place not only Primary Beacons, which had additional access to his new Emporium feature, but also Secondary Beacons that functioned simply as the old Beacons had, allowing authorized people to transport and extract items from his Storage. That was a neat new addition, and something Karys was over the moon about—Felix was much more interested in the brand new feature that had dropped.

Librarium Has Been Added To Elderthrone!

Librarium - Written records can be placed into any Beacon, and a copy of those records will be stored within the halls of the Librarium. These copies can be accessed by anyone with access to a Beacon, extracting a physical reproduction when-

ever they pull out said copies, allowing for the quick dissemination of information among your Territories. A private function exists as well, meant for valuable or dangerous texts, such as Skill Books (which cannot be replicated). Special permission is required to access the private function.

God, that's so cool. Felix had always loved books, and while the shelves of his Librarium were mostly empty, it was an awesome new feature. He had immediately sent word for every text in Elderthrone and Ahkestria to be placed into a Beacon, and if Felix took over any more Territories, he'd repeat that process.

Knowledge was power.

His Shadowgates had also earned an upgrade, though in their case, it had only been a surge of restoration. Pieces that had seemed broken or non-functioning had suddenly come back online, art repairing itself and the shadows strengthening. Karys was reasonably certain he could get most of them repaired within a few weeks, though their matching gates still needed to be restored for any of that to matter.

None of that helped him immediately, but in the future, the Shadowgates would save him so much time. As much as traveling to the Hoarfrost and claiming it had helped, it was a massive detour on what they needed to do.

Which brought him back to the voices, now in a full-fledged fight.

Alright. Been putting this off long enough.

Felix pushed off the balcony and into the open air. He fell, feet-first, while the wind whipped around his ears. Below, he could make out the gathering of giants in the courtyard, as well as a circle of Witches violently gesticulating at one another. He flared his Adamant Discord, speeding up just before landing.

He hit the ground in a burst of lightning and thunder that ground their arguments to a halt.

Reluctantly, the Kin took a knee before him. All of them, even that one flying Witch, though she was among the last to do so.

Kimaris was at the fore, and she looked at him with a grin. "Colossus. I have gathered the tribes here, as you requested. We have been discussing the role we shall all have in the governance of the Kingsrock."

"It is the way of our people that the Covens rule over the tribes," Naberius added. "We wish for that tradition to continue, my Lord."

"You want to cut up the pieces of the Kingsrock, divvying out the meanest portions to the other tribes," the flying Witch protested. Her name was Malva, and she remained kneeling, as all the rest, but her Spirit was heated.

"I simply said that the Covens should all have a piece that is equal to their strength," Naberius protested. "It is not my fault that you did not ally yourself with the Colossus before his rise."

Shouts met that proclamation, from Witch and Warrior alike. Felix snapped his fingers, the sound echoing like a gunshot in the wide courtyard. "I have claimed the Kingsrock, and the entirety of the Hoarfrost as well. Khalheim, the ancient nation once called the Unbroken Shield, is returned...and you are its people. I will not have you folks fighting over dumb shit."

When the giants kept themselves from arguing, Felix continued. "I am the Colossus of Khalheim, and I hold ultimate Authority here...but I am not one of you. I also cannot remain here, isolated within the ice fields. I need to appoint a Chancellor, to administer things in my place."

The silence grew fangs, each of the Witches around him almost leaning toward Felix in their eagerness to volunteer. Malva, however, was simply surprised.

"You will not reign here?" the floating Witch asked.

"No. I have other things to handle. My Chancellor will run things in my place, acting as my eyes, ears, and hands. She will retain a measure of Territorial Authority as well. Most importantly, she will be responsible for protecting the Hoarfrost and all of the people within its borders."

Malva frowned. "How? You are mighty, Colossus, but you have already said you shall leave us. How could one of us protect all of the north?"

"With this," Felix gestured, and a bolt of lightning pulled an icy comet down onto them all. Felix caught it easily, arresting the pull of his power as he did so, and the Razorspine statue gleamed in the afternoon light. Several Witches ceased breathing entirely, first at the show of power and then the presence of the artifact.

Felix had been sure to let the artifact's capabilities slip in casual conversation over the last few days, and it had done as he'd hoped. They were primed. "This is a Guardian, one that will protect our people from a great deal of threats. I will also provide resources and support from my other Territories. A Beacon has been installed within the Kingsrock, a sort of...doorway where we can trade goods between locations. I have similar Beacons in all of my cities."

"Trade. What could you trade with us that we could not simply take in raids?"

"We...are to cease all raiding, indefinitely," Kimaris said. It had been part of what Felix had told them, back when he'd claimed the Territory, and the tribes around him reacted just as the others had: poorly.

"No more raiding," Felix half-shouted over their protests. Silence descended. "Not the Dwarves or others outside the Territory, and certainly not amongst yourselves. In fact, I require that all members of all tribes are to relocate here, to the Kingsrock. It has more than enough space, it is protected by the Starfield Steps, and it has the resources to support every single one of you."

"What do we do for food?" Malva asked.

"There are deep caverns beneath us, filled with beasts to hunt and monsters to slay," Kimaris said. "And the Frostfather himself has relocated the Ironskin Domain there, for all of us to use and grow stronger."

That was of particular interest to the giants. An excited murmuring rippled among the crowd.

"Kimaris," Felix said. The Witch's head snapped toward him, as did many others. "Stand beside me."

The Witch swallowed and did so. He put his hand out, and she knelt before him so that his palmed hovered somewhere above her heart. "I would like to name you Chancellor of Khalheim. It will be a position of power but also responsibility. Do you agree to take on these duties?"

Naberius scowled and stepped forward, but Mother Vepar, the old crone, grabbed her by the arm. No one else moved.

Kimaris tried to speak, but no words came out the first time. She tried again. "Yes, my Lord."

"Then rise, Chancellor of Khalheim."

Congratulations!
You Have Chosen A Chancellor Of Your Territory!

Kimaris jerked to her feet as if she'd been electrocuted. Felix started, concerned for a moment before he saw what was happening. Power was swirling around the woman, congealing across her chest in great loops visible to his Manasight, all of it pressing into her center. Her core.

She was Evolving.

Kimaris gasped, eyes fixed on a middle distance. "My Lord, I—these notifications—"

Felix smiled. "Choose, Chancellor Kimaris."

She closed her mouth, pressing her lips into a thin, determined line. She reached out and touched her invisible notification…and the moment she did so, her skin began to glow. Several giants shouted, shielding their eyes, as Kimaris grew from nine feet to a bit over thirteen feet tall. Mana swirled, a storm now visible to everyone, centered upon her.

Kimaris reached up, into the storm, and frost flowered across her fingertips and hands, crawling across her arms until it reached her shoulders, where it thickened into a purple-white armor across her back and chest. Icicles like elegant blades sprouted from her back and studded her arms, looking wickedly sharp and twice as deadly. All of it, despite the added bulk, gave her a sleek, agile appearance that was both beautiful, regal, and undeniably deadly.

The storm ended, absorbed fully into Kimaris now. She stood up to her new, full height, and the weight of her presence unfurled into the crowd. Naberius, Malva, and even Mother Vepar gasped, while many others looked just about ready to bolt, like a herd of gazelle worriedly watching a lion.

"I—I have attained my next Evolution," Kimaris said. "I am a Hex Warden."

"You are the Chancellor of Khalheim," Felix reiterated. Kimaris raised a frosted fist to her heart. To the rest of the tribes, Felix raised his voice. "And you will also notice a new Title. Read it aloud for me, please."

Kimaris blinked then put a frost-coated hand up over her open mouth. She read. "'Magic of the Colossus. A leader is meant to serve their people. By boon of the Frostfather, all Kin sworn to the Colossus of Khalheim's service will gain a portion of their Intelligence, Perception, and Willpower.' My Lord? I—" She seemed to navigate through some other windows, and her eyes bulged in shock. "My stats, they're—"

"Yeah," Felix laughed. "It's a good Title. And there is another, meant for those following more martial paths, called Might of the Colossus. It is the same, except that it applies the boon to your Strength, Endurance, and Vitality instead." Felix met the tribes, eye to eye. "All you need to do is swear your fealty to me and to Khalheim."

Huh, he thought. *They kneeled a* lot *quicker this time.*

CHAPTER SIXTY-FOUR

Light, but this is excruciatingly boring.

The thought was inescapable as Mervin trailed behind the Dwarven Chanter Tzfell. She had requested some assistance from Loquis and had instead volunteered Mervin for the honor. Mervin was originally going to refuse—he had planned to get some extra training in with the other Blades—but that's when Loquis hit him with those dire hound eyes.

The things I do for friends, he thought with a scowl. Loquis had apparently made plans. *That Half-Orc better actually make a move on her, or I'll be so very cross.*

"Come closer, lad. I need to see this with the lantern," the Chanter said.

Can't you summon a magelight? Why do you need me? Yet Mervin walked up, holding the mage-wrought lamp up so that it cast its bright light over a wide mural. It had been hacked at with some sort of weapon, cracking the myriad tiles and sculpted shapes until it was almost unrecognizable. For all his bellyaching, Mervin did find the halls of the Kingsrock fascinating…and sad, too.

"So much beauty, lost," he said.

Chanter Tzfell nodded solemnly. "It is a travesty of the highest order." She ran her hands down the mural, following the brutal gashes in the stonework. "You can see here, where they heated their blades so it would disfigure the stone beneath as well. Tough to do, especially with high-Tier materials."

"The fires, the wanton destruction...it's like they were trying to make it worse for all who came after them."

"It was absolutely an intentional act. See here? This was a glyph once, an anchor for any number of wards that laced these halls. Tch. It is likely the invaders were chasing down protective enchantments and disabling them first and foremost."

He noticed she often referred to them as invaders, not Dwarves. Mervin wondered if she wanted to pull away from her connection with such heartless devastation, or if perhaps it had another meaning he was missing.

"Was there sigaldry here, or here?" Mervin asked, genuinely curious. He pointed to two other gashes that sliced down through the mural and into the floor itself.

"No. That—that seems to be a stray blow."

Mervin didn't know if he believed that. They had passed many places where things had been melted, burned, broken, or smashed in a way that seemed spiteful to him. The Chanter, however, was reluctant to admit that, though.

"Have you written down the mural and its description?" she asked.

He grumbled, but he shifted the ring handle of the lantern onto his wrist before retrieving the paper and pen he'd tucked under his arm. He started scratching out their location, *Tower 2, Floor 12, Passage E* before jotting down a quick summarization of the art. *Looks like a big soldier, maybe a giant, wearing full plate. Swirling colors surround the figure. Mountains, snow, and a setting sun in the background. Broken with weapons, slashed....eleven times by Dwarven invaders.*

That was the real reason the Chanter needed an assistant. She was cataloging things around the Stronghold, and had been doing it for days on her own, judging by the ream of paper on his board. Why was anyone's guess. Mervin figured she was compiling an account for the Autarch. *The Chanters work for him, right?*

"Oh. *Oh.* Lad, come closer. Down here." Chanter Tzfell was crouched low on the ground, apparently inspecting the breaks Mervin had pointed out. He crouched as well, putting the lantern to the floor. "See this? And this? What do you think this is?"

"More cracks in the floor?"

"No, no. These are too regular, too *perfect.* If you—do you have a way to visualize Mana?" She waved her hands at his blank stare. "Nevermind. It doesn't matter. There are sigils here, formed into the stonework itself. Hidden, like most Nymean enchantments. They cross the floor from the wall—from the mural—and end…here."

The Chanter scooted back until she was standing in the center of the mural alcove. Mervin followed her gaze, sweeping the mage lantern over until it illuminated a shallow depression in the floor. Three grooves met there, forming a nine-pointed star where they all intersected, as if the star was throwing off rays of light.

"Blessed Night," she whispered. "I see."

Mervin certainly didn't. It just looked like a weird tripping hazard. "What is—"

A chiming bell rang through the halls, clear as if it was hanging above his own shoulder, and Mervin pivoted to find its source. There was nothing, but it was followed up by a familiar voice, just as close and clear.

"Calling all Claw. The Autarch's expedition is leavin' within fifteen minutes. Minutes? Is that—? Ugh, why didn't you just say that. We're goin' in a quarter glass, folks! Wrap up your shit and get down to the Gloamin' Gate, or you'll get left behind."

"Evie—!"

The voices cut off abruptly, and Mervin's lips stretched into a wide smile. That last one sounded an awful lot like a certain Half-Orc mage. Then the content of the message settled in, and he just about sighed in pleasured relief. "Oh ah, we should get back then. Right?"

The Chanter, however, was fully engrossed in the floor. "I am not in a hurry. This requires study. I need to see if there are more, and how many. I think—hmm."

She continued to run her hands across the floor, feeling at something. Probably doing magic. Mervin shifted nervously from foot to foot. "Are you sure? They said they'd leave us behind if we're not there in time."

The Chanter did not look particularly phased by that revelation. She was fully engrossed in her study, until she suddenly stood up and snatched the board from Mervin's hands.

"Hey!"

"I need to see—Ah. No. Not this. Not—yes. Yes." She flipped through pages, earmarking one and then three other annotations. "This is the fourth mural like this I have found. The flooring in the rest had been devastated by blunt tools, though. On purpose?"

A clarion shriek echoed through the halls from far away, and Mervin couldn't handle it anymore. "That's the Autarch's Chimera. They're leaving!"

"Hush child, it hasn't been a quarter glass yet."

Mervin ground his teeth. "Do you require my assistance any longer?"

"Hm? No, no, you can go. I need to—"

The Chanter kept speaking, but Mervin didn't hear the words because he was already off. He bounded down the hall and down the nearest staircase. The last thing he wanted was to be left behind from the action, *again*.

Getting out of the Kingsrock was a lot easier than getting in. Felix was pleased to find a familiar set of boundary stones located within the Stronghold itself. They were arranged strangely, the path between them describing a twisted loop twenty feet wide and more than three times that in length, and it descended to just above the entrance to the caverns below. It was, Felix had discovered, the normal path toward the underground areas, but if activated by someone with the proper Authority, it would instead lead them out into the greater Hoarfrost.

"This leads all over the Hoarfrost," Laur said, marveling at the diagram that had appeared before them at the start of the boundary path. It was like a System notification, only made of swirling gold and crossed with the shimmering colors of a glacier. It was a map, not just of the Starfield Step (which hovered slightly separate from the rest), but the Hoarfrost as well.

"Wow. This place is *big*," Beef said. "Where's Nagast? There?"

"Yeah, by that break in the mountains," Felix said. "This is awfully impressive."

"I mean, it's big, but don't pat yourself on the back too hard."

"No, Evie. I meant the access points to the Starfield Step. Look here and here," Felix pointed to points of serpentine and sapphire on the golden map. "These are the areas where the tribes entered the Step at the start of all this. Laur, am I reading this right? Does this path allow us to leave through *any* of them?"

"It certainly seems that way," the tall Elf said. He traced several fingers through the map, disturbing it like a thick curtain of water. Colorful ripples extended from his touch, flitting across the map from the boundary points toward the Kingsrock at the center. "I am unsure of how this functions. The song of it…it borrows heavily from something other than Harmony."

"Dissonance?" Felix asked.

Laur gave him a sharp look. "Of course not. Using Dissonance would unravel any Harmonics it was placed within. Not even the mighty Nym were above the rules of the Realms."

Felix grunted. He didn't believe that, but it wasn't worth arguing. "Alright, so if these go all over, where does—aha. Perfect." Felix turned to his assembled team and the ice sleds that were beside them. Those were packed with supplies and drawn by a team of Hoarhounds that were cautiously sniffing at Pit. "Everyone! Follow me."

They started down the boundary path, walking with a steady, distance-eating gait. Most of the Claw were afoot, with only a few driving the sleds in lieu of their Frost Giant friends. Felix led the way, but Vess, Evie, Beef, Harn, and the Chanters were close behind. The path was lined with small stones, and it crunched beneath their feet, a steady counterpoint to the hum of the inscribed stones beside them.

"Will your new Chancellor have any issues with her duties?" Vess asked.

"Nah. Kimaris has a good head on her shoulders, and she's ambitious. She already made it clear to them that the Title they value so highly will be revoked if they break their Oath, and everyone seems eager to toe the line."

"It is an impressive Title, considering who it is drawing stats from," Vess admitted. "Do you have any clue what percentage it is?"

"Just about ten percent." Vess whistled appreciatively, and Felix grinned. "That's what they said."

The transition from path to elsewhere was a subtle one. The sound of crunching gravel faded as the hum of the stones increased, and the effervescent light slowly muted itself, until only a chill white sun shone upon them all. By the time Felix noticed that, he was standing among a collection of upthrust rocks. They weren't standing stones—though some sigaldry existed among some moss-coated nubs nearby—and instead seemed to be the remains of some ancient geological feature, worn by wind, ice, and time. Outside of the broken tor was flat tundra, unrelieved for as far as even Felix's eyes could see.

"Where're we now?" Harn asked. Tzfell climbed up onto the rock behind him, peering off into the distance.

"Much farther southeast than I could have hoped." Felix called up the golden map again through his Authority screen. He had puzzled that out while walking, and with an effort of Will, he added a series of dark tunnels across the map. "And if we walk about a mile south, we can hop a ride through a Dark Passage. C'mon."

A bit farther on, Felix tore open the face of reality to reveal a patch of star-drenched night. It felt a touch easier than before, though he wasn't sure how much of that was his imagination. He did know that Labyrinthine Wing had gained a level after claiming Khalheim, and instinctively, he knew it was because of that fact. The knowledge had beamed itself into his brain the moment he contemplated the issue, coming from the pattern that constituted his Skill, and any time he added more Territories, it would level again.

While it may not have been easier to open, it definitely was a larger opening than before. Now it could easily accommodate their oversized sleds, and his team filed into the Dark Passage with little issue. Felix grasped his hooked blade and sent a pulse of his Will through it.

"Karys, we're entering a Dark Passage now. Mark it down. I'll contact you when we emerge."

The sword buzzed, green-gold. "Of course, my Lord."

Felix and Pit were the last to enter, closing it behind them.

Inside, the normal pitch darkness was lightened; still Void-like, but now with a touch of gray. The mountains in the distance were more detailed, and the stone platform they entered upon even had the start of some sort of workmanship. It appeared ancient and dilapidated, brickwork worn by feet over a thousand years, pitted and cracked.

Hm. Is this a feature of Labyrinthine Wing's level up? Felix scratched his head as he entered, studying the changes. *Or was it just already here?*

Zara and others had told him that, when she had utilized the Dark Passages in the Verdant Pass, she had been forced to expend her Will and Mana to create a physical construct. A bridge, something that everyone could interact with so they wouldn't fall into the Void, never to be seen again. It had also been easily affected by the Wills of others, enough that many of the soldiers had required drugs to dull their senses.

His experience with Dark Passages had so far been wildly different, but then, Zara didn't have the same Titles as Felix. Chthonic Traveler was potent, indeed.

"Felix! Make the Sailwhale!" Pit shouted from ahead. He was already at the edge of the broken cliff, bouncing among the Claw. Several of the soldiers watched him with half-hidden smiles.

"Ugh. I thought we weren't calling it that?"

"Oh no, we're definitely calling it that," Beef said.

"Looks like a fish, flies like a fish…" Evie paused. "Something something Sailwhale."

"Great," Felix muttered. He mustered his Will, and the nature of the Dark Passage shifted to accommodate it. "Wonderful."

CHAPTER SIXTY-FIVE

The Sailwhale floated through an infinite twilight, its crystalline balloon thingy lighting up the dim darkness. The Claw moved calmly along the gunwales, patrolling in case of another Void beast attack, but mostly it was silent. There wasn't even a breeze, just the distant impression of mountains slowly growing closer.

Beef was settled against one of the masts, Bedlam across his lap, in a cradle of thick roots before they merged completely with the living deck. He was trying to meditate, but it was hard. The Sailwhale distracted him, as it had since the first time he'd laid eyes on it. His experience constructing Manaships had given him a deep appreciation for the rules and processes needed to build one—and the Sailwhale betrayed all of them. Forged of Felix's Willpower alone, it worked despite its strange shape and massive weight. It didn't even have an engine!

I knew magic was crazy. But this doesn't make sense. The Dark Passages were like core spaces in many ways, and those were bonkers, too. Keeping all the details straight was so hard, sometimes. *Wish I had a wiki.*

"Beef? Are you ready?" Vess asked. She was clad in her elaborate armor, and her matching spear was angled into the crook of her elbow. "Harn said you had finished his regimen for the day."

Beef groaned. "Barely. That guy is a monster."

To his surprise, Vess folded her legs and sat before him. She set her spear aside. "Harn's greatest strength is his commitment to improvement, whether that is fighting or smithing. It has carried him far, and I hope it will carry him further still."

"Improvement. Isn't that like...the point? Isn't everyone trying to advance?"

"Not at all. In your days in Ahkestria, were there people who stagnated?"

"Yeah. But, like, those people were miners. Slaves, basically. They didn't have any way to get stronger."

Vess' face pinched. "I have not forgotten. I have talked with many of those former miners. All struggled ahead, advancing their Skills in whatever way they could. It was their guards that often remained behind. They reached a point in their training that allowed them to exert their Will on the lives of others, and for them, that was enough."

Beef wrinkled his nose. "Gross."

"I agree. Yet, not all those who stagnate do so for such vile reasons. Some are simply content. Some are numb. Some are afraid." The lady laid her hands along her armored thighs, palms up. "It is vision and conviction that drive us to greater heights. Now. Shall we begin?"

Beef swallowed nervously and nodded.

"Good. Then we shall enter your core space together."

Beef no longer stood upon the Sailwhale, and the ground beneath him heaved. He stumbled, nearly losing his footing on the slightly rounded surface, but his hooves caught traction along a pattern of bumpy ridges.

"Gah. Terrible entrance," he muttered. "Dumb hammer."

Bedlam hung heavily across his back, and it weighed Beef down immensely. He clenched his jaw and frowned, flaring his Willpower so hard that his neck corded with tendons and veins. With a muted *pop*, the hammer vanished.

"Are you alright?" Vess asked. She stood a short distance away, poised upon a thin railing as if it were a ballroom floor. She was clad in her white-enameled armor, just as in the real world, but also had no weapons. A scarf fluttered across her shoulders, diaphanous and colored a pale blue edged with red-gold. "You look...ill."

Beef flushed. "I uh, I didn't want Bedlam on me. So, I had to get rid of it."

"Ah, yes. Altering your visualized projection is difficult at first." She tilted her head, and the dark-skinned woman's eyes flickered from golden brown to red to blue to bright magenta before returning to normal. "But that is part of what we are working upon today. Thanks to our Link with Felix, I can enter your space directly to refine your control with a few techniques."

"Right." Beef looked down at himself, studying his chitin breastplate and vambraces. "I've always wondered why I look like this when I come here. My armor hasn't looked like this for months."

Vess stepped gracefully off the railing and onto the curved floor. "It is a matter of perspective and identity. You are who you believe yourself to be."

"I'm a Minotaur." Beef grinned. He had appeared as his old self in his core space before, but that was back when he was upgrading it all. He hadn't lapsed like that since.

"Indeed." Vess gestured around herself. "Can you tell me about your core space? It is quite…unique."

"Oh! Yeah!" Beef walked over to the railing and threw out his arms. "This is the Golden Death Beetle!"

They stood atop the back of an enormous bug, a mixture of scarab and a rhinoceros beetle. The creature moved as if alive, scuttling across the landscape tirelessly. It was shaped like a tank made of green-gold plates, with a large structure built atop its back that resembled nothing so much as an enormous, sprawling mansion. The thick walls and oddly joined rooms were piled atop one another, like a fever dream of a house, all of them built of green-gold chitin, extending out of the beetle's back like they had been grown.

All around them was an endless field of golden grain and small trees, while above, the sky was blue touched by the faintest hint of sunset. The pervasive heat might have been too dry and overbearing, were it not for the cool, intermittent breeze that rolled across the fields. Beef had designed the place to reflect his favorite time of the day during his favorite time of the year: late afternoon in the heart of summer.

The ground shifted again as the Golden Death Beetle strode forward on its massive legs, forcing Beef to grab hold of the railing. Vess merely rolled with the movement, her concentration untouched.

"It's not as hot as summer in Texas, but I couldn't do that to myself, especially after the Scorched Expanse," Beef explained. He looked at the older woman, unexpectedly nervous. "Do—do you like it?"

"Beef, it is extraordinary. All of this detail! You clearly had a powerful vision in order to produce something so complex."

Pride swelled in Beef, washing away some of his jitters. "Yeah. Yeah

I did. The Primordial of Withering Dust helped. All that power from Felix and our Link was like…like a big uh, a big help."

Beef inwardly cursed himself for his clumsy words. The game-like stuff was easy to understand, but the more he moved away from simple RPG rules, the less he understood.

Vess didn't seem to care. "Yes, the Link has proven more of a boon than I originally estimated. But! There is always room for improvement, as you well know. What did you wish to focus on today?"

He chewed at his lip. "Follow me. Hallow? Take us to my Skills, please."

"Of course."

Hallow's voice rang out around them, sounding smooth and calm and exactly like his mom. Beef wasn't exactly a fan of that, but he'd yet to figure out how to change it. A massive, segmented leg lifted from the fields and bent unnaturally on itself, until it came to a rest inches from Beef's feet.

"Hallow, you are the beetle itself?" Vess asked.

"I am, yes. Welcome, Lady Dayne, to our core space."

Beef stepped forward, hooves finding purchase on ridges and thick spikes on the limb. "Hop on."

Vess did so, and Hallow immediately lifted them both up and over the mansion's outer walls. The wind howled in their ears, a refreshing gust that set his fur rippling across his arms and neck. In moments, they were deposited atop the tallest portion of the wild house, where a wide field opened up to the sun and sky. They hopped off.

"Interesting," Vess remarked as she took in the grass-filled area. "Each one of these is a Skill?"

"Yeah."

Surrounding them were a number of statues, each one depicting a unique object, person, or monster. A big hammer for his Bludgeoning Weapon Mastery. A suit of armor surrounded by insectoid legs for his Keratin Conception. The list went on. All were done up in a green stone so deep it was nearly black, except where the sculptures were the most detailed. There, they shone like transparent stars, glimmering with sparks of brighter green and hints of vibrant gold.

Beyond the overgrown field was another portion of his mansion, but this one was a little different than the others, if only in coloration. Beef scrubbed his hands against his leather battle skirt, but his hands remained vaguely sweaty. He ignored the building. It wasn't important.

Vess walked among them, through the overgrown weeds at their bases. "Is the detail representative of their respective levels?"

That took a second for Beef to figure out. "Oh! Yeah. Every time I level them up, they get a little better. I've got most of them up into high Journeyman now, except for one or two new ones. I don't, uh, really know why they get all shiny, though."

"It is a visual aid," Hallow said, her voice just a touch too loud. "The more detail, the greater the power that can shine through your Skills."

"And this?" Vess asked. She had come to one of his Skills that was represented not by a single statue, but many all clustered together. They rose up from the same base, as if exploding outward, reaching or clawing or lunging. "I sense this is all one Skill."

"Hallow Rise," Beef said. "The one we use to take over dead Bodies. Each figure is something that Hallow has Risen before, even if we don't have access to it anymore."

The statue was big, taking up a considerable portion of Beef's field, as well it should. A massive scorpion was there, the Multipede, too, as well as Sand Wolves, Paladins, and even the undead from the desert. Surmounting it all was the Homunculus, and that looked the least refined of all.

Vess bent down and parted the grasses near the Skill's base. "Weeds here, and the hint of something else below. What is it?"

Beef craned his neck over, curious. "I have no idea."

"Something to be discovered," Hallow said.

Vess nodded along. "Very good. The mansion below…what is the purpose of it?"

Beef cocked his head. "Purpose? Do I need one?"

"Usually. The way we visualize our core spaces speaks to our desires and dreams. What does this mansion mean to you?"

He hadn't really thought much of it, back when he'd forged the place. It had been done under extreme circumstances back in Khasma, as Vess well knew, and Beef didn't remember all of the process. He told her as much. "I think it's mostly that I wanted a home. My old space was…cozier. But I'd outgrown it. This is more my style, now."

"I can understand that. You have been through a great deal, Beef." Vess gave him a kind smile and patted a sand zombie on the shoulder. "Now, stand on one leg, and empty your Mind."

Beef did so, wobbling a bit on his narrow hoof. "How do I empty my Mind?"

"Calm your thoughts. I have found it helpful to focus upon a singular image or sensation and to let that fill the space of your Mind. Peace will follow, given enough time." Vess copied his stance, but she folded her lifted leg up and over her other thigh without issue. She settled in. "Do not be worried if it takes a while. It is a process."

Beef nodded and got to work.

CHAPTER SIXTY-SIX

The first thing Vess helped him do was clear up the grass in his field of statues. Some grass was left, but the vast majority was eliminated, and the ground below it resolved into a pattern of concentric circles. Each of the circles was made of a metal-like chitin, bright green in color and somewhat raised from the Golden Death Beetle's carapace. They looped between the Skill statues in convoluted knots, intersecting some but not all before they inevitably led to the center.

It was his center that was the problem.

His core, now a ring of blackened green light, had been buried deep inside his elaborate mansion. Safe, or so he had thought when creating his core space. With Vess' assistance, Beef realized that his layers of protection were actually hampering the flow of power in his core space. His visualization was too tangled in some places, too solid in others—his entire setup required an overhaul.

Hours went by as Vess and Beef practiced her visualization techniques. Together, they developed a sort of stepped well design, turning the flat field into a spiraling path that led inward and downward, with each of his Skill statues positioned at specific intervals. Vess inspired the design, but Beef was the one who shaped it, visualizing the specific bricks and steps in the new formation, all while maintaining the pattern of those metal-chitin loops.

He based the design on a specific type of well, a communal construction he recalled seeing in some sort of documentary. Deep in the center of the well, down in a thick darkness that reminded Beef of the Passages, was his core. It was a spinning ring made of blackened-green light and broken statuary. Arms, legs, and faces swirled among the ring, colliding and coiling through the light as they were slowly polished from dull stone to translucent gems.

It thumped like a heartbeat, driving the Golden Death Beetle forward and providing power through the looping circles of metal-chitin and into his Skills. Bright pulses swirled upward from the dark depths in time with that enormous heartbeat, regular intervals accompanied by strobe lights and a satisfying, almost imperceptible song.

As the last piece of brickwork clarified, Beef let himself sag backward. He dropped a leg, bracing his wobbling muscles as he marshaled his Strength…yet after a moment, he already felt stronger. Steadier. The fields around them blurred by, Hallow's steps a distant thunder, and he didn't even notice the beetle's wobbling.

"Excellent job, Beef! I am quite happily surprised. Normally, such changes would require a great deal of time to enact, but we have been at this for a mere four hours."

"That's fast?"

"Incredibly so. Perhaps sometime you can ask Felix how long it took him to learn my techniques."

Beef perked up. "He wasn't good at them?"

"A powerful Mind is not always a boon," she said by way of explanation. "Nor is advancement. My techniques were developed for those who have barely begun their path, and they grow far less effective when you have several Temperings under your belt."

"But I'm fully Tempered into Journeyman Tier," Beef noted. It had been difficult, changing parts of his core space, but not *that* troublesome. "Doesn't that mean it should be harder?"

"I—yes. Yes, it should." Vess hesitated, frowning into the middle distance. "I apologize if this comes off as rude, Beef. Please know I do not mean to offend you."

Beef winced. He knew it. Something was wrong with him. He was still so far behind Felix in strength, and he had no clue why…but maybe this was it. Maybe it was something about his core that was broken or faulty. "I can handle it," he said.

"Your Mind and Spirit are open."

"I knew it, I—" Beef blinked. "What? Is that a bad thing?"

"It means they are more malleable than I expected. You take to change far more rapidly than someone of your Temper should—partly,

I believe, due to your relative youth." She stared thoughtfully down into the newly made well. "In this case, it was a benefit, but as you advance, it is your solidity that will protect you. To reach the pinnacle is to accumulate a vast amount of significance within our Skills, then our Tempered Aspects themselves. If you remain too amenable to change, I do not know if you can handle the rigors of Master Tier and beyond."

Beef stared at the lady, his insides all churned up. He had felt so good a second ago, and now he felt like a failure again. "How do I fix that?"

"I do not know," she admitted, her tone apologetic.

"Bring the boy to me."

The voice echoed around Beef's core space, piercing in a way that Hallow's voice never matched. Vess looked up, startled. "Are you sure, Yin?"

The only response was a deep rumble, like distant thunder.

Vess looked at him. "It seems my Companion might have a solution. Would you care to see my core space?"

Beef's eyes widened. "I can do that?"

"The benefit of our Links to Felix. Come." She took his hand. It was so much smaller, but her grip was firm. "Hold on…and let go."

"What do you—AHH!"

They fell upward Into the Blue Sky. Azure turned to black as they passed the edges of Beef's core space. The Minotaur looked down, beyond his feet, to watch as his core space shrank below. It resembled a tiny orb, a toy world filled with golden fields of grain, rolling hills, and a proliferation of small, stunted trees. Blue clung to the air like a halo, and as they rose higher into the thick shadows, he saw his golden death Beetle scuttling across its surface like a small dog balancing atop a large ball.

Whoa.

His attention was drawn away from his core space as a new light hit them—twin stars, one shining red-gold and another blue-white. They fell between their radiance, and Beef's world twisted into incomprehensible chaos. Thankfully, that faded a half-second later, and suddenly they were falling across a new sky. A new world.

"Turn with me!" Vess shouted over the wind.

She moved, rotating her body so her feet were angled toward the approaching core space. Beef flared his Willpower and Alacrity, able to just about spin his bulky form as they streaked across night-touched skies and into a mountain range covered in clouds. Winds whipped at him, parting the clouds and stealing the breath from his lungs almost as much as the sudden appearance of a massive, golden maw.

Beef screamed.

They fell past it, and only then did he realize it was a statue. He was so embarrassed, he barely noticed as they landed in the midst of a wide, stone-paved courtyard.

The clouds were gone now, and he could see the structure ahead in all its glory. The Dragon was huge, a dozen times bigger than the Sail-whale and perhaps five times bigger than his Golden Death Beetle. Its wings seemed to spread across the entire horizon, blanketing the rocky peaks in a curious mix of shadow and reflected light.

Beneath the Dragon was a building that only sort of resembled a house. The enormous sculpture's legs were worked into pillars, its belly becoming the sloping roof, while enormous doors led within. Those were worked with green and white gemstones, polished to a brilliant sheen.

"This place…there's so much detail!" Beef marveled at the court-yard beneath his hooves. Each paving stone was so well-realized that they made his own efforts look like a baby playing with clay. "How did you do this?"

"A lot of trial and error over a great many years," Vess said. She looked proud, though, and swept her gaze around the windswept area. "Each peak is a Skill shaped to reflect my abilities. But this is where I keep my core."

The two of them ascended the steps and the white and green doors opened at their approach. Beyond the threshold, the floor became a polished expanse of marble, surrounded by fluted columns decorated with the spiraling shapes of serpentine Dragons. In the center of it all was a structure that looked similar to the base of a fountain, but in place of water, there was only a column of liquid Mana. The column split at the top, spraying outward as a fountain might before it flowed into a horizontal ring. Mana colored white-green and silver flowed through the ring, and the ring itself connected segmented pieces of yet another large metal Dragon. It was horned and bearded, much like the statue outside, and shared many similari-ties with her Companion.

Except size, Beef amended. *This thing is wider than my old house.* "Hey, that's kinda like mine."

Vess grimaced. "I noticed that, yes. I apologize. My influence may have left its mark on your core space."

"Nah, that's okay. I didn't have a better idea, and this looks sick as hell."

Vess frowned, casting her gaze over her core. "How—? Ah. I am assuming that means it is…interesting?"

Beef blushed. "Oh. Sorry. Like, it means, uh, it's cool. Awesome."

Vess' frown transformed into a wide smile. "Thank you. Come this way."

They followed the perimeter of the core fountain, around to a decorated alcove hidden in the back. There, between braziers of brilliant fire, a cat-sized golden Wyrmling was curled upon sumptuous cushions of embroidered silk. Yintarion of the Cerulean Skies lifted his head regally, and smoke curled from his nostrils. His crystalline horns caught the light and cast rainbow reflections, and his scales glittered like polished metal, but it was the objects beneath him that drew Beef's attention.

"Dragon eggs," he said, and couldn't help the shiver of awe that ran through him.

"Yes," the Wyrmling said, his deep voice strange coming from his tiny mouth. "Their eternal care is my penance for the dark deeds I once performed."

"That was not your fault, Yin."

A tiny, five-fingered claw lifted up, forestalling Vess' words. "Let us leave that familiar argument by the wayside, little Dragoon." He fixed Beef with his liquid gaze, gold on gold, without any trace of a pupil. "You were brought here to fix a deficiency in your Aspects."

"Oh. Yeah. My…malleability, right? It *can* be fixed?"

"It can. But it requires sacrifice."

Beef scrunched his snout. "Like…a virgin blood sacrifice?"

"What?" Yin asked, his regal pose disrupted. "Why would I—what does virginity have to do with this?"

"I don't know, you said it!"

"I did not!"

"Boys," Vess said. Her face was a weird mix of pale and flushed, and a smirk fought against her control. "Please. Yin, explain what you need from him."

"I was doing so before he interrupted me," the Wyrmling stated as he flowed back into his regal posture. "I have a method to fix your deficiency, but it cannot be attempted until I have advanced. Once I have, it will still require a great deal of pain and effort on your part."

"Okay. I'm not a huge, uh, fan of the last part, but 'no pain no gain,' right?"

"...Right."

"What exactly would be required of him?" Vess asked.

"He must help us. I have hunted down most of what I need to begin my Evolution; the elements churn within my belly even now. The last piece of it will come from the Dwarven mountains, and it will require your particular Skills to capture it alive. However, it was a unique sort of creature, rare even in my time." Yin sighed. "I do not know if its kind still lives."

"Hunt down a monster? I can do that." Beef was pretty confident of his battle capabilities, at least. Most of the time. "What then?"

"Then, once I have Evolved...once I can complete my penance... then I shall attempt to bind your unique Spirit to something truly exceptional."

"Truly?" Vess asked. "Yin, how?"

"Wait. What are you talking about?" Yin's eyes flickered downward. Beef gasped. "You're *kidding*!"

"I would not dare," the Wyrmling said. "If you aid me, Beefhammer, Minotaur and Unbound warrior, I shall bind your Spirit to a hatchling."

"Yeah!" Beef shouted in unrestrained glee. "A fucking Dragon!"

CHAPTER SIXTY-SEVEN

The winged ship was very big, and Felix had designed it to more than accommodate all of the people who followed him. Rooms for sleep, to eat, and most importantly: rooms to train. Two entire lower decks had been made, reinforced as best Felix could manage, so that the Claw could spar and practice their Skills with little worry. There had been a few explosions and incidents of elemental shenanigans, but it was easily repairable.

He commandeered the prow of the ship for himself.

Wild Threnody is level 88!
Hand of Calamity is level 74!
Meditation is level 80!
Manasight is level 90!
Manaship Pilot is level 46!
Multi-Cast is level 89!
Green Shaping is level 86!
Shadow Whip is level 74!
Rime Shaping is level 90!
Auroral Forge is level 84!
Abyssal Skein is level 82!

Illusory Double is level 55!
Journeyman Tier!

You Gain:
+10 INT
+10 RES
+10 PER

Ferric Shaping is level 37!
Apprentice Tier!
You Gain:
+10 WIL
+10 INT
+10 MIG

Mantle of the Infinite Revolution is level 75!
Adept Tier!
You Gain:
+15 MIG
+15 INT
+15 END

Storm Shaping is level 35!
Apprentice Tier!
You Gain:
+10 EVA
+10 RES
+10 INT

The past few hours had been intense for him. Left without responsibility for the first time in a while, Felix put all of his building frustration to work. His concern over Pit's injuries, the worry that he'd mess up his interactions with the Frost Giants, even his fear that he'd be too late to save the Gnome. He grasped all of it and burned it as fuel.

He trained.

Felix's Skill levels had grown, some by significant leaps, but most by small increments as he learned to leverage the patterns in his chest. His shaping Skills were growing especially well, though Ferric and Storm Shaping still had a long ways to catch up. He had put both of those Skills into his Shaping Array and was still hoping to combine them all together at some point, but it wasn't right yet. The patterns were just slightly off.

Interestingly enough, Abyssal Skein was also easier to use within the

Dark Passage. Conversely, it was also a *lot* stronger and actively fought against Felix's Will. He realized that it was affected by the proximity of the Void, the darkness inside his core space reacting to the darkness without.

The true Void hadn't worked like that, but the Dark Passages weren't really the Void, just as they weren't really the Corporeal Realm. Something about the in-between nature tried to destabilize the Skill whenever he tried to use it, like an explosion in a pressurized chamber. Felix hadn't tried to use it more than once, but ironically, his revelation was what bumped the Skill up several levels, going from seventy-seven to eighty-two all at once.

The Skills with the lowest levels were the easiest to advance; the advantage of having a powerful Body, Mind, and Spirit, he supposed. Anything below level 90 had advanced at least a little, while those above it were stuck in place. Felix knew he required a greater challenge, or perhaps greater understanding, to push those into Master Tier. It was still incredibly frustrating, though.

He had tried for hours to push Relentless Resolution up by a single level, racing across the forward deck like a madman in complex loops, leaps, and turns. The problem, as he saw it, was that his Body and Mind were too strong. Relentless Resolution was about turning thought into action, and only by pressing himself to his utter limits would he see more growth.

He tried, but when the deck had burst into flame and shattered, he was forced to tone it down.

Hours later, sweat dripped from Felix's brow as he settled against the foremost point of his ship. A great deal of his concentration and thought had gone into his training—he wanted to eke out whatever advantage he could from their time in the Dark Passage. Now, he just wanted to rest. Which, of course, meant a different kind of work: as he caught his breath, he thought about his bonus stats.

He had ninety bonus stats, a veritable windfall for anyone else, but considerably less for him. The eternal question was whether he wished to pursue a balanced build as best he could, or if he should emphasize his strengths.

Am I close to the next Threshold? When asked, Karys hadn't known if there *was* another Threshold after the third; Zara hadn't even heard of the third until Felix reached it. As with all power on the Continent, people who had as many stats as Felix weren't interested in sharing details.

He brought up his stats.

STR:4184
PER:3202
VIT:3240
END:2642
INT:3347
WIL:4254
AGL:2835
DEX:2957

Certainly not bad. His Strength and Willpower were his two highest, followed closely by Perception, Vitality, and Intelligence. But even his Endurance, Agility, and Dexterity were monstrous in comparison. From what Felix gleaned from his friends, few had more than one stat higher than a thousand. His friends were growing past that, though they remained fairly specialized.

Evie was focused on Agility and Dexterity, Harn on Endurance and Strength, Atar on Intelligence and Willpower, and Vess on Strength and Agility. Even Beef wasn't as far ahead as Felix, which he was certain was just blind luck; Felix had stumbled into his fair share of bad encounters. His greatest feat, in those early days, was that he kept surviving—if only barely.

Thankfully, their Link with him was hastening their growth. It was many times greater than the strange effect he was having on the Claw, which was already pushing them to advance their Skills just a touch faster. He knew, one on one, his friends were more than a match for anyone at their own Tier. Together? They were a walking bad day for whoever opposed them.

Karys had explained that most people in his Age were in the two thousand point range when approaching Master Tier…and then, only in a handful of stats. Specialization reigned even in the Golden Empire, apparently, though the old man claimed the opportunities for advancement and growth were far greater. "War," he had said, "is a remarkable accelerant."

Felix mentally clicked on the little feather icon in his display.

<u>Pit's Stats</u>
STR: 873
PER: 728

VIT: 910
END: 1152
INT: 894
WIL: 861
AGL: 2226
DEX: 1802

Even if Pit only had Agility and Dexterity as his primary focus, he would be faster and more nimble than most Adept Tier combatants. His other stats, however, meant he could fight several Adept Tiers head-on without much worry. Specialization was strong, but only until you met a counter. Balance was the go-to for anyone who had to fight alone. Balance would keep them alive.

And yet…

It's only ninety points, he reasoned. *I can earn those back pretty fast.*

Felix put all of them into Willpower. It was the stat that had gotten him to this point, after all.

WIL:4511

He took a deep breath as System energy spun through the funnel of his core space. It narrowly avoided being sucked up by his Hunger before crashing into his dual cores. The spinning rings swelled with their respective lights, turning the colorless potency into vibrant rays of power. It wasn't too many stat points, but Felix could feel his Mind clarify just a touch. With a slight press of his Will, he rose into the air.

I'll never get over that. Being able to propel himself via Willpower and Alacrity was the only thing Felix had ever missed about the Void. It was easier than ever, now.

He settled back onto the deck with a muted thump. *I suppose, since I'm making decisions, I should assign my extra Skill levels.*

The Title: Champion of the Long Night had granted him (and Pit) an extra ten levels to apply to a single Skill below Adept Tier. He'd held off, attempting to train what he could before spending the Title's bounty. Felix would rather spend the free levels on a Skill that was as close to Adept Tier as possible. But…what if the Skill was *too* close to Adept? Would the Skill levels push it beyond? Or would they be wasted?

Stupid opaque System. Still, he checked his status once more. A list of Skills too hard or too strange to level normally, closer to Adept. He could choose Fiendforge, but that could be trained and it was of no immediate use. Perhaps the Last Cry of the Chthonic Host, his life-saving trump card. It was an insta-heal ability, only able to be used once per month—the extra levels would surely reduce that cooldown, perhaps by as much as a day. He discarded that idea.

He knew what to choose.

Congratulations Champion!
You Have Added 10 Levels To Your Skill!

Unite the Lost is level 52!
...
Unite the Lost is level 61!

Aside from its help in fixing Pit, just in case this Mote of Frenzy didn't pan out, Felix had a feeling he would need the Skill a lot in the coming days. The System's word echoed in his memory, as clear and sharp as diamonds.

What Is Lost Can Be Regained.

He certainly hoped so.

Felix lounged against the gunwale, elbows up against the rounded railing. *Pit. How's training going?*

AH! It's good! Totally fine and safe!

Are you lying?

Why would I do that? Don't—Hey! Spread the fire evenly—Yeah, sure. There was a sound of crashing, and if Felix focused, he could hear the whoosh of wind from somewhere below decks. *Everything's fine. Don't even, uh, worry. Gotta go.*

Their bond dimmed, pinched tight by his Companion, and Felix rolled his eyes. He knew nothing was wrong with his friend—he could see the tenku's Status Sheet after all. What annoyed Felix was that Pit had begun downplaying a lot of the dangerous things he got into; a bad habit that he needed to shake, quickly.

At the very least, it was mollifying that he had been burning through the Skill levels as much as Felix.

Cold Resistance is level 70!

Long Blade Mastery is level 48!
BloodBloody Gnaw is level 85!
Hurricane Rasp is level 86!
Howl At The Dark is level 84!
Dawn's Advent is level 82!
Tempest Fugit is level 84!
Mantle of Tumult is level 88!

Poison Resistance is level 55!
Journeyman Tier!
You Gain:
+5 VIT
+5 END
+5 STR

Heat Resistance is level 42!
Apprentice Tier!
You Gain:
+7 VIT
+7 END
+7 AGL

Breath of the Wild is level 25!
Apprentice Tier!
You Gain:
+5% PER
+5% VIT
+5% END

Dark Glacial Guard is level 59!
Journeyman Tier!
You Gain:
+15 END
+15 STR
+15 VIT

Pit had also already chosen his Skill for the Champion bonus. Dark Glacial Guard was a tough one to level compared to most of his others. His friend had been fighting the other Claw members for hours, just like Felix, and it had barely risen five levels from the repeated attacks.

Adding the Title bonus pushed it right into Journeyman Tier and got him a solid stat boost, too.

The ship sailed onward through the tepid darkness, the occasional distant mountain peak their only sense of progress. Felix was fairly certain they were reaching the end of the Passage—knowledge from Labyrinthine Wing that rumbled through distant pieces of his Mind.

How much time has passed in the real world, this time? he wondered. With the Skill's increase in level, it had already changed a lot. He had been interested in using his Champion's bonus on it, but the Skill wouldn't take the extra levels. *Shame. But we'll get there, one step at a time.*

"Ah!" Beef shouted from further down the deck. Felix craned his neck, peering toward the living tree-mast and his bulky friend sat beneath it. "Oh, we're back."

"You needed the break," Vess said. She stood up and gave a languid stretch. "As did I."

Felix had been keeping an eye on the two of them for a while now. Vess was an exceptional teacher, and he truly hoped she had impressed on Beef the value of what she offered. The kid meant well, but he could be stubborn—he still hadn't even shown Felix his core space. Too shy, his Spirit reported. Felix didn't really understand why.

But he was growing. Already, there was a new, ineffable sense of strength about the Minotaur. He felt…grounded. Felix tilted his head at that; Affinity did more than sense emotions, it sensed the web of connections all around them. As Beef stood and started stretching, Felix could feel gossamer, unreal threads flexing and going taut. One was to Vess, but the biggest was to Felix himself.

Hopefully, that means he did well in there. All of his people were growing. Many had leveled during the trip across the Step, and Pit had helped the majority of them polish their Skills. Only six were patrolling the gunwales, while the rest were below decks. Something boomed beneath him, rattling the deck very slightly.

We're fine! Pit sent.

Felix rolled his eyes and settled in. He also sent the six patrolling guards to rest or train, as they wished. He could handle anything that lurked in the darkness.

Little did.

The Dark Passages had changed in many ways, but somehow the borders of it were far stronger. Felix could sense a few Void beasts lingering here or there, flocks of Harrowings, for instance. It was a sizable flock, numbering around a thousand, but he wasn't really concerned with them, not as he would have been once before. The real worry were the mountains, which had proven to host strange, tentacular beasts. But the few they had drawn close to were empty expanses of lifeless rock. Not even weeds grew on their gray slopes, and all were riddled with holes, worn through by acid or digging claws...but the dark dens were void of all life. Felix made sure of it.

The ship continued on.

Somewhere around the six-hour mark, Felix's Labyrinthine Wing alerted him to the approaching edge of the Passage. At the same time, his powerful Perception flagged a distant peak straight ahead.

Felix straightened, standing so that he braced his foot against the base of the spar. "Holy crap, that's a big mountain."

Though the ship didn't accelerate, the mountain drew closer way faster than it should have. Soon, the Sailwhale was before a mountain that made Everest look like an anthill, and people began to crowd the deck.

"Blood and ash," Evie cursed. Felix agreed.

Their hundreds-feet-long, blimp-like crystal cast enough light that their way forward was clear: through an enormous gate, easily ten times the size of the ship, bored through the center of the mega-mountain. It was open and empty, though Felix picked out the rusted remains of metal along its edges. It was otherwise shaped like a giant, nine-pointed star.

"You think that's Nymean?" Beef asked.

"Gotta be," Evie said.

"Wasn't here before, though," Harn pointed out. "Is that on you?"

Felix nodded but said nothing. He was engrossed in the details as they drifted through the first open gate. Another was beyond it, a half mile ahead, and he could see a third in the distance as well. Between each one were rotted and broken-down structures that had been carved into the sheer side of the mountain. From the pitted stone and cracked foundations worn to rounded nubs, they looked as if something had devastated them a long time ago.

Unlike their swift approach, moving through the gates was a slow affair. After perhaps twenty minutes, they passed through the third star-shaped gate to find a wide circular platform built into a deep, terraced mountainside. It was a caldera of sorts, empty now, but filled with the crumbling remnants of an ancient outpost or city. Nearest to them was an array of crumbling landing bays, and Felix had the ship guided to the one that looked the sturdiest.

He made sure to Stone Shape it back together, just to be safe.

"Down and out, folks!" Felix shouted. "I'm opening the rift very soon. Assemble there." He cast Illusory Double, and a shadowy shape manifested several dozen yards into the quay. A tumbled-down pathway of arches framed his illusion as it waved its hands.

"Move your asses!" Harn bellowed.

CHAPTER SIXTY-EIGHT

The rift opened up into a massive snowdrift, and his Claw members floundered in the heavy banks for several long seconds before Felix emerged. He used Rime Shaping to clear a path.

"Thank you, sir," said one of the scouts between shivers. "Just about drowned in all that snow."

"Don't mention it—"

Felix stumbled, his words failing him as a sharp screeching chord cut through his attention. A notification appeared, red-gold and edged with a pulsating black.

Quest Completed!

Delicious Devour I
Your Primordial Hunger has requested a reward for all of its hard work. Prey must be Tier V or higher if a monster, Master or greater if a mortal, or the equivalent in magical potency.
Rewards dependent upon prey devoured.
Reward(s): Doubled Significance, Varies

A conspicuous weight settled on him like a leaden vest, pressing his shoulders and chest down and inward. It expanded, doubling on itself until it was a small mountain, a Kingsrock-sized pressure that seeped into his very bones.

"Sir! Are you hurt?"

"He's in pain! Spread out! Find the attacker?"

That…took…a while. What's the deal?

Dead Too Long.

The Forge Knight? Felix barely got the thought out when a sizzling bar of flame ripped through his middle. Not System energy, which came from outside in, but from the depths of his dark Hunger. Red-gold flame surged through his core space, painting all of it vermillion for the briefest of instances before seemingly vanishing. That mountain had inundated his core space, but, by the heaviness in his gut, Felix felt it had gathered nearest the base.

Pillars Partially Reinforced!
Devour More To Prepare Yourself, Unbound!
Your Next Challenge Awaits.

He blinked, snow catching on his lashes. *What does that mean?*

Be Ready. Ten. The Last.

My tenth Pillar? You reinforced it?

Others. Give Me More. I Protect. We Grow.

Felix straightened, catching the concerned looks he was getting from the Claw members all around him. Several had pushed outward, climbing the snow banks in an effort to clear their line of sight. "I'm fine. Stand down. There's no attack."

Another notification appeared to him, and it was just as grating as before.

New Quest!

Delicious Devour II
Your Primordial Hunger has requested a reward for all of its hard work. Prey must be Tier VII or higher if a monster, Grandmaster or greater if a mortal, or the equivalent in magical potency.
Rewards dependent upon prey devoured.
Reward(s): Doubled Significance, Varies

Felix licked his lips and considered the new Quest. The completion parameters were more intense than the last, but he'd faced Grandmasters before. Maybe not full-strength Grandmasters, but they had been close.

If it can get me farther down the path, I'm all for it. He hesitated, checking his memory. *How many Grandmasters does the Hierocracy have?* Felix didn't know, but he shrugged it off. His Hunger adding reinforcement to his already crazy-strong Pillars—and potentially to his tenth Pillar—was well and good, but it still left him with the task of choosing the right Skill.

Felix still hadn't progressed very far in that process.

"You sound loud," Pit said, hopping through the rift behind him. Others passed the starry veil, their forms emerging through the liquid film. "...Oh. Did she finish digesting?"

"Apparently." Felix moved aside, idly Rime Shaping a larger staging ground for his people to occupy. The snow shifted, piled to the sides where it wasn't stamped down until it formed a thick surface of ice. "And I've got a great deal more significance built up, too. Maybe even enough to cleanse your curse."

Pit perked up at that for a moment before his tufted ears laid flat against his head. "Maybe? As in, maybe you'll hurt yourself if you try?" The tenku shook his head, firmly. "Best wait, just to be sure."

"That's fair," he said. Felix didn't like waiting—Pit was still in pain, all the time. But he was also older now. Smarter. His Companion could make his own decisions. "But the next hostile monster we come across is getting eaten."

"When hasn't that been true?" Pit chirruped.

"Where'd we end up?" Harn asked, shading his eyes. The sun seemed to have barely crested the horizon, but its light was brilliant against the accumulated snow. With an annoyed grunt, the man put his helm back on. "Too damn bright to see anythin'."

As his friends gathered around him, and the Claw secured their position, Felix brought up his Territory Map. They were at the south-eastern edge of the Hoarfrost, right before it joined with a thick forest to the east and a tall mountain range to the south. His Map stopped there, a stark edge to his Authority, but it was a bit easier to match the terrain with the few maps Felix had studied months back in Ahkestria.

"We're just about at the foot of the Rimefangs," he said, shaping the snow away from the southern face of their clearing. The powder split, revealing a bit of that dark forest. Beyond that, pressing into the sky like bared teeth, was a range of mountains that utterly dominated the southern horizon.

"Here, in one trip?" Vess' voice was quietly awed. "That had to have been a thousand leagues in the span of an afternoon."

"No clue on the distance, but…" Felix tapped his hooked blade. "Karys. We're out of the Passage. How long has it been?"

"A half-glass, my Lord," the man reported. "Or thirty minutes, as you reckon time."

Felix smiled. "Thanks, man. That's incredible. We're heading into the Rimefangs now. I'll touch base with you tonight." The sword-light vanished. "Let's get moving southward. We might have saved a ton of time across the Hoarfrost, but we're months behind. Keep an eye out. The Hierocracy is here, and they're on the hunt, same as us."

"When we find this Gnome, what then?" Tzfell asked.

"High-tail it back north. Cross into the Hoarfrost and hop a ride on the ol' Sailwhale," Harn said, not bothering to hide his amusement when Felix rolled his eyes. "We do that, nobody is gonna be able to keep up."

"That means the Autarch must remain with us," Laur pointed out.

"Nope," Felix said, slapping both Vess and Harn on the backs. He may have put a bit more oomph on the latter, for no particular, whale-related reason. "These are both my Exemplars. They can create lesser versions of my Passages. A little less safe, probably slower, but if it comes down to it, we have alternative ways out."

Tzfell studied the two warriors with interest. "And if we are stuck within the mountains? Unable to flee?"

"Then we probably got a whole host of worse problems," Harn added. Tzfell's mouth twisted, but she nodded.

As much as his people could have forged through the snow, time was of the essence. He kept Rime Shaping going at a low burn, an ever-present hum that gently split the worst of the snowfall from their path. It was an easy thing for him, the equivalent of scooping through foam atop a bubble bath—because the worst wasn't the hard-packed stuff at the bottom, but the six or so feet of loose layers at the top. With firm footing, his company made great time.

In a few short minutes, they had passed from the Hoarfrost and into the Rimefangs proper. That happened about a mile into the southern edge of the forest, right as the elevation started to change. Most of the Hoarfrost was flat, save for its sudden peaks, but soon they were climbing up and down small foothills covered in evergreen trees that looked an awful lot like pines. If pines were as thick around as a young Redwood. They were tall, too, which made the looming Rimefangs even more imposing, as Felix's sense of scale was thrown totally out of whack.

The scouts went on ahead, all of them agile enough that the snow was little impediment to their movement. They set the trail, marking the snow in a way that Felix could easily recognize before he wiped all traces away with Rime Shaping. The landscape steadily changed around them. The ground grew more rocky, the forest a touch thinner, while the incline steadily ticked upward.

Every once in a while, small, frost-coated ridges rose from between copses of firs and spruces. They avoided them, by and large, as it was clear that they hid dozens of monster dens. Not in the Domain sense, but simple dugouts where lone beasts or small family units were snuggled up against the cold.

The Claw were quiet for the most part, focused on staying in formation and eyeing their surroundings. Every once in a while, someone would run low on Stamina, however, and they were transferred to the back of Hallow's Multipede Body. Beef was up there, beside the perching Sharpwing Matriarch with the Homunculus wrapped around his torso like an armored vest. He made sure the Claw stayed aboard, summoning small, chitinous legs that latched onto legs and hips. Most of them didn't mind.

Felix found it kinda gross. It made Pit hungry.

Early on, the tenku had shifted into Dire Hound form and clambered up onto Felix's shoulders, complaining of "too much training" back on the ship. While it wasn't out of the ordinary for Pit to lounge around when he could, his drive had been amped to high levels in recent weeks. It wasn't until Felix spied Beef and Vess trudge through the snow—Homunculus and Wyrmling nestled comfortably on their back and shoulders respectively—that he realized his Companion was just a little jealous.

You could have just asked, he sent. *I wouldn't have said no.*

Of course not, Pit sent back. He flopped across his deltoid and nearly unseated himself. *Ah!*

Felix caught him with a quick Garment change; a small, boiled leather harness snagged around his russet butt.

Pit barked, the sound of it edged by a songbird's relieved trill. *Thanks.*

Don't mention it.

Perhaps two hours and a great many miles after they set out, a scout named Lenat dropped from a tree. She was Henaari and bore a pair of short spears at her waist. "My Lord. There is a settlement, just ahead."

Felix peered beyond their immediate surroundings, but another icy ridge blocked the direction she indicated. He flared his Perception, sorting through wind, creaking ice, and soft snoring monsters…and found the overwhelming smell of char. He wrinkled his nose. "What happened to it?"

"It would be easier to show you, my Lord."

"Lead on."

Their company met with the other scouts just outside of a walled village. Though the height of the stone construction meant they couldn't see into the town from their vantage point, it was clear that at least part of the wall had been broken. The scouts outlined what they had found, and it twisted Felix's stomach. Someone or something had attacked it, knocking down a large section of the wall and burning at least half of the homes within. There was no sign of the living, but quite a few bodies lined streets that looked almost melted.

Evie whistled. "That wall alone is fifteen strides thick. What kinda beast could break a hole in that?"

"Normally, I'd suggest Frost Giant raiders, this close to the border," Tzfell said. "But it is clear that whoever attacked used fire or heat magic. That precludes a Troll attack, too. They cannot abide an open flame."

Beef had Hallow lower her Multipedal head to their level. "Trolls? You're saying there are actual, real-life trolls here?"

Evie snorted. "As opposed to what? Fake Trolls?"

Beef lifted his snout into the air. "*Obviously*, you've never been on the SwordLore forums."

"Beef. In your short life, have you ever *tried* to make sense?"

"Don't see how that's relevant."

"Yes, well," Tzfell said, clearing her throat. "Giants and Trolls can be a problem in these border towns because they're generally left on their own by the clans."

"What about in the event of a raid?" Felix asked.

"The walls are so sturdy for a reason, but most of these towns are decently defended. Most have at least a handful of Journeyman Tiers in residence. If that wasn't enough, they would send word to the nearest outpost, requesting aid from the Ironclads."

The Henaari scout cleared her throat. "My Lord, there is a distinct trail headed southwest, farther into the mountains. It is clear that the survivors fled en masse."

Felix nodded. "That's good to hear. Any idea where they'd be headed, Tzfell?"

"Same place the Ironclads would have been dispatched from, Lord Autarch: the nearest Clan Hold." Tzfell peered at the town from a distance. "Look. That flag. Clan Red Shield. It means we're closer to our goal than I anticipated."

Felix knew that name. Clan Red Shield was where one of his earliest visions of Imara had taken place, where she had fought some Dwarves outside a mountain. He directed his next question to the scout. "Lenat, does your tracking Skill tell you how long ago they were made?"

"An approximation. Between four days and a week."

"Well, before I made them swear a cease-fire," Felix noted. "It could have been a Giant raid."

"Giants do not drive off the Ironclads with the mere mention of an attack," Tzfell insisted. "If it has been that long, then the Ironclads aren't coming. Something else is going on."

"Is it the Corrupted One?" Laur asked.

"The other Unbound lady?" Beef craned his neck, as if he could spot her somewhere in the distance. Pit shuddered against Felix's neck.

Imara. Felix looked around again, taking in the same details in a new light. "Those stones I can see are melted. Was it the same for the houses in town, Lenat?"

"The wall was collapsed inward, like someone just shoved their way through it. However, near the break, there is a wide span of empty stone. Only on the borders of that patch were there houses, and those were burnt to a crisp."

"That tracks for someone using heat, light, or fire Mana," Felix noted. "Any of them could melt stone and consume entire houses, if they use enough."

"So, either a dangerous Unbound or multiple battalions of redcloaks," Vess listed. "The Chanters did say this Imara was expecting reinforcements."

"Let's hope for the redcloaks," Evie said. "I barely got to stretch my chain in the frostlands, and they're good target practice."

"Redcloaks would be a damn sight better than a crazy Unbound," Harn agreed. "No offense, kid."

Felix snorted.

"These mountains are full of blind spots and narrow trails. I am not eager to meet either by chance," Vess added.

"Until we know better, we'll treat it as if it is the Unbound. Harn, Evie, gather the Talons and keep them tight. Lenat, you and the scouts stick close, too. I'll hold the company under stealth and pave the way. We'll follow the townsfolk toward this Red Shield Hold."

"Aye, sir."

CHAPTER SIXTY-NINE

It was far easier to hold onto his Abyssal Skein outside of the Dark Passage, even when Felix extended it across the entire company. Where before the ability squirmed from his control, now it merely felt as it always had: a cold, slithery sensation then a slick film that rolled across his skin and against his teeth. Unpleasant, sure, but it had grown familiar. He pressed it outward, manipulating the threads of connection to his company so that each one was affected equally. He had grown adept at that, too.

As Felix requested, the scouts remained close at hand, never straying farther than twenty yards away. It wasn't that Felix couldn't keep them hidden at longer distances—he could, so long as he had enough Mana and a proper connection to funnel his Skill across—instead, he feared for their safety. He'd faced the redcloaks too many times to underestimate them, even if Felix was personally stronger than any number of Paladins or Inquisitors. They were dangerous, especially in large numbers.

They followed the path worn by the fleeing townsfolk for an hour before they discovered their first hurdle. At some point, there had been a small avalanche, and it had wiped out all traces of the townsfolk. There were no bodies, but their footprints and cart ruts had been swallowed up completely. Added to the small but consistent snowfall, the trail became far harder to traverse. As uneasy as it made him, Felix ordered the scouts out farther to range ahead.

In the meantime, Felix forged onward, shaping out their trail in his best impression of a snowplow. Living in Florida, he hadn't actually seen one of those before outside of the news, but he did his best. He angled his Will, shoving ice and snow to either side of them like the bow wave of a boat, trying his best not to put too much power into the shaping. The last thing he wanted to do was draw attention to himself, and not even Abyssal Skein could hide fifty-foot-high waves of blasted snow.

His people followed behind him, weapons sheathed but close to hand. All had their senses pressed to the limits, hunting for the hint of crimson in the white alpine forests. Hunting for danger in general, really.

There was little to be had, thankfully. Monsters were far off, hidden in dens for the winter or perhaps just waiting for nightfall, and there were no signs of anyone else either. The snow fell harder, filling the space between them with thick, clumpy gusts. Felix shaped it away, but it affected visibility anyway, acting like white noise to their senses. Where he could, Felix guided them through game trails and rocky ledges, where the natural outcroppings protected them from constantly having to trudge through the elements. More opportunities to move in stealth, and he would often drop his Rime Shaping entirely.

Several times, Felix spotted structures farther into the mountains. They were distant things, occluded by weather and enough wards that even Felix's senses couldn't take in many details. It wasn't until they climbed a switchback trail that he got a better look at them, and then it was like a bucket of ice water down his spine.

What's that? Pit asked, nuzzled against Felix's neck. He was like a molten ball of heat inside the fur-lined hood, but Pit had no desire to leave. *Looks…I don't like it.*

"Yeah. Me either."

A dozen miles away, half-veiled by bruised clouds and the oncoming storm, was a large, unearthly statue. It had been built into the side of a mountain, carved from it, but at a size that made it rival Elderthrone's cliff.

The statue of a Dwarven woman stuck out, standing tall on the mountain with a single hand upraised. In her hand was a sickle, silver and glittering with specks of black, with the open throat of its curve pointed straight at the sky. The woman herself was carved with strong features, eyes the color of onyx, and hair like a silver stream. She was squat and square in the Dwarven style, but her clothing was a strange mix of flowing cloth and rigid stone, as if she had been only half carved from the mountain's face.

"The Birth of Noctis," Tzfell said in a quiet voice. "Goddess of the Night and mother of the seas."

"She was a Dwarf?" Felix asked.

"That is what my people believe, yes. The little we know of the old gods indicated they could be viewed however they wished, but that their true forms were unknowable."

Felix let a sour smile twist his lips. He knew how unknowable they were, after all. They featured in his nightmares, whenever he decided to sleep. "What is it? Is that the Clan Hold?"

"No. Just an artifact of an older time. The Dwarves are not monolithic, much as we pretend otherwise. Only some still worship the old gods, while others have abandoned them entirely to focus upon this world to the exclusion of all others. The Hinterlords, by and large, still worship in the old ways."

"Hinterlords?"

"Rulers of the clans. Think of them as mini kings, each with a piece of Authority over the Rimefangs."

"Great. Can I expect trouble from her followers? Noctis doesn't really like me. None of them do."

Just don't go telling them you ate a piece of their goddess, Pit offered, sleepily.

Thanks. That hadn't occurred to me.

Welcome. Pit started snoring.

"It may cause us some problems if you attract the attention of the Hinterlord or his hangerson."

"I plan to be the soul of discretion," Felix said. Behind him, someone laughed, but he couldn't tell who. Felix narrowed his eyes. "*Anyway*. Do we have to worry about them?"

Tzfell squinted up at the statue. The tattoos just above her eyes rotated slightly, as if they were tightening. "All I sense are the Dwarven Choristers who maintain the site. No redcloaks. No Unbound."

"And if Imara knows how to hide as well as I do?"

Tzfell bobbed her head. "I could be wrong. The temple here does offer a unique vantage on the valleys between it and the other peaks, but reaching it provides many challenges. There is a reason the Hierophant hasn't come and smashed it apart, much as she likely wants to."

She pointed. "The Clan Hold is south of us, and it is closer. I would suggest that we head there first before climbing across the peaks."

"Fair."

As much as stealth was still important, there was a storm gathering on the horizon. Distant thunder rolled and the winds began to whip, carrying a bevy of thickening flurries that promised to reduce their visibility to almost nothing. They had some time, and the peaks were likely to blunt some of its force, but Felix wanted to make it to the Clan Hold soon. They carefully clambered down one ridge and up another, until a scout returned.

They had found proper roads.

In ten minutes, his company was on a wide thoroughfare that had been excavated from the mountains. It was part of the High Roads, according to Tzfell, and resembled nothing so much as a narrow highway from Earth, if paved with segmented stone and marked by the occasional stone pyramid. Each of those was around five feet tall, three feet at the base, and made of a local stone called Felling's Blue. It was a Tier IV material, as was the Felling's Gray that made up the roadway. Both were durable, and according to Tzfell, the roadways had existed for over two Ages. Sigils were etched into the pyramids, and while most were dark, the innermost edges were lit up with a purple-white vapor that shifted to a deep, almost blackened blue.

Ice. Water. Shell. There's modification sigils, too. Felix studied the pyramids as they walked. Each one was the same, and his Perception could envelop them easily from a distance. *They're meant to keep the roads clear of ice and water. Oh. Oh, that's genius.*

Unlike heat wards, the pyramids were designed to repel ice and water Mana from their perimeters. Not all of it, just a majority, and focusing clearly on snow. Based on the limited details he could see (without tearing up the pavement), it used far less energy than it would take to constantly melt accumulating snow. Felix loved the design and made a mental note to write it down later. It was no wonder the roadways had existed for multiple Ages, if this is how they were being treated. The repelling of water and ice meant no freeze-thaw cycle inside the cracks of the road, which meant far less destruction over time. Add in its natural strength, and Felix expected the roads would last for a great many years yet.

Felix sped up their pace. Now that they were on proper roads, his team could really open up, and soon they were all jogging at a decent clip down the Dwarven High Roads. His company didn't complain, and many of them relished the chance to exert themselves. Moving across uneven countryside was one thing, but this was smooth and free of outcroppings and roots. They made good time.

At least until they heard the shouting.

Felix's scouts returned almost at the same time he commanded the company to a halt. "Lenat. What's out there?"

"A battle, my Lord. A group of locals are fighting off a pack of River Trolls."

"Describe the locals."

She did, and when she was finished, Tzfell cut in. "Those sound like Ironclads."

Pit shoved his head out of Felix's hood. "Like the undead guys?"

"...Correct. They are the most common soldiers of the clans, used for defending the Clan Holds and the outlying towns. They are the ones who should have been at that town, helping to repair it and keeping the people safe."

"Seems they're tied up with Trolls," Harn said. "How many?"

"Sixty Ironclads. Ten River Trolls," Lenat reported. The other two scouts nodded in confirmation.

Harn whistled appreciatively, and Tzfell cursed. Vess looked between them, lost as Felix. "Explain, if you please."

"Trolls are nasty, and it ain't just cuz they're big enough to punch above their Tier. They've got natural regeneration. A lot of it," Harn said.

"A single River Troll is enough to call down a full company, at least fifty to a hundred warriors." Tzfell swallowed and Laur put a hand on her shoulder. She leaned into it. "We need to help them."

Felix smiled. "Of course we do. Harn, get everyone ready. We're going in hot."

"Form up! Quick march into a battle! First Talon, prime yourselves!"

Harn's voice battered at Felix's Abyssal Skein, pushing the Skill to its limit, but Felix held it close. If the Trolls were as tough as Tzfell suggested, he needed them to remain unnoticed. Felix saw each of his friends readying their weapons and priming their Skills. They were ready to go.

He nodded to Lenat. "Scouts, lead the way."

CHAPTER SEVENTY

Captain Doric of the Stoneheart Vanguard watched his men die.

He'd seen many die before, whether it was to Frost Giants raids or the monsters of the Rimefangs, and had thought himself inured to it—the blood, the stench. Each of their deaths had been for a greater cause, a noble victory. Now, facing down a clutch of River Trolls gone rabid, Doric could not stand it.

"They're rising again, captain!"

The worst thing about Trolls wasn't their bite, which was filled with enough Status Conditions to drop an Apprentice Tier, and it wasn't their long limbs and steel claws. It was their regeneration. Limbs fell to axes and halberds, eyes were gouged out by sword and bolt, and even magic tore their powerful, fur-covered bodies to pieces. Yet, without fail, the Trolls rose back to their feet while his men remained in gore-soaked piles. The only way around it was to drench their wounds in fire or acid—only then would their regeneration fail them.

Yet the damn things were getting back up.

His lieutenant hissed in surprise. Her tattoos stretched with her shock. "The fire did nothing! They've Evolved!"

"Analyze," he muttered. His Skill flickered and fought against the power of the monstrosities before them. As before, it only brought up their name, but this time, the name was clear.

Name: Sun Troll
Type: Giantkin

Sun Trolls. Those were far worse than normal Forest or River Trolls. *Night save me.*

Sun Trolls were immune to fire.

"Stand your ground!" he commanded, brandishing his sword. It was wide and hooked at the end, as all standard issue blades were, and it had served him well for the last twenty years. It would serve him well for a little longer. "Nolva, do you have any acid? The fire rods won't work."

"Nothing more than two vials, sir! The Armorer was stripped bare!"

The Sun Trolls snarled, getting their feet beneath them once more. Their faces were contorted with animalistic rage, veins popping like cables even through their thick pelts, and steel claws drew sparks from the bottom of the rocky gully they'd been herded into. Doric hadn't much time. He turned to his warriors, all sixty that remained, and raised his voice.

"Men! These Trolls have gone rabid. Worse than that, they have Evolved beyond their weakness to fire. They are beyond most citizens of our Hold. If they reach Birchstone…I cannot allow that to happen. We cannot!" A ragged cheer met his words. A bannerman pulled his flag taut, three crimson shields over white mountains. The standard of Clan Red Shield.

"Look to that flag, Ironclads! Look at what it bears! Not one shield in defense, but all of them, held together! Lift your blades, and let your hearts be stone! The Stoneheart Vanguard does not flinch from our duty! Today, we end this! And if we die, we die as heroes!"

"Here, sir," Nolva said over the exultant cheers. She handed him two thick vials as his Ironclads unsheathed their weapons and readied themselves. Scratched and pitted shields were strapped tighter to bruised and broken arms, armor adjusted and helmets donned.

"Thank you, Sergeant." Accounting for the thick, alchemical glass, they contained enough to stall out the Trolls' regenerations, if for only a few seconds. *I must only time it right.* Doric slotted them into his gauntlet before turning a dial. The slots pulled tight, vials locking into place. "If you would."

"Aye, sir," Nolva said. "Take aim! Fire!"

Doric's Ironclads were warriors of grit and precision. Their crossbows were to hand in a half-heartbeat, bolts already loaded, and their shots flew true. Every one hit a Troll, until the stumbling creatures resembled nothing more than his wife's pincushions. Skills burst from those who bore them for projectile combat, ice and earth and shadow adding a brutal pop to each impact. Claws and jaws of Mana dug into red-stained fur, tearing free chunks of messy flesh.

The Trolls lolled back, limbs spasming, before they snarled to their feet. Blood and foam dripped from their wide, bestial mouths. There was no reason in their eyes, nor animal cunning; just hate and rage.

The Trolls began to run at them.

"Wards!" Nolva commanded. Shields were raised, and a pulse of shimmering brown vapor enveloped the warriors. "Forward! Half-speed!"

Traditionally, Doric led his men from the front, and today was no different. He charged down the gully's incline, Ironclads behind him, and smashed headlong into the clutch of Trolls. Claws met stone wards, High Steel shields, and powerful Journeyman Tier armor. The beasts were stronger than any one of the Ironclads, but even ten of them could not hold a candle to the might of the Vanguard.

The Trolls buckled, their mighty arms pressed back, and the Ironclads went to work.

Blood flew as swords, axes, and spears found purchase in thickened flesh. Trolls screeched, and slashed, their blows bashing Dwarves to the earth and breaking wards. Magic sizzled, popped into cascades of light as it discharged ineffectually. The Trolls pushed back.

Doric slashed through, lopping off an arm here, a leg there. His wide blade danced like a leaf on the breeze, a razor-sharp feather, trailing blood. The monsters crowded him, swinging at his head and shoulders, aiming to disarm him. Doric bullied through them all, each resolute step a powerful, immovable choice. A promise: he would stand until all the earth ground to dust. He would not be moved.

The creatures healed and came back, their unflinching bodies immune to pain. Foamy spittle drooled all over his Ironclads as madness leaked from their veins like blackened sludge. Doric pressed inward, opening space for his men behind him, until he came across their momentous leader: an enormous Troll, easily two heads taller than the others. Unphased, Doric slashed up, catching the biggest of the Trolls across the face and opening its snout to the bone.

As his fist reached the zenith of that attack, he squeezed the release on his gauntlet. Acid sprayed outward over the clustered group of Trolls as a thin, pressurized mist. It sank into hide and hair, eyes and mouths, sizzling against open wounds. The Trolls reared back, hissing.

He shouted. "Press the attack! Now, while their regeneration falters!"

Doric thrust, his blade sinking deep in the big Troll's belly.

It seemed, for a moment, that the world held its breath. Doric pulled at his sword, but it was stuck fast. Without warning, the big Troll laughed—a bubbling, wheezing thing that froze Doric's blood.

Status Condition: Frightened
You Have Been Frightened For Five Heartbeats!

Status Condition: Restrained
You Have Been Restrained For Five Heartbeats!

It wasn't enough! Oh, Night, they've grown too much, and it wasn't enough.

The fear spread, locking his men into terror the same as Doric. The Troll's arms ignited, filling with a golden-orange light like a mantle of infectious fury. Madness burned in its eyes. Doric could not move, let alone free his blade, so when the creature's hand closed over his, he could do nothing but stifle a scream.

Steel claws ripped into his forearm like forge-heated daggers. The light flared around the Troll, a cataclysm only bare breaths away from unleashing. The Troll bellowed—

And choked on needles of virulent green rain.

Doric blinked. The needles became daggers, and the daggers turned to swords, each as flat as a razor…and just as sharp. Holes sliced into the Trolls, cutting through skin and fur and muscle in an instant. It splashed, overwhelming them—yet leaving Doric and his Ironclads untouched.

Acid, he realized. *From the sky…magic.* "Rally, men! Cut them down!"

His warriors surged forward, screams ripping from beneath battered helmets. Their weapons lopped off fingers and forearms then cut into bellies and thighs, until the ground ran red with their ichor. The acid came down, relentless, unstoppable, and precise. It stymied the monsters' regeneration, and the Trolls screeched again. Not in madness or rage, but in fear.

They fell, hacked to quivering pieces.

From the messy pile, that biggest Troll surged forward without warning. It seized Doric by the throat before clutching him to its ruined chest. The captain screamed as the thing's magic engaged, that mantle of maddened heat blazing like the sun itself. His armor became an inferno, the metal softening before dripping onto the Dwarf's wide chest and belly. He tried to fight back, to push off, but the Troll was possessed of a vengeful strength.

Blows hit the Troll, and it fell, but it fell atop of the captain. Doric knew, then, that he would not live to see their city.

But the Vanguard will live. The dim thought let him hold on a moment longer. And then another moment. Nolva would tell his wife and kids what happened. *I…have no regrets. I am ready.*

I—

The heat was gone.

Doric blinked, but his vision was awash in spots. He could see nothing for several long moments, and when his sight cleared, he did not understand.

The Troll's head was encased in a writhing tendril of virulent green acid. It was twitching, but the thing's bones were dissolving in there, only inches from Doric's face.

Someone hauled the Troll's body off of him, and the acid fell to the wet stone. It sizzled and hissed violently, but only for an instant longer. Doric's medic knelt over him. "Stay still, Captain! We have you!"

"What…what happened? Who—?"

"Strangers, sir. They came outta nowhere."

Doric was lying on his back, but he saw them, standing on the opposite ridge. Close to fifty people, ranging in Race from Human to Goblin. Even a…bull-man. In the center, however, was a tall Human with a strange coat and too little armor. His eyes burned. No. That was only a trick of the light.

"Get this off me, and get me my spare set," Doric commanded, ignoring the pain of his burns. "Quickly."

"Aye, sir."

"Damn, that acid *was* effective," Felix said from the ridge. "Thanks, Tzfell."

"A pleasure to be of service, Lord Autarch."

Felix watched the Ironclads gather themselves. Many were injured, their armor scored or broken by the Trolls metal claws. The things had been sturdy, and his Voracious Eye pegged them at a solid Tier IV. Considering most of the Ironclads below were around Journeyman,

Felix was amazed at how long they'd lasted. From what Tzfell and Harn had suggested, it wasn't their power that made them rank so high, but their relentless regeneration. Hard to kill something that wouldn't stay hurt.

That's why Tzfell had suggested he use acid magic. Felix had opted for Rain of Cataclysm but had coupled it with Hand of Calamity to increase his precision and control. It had worked beautifully, allowing the Dwarves to fight back on their own.

Then that captain guy got pounced on. Felix had gone a little overboard in killing that Troll, but the Dwarf had survived, so that was all that mattered.

The Ironclads watched him right back, and from the song of their Spirits, they weren't afraid so much as alarmed and suspicious. A few were confused and relieved. Felix had made sure to keep himself and the Claw in full sight of the Dwarven warriors, their hands folded across their belts. He didn't want to get off on the wrong foot. "Sorry. What were you saying, Laur?"

"*I said*, before you killed them all, that the Trolls were maddened by a foreign Will. Their Minds and Spirits were in disarray, I could see it trailing off of them like a shroud—it is likely why they were so out of control. Such terrible wounds…I would think any sane being, beast or not, would have fled."

"Trolls ain't sane, son. Nothing that can regrow its brain from a piece of its tooth is gonna be," Harn said, taking off his helmet. "But yeah. Ain't never seen 'em act like that."

Evie looked him up and down. "You've fought Trolls before, Harn? When?"

"I wasn't always fightin' with your sister." Harn grunted. "Heads up. Looks like their leader's comin' this way."

A squat Dwarf had walked up the short switchback trail out of the gully. He had discarded his half-melted armor in favor of a loose chainmail shirt, and his head was bare of any helmet. His nose was large and hooked, like a hatchet attached to a rock, while a wide, square cut beard fanned out over his thick chest. The man was flanked by five Ironclads wearing dark metal armor that was covered in dents and bright, silvery scratches.

"Well met, strangers. I am Doric Stoneheart, Captain of the Stoneheart Vanguard. Who might you be?"

"We're merchants from out west," Felix lied smoothly. "Name's Silas Veil."

"West? Through the mountains? That's a hazardous trip, especially in wintertime."

"Profitable, too," Harn added. He tapped the side of his crooked nose. "If we can make it before the thaws, then we're guaranteed a profit."

Harn knows everything, Pit marveled from inside Felix's lowered hood.

"Fair enough," Captain Doric said. "You're headed to Birchstone?"

"Headed to the Clan Hold when we heard the trouble over here. Thought we could be of help, and luckily we've got a few acid-attuned fighters among my guards."

"Luck," the captain said with a snort. He winced and put a hand to his mailed chest. Bandages wrapped up along his neckline, and the skin looked angry and puffed up. "Those were Sun Trolls. Immune to fire. The only thing that could hurt them was acid. That's more'n luck, Mr. Veil."

Felix winced inwardly. He was glad he hadn't tried to use fire. In all the hubbub, he hadn't taken the time to inspect them with his Voracious Eye and relied on Tzfell's advice, instead. "All comes down to preparation, captain. As I said, we've been traveling a while. We're prepared for a fight."

"So I see. And if you'd encountered the Titan?"

Felix frowned. "The Titan?"

"So you don't know of her." The captain sighed. "She's a scourge on all the Rimefangs, Mr. Veil, though perhaps less so in other peaks. If you haven't heard of her already, you soon will."

"Her?" Felix asked, but he already knew. He'd earned a few nicknames, himself.

"A monster made of mithril and fire. A giant, but not a piddly raider. She's burned half the countryside to ash in her mad hunt, and none of us can stop her. We might be Ironclads, but it's all we can do to bring our people in from their towns and villages." Captain Doric clenched his jaw, angry but not at Felix. "I'm thankful you came along when you did, Mr. Veil, but I don't doubt you'll come to regret traveling into these parts."

Felix smiled and tried to keep it light and easy. It was hard. He wanted to check over his shoulder for the Corrupted Unbound. "I don't regret helping people."

The captain laughed and combed one of his gauntlets through his tangled black beard. "Aye. Neither do we." He raised his voice and addressed his soldiers. "What say we escort Mr. Veil and his team into Birchstone, eh?"

A vigorous cheer followed.

Felix's smile brightened. "That would be very much appreciated, captain."

The Dwarven warrior inclined his head. "It's the least I can do."

CHAPTER SEVENTY-ONE

It was hours yet to Birchstone, and at first the journey was slow and silent as the ever-increasing snowfall. Accumulation didn't bother them, not on enchanted roads that repelled the ice, but it did fill the air until their odd processional was marching through a column of white, cut only by the rarest glimpses of distant daylight. Golden sigils ignited along the forward-facing edges of pyramidal stones, painting the High Roads with just enough illumination to see where they were going. It was only midday, but the storm was thick with purple shadows and the sound of rolling thunder.

The captain and his Ironclads all rode atop pale-feathered Avum, their crested necks adorned with the standard of Clan Red Shield. The birds were large, but the mounted captain was no more than a single head taller than Felix was standing. The Claw, all of them posing as guards for his merchant company, kept pace and maintained the perimeter while the Ironclads got some rest.

Felix had spent some time chatting up the leader of the Dwarven warriors. He was a nice enough guy, all things considered. Honest, too. The man didn't say anything but what he meant, if Felix was judging his Spirit correctly, and the captain was appreciative of their help. He was more than happy to tell them what he could about their destination, too.

"Thanks to the Titan, Birchstone is bursting at the seams. I can get you into the city, Mr. Veil, on account of you helping us, but the Clan Hold is another matter." Captain Doric shook his head. "None are being let into the mountain, not unless you've got High Clan blood in those veins. Until the Titan is driven from the Rimefangs for good, they are the only ones allowed inside the ancient halls."

"Is that what you're out here to do, captain?" Felix asked.

"Fight the Titan? Are you mad?" Doric guffawed, but it was cut short by a grimace. "Ah, that hurts. Damnable Trolls. No, lad. My humble company cannot trade even a single blow with that nightmare. The Forge Knights themselves failed at that task—we would be snuffed out faster than a candle flame in a hurricane."

Forge Knights. So they still exist…and Imara beat a number of them. Felix nodded along with the captain's words, only half-listening. *Does that mean she's as strong as me? Stronger?*

A part of him—a part he didn't much care to acknowledge—was eager to find out.

"So you're out here for the Trolls, then?" he asked.

"Trolls and other beasts. Ironclad companies like ours are employed by the High Clans to act like guardians for their upland territories. Means we range the slopes, dells, and valleys regularly. When trouble comes for the villages, we respond." Doric blew a tight breath out of his lips, his square-cut beard bristling. "I'll tell you this for free, Mr. Veil: this winter has been the most troubling in recent memory."

Felix nodded, trying to convey a general sense of agreement. The captain barely noticed.

"Violence has been brewing in the city walls well before we packed it full of townsfolk. Cutpurses on every street corner, bending knee to the rat lords or whatever they call themselves. Then the Titan and her Hierocratic dogs put their noses in our business. And that *Gnome*," Captain Doric almost bit the word in half. "The Gnome has multiplied our troubles tenfold."

"How so? If you don't mind me asking," Felix said. "I heard some of this during our travels, but never the whole story. How'd it all begin?"

Doric tugged on his reins, drawing an indignant squawk from his Avum. "Ach. Sorry, Fini. The whole problem started when some precious bits went missing in Birchstone. Jewelry and the like. Had the guard up in arms for days, huntin' for the thief, but they couldn't turn up hide nor hair of him. Then a Pathless dog shows up, bloodcaped lackeys behind him, and says he can find the thief. Says he's got a hunter, specialized for it." Doric spat to the side, and Felix watched the spittle skip off the High Road and into the gutter.

"The Titan."

"Aye. The white skirt lickspittle let her loose in Birchstone, and he wasn't lyin'. She soon found the Gnome. Problem is, the Gnome was more slippery than a patch of spring thaw. Every time the Titan got him cornered, he escaped. Drove the woman mad, and she damn near destroyed half a district. Then, the thief got into the mountain."

Felix winced. He'd seen a bit of that, back when he was in Ahkestria.

"The Titan came up against the Watch, and she tore through them like decades-old sheets. Blood ran across the gates that day, and not even the mountain could stop her. She broke into Red Shield's Clan Hold by pure Strength and holy fire, lit up like a bonfire, until all that armor of hers was cherry red." Doric shuddered. "The Gnome kept runnin', and I don't blame him. The Titan was off to kill, no matter what her priestly minder said."

Jesus. "And she rampaged through the Clan Hold?"

"She did, lad. Many died that day, and most weren't even fightin' her. Folks burned just from bein' near enough, and her angry tread broke homes and businesses. Then, finally, the Gnome got away, somehow, deeper into the mountains. The Titan followed, and she hasn't been seen since."

Felix didn't have to fake the concern on his face. "How long has she been gone?"

"Months. We're hopin' the thief has her halfway back to the Hierocracy now. Let them deal with her rampage."

"But you aren't sure," Felix guessed.

"Not by a league, lad. But don't worry," Doric added, apparently remembering who he was talking to. "The city's safe. A whole net of scouts are keepin' a weather eye out for her comin'. The Titan ain't gettin' close without a whole hell of a ruckus getting raised."

"That is a relief," Felix admitted. He would appreciate a warning before he had to deal with her. "I hope you don't find this rude, but does Red Shield not have any warriors that can match the Titan? Perhaps not kill her, but drive her off?"

"No. Whatever trainin' that woman's been through has her Tiers above even the best of us." Doric scratched his cheek and cast a look back at his men before lowering his voice. "Word is, one of the Grandmasters of the Clan descended from the Undermount itself. Clashed with the Titan…and came out of it bloodied."

Felix clenched his jaw. "How'd the Titan fare?"

Doric shrugged. "It's all rumors. As captain of my company, I'm allowed inside the Clan Hold every few weeks to report, but I'm common as they come. No High Clan blood in these veins, and without that, you'll not get to the real secrets of the Undermount."

They walked a bit more, letting silence overtake their conversation. It wasn't uncomfortable, not for Felix and, judging from his Spirit, not for the captain, either. Felix had decided he'd liked the guy; he reminded him of Harn in many ways, or Rory even. The Ironclads were more of a mystery. They rode without much chatter, held separate from his Claw, heads low. Sorrow rolled through their Spirits, a distant dirge for their fallen. Felix was inclined to like them, too.

He'd been in too many battles, lost too many people, not to feel for them.

The High Roads wound in and out of valleys, lined by the occasional walled town or tiny hill fort. All were empty, their dark husks staring out of the storm like empty skulls. The roads ran past them, hung over by skeletal trees clogged with ice, and up inclines so graduated that even the lamest Avum could walk it without issue.

"How about yourself, Mr. Veil? How did you come into so many strong guards? Unless I miss my guess, they're all Journeyman Tier… and so are you. Most Human merchants are coddled and soft. You look ready to fight a Dire Wolf barehanded."

Felix laughed. It took a measure of Felix's Willpower not to fiddle with his Veiling Amulet—a small measure, but important nonetheless. "I'm glad you think so highly of me. My uncle thought it better that I knew how to handle myself well before I could go off on my own."

"Uncle?"

He nodded toward Harn, who had his helmet off and was talking to Evie. "Trained me himself. This is his company, and my first trip as the boss." He gave the captain a relieved grin. "So far, it hasn't been a disaster. Done well, even, by all accounts."

Deception is level 46!

Doric laughed. "Good on ya, lad. Times are tough. Imagine that's as true outside the Rimefangs as in it. My nephew's been struggling as a mason, but at least my nieces have been doing well with their tavern. Coin flows for good ale and a soft bed, after all."

"I imagine a packed city makes for even better business."

"You'd be right, Mr. Veil. Even the destruction has helped my sister's son, what with all the reconstruction, but he's a layabout. Rather soak himself in wine than sweat."

"We all try our best," Felix peered ahead to where the High Road disappeared around a bend in the mountains. They were following a ridge above a slate gray river hundreds of feet below, and though the path was wide and even, he didn't entirely trust the lack of guardrails. He wasn't exactly afraid of a fall, but an ill-timed landslide or monster attack could drive his people off the edge. "Those Trolls you fought. I hear they're common around these parts."

Doric grunted. "They are, but not so common for deep winter. They've usually had their fill of slaughter by year's end and found a deep cavern to sleep through the coldest months."

"What woke them up?"

"We don't know, but whatever it was had them riled up *bad*. Trolls are violent, gluttonous things at the best of times, but not like that. They normally hunt in smaller packs of two or three, not a near-dozen, and never during the day."

"I am quite surprised to see Sun Trolls at all, captain," Tzfell said from behind them. She had crept up on them at some point, her head fully covered and mouth swathed with a thick scarf. The Dwarf half-turned in his saddle, giving the Chanter a long look. "They only Evolve during the summer months, when the heat and fire Mana of the sun bakes the lower slopes. Do you know how such creatures came to be?"

"No," he said after a moment. "And that don't sit right with me, either."

Felix frowned at the Chanter, but she ignored him and started jotting notes down in a small, brown book.

Pit stuck his head out of Felix's hood and collar, shaking his floppy, crimson-furred ears. The disguised Chimera had fallen asleep over an hour previously, and now he pushed himself into a big, wobbly stretch.

"Morning, lil pig," Felix said, scratching the top of his head.

Pit let out a pleased chirrup. A strange noise to come from a dog, but the captain didn't seem to care. "Ach, Dire Hound, yes?"

"Hm? Oh, yeah."

"Used to have a Howler, m'self. A lot like hounds, Howlers, save for the shells, the claws, and the inflatable sacs along their necks. Ah, Lobber." Doric gave a deep, tired sigh. "I miss that old beast."

Felix tried not to squirm at the mental image the Dwarf had conjured. "Sounds like he was a great friend."

"Aye, he was. No offense to Fini, here," he said, patting his mount.

"But there's just somethin' to havin' a bond like that. You said it right, Mr. Veil. Not a pet, but a friend. A companion, even."

Pit wiggled his head, chin lifted. Felix snorted. "They're alright."

Pit stuck his tongue out at him.

Something shifted as they rounded the bend in the mountain, and Felix heard it as a sudden, sharp whine in the wards. Without warning, a cascade of vaporous lights arced around them and a stream of violent wind tore across the path as if it had been waiting for them. Thunder rolled, a sharp explosion of sound that buzzed against his teeth and shook Felix's insides as a gale tried to rip the cloak off his back. Pit squawked indignantly.

"Damnable storms! Hold the line, men!" The captain shouted, and his Ironclads hunched their shoulders as Doric lifted an amulet into the sky. It blazed white-green, the color of air Mana, and those pyramids flickered. New inscriptions lit up, and the wind died down to a dull roar.

"There," he panted, tucking the amulet back away. "Didn't expect the storm to hit us so badly. Had to reattune the High Road, or else we'd have ended up plastered against that ravine."

Storm Shaping is level 36!

"I'm fine," Felix said mildly. After a moment's surprise, he had bent the wind around himself and Pit with a touch of his new shaping Skill. It hadn't been hard, but it cost him a decent chunk of Mana. That storm above them was no joke. "Bit stunned, though."

Doric grunted. "Wards on the roads are usually kept in better order, but I doubt anyone's run down this since we left. Still. The High Roads don't fail."

Felix hadn't meant that; accidents happened all the time. What had stunned him was that the High Roads even *had* adaptable wards. That was crazy complicated, and he was glad Atar hadn't come with them; the mage would have torn apart a dozen of those pyramids already. "I'm fine, just a little tousled. I—What's that?"

Through the swirling gusts of the winter storm, Felix could see the High Road winding down the mountainside, tracing the river far below until it dropped level just before the high walls of a city. Sturdy defenses and high, powerfully solid towers jutted above the walls, all of them built with sharp angles and an abundance of stone. Behind it, dominating the horizon, was a single mountain.

"Ah, we're not far off. That, Mr. Veil, is Birchstone."

CHAPTER SEVENTY-TWO

The warding around the High Roads faded considerably by the time they had reached the gates of Birchstone, and the storm had reached its fullest measure. The whipping winds and blinding snow flurries had gotten so bad that, at one point, Felix had been forced to shape it away. A difficult task, not only due to the amount of Mana it burned through, but because he made an effort to be subtle about it. They still ended up pummeled by sleet and a bitter, northerly gale, but at least none of them were buried or swept into the nearby river.

Storm Shaping is level 37!
...
Storm Shaping is level 41!

None of the Ironclads had noticed his subtle manipulation. The low visibility coupled with the driving winds meant all of them had their faces buried in their thick, woolen cloaks. Captain Doric, meanwhile, was entirely preoccupied with the roads themselves.

"What is happening to the wardings?" he muttered, not for the first time. "They shouldn't be so bad, especially not near the city."

"What could cause it?" Felix asked.

"I don't know," Doric said. His jaw firmed. "But I plan to find out."

The walls of Birchstone loomed ahead, dark against the endless white, and bright sodium-colored flames atop strange, box-like torches.

Dwarves in heavy armor stood by a sixty-foot gate that looked carved from the bedrock of the earth. All of it, walls, watch towers, and gate appeared to be made of a single piece of mighty stone without join or break.

Shaped, Felix realized. *Or cleverly disguised like it.*

His Voracious Eye picked out several enchantments on the fortifications, mostly to repel would-be climbers or even sappers that tried to tunnel beneath. The stone itself was a Tier VI material called Deepstone, and was even more durable than the High Roads themselves. That put Felix at ease. An army of redcloaks wouldn't be able to breach it easily.

A circle of pyramids surrounded the area, and the wardings functioned perfectly there. Wind, snow, and cold were cut off as if they were encased in a glass dome, and it was wide enough that all of the Ironclads and Claw were able to fit in with space to spare.

Doric shook his cloak out, letting snow run from its folds. "Let me do the talking, Mr. Veil. The Watch is best handled lightly."

One of the guards lifted a hand as the two companies drew level with the gatehouses. "Name, rank, and purpose of your visit."

"Good evening Lieutenant Ulrich. Captain Doric, Stoneheart Vanguard of the Ironclads. Returning from patrol."

"I know ya, Doric. Go on through." Ulrich grunted and swung his gaze to Felix. "Name, rank, and purpose of your visit."

"Silas Veil. Merchant. Carrying goods for trade."

The guard nodded at two others who had emerged from the guardhouse. "Inspect those sleds." He stared at Felix through his barred visor, and his eyes flashed with some sort of Skill. "What sort of goods requires such a heavy escort? All Journeyman Tier, too."

"Rare alchemical reagents. Some metals and woods," Felix said, trying not to worry about the Watch approaching their supplies with long spears. They started to prod bundles of cloth and move aside crates. "Essence draughts."

The guard scoffed. "Really. Carried essence draughts across the mountains, have you?"

"Lieutenant, I can vouch for Mr. Veil's integrity. He and his guards saved us from a Troll attack not six glasses ago."

"Open those crates, boys!" the guard ordered. Felix heard wood splintering and forced his breathing to calm. Willpower was useful in many ways, he'd found.

"Lieutenant! This is unnecessary!"

"Leave off, Doric. Savin' your hide don't mean Howler spit to me. If he had essence draughts, then he'd have flown here in half the time it'd take to cross the lower peaks. Rich merchants don't walk," he sneered at Felix. "No, we're gonna strip these sleds. No tellin' what contraband's in here, let alone if he's smugglin' in that thief again."

Ah, that's why the tight security, Felix realized.

A sharp crack splintered the air and was followed by a terrified series of shouts. A wind tore through the area, trails of vaporous Mana suddenly visible to all like a swirl of glowing ink in water. It crackled, condensing into a storm cloud of flashing lights, pulled from inside the silent dome of wards until it clustered above the sled.

The guards fell backward, and the lieutenant shoved his visor up and away from his face in confusion. Beside him, Captain Doric's jaw dropped, and Felix allowed himself a tiny smile.

"What's in the crate, lad!" the lieutenant snapped, his self-satisfied annoyance crumbling. "Tell me, quick-like!"

"E-essence draughts, sir!" his subordinate stuttered. "There's crates and crates of 'em!"

"As I claimed," Felix said, calm and measured. "Do you believe me now, lieutenant?"

Ulrich looked at Felix then at the cloaked and armed Claw that backed him. At some point, they had completely surrounded the Watch, and the Dwarf was keenly aware of that fact. "Aye. Still gotta do my duty though, don't I?"

"Of course."

The lieutenant gathered himself up, breathing so hard his mustache quivered. "Anything else, men?"

"N-no, sir."

"Right." Ulrich proffered a wooden token to Felix, who took it carefully. "Take that to the Watch's bursar down Mended Way. He'll… compensate you. For the crates."

Felix smiled. "I appreciate it."

The lieutenant only grunted before half-turning to the guardhouse. "Open the gate!"

Entering a new city was always an interesting experience for Felix. Each time he was accosted by something new, something different, even if most of the cultures were largely similar. Birchstone was built along the lines of Haarwatch, only on a much larger scale. The gate had opened and let their two companies in, but reaching Birchstone was a process.

They had to walk through a hundred-foot-thick tunnel absolutely festooned with enchantments and defensive measures before emerging into an open air pathway between the gate and *another* wall. The team was led by intense-looking Watchmen to the right, where they followed the curving defenses until a second gate and tunnel was revealed.

This happened two more times.

Finally, at the end of a much shorter tunnel of only twenty feet, Felix emerged into a wide, bustling metropolis. He was immediately accosted by the smells of wet earth, stone dust, and the sharp tang of metal while hundreds of Dwarves walked, drove, or hustled through the wide plaza. The air was alive with a symphony of sounds, too, from the raised voices of market-bound merchants hawking their wares, to the anxious griping of an older man and the squeal of children running underfoot. Smoke from a thousand chimneys rose up like flags, adding char scent to the tang of metal, as well as a touch of baking bread. Several nearby street vendors sold hearty meat skewers and mouth-watering mini pies.

Towering stone architecture was everywhere Felix looked, built into even the most mundane of structures. Here, a tavern filled with patrons, but featuring a massive arch covered in angular knotwork patterns and a depiction of some ancient battle. There, a private home, flanked by the beveled edges of a pillar that had once supported a great statue, of which only the hobnailed boots remained. All over, there was a sense of age and weight to the large, stout buildings, everything built with a thousand purposes all layered atop one another.

It was amazing.

"This is where we part, Mr. Veil," Captain Doric said as the two companies claimed a portion of the square. Crowds parted around them, curious eyes roving their cloaks and armor, though they mostly ignored the Ironclads.

"I appreciate the escort, captain," Felix said. His Claw formed up around him and their sleds. "And the conversation."

Doric barked a laugh. "Been a while since I talked so much! But duty calls. My Ironclads are bound to report to the Anvil. I'll need to tell them about the Trolls and their nasty Evolution." He nodded to the ice sleds. "Guard your wares well, Mr. Veil. Much as I hate to admit it, Birchwood is thick with thieves. And they're bold, too. Given the chance, they'd steal the beak right off my old Fini, here."

His Avum gave a confused squawk. Pit snorted. Quietly.

"Any good inns with vacancies, Captain?" Tzfell asked.

"Take the Mosslane there down a quarter league, to where the river slows. You'll see the statue of the Rockshaper, and two squares west is my nieces' place. The Torrent's Rest. Hard to miss it, accountin' for the bloomin' tree up the middle. Give her my name. Last I heard, she had some vacancies, but if she doesn't, coin talks."

Doric gave Felix's sleds a significant look.

"Plenty of stock, but no buyers yet," Felix admitted. "The Watch Lieutenant was right. If I had the money, I would have taken a Manaship across the mountains. I hope I can change my fortunes here, though."

Deception is level 47!

"The Golden Scale, alchemist's guild, will be breathin' down your neck," Doric warned, sliding into a sharp grin. "But, if you handle them as cool as you did the Watch, you'll be just fine."

Felix laughed. "I appreciate the warning."

"Glad of it. Hope you'll appreciate this one just the same," he said, lowering his voice. "Watch yourselves as much as your wares. The Watch and I both got our duty, and over fifty Journeyman Tiers ain't gonna go unnoticed for long."

"You're saying the Watch considers us a threat?" Harn asked.

"Aye."

Felix put his hands on his hips. "Well, I can nip that in the bud. You said the mountain was closed off to everyone, right?"

"Just about everyone. The High Clans come and go as they please, and those that're in good favor with the Hinterlord."

"I have business with them all. What do I have to do to get an audience with him? The Hinterlord of Red Shield."

The captain ran a gauntlet through his beard, tugging on it. "Can't guarantee anythin', Mr. Veil. Considerin' the trouble you had with the Watch, I'll do what I can. Been around a while, Stoneheart Vanguard. Might see what pull I still got."

Felix let loose a relieved breath. "Thank you, Captain. That would solve a lot of our problems."

"Happy to help…but I have a favor of my own, Mr. Veil."

"Oh." Felix steeled himself. The Dwarf looked downright nervous. "What's the favor?"

"The Ironclads are many, but I don't much like our chances if the Titan comes back. If she does, if she attacks this city, can we count you among the defenders?"

"Is that a worry?" Vess asked. "Your walls are quite impressive."

"She attacked the city once before, but then her focus was on getting into the Clan Hold. Against her unnatural power…I truly do not know if our wards will hold." Doric clenched his jaw, and a vein slowly pulsed across his forehead. "All able hands would be appreciated."

Felix put out his hand, grasping the man's forearm in a tight squeeze. "We will do what we can."

"That is all I ask," Doric said, squeezing right back. He looked like a weight had been shifted from his chest, and a tight smile spread his beard. "Be well, Mr. Veil. 'Til we meet again beneath star and stone."

"Be well, Captain."

CHAPTER SEVENTY-THREE

Finding the Torrent's Rest was just as simple as Doric had promised, though perhaps they had an easier time of it than most. The ice sleds drew interest in the packed streets, but the Claw had grown into a fearsome bunch. The vast majority of the crowds were Apprentice Tier or lower, and while most people couldn't identify one's advancement at a glance, Felix's company walked with the casual confidence of those who had been forged in battle.

The masses had split before them without a single word.

The inn itself sat inside a calm bend in the Swiftsteel River, perched atop a piece of land pinched between its fast-coursing length and marked by the enormous statue of a regal-looking Dwarf. Here, the river was wide, nearly double its normal size, and it seemed to crawl by, compared to the white waters farther upstream. Tall homes and apartments clung to the far bank, dotted with winter-bare parks and snow-piled lawns, while inside the bend, there were several high end shops in addition to the Torrent's Rest. It was a busy place, but was clearly more exclusive…and expensive.

Felix felt that particular pinch when they had arrived. Despite a recommendation from their "most beloved uncle," the twin sisters who ran the Torrent's Rest were adamant about their lack of vacancy. Times were quite busy, with the influx of folks from the border towns, leading the more well-off to come seeking their refined establishment. When Felix offered enough crowns to pay for his entire company for the whole week, however, their tune quickly changed. The entire fourth floor was emptied, their occupants ousted, and meals whipped up from seemingly nothing.

He only felt a little bad for the townsfolk put out on their rears. Most of them, he was assured, had only paid up through the morning and couldn't afford a single second more. Refugees, they had spent what little coin they had on expensive lodgings instead of opting for a lesser establishment and had already started begging for whatever clemency the sisters were willing to give. Dwarven businesswomen, it turned out, didn't know the meaning of the word.

So Felix found himself ensconced in a fine room at the very top of the Torrent's Rest, settled into a comfortable chair so solidly built it even handled his exceptional weight without a creak. His room was an entire suite, in fact, consisting of four separate chambers and only one of them containing a bed.

Said furniture was a four-post monster that could easily have swallowed ten Dwarves and was draped in sumptuous silk sheets and curtains stitched with sigaldry to maintain a pleasant sleeping temperature. The sitting room, where he and the others relaxed, was filled with seating, low tables, and two large fireplaces shaped into the likeness of some yawning Dwarven warrior. A merry fire crackled in their mouths, the warmth pleasant after their long, wintry walk.

"That's an oxbow," Harn said.

"What is?" Beef looked back out the window. "All I see is water."

Felix looked up at them both, arcing his neck to see outside to the river. His suite had a great view of the bend in the Swiftsteel, apparently.

"The river. It's the bend. The shape of it is called an oxbow. Named after an old story my uncle told me." Harn's gruff voice was strangely wistful. Felix would have listened for that alone. "A great hunter, a bull-man. Minotaur. He shaped a bow from the corpse of a monster. The greatest beast on land, they said, provin' that he had no equal on the Continent."

Harn scratched his cheek. "Dunno how accurate that all is, but it's what they say. Anyway, the Minotaur saw a huge bird, a Roc, and shot at it with his bow. Not a normal bow, though, was it? Its arrows curved, chasing its prey, and it struck that great bird right in the rump. And what'd the bird do? It grabbed that bullman and dragged up across the sky."

He chuckled at Beef's wide eyes. "The hunter shot arrow after arrow, but somehow they all missed. Damn things hit the ground, carvin' rivers all over the Continent. Wherever it hit, the rivers turned, curvin' on themselves. Eventually, the Roc flew so high they got lost in the stars. Stuck. Now they're still up there, fightin' forever."

Harn pointed up into the sky, where a dim grouping of stars could be seen through the haze of smoke and light pollution.

Beef was enraptured. "Sick."

Felix couldn't help but smile and try to enjoy this moment of peace. Pit snuggled deeper into his lap, demanding belly rubs, and Felix obliged. Vess was to his right in a similar chair, sitting with her legs tucked beneath her and two books balanced across her unarmored knees. Her hair was loosened a touch after their long journey, and her gambeson was unbuttoned as she turned pages.

A blue, high-collared blouse peeked out from beneath it as she stuck the end of her tongue out of her mouth and jotted down a note. The proprietors had a fair collection of books, and Vess had charmed her way into their private library soon after hearing of it.

Evie was lounging on the very wide bed, her boots pressed up against the headboard as she snacked on something or other. The Chanters were gathered before the crackling fire, nearly fifty feet away, poring over a map of the city.

The lot of them fit easily into the wide sitting room—the place was built for twice their number. It was quite nice and certainly more room than Felix needed.

"Alright. Everyone's had food?" he said.

"They have. The Talon leaders made it a priority, along with some relaxation in the tavern," Vess reported. She nestled a leather bookmark into her tome before shutting it. "As ordered."

Evie just held up a half-eaten roasted drumstick. "What's the point of bein' in an inn if we can't take advantage of it, eh?"

Felix nodded. "Good. They could use the break. All of you could—but first, we've some planning to do."

"Find the Gnome," Harn said, settling down against the Dwarven mantle.

"Keep him away from Imara," Vess added.

"And," Felix said, lifting a finger. "Access the Dwarven vaults."

"What? Why?" Tzfell asked.

"They have something I need." In his lap, Pit gave a firm nod. "And I'm willing to trade for it. That's why I brought so many Spirit Fruit and essence draughts with us."

"Gaining access to the vaults requires entry to the Clan Hold and an audience with the Hinterlord," Tzfell said, understanding dawning on her. "Which is why you asked Captain Doric for an introduction."

"Yeah. I don't know if that'll work, or if we need to figure out another path, but I figured it couldn't hurt. There's a treasure somewhere in these mountains, and I need it. Tzfell, can you look into what treasures Red Shield might have to hand?"

"They don't exactly keep a public list. What are you looking for?"

"The Mote of Frenzy," Felix said. A nervous energy spiraled through him. They were so close. "It's powerful, said to heal any injury to the Aspects."

"I've never heard of it," Laur admitted.

"Neither have I, but that is not unusual, especially if the Hinterlords have had it for any length of time. What goes into their vaults rarely comes back out again." The Dwarven Chanter tapped her lips with a pen. "If it is as powerful as you say, then it is likely in the hands of the Hinterlord himself. Reaching such an object would be difficult even in normal circumstances, let alone when the entire Hold is on lockdown."

"Let me worry about getting into the Hold. I don't even know if the Mote is here or in some other mountain. My source only said that the Dwarves took it into the Rimefangs, nothing more."

Tzfell adopts a thoughtful look. "My order has some ears among the Dwarves. I will see what I can find."

"I appreciate it." Felix ruffled Pit's floppy, russet hued ears. "Our first priority, though, is to find the Gnome."

"He could be anywhere, right?" Beef asked. "That Titan lady is chasing him. If she's anywhere as scary as everyone says, then I don't see why he wouldn't be halfway across the Continent by now."

"But she's still hunting for him in the Rimefangs," Evie pointed out. "The Dwarves said as much. Why would she do that, if he'd run off?"

"Maybe she's bad at her job?" Beef suggested.

"We have seen a clue already, I think," Laur said. "Those Trolls were suffering under the effects of a Mind Skill. Something had stirred their thoughts until they were soup—not a far stretch for a Troll, I admit. It was likely why they were so aggressive and acting out of ordinary."

"Like being active during the day," Felix said.

"Precisely."

"Do we think it was Imara?"

Vess frowned. "What benefit would that have? Wouldn't that make her own hunt harder, if Trolls were out and about attacking things?"

"Then was it Archibald?" Felix asked.

"Possible. We know the Corrupted is powerful, but we haven't a clue on the Gnome's advancement, other than his penchant for escape," Tzfell said, exchanging a look with the Elven Chanter. "Can you lock him down with wards?"

The Elf chewed his lip. "Possibly. I don't know what Skills he is using to evade capture, so crafting a ward to counter them would be like firing an arrow into the dark."

"I tried to locate him using our connection, but other than knowing he was somewhere in the city, I couldn't get more details. Either someone is blocking my access, or he's learned to do it himself," Felix said.

"If he's been on the run from the Corrupted for so long, it is likely he has ways of fouling tracking. Even methods utilizing the Grand Harmony."

"Which makes the Troll tactic make more sense. He scrambles up some monsters and conceals his trail." Felix nodded. "We'll have to search the city on foot, then."

Beef and Evie both groaned.

"Can't imagine that'll be easy. Fella sounds slippery."

"Yeah. Small, too. Everyone's so small in this place. I'll have trouble spotting anything in these crowds," Beef pointed out.

That was something Felix had noticed, too, but it was worse for the teen Minotaur. At least Felix retained relatively normal dimensions, despite his six-and-a-half-foot height. Beef was a bit over seven and built like a champion bodybuilder covered in fur.

"You can work with me, Beef," Vess said. "I've some business to attend to myself, and the Claw will have enough eyes walking the streets."

Beef's forehead unknitted. "Oh. Okay, I can do that."

Felix tossed a grateful smile to Vess. She smiled right back. "Harn, I'll need you to run point with the Claw, then. Fifty pairs of eyes will help a lot, but I don't want to draw too much attention. Pick the groups, and keep them low-key."

"Sure, kid. The Henaari are canny enough for that, though they're pretty distinctive."

"That's what cloaks are for," Evie said. "It's warm here, what with all the forges and stuff, but it ain't spring. No one'll bat an eye at someone with a hood up."

Harn grunted. "Good. You'll lead the first shift, then."

"Yyero's boiled nethers," Evie muttered. "Outstandin'."

Felix drummed his fingers on the arms of his chair, running through the details. He stood up. "We'll start first thing in the morning. Relax for the night."

"And you?" Vess asked as Felix walked to the door.

"Not tired. I'm going to take a look around."

"Alone?" Laur asked. Then, less sharply, said, "Are you sure, Lord Autarch?"

"I'll be fine. Stay. Rest up." He opened the door latch and paused at the threshold. "Pit?"

The Dire Hound scratched his neck with a hind leg. "I'll stay, too. Wasn't there something about food being sent up?"

"Already sent food," Harn said.

Beef's very large stomach growled. "I could use another plate. Think they got more in those kitchens?"

"Great heaps of it, I bet," Evie said, wiping her lips. "What say we three take a gander?"

"Ooh." Pit's golden eyes sharpened, and his ears pricked forward. A fox on the hunt. "I like that."

Felix snorted. "I'll be back soon. Don't break anything."

A chorus of assurances followed him out as he closed the door tight and walked down the hall.

The Sun Trolls died slower than the rest, but they could not resist the Light.

Imara stood among their smoking corpses, her armor still cherry red. Superheated air met frozen storm winds and boiled around her in a furious cyclone, but that faded as her armor did. Soon, she stood in the snow, weapons unbloodied and armor a dull, listless gray.

Another group, more rabid than the last. He's getting desperate.

A grim pleasure rippled across her chest, tingling across her core before fading away. She could almost taste the end of her hunt, and the great rewards she was promised. The Gnome had sent fewer and fewer clutches of Trolls at her as the days rolled on, and each time she killed them, she came that much closer to catching him.

Imara sat down, the melted stone already hardened into a wavy slag.

"Light guide me," she said, her voice even and untouched by the strain of her fight. Pure. "Unveil my path."

Within her core, where the Light pooled like a captured sun, Imara grasped at the rays. They spun, rings within rings, dripping gold upon her hands like molten metal, but she held on. She pulled them, dominated them, and she saw.

A dusty-brown beam flecked with purple hovered into view. Imara reached for it, but it skipped away, just beyond her grasp. As slippery as its bearer, the beam could not be held still or contained, no matter her Willpower. The Light washed against it all, fading the beam from view, but she preserved. The Pathless' power was great, so much more than hers, but Imara would master herself. She must.

She *reached.*

There. He is there. A dull satisfaction pulsed in her middle. *I can see—*

Something else was there. Another beam.

Once she noticed it, Imara wondered how she'd ever missed its presence. It loomed large, bigger than the Gnome's trace by several orders of magnitude. It pulsed, red-gold and blue-white tangled around a core of deepest darkness.

Anathema...

The word was whispered into her Mind, but it resonated with her core until it filled up her entire world.

Trackless One, she sent, breathlessly. *What is this?*

Danger.

Danger? Has one of the Dwarven champions made a move?

No. You Must Tread Carefully, Child. A Finger Is Upon The Scale Of Fate.

The Pathless couldn't see the future; the potency of His own Light clouded His vision. This is what she had been taught. However, things that affected Fate, as He called it, had a resonance in the Light.

He Is Near...

Who is, Trackless One?

The Fiend.

A thrill of excitement ran through Imara, tingling down her spine and down every limb. Her heartbeat sped up, and her mouth went dry. Word had spread of that man, though no one told her of him directly, save for that Henaari Windcaller. She'd had to learn mostly from fearful whispers among the faithful. *He is powerful?*

There was a profound silence as the Fiend's beam filled the entirety of Imara's vision. It swelled, becoming the horizon. The sky itself. The red-gold and blue-white split, opening to reveal the yawning shadow. An endless…nothing.

Something inside her quailed, and she called upon the Light.

Golden radiance answered, welling up from within her. From without, as well. Light banished the dark, occluding her senses and the beam of this…Fiend.

Her fear faded. Vanished. Until she was calm and empty once again.

Child. Find The Gnome. Beware The Fiend.

I do not fear, she sent. It wasn't a lie. Her fear had gone, utterly. *I will conquer all for you, Pathless.*

Time Is Short. Trust In The Light.

Always.

She opened her eyes and stood, gauging the angle of the risen moons. Night had fallen during her communion, and the storm had not abated. Winds whipped and snow swirled between her and her goal.

"The Light will return, and it will cleanse this place," she said. The words were a ritual, one the Hierophant had taught her to embody. *"The dawn always arrived,"* she would say. *"Let us meet it with open arms."*

Imara strode into the squall.

CHAPTER SEVENTY-FOUR

"That is a very big statue," Felix said to no one in particular.

He stood at Shaper Square, as it was apparently called, just on the other side of the squeeze of streets that led away from the Torrent's Rest. It was full dark, but lamps sat at steady intervals down every thoroughfare and side alley. Their light was buttery yellow bordering on orange, and mingled with the press of people, their noise and smell, Felix could almost believe he was back on Earth. At least, until he actually paid attention.

Dwarves, Goblins, and even a few Korva filled the streets, filling the night with idle chatter, nervous conversation, and everything in between. The crowds weren't much affected by the forced relocation into Birchstone, at least not their attitudes. They drifted among shops and through small parks, eating steaming pastries or sipping on drinks. They weren't all rich, either, despite their surroundings.

Felix spotted more than a few Dwarves with threadbare jackets and well-patched trousers, often with entire families in tow. They stared about the city, taking in the hustle and bustle with overwhelmed wonder.

I know how you feel, folks. He looked back up at the statue that dominated the square. *A Dwarven city. Awesome.*

It was why he'd come out, really. Visiting a new city after months of snowy Nagast was fascinating and intoxicating all at once. So many things were going on, and he'd only seen a tiny portion of one section of Birchstone. Felix had no clue how quickly they would find the other

Unbound, but he wanted to explore while he could. Which brought him back to the statue at the center of Shaper Square.

The statue was of a very wide Dwarf, but unlike some of the more martial carvings he'd seen around the city, this one was wearing soft, flowing robes and holding a baton or rod. It was big, at least fifty feet tall, and Felix imagined people could see it from streets away. A thick belt covered the statue's torso from sternum to hips, and a number of symbols were etched into it. Not an array, but letters of some sort.

A young Dwarven woman was set up against the statue's base, patiently tuning some sort of stringed instrument. A lute, he was pretty sure. An open case sat next to her, empty except for a dirty rag. Felix turned to her. "Excuse me. Sorry. Can you tell me what this says?"

The woman blinked at him once before her uninterested face came alive. "Oh! The Rockshaper? It's a list of his accomplishments."

"Accomplishments? What did this Rockshaper do?"

"New here?"

"What gave that away," Felix asked with a smirk.

The musician strummed a few chords. "You're very tall, even for a Human."

"I eat my vegetables. Have you played for long?"

"All my life," she said proudly. "You interested in a song? Two stone, and I'll play your ears off."

"Tempting. More interested in this statue and what it says, though."

The woman smiled, revealing several missing teeth and a scar across her lips. "What say we split the difference? Toss me some copper, and I'll tell you the tale. Better than some stuffy list."

Felix pulled two coppers from his pouch, tossing them into her instrument case. "Fair trade."

The Dwarven busker lowered her head, her mouth moving silently. Felix's first instinct was to rush her, to disable her before she could use a Skill—but he suppressed it. She seemed to be repeating something. Reminding herself. When she was done, she changed her fingering on the frets of her lute and strummed once.

A chord rang out into the square, pure and almost sweet-sounding. The crowds slowed, stilled, turning toward her as her voice followed. It lilted, drifting through notes with enviable agility, before settling on a steady harmony. Words formed, first in what he assumed was Dwarven, then switching to the common tongue.

"In ancient days of yore, a tale we sing,
Of Rockshaper, the mage, earth's sacred king.

Ancestor of Red Shield, revered with pride,
Master of elements, his power amplified.
The Troll King, imprisoned in depths below,
By Rockshaper's might, dealt a crushing blow.
Foundations laid, through shadow and flame,
Undermount emerged, hidden realm claimed."

The words went on, a song worthy of a hero of legend. Felix filed away all the details, though he was sure some of them were likely made up. He definitely hadn't heard of anything called a "nevermind" or an "aberrant terror." At the very least, they were probably exaggerated by countless retellings. His own growing fame was proof of that—many of the "miraculous feats" he was credited with were impossible, even for him.

The musician—bard, he supposed—ran out of verses a few minutes later, and the tumble of chords became something uplifting.

"So raise your voices high, with hearts alight,
To Rockshaper, the mage, in eternal Night.
His story lives on, through the ages told,
A Dwarven legend, noble and bold."

The crowd applauded, some quite enthusiastically, the moment she finished the last note. Coppers rained down on the bard, most landing in her lute case. She thanked them all with a seated bow and a wide smile.

"Your voice is very good," Felix said through the crowd.

"Well, thanks Tall Man," she half-shouted. Several of the Dwarven families, the ones clearly from the evacuated towns, leaned in to praise her voice.

"What's the Undermount?" He'd heard of it in passing before but hadn't given it much thought. "Is that what they call the Clan Hall?"

"No, Tall Man. You really are new. It's a mountain that hangs from the bottom of the world. My thanks," she said, as another farmer dropped a coin into her case. "The Clan Holds all connect to it, and it's where the Highbloods all hobnob with the Hinterlords. Or try to, anyway. Mostly, they just host parties so depraved that it'd curl your hair."

Connected to all the Clan Holds, he mused. *Sounds like another liminal space…and the perfect place to keep valuable treasures like the Mote of Frenzy.*

"Is Undermount dangerous? It seems this Rockshaper dealt with a lot of mighty things, but your song barely mentioned it."

"Oh it's dangerous, alright. Filled with monsters and guardians.

Creatures born of the mountain, slaved to it. Sworn to guard its secrets for all time. And it's got plenty of those. Treasures like you wouldn't believe in tombs bigger than this whole city. Rockshaper himself got buried there, I hear."

Something danced across his senses, and Felix focused on it as the bard kept talking. His Perception had flagged a figure moving through the crowd while the bard was still performing, but he'd ignored them at the time. Just another body, after all. Now, as the crowd jostled on its way, they were a touch more obvious. As was the muffled jingle of coins at their waist. Too many coins.

A thief. What do they call them here? Right. A cutpurse.

He focused again on the bard, who was still talking about the horrors and treasures of the Undermount. She very pointedly never looked at the thief, even when the slight figure passed nearby, which settled Felix's thoughts. And it gave him an idea, one that might even save him some time.

The woman shivered, her litany of dangers petering out, and Felix could tell it was an honest reaction. "Some folks dream of climbin' the heights, braving the air that wants to kill you and the tombs filled with living shadows…me, I'd be happy with a simple roof over my head and steady meals."

"That sounds wise." He dropped a handful of gold crowns in her case and kept his smile mild when her eyes widened in surprise. "I appreciate the song. And the help."

She sputtered something that came close to "thank you," but was mostly noise.

"Don't worry about it. But tell me: where do you go to get a drink?"

"Rich man like yourself, the Torrent's Rest is about the only place 'round these parts."

"What if I wanted something rougher? More…down to earth?" His hand snapped to his waist, where his pouch dangled. He'd caught a thin, overly pale wrist attached to a slender Dwarven girl. She squirmed hard, trying to free herself. "A place where *you* fine folks might frequent," he continued, emphasizing the right words. "I'm looking for a job."

The bard looked at him in fear, trading glances with what was clearly her accomplice. As he hoped, she spoke quickly. "Go to the Cask. It's northwest, over the river, near the first wall. Ask for Quarro. You'll, ah, you'll find it exactly as you hope."

Felix let the Dwarven thief go, and she retreated, rubbing her wrist. "What do you need a job for? You ain't no rat lord."

"Misha," the musician warned.

Felix chuckled. "Sorry if I squeezed too tightly. And please, don't rob the refugees. Focus on the rich ones."

"Like you?" the thief snapped back.

"Quiet, Misha!"

Felix just smiled, letting his Sovereign of Flesh sharpen the edges of his white teeth. The two thieves stumbled back, pale and shaking. "I think you know the answer to that, Misha."

They both ran.

Felix watched them for a moment before heading in the opposite direction. Northwest, toward the river.

"And so you scared them?" Karys said, somewhat incredulous.

"They were trying to rob me," Felix muttered, only a little defensive. Mostly, he felt bad for freaking them out. They hadn't even been Apprentice Tier. "I'm not *super* proud of it, but hey, it got me some interesting information."

"Hm." The sword at his waist buzzed with disapproval, life Mana seeping out around it in a cloud. The vapor was invisible to everyone on the street, though most people still gave Felix a wide berth and worried stares as he strode past. Compared to almost everyone, he was practically a giant. It was slightly disorienting after his stay among the Risi.

"This Rockshaper is intriguing. Based on that lady's song, he probably had Stone Shaping, like me. Might be some Dwarves here know about shaping Skills and could point me in the right direction."

"For your tenth Pillar?"

"Maybe. I'm still aiming to combine all my shaping Skills into a singular Skill, something with a high rarity. Something powerful and with a lot of utility." He'd already incorporated his newest one into his Shaping Array, and Storm Shaping had slotted into place without a single twinge of pain. "If it's Tri-Aspected, then yeah. That's the goal."

"Remember, Felix. What you need is balance. Power and even utility is secondary."

"Right." He hadn't forgotten; focusing on Tri-Aspected Skills was part of his decision-making process. He looked up, spotting a soaring wall at the end of the next street. "I gotta go. I'm here."

"Do be careful," Karys insisted. "I would ask that you come back with your allies, but I know you won't. So instead, I'll only say this: many lives depend on you. Do not walk into needless danger, Felix."

"Hey. You know me."

Karys sighed, and their connection fizzled out.

The city of Birchstone was split into segments, much as Haarwatch was, though the Dwarves had designed the mountain city like a series of nested circles. Each one rose higher as they neared the grand expanse of the mountain itself. The huge walls were incredibly thick and sported guarded gates between. He'd seen traffic moving between districts, but the gates were closed at night, likely for security reasons.

Down at the end of the street, perched against the soot-stained wall, was a ramshackle structure. Though the tavern didn't climb even a quarter of the wall's height, it was still three stories tall, each level seemingly made by a different hand until the entire thing leaned drunkenly against the battlements. A sign hung above a stained and time-worn door, depicting a wine barrel with a big skull and crossbones covering its side.

The Cask, I assume. As far as branding went, it was pretty spot on.

Compared to the Torrent's Rest, the Cask looked to be held together by wishes, dreams, and pigeon crap. Windows sagged in their frames, the small panes of glass so soot stained that they might as well have been painted over. A tottering porch rose to meet an off-center wooden door, worn pale by years of rough, ungentle hands. Felix pushed it open. Inside, it was both dark and smoky. Worn and splintered tables and chairs filled the tavern, stained and sticky in the wan light. A dozen Dwarves, Goblins, Orcs, and Hobgoblins were seated or standing, and all of them looked up at him as he entered. Not a single Human. No Elves or Gnomes either, though perhaps the latter weren't much appreciated around town anymore.

"Evening," he muttered.

Everyone went back to ignoring him.

Felix walked through, ducking his head as he passed a particularly low ceiling support. All around, the patrons pulled on their pipes and drank ironbound mugs of foamy ale. They were settled into the thick shadows that clung to the dingy little place despite the fire that burned in a hearth at the far end. Felix imagined someone with a lower Perception would find it all pretty unnerving. As it was, he could see them all just fine, and he made special note of all of the weaponry hidden just out of direct view.

"Tall bastard, ain't cha?" said the grizzled bartender. He was a

Dwarf with a wild gray beard and an eye patch painted with a small green snake. "Don't see many Humans 'round these parts, not 'til recently, anyhow. And not fair-haired, pretty boys like you. What's yer business, boy?"

Deception is level 48!

Felix managed not to touch his head at the comment. He was using his Glamulet to form an illusion around himself; to others he appeared as a normal Human man, with ordinary hands that definitely weren't claws. He was blond now, with a slightly too-big chin and a crooked nose. The look of a laborer, but someone who clearly specialized in Strength. His height made him conspicuous, but there was little he could do about that.

He coughed, putting some rasp into his voice. "You're right. I'm new to Birchstone and got no connections. Need a job. Some friends told me to come here. Ask for Quarro."

The bartender squinted at him, and Felix felt a faint shiver against his Spirit. "What's yer name?"

"Mervin."

"Already got a bouncer, Mervin, and he lifts all my stock when needs be. Ain't got work for you, kid."

"No no, not that. I'm strong. Got a good back and decent vision. I wanna work." Felix lowered his voice, looking around the bar suspiciously. "For the rat lords."

A crossbow beneath the counter was lifted enough that Felix could see its knocked bolt. "Show me your stats."

Felix sent them—veiled, of course. The bartender grunted again, but this time Felix got the impression he was impressed. His stats was still impersonating a Journeyman Tier with a Strength specialization, but he'd made his Endurance and Vitality look good, too. His Veiling Amulet had a considerable amount of versatility if used by someone with enough Willpower and Intent—Felix just had to focus hard on what he wanted to show.

"I just need somethin' to do, you know? Keep silver in my pocket and food on the table. I'm strong, and I ain't picky about how I use it."

Deception is level 49!

"Alright. Might be we have a use for ya," the bartender admitted. "Come with me."

The grizzled Dwarf flipped open a length of the bar and sauntered out and around several patrons. Felix followed, stepping around snoring patrons and a few who sent more inquisitive shivers across his Spirit. Analyzing people without asking was considered rude, but he supposed no one at the Cask much cared about manners.

The bartender brought him down a short hall that ended with a stone wall. It was the same stone wall as outside, the warded ones that separated the districts. Felix raised an eyebrow, but the Dwarf merely reached out and ran his fingers across a particular section. Sigils formed beneath his hand, dusty brown and silver, before fading. In their place, something mechanical clicked and ratcheted, muted by feet of dark stone, until a Dwarf-sized door slid smoothly open.

"C'mon, boy, and don't lag behind." The bartender vanished into the door, footsteps loud but fading fast.

Felix took a breath. *This is probably stupid.*

He followed, folding himself almost in half to fit beneath the lintel, and shuffled off into the dark.

CHAPTER SEVENTY-FIVE

The low passage was uncomfortable, but it didn't last long. After twenty or so strides, they came to a set of stairs, and the ceiling there was far taller, allowing Felix to unbend his considerable height. The steps themselves were odd, built for shorter feet, but that just meant Felix skipped three at a time. A good thing, as the eyepatched bartender hustled up them faster than he expected.

Soon they came to another door, but this one wasn't hidden behind wards and magical mechanisms. It was made of simple iron-strapped wood. It looked new-built—it lacked the dirt and wear of a thousand hands like the tavern's front entrance—and when the Dwarf pushed on it, the door swung open without a sound. Strangely enough, the room beyond was just as quiet, which threw Felix at first.

Men and women of many Races mingled and caroused across a cramped series of rooms carved from the dark stone walls. Fine tiles had been laid, pillars sculpted with sharp angles, and more than one bas-relief sculpture dominated the walls. Well-polished if mismatched furniture divided the rooms up into smaller congregations; here a card game, there a number of masked individuals arguing over several reams of paper, and closer still were scarred Dwarves and Goblins throwing back shots of something that bubbled viciously.

"C'mon boy. Don't got all day," the bartender said, stepping into the room.

Felix followed, and the moment his foot crossed the threshold, the sound reinstated itself like a bubble popping inside his ears. He glanced down and back, noting the deftly hidden strip of sigaldry just inside the door frame. *Sound ward. Highly advanced, too. These people are* loud.

Shouts buffeted him from powerful lungs as he wound through the eclectic collection of tables. Briefly, Felix glimpsed a rough iron cage that featured a number of burly figures tussling with a large Golem. The cheers escalated when one of the Dwarves was pinned by an enormous wood and steel hand, so much that the ground itself shook.

As if the secret doors and hidden wards weren't enough evidence, one look at these folks and Felix was certain he'd come to the right place.

Eyepatch led him on through a well-constructed archway and into a wide room almost totally filled by a long stone table carved so it appeared to have long, serpentine dragons flying around the edges. Atop it were the remains of a mighty feast. Little was left except platters of bones and gristle, save for the platter before a very wide Dwarf.

Felix flared his Perception and Affinity even before they entered, sorting through the countless impressions all around him. The room was mostly empty, but he could hear the steady breathing of at least three people hidden behind two separate secret doors. Guards, he assumed, their Spirits vibrating in a choppy sort of irritation. They were bored.

They crossed the archway, and the noise of the hidden bar was muted to a dull, distant roar. The breathing in the walls grew more pronounced.

More sigils. Despite his Adept Body, passing through that was a balm to his ears. He sighed in relief.

"Loud bastards, ain't they?" said the man behind the table. He was busy sucking the meat off of some sort of fowl, uncaring how the grease and juices spilled over his wide, plaited beard.

"Uh, yeah," Felix said.

"This one is looking for work with the crews, Thrumm," Eyepatch said. "Said he's a strongarm, and his stats look solid."

The wide Dwarf eyed him, and Felix felt that tell-tale shiver across his Spirit. "Name's Mervin? You don't look like a Mervin, kid. Too tall."

"Take it up with my parents," Felix said, before snapping his lips closed. Thrumm, however, just laughed.

"Aye, that's the way, innit? In my experience, though, men such as us have a way of earnin' our names. Might be you work for me, and if that happens, we'll see about findin' you a name what suits you better, eh?"

Felix forced a smile. "I'd like that."

"Take a seat, I'm tired of lookin' up at ya." The rat lord—for that is what he must have been—looked Felix over. "Strongarm. I can see that. Done any protection gigs, Mervin?"

"Some. Kept friends alive more than once."

Thrumm grunted. "Friends. Rare to be runnin' jobs with folks like that. Can't guarantee you'll be workin' with those you like. Might be those ya hate, if the job calls for it. Can you handle that?"

Felix shrugged. "I need money. I can't afford to be picky…but I knew someone that said they were coming out here to work. If he works for you, maybe I might not be so bad off."

The rat lord frowned. "Got a name?"

"Archibald."

One of those heartbeats sped up.

"Never heard of 'im," the rat lord said. His Spirit tightened like the head of a drum, as a tattoo of rapid anxiety beat out loud.

Liar. The quickening heartbeat was to the right, hidden neatly by a faux wine rack. Strangely, he couldn't sense anything about their Spirit.

"Really?" Felix sighed. "Well, if you see him, tell him his old friend from Earth is looking for him."

"From earth, eh? Strange way to put it. You don't look like a Dwarf."

Felix smiled. "He'll understand."

"I'm afraid I don't," Thrumm said, his anxiety turning sour. "Why don't you explain it to me?"

"Not sure I have the time for that."

"Make the time."

Felix laughed. He was surprised at how tired he was of pretending already. "No."

Thrumm regarded him levelly, and the rhythm within him sped up all the more. It had turned ugly, too fast, too chaotic. "Who are you?"

Smooth as silk, hidden panels opened, and two Dwarves and a Hobgoblin surrounded Felix. They held black knives low at their waists, but stayed out of his reach. Voracious Eye swept among them all, stopping curiously on their enchanted blades.

"I told you. A friend." Felix stood up calmly. Their knives tracked him. "I'd appreciate it if you could pass along my message."

Felix made to walk out, but Thrumm's deep voice stopped him. "I don't care who you are, Mervin. No one orders me around. Not here."

The rat lord whistled, and the killers lunged for Felix, their blades suddenly sparking with brilliant green vapor. They were fast, silent, and committed to killing him.

Every single one of their weapons stopped a foot from Felix's flesh.

Idly, he plucked one of the knives from the assassin's grip. The acid vapor around the blade bent to his Will and Hand of Calamity, with a little touch of Ferric Shaping. They were High Steel weapons, but iron was in there *somewhere*. "Cool knives."

He kept walking. The assassins, letting go of their stuck-fast weapons, looked worriedly between him and their boss, but Felix paid them little mind. His attention was taken up by the figure hidden behind the wine rack. They were as still as a statue, and only their hammering heart and rough breathing gave Felix any indication they were even alive.

"Remember," he called back without turning. He headed for the exit. "Friend. Earth. Want to talk."

No one tried to stop him again.

That might've been a little hasty, he admitted later, kicking his feet over the edge of a third story roof.

Shortly after Felix had left the Cask, the rat lord's men had boiled into the street, hunting for him. His display with the acid-enchanted knives hadn't been enough to scare them forever, just enough to make Thrumm consider his options.

He'd been smart about it, though, immediately dropping his Glamulet's illusion and activating his Abyssal Skein. Once he'd relocated to a high vantage point, Felix had watched as the rat lord's men searched ineffectually for signs of his passage. It had been a close thing at first, but not because of speed or ability.

Instead, Felix had to find a slower route to the rooftops, as anything faster was either blatantly obvious or would leave shattered cobblestones in his wake. Dense as his Body was, it did not make it easy to sneak around, and he no longer had Cloudstep to cushion his weight. Storm Shaping might have lifted him—Felix hadn't tried that yet—but its level was still too low and thus his control was lacking, too.

At least the Dwarves build things sturdy, he mused, not for the first time. *I only cracked two roof tiles.*

Felix wasn't exactly thrilled to have angered a whole thieves guild or whatever, but it was a calculated decision. Now, shrouded by his Void

Skill, Felix watched as the last of the rat lord's men gave up searching the local alleyways. The streets around him were as quiet as cities got, with only the ambient noise of folks living their lives as evening turned to true night.

Any minute now.

An hour passed. Two hours. Felix sat, shrouded and bored out of his Mind while snow fell steadily. He'd just about stared a hole through the Cask and the dark wall it leaned against. Had he made a mistake? Or did he miss something? The Casks' secret rooms extended into the warded walls themselves, so maybe there was another exit. If he—

Abyssal Skein is level 83!

Felix perked up. Someone was searching for him. Someone with *very* good Perception to press his Abyssal Skein up another level. He scanned the streets below, flaring his own Perception and Affinity to their limits.

A short figure crept from behind the Cask, peering cautiously down the maze of back alleys before walking out into the snowfall.

Felix stifled his excitement and got moving.

Archie clung to the shadows as best he could, but there was limp in his step and a fire burning in his brain. Thrumm had torn into him for the past few hours, demanding to know everything he could about this mysterious bruiser that had shown up at the Cask. Archie hadn't known anything and admitted as much…but the rat lords didn't get their power by being kind.

Status Condition: Sprained Ankle
Status Condition: Bruised Ribs (x2)

Thrumm had roughed him up after that tall stranger left, asking for everything Archie knew about the guy. Which was nothing, of course.

Asshole. He knew coming back to Birchstone was stupid, but it was the only real option he'd had. He'd bought some time with all those Trolls, but they wouldn't keep his personal monster at bay forever. Archie had thought working with Thrumm and his crew would save him time—but all he'd done was lay low while the rat lord "read the lay of the land."

He'd realized that night that Thrumm wasn't going to help. No one was.

And now I have this Mervin guy saying crazy things. Hunting for me. Fuck.

"Archibald."

Archie pinpointed the source of the words in a half-second, his Perception flaring even as he braced his feet to run. He looked to his left, where another narrow alley met up with his own...but couldn't see anyone. It wasn't even his tinted goggles at fault, either. His Blindsense found nothing at all. "Who's asking?"

"A friend."

The voice echoed around him now, somehow sourceless. Archie did a little half-spin, hunting for the guy. "Ain't got many of those." He spat, if only to cover up his fear. "You Mervin?"

The voice laughed. It was...kind, and even sounded a little embarrassed. "No. That was a fake name. First one I could think of, actually."

"Who are you, then?"

Something...shifted. Archie's Perception screamed at him, and he danced back, putting a dozen feet between him and a huge guy standing in the middle of the alley. He was similar in size to the blond man in the Cask, but his hair was black, his face different, and his eyes... Archie's heart hammered and sweat sprang up across his back despite the cold. "What the fuck? How'd you do that? I've seen Stealth. That wasn't Stealth."

The guy waggled his fingers. They were covered in some sort of dark gloves. "Magic."

"God, I'm so sick of magic," Archie muttered. He sidled closer to the stone wall, his core spinning. "Well, Not-Mervin. What the fuck do you want?"

The guy blinked and lowered his hands. "I wasn't lying before. Well, I was. We're not friends, but I'd like that to change."

"You said that in the Cask. Not a fan of friends," Archie admitted. "Doesn't end well."

"You seemed pretty chummy with all those folks back at the Cask."

"They owe me favors. Or I owe them." Archie ran his hands across the wall, and the stone helped him calm down. He could run...but he was curious. "What's your angle?"

"My name is Felix. I'm from Florida."

"You—wait. What?"

"And I'm Unbound, too."

Archie swallowed, forcing breaths through his nose. His core spun wildly, but his Skills felt unstable, unready. *Just like me. Like* her. *I—I can't fight two of them.*

"Hey, calm down," the guy—Felix—said. "I'm not here to fight you or capture you or kill you."

The guy smiled, and his teeth were bright white and perfectly aligned.

"I'm here to save you."

CHAPTER SEVENTY-SIX

"This is the place?" Archie asked, his thick eyebrows lifted to the brim of his cap. "Swanky."

"Mm," Felix grunted. "Cost an arm and a leg, too."

"Oh? So you're rich, huh?"

Felix just smiled and gestured across the courtyard, leading his shaky ally onto the wide steps of the Torrent's Rest.

Getting Archibald—he preferred Archie—back to the inn hadn't been easy. Felix had been quizzed by the Gnome repeatedly on Earth-based trivia, pummelled with question after question about where he came from. It was harmless, and it apparently put the guy at ease, so Felix answered as best he could. Whenever the guy dipped into pop culture, though, Felix could only vaguely guess. He'd never paid enough attention to all that stuff.

In contrast, Archie answered very little. Other than operating in some sort of vaguely criminal capacity and running from the Titan, he didn't go into his life on the Continent or back on Earth.

All Felix really learned was the guy's appearance. He was short, a hair over three feet tall, with a build that was lean rather than portly, like many Gnomes Felix had encountered. He had a curly gray mop of hair beneath a floppy sort of newsboy cap, pulled low so that it practically met his eyebrows. His square face was dominated by a bulbous nose and a pair of thick, heavily tinted goggles, while his jawline was framed by a neatly groomed black beard. Handsome, in a Gnomish sort of way.

Other than a set of flexible leathers that were steeped in earth Mana, he wasn't carrying anything particularly powerful on his person, either. Pouches at his waist were full of thin rods and hooks—thieves tools, if Felix had to guess—and a smattering of silver coins. There were also the dark goggles he never removed, but they weren't enchanted—Felix could tell that much even without using his Voracious Eye. And he wasn't going to, at least not yet. Light as his Analyze Skill was, his consideration could be felt. Archie was skittish enough already, he didn't want to chase the guy off. It was easier and more polite to just talk, for now.

They entered the inn to the sound of a rowdy song being belted at the top of powerful lungs. It was a wall of pure noise, clad in only the barest veneer of melody. The crowd of patrons singing were still primarily wealthy merchants, but they were supplemented by a core of cloaked figures bearing a burning eye upon their backs. At the center, however, perched atop the bar and howling with every ounce of their souls, were three very familiar faces.

"Is that a Minotaur?" Archie asked.

Felix groaned. Evie, Beef, and Pit crooned to the dulcet tones of a Hobgoblin bard near the fireplace, their singing almost a crime against the very concept of sound. The crowd was not much better.

Beef met his eyes first, flicked to the side, and his giant mouth abruptly snapped shut. He fumbled, smacking into Evie with a meaty fist, which caused her to almost tumble off the top of the bar. She shouted something inaudible over the racket, but Beef grabbed her cheeks and pointed her face at Felix and Archie. She cursed.

Felix could almost hear the words. *Noctis' tits.*

Pit was the last to know, and he kept howling even after Evie picked him up and carried him with her across the tavern. The Claw and other patrons slowed for a moment, but then the bard struck up a new song, this one faster and wilder than the last. Cheers and clinking mugs filled the air, and no one bothered to look toward Felix and his guest.

"Friends of yours?" Archie asked as the three neared.

"Yes." Felix started up the stairs. "Come on. My rooms are on the top floor."

Archie followed, eyes almost boring into Felix's back, but he hustled a bit when Beef and Evie brought up the rear. After a single flight, the sound below was muffled to a dull roar, and after the second, it had vanished completely.

"Out for some night huntin'?" Evie asked. Pit wriggled out of her grasp, landed heavily on the ground, and ran to Felix's feet.

"Had a lead. Took a chance," Felix said with a shrug. "Evie, Beef, Pit. Meet Archie."

The Gnome raised his eyebrows at the introduction, perhaps at being introduced to a Dire Hound, but he pivoted smoothly. "Charmed. Enchanted, even. Evie. That is a beautiful name to fit a beautiful woman."

Evie snorted. "He's got a mouth."

"More than that, sweetheart. They call me Silvertongue for a reason."

Evie produced a dagger from somewhere, letting it dance across her knuckles. "Wanna lose it?"

Archie blanched, but his Spirit remained undaunted. Intrigued, even. Felix rolled his eyes and resumed walking upstairs.

"This the guy?" Beef asked.

"This is the guy," Felix confirmed. "No more questions until we're in my room."

Wait up! These stairs are hard in this form, Pit complained.

Then change back.

Not enough room. Oh! Idea.

Pit suddenly scrabbled past them all, and Felix felt a curious echo in his gut.

"What the shit is that?" Archie all but screamed, shoving a glowing hand toward Pit.

Felix grasped his arm, lifting it up. "That is my friend. Don't harm him."

"That—that isn't a friend," the Gnome hissed, unable to take his eyes off the Chimera. "That's a nightmare."

"What?" Pit asked, looking down at himself. He resembled nothing so much as a dog crossed with a cursed insect. He'd used Sovereign of Flesh to fashion strange, temporary limbs that looked an awful lot like Felix's scaled arms. "This is faster, and I'm still small. Win, win."

"It can talk?!"

Claw members peeked out of their rooms, eyes widening at the procession. A few saluted as Felix passed, but most were watching the Gnome, and their Spirits soared with confusion, alarm, and, eventually, triumph.

"Enough. Into my rooms, everyone."

Felix ushered them across the fourth floor and into the wide door to his suite. He breathed easier once it clicked shut behind him. He looked to Pit, who had returned to his normal Dire Hound form.

What was that? I thought you couldn't use my Sovereign of Flesh well?

Been practicing. Pit let out a little whine, his golden eyes half-closing. *Hurts, though. Can't shake the wounds, even with your Skill.*

That soured the excitement Felix felt, but only a bit. *Well it's good news, anyway. You—Did you use my stockpile of Essence?*

Pit just gave him a wide, doggy grin.

"Are you going to introduce us to your new friend?" Vess asked.

Felix wiped the frown from his face and focused on everyone else in the room. Archie was standing only a few feet from him, trapped between the door and an array of strangers. Aside from Pit, Evie, and Beef, who had spread to either side, Harn, Vess, and Laur had stepped away from a low table near the fireplace. Vess was still wearing only her gambeson, but her fingers twitched uneasily, and Harn's scowl was loud enough to wake the dead. Laur, on the other hand, looked elated.

"Everyone, this is Archie. Archie, everyone."

The Gnome gave a small, humorless grin. "Lotta people in here."

"Big rooms," Evie quipped.

"Is he—?"

"He is, Laur," Felix answered quickly. "Archie is the Unbound we've been looking for."

Harn grunted. "That was stone simple. You trip over him on your walk?"

"Is that a jab at my height, ugly?" Archie shot back. "Or—no. Face that busted up means you're real familiar with tripping, I'd guess."

"Hah," Harn barked. "If you're going for a dig, best bring a shovel, kid. Or else I'll bury ya."

The Gnome snorted, letting the comment slide. "So you're the heroes set against the mighty Hierocracy?"

"I never called us heroes," Felix said. "Just people trying to do the right thing."

"And that means fight the big bad fascist theocracy?"

"Yeah. It does."

Archie scoffed. "Right. Well, anyone willing to shield me from the Titan is worth giving a chance."

"A chance?" Vess asked. "Felix?"

"We've talked. Archie is interested in hearing us out before he makes any large, life-altering decisions."

"That is…fair." She regarded the Unbound with her gold-flecked eyes. "What do you need to know?"

Felix stood a bit apart from the group as Archie spoke with each of them in turn, learning more about Nagast with every question. The night had still been young when they'd arrived, but now it stretched closer and closer to midnight. The Gnome was sitting close to Evie and Vess, with Laur practically hovering over him. If that made Archie uncomfortable, Felix couldn't tell, but what was clear was his nervousness around Pit. The guy kept his distance from the russet-furred pup, his goggled-eyes twitching toward Pit every few minutes. Pit thought it was funny.

Next to Felix, Harn stood and regarded their new arrival, his eyes hooded and a finger to his lips. "I don't like him."

"I gathered as much. Why?"

Harn grunted, letting his hand drop to his side. "He's shifty. Nervous."

"I'd be, too, with what he's been through."

"It's more than that. He's workin' an angle."

Felix frowned. "What angle? He either comes with us, or he doesn't. That's pretty cut and dry."

"To you, maybe. But I've seen folks like him before. He's cornered, and he knows it." Harn picked up a drumstick of some monstrous bird, long gone cold, and bit into it. "He's eyed the windows and door sixteen times in the last quarter glass."

Huh. Felix wasn't exactly ready to trust the Gnome with his life, but he'd felt the man was fairly straightforward. Cautious, certainly, but that was reasonable. On top of that, the Gnome's Spirit had remained steady all evening, with only the faintest of notes to indicate curiosity, annoyance, and amusement. He seemed more or less at ease.

Across the room, Laur leaned over the Gnome, his wide Elven eyes intense. "You are remarkably in tune with the song around you, Archibald. Are you using a Skill right now?"

"...No."

"Fascinating."

<<He is lying,>> Vess signed to Felix.

Felix narrowed his eyes. Archie, however, continued to speak. "I noticed your map, there. You all got plans for Birchstone?"

A map of the city was laid out on one of the low tables, and impromptu wooden markers—chipped off pieces of firewood—were set around it.

"Just plottin' out a nice stroll," Evie said.

"Planning on walking into the mountain?" The Gnome picked up one of the wood chips, which was situated at the apex of the city. "Sad to say, they've gotten real tight on security there. Won't let just anybody in. Though…you're a king, right?"

"Territorial Lord," Felix corrected.

Archie waved his hand dismissively. "Sure, that. Gotta believe the Highbloods wouldn't wanna turn you away."

"Could be."

"They'd be dumb if they didn't. Felix is like, mega important," Beef added. "We might be strong, but he's doing straight-up endgame content."

Archie gave the Minotaur a tight smile, and Felix could practically see the gears turning behind his eyes. "Endgame, huh? So you're after something in the Clan Hold?"

Beef opened his mouth to answer, but Felix cut him off. "That's not important right now."

"Sounds important to me. And, considering the protection you're promising me, I think that means I should at least have an inkling. Right?"

"It's unrelated to you or the woman hunting you," Felix insisted, firmly. He was fine with Archie asking questions, but until he joined up with them, Felix wasn't in a hurry to share everything.

Archie raised his hands, reading the mood. "Answer me this, at least: how'd you find me? I put a lot of effort in staying out of sight. Maybe that'll answer how that enormous bitch keeps tracking me down, too."

"We're connected," Felix said.

Archie raised an eyebrow. "Like…our horoscopes? Sorry, but I don't believe in that shit."

"Believe or not, there are things here that don't have much in the way of Earthly explanations. I found your general location through our connection. If Imara is as capable as I believe, she might have a similar ability."

"Wonderful," Archie said, dryly. "I spent a fistful of crowns on enchantments to keep me hidden. Glad to know I wasted my money."

"I wouldn't say that," Felix said, new details slotting into his understanding. "Our connection is fuzzy and dim, like a bad phone call. So they're doing something."

"That's…comforting, I suppose. But that means the Titan could find me at any moment, right?"

"I doubt it, or else she would have already," Vess said.

"Hasn't she burned down like a grip of towns? She ain't subtle."

"As subtle as a hurricane," Archie agreed, somewhat grimly. "So, she'll find me, sooner or later. Cart me off to the Hierophant and whatever bullshit they want."

"Not if I can help it," Felix said, stepping closer. Archie flinched ever so slightly, eyes turning toward the fireplace. "We're fighting against the Hierophant and all of her plans. That's what we've been doing for months."

Beef puffed up his chest. "We save people."

Felix nodded. "If you agree, we'll bring you with us."

"To Nagast. This magical safe haven." Archie's eyes widened, and he snapped his fingers. "That's where I know your name. You claimed a Territory."

"That's me, yeah."

"How safe is this Territory?" the Gnome asked.

"Safest place around," Evie confirmed. "Hierophant is pissing her robes thinkin' about attacking us again."

"An exaggeration, but not without merit," Vess said. "The protections of Nagast are many, not the least of which is a powerful and growing army."

"And some sorta Unbound powerhouse, eh?" Archie said, eyeing Felix.

"Two," Beef said, chest still puffed out.

The Gnome looked at the Minotaur. "Huh. You…?"

Beef flexed, his shoulders and biceps bigger than Felix's head. "Oh yeah."

"Shit. I knew I shoulda picked a brawnier Race. Instead, I got this," Archie said, holding his arms out as if to display his small form.

Harn grunted. "What's wrong with bein' a Gnome? Smart, clever with magic, and fast, too. Coulda gotten a lot worse."

Archie frowned. "I'm not a Gnome."

CHAPTER SEVENTY-SEVEN

"Huh." Felix said. "Do you mind if I–?"

"Analyze? Sure."

Voracious Eye.

Name: Archibald Ross
Race: Delven
Level: 72
HP: 4482/4482
SP: 3347/3347
MP: 3266/6533
Lore: A Lost Race, the Delven were early ancestors of the modern Gnome. They are a slim people, with prominent noses and an easy mastery over elemental magics, specifically earth, life, and water. Little else is known.
Strength: More Data Required
Weakness: More Data Required

The man was well into his Journeyman Tier, and his Aspects felt fairly potent, skewed toward speed and strength rather than durability. Felix got the immediate impression that the man was something like a glass cannon—lots of offense, little defense.

Archie shivered. "Christ, that's strong. How leveled-up is your Skill?"

"You're Delven," Felix said, not answering the question. "Another Lost Race."

"Dunno what that means, but yeah, that's what it says. I tried looking them up in a library once, but I couldn't find a single mention of it."

"A Lost Race is one that was eradicated by the Ruin at some point," Vess explained.

"Ruin?" Archie's face screwed up. "Is this a magic thing?"

"A long story, but we'll get into that soon," Felix promised. "Laur? What do you know about the Delven?"

Laur lowered his hand from his mouth. His sharp ears were almost quivering in excitement. "The Deepsingers once maintained an empire of their own, far below the earth. Little is known of them, as they were Lost before the Golden Empire began. In the First Age."

"That old, huh?" Archie said. "I'm a fossil."

"So you picked this Race? You didn't—have any issues with that?" Felix asked.

Archie scrunched up his nose. "Issues? No. But I don't know anything about this game shit, and that list was stupidly long. So I picked the one that seemed the most useful. I didn't know I'd be forced into a child's body for the rest of my life, though. That part sucks."

Felix nodded slowly. He could understand that. "Most useful?"

Archie shrugged, his eyes hidden behind the dark surface of his goggles. "Level-up perks are nice. Got some good senses, too; it's why I can wear these without any issues. Don't even need to look at stuff, technically. Called Blindsense, and it's based on vibrations."

"That *is* useful," Beef said. "Lotsa monsters in SwordLore had blindsense, and they were a bitch to fight."

"SwordLore. Isn't that a kid's game?"

"No. It's rated T for teen. That's not kids."

"...how old are you?"

Beef clammed up there. "Old enough."

"Oh Jesus. Can you even drive?"

"Never really liked racing games."

Archie groaned. "Please. Felix. Tell me you're old enough to drink."

Felix fought back a smile. "I was, years ago. Don't be fooled by Beef's age. He's smart, strong, and brave."

"Yeah," Beef echoed. Felix didn't miss the kid's blush of embarrassment, though.

Before he could course correct, however, the door to his room clicked open. Tzfell stepped in. She smiled as she saw Felix. "Ah, you've returned, Lord Autarch. That is good. I've news on the Hinterlord, his treasury, and more importantly…"

She gestured behind her, and an old man in a nondescript woolen cloak entered. His face was heavily wrinkled, but his eyes were sharp and clear. A hint of white and gold could be seen at his sagging throat, but little else. The door closed behind them.

"I wish to introduce you to an important contact here in the city," the Chanter said.

"My Lord," the old man croaked out. His voice was rough, not deep but wounded, as if he were gargling gravel.

"Hi," Felix said, bemused. "Who's this, Tzfell?"

"Bastard!"

Felix whipped his attention back to Archie. He stood like a cornered animal, a single arm outstretched, Mana glowing off the dagger he'd produced from somewhere.

Evie slapped her hand to an empty spot on her bandolier. "Hey, that's mine!"

"Archie. What's going on?" Felix asked, slow and steady.

"You tell me!" the man yelled. His Spirit was in a disarray. "What is this? Why is *he* here?"

Felix glanced between the old man and the Unbound. "Dude, calm down. I don't even know who he is."

"He's the douchebag that brought the Titan here!"

In the silence that followed, there was only the crackle of the fire for a long, strained moment.

"Felix." Vess broke the silence by manifesting a Spear into her hands. She pointed it at the priest. "It has been a long time, but I know him. Archie is correct. He is a pawn of the Hierophant."

Felix turned his gaze onto the Dwarven Chanter and her guest. "Is this true?"

The old man pushed back his hood, revealing white, thinning hair. Around his throat and shoulders was a white jacket or robe, elaborately embroidered with thread of gold. "I cannot lie. There is truth to what all have said, my Lord."

Felix pulsed his Voracious Eye, placing the man at the upper reaches of Master Tier. "Kellis Faer," he read off. "Hierei of Calumb, Pax'Vrell, and Sao'thun. What the hell are you doing here?"

"And what the hell is a Hierei?" Beef asked in a low rumble.

"It's a big boy priest," Evie hissed. "Hush."

"Kellis is our contact, my Lord," Tzfell said. "He is a Chanter himself."

"Impossible. Hierei Faer has been the Pathless' high priest over our Territory for longer than my grandfather has been alive. I was slow to recognize him, but I am certain of that fact." Vess tightened her grip on her Spear. "How could he be both a Chanter and Hierei? The Hierophant would slaughter him on sight."

"I have worked very hard in that regard," the old man said, and the words all but dripped with exhaustion.

"Kellis has been undercover almost his entire life," Tzfell added. "When we were chosen for this mission, Mauvim told me of him and his history. He is the reason why we even knew the Corrupted had yet to find Archibald, here."

"She did not tell *me*," Laur protested. "Which means it is a grave secret. What has changed?"

"Imara," the old priest said. The name alone sent a shiver through Archie. "She is unhinged, and I cannot predict what she might do next. I sent a missive to Mauvim under ward, in the hopes that we could salvage this situation." He bowed, his Spirit unfurling like a soft arrangement of woodwinds. It sounded of gratitude and no small amount of fear.

Not fear of him, which was a surprise. It was directed elsewhere. Outward.

He's afraid of Imara. With every bone in his body. A thrill of nervousness shot through Felix's limbs.

"I visited with him in the hopes that he could provide greater information on our task," Tzfell explained. "He also—"

"Okay, wait," Felix put his hand up, black scales catching the firelight. He recognized the man now, too, from his earliest visions of Imara. He was the one pleading with her to restrain herself. "You have inside men with the freaking Hierophant?"

"Too few, but yes," Laur said.

Tzfell sighed but nodded. "In fact, Kellis was the one to tell us about the Unbound summoning ritual. The reason we could react at all."

Felix's Mind whirled, putting new pieces into place. "Okay. Okay, then. Why does—"

"No no, enough talking. Why should I stay here if *this* guy is your ally?" Archie asked suddenly. The guy had maneuvered himself until he was practically standing in the giant Dwarven fireplace. "He sicced his rabid dog on me! He's the reason I'm—he sucks! Clearly!"

"Imara was only ever instructed to capture you. The plan was to secret you away in transit…but the bonds upon Imara's being are too tight. Too…all-encompassing." The priest bowed, this time to Archie. "I humbly apologize, Unbound. None of this should have happened."

"No. Don't care. You sent that bitch after me. I'm done here."

"You go out there, and Imara will find you," Felix insisted. "It's just a matter of time. Come with us. We can figure this out."

Archie scoffed and tucked his stolen dagger into his belt. "Wars. Politics. I'm not getting involved in any of that, man. You can have this Continent and all these nutjobs doing wetwork for gods. I only wanna go home."

"To Earth?" Beef asked, incredulous.

"That…might be possible," Felix said slowly. "It's something we're looking into."

"I don't need your help. I got one last job here, then I'm done. I'm out."

Beef snorted, folding his thick arms. "Oh yeah? How're you gonna do that?"

"You bigwigs aren't the only ones with smarts. I found records of a ritual that was sealed away by the Hinterlords a long-ass time ago. Read about it at some lordling's ball, when I was…information gathering for some friends."

"A ritual to do what?" Tzfell asked, suspicious.

Archie ignored her. "I know it's real. I got diagrams, but they're patchy. Incomplete. I need the real thing, and that's stored away. Hidden in the Undermount. In the damn Vault of Nine Kings, if you can believe it." He scowled at the priest. "And ever since *someone* showed up, they're on lockdown. But I can manage that. All I need is *time*."

"A ritual to do what?" Tzfell repeated, her voice tight.

Archie put his hands on his hips. "We got summoned, right? Well, we can get banished, too."

Stunned silence filled the room like too much water in a cup. Felix's Mind raced, piecing together details and possibilities.

"Felix," Beef said, breathlessly. "We could go home."

A deep tremor shook the room, raining dust from the rafters and shattering the silence with groaning stone and timber. In the distance, big brassy gongs and rapid drums began to sound.

Alarms.

"Something is at the gate," Tzfell said. Tattoos squirmed across her temples.

Without warning, the glass in the windows *shattered.* Felix threw himself over Vess and Pit, Storm Shaping a violent gust to blast the shards back outward. Beef had done the same for the Chanters and Evie, erecting chitinous barriers.

Archie climbed back to his feet, left arm bloody. "What the hell?"

Harn stepped to the empty sills, axes already aflame and stared into the night. He grunted. "Time's up."

A voice ripped across the night, each syllable shaking floors and splintering walls.

"TREACHEROUS GNOME!"

CHAPTER SEVENTY-EIGHT

"No no no no." Archie was pressed up against the fireplace, its carved beard pressing hard into his spine.

"Archie, it's gonna be fine."

"No it's not. You haven't seen her, man." The Gnome—Delven—was taking large, gulping breaths. "She's unstoppable. She's like—like death walking."

"Kid."

Felix looked away from Archie to where Harn was standing by the window. Garish orange painted his dented armor in blooms of light. Harn jerked his chin toward something in the distance.

"Siva's Grace," Vess cursed with a sharp gasp. "The walls are aflame."

Felix moved swiftly to another window and pulled away the now-tattered curtains. There, just around the edge of the inn, he could see the city gates, and they burned like a giant's bonfire. Flames bigger than houses roared into the night, belching dark smoke and enough sparks to contend with the snow that still swirled down. He didn't have direct line of sight on the entry point—too many buildings blocked the way—but his Perception picked up the familiar clash of metal, flesh, and panicked shouting.

"Damn it." Felix spun toward the door.

"What're you doing?" Archie demanded.

"If Imara is in the city already, the Watch is going to get killed. I'm not letting that happen."

"Don't be a hero! She'll kill you! A whole army tried stopping her, and they could barely slow her down!"

Felix smiled and put a hand to Archie's shoulder. "Just stay here. My company will keep you safe." He straightened up, a plan forming. "Pit. Vess. Beef. You're with me. Evie, Tzfell, and Laur, stay with the Claw and listen to the commander. I'll need you all on high alert. Harn, if you see her coming this way—"

"We'll run," the man finished for Felix. "Ain't stupid enough to let pride kill me. I'll keep 'em safe, kid."

"Thank you." Felix spun on his heel and threw open the door, his friends close on his heels.

The streets were full of chaos. Gone was the idle bustle, and in its place were screaming throngs of men, women, and children. Panic gripped them all, spreading fires pushing some to stampede down narrow alleys while others were frozen in place by the titanic sounds of battle…and an incredible amount of spiritual pressure.

Felix and his friends ran across the rooftops, easily managing the gaps between wide thoroughfares as easy as narrow side streets. As he moved, he seized every fire he spotted with Cardinal Flame, smothering them all without mercy. Vess sent spears of silver flashing outward, pinning through rock and timber before structures could collapse on fleeing innocents, while Beef's conjured walls of chitin diverted them away from the worst of it ahead.

"So many people are hurt," Beef shouted from atop his Multipede. Hallow's Homunculus form was wrapped around his chest and the Sharpwing Matriarch flew just above them. "Should we—?"

"We need to stop the Unbound first," Felix insisted.

Pit had long ago changed back into his tenku form, his lithe body bounding from roof to roof with ease. "I see something!" he shouted.

Five streets down, Felix saw it, too. The gate into the city was still burning, and in the wide cobblestone square before it, Dwarves in dark armor fought against monstrosities.

"Are those Trolls on fire?" Beef asked.

"Look how they are grouped, how they run…They are fleeing something," Vess said.

"My bet is on Imara." Felix flashed his Voracious Eye, confirming his suspicions. "Sun Trolls. The fire isn't doing anything to them except making them more angry. Everyone, stop."

They landed atop a third story terrace at the edge of the fighting, and Felix drew deep on his Mana. Two Skills sounded within him, accessed with his Affinity and shaped by his Intent. He wanted to use Chanter techniques for this one. Acidic Mana streamed from his palms and mouth, swirling and congealing in the air above the battle, until a cloud of virulent green formed. It flashed once before letting loose a deluge of acid rain.

Rain of Cataclysm!

Hand of Calamity!

He shaped the falling rain, directing the liquid destruction directly upon the Sun Trolls. They screamed as it ate into them, extinguishing the flames in their fur but eating into numerous wounds just below.

"Unleash!" Felix commanded.

Golden crescents, silver Spears, and crystalline daggers inundated the Trolls. Ichor gouted into the air as limbs were severed and bodies impaled or straight up blown apart. Beef went so far as to land among them, smashing Bedlam into the earth. The ground trembled, casting several Trolls to their knees just as Hallow's Multipede smashed into their ranks.

In seconds, the Trolls were obliterated.

The Ironclads and the Watch fell back, their warriors exhausted and bewildered by the turn of events. Felix and friends landed among them, quickly catching the gaze of a familiar captain.

"Mr. Veil?" Doric shouted, pushing past his men.

"Here to help, Captain. As promised."

"Aye, sir. I can see that." The captain huffed a laugh. "I hadn't expected—"

The alarm gong rang once again. Someone was beating it rapidly, almost chaotically, as a sharp whistling sound filled the air. Felix jerked back, and Beef shouted.

"Down!"

The watchtower exploded as a ball of liquid sunlight hit it from beyond the wall. Stone, shingle, and Dwarves were evaporated, leaving nothing but a melted hole in its place. The alarm had been silenced forever.

Doric swallowed. "I hope the rest of your men are on the way."

The gate finally succumbed to the flames that ate at it, falling in an avalanche of charred wood and melted stone. Through that hellscape walked a figure, her armor cherry red where it splashed carelessly through molten stone. The armor itself was spiked and bladed, bristling with weapons at hip, chest, back, arm, and legs. She was…huge. Taller than Felix or Beef by several feet, she was built like a mini giant of steel.

Whoa, Pit sent.

Felix silently agreed. Imara had a greatsword slung casually over her shoulder, held in a single enormous gauntlet. The blade rivaled Darius' barn-door-sized sword for width and had to have been at least eight feet long. He couldn't see her face—it was covered by a full helm that only had a slot for her eyes—but her attention wasn't even fixed on them. Felix could sense it in the air, an Intent so focused it was all but palpable. An insane pressure followed her, doubling the feeling that blanketed this section of Birchstone. It shoved at all of them like a mountain had climbed onto their backs. The Watch and Ironclads fell to their hands and knees, while Felix and his friends grunted with strain.

"No wonder they call her Titan," Vess grunted through her teeth.

Voracious Eye!

As happened infrequently when he Analyzed stronger beings, there was resistance to his Skill. This was…more than he'd ever experienced before. It lashed out, as if alive, attempting to dig claws into his Mind, but Felix shoved it right back. A deep, sonorous howl tore through him, something he knew he could only sense in his Mind—and the world burst into gold. A flash of light and concussive force blasted at him, exploding like a tiny bomb in his face.

Felix jerked back, pain surging across his Body as his Mind reeled.

Name: L032 ERROR_FOUND
Race: Gigas
—ERROR!

Voracious Eye is level 95!

No name. Just a Race. Gigas. Everything else was beyond him and his Skill, even a true estimate of her advancement. He had only grasped the edges of it, but she was clearly beyond any Grandmaster he'd faced.

Felix threw a handsign for his people but shouted for everyone's benefit. "She's too strong, everyone back up! Ranged support only!"

Vess, Beef, and Pit gave him firm nods before retreating. The Watch ignored him altogether, clumped around their lieutenant. The Ironclads, however, looked to their captain.

Doric was breathing heavy, the incredible spiritual pressure weighing on him. He was having a hard time standing. "You're staying? To fight her alone?"

"Yeah." Felix didn't take his eyes off the Titan. She had stopped advancing and was waiting with her sword held in a low guard. "I have to."

Doric nodded. "Men! Pull back! Ranged attacks only!"

"Aye sir!"

The Ironclad pulled back as orderly as they could, though some struggled to stand at all. After a dozen paces, they moved more freely. Felix noticed that the captain, however, refused to back away.

"Doric—" Felix started.

"We bring the fight to her, yeah?"

Felix met the captain's eye. The guy wasn't going to back down. "She's a Grandmaster," he said. "Maybe stronger."

"I don't see you running, Mr. Veil."

Felix gritted his teeth. "I—"

"Fire!" the Watch Lieutenant shouted, and his men unveiled a ballista that they'd rolled out of somewhere. A massive, spear-sized bolt screamed through the air, so fast it left a trail of silver metal Mana gleaming behind it. It took the Titan directly in the chest.

"Charge!" The Watch Lieutenant screamed, and his people ran. Their armor must have boosted their speed, because they moved faster than Felix expected. Pikes, halberds, and spears converged on the enemy, all of them wielded with a fury so strong it stained the air with its song.

They didn't even reach her.

Felix's Perception strained to keep up, but he saw it all. That greatsword shone gold as Imara met the first ranks with a horizontal sweep, decapitating all of them. Then, ignoring the ballista bolt embedding into her armor, she thrust her sword up into the air, which sent golden yellow rockets of light and heat outward. They shot out in perfect, straight lines that ripped through their armor and chests, leaving only gaping holes behind.

To everyone else, the Watch fell as one. Dead.

"Go," Felix insisted. A frigid chill tore up his spine as he considered Imara's power. "I've got this, man."

The captain's jaw clenched so hard Felix was afraid the guy would bust a tooth. "Fine," he said, backing up. "We'll support from the back. Archers! On my command!"

Behind them, the Ironclads hadn't been idle. Each and every one of them bore monstrously heavy-looking crossbows, each one almost as big as a single Dwarf. They lined up their shots, arrows gleaming with swirling magic.

The Titan advanced, stepping carelessly on the corpses of the Watch. She crushed them to paste beneath her armored boots.

"Now!"

A cascade of light fell onto Imara, each one bearing a heavy steel quarrel behind its magic. The few remaining Watch members even managed to shoot another ballista bolt. All of them hit, each erupting into binding vines, clinging frost, dark jaws of shadow, or sharpened spears of metal. The Titan's form was obscured by the chaos of so much Mana, but it was clear she lurched to a stop.

Doric lifted his hand. "Archers! Reload!"

Without warning, the Titan moved.

Holy shit, she's fast.

Felix barely had time to act before she was on top of him, her sword swinging around him at the Dwarven captain. Her incredible reach plus the six-foot blade made it easy…but Felix wouldn't. He shoved his palm upward, smashing into Imara's elbow and forcing her blow askew. It tore through the air, whistling and sizzling with magic, but missed Doric entirely.

"No," he growled, and his eyes surged with crackling light. "Your fight's with me."

CHAPTER SEVENTY-NINE

"The Fiend."

For the first time, Felix felt something from the enormous woman. It stuck to him, a cloying heat between green summer shadows. Curiosity.

"You know me?" he asked.

"The Pathless does. And through Him, all things are known." Imara brought her greatsword back around, still glowing with an intense amount of Mana. "Stand aside, Fiend. I am not here for you."

"No, you're here for Archie." Felix let black scales ripple up across his chest and shoulders, stretching up his neck and jaw. "But that's not happening."

"The Gnome."

The woman's words hummed in the night, buzzing uncomfortable against Felix's teeth. There was a weight to them, as if her words were solid and—something else. A familiar, sharp-toothed growl. A hunger.

"Why do you want him? No," Felix corrected himself. "There's something in you that—Why do you *need* him?"

The eleven-foot-tall warrior stared down at him impassively. "Because I am commanded to."

"By who? The Hierophant? You don't have to listen to her—"

"By the Trackless One Himself," she all but shouted. "I am the Chosen of the Pathless, Fiend. A Title that holds a far greater Authority than the King of Nagast."

Felix grimaced as something beyond her Spirit pressed down on him. The vibrations of the world around him—normally ever-present—stilled for a single, terrifying moment. He ground his teeth so hard he felt one snap…but the silence faded. The world resumed.

"You." He took a deep breath, as if assuring himself that his lungs still worked. "That wasn't you. You're from Earth, right? Just like me."

"I am nothing," she stated. "And you are in my way."

The barest shift of her hips was all the warning Felix received before a glowing greatsword slashed down at him. He dodged it, but only just—his jacket sleeve and a fair bit of flesh and blood were severed from his shoulder. All of it burnt up before it ever touched the ground, even his scales.

Dodge is level 84!
Relentless Resolution is level 96!

Felix unsheathed his Inheritor's Will, deflecting the upward swing of her next strike, but it was so hard it split open his wounded shoulder. Imara didn't stop however, flowing seamlessly into another swing. He flared Sovereign of Flesh, letting scales climb back over the healing wound, and met her next attack head on. The ground beneath them splintered, cobblestones tossed away from them in a maelstrom of wind.

Back!

Flaring his Relentless Resolution, Felix disengaged with the enormous warrior just as she was bombarded. A claw made of a dozen chitinous legs wrapped around Imara's form as spears of ice and Spears of silver metal slammed into her, both of them exploding into electrical tempests before golden crescents and bronze discs followed.

Imara roared, and a corona of golden light engulfed her for the briefest of instants. All of the attacks vanished, flash fried into nothing. She surged forward, trailing golden vapor away from Felix and toward the Ironclads and his friends beyond.

Toward the inn.

She can sense Archie, somehow! Keep her off-balance!

We're trying! Pit sent back just before a volley of Tempest Fugit spears hit her. She shattered them with a casual backhand, ignoring the lightning that chained across her armor. *Help!*

Felix rushed the woman, summoning ice and water to match the sizzling light and heat that hovered around her like a cloak.

Rime Shaping is level 91!

Storm Shaping is level 42!

Steam bloomed where his magic met hers. Imara pulled back, her vision obscured. “You cannot harm me with this!”

Felix kicked the back of her knees.

Imara fell, toppling like a redwood before slamming her enormous gauntlets to the cobbles. Cracks spread in concentric circles from her hands and knees, sending stone chips flying. Felix’s next kick caught her in the gut, and it sent her spinning to the side.

“Fuck!” he cursed. His silver boot and greave was crushed and mangled against his foot and shin, and dark blood oozed from one of the rents. He ripped both boots off, flexing his clawed feet against the cold street. “You’re sturdy.”

Imara stood up, hand to her gut. When she removed it, there was a sizeable indent in her armor…for all of five seconds. Mana mobilized within the metal, and it popped back into its original shape.

Damn. He looked down at his shoulder, where his Garment had already repaired his torn jacket. *That’s unfair.*

“Our greatest trial approaches.” Her eyes blazed gold, and that corona reappeared, a gilded disc behind her head and shoulders. “I am the rock upon which the Continent will depend.”

“Uh-huh.” Felix hefted his blade. “Kinda full of yourself, too.”

Without another word, she charged.

Dodge is level 85!
Wild Threnody is level 89!

He dove over her horizontal slash and brought his hooked blade up to parry her quick reversal. Acid Mana surged through the sword, combating the golden heat of her own before both weapons shrieked. Felix and Imara staggered back, both wincing, but Felix recovered first. He thrust, catching the woman across her inner thigh and drawing a cascade of sparks…and blood.

Imara shrieked, but it wasn’t in pain. If before her words had weight, then her scream was an avalanche. Her Spirit bashed into him, and light coursed outward like a living sun.

Felix’s clothes caught fire, his movements slowed, but he struck again. And again. Six times in rapid succession. Imara met him at every one, deflecting his attacks with more technique than he had ever managed. On the seventh, she caught him square in the chest, smashing him down and back. For the first time in a while, Felix was thrown bodily by an opponent's blows, and he cratered the ground when he landed.

Armored Skin is level 94!

"The Trackless One told me to be wary of you, Fiend. But you cannot even stand before the Light."

A deluge of arrows, ballista bolts, spears, and chitinous conjurings slammed into the Titan, but she moved through them all as if wading through a fierce but impotent storm. She advanced on Felix, her steps shaking the earth. Her eyes shone, and it was all Felix could perceive of her face beneath that full helm. They were like hollow tunnels into the heart of the sun.

"I'll admit," Felix groaned, spitting out a wad of blood. His chest was torn and broken, and something had cracked in his back. Things were stitching up, but it wasn't fast enough. "You're really strong. But you're not all there, are you?"

The woman didn't answer, just stepped slowly forward under the barrage, until she came up to the edge of Felix's dip in the road. He was having trouble making his legs work right.

"I can hear it," he grunted. "Or rather, I can't. Your Spirit is empty."

Imara lifted her greatsword like an executioner's blade, and that golden disc behind her flared. "I am filled with His Light. It is all that is needed."

"What about situational awareness?" he asked, looking behind her.

The Titan hesitated, casting her Perception backward, for no more than a half second—but that was an eternity in battle. Time enough for Felix to shove his wobbly legs beneath him and lunge.

Sovereign of Flesh!

Wild Threnody!

Shadow Whip!

With Shadow Whip channeled through Wild Threnody, Mana flooded through his palms without shape or form but with an intensity unmatched by the original Skill. The darkness briefly smothered the light as Felix flared his Will and Intent, matching Imara's, before his entire arm grew three times its normal size. He slammed his fist directly into her wrist. Something crunched, and the Titan lost grip on her greatsword.

His second fist came down, crashing into her shoulders, almost buckling the woman's knees—but the light burned through the dark.

Imara hissed, and golden vapor poured from her mouth and nose.

She charged, and Felix met her, blow for blow. A ripple of air tore outward from their impact, crashing into a guardhouse and toppling a tavern that had been weakened by fire. The cobblestones sundered, cratering beneath their feet before exploding into shrapnel little bigger than pebbles.

Stone Shaping!

Rime Shaping!

Green Shaping!

Cardinal Flame!

The floating shrapnel stopped, seized by Felix's Will to flow in a flash around Imara's limbs. His other shaping Skills congealed together, forming a matrix of familiar elements that others called Fiendstone. Blue rock, veined with red-gold, solidified across Imara's legs, hips, and arms, holding her perfectly immobile.

"Stop breaking things!" he shouted. "And stay still."

Felix couldn't make out the woman's features beneath her full helmet, but he could see some of her heavy brows and dark eyes.

"No." She flexed, her metal armor groaning.

"Stop. That stuff is hard as hell. You can't—"

Imara didn't listen. Didn't stop. The Fiendstone didn't crack.

It shattered.

Light followed, blindingly bright, and Imara was on its heels. She swung for him, and he barely dodged away, a dance through scintillating gold that stirred the air into a cyclone peppered with shards of cobblestone. Felix could see nothing, but that didn't stop him.

Blind Fighting is level 79!

...

Blind Fighting is level 85!

Dodge is level 86!

...

Dodge is level 91!

Relentless Resolution is level 97!

Fast as he was, however, the Titan carved him up. His scales provided little protection against her might and magic, and his dark blood burned.

Sovereign of Flesh is level 96!
Armored Skin is level 95!

Wounds healed and scales reformed, but Felix's store of Essence was vanishing fast…and Imara looked unflagging and indestructible. A lie, he reasoned, but Felix was increasingly certain a fair fight between the two of them could take hours—but the city wouldn't.

Inheritor's Will leaped to hand, deflecting the woman's potent haymaker and dragging it down. She pulled forward, her other arm already moving, but Felix didn't waste time. He punched with his left hand, and this time caught her full on in the face.

Imara's head rocked back, but her body was unphased. Her metal-plated arms wrapped around him, turning his attack into a dire grapple. Felix kicked out, clawed feet scoring sparks against her abdomen and thighs, but it did nothing to hamper her incredible Strength.

"You are not required, Fiend," she stated, deadpan as a corpse.

She squeezed, pulling Felix so close he could smell breath behind her dented helm. It was honeysuckle. The dents in her helmet swelled and popped, restoring itself. Felix, by contrast, was being broken down. Skin ripped and muscle tore as she squeezed. He fought back, but she was impossibly strong.

"L-look out," he groaned around the sound of his bones creaking.

"I will not fall for your petty tricks again—"

Pit hit her like a speeding semi, Blade of the Fang held within his beak. It slammed into her lower back, yet the Titan didn't budge an inch, and the Fang didn't even dent her armor…until Felix pressed his foot against the bone-white blade. He hurled Essence down his channels and into the Fang, which glowed with sudden, brilliant sigils.

"Get fucked."

Pit wrenched the Fang aside, and it cut through armor and flesh like paper.

CHAPTER EIGHTY

Imara screamed.

There was a savage pain in the noise. A rage. The Fang had bit deep enough that her spine should have been severed—but instead of blood and viscera, there was a corruscation of golden radiance. Sparks spat from the wound, and Felix had only a moment to marvel at it before Pit and the Fang were blasted away by an eruption of light.

Pit!

Still clutching Felix tightly, the Titan spun toward the Chimera but was immediately bombarded by brutal projectiles. Spears and discs and arrows honed in on her injury, most unable to breach the searing light or her incomparable armor.

All of it a distraction.

"Lights out!" Felix growled.

Wild Threnody!

Shadow Whip!

He grabbed her head. His hands crackled, black scales turned to pure midnight as suffocating shadow inundated them, snuffing out a portion of her power. Imara howled, that empty Spirit filled with pain for the very first time, and she tried to throw Felix away.

"No you don't!" Beef cried from far away.

Chitinous legs seized her arms, stopping her for a brief moment before a savage twist splintered them. Snapped them. Beef screamed in pain.

Imara flared her power, and light burst through Felix's shroud of darkness. A beam of incandescent fury shrieked from her eyes, blasting Felix full in the chest and face from inches away.

Auroral Forge!

Face burned and hair aflame, Felix seized the Titan's attack with his Skill and Willpower. It split, curving around his head to drill into the street twenty feet away.

Auroral Forge is level 85!

...

Auroral Forge is level 90!

Holding onto the Skill was difficult, though not due to pain. Agony was an old friend. Instead, it was the sheer volume of Imara's power. Handling it was like grasping a wet bar of soap—slick and unsteady. The light fought against him as if alive.

Felix held on, skin flaking off his grimacing cheeks as they slowly healed. "Stop! You're fighting for the wrong side!"

"No!" The word arrived like a gunshot. Her Spirit was unsteady, still filled with a chorus of rage and pain. "There is only the Light!"

A third beam shot out of Imara's mouth. Felix frantically bent it away, shaping it into the sky. Clouds of steam pooled around them, heat against winter's chill, until it was like they were struggling within a dream.

Felix!

Pit careened into the steam clouds, a storm wreathing his ice-armored form. His huge, dark ice jaws came for the Titan, but Imara kicked out and shattered his armor with a single blow. Pit yelped and spun off into the mist.

"Pit!" Felix shoved his claws against Imara's chest and felt her arms slip…but his attention split from Auroral Forge. Light hit him, cutting burning swaths through his chest and shoulder.

Damn it! He refocused on the Skill, diverting it again.

Imara only crushed him harder. Her immense Strength was only held back by Felix's incredible Endurance and Vitality.

"Imara! You have to let go!"

"You will die here, Fiend," she said.

"No I won't," he said. "Now, wake up!"

Felix hurled all of his Affinity and Intent at the swirling pattern within him, urging it to blaze. "Unite the Lo—!"

The light he'd held at bay rippled, and Something Else pushed through the Titan. Felix's tentative control over her eyebeams was cast aside by a vast, casual backhand as a towering voice shook through him.

BEGONE, FIEND!

Unite the Lost was snuffed out, his store of significance unspent. Deep within, Felix's Hunger snarled in hatred and recognition.

Anathema, the familiar voice continued. **You Are Unwelcome!**

Felix refused to bow before the golden power that assaulted him. It shoved at him, burning at his chest and face and—he was lifted from Imara's arms by a cage of blazing light. His connections to the ground—to gravity—were severed. Burnt away in an instant.

BEGONE!

"*I…refuse*," he growled. "Coward in White!"

The Call of Defiance is active!
+25% Willpower When Contested By A Foe Of Divine Or Greater Advancement!

The force multiplied, but it could not touch the core of him. His foundation, made of opalescent crystal and the threads of Divinity and Primordials alike, was too strong. His Will before Imara was strong, but before a fragment of the gods, it was indomitable. Dissonance and Harmony roared from his heart, and a deep, unconquered darkness quenched the light.

Consumed it.

Imara stumbled back, holding her head. Around her, that aura of twisted golden light flared and popped, like static.

I Remain! Hunger cheered. Felix fell to the ground, his knees weak. **We Remain!**

It's not over yet.

The Titan reached for Felix, grabbing blindly with her shattered gauntlet. Instead of dodging, Felix darted inward, well within her enormous reach.

"Back off!" Felix punched upward, caving in Imara's breastplate and throwing her into an ungainly backward leap.

She touched her bent armor, and a glimmer of emotion threaded through her Spirit. Confusion, worry, and fear. "You…ate His light. How?"

Felix breathed hard, Mana and Essence surging through his channels fast enough to make the cyan markings on his scales glow bright. "Imara…you need to listen to me. You are being controlled—"

Leave The Fiend! Find The Gnome!

Felix growled. The voice rang through her Spirit like a shout down an emptied hallway, echoing and distorted, but powerfully loud. It cut through the fire of her burgeoning emotions, battering them into smoldering embers.

Imara hesitated, that confused jumble trying to catch flame once more…before a burst of Light within her forced her to a single knee. She was shrouded in it, all but obscuring her form.

Felix rushed ahead, Unite the Lost singing in his chest once more. *She's fighting the Pathless and whatever was done to her.* It was his chance. He just had to touch her again and—

"Mr. Veil!"

Doric leaped in front of him, heavy shield outstretched, as a smaller blade stabbed forward from the haze of golden light. Metal shrieked and popped as the shield was cut through. Felix, too late, pulled back only as the Dwarven captain was hit with a second glowing weapon that sent him rocketing across the square. Doric didn't stop until he bashed into and through a solid stone storefront, which collapsed in his wake.

"Doric!" Felix whipped his attention back to Imara, who was standing again. The haze had faded, along with her previous Spiritual pressure, folded somehow into the woman—contained until it pulsed like a miniature sun around her shoulders. She bore a glowing longsword in one hand and a flanged mace in the other, both of which sizzled with the last traces of crimson blood.

"You—"

Her voice was cold and dead once more. "You are all meaningless. Step aside or die."

Lightning burst alight in Felix's hands. "No."

"Then die."

Relentless Resolution is level 98!

Without the weight of her Spirit pressing down on him, Felix moved like the wind. Imara brought her weapons down with titanic Strength, uncaring that he was already before her; he'd only managed to push her back before.

"See you soon, asshole," he growled.

Setting himself, Felix punched upward with both fists. Adamant

Discord surged through him, settling upon connections so complicated and vast that they were less like metal cables and more like steel hawsers—a dozen feet thick and woven with a depth that he could barely parse. Their Unbound connection howled, ignited into sudden, electric fury.

Imara didn't even have time to scream.

She shot into the sky, hurtled along the path of a bolt of lightning the width of Birchstone itself. Golden radiance flared, spilling light into the sky like the sun, but she had no purchase. She was in Felix's domain. She flew up and up, arcing into the distance before vanishing behind the peak of another mountain.

Adamant Discord is level 92!
...
Adamant Discord is level 96!

The Song of Absolution is level 97!

You Have Defeated Imara, The Chosen Of The Pathless!
XP Earned!

Felix dropped to his knees, both arms broken and crawling with residual electricity. His Body burned, strained in a way he hadn't felt in months. Felix held back a pained gasp, forcing it down and into his Hunger. It faded immediately.

Doric. He stood up and staggered into the nearest collapsed building. Within the broken masonry and shattered walls, was a pile of debris that half-buried the man. He was bloodied and beaten, and Felix's Voracious Eye told him more than he wanted to know.

The man was dying.

Pit! I need you! He sent, before awkwardly kneeling beside the Ironclad captain. "Hold on, man, hold on!"

Doric blinked up at him, his dark eyes focusing on Felix. "Veil…? Then…is she—?"

"She's gone," Felix said. "For now. Knocked her into the mountains."

Wheezing breath, gurgling blood. "You—you're not really a merchant, are you?"

Felix clenched his jaw. "No."

"Kn-knew it. T-too nice for tho-those vipers." Doric closed his eyes in a slow blink. "Damnable Night. I had hoped she would die—My men, are they—?"

"They're fine," Felix said. *Most of them.* "Focus on yourself. We have to get you back up and moving."

Pit scurried into the room, scratches and wounds across his chest and rump, but he didn't hesitate to unleash his Breath of the Wild. A wave of shimmering life Mana pulsed, sinking into all three of them. For a second, Doric breathed easier…but his Health didn't budge.

"Ain't gonna work. Can't save me." He coughed. "My Body…I can feel it. Somethin' she did broke me. It's all just…drainin' away. Water—water from a shattered jar."

Pit whimpered, and Felix clutched his blackened hands together. He reached into Pit's saddlebags and withdrew some Health Potions anyway.

"Drink this. You saved me," Felix said. "I gotta return the favor."

"Useless." Still, the man did as he was told. "Focus…focus on the Titan. Kill her."

"I don't know if I can."

"Find a way."

"She's strong. Stronger than me, and now she knows what I can do." Felix shook his head. "Best option I have is running. Leading her away."

"The—the thief? You—" Understanding dawned on the Dwarf. "No merchant at all. A warrior."

"More of a meddler," Felix said, trying to stay calm. Even with the potion, the guy's Health was less than ten percent now, and his Stamina had just about bottomed out.

"I saw you fight. Yo–you're a warrior, and you don't…you don't seem the type to run," he wheezed. Another wash of Pit's Breath hit him, but it did little.

"Yeah. I can be stupid like that."

"Could be…this town could use a little stupid." His eyes rolled, unable to focus, but seemingly searching. "Stone. All stone. I–I don't see the stars, Silas."

"They're there, just outside."

Doric's breath came faster. "Be well, Silas. 'Til we meet—"

Without warning, the man's breathing shuddered to a stop.

"Doric?" Felix flared Unite the Lost. It burned, vibrating the pattern with all the Affinity and Intent he meant for Imara. Significance mobilized within him, enough to restore Primordial-tained abominations or Temples from the brink of collapse…and all of it hit a wall.

Nothing happened.

"Til we meet again beneath star and stone, Captain." With the tips of his dark fingers, Felix closed the Dwarf's sightless eyes.

"What's happening?" Beef asked. "Where'd he go?"

Vess swallowed. She had watched Felix follow after that Dwarven captain, and she didn't need high Perception or Affinity to know how that was likely to go. "He will be a moment."

The young Minotaur looked into the sky and licked his lips nervously. "Think she'll be back? He hit her really hard."

"Yes." There was little doubt. If their fight had offered them anything, it was a greater understanding of their foe's capabilities. The Titan was powerful, certainly, but something else, too. "She will not stop. She is like Felix."

Beef swallowed audibly. "Crap."

Down below, the Ironclads had gathered near the collapsed building, their reduced numbers staring at the darkened interior. Vess could feel their trepidation, their preemptive sorrow…and she felt when it was overwhelmed by fear and awe, as Felix and Pit emerged. They carried a bundle, wrapped in tattered cloth.

Felix said something, handing them the bundle. The body. That sorrow returned, and this time it was as intense as the Titan's golden light. Vess shied away, squeezing her Affinity shut as best she could.

"Look. Those other guys are coming up," Beef said. He pointed to the far side of the square, where members of the Birchstone Watch were advancing on Felix with spears and axes. The Watch loudly demanded his identity. "Felix should—"

Autarch and Chimera vanished.

Moments later, they reappeared right next to the Minotaur, making Beef jolt in surprise. "Ah! Don't do that!"

Felix's eyes were burning, but he looked tired. "Back to the inn. Now."

Vess reached out to him, touching his shoulder. "Are you okay? Is she—?"

"Save it for later. We need to run."

Pit dissolved into white light, and Felix all but vanished again, his form blurring into a streak of lightning in the sky.

Felix landed in the courtyard of the Torrent's Rest, collapsing part of it with a bad landing. Cracks splintered the yard, spitting dust and stone chips up into the air around him. He silently cursed his Body as his leg twinged painfully, before feeding the ache to his Hunger again.

People of all sorts scattered with his landing, and more ran when they met his burning gaze. The courtyard was lit by flickers of blue-white and red-gold.

He rushed into the inn, through the tavern, and up the several flights of stairs. The fourth floor was in chaos as his company were hurriedly strapping their armor back on and readying their weapons.

Harn met him at the door to his suite. "You're back." He frowned. "You're hurt."

Felix pushed past the man. Inside the suite, everything was a mess. Papers were scattered, and furniture was overturned.

"What happened? Were you attacked?" His senses brushed against everything in the room instantly. "Where's Archie?"

"No attack," Harn said. "Kid. He ran."

"Sucker punched us and zipped through the fireplace like a fish in water," Evie said. She was sporting a black eye, and Tzfell was healing her arm. "The little bastard's probably halfway to the next mountain right now."

Felix's hand crushed the doorframe, his Mind whirling through everything the Delven had said. All of his looks and gestures. A picture formed, and it calmed Felix's speeding heart. "No. No, he hasn't left town. He still has a job to do." Felix pried his hand from the broken timber frame, pieces raining down onto the floor. "Gather everyone. Now."

"Aye," Harn saluted and walked out.

"What is going on?" Laur asked. "You're wounded. Did you—"

"Set up the table and spread out the maps again," Felix ordered. "We have plans to make."

CHAPTER EIGHTY-ONE

"Priest," Felix growled as the door clicked close behind him. "What the hell did you do to Imara?"

The others had only just set the large table back onto its feet, and they blinked owlishly at Felix as he stalked forward. The priest, for his part, only looked tired.

"The Hierophant trained her directly. The methods are known only to her and the High Guard, but I know they were…intense. Brutal. The power I have seen her put on display is greater than mine by an order of magnitude…and I am frankly surprised that you are still standing, Mr. Nevarre."

"She's very, very strong, and I've tangled with some real nightmares. All I've done is put a pause on her attack for now, but it'll resume before long. When that happens, I need to know what's going on with her. Her Spirit. It's wrong."

The priest nodded.

"You're aware?"

"I am. She…the Hierophant did something to the girl. I don't know what, but it deprived her of all emotion. All desire. The only thing that remains is the need to follow her orders."

"Empty Spirit?" Beef asked. "Like Hallow?"

"Not like yours," Felix explained. "You externalized your Spirit. Whatever was done to Imara has stripped her almost completely."

"Almost?" Faer asked. "I traveled at her side for months and felt not a ripple of emotion outside of her daily ablutions."

"Her daily what?" Evie asked. Tzfell had finished healing her arm, and she rotated it slowly.

"She would ruminate upon the Light of the Trackless One, and…" Faer swallowed. "She would commune with Him."

"Talk? To a god? That's not normal, right?"

"No, Beef. It is not," Vess said firmly. "The Pathless is said to only speak to the Hierophant. It is a part of her power."

"Not any longer. Imara is the Chosen of the Pathless, and a piece of His power flows through her." Faer shivered. "That emptiness…it is not truly empty. There is no 'her' remaining, but she is filled with the Light. It…consumes her from within, powering her advancement and Aspects."

Felix ran through his fight, recalled in perfect, excruciating detail. The woman all but bled golden light, and when he attempted to use Unite the Lost on her, the Pathless had immediately blocked the way. "Can it be blocked? Stopped?"

"Can you snuff out the sun?"

Deep inside of his gut, there was an eager rumble. Felix ignored it. "Not yet."

Faer raised an eyebrow. "The Pathless is a font of infinite power. So long as He remains, I suspect that Imara will continue on, fighting for Him. She has been emptied of all that was once mortal. There is only the Pathless for her, now."

"No one's beyond saving," Felix insisted. "My Skill…it would've worked, if the Pathless hadn't interfered."

"He…directly intervened?"

"Talked and everything," Pit confirmed.

Faer clearly didn't know what to make of that. "That is not— That would make you the third person He has made contact with directly. But more importantly, that worries me. To speak through someone…I do not think enough remains of her for you to save, Lord Autarch."

An instant image, recollection gone sour, assaulted Felix's Mind. Captain Doric, bloody and trapped beneath the rubble. Felix clenched his fists until blood poured from between his scaled fingers. It was only a single man, someone Felix didn't even know that well…but it clung to him like a stain.

A warm hand slid across his shoulder, gripping him gently. Vess was at his side, her soft brown eyes staring into his. "You did what you could."

"I—Yeah." *And it wasn't enough,* he finished for her.

Harn cleared his throat, just returning to the room. "Tell us, kid. Are we runnin' from this Titan or not?"

"Beef, can you explain the battle?" Vess asked, speaking before Felix could open his mouth.

"Me? Sure. I saw it all. We got to the gate and it was melted, and all these Sun Trolls were attacking…"

The explanation went on for five minutes, Beef giving a blow-by-blow of the fight from his perspective. A part of Felix was impressed; the kid really had paid attention.

"Then he punched her so hard, she vanished," Beef finished excitedly. All of them were crowded around the table now, the leaders at least. Outside, the Claw was hastily putting their caravan back together.

"She's dead?" Evie asked.

"No. But I put every ounce of Strength I had into that hit and my Skill. The System marked her as "defeated," so hopefully that means she'll be wounded…and she's at least an entire mountain away from us now. She doesn't have a way to fly, otherwise she would've fought my Adamant Discord better, so that means we've got a little time." Felix frowned, running his scaled hands across the map before him. "Not a lot, but some. Time enough to carry out my plan."

"And that is?" Harn asked.

"We need to get Archie, whether he likes it or not. To do that, we need to find him."

Loquis, one of two Claw members present, cleared his throat nervously. "Sir—Lord Autarch, that is—how can we catch him? I understand the last plan was to canvas the city with our people…but, by your own estimation, we don't have time for that."

"Stone-solid point, Loq," Evie said, causing the Half-Orc to straighten slightly. Beside him, Mervin rolled his eyes. "We can't track him, true enough. Laur said he wiggled through that rock, so good he's lost. Plus, you can't find him with your Unbound locator, Felix."

"You're right. But we know for certain where he will be." Felix tapped the map, which showed the mountain gates into the Clan Hold.

"You're kidding," Harn said with a sharp laugh.

"What?" Beef asked. "Where will he be?"

"The Vault of Nine Kings," Vess said, her voice disbelieving. "That is the plan?"

"Yeah. I'd wager all my Territories he's on his way there now." Felix stabbed his claw into the map and through the table. "But we're gonna rob it first."

"Avet's teeth," Evie said with a grin. "Now *this* is excitin'."

"Do you truly think he will persist with a foolish heist when things are so dire?" Vess asked.

Harn grunted. "He will. He's a rat fleeing a sinking ship...but he thinks the way out is through there."

"The ritual. The one to take us home," Beef said. He looked at Felix. "We gotta get it."

"Eager to leave, too?" Evie asked.

"Leave? No, I—no. But we should have it. Just in case," Beef finished lamely.

"The plan is to corner him at the Vault. Failing that, so long as we get the ritual, then Archie will come to us," Felix pointed out. "The real problem is Imara. She won't stop until she captures him, and I'm not letting her do that."

Vess frowned. "How do we reach this vault?"

"If we've access to the Clan Hold, then there are two access points that I am aware of," Tzfell offered. "Reaching them, however, is problematic. They are both within the Nightfall Palace."

"The Hinterlord's home, you mean?" Laur asked.

"The same."

"So, the plan is to break into a king's castle, sneak into a magic vault, and steal everything?" Evie spun a knife in her hand, idly. "I'm likin' this idea more and more."

Felix smirked, but there was no humor in it. "That's the sum of it, yeah. But we've got a few flies in the soup. The first one is time. We need to get this done in the next day, or we risk Imara's return. The second is getting into the Clan Hold in the first place, and the third is getting back out. I had hoped—" he cut himself off. He'd hoped for Doric to reach his contacts in the Hold on the pretense of trading... "It doesn't matter. We need a new way in. Any ideas?"

"Perhaps," Laur said, lifting a slender hand. "The Unbound, when he departed from us, slipped through the stone like water. Likely a power inherent to his Lost Race. But," the Elf strode to the fireplace in question, pointing a long finger at a portion carved to resemble an immense Dwarf's beard. "Here. And here. The matrices of the stone remain disturbed."

"Meaning?"

"It was rippled, as if vibrated at an extremely high speed. In the chaos, I recall hearing unfamiliar strains of Harmony, but at the time, I could not place them. I believe Archibald's Skill uses the Chant intrinsically, manipulating the Grand Harmony to move through solid stone."

"So we can track him by the ripples he makes?" Vess asked.

"Well, yes, I suppose so. But doing so would be the equivalent of finding a snow hare in a blizzard. No, what I suggest is more…actionable. I have seen this rippling before: the wards of the High Road and near the walls of Birchstone bear their likeness."

"Likely where the guy tunneled through to get into the city again," Felix said. "Wait. Is that why the High Road wards were failing?"

"Precisely! Or, that is what I am hoping. If so, then there is a weakness we can exploit." The Elf tapped the fireplace. "I just need to study the ripples again, and I might be able to learn more."

Felix snapped his fingers. "That's perfect. Mervin, you and a contingent of the Claw go with Laur to investigate the wards around town. The sooner, the better."

Mervin saluted and hustled from the room, the Elven Chanter following with a touch more grace.

"That's the way in set," Evie said. "What about the way out? I don't fancy walkin' into a death trap more than a few times a year."

"I have an idea for that, and you are the perfect person to handle it, Evie." Felix pointed at a portion of the map that was close by, if quite near the next district. "Go here. Take Beef for backup, and hire—wait, lemme just write it down, that's easier."

Felix scribbled a note on a blank piece of map before ripping it off. Tzfell gave a pained gasp, and Pit practically radiated disappointment at his cavalier treatment of the maps, but Felix didn't much care at the moment. "Here. Find that guy, and don't take no for an answer."

Evie glanced over the note, and Beef did the same over her shoulder. She grinned. "What if they get all feisty?"

"I trust you to do what you do best." Felix looked to the teen Minotaur. "Beef, keep her safe."

"We will," Hallow said, her Homunculus form still wrapped around Beef's chest.

"Uh, yeah, sure. But…I told you I'm not old enough to drink. What if they don't let me in?"

"C'mon, meathead. Let's go."

Evie all but hauled the seven foot Minotaur out of the door, and Felix could feel Hallow's other forms soon mobilize from the stables out back. Felix ran his hands through his dark hair, the stress building up across his chest and shoulders.

"Right. That just leaves information gathering, which I've already assigned to you, Tzfell. Vess, please assist her in finding out everything we can about the Undermount in as little time as possible."

"Certainly," Vess agreed, and Tzfell nodded.

"I do know a bit about the Undermount," Faer said, his sad voice gaining some strength. "My time with the Hierocracy has made me privy to a great many things, and I once read a first-person account of a foreign dignitary's visit. I recall it quite well, and I can summarize at least the first few levels of the place."

Vess reached over and handed the man a scroll of vellum and an ink pen. "That would be wonderful, Hierei Faer. Please jot down all you remember."

"Please, call me Kellis."

"As you wish," she said with a diplomatic smile.

"Last, but not least, is our task," Felix said, looking at Pit, Harn, and the Half-Orc, Loquis. "We have to figure out a way to combat an Unbound stronger than me, with enough firepower to level this whole city."

"A tall order," Harn said. "What'd you have in mind?"

"Keystones. As many as you can make."

Harn's head rocked back. "Huh. Yeah. Could work. Same schematics?"

"Yeah, but focus on Stamina and Health. Mana is gonna be pointless."

Harn grunted in confirmation. "Array only supports thirteen. Works best that way."

"Then try for a full set."

"Aye."

"I'm sorry, what are we making?" Loquis asked.

"Contingency plan," Pit chirruped.

"That is…remarkably unhelpful," the mage said.

"Heh. Anyone know of a Domain around here?" Felix asked.

Tzfell raised her head from the books she and Vess were already pouring over. "There is one farther down the mountain. It's strong, though, and is suppressed regularly by the Forge Knights."

Felix tapped his lips. "That'll have to do. Right," he slapped the table. "Get started on those, and I'll be back as soon as I'm able."

"Aye. Loquis, let's round up my apprentices," Harn said, grabbing the mage by the arm and heading out the door.

"Pit, it's just you and me on this one. It'll be faster than dragging anyone else along."

"Just like always." Pit hesitated, thinking. "If it'll take a while, we should pack snacks."

Felix forced a smile. "I'll pass. I think I'll have enough on my plate."

Pit trotted across the room, beelining straight for the leftovers.

"Felix."

"Vess? What's up?"

"Are you…well?"

"Oh. I'm fine. Imara strained my Body Aspect, but it's nothing I haven't dealt with before." Across the room, Pit stuck his beak onto platters and shoved things unceremoniously into his saddlebags.

"That fight with Imara was tough, there is no doubt about that. But…I am speaking of other things. Of the captain."

Felix clenched his jaw and didn't answer.

"I saw it happen, though it was almost too fast for me to perceive. He…he saved your life."

"I could've survived," Felix whispered.

"You don't know that—"

"I've survived so much worse than a hot sword through my middle," Felix said, a bit too loud. His head felt like it was stuffed with cotton and set on fire, all at once. "Imara, she—and Doric just jumped in. No thought."

Vess was quiet for a long moment as Felix struggled to master himself. It was stupid, he told himself. He barely knew the guy. And yet…

"Imara killed him, Felix. And, perhaps I overstep myself, but it would not sit right with me if I remained silent." She took a soft, unsteady breath, as if she were rushing her words. "Do not seek vengeance."

Felix blinked. "What?"

She nodded to the corner, where Yintarion slept curled near the fire. "When I faced down my people's hated enemy, a Dragon, it took everything in me not to seek its destruction. It let me down some…unwise paths. With the aid of my friends, I found my way to the right of things. Vengeance is a dull stone; handle it too much, and it will blunt your edge."

They stood there silently for a time, regarding the fire. The logs popped, shifting as pieces of them were gnawed away.

"I have seen so many die," Felix said at last. "Too many."

So many had died while following him. His cause. Doric had died saving Felix. Just like Magda.

"Never again," he told Vess. "Never again."

Pit returned to his side, and the two of them walked out of the suite.

CHAPTER EIGHTY-TWO

The air stank of unwashed bodies and sour, spilled ale when Evie stepped into the Cask. She breathed deep and sighed. "Ahh, my people."

The eclectic gathering of smugglers, cutthroats, and drunks turned toward her voice and many turned back to their drinks. Some, however, seeing nothing more than a slender woman at a bar of ill repute in the small hours of the night, got certain ideas into their head. These fellows stood up and walked closer.

"Oh, look, they're comin' to me. Wonderful." Evie smiled wide as the first Dwarf lunged at her, stepping aside and letting the fool bash his head into the doorjamb. "I'm sure you were very agile, once. Sadly, those times have passed."

The bartender, a Dwarf with an eyepatch, lifted a heavy crossbow from beneath the counter. "Back off, damn drunks, unless you want me to put a hole in those wineskins you call a gut."

The drunks and scoundrels hesitated, and a few even sat back down. Four, however, charged.

A hammer made of ice and steel took all of them down as Beef busted through the too-small door. Timber and old plaster rained atop the sticky floorboards, now even stickier as the fools' blood spilled out.

Evie stepped over them. "Bartender! Do us a favor and summon your boss."

Old Eyepatch scowled, still hefting his crossbow. "I don't take orders—"

"Hold now, Brak. Let's hear what she's got ta say," said another. From the shadows at the back of the bar, the widest Dwarf Evie had ever seen stepped into view.

"You Thrumm the Rat Lord?" she asked.

Unsettled mutters filled the room, but none of the louses even so much as moved from their tables. The Rat Lord smiled, revealing several missing teeth. "I am. And who might you be, waltzing into my establishment and killing my clientele?"

"They're not dead," Beef pointed out, a bit defensively.

Thrumm craned his neck. "Tch. Pity. Gives you less leverage, too. How am I supposed to be afraid of a strongarm that can't commit?"

As if signaled, another Dwarf rushed from the side, two foot-long knives gleaming in his hands. Beef backhanded the man, and he crashed through two tables and a wall.

"Then again, there's somethin' to be said for restraint," Thrumm said with a nervous smile. "How can I help ya, ma'am?"

"It's stone simple." Evie spread her hands guilelessly as Beef loomed behind her, a dark shadow lit only by the flickering light in his oversized hammer. "I'd like to hire you for a job."

"The ripples, they're so similar but not entirely," Laur reported. "The pattern suggests directionality…perhaps a relic of Intent…"

Mervin nodded absently. The Chanter had said similar things at the last six places they'd stopped at, and by this point, he'd grown numb to the magical babble. Mervin had found it all very interesting, once upon a time, but the Elf was speaking in realms that Mervin couldn't comprehend. So, instead of worrying about that, Mervin checked their surroundings again.

His team of ten was arranged in a loose circle around the Chanter, all of them on the alert for any sort of attack. Considering the damage to this area of the city, it was far more likely that a building would collapse on them. There were very few people around, and most of them were covered in soot and carrying their meager belongings in their hands.

I can't do anything for you, he thought with an aimless sort of ache as another few Hobgoblins scurried past, rags on their backs. *So much incredible suffering…how could she be a Chosen of the Pathless?*

That detail had stuck with Mervin more than any other. He'd fought to keep from voicing his concerns during the Autarch's meeting, but it had been difficult. He had hoped when he saw the Hierei that perhaps there was something worthwhile to the Pathless, something to account for all the good memories of his childhood…and he heard only atrocities.

Purity. Order. Strength. And yet you hold to none of them but the last. Mervin gritted his teeth. *I cannot—*

"I see!"

Mervin spun back toward the Chanter to find the tall Elf running his hands through his long hair like a madman. "You see what?"

"The purpose! The flaw!" Chanter Laur grasped Mervin by the arm and pulled at him. "Come. We need to see the gates next!"

"The ones that are still on fire?" he asked.

"While they're fresh!"

Commander Kastos' crystalline hammers drew a cascade of sparks from the Leviathan bone. It was fixed by his Will atop a plain black anvil, and Mana was folded into its shape with every strike. Not his own, Loquis was fascinated to learn, but Mana stored within the hammers themselves. The commander switched between them liberally, applying ice, fire, and even shadow Mana to the piece of shaped bone.

Loquis still hadn't a clue what the man was making. His instructions had only gone so far as to secure a forge and guard it from passersby. The Torrent's Rest had a small smithy off to the side of their main building, and it had only taken a handful of crowns to convince the smith to go to bed with a wineskin. As far as passersby went, the place was deathly quiet in light of the Titan's attack and the fact that it was well beyond midnight.

He blinked at that, more tired than he realized. All of his men were, though they hid it well enough.

Late hour or not, Commander Kastos' work continued, unabated.

Leviathan bone was replaced by ice ore, each bent and flattened by heat and strange flows of magic. The commander's Skills with the forge were remarkable, and honed over the last few months back in

Elderthrone. Loquis watched, fascinated, as his commander's designs took shape.

With a heavy breath, the commander placed the final piece into a bucket filled with a thick, opalescent liquid. It boiled as it entered, but instead of steam or shrieking steel, all Loquis heard was a jubilant crescendo of unearthly music. It quickly silenced, and the commander fished a plate-sized hexagon from the bucket.

"Damn near perfect," he muttered. The commander was sweating, his chest pumping like a bellows, but he looked pleased. On his scarred and broken face, it seemed more like a snarl. "Set it with the others."

Loquis took the hexagon in hand, fighting back a flinch. The object wasn't hot, in fact it was bitterly cold. Part bone, part uncanny ice, the strange tablet was a swirl of black and deepest blue-purple. He set it atop twelve others and gestured to his men to pack them up.

The commander packed up his hammers and gear, but Loquis spared a glance at the anvil. It had grown white hot across almost its entirety. Normally, Loquis would have supposed the structure of it would have failed as the metal turned to mush, but other colors chased the white radiance across the heated anvil. Magic seeped into it as much as the Leviathan bone and ice ore, except, in the anvil's case, the working was unstructured and wild. Dangerous.

"Make sure to tell the blacksmith to throw this anvil out," Loquis told the Goblin packing up the tablets beside him. "And make sure it's not melted down. Stress how perilous that could be."

"Aye sir."

In the distance, a faint bell sounded, and the commander looked up in surprise. "Dawn already, eh? Damnation. Pack it up, boys, and get what rest you can." He slung his satchel of tools over a broad shoulder. "That's an order."

"Aye, sir!" they all shouted in unison, before Loquis sent them scurrying about, cleaning up their presence in the smithy.

All of them would sleep hard. No order required.

Felix flowed through the open window, still devoid of glass, and landed in a roll on a plush rug. Pit came through another, though his wide torso ended up taking a new chunk out of the casement.

Startled, Hierei Faer, Vess, and Tzfell stood from a pile of books. Vess smiled. "You've returned."

Yintarion hovered in the air above Vess' head. He fixed the two of them with his depthless golden eyes. "Successfully?"

"Was that ever in question?" Pit asked, beak tilted up.

"Domain's done." Felix set a shimmering black crystal stamped with whorls of gold onto the table. Two others followed, but they were smaller. "Took longer than I expected."

"You've only been gone three hours," the priest said, alarmed. "You sped through an entire Domain?"

"No. We emptied it out."

The priest stared at him, sagging jowls quivering. "You—?"

"I was there to take the Domain's primary and sub cores. That collapses the whole thing. Pressed for time or not, I'm not setting loose several thousand little monsters on the mountain." He looked to Vess. "Can you get Harn up here?"

"Of course."

Vess rose and went to the door, moving deceptively fast. Yintarion stayed behind, curling atop invisible waves of air and fire Mana.

"I still don't—even for a Master Tier, clearing an entire Domain requires days of work. The bodies alone would need to decay long enough to let their Mana settle, otherwise it'd breach the liminal envelope."

"The Autarch is possessed of unique…capabilities," Tzfell said.

Yintarion gave a low, throaty chuckle. Faer looked up at the Wyrmling, clearly nervous.

Felix only grunted and took a seat beside the fire, uninterested in parsing whatever was going on among them all. He *had* cleared the Domain, but it wasn't nearly as simple as he had suggested. Felix was strong, true, but he was constantly reminded of how little time he had remaining. That had forced him to use more brute force than might have been strictly necessary, and now his Adept Tier Body ached all the more.

Still, the Domain was done. He'd conquered it mostly with area of effect Skills like Rain of Cataclysm, but he'd also made sure not to waste the opportunity to push another Skill as high as he could: Shadow Whip. Its darkness element had been useful against Imara when funneled through Wild Threnody, and Felix wanted to see it evolve. It was on the cusp of Adept Tier now, but the Domain monsters had died too easy. It was Adept-ranked as well, but it couldn't handle Felix, let alone Pit, too.

Chthonic Tribute had taken care of the rest.

Felix leaned toward the fire. He was cold, and not just from the long fights. He'd spent hours demolishing hordes of spiders, wolves, and lizards with twisted humanoid faces, but all of it had only occupied a piece of his attention. The hours had given him enough time to contemplate his plans, turning them about in his Mind, examining them from every angle. He knew there were more than a few failure points in his scheme…but he couldn't think of anything better.

He hoped it would be enough.

Across the room, the door opened, creaking slightly.

"That was fast, was he waiting—" Felix stood when he saw Vess' face. Felt her Spirit. "What's happened?"

"You have a visitor," she said, holding a rapid handsign. <<Calm. Safe. Careful.>>

Vess stepped from the door, and Felix saw a Dwarven woman wearing an outfit that could only be described as rocky. It was formed entirely from stone, specifically a blue-gray granite, broken into uneven chunks and held together by either fabric or perhaps metal. A necklace of blue sapphires hung around her throat, accentuating the red hair that filled the inside of a beaded caul. Bright eyes, a proud nose, and a smattering of freckles gave her an innocence that was belied by the Master Tier presence she exuded.

And behind her, twenty armored Dwarves that were just as advanced. Felix recognized their distinctive armor and the hammers at their waists. Forge Knights.

"Mr. Silas Veil?" the woman asked.

"Yes," Felix put himself ahead of Vess, blocking the door with his wide shoulders. "How can I help you?"

"You are cordially invited to the Hinterlord's Grand Gala." A scroll sealed with red wax and dangling with ribbons was presented to him. He took it, careful to flex Sovereign of Flesh and hide his claws.

Felix turned it over in his hands. "What for?"

"It is a celebration!" she announced with a bright white smile. "The vile Titan has been expelled from the city, and Birchstone shall hail its newest hero!"

When Felix stared at her, uncomprehending, the courier's smile somehow grew even wider. "That would be you, Mr. Veil!"

CHAPTER EIGHTY-THREE

Bellar sat atop the cliff, crimson cloak held close, and considered their path.

The night was dark. No moons shone upon the mountain, but the thick layers of snow and ice reflected the paltry starlight well enough. It was the bitter cold, truly, that hampered their movements, as it had hampered the engines of their Manaship. Forced to land within the foothills of the western range, they had trudged with indefatigable steps over hill and dale, battling Trolls and beasts the likes of which he had never seen.

The retreating storm even now buffeted them with its fury, but his men were hardy, and their armor was heavily enchanted for the bitter cold. They had trudged across half the world to reach this point. They wouldn't be put off by some snow.

When his scouts witnessed a bolt of lightning from the heavens, they had been astounded. The potency of it had even lifted the hairs on Bellar's neck, and he had only viewed it from the pine forests below. He'd immediately ordered them to follow the bolt and was rewarded when it hit a nearby mountain. The impact of it had shaken the ground beneath their feet—causing an avalanche in an adjacent valley—but what made his people eager was the conflagration of golden light that had spilled from the crater it left.

Holy Light.

"Lord Inquisitor! Over here!"

Bellar stood from his improvised throne of stone and strode across the slanted ice. Golden Mana flared beneath his feet, enchantments worn into the armor that melted the ice just enough to secure his footing. Bellar walked across the mountain and down into a crumbling slope at least seventy strides wide. The rock and snow at its center had been painstakingly removed, and now they revealed an armored giant, half-trapped beneath the mountain.

"The Chosen," Bellar whispered. He gestured furiously. "Get her out of there! Now!"

His men got to work, their blood-red cloaks nearly black in the moonless night. Soon, however, the sun would rise.

Dawn came as Felix and company rushed to answer the Hinterlord's summons. The contingent of Forge Knights and the fancy courier all waited as they did so, posted up in the courtyard of the Torrent's Rest for all to see. The sun rose, and smoke darkened the sky, while a crowd of onlookers gathered.

Felix took his time to ensure his people were organized and secure, much to the chagrin of the courier. She grimaced at each delay, though she refrained from speaking against Felix's decisions. His role as the Hero of Birchstone apparently had some weight, and he planned to make it work for him.

When they finally emerged, it was with everyone as shined up as they could be. Armor, weapons, their bodies, all were washed and polished. Even Harn's battered set was buffed to the best of their ability, though the man wasn't too happy about it. He was still grumbling as they descended the steps of the inn and into the courtyard.

"The dirt adds character," he growled.

"Uh-huh. You had enough blood in the grooves of your gorget to make half a man," Evie pointed out.

"Character," he grunted.

The Claw had already brought around their ice sleds and crates of goods, and Felix ran his Perception over the lot of them. They had cleaned up as well but still wore their fur-lined cloaks that covered most of their Leviathan bone armor. Loquis and Mervin were at their head, and they each gave Felix a firm nod as he passed, heading toward the courier.

The courier brightened at their approach. "You are ready, Mr. Veil? Is—is that a Dire Hound?"

"We are. And yes," Felix gestured ahead with the hand not carrying Pit. "Lead on."

Had his company tried to push their way through Birchstone alone, getting through the outer district would have taken them hours. The streets were crowded with people, locals and refugees alike, many of whom were covered in soot and carrying their belongings on their backs. All of them stepped aside for the Forge Knights carrying the Red Shield banner, and the courier was none too shy about summoning a shield of force Mana that she wielded like a plow. Those who were too slow were shoved aside.

Felix grimaced internally but schooled his face to stillness. They only had one shot at their goal, and this invitation was a windfall—he wasn't going to screw it up now by protesting the Hinterlord's men. Not yet, anyway. Still, people around them were injured, many burned, and that tugged at his heart.

Half the district had caught fire during Imara's assault, and the Watch had been entirely too slow at putting it out. Birchstone watched them march through the district, fear and anxiety and anger roiling around their Spirits like a nest of snakes. Felix fought to keep his breathing steady as they moved through them all. Their stares felt like an accusation.

He could have easily ordered the Claw out to put out fires and help people, but instead Felix had focused on their task ahead, at the expense of everything else. It was a good excuse, but that's all it was. An excuse.

Hero of Birchstone, he mused sourly. *Some hero I am.*

A wave of green-gold life Mana waved outward in a rushing breeze. It passed his company without much effect, but it spread powerfully over the crowds. People looked around in shock, hefting their burdens easier, and even some of the worst burns visibly healed over.

Pit's Breath of the Wild is level 30!

"Pit…" Felix ruffled Pit's russet ears. "Thanks."

The little tenku said nothing, focusing on expelling a great lungful of air to keep the Skill going. Whenever he ran out, and the Skill faded, he took a huge breath and immediately recast it. So it went, as the courier led them through the district, until they passed through the gates and into the second district of Birchstone.

Pit's Breath of the Wild is level 42!

Pit settled into Felix's arms, out of breath and thoroughly exhausted. There had been a great deal of injured people on their path, and everyone who received his temporary boon had helped push the Skill higher and higher. Felix gave him an appreciative belly rub as they strode down newer and far wider thoroughfares.

The streets weren't nearly as crowded there, most of the foot traffic belonging to liveried servants purchasing sundry goods from the assorted shops that lined their route. They walked up a perfectly straight road for almost a mile before it began to ascend, leading to yet another district gate. They passed through without a moment's hesitation and found themselves climbing a switchbacked thoroughfare up the side of a cliff.

Structures were built into the cliff, stout, sturdy, and ornamented with gold, silver, and precious stones. They were homes of the wealthier merchants, Tzfell informed him in a low voice, positions of renown second only to the mansions within the upper district or the Clan Hold itself.

They saw those soon enough, as the winding road once again straightened out and flattened itself. Walled estates extended in every direction, most with extensive gardens and lands. Occasionally, they would pass a pair of guards, each wearing distinct livery. They saluted sharply to the Forge Knights before resuming their duty.

Beyond the walled mansions and snow-clad personal forests, there was the mountain. It loomed above them their entire trip, a star shadow in the early dawn light, like a piece of midnight tossed to earth. As the sun rose farther, details could be picked out. Massive carvings of Dwarven faces, each a hundred feet high, flanked a massive fortification that easily outstripped them in size if not artistry. It was bulky and blocky, its high, seamless walls a testament to defense rather than ostentatious design.

They approached the fortress and found themselves surrounded by well-dressed craftsmen, merchants, and various rich folk from the city. They were jostling among one another, all of them shouting questions for the well-dressed men and women who stood before the gates. Another company of Forge Knights stood with them, just as silent as they waited.

"When can we reach the High Clans again? I have an exclusive contract with—"

"What of my family? They are within the Clan Hold! I should be able to join them…!"

"—lit up the sky with gold! You all saw it! We are not safe!"

"In the name of the Hinterlord, stand aside. I bring with us the Hero of Birchstone!"

The voice of the courier tore through the throng, loud as her impressive Body could make it before she started hurting people. Still, Felix saw some wince and shield their ears. The crowd turned almost as one to stare at them, but only a few began to move. The courier cleared her throat, and once again, her shield of force Mana slipped among them like a glowing blue worm. Few could see it, but it hung there, ready for the courier's Will to activate it. "Do I need to repeat myself?"

Reluctantly, the opulent mob stepped aside. The courier smiled brightly and led them ahead, passing through the cordon of Forge Knights. Felix frowned, taking in the crowd's Spirits. Impatience and a strange sort of eagerness flickered among them, sharp and staccato, but it rode atop an undercurrent of dread. A few seemed confused and peered at Felix's party with bright curiosity. Whispers followed him, the word "hero" bandied around, just as the courier no doubt intended.

"Open the gates!" came the call, echoing from one Forge Knight to another. By the time it faded, the gates rumbled open.

They entered, passing into a winding, mazelike entryway that was shrouded in gleaming sigaldry. It was so thick Felix could feel it press against his skin, like a wave of thick oil. It clung to them, growing in pressure with every step, but never so much that it slowed their progress.

The courier led them on through bladed battlements and beneath vaulted arches dotted with inscribed murderholes, all of which was manned by a battalion of hardened warriors. Though he kept his Voracious Eye to himself, every warrior was at least at the upper edge of Journeyman Tier. Some were Adept as well.

"I see you admiring our fortifications," the courier said, once again flashing that wide smile. "Many of these are new, and the enchantments have been layered by Master Tier inscriptionists."

"Are they new because Im—the Titan broke the last set?" he asked.

The courier's smile faltered. "Yes."

"Hm," was all Felix offered. He ran his gaze over their defenses, judging them all. They were strong, he could tell that, and a lot of traps were worked into the arrays he could see. He imagined more existed in hiding, ready to catch any invaders by surprise. The bones of the mountain were strong. He hoped she was right.

"Ahem. The soldiers stationed here normally protect highly important places within the Clan Hold, such as the Hall of Ancestors where the Highblooded meet, or even Nightfall Palace. In his infinite wisdom and compassion, the Hinterlord moved all the men he could here, to protect us against the new onslaught of the Titan."

As she spoke, they finished their winding, serpentine journey and walked out into a wide platform. It was very large, clearly designed to accommodate far more traffic than their relatively small group, and it was ringed by a stout ornamental railing. Several paths led off of it, all of them winding downward toward a glittering vastness below.

"Siva's Grace," Vess whispered. "Incredible."

Others gasped as well, clearly overwhelmed. Before them, a city many times the size of Birchstone sat within a cavern that stretched for miles in every direction. The ceiling itself was so high that swirling clouds obscured it from view, intersected only by dark pipes that seem to hang unsupported in rigid formations.

Below, colorful lights twinkled among palatial mansions, enormous gardens in full bloom, and streets that looked to be made of literal gold. Statues of Dwarven figures abounded, most between fifty and a hundred feet tall, and all worked from the midnight stone all around them.

The courier flung out her arms dramatically. "Welcome, Mr. Veil, to Red Shield Hold!"

Exploration is level 75!
Adept Tier!
You Gain:
+5 PER
+5 INT
+5 FEL

Felix shoved aside the notification and tiny surge of System energy, only missing a part of the courier's speech.

"—from here, and the golden roads of Red Shield will lead you to the vast Crimson Bazaar, where any number of curios and delicacies can be found. There, by the copper domes of the Grand Assembly, is the temple district, where the worship of our Revered Mother Nocits and her wayward siblings still holds strong."

Felix scratched his jaw, looking for a thread of conversation to latch onto. He definitely didn't want to talk about Noctis. "This is all very impressive. Does this city take up the whole mountain?"

"Of course! Red Shield Hold itself is quite expansive, but there are also dozens of layers beneath our feet that spread through the Rimefang Mountains with unchallenged range. A connection between our cities is truly what separates our proud nation from the mewling sun-worshippers."

"Interesting. Are the paths between cities traversed by foot?" Felix asked.

"They are, but the distances are vast," she said, leading them down from the wide entrance platform down one of several sloping streets. "Even within the city itself, getting from one place to another is quite a chore. So, we have developed a true marvel. Behold!"

She stopped at the first curve in the path, where a rectangular building carved with intricate geometric knots jutted out of the cavern wall. Some of the dark pipes he'd seen in the sky traced directly to the squat building, passing through the short end and into the interior. They were notched in such a way that tugged at Felix's memory, but it eluded him. The building was lit by a number of blue-green magelights but was otherwise quiet and decidedly empty.

"What am I beholdin'?" Evie asked.

"Ahem. Grom, if you would."

One of the Forge Knights stepped forward and threw open the doors to the squat building. The wide entryway revealed a large space that looked remarkably like a bus station, with an open floor plan, some seating clustered along the walls, and a single desk manned by a very tired-looking Dwarf.

The Dwarf, a man with a floppy hat and a thick black beard, jolted awake. He scrabbled in his seat, flapping his lips without effect for a second before he found his voice. "Welcome! Honored guests! To the Cloud Chariot!"

Light came alive, swirling along the ceiling to reveal a long steel box the size of a single train car. It was shaped like one, too, long and rectangular, except it was suspended from the notched pipes that entered through the open end of the building. Several silver-green clamps and gears held the thing to the pipes, and they shimmered with sigaldry. More evidence of an advanced array was apparent across the metal chassis, but the bulk of it was hidden from view. Glass windows covered the front and back with smaller portholes along the sides, except where a door was situated.

"Uh, we're supposed to get in that?" Beef asked. "It's not really made for…people my size."

A Forge Knight pressed a triangular piece of crystal to the side of the Cloud Chariot, and two wide doors opened up with a hiss of silver Mana vapor.

"Built of high steel and reinforced by the very best metal mages this side of the Continent, the Cloud Chariots were designed with the intent to haul large amounts of cargo, sir. You will be quite safe." The courier stepped within and jumped up and down twice. The steel railcar didn't so much as quiver. "As you can see, it is quite sturdy. Now."

She clapped her hands, and her smile widened even farther. "Who would like to soar the heavens?"

CHAPTER EIGHTY-FOUR

I like *it!* Pit declared a few minutes later. He had insisted Felix stand at the front, so he could see properly out of the large window there.

I'm afraid Beef is not a fan, Felix noted. The teen was standing in the exact center of the structure and had to bend himself almost in half to keep his tall horns from colliding with the roof. He had been right; the Chariot was not created with Minotaurs in mind. Even Felix felt his hair brushing up against the metal roof where it curved near the leading edge.

At least what the courier said had been true; the Chariot *was* built for hauling heavy materials. It hadn't shaken at all when Beef entered, nor when the Claw all piled in along with their supplies. When Felix stepped inside, however, it had given a little groan, but it wasn't too bad.

"Maybe cut back on all the eatin', eh?" Evie had said under her breath.

Felix had given her a mock smile. "Hilarious."

Evie chuckled. As did Vess and Harn.

They've all betrayed me, Pit. What am I gonna do?

Pit scratched his ear. *When I'm betrayed, I like to eat a snack.*

You always like a snack.

Yes. Do you have anything?

Felix fished a winter-withered fruit from his pocket he'd taken from the inn that morning. Pit took it between his puppy teeth and started munching away.

"Doors are closing; please watch your arms and legs," the Dwarven man said, his floppy hat dangling in his eyes. He swiped it away in annoyance. "You'll feel a bump, please brace."

The doors closed, a seam of metal Mana slipping across the surface like a lock, and the entire cabin jolted. Felix braced himself against the front window. He could hear Beef quietly muttering to himself.

The Cloud Chariot surged forward and out into empty air.

"Whoa."

Red Shield Hold opened up below them, and it was like looking down at a dark countryside from an airplane window. Much like from the entrance platform, they could see twinkling lights throughout the city and streets of golden bricks marking bright pathways between the dark stone buildings. Like arteries pumping vital blood, throngs of people moved across those thoroughfares, shopping, selling, and conversing. Bridges and walkways spanned a subterranean river, likely the same Swiftsteel River that flowed through Birchstone, except here it had been altered and split, terraced into waterfalls and elegant pools. Well-dressed figures walked those paths, strolling the water's edge as if they hadn't a care in the world. It was a far cry from those just outside the Hold's gates.

They rose higher until clouds interfered with the view as the rails pulled them farther toward the distant ceiling.

It's like flying again, Pit sent softly.

Felix looked at his friend, but the tenku-turned-hound had his eyes fixed on the clouds. *We're gonna fix your wings. No matter what.*

I know. But… Pit huffed a doggy sigh. *It's okay if we can't. If it comes down to it, we gotta get Archie and go—*

We'll fix them, Felix promised yet again. *No matter what.*

Pit only nodded and nestled into the crook of Felix's elbow.

The sky train clicked and clacked every few seconds, but it was a remarkably smooth ride. Felix was surprised. He'd seen Manaships and many fascinating things achieved through ancient magic, but little on the Continent had ever reminded him so much of Earth tech. It was clearly fashioned by Dwarves, evident in the intricate styling of the high steel around them, but it was designed by someone with an enterprising Mind. The Hold was huge, but at their rate of speed, Felix didn't doubt they could cross the entire thing in thirty minutes.

"Are these designed to travel between Holds as well?" Felix asked the courier.

"Ah, no. Currently these are only constructed here, in Red Shield."

She picked an imaginary piece of dust off of her shoulder and flicked it away. "Though it would make all of our lives easier, and increase the wealth of all...the other Holds have proven intractable on that front."

Likely they don't want to give another Hold easy access to their center of power, Pit said. *Isolation as defense.*

Felix blinked at his friend. *Where did that come from?*

Pit grinned. *Books.*

The clouds thinned just as they passed over a series of large copper domes. The Grand Assembly, Felix believed the woman had called it, whatever that meant. More startling was the vast figure staring up at them with wide, vacant eyes that glimmered with captured light. Felix tensed, but it was only a statue. A massive one, carved of the same midnight black stone of the mountain and flecked with pieces of diamond.

Noctis. He recognized her from the mountainside depiction they had seen previously. The others beside her were unfamiliar but could be guessed through context. *The two identical ones in Felling's Blue stone must be the Twins. The pale one in the dress is Siva, and that—huh. They made Vellus quite tiny.*

A gray statue half the height of the towering Goddess of Night, Vellus clung to the woman's skirts like a wayward child. There was no sign of Yyero, Avet, or the Pathless. He said as much to Tzfell.

"Yyero is reviled, as you can imagine how fast sickness can spread within an underground society." She shook her head. "But even he has a small temple of bronze-robed mendicants. There, by the foot of Siva. Only Avet and the Pathless have no presence there."

"Avet has little presence anywhere," Vess added. "Most are not keen on the prospect of change."

The courier nodded in sharp agreement. "The fires of violent upset have no place among the Holds."

Felix scratched the back of his neck, and the Chariot sped on.

Winds buffeted them but never enough to do more than slightly tilt the cabin, and even some intermittent rain pattered down atop the high steel and glass. The clouds continued, thickening so much that Felix began to wonder how they had formed. He didn't know much about meteorology—or if clouds even fell under that discipline—but he was pretty sure it had less to do with nature and more to do with magic. When they did clear, it was sudden and dramatic, revealing a number of similar tracks converging on a single point ahead.

"What is that?" Vess asked.

"Looks like one of those stalagmites," Beef said.

"Tites. Stalactites hang down, mites rise up," Harn corrected. "And that ain't no drippin' rock."

"Too right!" the courier said. She gestured ahead to where the clouds framed a dark structure. "Welcome, one and all, to Nightfall Palace."

It was built entirely upside-down, exactly like a stalactite from the roof of the cavern. Layered towers and walls and wide fortifications were all seemingly carved of a single, gargantuan piece of midnight black stone, dotted with diamonds that resembled nothing so much as a field of stars. Fluted towers, battlements, walkways, all of them were built upside down so that people could walk normally among them. Hanging gardens proliferated, the greenery as vivid against the dark rock as the swirling clouds of Mana vapor. Those seemed to pulse around the palace, spreading outward only to spin inward again later, as if the whole, magnificent structure was breathing.

It's like the Kingsrock, just...flipped, Pit noticed. *And black. That's weird.*

"Holy moly," Beef said, leaning toward a side window. They had come close enough that the palace dominated the entire right side of the Cloud Chariot. "That's someone's house?"

"The Hinterlord of Red Shield," Tzfell muttered. "This was far smaller the last time I was here."

"An addition was completed last decade, allowing for the Consort's bountiful gardens. They are said to contain a seed from every plant in the eastern Continent, you know."

The Cloud Chariot raced closer, not slowing down at all, but the palace's immense size made it seem to linger always out of reach. It wasn't until a number of metal rails converged alongside them that the Nightfall Palace loomed like the miniature mountain it was, and its upside-down towers and bridges whipped by overhead.

"They say it was designed to mimic the Undermount," the courier said, just as they lost sight of the fullness of the palace and entered the Cloud Chariot station. "The foundations were even laid by the Rock-shaper himself!"

"Really? The guy who made the Undermount?" That was intriguing. He kept hearing about that guy, and it tickled at something in his brain. Felix set it aside for now, as the Chariot came to a stop, and the doors once more hissed open.

"Oh, you know your Dwarven history! The very same." The courier hopped out. "If you would follow me, Mr. Veil."

"Are we to see the Hinterlord now?" he asked, stepping carefully out of the train car. The whole thing lurched a little, jostling his people. Beef looked like he was going to be sick.

"Come along!"

The Forge Knights gently prodded Felix and his people into moving. They followed, but Felix was wary. She led them down polished halls of dark blue marble and gorgeously stained wood, flanked by stout statues in the Dwarven style as well as delicate paintings of nature. The place was built on the scale of giants rather than Dwarves, all of it vast and wide with exceeding amounts of empty space.

"Damn," Evie whispered. Even that felt loud in the quiet hallways.

"What? What happened?" Laur asked, looking around. The Elf was sweating.

"This whole place was upside down, which was very interestin'. Somethin' I've never seen before. But we got in, and it's just…normal."

"Did…did you want us to be struggling across the vaulted ceiling?"

Evie's eyes drifted up, and she sighed. "Forget it."

Eventually, the courier stopped at a pair of overlarge doors made entirely out of silver. Elaborate, geometric designs were etched into the metal along the edges, while the centers were embossed with three shields. "Your rooms."

With a single finger, she pushed open the doors.

Beyond was a mansion in and of itself. The large central room was floored in polished stone and inlaid with silver and precious jewels in elaborate, knotwork patterns. Plush, Troll-fur rugs broke up the expanse into a sitting area and a sort of extended dining room while a grand fireplace decorated an entire wall, the mantle carved to depict some ancient Dwarven battle.

Another wall was entirely glass and led out onto a balcony so big Felix could have fit his old studio apartment on it three times over. At the far end, a deep pool was dug into the stone. A short waterfall dropped water from above, filling the pool with a constant roiling current that smelled of sharp minerals. No less than ten doors—each half the size of the entrance—dotted the main room, no doubt leading off to other chambers.

Felix and his people walked slowly into the chambers, many of them goggling at the lush surroundings.

"Your guards and attendants are encouraged to freely explore the Hold. The Cloud Chariots are at their service. However, the feast honoring your bravery will commence shortly."

"So early?" Felix asked, a bit surprised.

"For the Hero of Birchstone? Why, this is to be an entire day of celebration!" The Dwarven woman laughed, and if it weren't for his Affinity, Felix honestly wouldn't have been able to tell if she was being sincere or not. She must have had a Deception or Acting Skill at very high levels.

"How…great," Harn said, his own cheer falling far below the mark.

The courier either didn't notice or didn't care. "Simply pull that cord once you are ready, and an honor guard will lead you to the Hinterlord's presence. Ah, so exciting!"

The courier left, all but squealing.

Once the double doors shut, Felix let an appreciable amount of time pass for the Forge Knights to march away. Once he no longer heard them, Felix signaled Laur. The Elven Chanter immediately threw up a multi-layered ward to hold in all sound. Once it was in place, and the Chanter confirmed it was tied down to the room, Felix wasted no time.

"Claw, this is going to be dangerous, but you're all highly capable. You've proven it to me on this journey, again and again." Felix met each of their eyes as he spoke, all fifty of them. "You need to stick together and listen to your captains, alright? Do that, and we will win this."

"Aye, sir!"

"Laur, Tzfell. Go." The Chanters nodded and slipped out of the chamber. "Evie, Beef, Harn. You know what to do?"

"Yup, though it cost us a lot."

"They better be worth it," Evie muttered.

"Stop yappin' and start movin'. Ain't got time." Harn headed out, gathering a third of the Claw with him. Evie and Beef left, too, each with their own third.

"That leaves us." Felix tugged at his collar and fed his Will into his Garment. It transformed, turning from his rough blue jacket into something far darker, and his tunic whitened until it shone bright beneath a bottle-green vest. Fancy clothes, as best he could figure, though the look was spoiled a bit by the russet puppy that jumped up into his arms.

"You can't walk?"

"He isn't," Pit objected, shoving his wet nose toward Vess.

Vess had clearly changed while the others organized. Her armor had, of course, been polished earlier, but now her dark locks were put up in a stylish cascade of wavy curls. According to Tzfell, the Red Shields were a martial clan that encouraged appearing as if you were ready for war. All she had added was a short half-cape made of some glittery gold fabric that acted as camouflage for her Companion. The Wyrmling was coiled around Vess' shoulders like a stole, so still that he might have been a sculpture.

"Walking is for lesser creatures," Yintarion agreed.

Felix sighed. "Alright, alright." He settled Pit into his left arm. He offered his right to Vess, and she looped her arm eagerly. "Ready to party?"

"Quite."

CHAPTER EIGHTY-FIVE

"This is nerve-wracking," Felix muttered.

They stood at the bottom of a pair of black stone stairs, which swept upward out of a diamond-shaped antechamber. Behind them, a statue of four dour-faced Dwarves sat amidst a fountain of vivid blue water, their hands holding a rod, sword, orb, and a chunky piece of what Felix guessed was metal ore. Behind *that* extended a line of other attendees, all of them waiting impatiently to enter the grand ballroom up at the other end of the staircase.

"You might be comfortable in combat, but this is my battlefield. Follow my lead, and we will prevail," Vess said, patting his hand.

"You're good at fighting, too," Felix pointed out.

"So I am."

"Seems unfair."

Vess gave him a dimpled grin. "If I were to list out how many unfair advantages you benefited from, we would miss the gala."

Felix laughed, and they progressed up the dark steps. After leaving their room, an Untempered servant had guided them through Nightfall Palace to the antechamber behind them. The place was filled with sound wards that expanded and dissipated like a field of soap bubbles as Dwarven nobility gossipped. Felix hadn't any interest in what they spoke of, but judging by the many looks his way, it was likely him.

As he'd been reminded over and over again, a six-and-a-half-foot Human stood out in Dwarven society, and that was never so apparent as when he stopped atop the dark staircase next to a thirty-foot-tall door made of solid gold.

"Your card, sir?" An impressively fancy Dwarf stood off to the side, his beard and mustache waxed to a point.

Felix stared blankly at the guy until Vess nudged him lightly. "Oh. Right."

He handed over a small square of cardstock the Untempered servant had left them before he had scurried off. It bore two names on it, written in silver ink and bordered by an interlocking maze of geometric patterns. The majordomo lifted the card to his eyes and gestured for the two of them to begin walking forward.

"Ready?" Vess asked him.

"As I'll ever be."

They stepped across the threshold of the golden door and onto a pristine white landing as bright as the anteroom was dark. Spread out before them was another set of stairs sweeping downward into a vast ballroom of elaborate inlaid flooring polished to a mirror finish and filled with hundreds of Dwarves. Huge, twenty-foot-thick pillars lined the outskirts of the chamber before joining with a vaulted ceiling at least a hundred feet high. Fifty-foot windows filled the gap between each pillar, with rich, textured curtains drawn open to reveal all of Red Shield Hold spread out below them like a sea of golden rivers and twinkling lights.

At the far end, a raised dais displayed a ceremonial seat that looked exceedingly like a throne. It was empty. Felix was about to make a comment about it to Vess, but the majordomo's voice outstripped his by several orders of magnitude.

"Mr. Silas Veil, Hero of Birchstone, and Her Grace, Vessilia Dayne of Pax'Vrell!"

The entirety of the crowd turned to watch them, drink paused halfway to mouths, and the soft buzz of conversations cut off completely. Felix stiffened, and only Vess' gentle guidance reminded him to keep moving down the stairs.

"We expected them to know me. We are fine," she murmured.

"Just startled me," Felix admitted. He kept it to himself how uneasy the sudden stares all were making him and finished walking down the interminable white steps. By the time they reached the floor, however, conversations had resumed, and most of the attendees no longer stared so openly.

Most.

"Brace yourself," Vess whispered.

The Dwarven nobility came for them. First in a trickle, as one or two cozied up next to them, but then a flood as the others grew more bold.

"Good evening, Your Grace! What a delight to have a representative of Pax'Vrell among us."

"Mr. Veil! The hero himself! What an honor to have you within the Hold!"

"Pow! Then you struck the Titan! When I heard that I—"

"—lost a thousand crowns worth of property due to the rampant fires! Can you believe that? The Hinterlord must invest in more water-attuned mages, or else we're all poised to lose our shirts!"

"Do you have Dwarven blood in you, Mr. Veil? Your broad shoulders suggest you must!"

"—did you see them as you came in? Crowding the Clan Gate? Pitiful upstarts."

"Hopefully the Titan's defeat will mean a return to normal—"

Vess handled all of them with remarkable poise and charm, answering very little of their questions and deftly turning their conversational points back onto the askers. After only a few short minutes, she had most of the nobles in the palm of her hand, commanding the flow of conversation. She did all the heavy lifting, while Felix mostly smiled and nodded where he thought was most appropriate.

While more and more people were loudly introduced by the majordomo, their audience dwindled in number until there were only three well-dressed individuals engaging their time. A Dwarven woman, Rosalind Uterre, was their de facto leader, as they deferred to her whenever she spoke.

"I have always wished to summer in Pax'Vrell, my dear. I hear it is a temperate clime but leans quite warm."

Vess laughed. "Our warm summers are excellent for our wine sellers. The grapes ripen beautifully on the vines. You should visit for the wine alone; my father would be proud to have such esteemed guests."

"Perhaps I shall," the older Dwarf tittered, as if the idea of it amused and appealed in equal measure. "And you, Mr. Veil. Where do you hail from?"

"Around."

"...it must be renowned for its warriors, for I hear the Titan was no easy opponent. How did you defeat her? Previously, it required a great deal of the Hinterlord's personal resources to keep her out of our city."

"I'm lucky, I suppose," Felix said.

"Would that I had such luck. Handsome, strong, and with the arm of a Duchess. Are you a noble in your home, Mr. Veil?"

"I'm no one special," Felix said, before floundering. "Vess and I are...ah..."

"Associates," Vess finished for him, a smile on her lips. "And you, Lady Uterre? What is it you do in this wonderful Hold?"

"Please, call me Rosalind, your Grace."

"Rosalind, then."

"To answer your question, I am in charge of the well-being of the entire Hold. I would dare say my responsibilities vie with the Hinter-lord's own—for how far would our Hold fall if the Untempered were mismanaged?"

"Untempered...You manage the servants?" Felix asked.

"Servants, skilled and unskilled laborers, even many merchants. All live within my district, where they are provided for according to their needs."

"Where they are stuffed into overflowing tenements and given the bare essentials to survive, you mean."

A well-dressed Dwarven man had stepped into the trio of nobles. He had a black beard streaked with white and his hair was the same, save it was pulled back into a plaited tail. He grinned around a long-stemmed pipe as he settled between Rosalind and Felix, punctuating his statement with a cloud of blue-green smoke.

"Lord Oslo," Rosalind said icily. "You presume much, as always. I take care of my vassals, and you cannot prove otherwise."

"Of course, Rosalind. There is always more to know than one can prove. For instance, I know the Untempered that you so lovingly tend to are malnourished and are given less leeway than the meanest of Howlers."

"You care only for yourself and your 'art,' which is why you cannot begin to understand the magnitude of my responsibilities. The grand design of my Lord husband." Rosalind drew herself up, her Spirit as sharp as her glare. "Landless nobles should not speak to their betters."

"To be considered my better, you would require both a fortune and a conscience, Rosalind." Lord Oslo tapped a finger against his pipe. "I don't think your lord husband can afford both."

Rosalind gave an exaggerated huff, almost a hiss, and stomped off. The two lackeys followed her with worried words of comfort.

Lord Oslo chuckled. "Damnable harpy. Sorry about that, Mr. Veil.

Your Grace. I simply cannot stand worthless people." He put out his hand and, amused, Felix grasped forearms with the stocky Dwarf. "Lord Bron Oslo."

"You already have our names, it seems, but it is a pleasure to meet you," Felix said.

"I agree, Lord Oslo," Vess said.

"Please, call me Bron. You two appear to have solid heads on your shoulders, and that is a refreshing thing at events such as these." The noble bowed over Vess' hand, kissing the back of his own thumb as he held her wrist.

"To control the supply of servants and laborers in the Hold is quite potent." Vess lifted an eyebrow. "Is it wise to antagonize such a powerful player?"

"Rosalind? Hm, perhaps. But then, I am not one to play games among the Highbloods. Clan Oslo is small and landless, controlling no district of the Hold like some others, but we are mighty. I also do not employ servants. I think I can handle Uterre's insipid vitriol."

Felix liked the guy immediately. He was a breath of fresh air compared to the unctuous nobles that had introduced themselves to the pair of them, and even Pit roused from his nap of boredom. *What do you think, bud?*

His pipe stinks. But I like his beard.

"What does Clan Oslo specialize in?" Vess asked.

"A unique resource in our underground kingdom. Our fortune is not in soldiers, mines, or forges, but art. My family has long been a prolific patron of the arts, but in my earliest years, I set about fostering it as best I can across the Dwarven Holds."

"Art? That's noble."

"Thank you, Mr. Veil. The other nobles would not agree, but then anything that does not glitter holds little value to them." Bron snorted, a stream of blue-green smoke firing out of both nostrils.

"What sort of art?" Vess asked.

"If you but wait a while, you shall see," Bron said, waggling his eyebrows. "The Hinterlord has commissioned my clan for a performance today and—" a series of deep horns rang out from behind the dais. "Ah. Call the Unbound, and they shall answer. Excuse me, Mr. Veil. Your Grace."

Felix gave the man a sharp glance, but he was already off, hustling through the crowd toward the throne. The deep horns grew louder, gaining a brassy accompaniment as the doors at the far end of the chamber opened up. The majordomo, now somehow beside the throne, opened his arms wide and spoke words that buzzed against Felix's inner ear.

"Stand now, for Kragan Red Shield, Patriarch of Clan Red Shield, Protector of the Undermount, Honorary Grandmaster of the Hidden Night."

A number of armored Dwarves marched from the golden doors, all of them bearing tall halberds and banners displaying the three shields of the Hinterlord's clan. They split as the majordomo finished speaking, and a rotund figure in custom, golden-plated armor stepped from their midst. He had the gait of a warrior, but one far past his prime, for all the vigor he mustered in keeping his bearded chin high as he strode to the top of the dias.

"Honorary Grandmaster?" Felix asked.

"A tradition among some cultures," Vess explained. "Silly perhaps, but it conveys a societal authority—just not a true one."

"A false king," Yintarion whispered, his voice barely audible. "Wearing false gold. Fitting."

Felix activated Voracious Eye, focusing on the Hinterlord's armor and not the man. It came back as gold-plated mithril and was heavily enchanted with a slew of defensive measures. The circlet around his head, a number of amulets, rings, and earrings inundated him with even more. So many that it was hard to parse one from the other, or even the Dwarf underneath. Without focusing harder and betraying the fact that he was Analyzing the ruler of this little kingdom, it was difficult to even identify the Hinterlord's advancement.

I bet he's weak. Why else does he need so much jewelry, Pit sent.

Fair point. But I'm not taking any chances.

The Hinterlord stood before his throne, arms akimbo as if to let his people survey his shiny armor and flowing auburn beard—and to survey them in turn. Felix's Spirit prickled under the scrutiny, the Hinterlord's Analyze hitting a great many of them all at once.

"Welcome, one and all. This day of celebration was originally to usher in the dawn of spring as it slowly crawls over the land and a return to days of plenty as the villages upon our peaks turn in their tribute of grain and fish and ore. Instead, we have gathered to celebrate a new event, one that puts the advent of spring to shame: the defeat of the wretched Titan!"

The ballroom shook as the nobles gave an extended cheer. All of them seemed very pleased.

"We have gathered to herald the rise of a hero! The one who fought down the Titan and lived, while so many others died or were beaten to submission. The Hero of Birchstone, Silas Veil!"

Once again, Felix found himself the center of attention. The braziers near him surged with flames, illuminating his every angle, and the nobles cheered all the louder.

"Now," the Hinterlord said, cutting off the din as if he'd strangled them all. "The hero deserves a feast!" Kragan Red Shield clapped his hands. "Bring out the feast!"

All at once, an army of servants clad in black and white livery came streaming from smaller doorways along the ballroom's length. Dozens. Hundreds. All of them were carrying tables, chairs, linens, and gleaming utensils. Porcelain followed, along with steaming platters of roasted meat, vegetables, and sumptuous sweets and breads. Great trestle tables were set out in seconds, laden with delicious smelling food, and the nobility descended on them.

Felix watched with quite a bit of shock. There was no civility or niceties when it came to the Dwarven nobility and their food. The last servant had barely scurried away when the first Lord was elbow-deep in some roasted ham hock. Juice and grease dribbled down braided beards with abandon.

"Dunno if I'm all that hungry," Felix admitted. Vess only nodded mutely, her dusky skin paler than usual. Pit's stomach gurgled loudly.

"Would they be upset if you threw me onto that table?" Pit asked.

"I'm not doing that."

"But look at all that food!"

"Indeed," Yintarion said. "Each and every dish I can see has been harvested from potent monsters. No wonder they eat with such abandon. I, too, would like to partake. Can you get closer, little Dragoon?"

"I refuse. I apologize, Yin."

"Fah."

The four of them made their way to the sidelines, intending to stay out of everyone's way, but instead found another trestle table being set up at their side. Liveried servants hustled, carrying chairs and food at rapid speeds, before bowing low and gesturing to the spread. "Please, hero. Break your fast with this feast."

Felix smiled at them and gave them a bit of a bow in return. Several of the servants were breathing heavily, most were sweating, but that was to be expected. All of them were Untempered. "This is very impressive. Thank you."

The Dwarven servants grinned and, seeing that Felix and Vess were sitting themselves, soon scurried off.

For a time, they ate. It was really good food, though Felix only gave it a nibble. He was still rather full from the Domain. Vess put in the effort, but her attention was too wrapped up in their surroundings for her to enjoy a meal. Pit and Yintarion, then, took it as their duty to make up for their Companions.

The feast didn't stand a chance.

A quarter hour later, the horns sounded once again, and Hinterlord Kagan slammed a diamond-encrusted staff of office upon the dais. It echoed throughout the ballroom like thunder.

"While you enjoy your feast, we must have entertainment!" he bellowed. His own face was a bit stained by wine and the greasy remnants of a monster haunch. "Lord Oslo!"

"Yes, my Lord?" Bron was still at the foot of the dais, waiting patiently all this time.

"What of our entertainment?"

"But of course, Hinterlord! But of course!" Bron rushed off, back through the golden doors behind the throne. In less than a minute, he returned, and this time, he was dressed in robes that made him look like a very fancy mage.

"By your Will, Hinterlord, I have gathered today the greatest talent upon the face of the Continent! They have composed a new performance for you, my Lord, special for this glorious day. Please, allow me to introduce the Flight of Elegance!"

From behind him came a flash of brilliant light and colors as Skills fired off all at once. Illusions, shadows, and swirling air Mana surged around Lord Oslo in a vibrant, glittering display. From within it, lithe figures emerged mid-air. Wings of earthen hues spread, gliding down from above in smooth pirouettes as a troupe of bird-like Korvaa alighted in a triangular stack. With a delicate chirrup, they dove aside, the triangle splitting open to reveal three angular, Elven figures wearing diaphanous robes and bearing weapons.

"Felix," Vess said, eyes wide. "Are they—?"

"Yeah," he said. His gaze was riveted to the dancers. Upon their backs were brilliantly colored wings. Wings he'd seen only one other time.

On the back of another Unbound.

CHAPTER EIGHTY-SIX

Voracious Eye!

Name: Narin Saaf
Race: Sylphaen
Level: 43
HP: 2433/2433
SP: 6699/6742
MP: 4345/4345
Lore: The Sylphaen are a precursor of modern Elves and have deep ties to the Supreme Elemental of air. As with many Races in the early Ages of the Continent, the Sylphaen carry part of that elemental power with them. Many of their core spaces are air attuned, which makes them particularly adept at flight with their vividly colored wings.
Strength: More Data Required
Weakness: More Data Required

The other two were Mosa and Idin Saaf, relations of some sort, and all of them lower-leveled than Narin. Felix checked his memories, comparing them. They looked as gaunt as the Winged Elf in Felix's visions, but their hair color was different, as were their wings. The Unbound had wings of many different colors in a sort of gradient of hue, while these Sylphaen bore feathers almost entirely of one color, with only a smattering of others along the inner portions and top edge.

Felix checked his connections to the Unbound. It was dulled, as it had been for a while, with Archie and Imara somewhere relatively close. Beef was moving above him, somewhere in an upper level, and the rest were scattered far and wide. The cord he associated with the Winged Elf was dim and distant.

"What is wrong?" Vess asked. Only then did Felix realize that he'd crumbled one of the forks in his hand as if it were made of aluminum foil.

He set it down gently on the table. "Nothing. I thought—nothing."

While the dancers certainly noticed Felix's analyzing them—he could tell by the deep flinches during their movements—the Flight of Elegance were professionals. They continued their dance as the shorter Korvaa around them rotated into a spin, their earth-toned wings flared outward. Soon, the Sylphaen moved as well, leaping between the gathered Korvaa as if jumping across a wall. The Korvaa fell backward, tumbling head over heels before fetching back up onto their clawed feet.

Magic swirled, shadow, illusion, and light Mana pouring from palms and elbows until the dancers were obscured by a veil of seeming. Snow looked to fall, until it appeared like a frigid squall had erupted within the ballroom. The fallen Korvaa had become walls and buildings, the Sylphaen fire, and all of it raged. In their midst, white figures bathed in flame stormed the walls. The Korvaa swept forward, wings held out as if bearing mighty weapons, and met the dangerous tide.

Trolls. Trolls versus the Watch and Ironclads, Felix realized. *They're reenacting the fight against Imara.*

When one of the Sylphaen appeared garbed in golden light and the illusory sheen of metal armor, another stepped out of the wreckage. A figure in a dark coat with bright blue eyes. Felix's stomach sank as they danced around one another, their movements in sync as only a pair of dancers could be. Overly dramatic movements were attacks, knocking each other around and to the ground, but it was clear from the outset that the Titan was on the backfoot.

The fight continued, a strange, floating dream before Felix's eyes. It conjured memories as he watched, too close to reality for comfort and too strangely surreal to take it seriously. He was left in a strange limbo, consumed by the magic of their performance as the inevitable played out.

And it was magic, Felix was surprised to note. Humming threads of the Grand Harmony sang from them, hidden within the fabric of the world but expressed by their pure movements. It was beautiful, in a haunting sort of way…which made the end all the more jarring.

"Felix" struck the "Titan," and the dancer flew away, propelled by spiraling illusions off into the snowy distance. Yet there was no Doric. No sacrifice. As if the man's final act meant nothing, the performance ended, and the ballroom went dark.

Applause erupted, great and booming cheers following calls for more. At his table, Felix was jerked from the spell, his unsure enjoyment turned abruptly sour. Warmth enveloped his hand as Vess took it, and Felix blinked at her. She said nothing, and Felix was thankful for that. He wasn't sure he had the right words to say, anyway.

"I wasn't even in that," Pit protested.

Unbidden, a chuckle escaped Felix's lips. He ruffled Pit's doggy ears and pushed another plate of steak at him.

The performers basked for a bit longer in their applause, but soon they departed, this time through the doors of the servants. Musicians were ushered in to replace them, and they soon began a series of relatively sedate songs. Felix frowned. It was like elevator music gone medieval, and all the worse for the transition.

Lord Oslo emerged from behind the throne, once again in his normal clothing and smoking his long-stemmed pipe. He was grinning widely as he sidled up to their table. "What did you think, Mr. Veil? Was it not glorious? Not an exact replaying of events, but such is art!"

"It was…" Felix cleared his throat. "It was great."

"The magic was quite dazzling," Vess agreed, amping up her own enthusiasm to cover for Felix's flat delivery. "How did you come across this troupe?"

"By thinking beyond the rigid mindset of my people. Too many Dwarves are mired in past glories to reach for something new, but not I. The Flight of Elegance is renowned in their own Territory, and when I chanced upon them during my travels, I was delighted. I've hired them on for the next year, as I have done for a great many artists, in the hopes that they can bring a little outside perspective to the Hold."

"Their Territory…where would that be?" Felix asked.

"Hm? Oh, they hail from mysterious Sunara! Where the stones stand as high as mountains, worn to pillars beneath tempestuous winds and the very waters boil beneath their feet!" Bron laughed. "A fanciful description for patrons. But it is truly an inhospitable place to Dwarf or Human, and only those blessed with flight may traverse the land."

Vess laughed along with him, and her brown eyes flashed gold. "I have heard of it, that is north of the jungles of Jaast, is it not?"

"It is! You are a traveler, too?"

"Only in my dreams. My father has a grand collection of maps." Vess tapped her dark lips. "Sunara. I have heard they are fiercely isolated. How did you even find them?"

"By lucky chance, as I said. I have journeyed far and wide across the Continent and hope to one day see it all. One benefit of being a landless clan," Bron said with a wink.

The garrulous man kept going for a bit longer, but it was all pleasantries and nonsense to Felix as he marked down the Territory of Sunara in his impressive memory. Even if the Sylphaen here had nothing to do with the Winged Elf, Felix had a new place to check. Still, as Bron departed to speak with other waiting nobles, Felix couldn't help but eye the door the troupe exited.

"We need to talk to them. Those dancers were the same Race as the Winged Elf," he said to Vess in a low whisper.

She clenched her jaw but nodded. "What do you wish to do about it? We cannot leave, or else we may miss our chance to speak with the Hinterlord."

Felix growled, yet barely noticed the noise, even as the dishes around him rattled. Vess stilled them with a touch. The downside of being a "hero" was that everyone was watching him, even as he did nothing more than sit and stare into the middle distance. People would notice if Felix or Vess left to speak to the Sylphaen.

"I can go," Pit said. "I'll sneak my way through."

"An excellent idea," Vess agreed.

Felix bit his lip before nodding. His friend would be safe enough in the palace. "Right. Go fast, keep hidden, and stay in contact."

Pit hopped down off his lap and under the table. There, Felix felt Gloaming Shroud activate, coating Pit in a mixture of shadow, light, and earth Mana. When he scampered from beneath the table, he was barely visible, and that was with Adept eyes and knowing where to look. Before long, he vanished into the opposing tables where the nobility still stuffed their faces.

Tell me when you're there, Felix sent.

I know. I got it.

The doors across the ballroom opened and closed as servants picked up used platters and dirty cutlery. He couldn't tell exactly when Pit made it through, but the sudden swell of triumph across their bond was a good general indicator. Felix waited, drumming his fingers on the table.

"You should relax, Autarch," Yintarion suggested. His form was still bundled up in the golden cape/shawl combo Vess wore, but his eyes shone through the diaphanous material. "Worrying will not solve our many dilemmas." The music swelled as the staid and sedate songs were replaced with something more lively. "This is a ballroom. My many years among you mortals has shown me that you love little more than a chance to dance. It will improve your mood."

"An inspired idea. Our Companions are quite brilliant," Vess said. She stood and offered Felix her hand. "Will you join me?"

Felix sighed but managed a wan smile. "Yes. Of course, I will."

Together, they swept out onto the center of the ballroom, where a number of Dwarves had already started dancing. Vess led, her steps sure as she adapted to the music, and Felix just barely kept up. His Skills and stats were great and powerful, but dancing hadn't ever been in his wheelhouse. The third time he stepped on Vess' foot, he grew frustrated.

"Here, watch my feet," Vess offered. She performed a sample step, placing her feet just so before turning and repeating the process. "This is a simple one."

Felix burned the pattern into his brain and took up her hands again. This time, he made no mistakes. He smiled. "Huh."

"Now to make it complicated," Vess said with an impish smile.

"Wait, why—"

She took off, giving Felix little choice but to flow with her or be left behind. Her steps followed the same pattern as before, but every other turn she added more flourishes and movements.

"This was how my first instructor taught me my movement Skill," she said, a flush of color on her cheeks as they moved together. "This is a battlefield, just as any other. Treat it as such, and it becomes far easier. Right?"

Felix, who was matching her step for step, gave a rueful grin. "Such a simple change of perspective, and it helps so much."

They danced, and their display did not go unnoticed. Other couples moved to the floor, their movements just as graceful and studied, until the ballroom was packed with those dancing. The songs turned happy, bouncy, and invigorating, pushing all of them to greater heights.

More than a simple distraction, Felix found himself having fun. There was a joy in movement, something often forgotten in his drive to train and improve his Skills. Holding Vess close, they whirled about the dance floor, complicated steps weaving among the crowd. She was warm, even through her armor, and the laughter in her eyes was a balm to his frazzled nerves.

At some point, the songs slowed and their pace with it. They stood among many, carefully navigating a measured pace, and Felix's thoughts caught up to him.

"I'm sorry," he said.

Vess raised an eyebrow. "For?"

"Before. With that Rosalind lady. She asked if we—I hesitated. You called us 'associates.' I don't know what we are, yet, but that felt…lesser."

She cocked her head, and a curl tumbled loose from her temple. "Did you think I was angry?"

He winced through his smile. "I mean, I thought you thought it might have been rude—"

"Felix. You have an ability to read my emotions. Do I seem angry now?"

"Well, I usually don't use that on you. It's invasive, and…oh, no you're not." He paused. "If you're that amused by me, I guess I'm a lot funnier than I thought."

"You can be, but no. You are an incredibly frustrating man, but you are also good. Compassionate to a fault and willing to make hard choices for your people. You deny it and cast aside crowns and scepters, but you are a king, Felix. It is baked into your bones."

"I'm all that?" Felix asked, a little nonplussed.

"You are."

"And you're not mad."

A smile quirked her lips. "I am not. I—if I were being honest, 'associate' was only a balm to my wounds. I did not wish to presume that—we shared a meal and a kiss, and I, too, am unsure. Of where I stand."

Felix held her a bit closer to him as the music swelled. "You stand with me."

That dimpled smile blossomed. "So I do."

"Still, it is worthwhile to make our Intent clear, is it not? I would officially court you, if I could, Felix Nevarre." She looked up at him, the gold in her brown eyes catching the light. "Would that be…pleasing to you?"

"I can't say I've ever been courted before," Felix admitted. "It's fancy."

"Evie says I am the fanciest." Vess bit her lip. "What do you say?"

In response, Felix kissed her.

Yintarion snorted out a little bit of smoke. "Mortal courtship. Bah. A silly tradition."

"Mr. Veil?"

Felix and Vess stopped in their tracks, their dance interrupted by a familiar woman flanked by two Forge Knights. The courier, except now she was wearing an elaborate formal gown.

She curtsied. "The Hinterlord would like a word."

CHAPTER EIGHTY-SEVEN

"Silas Veil. Your Grace Vessilia Dayne. I am honored to host the daughter of the Howling Hurricane, but I must admit a certain fondness for you, Mr. Veil. The Titanslayer himself."

The Hinterlord Kragan Red Shield lounged on his throne. Up close, the man wasn't as portly as Felix had thought. His golden-plated armor was ill-fitting around the neck and belly, as if he'd lost weight fairly rapidly, and his armorer hadn't had time to make adjustments. His beard was splayed over his chest, hiding most of his weight loss beneath its volume of braids, gold fasteners, and gems. A diamond-studded goblet of wine dangled from his hand.

"Titanslayer?" Felix asked, trading a look with Vess. "You think she's dead?"

"I have heard the reports of your fight. If she has survived your powerful attack, she would be a fool to return. And if she does, then I have the Titanslayer here to fend her off, aye?"

Felix inclined his head but said nothing.

Kragan set his goblet into the hands of a waiting servant and leaned forward. "I also hear that you originally came to this Hold in order to establish trade with my clan. Is this true?"

"It is."

"Red Shield Hold does not often form trade agreements with foreigners, no matter their bravery, but…as you have done my realm a service, I shall at least inspect your wares. Do you have them with you in your apartments?"

"Better. I have a sample here." Felix reached into his coat and withdrew a stone bottle corked and sealed with inscribed wax. "This is an Essence Draught attuned to earth Mana."

The Hinterlord gestured and a servant scurried forward to take the bottle from Felix and bring it to the Dwarf's outstretched hand. He turned it over twice, inspecting it from all angles. He even brought it to his nose and sniffed it. With a flick of his wrist, the Hinterlord broke the wax seal, releasing a cloud of dusty brown infused heavily with pale, undifferentiated Mana. From all around, the ambient power in the room was drawn forward, gathering in heavy clouds and shimmering auras around the bottle's open mouth. The music halted, the dancers paused, and all conversation died away.

The man blinked, throat working for a second before any sound came out. "Powerful. Truly, magnificently powerful. Distilled from the Spirit Fruit of the Atlantes Anima. What is that?"

"A Spirit Tree."

Kragan Red Shield blinked again, then he laughed. "Stones and stars. You speak the truth, Mr. Veil?"

"I do. My source distills these draughts directly from the Tree itself."

"Astounding." The Hinterlord handed the bottle to a servant, who held it away from themselves as if it were a bomb. "These could be a mighty boon to anyone who trades with you, Mr. Veil. Have you established contact with anyone else?"

"I have not. You are my first, Hinterlord."

Kragan rubbed his chin. "I would offer you a grand sum of gold for the shipment you have with you...but if you have not approached any others as of yet, that makes me question why."

Felix smiled and spread his hands. "For future trade, I would be more than happy with gold. However, for now, I am looking for something more important. An item to heal a friend."

"Far be it for me to spurn coin, but that would be a simple solution not suitable for a trade of such opulence. Red Shield Hold claims the allegiance of many great alchemists and herbalists. They are able to concoct any number of remedies that could easily heal your friend."

"It's not a Status Condition or an ailment," Felix said. "It's a curse wrapped around my friend's core space."

Kragan sucked at his teeth, thick fingers tapping at his lips. "A dangerous thing. Few could cure that…and fewer still would try without great urging. To fail would have a terrible cost."

"I have heard a great deal of the treasures the Hinterlords possess. One such item has been mentioned to me in my travels." Felix took a bracing breath. "An artifact that could heal anything, Body, Mind, and Spirit. The Mote of Frenzy."

The Hinterlord dropped his hand, gripping the golden arm of his throne. "I am aware of that artifact…and I am disappointed. Not because what you say is untrue, but because it is a treasure I cannot offer."

Felix's gut dropped, and a curious heat crawled up his back. "Why?"

Kragan narrowed his eyes, perhaps at Felix's tone, but he answered. "It is a clan treasure, one passed through the Ages from one Hinterlord to the next. They are sacrosanct, not to be touched by any but the Hinterlords themselves, and even then, only when it would strengthen the clan."

"The Essence Draughts would greatly benefit your clan," Vess pointed out. "It would empower your people with potent Aspects and solidify their foundations. In time, with our draughts, the Red Shield clan would strengthen its base tenfold."

Kragan grunted. "You'll forgive me for not taking you at your word, Your Grace. The Hierocracy, who your father serves, has been attempting to grasp the treasures of my people for many long centuries." The guy blew a deep breath out of his lungs, setting his mustache fluttering. "However, for the Hero of Birchstone, I am honor-bound to do something. Bring your friend to me, and I'll have my finest healers look into their curse. Perhaps they can find a solution."

"That's…generous," Felix said. It wasn't the Mote, but it couldn't hurt. *If only we had more time.*

"In return, I would ask that you stay in the Clan Hold until the summer begins. Your prowess would be a potent solution to our current issues of security and—"

A Dwarf with an iron gray mustache stepped up to the throne, a conical helmet set with scrolling gold knotwork upon his head to match the mithril armor he wore. "My Lord. A development."

"Hm. My Marshal-General beckons. In the meantime, please enjoy yourselves at the gala. It is for you, after all. I will have your answer later, Mr. Veil. Your Grace."

With less than a nod, the two of them were dismissed from the dais. Forge Knights led them back down to the polished floor before they returned to the throne. Felix chewed at his cheek, considering their options as he mindlessly returned to their original table. He turned and studied the dancing nobility, watching them fake laugh through song after song, their Spirits belying their savage dislike of one another.

"We tried," Felix muttered at last. "He won't trade for the Mote and clearly won't give us access to it."

Vess took his hand, giving it a squeeze. "Do you think his healers would be able to accomplish anything?"

"We don't have the time to figure that out," Felix said with a sigh. "Archie. Imara. It's all coming to a head. Soon—"

A piping voice interrupted his thoughts, as Pit's excitement rippled through their bond.

Felix? I found them.

Where are you? Felix asked.

Just outside the servants' quarters. I made… Pit paused, tracing his thoughts back along the path he'd followed. *Lots of turns to get here. Not sure how far.*

The Flight of Elegance was ahead, and Pit watched them from around a corner. Their door opened, and all of them started piling in. Pit danced indecisively, his little feet shuffling. *I'm gonna go for it!*

Wait, go for what?

Pit didn't answer and instead rushed the open door. Thankfully his stealth and small size was more than adequate to squeeze through unnoticed.

Inside, it was modest, clearly designed for servants and a bit too small for the entire troupe. The Korvaa started chatting among one another, while the three Sylphaen gathered in the far corner. Pit hopped up onto a narrow bed and dropped his Gloaming Shroud.

"Where—? Did someone get a dog?" a falcon-like Korvaa asked.

"What? No. Where did that come from?"

"Musta snuck in."

The Sylphaen were looking at him, but their heads were tilted to the side, as if Pit confused them somehow. A bulkier Korvaa approached carefully.

"Come here, little fella. We'll get you back out of here."

The guy looked like he was going to grab him, so Pit took away the option. He shifted from Dire Hound to tenku. His body spread out in a flash of light, tail bumping against the headboard while his forepaws and head just about hung off the end. Everyone in the room jumped back, startled and cursing.

"Hello," he chirruped. "I'm Pit."

That's one way to introduce yourself, Felix said.

There was a beat of shock, but to Pit's surprise and delight, every single person in the room dropped into a bow.

"Honored Tenku," Falcon said. "How are you here…Are you trapped by the Dwarves?"

Pit laughed. "What? No. I came here with my Companion."

"Companion?" The Korvaa and Sylphaen exchanged surprised looks. Maybe even alarmed, but Pit hadn't a clue why that would be. His Etheric Concordance was one of the best things that had happened to him.

"Yup. Anyway, we had some questions."

"What sort of questions?" Falcon asked.

Ask them if they know of a multi-colored Sylphaen, Felix sent. *She would have shown up a year ago and—*

"Why do you call me Honored Tenku?" Pit asked instead. "I met some Korvaa once in the Void, and they called me the same thing. Is it like…a cultural thing?"

Falcon slowly considered Pit's words, likely because they were so incredibly wise. "The Chimera are to be honored. Such is our way. Such is our truth."

"Uh-huh. Okay. That doesn't really answer anything. How do you even know what Chimera are?" Pit twitched his ear tufts. "We're not common."

"In Sunara, tenku and wyverns are known to fly the Tempest. They are powerful and worthy of our respect."

"There's…more tenku?" Pit sat back on his haunches, stunned.

"We have seen only a few during the worst of the seasonal storms, but yes. There are Chimera in Sunara." Falcon gave him a look that Pit couldn't interpret. It was…misty-eyed. "Where are you from, that you've been so isolated, Honored Tenku?"

Pit?

I'm fine. I just didn't think… "I'm fine. My Companion wanted to ask the Sylphaen a question."

The Elf-like people tilted their heads again, this time their mouths opening to release a trilling song. Pit frowned. Falcon answered for them.

"The Sylphaen cannot speak the common tongue. Their mouths are not right for it. But I will speak with you, Companion of the Honored Tenku."

"Do you know of a woman with multi-colored wings? She is a Sylphaen, like you guys."

The Sylphaens straightened, their curious body language suddenly guarded. The Korvaa spoke to them in their fluting language, but they only replied with a series of terse notes. "Sorry. They will not speak on it. They say it is forbidden."

"Why?"

Without warning, the Sylphaen gave Pit another bow of respect, before they walked out of the room entirely.

Falcon sighed. "Honored Tenku or no, their people hold Oaths to be powerful. I am sorry." He and the other Korvaa looked to Pit curiously. "Do you have any other questions?"

...Felix?

Annoying. Yeah, let me list a few off for you.

After giving Pit a list of questions to ask the Sunaran troupe, Vess had dragged Felix back onto the dance floor.

He'd never been a big fan of it back home, but he had to admit it was quite fun, so long as you had the right partner. Matching Vess' impeccable footwork was tough, especially as the steps grew more and more complicated, but it was a satisfying challenge. And it kept his Mind from worrying at the plan.

"They have returned," Vess whispered.

Felix completed a half-turn with Vess in his arms and saw a Dwarf and Elf hustling down the pale stairs of the ballroom. The Chanters scanned the room for only a second before they made a beeline straight for them.

"My...Mr. Veil," Laur said, panting slightly. Felix raised an eyebrow at that; for a Master Tier to get winded meant they had really pressed themselves. A bubble of wards surrounded their group, cutting off any eavesdroppers. "I have traced the faults from the High Roads into the Clan Hold, and, following the patterns, have developed a method to identify the disruption in—"

"We found the way into the Undermount," Tzfell finished, her own excitement mounting. "It's close, as we guessed."

"Oh good." Pit, fully stealthed, leaped into the air and landed on Felix's shoulder. He dropped a rolled-up scroll into his Companion's hands. "I'm done, too. After all those questions, the dancers drew a map."

Felix unrolled it, glancing over the hastily scribed mountains and what looked like water. "Excellent. Laur, send word to Loquis and Mervin. Have them engage their distraction. We've exhausted our efforts here."

As if waiting for Felix's words, alarm bells rang out. They were distant at first, a sparse far-off ringing, but they grew closer and closer until even the ballroom of the Nightfall Palace shook with their warning.

"The Hinterlord is gone," Vess said.

"The Marshal-General with him." Felix scanned the crowd. The nobility had frozen at first but now they gathered in fast-talking clusters, glancing worriedly out through the vast windows.

"Is this us?" Pit asked. "The distraction?"

"No." Tzfell's tattoos squirmed, a sign of her fear, Felix had learned. "Someone has breached the city gates."

"Again?"

One of the many stone braziers around them flared with fire, popping as it consumed whatever fuel it ran on. In that noise, Felix's Affinity tangled with something else. A voice, just on the edge of hearing.

The Pathless' Chosen Has Arrived.

"Did anyone else hear that?" he asked.

"I cannot hear anything over these forsaken *bells*," Yintarion grumbled.

It wasn't his Hunger. The voice was old, grandfatherly even…and distantly familiar. *Does it mean Imara?* If it was true…Felix licked his lips, sorting through his options. Evie, Beef, and Harn weren't back yet, and the Claw might not have moved onto their second phase. They had to move fast.

"We need to act now. Stick to the plan," Felix said. "Go."

CHAPTER EIGHTY-EIGHT

"We hold here! Hold it, or else we lose the district entirely!"

Kossryn, Captain of the Watch, rode down the line on her Avum. Her sword was high and her armors scuffed, but they had survived the enemy's initial thrust into Birchstone. The city gate had fallen, but then it had not yet been truly repaired. The watchtowers themselves were still slag, and much of the wall itself. There was nothing to stop the bastards from charging through the breach.

Hundreds of the Watch died to their golden blades, cut through just as easily as the laborers hauling stone. The people had run, funneled toward the district gate as fire rampaged across the streets. Many more had died to panic than enemy Skills, but the how meant little to the bodies strewn across the cobblestones. Smoke clouded the skies now, and though it was mid-morning, the city remained shrouded in false night.

Above, the smoke split into concentric rings to reveal a bright blue sky. Through those gaps, sunbeams filtered through, warm and bright as summer, as the tromp of heavy boots echoed across the chaotic streets.

They had come.

They marched through ash-choked streets, across burning courtyards, but they remained untouched by filth or flame. Their armor was white, but their cloaks…those told the true story, stained by the blood they had spilled. Two thousand, four thousand, eight. Ten. Ten thousand Inquisitors, the least of them advanced to high Journeyman Tier.

Many were bathed in the golden glow of the sun, while others wielded swords of flame, and a few at the front shimmered with a radiance that was blinding to look upon. Those were the Inquisitors, possessed of far greater powers than any among the Watch.

Her only hope was the wall at her back, unbroken and layered with defensive enchantments. All that remained of her battalion stood strong before the locked and reinforced inner gates. They could not let the redcloaks into the next district. Too many citizens crowded within. The fires would… Bile rose in Kossryn's throat, sharp and acrid, but she muscled it back down. She would not falter.

Kossryn gritted her teeth at the redcloaks' approach, the leather interior of her gauntlet grown slick with sweat. She tightened her grip on her sword, lifting it one more time. "For Birchstone! For Red Shield!"

Others took up her battlecry. "For Birchstone! For Red Shield!"

The redcloaks surged, and the Watch met their charge with the clang of steel and flash of discharging Skills. Dwarven voices roared defiance, and the Inquisition met them with sunlit flame. Kossryn slapped aside an Initiate's blade, scoring a strike against their groin and bringing another to their knees. All along the line, the Watch held.

"Enough."

Kossryn had barely registered the voice when she was blinded. Darkness consumed her vision, followed closely by the savage pain of melting high steel armor. She shrieked, unable to bear it, but the molten metal clung to her no matter how furiously she cast off parts of it.

"We waste time," said the voice again.

A roaring note cut through the fog of her pain. The voice spoke again, but Kossryn couldn't make out the words. All she felt was heat.

And then nothing.

"They are defeated, Lady Chosen!" Bellar cheered as he marched from the front lines. He was spotlessly clean, as were all those blessed by the Light, and he flashed her a broad smile. "Your power turned them to little more than char, Lady Imara, and those that remain have scattered, soon to be picked off by our forces. You have taken the first district."

"We waste time here," she repeated.

Bellar nodded, the epitome of gracious understanding. "Indeed. But the city must be expunged before we can take the Clan Hold properly. What if the Gnome is hiding among them?"

Around her, small fires sprang up atop the slagged cobbles, burning without fuel. The sunlight that streamed between pillars of dark smoke brightened until the glare of it was too much even for Bellar to withstand. Imara felt a dark pleasure at seeing him wince.

"We are wasting time," she repeated, lifting her bare left hand. The gauntlet had been lost during her impromptu flight, and it exposed heavy scars and too-pale skin before it welled with a golden radiance brighter than anything else the paltry Inquisition could muster. It resolved into a beam of near-white light, tearing through the reinforced gate like flame through paper. Wards snapped, stone caught fire, and wood turned to crumbling ash as she guided the beam in a zig-zagging line.

The gate fell, cut into burning chunks.

"Come, Bellar. Or be left behind."

Imara marched through the flames, heedless of their fury, and directly into the path of a force of Ironclads and Watch members. They hesitated upon seeing her, craning their necks to meet her hidden gaze, and a few even turned and ran.

"Flee, Dwarves. Flee and have your lives. I'm only here for the Gnome." Then, in a rumbling growl, she added, "And the Fiend."

Many scattered, but not all. Those who stayed drew their weapons and readied a variety of Skills that cast their own, impure light.

"Very well," she nodded. "Then die."

<<Now,>> Felix signed.

Vess moved like liquid silk, her armor making not a single sound as she sped toward the trio of guards. She was upon them in a fraction of a second, her bare hands making contact with two of their skulls before striking the third directly below the sternum. Armor or not, the guards were Journeyman Tier, and they folded to Vess' Adept Tier Strength. She caught them all before they could clatter unconscious to the ground.

"Great job," Felix said as he and Pit hustled forward. He took two of the stocky Dwarves from her, hefting them by the back of their plate armor. "This is the third storage room, right?"

"It is." Vess rustled along one of their belts and pulled free a ring of keys. "Quickly. Through the door."

She opened the doors with the keys and slipped inside. Pit and Yintarion followed, padding across the ground and flying through the air, leaving Felix to carry the unconscious guards with him.

He shut the door just as the thunder of booted feet approached down a separate hallway, engaging the lock with quick fingers before all four of them all but froze in place. The steps grew louder, more frantic, but then they faded as the group of guards kept moving.

"Not Forge Knights." Felix let go of his pent breath, and Pit basically melted into the ground with relief. "That was close."

"The guards are swarming across every inch of this place," Yintarion said, alighting on a stack of dusty bottles. Aside from the light that leaked under the door, it was dark within the storage room, but that wasn't a problem. "We are lucky most have been too preoccupied to notice us."

"They are afraid," Vess said.

"They should be." Felix stretched his Perception out, through the door and into the halls beyond. The four of them had traveled through miles of corridors and pass-through chambers in order to reach their location, but still the ballroom was only three floors below them. Thanks to the high-tier materials the palace was made from, Felix's senses were limited to a smaller scope than normal, but even that was enough to know the place had been thrown into utter chaos.

The moment those bells began ringing, Forge Knights had appeared to usher the nobles to saferooms. The Hinterlord himself had never returned. Thinking fast, Felix had shrouded all of them in his Abyssal Skein and followed Laur's directions to get them away from the ballroom as quickly as possible. That, however, was where their paths diverged. The Chanters had left to contact their scattered team, and Felix and Vess were tasked with securing a path to the fault in the wards that Laur was so certain of—a path that grew more crowded the farther up the palace they traveled.

Felix listened a while longer, fingers twitching as they waited. Tzfell had told them of this storage chamber and suggested it as a meeting point for their team. "I can't sense many more guards in the halls nearby. One, maybe two but—wait. No. They left, too."

"Where are they going?" Pit asked.

"I don't know. To defend the Clan Hold gates?"

"Those gates were strongly defended. I doubt the Hinterlord would divest himself of his private army just to give the Hold a few more defenders." Vess was pacing now. "Where could they be going?"

"Either way, it's good news for us. Our friends' path will be clear—oh." A weight lifted from Felix's chest. "They're here. Same floor, closing fast."

They had to wait a minute or two, but soon there came a familiar rhythmic knocking on the thick door. Felix suppressed a disbelieving laugh before unlocking and opened it enough to let Beef, Evie, Harn, and the two Chanters into the cramped room.

"Shave and a haircut?" Felix asked.

Beef grinned. The guy was draped in a long, dark cloak that only kind of hid his massive horns. "Two bits. Heard it in a really old movie once." His grinning stopped as the door shut. "Why's it so dark in here?"

"Up your Perception stat," Harn said. "What's the move, kid? I don't wanna be locked in here long."

"We find the weak point in the Undermount's wards, we go in. The Claw is set?"

"Yeah. Set 'em up nice with their escorts and all our supplies. Beef put a little fear into the smugglers, though. Should keep 'em on their toes should any of 'em get ideas."

"Plus, Hallow's Multipede is waiting for them on the other side."

"Good." Felix grunted. "Laur?"

The Elven Chanter's face was flushed, and his hair was a mess, but he straightened his robes before striding to the door. "Follow me, and please move quietly. The weak point is above us."

Abyssal Skein!

The cold, oily touch of Felix's Void Skill settled on them all, driving a shiver from most of them. Especially Yintarion.

"I dislike that greatly," he said with a basso rumble. "It feels…unnatural."

"Learned it from eating a Void beast. It's not natural, but it's our best defense." Felix looked at them all. "I'll hold Abyssal Skein as long as I can, but everyone who has one, use your Stealth Skills." After flaring his Perception for a moment, Felix unlocked it and pulled it open. "Lead on, Laur."

CHAPTER EIGHTY-NINE

"Imara!"

The second district of Birchstone was blazing beneath the benediction of a holy inferno when the voice accosted her. Imara looked up from the corpse she had just torn apart and let their armored halves clatter to the uneven flagstones. "Faer."

The old man hobbled from a side street, his white robes identifying his position to the Inquisitors who now filled the entirety of the district. Those closest bowed as he passed, as was befitting his rank beneath the Hierophant. "What have you done?" he demanded.

Imara frowned. "Done? I have done what is right."

"Right? You have killed hundreds! Thousands! This—this will incite a war not just with the Red Shield Hinterlord, but all of the Rimefang Clans. The Hierophant did not give you the authority to—"

"She gave me the authority to do what needs to be done," Imara said, cutting off the old man's blathering. She felt a bit of heat in her chest, but it vanished moments later, consumed by the Light.

Faer looked at her as if he'd been told *he* was being put to the torch. "No. I cannot believe that."

"War is inevitable," Bellar stated. "The Light must reach all, and the Dwarves have refused it too long. It is time we cracked open their mountains."

"Bellar." Faer's mouth twisted. There was little love lost between the old priest and the Inquisitors. Imara had learned that during their travels. “The Pathless does not seek war. Order. Strength. Purity. This… chaos does not serve Him.”

His wrinkled face was smudged with soot, and his hands were red with burns, something that immediately leaped to Imara’s attention. That spark of anger reignited. “You’re injured. What happened?”

She did not appreciate Faer’s constant objections, but to hurt a Hierei was to damage the Pathless. He waved aside her concern.

“I am fine. I stopped to offer aid to those who needed it.”

Bellar rolled his eyes. “Pointless. They are god-touched heathens.”

Faer’s dull eyes flashed with anger. She could almost…hear it. “If you wish to bring the Light to the Dwarves, the population must survive your arrival.”

Bellar clucked his tongue. “They were given a chance. The Dwarves have refused our offers of mercy.”

“Imara. Child. Please rethink this. The Hierophant—”

“The Hierophant willed this,” Bellar interrupted. “We have explicit orders from the Voice of Light to bring back the Gnome…and to secure the Hierocracy’s foothold in the Rimefangs. Soon, she plans to claim all of them entirely.”

Faer blinked, his aged face gone pale. “Madness…”

“It is the Will of the Pathless,” Imara stated, her voice as unyielding as her burning gaze. The spark of anger had died once again, and she felt steadier. Stronger. “I am to carry out that Will. I am Chosen.”

Tears welled in Faer’s eyes. “My child. I–I have failed you—”

Stretching her arm out, Imara caught a descending hammer moments before it impacted the old man’s skull. He blinked at it, but she merely turned toward the street ahead. Through the charred remains of a nearby stables, thirty Dwarves in matching armor walked into view. Tabards of black and white with three red shields in the center, and in their hands were short hammers.

“Titan,” the one in the center said. “Leave our city and never return.”

The hammer tried to retreat across the air, but she held firm. It glowed and sparked and steamed…and went nowhere.

The Gnome! You Need To Reach Him!

Imara shivered, the burning heat in her Mind making the inferno around them seem chill by comparison. “You cannot stop me.”

One of the Dwarven knights stepped forward. “We must try.”

All at once, the Forge Knights unleashed their Spirits. A powerful pressure descended on them all, shoving many of the Initiates to their knees and even the Inquisitors trembled. To Imara, however, it was less than a soft breeze.

Begone, Insects.

All at once, their Spiritual pressure vanished. It was overwhelmed and subsumed beneath a tidal wave of godly might. Imara felt it flow through her, as if her flesh were a conduit to something bigger than she could ever hope to become.

The Forge Knights recovered faster than Imara expected. They flashed forward, all of them lifting thick heater shields that glowed with Mana. Imara surged forward as well, arms spread to meet them. She laughed, and all but felt Hierei Faer glanced at her in surprise.

Where they met, the world descended into fiery chaos.

Great gongs and horns echoed through the palace, now going off constantly. They dashed by a wide window, and Felix saw a slew of Cloud Chariots zipping across the cavern ceiling toward the gates, each one filled with armored soldiers.

"She's reached the mountain," Tzfell announced. "Those signals… they're too frequent to mean anything else."

"Running outta time," Harn said.

Evie grimaced but picked up her pace. "Let's not dawdle, then."

Ahead, the corridor stretched onward toward a wide, open doorway framed by silver-green mithril. Laur pointed at it. "There! We need to go in there and ascend to the base of the palace."

"Thought you said it was close?" Beef shouted in annoyance.

"Relatively close."

Vess sucked in a sharp breath. "The door!"

Ahead, the open doorway closed as a smooth mithril door slid down from above. Or tried to, at least, as it met two Spears and a clutch of chitinous legs. Their group rushed forward, slipping beneath the halted door and onto a narrow walkway that terminated ten feet into the chamber. Beyond that, the room opened up into a wide barrel of a room that extended both up and down into darkness.

"Uh, what now?" Evie asked.

"Huh. It's an elevator shaft," Felix said. *First elevated trains, now this.*

Beef looked around, careful not to shift too much on the narrow platform. "So, is there like a button to call it?"

"A moment." Tzfell gestured, and a wave of her Mana spread

outward. Liquid shaped like silver geometric shapes snapped onto the walls, configuring itself into odd, shifting patterns. "The enchantment requires a keyform, but I'm forcing it to engage."

A humming grew until angular, Dwarven sigaldry shimmered into visibility, and a stone platform formed at the end of their walkway.

"Climb aboard, quickly," she said, strain evident in her voice.

Everyone did as they were asked, with the Chanter stepping on it last. Once there, she grunted, and the geometric shapes all rotated thirty degrees before a new thrumming began. The stone platform rose up, slowly at first, but gathering greater and greater speed. Tzfell trembled, her magic barely holding onto the strange interface she created, and Felix could do nothing but wait.

The stone walls flashed by, so precisely machined that it barely seemed they were moving, were it not for the occasional walkway that whipped past—and the intense amount of wind. The air pressure was a literal weight, growing with every floor they ascended, until Evie and Laur hunched their shoulders against it, and everyone else had to shield their faces or else be unable to see or breathe. The weight slowed them down, increasing Tzfell's trembling tenfold. That, at least, Felix could remedy.

Storm Shaping!

The wind split around them, seized by his power so that they rode within a fluctuating bubble of calm. It was simple enough, as it was just normal air, but it made all the difference as they reached the final floor, and Tzfell collapsed. The geometric patterns flickered out, and the stone platform immediately dropped…but not before Beef summoned giant insect legs from the walkway itself. They grasped the platform at an angle, but prevented it from falling back down the shaft.

Everyone leaped off, Felix with Tzfell in his arms, and they crowded onto the small walkway. "Another door," he said.

"Shut tight, too." Evie tried to shove a dagger beneath the metal. "How're we openin' this?"

"I'm fine, Lord Autarch," the Dwarven Chanter protested. Felix set her down, and she straightened her robes. "Thank you."

Felix inclined his head. "Laur. Is the weak point close?"

"Beyond this door, within a thousand strides." His eyes flashed, Mana swirling in them like chromatic pools of oil. "The patterns ripple from here, and they have not shifted."

"Alright." He walked up to the door and set his hand against it. The metal was hard and cold, but he activated his Manasight and saw *into* it.

The flow of it, the vibrations of its hidden structure. He couldn't see through it, the material was too high-Tier for that, but that wasn't required. "Chthonic Tribute."

The mithril fought against him. Not like Crescian Bronze with a Will of its own, but like all things, it had a certain inertia. A persistence of form, one could call it. It bucked against his control, and sigaldry around the chamber activated...but Felix spread his Intent. The sigaldry was snuffed out, its relatively weaker Mana consumed, until the door was undefended. The metal buckled beneath his Will and turned to a thick, silver-green liquid before vanishing into his bottomless Hunger.

They stepped into a wide corridor, and Harn whistled. "If we weren't already breakin' and enterin', I'd say we ain't supposed to be in here."

The floors, walls, and ceiling were all of that midnight stone flecked with diamonds that made up the exterior of Nightfall Palace, and they appeared to have been cut from a single piece. Or perhaps the corridor had been bored out from the stalactite that hung from the Clan Hold's ceiling. Geometric knotwork patterns abounded, framing the path, light fixtures, and large doorways—all of them made of gold that had been inlaid into the black stone. Statues of serious-looking Dwarves filled the alcoves between doors, each one at least twenty feet tall and set with hundreds of lit candles at their bases.

"These are the Hinterlord's private quarters," Tzfell said. She'd composed herself and peered around the area. "Laur?"

"This way."

The Elf led them down the hall, past several intersections and through three adjoined chambers, stopping every hundred feet to peer at the walls and feel the air. Strangely, the halls were utterly empty, as if the Hinterlord and all his staff had evacuated his own palace. It was quiet, the only sound was the tread of their boots and hooves on the stone...and even that was heavily muffled by his Abyssal Skein.

"The weak point is...there."

Laur gestured to an utterly nondescript wall between a large potted tree with orange leaves and a painting of some pinch-faced matriarch. The wall was smooth and unmarked.

"Judging on the resonance of these patterns, the official entrance to the Undermount is close. It is likely heavily guarded, however. Archibald must have exploited the proximity and used his unique Skill to bridge the gap, leaving us this tunnel." The Elven Chanter peered at the empty wall, his eyes swirling with Mana again. "Fascinating. The ripples are moving, as if it were a liquid and not a solid. I think—"

"We're wasting time," Felix said. "Laur, how do we get in?"

The Elf blinked. "We must force the weakness open to allow us to enter."

"Force it?"

"Feel out the edges of the pattern with your Affinity. Do you feel it?"

Concentrating, Felix did as Laur asked and, after fumbling for a minute or so, he sensed the first flashes of a strange, jagged design. "I think so."

"Find the center. Place your Intent squarely upon the point of confluence, and apply your Willpower to leverage the wards apart. When you are ready, I will craft a temporary opening through this tunnel."

Felix found the center. It was like a swirling whirlpool, those jagged waves rushing toward it before pushing back out again. "Ready."

He shaped his Intent into a sharpened point and thrust it through the center…before hurling his Willpower in all directions. It was surprisingly easy, like twisting off the lid of a pickle jar someone already loosened. The whirlpool widened, pressed apart by the sheer mass of his attention, and the wall before them buckled and snapped. A hole large enough to drive a bus through collapsed *into* the wall, as if the stone were falling sideways instead of down, and a frenetic surge of crackling Mana filled it.

"You—what is happening?" Vess asked, alarmed.

"The Autarch has done something impossible again," Yintarion said thoughtfully. "Has anyone kept a tally?"

"This shouldn't have occurred. My Lord, you cannot rip the weak point open yourself! The wards won't—!"

All around them, new alarms blared. Horns of a higher pitch sounded from what seemed only feet away, before they turned tinny and vanished. Magelights flickered and went dark, leaving their party standing before the blue-white light of a crackling vortex.

"Is it open?" Harn asked.

"It is, but—"

"Everyone in!"

They all piled through, Vess and Yintarion first, followed by Pit, Evie, Beef, and the rest. Felix brought up the rear, his attention the only thing keeping the vortex open.

He leaped through, and it snapped shut.

Across the mountain, standing amid the confusing tunnels of the Clan Hold's defenses, Imara perked up. Ballista bolts, concussive pillars of force, and blades of mithril had rained upon her army for what seemed like hours, but now they stopped. In fact, the wall of shimmering lights before her shuddered and winked out, as did a thousand other enchantments within range of her senses.

The Dwarves stared, all of them looking around in mounting horror. Their defenses were utterly compromised.

Imara pressed her hands to her chest. "Thank you, Pathless, for your aid."

The glow of gold around her brightened to a blinding inferno, and she lifted her bare hands to the sky. "Inquisition! Advance!"

CHAPTER NINETY

The vortex resolved quickly into a dark and somewhat damp cave. Felix stepped out of it just as it closed with a wet gurgle, like water down a drain filled with electricity.

Not a great comparison, but apt. Felix shook himself a bit and flared his Perception to gather his bearings. The cave was filled with luminescent mushrooms, hanging vines, and a lumpy sort of terrain. The floors, walls, and ceiling were all covered in bulbous stone outcroppings, as if hundreds of stalactites and stalagmites had been worn by years of running water. The craggy stone itself was riddled with holes, large and small, like pumice or some other volcanic rock.

His team was spread out a bit, filling a sizable depression between lumpy stone hills. Mushrooms dotted the floor around them, wide, dinner-plate-sized things that looked oddly moist. Felix stepped across the rock, avoiding the mushrooms and vines as best he could in order to get a better vantage.

"There," he said, indicating a point of light through one of the many porous paths. "We need to move fast, but stay on your guard. We don't know what to expect here. Vess?"

"Yin, scout ahead, if you please."

"Hm. Yes. Wise, little Dragoon." The golden Wyrmling flew ahead, entering the tunnel ahead of them all.

"The lizard? Alone?" Evie scoffed. "He'll miss six outta a half dozen. I'm goin', too." She vanished into the tunnel, seconds behind Yintarion. Vess and Harn both sighed.

"Where are we?" Beef asked as they stood there, waiting. He looked up at the uneven ceiling and glowing vegetation like it was going to fall on top of him. "Deeper in the mountain?"

"The Undermount," Pit said.

"Where's that?"

Pit paused, head cocked. "I dunno."

"The Undermount is a place between Realms. Much like the Kingsrock," Tzfell explained. "We are beyond the world. Beside it."

"Like a soap bubble clinging to the edge of a much larger soap bubble," Felix added. "Hopefully we don't go pop."

Beef's eyes widened. "Is that a thing that could happen?"

"No," Felix admitted. "Probably not."

"It is highly unlikely," Vess said, shooting Felix a glance. "The Dwarves built this place at least an Age ago and store their most precious treasures here. Even disregarding that, the Dwarves make structures that last. We are in no danger."

"Not from monsters, anyway," Harn added.

Beef tightened his hands around the haft of Bedlam and stared into the many dark tunnels around them.

Felix frowned, turning back toward the lit tunnel. Evie had returned, and her heart was racing. When she appeared, her face was flushed and eyes wide. "No monsters or nothin' but…you gotta see this."

Without a word, they all followed her into the tunnel.

The slightly brighter tunnel was filled with more of the same mushrooms and moss, though less of the latter. Felix and Beef had to duck on some of the larger protrusions on the ceiling, but it wasn't terrible. Even the footing wasn't bad, as the porous rock was wet yet heavily textured; it practically gripped the soles of their boots.

The path kept descending over that lumpy ground, until it felt like they'd walked a half mile beneath the earth. Passages zig-zagged across their tunnel, many of them dead ends that Felix's Perception quickly mapped out, while others extended far enough that he lost track of them. Evie hustled ahead, footsteps light as only she could make them, moving with a peculiar eagerness.

Finally, they reached the end to find Yintarion swimming in an anxious circle. "You are here. Good. Perhaps you can make sense of this oddity."

He nodded toward the side of the tunnel. Like a weird set of windows, the porous stone had expanded the holes into dozens of fist-sized windows into seemingly empty air. Through them, Felix spotted a strange and dizzying sight, and every single person in the party sucked in a sharp, surprised breath.

A mountain rose in the distance…or rather, it descended. Their tunnel just barely emerged from the roof of an incomprehensibly vast cavern, a thousand times bigger than the Clan Hold—ten thousand times bigger—and the mountain was suspended from the ceiling. It was remarkably similar to Nightfall Palace in shape and general composition, if not scale. The mountain-stalactite before them was incredibly large, on par with the mountain that housed Red Shield Hold, and it was filled with an eclectic mix of structures, forests, and distant waterfalls. Far stranger, however, was that those waterfalls fell the wrong way.

"The Undermount," Tzfell whispered. "It is as they say. A mirror to the greatest of Holds."

Below the impossible mountain was a swirling storm. Clouds and atmosphere swirled below them like an inverted sky, broken only by a howling wind that revealed a deep darkness.

Felix's Hunger rumbled at the sight, and he felt a certain connection to what lingered behind the clouds. "The Void. It's a whole mountain hanging above the Void."

"How do we get there?" Laur asked.

"Walk," Harn grunted, starting down the tunnel. "These tunnels gotta lead there at some point."

"Hey, no bargin' ahead. I'm scoutin', old man."

Evie and Yintarion took off while the rest followed at a more sedate pace. At the front of the group, he missed Tzfall's first beckoning motion, but definitely noticed when the Chanter grasped his arm.

"Lord Autarch. A word, before we enter the Undermount."

With enough Agility and Perception, finding their way through the porous tunnels was a simple matter. In less than five minutes, they had navigated all the way to the base of the Undermount…but had then encountered a problem.

"We just…step out?" Felix asked. He stood before a wide opening where, in a normal world, the tunnel would have opened up to the surface. Here, however, it was simply a wide breach along the ceiling. If he were to step out, Felix was convinced he would fall into the storm and the Void beyond.

"Yes. The mountain will take care of the rest."

That's what I'm afraid of. Felix leaned out, looking down. "Alright, let me test it first."

Not giving himself any further time to think about it, Felix jumped out through the hole…and was sent into a barreling roll as gravity switched direction. No longer falling down into the Void, Felix instead fell back onto the cavern ceiling and managed to just barely rotate his feet under his body.

"Whoa."

"Is it safe?" Beef asked.

"Yeah. Come on out. Just be careful, landing—" Before Felix could get the words out, Beef had shot up out of the tunnel and face-planted onto the rocky ground. "Landing is tricky."

"Eurgh."

The others came after, some like Laur and Harn having a bit of trouble, but the rest navigated the strange gravity with ease. Pit even executed a double somersault, while Yintarion simply flew out.

"I feel like you're just rubbing it in now," Beef muttered.

Felix helped the teen to his feet and patted him on the back. "Come on. That's not likely to be the weirdest part of all this."

They walked onward, Yintarion and Evie acting as scouts, and they discovered how true Felix's words were. A sourceless light covered everything, as if the midday sun shone upon them constantly. The cavern ceiling—now the ground—stretched onward as normal for perhaps five hundred feet. After that, grasses and plants sprouted, thick enough to carpet the area before trees appeared. A forest, verdant and lush, spread out ahead of them, rolling over two low hills before descending into a valley filled with a dark lake.

"A lake. On the ceiling," Vess said, perplexed. She looked up, where storm clouds rolled across the sky yet dropped not a single bit of rain.

"Looks like another palace, too," Harn pointed out.

On the edge of the dark lake, just as Harn had said, there was a palace. Unlike the Hinterlord's home, it was a sprawling piece of architecture extending for miles. Just beyond it, so large that it dominated the horizon, was the Undermount itself.

"The Havenhold," Tzfell said. "Once the proud seat of the Dwarven kings, now a debauched pleasure palace to the Hinterlords and the Highblood Clans. It is well-guarded and fully staffed at all times.

It represents our first barrier. We must move through it in order to reach the steps of the Undermount."

"Won't some of the guards be missing? Due to the whole attack?"

"No, Beef. The Havenhold is manned by the guards of all the Dwarven Holds. All of them have access to the Undermount, and it is likely that the Hinterlord himself retreated here when they heard the attack."

"So, we cut our way through?" Evie asked.

"We're not killing people when we don't have to," Felix sait, cutting her off.

"I'm not keen on hurting folks myself, scaleboy, but how else are we gettin' through?"

Vess put her hands on both of their shoulders. "Can we not circumvent the palace entirely? Why not go over it?"

Beef pointed at her. "Ooh! Yeah! Where's the main vault thingy? Why not just fly all the way to the top?"

Laur cleared his throat. "The storm. Threads of it are woven into the mountain itself, sealing off the air across the entire Undermount. Leaping several strides from the earth now would do little to agitate those threads…but too high, and you would call down the fury of whatever lies within that darkness. And it grows the higher one climbs." He shuddered. "I cannot parse the fullness of it, but it is a danger to even you, Lord Autarch."

"Right. Couldn't be that easy," Felix muttered. Then his expression brightened. "How bad would," he quickly counted the rows of windows. "Six stories be?"

"It would doubtlessly hurt and likely do far more. There is a reason Havenhold wraps around the entire base of the Undermount, a reason why it stretches no higher than it must." Tzfell considered the squat but ornate architecture in the valley below. "You could cross, perhaps. But I fear for the lives of the rest of us."

"Can we like, test it?" Beef asked.

"Test?" Evie raised her eyebrows. "You gonna jump into the storm yourself?"

"No, I just mean—I saw Felix take hits from the sandstorm 'round Ahkestria, full on. He didn't even flinch. If he can handle that, then he can handle this. But we won't know how until he tries. So…test. You've got that Abyssal Skim thing right?"

"Skein. Yeah."

"Sure. Just use that and slip over the top. The roofs shouldn't be deadly territory, right?"

Tzfell furrowed her brow. "The roofs should be well warded against intrusion…but no, I imagine the danger to the Highbloods would be too great if the very tops of the palace were affected."

"That assumes whoever built this cared," Harn pointed out.

"From this distance, I cannot be certain, but if there is a gap, it is a narrow one. Lord Autarch, if you attempt this, you must be ready to bail out as soon as possible."

Felix smiled. "Of course."

CHAPTER NINETY-ONE

Exploration is level 76!

Utilizing Abyssal Skein, the group was able to skirt the edges of the dark lake and steal up onto the grounds of Havenhold with little issue. There were some Dwarves wandering a few of the gardens nearer the lake, but they were few, and most were awfully…preoccupied with one another. They were easy to evade.

Once they reached Havenhold proper, they came upon open verandas filled with stout furniture, an elaborate wet bar, and a crackling fire pit in the shape of a pair of cupped, blocky hands—all of it beneath a long stone roof carved out so that the negative spaces resembled a star-filled sky. The terrace extended across a substantial section of the palace, overlooking a statue garden interspersed with exotic plants that shimmered with visible Mana vapor. Dwarven nobles lounged upon the furniture, drinking from goblets that burned, crackled, and smoked in equal measure. Lively, relaxed conversation rang out, the Highbloods laughing as they relaxed, as if they hadn't a care in the world.

None noticed their party, though Felix walked fairly close to the retaining wall holding up the nearest portion of the veranda. A noble even looked directly at him but seemed to see nothing but a grassy knoll.

Yintarion flew down from the lip of the veranda. "I see ten Dwarves and beyond them a series of glass doors leading inside this mansion.

There are many more within, including a number of other mortal servants and armored soldiers."

Evie scowled. "So, no going through the palace…unless the killin' thing is back on the table?"

"It isn't." Felix studied what he could through his Perception stat, marking the position of the nobles. Several of them carried things that sparked across his awareness. Enchanted items, no doubt, though he couldn't tell what they were from his blind vantage. His Hunger rumbled regardless. "Why are they all just…hanging out?"

"It is the pleasure palace," Tzfell said, as if that were explanation enough. When she saw Felix's annoyed stare, she kept talking. "The Havenhold was once the seat of our king…but that ended long ago. Now, it is home to the Highblood Clan families that hold the greatest sway over the Dwarven Holds. Within are all the pleasures mortal Minds can conceive, or so it is said, and some Highbloods never leave except for their most pressing duties."

"Oh. Ew," Felix said.

"Indeed."

"What of the nobility we spoke to at the Hinterlord's gala?" Vess asked.

"Lesser branches of the High Clans. They take up the responsibilities so that the real powers can govern from within this place."

"My sympathy for the nobility is dwindling by the second," Felix said.

"I see a path we may take," Yintarion said. His eyes shimmered bright gold, reminding Felix briefly of Imara's. "If we can move past these few and the glass doors, the roof would be ours."

"Perfect. Be ready to rush on my signal." Felix lifted his hand and activated one of his newest Skills. *Quiet Cacophony.*

A strange, buzzing puff of power poured from Felix's mouth. It condensed as it flew, unerring to a point within his Perception, before it splashed down like a geyser between the nobles. To Felix, it felt like his Will was suddenly inundated by ten separate forces, each pushing against him unconsciously. The Highbloods fought back, their Minds instinctively rejecting the effects of his Skill…but Felix's Will was beyond theirs, and his Intent could not be denied.

Dwarven Highblood (x10) Have Been Affected By Disorientation!

Dwarven Highblood (x10) Have Been Affected By Disquiet!
Dwarven Highblood (x10) Have Been Affected By Disgust!

Quiet Cacophony is level 2!
...
Quiet Cacophony is level 34!
Apprentice Tier!
You Gain:
+5% INE
+5% ALA
+5% WIL

"What was that?" one shouted.

"Watch it!"

"Did you spill Thacarin red on my husband's coat? You absolute fool! That stain will never come out!"

"I did not! I was standing here, and my wine is white!"

"Who else?"

The mild argument escalated quickly, and Vess shot Felix a look of surprise as actual fighting broke out among the Highbloods. He could only shrug.

"Good Skill," Harn grunted.

Yintarion floated back up. "I believe they're adequately distracted."

"What the lizard said," Evie agreed. "Time to run?"

Together they ascended the steps to the veranda, skirting the edges of the now-brawling nobles and onto the palace proper. The glass doors extended for quite a while, but the crowds within could not spot them through his Abyssal Skein. Or, so Felix hoped.

They took a corner, hugging tighter and tighter to the palace's dressed stone walls, before they came upon a narrow recess between two protruding sections. It was twenty feet wide and twice that deep, and it ended in a dark metal door without a latch or lock.

It was perfect.

Felix hissed as they came to a stop, a sudden sharp pain ripping across his core space. He felt a Skill within him still, its thrumming pattern cutting off so suddenly he feared it had been sundered entirely.

"Eugh, man, why'd you do that? Warn me next time you're shutting off your Skill," Beef said. He shivered. "That feels like getting dunked in cold oil."

"What happened?" Harn asked, helping Felix stand up straight.

"Skill got cut off." Felix glanced around the relatively small area, Manasight flaring without issue. Though Havenhold shined like a bonfire at midnight, he could still make out the filmy ward they'd penetrated…not so much meant to keep them out as to strip them of options. "The palace is interfering with my Stealth Skill."

Evie frowned. "Me, too. Can't even spin the damn thing."

"There's a wall between me and my Shroud," Pit added. "It's tough. But I think I could break it down."

"Don't!" Laur warned. "There are doubtless contingencies in place for such an act. Punishments, even. If we wish to remain undetected, it is better to go without than to batter down the door."

Harn nodded. "Now or never, then. To the roof?"

Felix assessed the thirty-foot wall ahead of them. "To the roof."

Rime Shaping!

Though the outside world was locked down by the Havenhold, it could not stop Felix's Mana from venting from his channels. Ice Mana poured from him, creating a frozen, purple-white lattice extending from the ground to the top of the nearby roof. Without a word, the others climbed up, Laur in the lead.

Felix repeated the process two more times, each improvised ladder getting them higher and higher, until they'd attained the topmost level. Here, Laur held out a hand. "Stop. The influence of the Undermount's storm is here. It touches down ten strides forward, but at seven strides, you would hit the angled side of it."

"It touches the roof? All of it?" Felix asked. The roof may have seemed ordinary, but it was the top of a palace. It extended for almost three hundred feet at the narrowest point ahead.

"No, but it is close. Too close for someone to slip through, unless they are far flatter than is healthy."

"Give me a second." Felix stepped forward, activating Manasight again. He waited while a chaos of light and sound and sensation reigned around him, patiently focusing until just the warding Laur mentioned came into view. Everything else was white noise.

Manasight is level 91!

The Elf was right, he thought, tracing the lines of almost-solid light that extended up into the sky. *The mountain is covered in this thing. Like a… laser dome. What would happen if I touched one—?*

Before he could try anything, the entire palace shook. It was a mild vibration, but enough that large waves suddenly kicked up in the lake. The fighting nobles, who Felix could only distantly hear, suddenly clammed up.

"What was that?" he asked.

Laur looked at him, face pale and jaw clenched. "I thought you touched the wards. Did you not?"

Felix lifted his hands innocently. "I would never."

"Laur, look," Tzfell said, pointing to something across the tiled roof. A crack ran across the palace's wall, the dressed stone split with a dark crevasse.

The Elven Chanter hummed, pulling something from between his palms. It looked like a series of strings made of liquid light, and he twisted them together twice before they winked out. "I left markers where we arrived, to keep track of our exit in case—" he shook himself. "The barrier between here and the Nightfall Palace seems to be…unraveling."

"Unraveling? How?" Vess asked.

"Something is agitating the Grand Harmony," Tzfell said. "The Undermount provides entirely too much interference to be sure, but it sings to me of heat. Of light."

"Give you two guesses on that one," Evie muttered. "First one doesn't count."

Damn. How'd she get here so fast? Felix spun back to the barrier. "Get ready. When I give the word, I need all of you to run through as fast as you can."

"What? We cannot. The wardings are too elaborate, it will—"

"Kid knows what he's doin'," Harn said, grabbing Laur by the arm. "Just be ready."

"I—right. Of course."

Felix reached out, until his hand was an inch from the barrier…and he grasped it with his Will. "*Chthonic Tribute.*"

Power rushed into him, the piece of ward siphoning off into Felix's open mouth before being replenished. It was like drinking the ocean through a straw.

More.

Felix pulled harder, forging his Intent into a funnel through which the barrier's magic could flow. It surged into him, so many Mana types that it would burst a normal man. Or several normal men. The magic went wild, fire and wind and lightning burning through him while earth, ice, and shadow tried to freeze and crush.

No. Quiet.

Instantly, the power was leashed. It fell, pulled by an inexorable grip into the swirling dark beneath Felix's core space. Ahead, a narrow section of the mountain ward flickered…and failed.

"Now!" Felix commanded.

Evie, Vess, Harn took the lead, followed closely by Tzfell and Laur with Beef and Hallow taking up the rear. Pit lingered at his side, but even he was sent running when Felix nudged him. He shifted to tenku form to catch up to the others.

Felix followed, one slow step after another.

The wards tried to close their tiny breach again and again. Each time, the mountain sent entire rivers of Mana against him. Felix and his Hunger roared as he walked, their maw opened wide, letting the power spiral into them without friction or fear. The last part was hard. So hard.

Felix's friends were almost through. He didn't even breathe—there wasn't the space for it. He just had to eat and walk. Step by step.

The palace shook again, and the roof cracked. Somewhere, screams echoed into the false daylight…and Felix stumbled.

The ward swelled, as if the storm above could sense his weakness. It fell upon him like a tidal wave.

"Pit! Run!"

His Companion was barely halfway across the roof when the warding fell on top of him. He squawked in alarm, and in a swirl of color became far, far smaller. The threads of discordant power surged through where his Body once resided, but even a Dire Hound pup was too tall. Pit froze, his bright eyes wide.

"Convergence!" Felix gasped, leaping forward. The roof buckled beneath him, shattering into a spiraling pattern of debris as he launched ahead horizontally. "Chthonic Tribute!"

Etheric Concordance is level 85!
Manasight is level 92!

Pit vanished into light that settled in Felix's Spirit moments before the wards slammed down…then Felix whipped by with his fangs bared, and the world *bent* around his howling maw.

Rivers of Mana flowed into him. Lakes of it, as the storm thundered above. His friends had vanished at some point, but Felix couldn't sense them. He could barely see through the riot of color, heat, and chaos. Dissonance buzzed against him, soaring for a brief, terrifying moment.

Chthonic Tribute!

Felix redoubled his Will and Intent upon the Skill just as a lightning bolt hundreds of feet wide came crashing down upon Havenhold. Felix took it in, but like drinking straight from a firehouse, it overwhelmed his Hunger. Lightning spilled outward, into his Body, his Mind, and his Spirit.

Within him, Pit shrieked.

The world went white. Time ceased to have meaning, and for an interminable Age, Felix floated amid a sea of horrendous sensation. There was a soundless howling, like of a great and terrible beast, but it was sourceless. Felix simply was…until he was no longer.

A rush of brutal cold broke upon him, streaking his reality with deep blues and striations of cold green. Felix woke up surrounded by the long roots of some underwater plant, tangled about himself tighter than ropes or chains. Blinking rapidly, Felix ripped free before kicking his legs and hurtling to the surface of a small pond.

An army of bright purple frogs fled from his mighty waves, leaping across oversized lily pads and announcing their displeasure with tiny, sonic attacks. Felix growled, and every single frog went silent…as did the Dwarven nobles who surrounded the pond.

Warning! Your Health Has Dropped Down To Ten Percent Of Maximum!
Seek Healing Immediately!

Chthonic Tribute is level 99!
Armored Skin is level 96!
The Song of Absolution is level 98!
Sovereign of Flesh is level 97!

"Who are you?" one of them demanded. He had a forked beard the color of slate and wore a shirt made entirely of faceted ruby. Imposing, but he was no more than Adept Tier. "Your name and advancement, brute, or in the name of the Uncrowned King, I shall slay you here and now."

"Felix!" Beef shouted. He and the others were beyond the pond, where the rolling hills of the Undermount gave way to steep cliffs. "C'mon!"

"Felix?" someone said. Their doublet was made of sapphires. "Nevarre?"

"I know of no others," said a woman wearing a gown of opal.

"The claimant of Nagast."

Great. Felix said nothing but flared his Agility as he kicked off the ground. He was gone before the Highbloods could blink.

CHAPTER NINETY-TWO

Felix joined his team just as they reached the base of a huge set of stairs. The others were a little singed, but basically fine, and had already downed at least one Health Potion. Beef started talking as soon as Felix came to a stop.

"God, Felix, I'm sorry! I shouldn't have said your name."

"Stop. It's fine." With a flash of light, Pit emerged from Felix's Spirit in tenku form. "Pit, buddy. You okay?"

The tenku limped a little, and his tail was smoking, but his Health was barely below ninety percent. "Could be better. You?"

"I'll live," Felix said. Already, Sovereign of Flesh was stitching his Body and Health back together, and all it cost him was a bit of stolen Essence. He still had plenty. "Guards are following, folks. Are these the stairs up, Tzfell?"

"Yes. The Serpent's Coil. They wind from the base of the Undermount to the very top."

Felix gazed up the long, serpentine set of stairs, noting that they were made from a pearlescent stone and inlaid with what looked like copper and iron. "Talk as we walk. What can we expect?"

Everyone began to ascend, taking steps two or three at a time.

"Beyond the pleasure palace are the Lesser Mausoleums. They are the final resting place for the great heroes of my people, and are guarded."

"Guarded by what?"

"Shades."

Harn spat. "Nasty things, Shades. Range from Tier II to Tier V on the worst end. But they won't tangle with us if we don't interfere with their territory."

"A true statement, yet functionally useless. The Shades aren't bound to singular mausoleums, but to the entire Necropolis, which encompasses the first two landings on the Serpent's Coil."

"What if we stay on the Coil?" Felix asked.

Tzfell shook her head. "Those that are near will come for us, and it could be hundreds. We must be prepared."

"I am very fast," Evie pointed out. "But…I've never fought a ghost before. Curious how it'd be…"

Harn waved his hand, cutting her off. "You don't wanna, kid. They're immune to physical attacks and most types of Mana. Light and life Mana put a dent in, but it's less than you'd expect."

"We don't have any of that," Beef pointed out. "Well, save for Felix and Pit…and Yin. Right? You've light and water-attuned Skills?"

"Indeed. Once, I would destroy entire armadas across these tempestuous skies." The Wyrmling hesitated. "In my current state, I could handle…considerably less."

"The Coil is not safe unless you've acquired a pass from one of the Hinterlords. Since we've no way to get those, nor the time, we are playing it loose with the rules," Laur said. "I will break down the wards on each landing as we reach them, but it may take time. I will need you to defend me while I unlock our way forward."

"We'll handle it," Felix promised.

Exploration is level 77!

It took ten minutes of all-out running for Felix and his team to reach the first landing. The Serpent's Coil was true to its name and wound in circuitous patterns all across the Undermount which, from so close, seemed at least ten times the size it was before.

Small shrines and graves decorated with burning lanterns covered the lower slopes, interspersed by trickling streams, blooming trees no bigger than Felix's waist, and empty bowls before each of them, filled only with dirt and leaves. Each one marked those who were somehow prized by Dwarven ancestry but not important enough to earn their own mausoleum. According to Tzfell, they were all for poor soldiers, folks the Highbloods clearly didn't care about. All the markers were in disrepair in one way or another. It was honestly a little depressing, and Felix was almost happy when the Shade showed up.

At first blush, the thing looked like a skull in a flowing cloak, hovering across the ground like a ghost. There was no cloak, though—the thing was made of shadows and thick, undulating strips of flesh. The skull was accurate, but it was far too large to be a Dwarf or even a Human. More giant-sized, really, as were the yellowed, skeletal arms that hung uselessly from its sides. It meandered a hundred feet away, but didn't attack or even look their way.

"Tier III. Guess this guy wasn't too important," Beef said, tapping a grave.

"Don't touch them. The Shades will get stronger the higher we ascend, as will the pressures of the Void above."

"Cheery," Evie muttered.

They walked the Coil, keeping an eye on the Shade all the while. At first, it simply hung near its small mausoleum, like a tired guard doing an overnight shift. The problem with the Serpent's Coil, however, was that it wound too lazily among the cliffs. When the Coil drew them too close to its position, that great skull tilted like a dog with a scent. Tier III or not, the speed at which it moved from aimless floating to all out attack was incredible.

"*Skyflare!*" Yintarion announced, and from his mouth emerged an orb of dense, golden Mana. It rocketed outward and impacted the Shade, where it burst into a conflagration of light. The Shade was burned up immediately.

"That was disappointingly easy," Evie said.

"Perhaps," Yintarion said between panting breaths. "But the Skill is a remnant of my greater stature, and it takes a great portion of my Mana to utilize. Too many, and I will be useless until my Mana regenerates."

Evie poked the Wyrmling. "Thought you were getting stronger. What's all the food been for?"

He curled away from her fingers, a scowl above his white-tufted chin. "Preparation. I need more time, you chain-swinging brute."

"Evolutions are hard," Pit commiserated. "Took me *forever*."

"We must keep moving," Tzfell said. "The Shades will gather if we tarry too long. Each one we engage with has the potential to attract a swarm."

Abyssal Skein. Felix tried to activate the Skill again, but it fizzled before it could spread out of his core. The wall was still there. *There goes the stealth option.*

"Pit and I will help you, Yin. My Auroral Forge is less concentrated than yours, but Pit's is mighty. Together, we'll cut the path. Vess, focus on giving Yintarion as many Mana Potions as he needs. Everyone else: go. Stay in the center of the stairs and move fast."

They took off, single-file, Felix in the lead. Around them, the mausoleums grew in size and complexity from small huts to elaborate, miniature houses. The Shades increased as well, their numbers swelling until the mountainside was crawling with thick, fleshy shadows. Most didn't notice them at all, and the few that did were quickly dispatched by Yintarion's Skyflare.

Felix set a brutal pace, driving all of them to sweat and pant despite their Adept Tier Bodies. Ironically, with a Journeyman Body, Beef was handling it better than Vess or even Harn. Around thirty miles of stairs had passed beneath their fleet feet, but the Minotaur was still running with an ease only surpassed by Felix himself. Wrapped around his torso, Hallow's Homunculus was whispering encouragement all the while.

The mausoleums grew and so did the trees. Huge, beautiful trunks colored a myriad of hues, adding to a widening canopy that cast emerald shade onto the tombs and Coil. When the team drew too close to that shadow, though, they were attacked. A handful of Tier IV Shades burst from the darkened edges of a small copse, fleshy tentacles grasping and huge skeleton heads shrieking so that a frigid chill stabbed at them all.

Beef met them with an earth-shattering hammer strike. No Skill, just brawn and a little magic from his weapon Bedlam. The potent artifact shook the earth and sent the Shades scattering, but most importantly, its special ability disrupted their shadow magic entirely.

Evie's chain came next, followed closely by exploding Spears and slashes of Dawn's Advent. The latter was the most useful, being light Mana, but it did little more than cut through their thick appendages. The Shades advanced through the hailstorm of violence until another Skyflare took one out.

"Potion!" Yintarion shouted.

In the breach, Felix lifted his hands and unleashed his own Skill. Spikes of gold condensed out of the omnipresent light all around them, stabbing through enormous skulls and pinning thick tentacles all at once. A dense field, four feet long and sharp as razors, they sizzled where they touched the shadow-stuff of Shade flesh.

Chthonic Tribute!

All six Shades resisted for only an instant before they burst into dark smoke and were devoured.

Weak. Delicious.

It'll do for now, Felix told his Hunger. The lesser Shades went a good way toward replenishing the Essence he'd spent on healing himself. *There will be plenty more to come.*

Good.

Abyssal Skein. Like a bubble bursting, the barrier between Felix's Skill and the world vanished. The cold oil sensation flowed outward, fading his presence from the world and his party's Perception…until he spread it across their connections as well. They gasped, taken aback.

"This will help a lot," Evie said with some relief. "Shades won't see what's comin'."

Vess hefted her partisan and grinned. "Let us put it to the test, yes?"

The team moved on.

Abyssal Skein is level 84!

…

Abyssal Skein is level 88!

The Serpent's Coil slithered further, winding through barren cliffs and forested hills, navigating the ever-growing necropolis around them. His stealth held up, and with Evie, Harn, and Pit each contributing their own Skills on top of it, their party remained unnoticed eighty percent of the time. Those that could notice them, however, were strong.

Tier IV Shades became more and more common, crowding the pathway as the small crypts became larger and larger, until Tier V creatures swarmed the edges as well. Those were the true threats so far, the equivalent of a Master Tier, and more than most of his team could handle.

Felix changed tactics. Stealth was the watchword, but where that failed, they went into immediate and full offense. Blades of light and orbs of destruction rained upon the Shades, obliterating the weaker ones while the stronger were at the very least stunned. Before the Tier V monsters could retaliate, Felix unleashed his Hunger. Again and again, their Essence funneled into his core space, until nothing stopped their ascent up the mountain.

The ground shook.

The Shades had just begun to thin out, and the mausoleums had transitioned into truly huge structures, fronted by old growth forests that obscured their view of the distant peak. Those branches swayed with more than the wind as pebbles and ill-kept tombs tumbled down the slopes.

"What the hell is that?" Beef asked.

Felix looked back down. They were far away from Havenhold, and much of the Undermount itself was in the way, but in the hazy distance beyond the strange forests, he thought he saw something flicker.

Flames.

CHAPTER NINETY-THREE

Abyssal Skein is level 89!

Felix squeezed his Void Skill for every ounce of magic stealth it could provide and no longer took the same amount of care as they accelerated up the Coil. Shades came and went; most were avoided and left behind, while others piled onto their path—only to be bludgeoned aside by hammer, chain, spear, axe, and furious light. The dead turned to dust and smoke.

Survivors were devoured.

Their first stumbling block came two miles higher where, between one step and the next, a terrible pressure descended on them all. They trembled, the weight almost a physical thing as it attempted to push them to the ground. None of them succumbed.

"We have entered the next segment of the Undermount," Tzfell announced in a thin whisper. "The Greater Mausoleums await."

Exploration is level 78!

They rested for a time, allowing for each of them to grow accustomed to the new pressure. It was more of a shock than anything else. Beef, the least Tempered among them, was fine in a few minutes. Vess passed around a few Stamina Potions and shook out the aches that had started building in their legs, and Felix paced.

"Calm down, kid," Harn said, putting his axes away after an inspection. "You're makin' me nervous."

"*I'm* nervous," Felix admitted.

"Can't say I blame ya."

Felix stopped pacing. He laughed. "I appreciate you, Harn."

The man shrugged, his battered armor moving smoothly despite what looked like a decade of wear and tear on it. "I call it like I see it. But we got a plan. That counts for somethin'."

"Think it'll work?"

"Probably not." Harn stood up. "Don't mean we shouldn't try."

Rested, Felix restored his Abyssal Skein on everyone, and they set out once more with new vigor in their steps. Around them, the Necropolis expanded, overwhelming the trees around them until only rare patches of weeds remained between the towering mausoleums. Tombs spread outward, pressing into the very air as they hung precariously over terraced cliffs or climbed vertically beside statues of stolid Dwarven figures.

The monsters changed as well, the Shades replaced by heavily armored Death Knights. Dwarven in proportion but twice the size, they wore suits of rounded armor made of that same, unidentifiable black stone from the Clan Hold. The Knights were Tier IVs, but every one was planted in silent vigil before specific tombs. They did not stray from the sealed doors, their ivy-coated swords thrust firmly in the stone at their feet, even when Felix's party was forced to draw close to them. They were Felix's favorite.

Less of a favorite were the Grave Trolls. Those gray-furred monsters ran in packs around the Grand Mausoleums, three or four of them at a time, and like their brethren, they possessed incredible regeneration. More than once, their party was surprised by the Grave Trolls' speed and stealth, engaged in a battle often before they had time to shout a warning.

Tzfell said they were an evolutionary offshoot of the River, Forest, and Sun Trolls they had faced previously. Trapped in the Necropolis by Dwarven ancestors, they had adapted and Evolved into a new form better suited to their environment. "It is likely due to their healing abilities. I believe they consume parts of themselves to power it, which requires them to eat more to survive. The eating is compressed into their cores and directly affects their abilities. With mostly shadow and necromantic Mana in their diet, they soon changed."

"Fascinating," Vess said.

"Uh-huh." Felix speared three more of them with swords of forged light. They crumpled to the ground. "At least they're weak to light Mana."

Harn chopped off their heads with a blazing swing. "Still hate 'em."

The Trolls were a constant, roaming threat, but the Tomb Guardians were the worst. The pinnacle of monstrosities in the Necropolis, they were massive amalgamations of worn, ivory skeletons that had been broken and bound together with intense amounts of necromantic Mana. They reminded Felix of the Shambling Horror, a creature Felix once fought within the Haestus Temple that had gone toe-to-toe with the Deepking. Luckily for them, despite being Tier V monsters, the Tomb Guardians weren't nearly as strong as the Horror had been.

They did, however, get in the way.

"Keratin Conception!" Beef shouted, seizing the third Guardian in the last half hour. It already had several gaping wounds from Harn's axes, but the thing remained upsettingly fast. Chitinous legs just barely grasped the bone monster's limbs, locking it down for a moment. "Seismic Shatter!"

Bedlam met a screeching skeletal face and slammed it into the earth. Its jaws snapped shut so hard they cracked like a gunshot, but the thing still struggled mightily.

"Dawn's Advent!"

"Bonds of Dominion!"

Golden crescents sliced into the monster's neck and chest, splintering bone and forcing it to flinch away from Beef's restraints. Ethereal purple chains followed, each one locking onto a portion of the nightmare beast's form, until it couldn't move at all. Evie landed on its back and brought her spiked weapon down hard, twisting it last-minute to snake its length around the Guardian's bony neck.

"Tooth and Claw!" she shouted. The chain bucked in her hands, the new spikes along its length spinning independent of the chain itself and chewing through gristle, bone, and magic.

The Tomb Guardian screamed, and its skull was split by a single silver Spear, exposing the malformed blackened-green core. A second Spear shattered it into pieces.

You Have Killed A Tomb Guardian!
XP Earned!

Experience trickled out to each of them as the monster faded into dark smoke, and his team took a moment to rest. Felix didn't care much about the experience—the creature barely made the needle move on his own level. He was far more interested in other things: he ate the remains, letting its significance trickle into his core space.

Good. Need Bigger.

He ignored his Hunger. Not because he didn't agree—they'd need all the significance they could get—but because of a glossy black feather that fluttered across his field of vision. Felix blinked, disbelieving, but the feather was very real and quite large—like one of Pit's pinions. It landed on a flat area of stone, just as the last of the Tomb Guardian vanished into Felix's belly.

"Is that—?" he stepped forward, only to be interrupted by a sharp crack. The stone floor split at his feet, trembling as a long crevasse opened up across the cliff and rocks tumbled down into a yawning blackness. Felix hopped backward, away from the traitorous edge.

"What happened?" Yintarion asked. "Did you break the ground, Autarch?"

"No," Felix said, frowning. "But someone did."

A cawing came from within, so faint that Felix questioned whether it had happened at all. No one else seemed to have heard it, except Pit.

That's the bird lady.

The Raven.

Right. What does she want?

"Looks like a cave-in," Vess said, leaping over to the edge of it. She peered inside. "Something glimmers within."

Felix hopped up, balancing on the tumbled edge where the stone had sheared off. Just within the short, dark tunnel was a sculpture. It was similar to many that they had seen across the Undermount, and especially in the upper levels of the Necropolis. A Dwarf in armor with an impressive beard. What struck Felix, however, was this one looked familiar.

"Hey I know that face," Felix said. "That's the Rockshaper."

"A blessed ancestor," Tzfell confirmed after climbing up herself. She put a hand to her mouth. "I cannot believe we've chanced upon this. His tomb was hidden by the ancient kings."

Felix leaned down and picked up a black feather lodged between stones. "Yeah."

"Sounds like a place for treasure," Evie suggested. "I wouldn't mind takin' a look."

"Ooh, loot. I love loot."

Laur smiled. "You play? I never knew."

Beef scratched his head. "I–what? Play what?"

"The lute."

"Uh…I mean, I don't play for loot exclusively. Like, I enjoyed the other parts of games, but loot is good. Who doesn't like some good magic items?" Beef shrugged. "Anyway, this isn't a game, right? But loot could help us. We should check it out."

Laur's smile had turned stiff and somewhat confused the longer Beef spoke. It would have been funny to Felix if he hadn't been so stressed. "We'll check it out. Tzfell, Pit, Vess, with me. Everyone else, keep an eye out."

Evie mock saluted. "Aye aye, your kingship."

The four of them slid down into the hole, traveling only thirty feet downward before the rubble and the natural floor turned level. From there, they saw the full statue of the Rockshaper, at least twenty feet tall and buried up to his knees in debris. One squared hand was curled over his chest as if he were clutching something, while the other pointed into the distance.

Tzfell ran her hands over the statue. "Incredible. The techniques here…this wasn't carved. It was shaped. Yes, that maker mark. He made this himself."

"Is Stone Shaping a common Skill among Dwarves?"

"Quite rare. Only one or two in a generation might see the talent awaken in them."

"Huh." Felix considered his hands. He'd learned the Skill from a big monkey. "So, the Rockshaper made this place?"

"It is likely, yes."

"There's a door!" Pit said from farther in.

Felix and Tzfell walked over, finding Pit and Vess standing next to a simple lintel carved into the natural rock wall. Right where the statue pointed.

"I cannot find a handle, but I also cannot detect any sort of traps or hidden catches." Vess gestured at the rough, uncarved door. It looked like a piece of the wall had been framed. "It seems to be a useless slab of stone."

"The Rockshaper was known for hiding things in plain sight," Tzfell said. "Surely we have just missed something."

"Perhaps."

Felix reached out and pushed on the wall, but it didn't budge. Vess gave him a look, and he laughed. "What?"

"Do you think we neglected to *push*?"

"Listen, I dunno—" Felix cut himself off, his hand still on the supposed door. He felt a thrum of…something. "Wait. Wait. This is a lower-Tier rock than the rest of the wall. *Stone Shaping.*"

Felix's oldest shaping Skill unfurled from his core and struck the rough wall. The door melted away.

Exploration is level 79!

"Whoa." Pit chirruped. "Big room."

Felix stepped in first, Manasight flared in case of a trap. He saw nothing of the sort, but instead was inundated by the sheer volume of sigaldry inlaid all around them. It was only a single room but was quite spacious, with high ceilings supported by sturdy stone columns. Shafts of sunlight pierced through high, narrow windows despite being underground, catching swirling dust that was displaced by Felix's entry. Between the columns, there were eight walls, and each was adorned by bas relief sculptures in a variety of minerals and precious ores.

"Not a tomb," Tzfell said in wonder. "An atelier! His workshop!"

Workbenches and shelves filled the space, covered in a thick layer of dust. They split the wide floor into discrete areas. To the left were a collection of polished chisels, hammers, and sculpting picks along with piles of uncut stone. To the right were rows of shiny gemstones, along with a number of rotted rags. The gemstones' facets caught the enchanted light and refracted it into rainbows across the nearest walls.

The centerpiece of the workshop, though, was a massive stone platform upon which rested a man-sized chunk of midnight rock studded with flecks of diamonds. Veilstone, it was called. The same material was used so often around the Clan Hold, but this was an unfinished sculpture. It bore chisel marks and the grooves of what looked like fingers, until the rock appeared to be a wave frozen in time. Unfinished, perhaps, but strangely beautiful.

"He was a true artisan, known to utilize sculptor's and mason's tools in addition to his prodigious magical Skill." Tzfell stepped closer to the sculpture, her hand twitching to touch it but never quite crossing the distance. "Even half-done, this is worth ten times its weight in gold."

Felix walked the room, careful not to touch anything as he traced out the hidden inscriptions with his Manasight. Someone, perhaps the Rockshaper himself, had inscribed complicated arrays around the room, and Felix took the time to translate them as best he could. It was in the more angular Dwarven script of course, but a large portion of the array was to mimic sunlight and shine it through the upper windows. Other portions were to preserve his tools—each glyph tied to the racks the chisels and hammers hung upon—but the rest seemed useless. Empty space meant for further additions.

"Well, this is a bust. I guess we can take the gems, but they're just rocks."

Vess plucked a fist-sized emerald from its stand. When nothing happened, she placed it in her pouch, along with the others. "We can sell them. I know Elderthrone is making a lot of profit, but gemstones trade far easier with some people."

"Plus, they're shiny," Pit added. "Pretty."

Tzfell pursed her lips, but she said nothing as Vess took all the remaining gemstones. When Felix stepped up to the tools, she cleared her throat. "Lord Autarch, I do not see the use these tools have for you. They are not enchanted and are only made of high steel. They would not compare to the implements your own craftsmen possess and…I would ask that you leave them. To honor the Rockshaper's memory."

Felix studied the Dwarven Chanter before nodding. "Sure. I don't need them, but I wanted to see the glyphs behind the racks a little closer."

He reached up and pushed aside a pair of rasps, only to find one of them stuck fast to the wall. Felix frowned and pushed a little harder. It remained unmoved, and he pushed harder. When a faint groaning came from the rasp, he realized the tool itself was bending rather than shifting position, and he stopped altogether.

He flared his Manasight.

The wall behind that section of tools was layered with inscriptions, some being the preservation array for the metal and wood implements, but the rest was that useless series of placeholder sigils. It spread like creeping vines all over the wall, the columns, and behind the bas relief sculptures in between.

Wait a second. Felix walked to the primary sculpture, following the flow of nonsense sigaldry as it reached a strange…knot was the only word Felix could think to describe it. Not a glyph or array, just a jumble of etched symbols traced with just the lightest touch of active Mana. In fact, it almost resembled—

"Oh. Oh, that's neat," Felix said. He slipped behind the unfinished sculpture and sounded a nearly identical pattern within himself. "Stone Shaping."

This time it wasn't *his* Will that commanded the stone to move, but another's. That pattern of sigaldry hidden within resonated with his Skill, and a delicate tracery of magic spread throughout the entire wall in an instant. It melted away to reveal a smaller chamber, almost an alcove, filled with a soft green light.

"How'd you know that was there?" Pit asked. "Wait, is there more behind these walls, too?"

"Not that I can figure, but feel free to poke around, dude."

Felix stepped into the alcove. Again, there were no traps or wards, just perfectly polished floors that sprouted organically into a table, shelf, and framed a large, circular window. The window was at head height and easily ten feet in diameter. It was stained glass, cut and leaded between panes to illustrate a high mountain surrounded by storm clouds. The Undermount, Felix surmised.

Light shone through, enough to illuminate the space completely... and this time, the light wasn't fabricated. Felix reached up and found a catch on the side of the window, and he opened it up. The circular frame swung outward into an odd, underground grotto, where very large green crystals gave off a brilliant shine.

"Is that inside the mountain?" Vess asked. She reached up and pressed her hand into the space, then quickly withdrew it. "It's freezing."

"I don't think it's inside the mountain. It looks like...yes. Look, there," Tzfell pointed to something just beyond the large crystals. There was a distinct golden pattern inlaid into the far wall, ornate knotwork and a truncated series of Dwarven words. "This is on the Low Road. I am unsure where, but it can be nowhere else."

"It's an exit?"

"Yes. It crosses out of the Undermount and back into the Continent, only...I am unsure how. I sense no dissonant tearing, as with the portal we used to enter."

Felix's Mind spun, adding the new information to the slew of calculations he'd been running constantly. He looked down, and for the first time noticed a thin book nestled between empty shelves on the desk. It was bound in wooden boards and wrapped in leather, very old but bearing no title or marking of any kind. Felix flipped it open, finding extremely thin, nearly transparent paper absolutely covered in a small, blocky scrawl. It was clearly in Dwarven script, but he'd already started piecing together some of their language.

"Basic Will...Sculptor...Melding," he translated. Tzfell gasped.

"That is a handwritten journal," she peered into his hands. "Written by the Rockshaper himself!"

"Can you read this?" he asked.

The Chanter shook her head. "It is in an older dialect. Given time, I could aid you in translating it. But the title here, I can read that. It isn't whatever you said. These mean 'Essence of Will: Shaping Unity.'"

"Shaping Unity," he murmured. He really hoped that meant what he thought it meant. "Is it a Skill Book?"

"No. Those are quite different," Vess said. "It appears to be a simple journal."

"I doubt there is anything simple about this book. The Rockshaper is so highly regarded for a reason. He was a genius, and it is only from his efforts that the line of kings was formed. I have seen your shaping Skills, Lord Autarch, and I cannot stress how helpful this journal might prove to be."

Felix had to stop himself from clawing the book back and settled for carefully lifting it out of Tzfell's hands. He formed a thick leather pouch out of his Garment and settled the journal into it, carefully strapping it down so it couldn't shift during a fight. He closed the ornate window and jerked his thumb over his shoulder. "Let's get back."

Far happier than when he'd entered, Felix hopped out of the collapsed tunnel with the others just as the mountain shook again. The ground broke just a bit more, rocks tumbling onto the carved face below, as lightning flashed across the sky. Ten bolts, each one brighter and larger than the last, seared into their vision as it slammed down onto the ground in the far distance.

"What is happenin' down there?" Evie asked.

"I see redcloaks," Vess said, fury thickening her voice. "How did they get in?"

It was true. The mountain blocked their view of the pleasure palace, but swarming across the grassy hills just beyond, they could make out ant-sized figures in white and red. The lightning landed among them, eradicated entire swathes of their army, but more poured from between the trees.

"There's *thousands* down there," Beef whispered. His hands were shaking. Hallow pressed her lumpy rock face against his cheek.

A mammoth bolt of lightning tore from the clouds, slamming into the rear of the army, only to be met by a brilliant golden radiance. Thunder tore across the sky, and the lightning cut off. A figure in brutal armor visibly larger than all the rest strode from the blackened earth, seemingly unharmed.

Imara.

Felix growled before shaping a layer of stone over the secret tunnel. "Rest is over. Go. Like our lives depend on it."

He was pretty sure they did.

CHAPTER NINETY-FOUR

While he couldn't move as fast as he wanted, Felix drove them up the mountain with a single-mindedness that left the others gasping for air.

By the fifth mile through the Greater Mausoleum, Pit Converged with him to conserve his Stamina, while Beef ended up physically carrying the two Chanters on his wide shoulders. Evie and Vess both managed in their own way, one utilizing her Born Trait to lighten her every step (and reduce her Stamina cost), the other leaning into her Dragoon training. Vess' confusing and powerful movement technique propelled her forward at a blistering pace—enough to match Felix's reduced speed.

Harn, too heavy to carry and too stubborn to accept it, simply muscled through. His Running Skill was Adept Tier, and despite being of Common rarity, the efficiency of his Stamina consumption was incredible. The man knew how to move.

Quick as it began, the Necropolis came to an end. Sprawling tombs and elaborate statuary were enveloped by fog as the Coil ascended, until the fog resolved into deep, thunderous clouds. As before, the Spiritual pressure of the Undermount increased, redoubling as their senses were swathed in moist cotton. Beef was driven to his knees, and the stone shattered under his weight. Evie, Harn, and Vess were not much better off.

"We have reached the Voidstorm!" Tzfell shouted over the crashing thunder and sudden, swirling wind. She clung to Beef's rocky pauldron so hard her knuckles were white. "We must all of us brace for its judgment!"

Lightning skittered across the sky before blasting onto the steps ahead of them, narrowly missing Beef.

"Gather close! Behind me!" Felix commanded, stepping ahead of everyone else. He set his Affinity flaring through two of his Skills. One old. One new. "Adamant Discord! Storm Shaping!"

A chaotic tangle of connections appeared in his vision, threads of influence between storm, sky, and mountain. As he watched, the dim lines between Harn and the sky swelled into a brilliant bar. Felix reached out, grasping at the connection with Adamant Discord…and at the lightning with Storm Shaping.

A waist-thick bolt of electricity surged downward toward the warrior, but it was diverted at the last minute into Felix's hands. Lightning coursed across his scaled hands and arms, burning away his Garment and exposing his spasming muscles before he guided it down and toward his open maw.

Chthonic Tribute!

Storm Shaping is level 43!

"Felix!" Vess stepped close, only to be warded off by one of his midnight hands. "How much of that can you take?"

"As much as necessary," he said.

The ascent continued, but this time it was like the world had turned against them. Bolts attempted to slay them where they stood, while gale-force winds and torrential rain tried to rip them free of the mountain. His team hunkered low, using chains and axes, chitinous legs and conjured spears to anchor themselves, stride by resolute stride.

Each blast of lightning was timed randomly, but Felix saw each of them coming, thanks to Adamant Discord. He stole them all, and while it didn't hurt nearly as badly as the mega-bolt from atop the pleasure palace, they weren't helpful for his already-strained Body.

Storm Shaping is level 44!
…
Storm Shaping is level 58!
Journeyman Tier!
You Gain:
+30 EVA

+30 RES
+35 INT

Step after step, Felix covered for his team. It grew increasingly easier to master the energies around him as Storm Shaping leveled, though he could do nothing against the Voidstorm itself. It hung above them like a god, boiling above the tear into the Void as magic and weird dimensional physics combined to make a nightmare come alive.

Thankfully, only a piece of the Voidstorm touched down around them, and eventually, it spat a final, anemic bolt. The winds flagged, blowing the smoke and steam from Felix's shoulders as the others staggered forward onto calmer ground. Between one step and another, the Voidstorm vanished, and his team passed into paved streets only faintly littered with fog.

"The Lesser Vaults," Tzfell said. "Each is a repository for the riches of the Highbloods. We will find greater guardians here, but they will remain bound closer to their structures."

Harn removed his helmet, letting rivulets of water stream down his chest. "Makes sense. Guards ain't useful if they leave their posts."

To either side of the paved street towered beautiful structures that were far removed from the grim iconography of the Necropolis and the gloom of the Voidstorm. Pale yellow towers, crimson manses, and vibrantly blue fortresses abounded, their architecture decidedly Dwarven despite the hues. Wards filled the spaces between them, overlapping in so many places that the interference created a shifting rainbow of radiance that flowed among the Lesser Vaults like visible air currents.

The Serpent's Coil continued, here and there flattening out into gently winding roads, splitting off into four, five, or even ten way intersections as they approached each Lesser Vault. In fact, as they jogged through the damp streets, it grew increasingly obvious that the Coil was lingering there.

"This is useless. We can't stay on the path, not if we wanna get to the top before we die of old age," Evie said.

Beef leaned over a railing, staring down a narrow alleyway between stout structures and glimmering wards. "We need a shortcut."

Tzfell clucked her tongue. "We cannot. It will draw the Arcane Sentries down upon us."

"Worth the risk," Evie decided. "I ain't doin' another race across… all of that."

She gestured toward the Serpent's Coil ahead, where they could see it split into four different roads, many of which split again and again. Felix chewed his lip, thinking. "Are the Arcane Sentries fast? Strong?"

"Tier V and perhaps Tier VI creatures. They're constructs built by our ancestors, and I don't know their capabilities other than they are tough."

"Evie and Beef are right," Vess said. "We cannot tarry on these roadways. We must ascend."

"Right." Felix flared Abyssal Skein, refreshing the Skill across his allies. "Mount up or keep up. We're not stopping 'til we hit the top."

Felix leaped from the elevated Coil, landing on a strip of soft loam and brightly colored flowers. Inside, Pit peered curiously from behind Felix's eyes as the world whipped by them at speed.

All these fancy houses. How many have magical treasure?

All of them, I'd guess. Felix leaped over a large urn planted with some sort of reed. *We can't check, though. You know that.*

Pit grumbled. *I know.*

Ahead, directly in their path, was a creature that looked like a wolf but made entirely of stone. A construct, clearly. Aside from being made from midnight veilstone, the wolf looked almost lifelike—if real wolves were the size of elephants. There was no easy path around them, as Felix sensed similar constructs around the sides of other vaults.

Felix glanced back. The others were following, but he had a sizable lead on them.

The only way is through.

Need my help? Pit asked.

No. I got this.

Felix flared his Agility, zipping ahead hard, and drove his bare fist into the stone wolf's side. Cracks splintered across its torso, and it let out a resounding yelp. The construct didn't simply take it though, it moved with the strike, acting so fluidly that Felix had to focus to dodge its slamming claws. He did, but not the shock of earth Mana that surged out from the impact. Spikes of stone shot up, bashing into his chest and thighs hard enough to drive him back a few steps.

"Strong and smart," he muttered, rubbing his chest.

The Sentry opened its stone jaws and spat out a gobbet of acid and flame. Felix grasped both, flaring Hand of Calamity and Cardinal Flame to divert the attack entirely. The combined Mana slapped into a nearby ward and sizzled out.

Hand of Calamity is level 75!
Adept Tier!
You Gain:
+5% MIG
+15 END
+5% AFI

"Three different elemental attacks. That's impressive." Shaking off the sudden boost to his stats, Felix set himself, shoulders squared against the crouching enemy. "I just need the one."

Wild Threnody!

Stone Shaping!

The construct's veilstone body was too strong for Felix to seize control of it, but that didn't stop him. The Sentry lunged, a corona of power flaring atop its spiky ruff, but Felix met it head-on. His Mana flowed out, congealing into rock around his fist.

He caught the Sentry by the snout, while his second arm snaked around the construct's neck. Felix twisted and slammed the thing into the ground. Dirt, grass, and dust exploded into the air. The Sentry thrashed, and Felix caught its hind leg before exerting all of his Strength against it. The limb tore right off, releasing a geyser of green, orange, and dusty brown vapor.

"Stop moving," he said. "Your skin is *tough*. Where is your core?"

The Arcane Sentry laid on its side, panting heavily, all but broken, and Felix hesitated. Its chest was glowing and it sounded…bad. More than bad. Discordant.

Voracious Eye.

Name: Arcane Sentry
Type: Elemental Construct
…
Lore: A construct built by the Dwarves of Ages past, each Sentry is a combination of at least three Lesser Elementals. The elementals are bound together with stringent Oaths and potent arrays to keep them trapped in the construct and dedicated to protecting their territory.

"Oaths?" He ignored the less-relevant parts of the thing's information and focused on the lore. "Are you…trapped in there?"

There was no answer. Of course there wasn't. So Felix shoved his fingers carefully into the side of the Sentry, and with a grunt, ripped free a chunk of stone from the wolf facade. Within was a cage, but not a ribcage, a literal cage inscribed with bright sigaldry. Inside of that cage were three swirling lights: Lesser Elementals, one of flame, one of acid, and one of earth.

Adamant Discord.

Skein of Fate.

Electric blue connections popped into his awareness, a great web of things that he ignored about ninety-nine percent of and focused on the construct before him. The earth elemental was tied to the stone skin, the fire element was tied to the sigaldry directly, while the acid elemental was linked to a river of green power that circulated throughout. All of them, however, were bound to a core of beaten metal by three silver wires. Those he saw with his Skein of Fate.

Those were Oaths.

They're so thin. They were anemic compared to the Oaths his people had sworn to him, like thread next to a steel hawser. They also floated up out of the Sentry, traveling some distance away before vanishing behind the corner of a nearby structure. Dissonance wafted off of the Oaths like a bad stink. Through his Skein of Fate, he could tell that the Oaths were not given in good faith. "You were tricked into this form, weren't you?"

The three lights surged, and the wolf tried to snap at him again. Pit manifested from his Spirit, landing atop the Sentry's head and pinning it. The Oaths shined brighter and brighter as the construct struggled to attack. The sound of Dissonance stained the Harmony all around them, a buzzing roar among a trumpet blast.

Felix reached down and, with a minor effort, snapped the Oaths apart.

The Arcane Sentry went rigid. Whatever power animated its stone form vanished, as did the lights within its eyes and claws. Without fanfare or display, the three Lesser Elementals zipped off into the distance. Free.

You Have Defeated An Arcane Sentry!
XP Earned!

New Quest!
Break the Bonds!

Sever the Oaths the Lesser Elementals were tricked into and free them from their imprisonment! Find the source!
Rewards: Varies

"Huh." He accepted the Quest.

Vess and the others reached him moments later as Felix stood, dusting off his knees. "These things are slaved elementals."

"'Kay," Beef said, breathing hard. "That's…bad, right?"

"It's not great. But I got a Quest." Felix told them the gist of it. "We find this source, we could maybe put all of the Sentries out of commission at once."

"And free up our path," Harn said. "Good plan."

Evie shrugged. "Where're we goin'?"

They started running again, and soon enough, they found another Arcane Sentry. Two of them, in fact. Felix stopped just shy of their position and flared Skein of Fate. Now that he knew what to look for, he could make out the silver gossamer that floated away from both of their stone bodies.

"This way," he whispered and took them off to the right.

Across gold-worked platforms, obsidian pillars, and sapphire studded archways, Felix found more and more of the Arcane Sentries. They prowled their lonely posts aimlessly, their attention trained to their own vaults and no others, making sneaking through a relatively easy task. It was just slow. Still, within twenty minutes, they came upon a cliff that overlooked a large depression in the mountainside. Inside was a large octagonal building with bronze pillars built on top, creating a deeply shadowed portico. The pillars were draped in a thick silver canopy of gathered threads as the Voidstorm thundered far above.

"The threads all lead…here," Felix said, not quite believing his eyes. Below, just ahead of where the silver threads all joined together, was Archie.

He was hemmed in by six Dwarves…each of them suffused with an aura of intense power.

"Grandmasters," Harn said in alarm.

"No. No, but they are very close. Too close." Tzfell cowered low behind the edge of the cliff. "They have him cornered."

As they watched, Archie tried to dive into the ground…only to be forced back by a pair of Dwarves that shimmered with dusty-brown Mana. Archie backed off until he was up against the octagonal building where the Oath threads all gathered.

Above, Vess clutched her partisan. “We need to do *something*.”

“Do what?” Harn asked. “We go down there, not all of us are comin’ back out.”

Felix crouched atop the cliff, thinking, but his time for that was running out. Then he caught movement out of the edge of his senses. Focusing his Perception, Felix slowly smiled. “I have a plan.”

CHAPTER NINETY-FIVE

Archie was trapped. He wasn't used to it, but then again, there was little he was used to in this screwed-up world.

He had almost made it up the mountain when he'd had to slow down because of the stupid Arcane Sentries. He'd even been forced to fight one, and it was tough. He beat it, sure, which got him that damn Quest to destroy them all. That had been too tempting to pass up. It would've meant he could race through this last area with impunity.

So he followed the things, tracking the slow movements of Sentries before catching a weird rhythm coming from this place. His Blindsense told him there was a big creature nearby…but all he found were the damn Vault Wardens.

"Listen, I've had about enough of the beard brigade. I'm just passing through, okay?"

"Your trespass stops here, child. We have locked down your curious gift," one of the Wardens said. "Do not fight us."

Archie rubbed his nose. He had bruised it when they stopped his Stoneswim from functioning. "Yeah, thanks for that."

The mountain shook, and the Wardens traded glances. They looked afraid, and it was definitely not because of him.

"The Hierocracy threatens our sovereignty. You will come with us to fix it," another said.

"Threatens you how? Fix it how?"

"The Titan ascends the peak."

For a second, Archie's heart felt like it wanted to claw up his throat. "What?"

"She and an army of sycophantic light-lickers have invaded our most sacred realm," another Warden spat. "She will stop when she has *you.*"

The mountain shook again.

"She is coming regardless of what you decide…and we are not enough to stop her. At least this way, you help someone with your miserable, thieving life before you are taken."

"So, I just roll over?" Archie barked a nasty laugh. He licked his lips, eyes still scanning for an opening in their guard. He needed to get out of there. "Never done that before. Don't see a reason to start now."

"Then you will die."

Archie bolted, flaring his measly Agility as hard as he could, but he wasn't fast enough to outrace a sudden wall of molded earth and slammed face-first into it. "Fuck! My nose!"

Before he could do more than reel back, a flash of blue-white lightning surged across the sky. Archie flinched, fearing the storm had opened up again…but nothing came of it. Until he realized that none of the Vault Wardens were doing anything, and he glanced at the bearded bastards.

All six of them were staring up above the weird building behind Archie with expressions that ranged between angry and terrified.

"You fool! What have you done?"

Archie looked up just in time to see a massive, house-sized spider leap from atop the roof.

Holy shi—Hey! I know that guy!

Felix quickly learned that there were two things massive mithril spider constructs don't like. The first is when someone messes with their web. The second is when you punch them very hard in the eye. In order to get its attention, he had done both.

It worked.

Was this the best idea? Pit asked, still riding shotgun in his Spirit.

Nope!

Felix straddled the enormous construct, arms clutching at a delicate seam between its thorax and abdomen. The thing bucked and slammed itself into the bronze pillars around its ethereal lair, trying to dislodge him with all of its might. It was only when he snapped a second Oath thread that the thing skittered out of its dark den and leaped into the light.

Directly onto the Vault Wardens.

Before Felix had soared over Archie and the Dwarves, he'd spotted the spider construct hiding in its little nest. His Voracious Eye had told him many things about it, like that it was called an Oathweaver, that it would defend the Oaths under its care with a wild ferocity, and that it was a Tier VI construct.

Or, in mortal terms: a goddamn Grandmaster.

The Wardens raised shields and summoned fantastical metal and stone armor around themselves, bringing all of the power of their high Master Tier to bear. When the Oathweaver landed, its careless legs slammed into only one…and ran the man through, killing him instantly.

You Have Killed A Vault Warden!
XP Earned!

The Dwarves rallied, their screams less frightened and more pissed off. Spells and Skills surged, ricocheting off of the Oathweaver's carapace as they tried and failed to hit Felix. Ducking his head so he didn't get it blown off, Felix reached back to his belt, fumbling with a buckle before realizing he could simply will the strap to dissolve. When it did, he grasped the horn of a large, monstrous skull and slammed it down onto the Oathweaver before funneling a stupid amount of Mana through it.

The Vault Wardens screamed, and the air positively vibrated with their fear as the giant mithril spider split into four identical copies. Each one was just as imposing as the real thing, carrying the weight of its presence that confused even Master Tier senses.

Skein of Fate!

Felix snipped another handful of threads, and the Oathweaver—and all of its copies—went absolutely nuts.

Dwarven curses split the air just as readily as blazing Skills and conjured boulders. The Oathweaver started leaping about and rolling, trying with every ounce of its being to kill Felix. He held on grimly, claws digging into metal with a tortured screech and healing the brutal damage each slam and roll did to him.

"They are false copies! They have no substance!" one of the

Wardens shouted. The ruse was up, but then, it was never about fooling them. It was a distraction.

"AAGH!" another screamed as the sound of electricity and crackling ice pierced the general tumult of a raging spider. Felix got a look as the Oathweaver reared back again, and he grinned through the blood on his face.

"Array keystones are on!" Harn shouted. "Light 'em up!"

Felix activated his suppression array.

Theurgist of the Rise is level 93!

...

Theurgist of the Rise is level 95!

Cardinal Flame is level 95!

On the back of each of the Vault Wardens, a dinner-plate-sized hexagon of Leviathan bone and ice ore seared into their flesh with light and a debilitating Intent. Sigils spread out along the ground, circle after concentric circle centered around the Dwarven Masters. Immediately, the auras around them flickered, and one even stumbled as if dizzy.

"Now!" Beef yelled and zipped forward in a reckless charge. The Warden took the hit in the chest, his rock armor splintering, but recovered quickly. Others hit their own targets, Spears, chains, flames, and crystalline darts all harrying the powerful warriors. Chanted spells and blazing axes met shields of stone and steel, denting them if not breaking them apart.

His friends were strong, but the Vault Wardens were still Master Tier, after all. Except, as the suppression array wore on, draining primarily their Health and Stamina, they couldn't recover as fast.

The fight was on.

Felix couldn't watch, though, because he had a separate issue as the Oathweaver slammed him into the bronze pillars of its home. That one hurt far more than the rest, and Sovereign of Flesh had to pull a great quantity of Essence to heal himself.

I can't keep this up. His only saving grace was that the construct wasn't very smart. It had all the power of a Grandmaster and nothing to do with it except slam and trample. *But I don't need you anymore.*

Skein of Fate!

This time, Felix reached up into the glistening silver canopy of threads above him and spread his Will across all of them…and tore them apart.

Skein of Fate is level 69!
…
Skein of Fate is level 81!
Adept Tier!
You Gain:
+10% RES
+10% REI
+10% FEL

A great cacophony sounded around them, like an entire orchestra falling down a mile-long flight of stairs. Dissonance surged, the buzzing stink of it tearing across Felix's senses. The Oathweaver seized up, its cold metal body losing the little flexibility it had as it stiffened and fell over. The clang of it hitting the stone building below hurled Felix from its back like a sedan hitting a telephone pole. He smashed into the far wall, his flight cushioned by bronze.

You Have Defeated The Oathweaver!
XP Earned!

Defeated, not killed, he mused, wincing as he found his feet again. Felix supposed the thing had never really been alive. It had clearly been powered by the active enslavement of Lesser Elementals, all of them… feeding Mana back into its body. His hands itched, wanting to pull apart the Oathweaver and see how it functioned…but they didn't have the time.

Quest Complete!
Break the Bonds!
Sever the Oaths the Lesser Elementals were tricked into and free them from their imprisonment! Find the source!
Rewards: Varies

Reward Increased Due To Finding The Source!
Reward Increased Due To Freeing 10,000 Arcane Sentries!
…
Reward Increased Due To Freeing All 30,000 Arcane Sentries!

New Title!
Bondbreaker (Unique)!
An evolution of Chain-Breaker, you have spat in the face of Fortune once again! Your defiance is seen and recognized, Felix Nevarre! Those that are bound against their Will are easier to spot for you now.
+1 Skill Evolution

Now that's *awesome.* Felix picked up the horned skull. It had fallen after the spider had died. Tucking it back into the straps at his waist, he helped Pit back to his feet, and they walked to the edge of the building together. *You get that, too, dude.*

Pit trilled happily. *Hell yeah!*

Language.

Hmph.

Down on the ground below, each of the Master Tier Vault Wardens had been killed. He winced not only at their needless deaths but also at having used up five of his array keystones. The additional bindings Felix added apparently meant that the hexagonal constructs were essentially one-use items. *Only eight left. Shit.*

Language, Pit sent.

Despite the suppression array, they had clearly not gone down without a fight, as the flagstones were torn up into spikes and grasping hands, while other parts were scorched black or even still glowing with heat. His friends were gathered close, almost all of them sipping on Health and Mana Potions in equal measure.

Archie was there, surrounded on all sides by weary and fairly angry people. Felix had to admit that it was cathartic to see him pale when Beef snorted and Yintarion growled.

The guy all but crapped himself when Felix landed nearby with a thud.

"Oh hey, fancy, ugh, fancy meeting you here," he said weakly.

"Uh-huh."

"Listen. Thanks for the assist, I'll admit I wasn't gonna escape those guys alone—"

"You would've died," Evie said.

"Right. Right, exactly. So I owe ya. I do." Archie swallowed. "But I can't leave. Not until I've gotten what I came here for. It's too—"

"I agree," Felix said. "That's why I'm gonna help you rob the vault."

"I—oh." Archie brightened, thick eyebrows lifting above his dark goggles. "Really?"

"Yeah really. So put your game face on, dude, because we've gotta run fast." Felix rolled his shoulders. "The path is clear of Arcane Sentries now; I've completed the Quest. So the straight shot to the top should be a lot easier now."

Archie gaped. "That was you? I saw it was complete…but I didn't get anything."

"Did you actually help?" Vess asked, voice harsh. "Or did you cower while we did the work?"

"Uh, I couldn't, um…"

Felix sighed. "That doesn't matter. We're going. Now. Archie, how fast can you run?"

"On the ground? I'm slow as hell. But my Stoneswim can keep up."

"Good. I'm not holding back anymore."

"Wait, wait. That guy," Archie said, pointing to one of the Dwarves. "He said the Hierocracy was here. On the Undermount. Is—is it her?"

"Yeah. It is."

Archie deflated. "We're dead."

Felix pulled the guy up onto his feet. "I have a plan for that, too."

The mountain shook, and Imara fell to one knee, forced to plant her bare hands onto the cold stone steps so she wasn't thrown free. Behind her, the Inquisition forces staggered, many falling to their deaths hundreds of feet below. Others fell to the Grave Trolls that hounded their steps in ever-growing packs or the far deadlier Tomb Guardians that lunged out of the shadows.

"Chosen! We must regroup!" Bellar said, not for the first time. He eyed the low layer of clouds ahead with blatant fear. "We do not know what lies within, and my people are too spread out along the mountain, we must—!"

Imara grabbed the Inquisitor by the neck, her hand more than large enough to wrap entirely around it. His words—his breath—cut off. "The only thing *we* must do is find the Gnome. All else is inconsequential."

Bellar pulled and pried at her hand, unable to budge it. "If–if we die, then the Gnome will escape! The Fiend will interfere!"

"No. The Fiend knows my power. He will—"

"He hurled you across the sky!"

Imara sneered and dropped the man. He clattered to the steps. "A display of desperate strength. He cannot withstand the unveiled might of the Light."

"Are you…your voice—" Bellar stood up slowly. "You're angry."

She stepped closer to the man, and he flinched, but he didn't back away. "I hold nothing within me but the Light. And we waste time here." She marched up the steps again, feet barely fitting into the ill-sized stairs. "I should have kept Faer with me. At least he holds to his convictions."

"Halt!"

To the right, one of the Inquisitors thrust out their hand and translucent golden panels manifested atop one of the mausoleums. Caught within that golden glow was a squat figure with dark goggles, a black beard, and a vicious, mocking smile.

Seemingly without effort, the Gnome vanished into the mausoleum beneath his feet.

"THERE!" Imara shouted and braced her legs—before another Inquisitor spotted the Gnome. And another. And another.

"Illusions!" Bellar snarled. "They're false trails!"

"They do not feel like illusions. All of them feel true." Imara spun, her powerful vision piercing through the gloom and catching double after double. "He must be among them…but which one?"

Ahead, just below the bank of clouds, the Gnome stood. He grinned and waved before scurrying up the stairs and into the fog.

"Chase them all!" she demanded before following her own advice.

"Chosen! No!" Bellar screamed after her. "Imara!"

Yet she had already plunged into the storm.

CHAPTER NINETY-SIX

Exploration is level 80!

The Vault of Nine Kings more than dominated the top of the Undermount.

It *was* the top of the Undermount.

The Serpent's Coil terminated there, twisting upon itself at the very last landing. The ground was made of orichalcum polished to a mirror finish, so that it looked like they walked atop a perfectly still, red-gold pond. To complete the illusion, strange, whiskered fish swam just beneath the surface of the metal, made of silver-green scales and possessing deep, haunting blue eyes. Plants and flowers abounded, organized into ornate pots and vases or grown across knotwork trellises. The path beyond the Coil was a series of squared stones, each one twenty feet in diameter and as dull as the metal was shiny.

"Bones of the mountain," Tzfell said in a voice of quiet reverence. "We walk this way to reach the entrance."

She pushed to the fore, leading their group swiftly across the strange terrain. Before long, they came to a structure that looked half palace and half mountain, with polished metal towers and walls that wove in and out of the craggy peak. A door, huge and circular, loomed ahead. On its face was carved an enormous, many-headed monstrosity, bordered by a series of large Dwarvish sigils. It, too, was made of orichalcum as well as mithril and veilstone, the red, silver, and black coloration working to almost bring the beast to life.

"Is that—?" Beef asked.

Evie whistled. "Noctis' tits."

Archie said nothing, but sweat visibly beaded across his forehead. Tzfell and Laur flanked him, prepared in case the guy bolted, but even they were distracted by the sheer presence of the Vault of Nine Kings.

"The Dwarves call it the biggest storehouse for treasure in all the Continent," Tzfell said, voice quiet. Reverent. "It contains the riches of Ages."

"Stolen riches," Yintarion said.

"The wages of war," the Chanter shot back. "But yes. Most of it was claimed during the Dwarven conquests. Centuries of fighting over the Rimefang range and beyond."

"Big door," Harn said. "How do we get in?"

"Laur?" Felix asked.

"Oh! Yes. Right." The Elven Chanter hustled forward, crossing the short distance to the viscerally real bas-relief sculpture. He stopped short of the dais before the door proper and ran his hands through the air. A rainbow of colors dragged through his fingers. "It is...quite complicated, as you can imagine. Already I've sensed four—no, five—seven! Seven layers of wards." He shook his head in disbelief. "And that is just on the outside."

Felix flexed his hands, and his Hunger rumbled. "What if we tear the wards off?"

"You mean...eat them? That wouldn't work. Or it would, but the result would be that this door's security measures would activate. The vault would seal itself...permanently."

"It's an enshrouded shield," Archie said. Everyone turned to look at the guy, and he puffed up his chest. "Studied up on this. I know how to break through." He looked pointedly at Tzfell. "You just gotta let me walk more than ten feet away from you."

"The last time we tried that, you ran away," the Chanter said.

"Through the fireplace," Beef added.

"After you sucker punched us," Evie said, gesturing to her eye.

"Okay, that's...fair. But this is what I came here to do. To get in there. I *need* this." He licked his lips. "I'm not gonna run."

Felix nodded. "Do it."

Archie walked up to the massive door, his heart hammering loud enough that Felix barely had to strain to hear its thudding. Archie stepped forward onto the segmented dais right before the vault door and shook out his hands. Felix watched the guy closely, but not because he was worried he'd run away. It was the door itself.

That monster carving is way too realistic, he sent to Pit.

Hm. Its necks look weird.

Oh? Felix focused on that part of the beast. The thing was crafted with such incredible detail that he could make out individual scales along the thing's necks…and just as Pit said, there was a point where they didn't quite meet up properly. *They're misaligned. Like they can move*—!

Between one second and the next, the vault came to life.

Archie stumbled, the segmented floor giving way beneath him as hidden sigaldry activated. The stone softened, sucking in his feet before hardening again, while above, the bas-relief beast pivoted. Its many heads struck like vipers, jaws somehow pulling free entirely from the surface of the vault to close around the would-be thief. Archie screamed, but the mouths were too fast even for Felix's ridiculous Agility.

The beastly jaws crashed to the floor, utterly burying the Delven Unbound.

"No!" Felix rushed forward, but it was no use. Six of the enormous, angular heads were fully emerged from the vault and piled around where Archie once stood. Horror welled up in him, and guilt.

"I couldn't have missed that," Laur was saying. "It wasn't there before!"

"The sigaldry moved?" Beef asked, eyes wide. His hands shook on his hammer. "A–a moving trap? That's OP."

Faintly, like an echo down a mine shaft, Felix heard something. "Wait. Shut up!" he told everyone. Felix stepped closer.

"Felix," Vess warned.

He held up a hand and put his head up against the now-immobile statue monster…and jerked back.

"Holy shit, he's still in there." Felix reached forward and slammed his hands into the metal beast. A sound like the loudest gong in the world went off. His hands stung from the force of the blow…and the metal was unmarred.

Wild Threnody!

Ferric Shaping!

Hand of Calamity!

Cardinal Flame!

Four Skills rang out within him, each one vying for his attention, but

Felix had enough to go around. Affinity sang through their patterns and his Intent shaped them to his Will, as metal, acid, and flame came to call. His hands were subsumed in a swirling haze of light that clung to him like viscous oil, and Felix pressed them carefully into the sculpted skull.

Metal screamed, as if the beast itself were howling in agony, and steam erupted into the air. The surface began to melt, but the area was no bigger than the tip of his pinky finger. Felix flared his nostrils and bore down, pushing more and more of his Mana into the mix of spells he was casting. Power pulsed through him, heating up his channels until his skin started to faintly glow from beneath, traceries of magic shining through his forearm scales and biceps, like LED lights under cloudy resin.

A frantic knocking came from within.

"Get back!" Felix shouted and began to shove with all his might. The metal groaned, its screams turned deep and hoarse, and the molten metal dripped onto his fingers and palms like streamers of pure agony. Regardless, Felix did not stop. He pulled and pried back, widening a hole into the sculpted beast as if he were digging in mud.

Wild Threnody is level 90!
...
Wild Threnody is level 93!

Ferric Shaping is level 38!
...
Ferric Shaping is level 55!
Journeyman Tier!
You Gain:
+15 WIL
+15 INT
+15 MIG

Hand of Calamity is level 76!
...
Hand of Calamity is level 81!

Cardinal Flame is level 96!

With a final burst of Strength, Felix wrenched the thick sides of the false head open…to reveal a stunned Delven man, pinned between teeth the size of swords. Most had missed, perhaps due to his size, but two of them had run Archie through.

"Are you hurt?" Felix asked frantically, then answered his own question by running his Voracious Eye over him. He sagged in relief. "You're fine…How?"

"Stoneswim, baby," Archie said through his teeth, patting the fangs that passed fully through his chest.

"Then how are you pinned down?"

"The metal…I can't, ugh, move through it easily." Archie pushed at the giant, silver-green teeth and slowly passed one trapped hand through its length. As he did, his limb took on the metal's color and luster. "Mithril's about the toughest stuff I can affect, but it takes too long."

"I can't try to eat the metal, or I might set off the wards. Can you get through this opening?"

"Y-yeah. Gimme a sec."

It took almost three minutes, but Archie slowly phased through the rest of the mithril teeth holding him down, including the two in his chest. Other than looking tired, he was none the worse for the experience, and Felix helped him climb out of the melted opening and back to safety.

"Impressive," Evie said, clapping. "I really liked how slow it was. Glad we don't have a murderous crazy lady after us."

"Yeah. Right." Archie squared his shoulders and walked around the descended heads of the vault beast. "Second attempt."

"You sure about this?" Felix asked.

"I was just surprised. That wasn't in the plans I stole…but if I can make this jump, then I can bypass it entirely."

Laur stepped up, holding out his hands. "I will disrupt as many wards as I can."

Felix patted the Elf on the back. "Good man."

They tried again. This time, with Laur playing interference, Archie got to the vault without issue. Felix sensed a few sigils start to engage, but Laur was on top of them, holding them at bay. For his part, Archie removed his goggles for the first time. Eyes like faceted rubies glanced at Felix nervously before honing in on the job ahead of him. He pressed his hands against the largely mithril vault door, as if feeling for something. After a handful of seconds, he nodded to himself.

"Here we go. Easy peasy."

With agonizing slowness, his hands and forearms sank into it. Then his feet and legs up to his knees. Last was his torso, and most horrifying, his face. Magic or not, it was awful to watch the man slowly press himself into solid metal, and Felix found himself holding his breath more than once. Eventually, the last trace of him vanished into the vault door, leaving the rest of them standing.

Waiting.

"Takin' him a while," Harn said.

"How thick is this door?" Beef asked. He rubbed his chest, making Hallow shift across his torso. "Does he…is he holding his breath?"

"Never asked. Laur? How're you holding up?"

"Just fine, Lord Autarch. But…I do wish Archibald would move faster. He is slipping through most of the wards, but there are several that I am holding back from engaging." The Elf licked his lips, and sweat dripped off his nose. "They are swiftly becoming too much for me."

Yet there was nothing they could do. Felix could only watch as Laur began to shake, his hands trailing rainbow afterimages as he wove his magic. A song of long pauses and tumbling refrains. An abeyance to hold the flow of wards aside…one that failed, note after note, as seconds stretched to three minutes. To five. Ten.

"I cannot hold this much longer," Laur gasped.

"Another minute," Felix urged.

"A what?"

"Another—portion of a glass. Just hold!"

"I—" the Elf's magic burst from around him, a corruscating aura of shimmering colors. "I cannot!"

Dammit! Felix let his Hunger roil, feeling its—her—immense emptiness as he traced the patterns of Chthonic Tribute. *Chthonic Trib—!*

A deep bell tolled, bright and cheery, and the beast heads lifted on their sinuous necks until they had retreated back into the vault door. At the same time, the massive ring of sigaldry around the edges began to rotate. The grinding sound of stone on stone outstripped the noise of the bell, and a great resounding *click* boomed through it all.

The vault door swung open to reveal a small man with his arms akimbo and head held high. "See? Easy."

CHAPTER NINETY-SEVEN

All of the wards were down, disabled by Archie as he released the vault door. Apparently, opening it from inside was as simple as pulling an ornate lever, for which Felix was immensely grateful.

Within the Vault of Nine Kings was a short corridor lined with fifty-foot statues. Eight Dwarven men and women stood, some in armor, some cloth, others in barely anything at all, but all of them bore crowns upon their heads. These, Tzfell had explained, were the ancient kings that had reigned over the height of Dwarven civilization.

The corridor ended in a split hallway leading into two half-circle staircases around the ninth king that Felix recognized. "The Rockshaper. He was a ruler of the Dwarves?"

"The first, many contend," Tzfell said.

The hall may have split, but both stairs led to the same place: a chamber that was far larger than anything they'd seen so far. Stretching as far as they could see, the vault seemed to be an endless expanse of orichalcum, mithril, and midnight stone. Supported atop gargantuan pillars, the ceiling was hundreds of feet high and held aloft by beams of metal that crisscrossed in intricate, almost dizzying patterns.

Twenty feet above them, a balcony stretched along every wall, until a second level was formed, with a great many silver-green doors bearing glowing locks. Felix counted at least thirty more before he stopped, each one with doors and supposed riches hid within. The floor was heavily patterned, golden knotwork bordering large slabs of veilstone, but little of it could be seen, due to the literal piles of treasure that filled every inch of the chamber.

"Siva's Grace," Vess whispered.

Shelves, cages, boxes, and racks organized all the riches before them, which were tidied into towering stacks. Precious artifacts, reams of books, carts of raw ore, and smelted ingots, and even the tools to work them. And literal piles of silver, gold, and platinum coins that were spread artfully across entire portions of the vault floor.

"Any traps or wards we should be worried about?" Harn asked.

Laur shook his head. "No. All of the constructs I sense are wound through the walls and those far-off windows. The rest is entirely safe."

"Unless we get more of those secret arrays," Evie pointed out.

"Then be careful," Felix said. "We need to find Archie's banishment array and the Mote of Frenzy. I've told you what it looks like, but don't grab it yourself. We don't have much time to search. Go."

Evie, Beef, and Harn took off, with Hallow craning her neck from the Minotaur's shoulder. Tzfell and Laur moved more cautiously, but with the same amount of excitement. Vess and Yintarion leaped over the balustrade and landed among the dark pathway between mounds of gold.

"Mote of Frenzy?" Archie asked. "That's what you've been after all this time?"

Felix shrugged, eyes scanning across the room. He kept his Voracious Eye humming in his chest, letting his eyes skim over the information that popped up. "Not the only reason. I meant what I said before. I want to keep you safe and out of the Hierophant's hands. Coming here…well, we had to catch you, right?"

Archie snorted. "Well, you did that. What's this Mote thing for?"

"To heal my friend."

"Friend? The cute one or the serious one with the spear?"

In a flash of light, Pit appeared next to Felix for the first time since Archie had joined them. "The cute one," Pit announced.

The Delven jerked in surprise, hands glowing with some sort of Skill before he dismissed it. "Who is—is that a…bird-dog? Where'd you keep it?" He peered closer. "Why didn't I know you had a bird-dog?"

"You've already met him," Felix said.

"I was smaller before."

Archie blanched. "The creepy dog."

Pit looked hurt. "Creepy?"

"Er, sorry. Not used to talking pets."

"Pet?"

Felix stopped scanning the room for a second, surprised by the change in the Delven's Spirit. This whole time, the guy had been suspicious, anxious, and more than a little angry. Now though, it was like his entire mood had been smoothed out. Calmed. "Did something happen? You're very calm all of a sudden."

Archie laughed. "Can't say I've ever seen altruism in action before, so you going all white knight on me, helping me out? That's suspicious. But if you're here for something, too...I get that. Respect it."

"You don't trust anyone, do you?"

"Not if I can help it."

Felix grunted and returned to scanning the treasure piles. Soon, he narrowed his eyes. "I see something. Hold on."

"To whaaaaa—!"

Archie screamed as Felix grabbed him and leaped into the air. They hurtled high and fast, describing an arc headed toward the middle of the orderly treasure pile, and he landed with a muted crash. A few precious stacks of gold tumbled to the ground, while a handful of jewel-encrusted swords clattered off their rack.

Archie staggered from Felix's grip, spreading his arms and legs as his balance returned. "What the hell, man?"

"Faster that way," Felix said. Pit appeared a second later, landing beside them far more gracefully than Felix had. "Both of you, help me search. I saw something weird over here."

"Weird how?"

"Looked like metal, but it kept changing colors…and my Eye couldn't identify it."

"Little Dragoon! Come here!"

Vess slipped between a block of stacked veilstone and vases so thin that the sourceless light made them almost transparent. On the other side, Yin was swimming in the air like an agitated fish.

"Ah, yes. Perfect. Look at these!" He floated closer to a shelf, which contained a number of jars all sealed with wax and sigils. However, among the jars was a single, battered book.

"A book?"

"Not just a book! A Dragoon book." Yin swam forward and clutched the tome with his little claws. "Look here! This seal is the mark of the order. I have seen it a thousand times. Rana would sign her letters with it, and it marked the binding of every book they produced."

Reverently, Vess took the book from Yin and turned it over in her hands. The cover wasn't nearly as bad as the binding appeared, but there was enough warping and discoloration that she could no longer tell what had been inked onto the front. Within, however, the pages were a rich paper covered in a blocky script.

"This is a shipment manifest," she said after reading it for a moment.

"Ah, well, hardly exciting. But if there is one, there should be more. Come, come!"

They had wandered through rows and rows of cloth, metal ingots, and crafted leather goods. Many had zero enchantments, but they were made of rare materials, were high Tier, or both. Useful, certainly, but Felix wondered at why it was all there. *You'd think with a vault like this, they would only put the best of the best in it.*

"I think I found it," Archie said.

Felix turned from a collection of axe handles—not even full axes, just the wooden handles—and saw Archie waving from across the aisle. "Pit. C'mon."

"Hm? Oh yeah. Be right there."

Felix crossed the thin path and found the Delven thief standing in front of a tiny door that was mostly hidden by a large tapestry depicting some ancient battle. As he watched, the door shifted from a steel-gray color to a warmer wood tone, then back to a cooler silver-blue.

"This was hiding here, covered by that tapestry. No wonder we couldn't find it at first. Thing is warded up like crazy." Archie knocked on the door, and a ripple of blue, green, and red spiraled out from the impact. "I think it's trying to make us ignore it."

Frowning, Felix focused on the door with all of his attention. As if a film had been ripped from his eyes, the door was suddenly three times larger and made of a shimmering, red-gold orichalcum. Pit trilled in surprise.

"Can you open it?" Felix asked.

"Can't Stoneswim through it, but I got other talents," Archie said and produced a selection of lockpicks before turning back to the door. Moments later, there was a solid click, and the large orichalcum door swung inward. "Hah! I'm not Adept Tier in Arcane Lockpicking for nothing."

Felix grinned and clapped the Delven on his back. "Great job."

Exploration is level 81!

He stepped into the door first and froze. "Pit."

"Yeah?"

"Go get everyone."

"Is it—?"

"Go. Quickly."

His Companion ran off, vanishing swiftly into the hoard. Archie stepped up and around Felix's legs, however, and stared.

"What the hell is this?" he asked.

"I really don't know."

Before them was a large, domed room carved from the rock instead of built from fine materials. It was a cavern, save that its ceiling was cut in facets, almost like looking out from inside a dull gemstone. Pillars held it up in places, covered in typical Dwarven knotwork and patterns, they were the least interesting thing about it.

Chains and hooks and pulleys attached to far more arcane tools were everywhere, each clearly designed to secure and manipulate the gargantuan creature within its midst. Said creature filled the cavern with light, a hot, molten illumination that bled down the walls like oozing waterfalls.

"But I know that," Felix continued. "*That* is a Superior Elemental."

CHAPTER NINETY-EIGHT

Name: Scaldara
Type: Superior Elemental (Earth/Fire)

As with the Frostfather, the rest of its information was a collection of question marks…but its power was undeniable. It was a Tier VIII creature. High Grandmaster.

"The Dwarves did this?" Archie asked.

"Looks like it."

"That's brutal." Archie stepped closer and the elemental shifted. "It's still alive?!"

Strung up on chains the size of Manaships, the Superior Elemental was made up of stone and living lava. Unmoving half-molten limbs, dozens of them, were clapped in enchanted chains while vast hooks were jammed into the center of its burning body, and pieces of it were split and spread by twenty-foot-thick spikes. Like a bug pinned to a board. Magma poured from wide fissures in steady streams, but its non-humanoid form was hard to parse. Was that its blood?

"I think so," he said. Felix couldn't tell how hurt the thing might have been, but it was clear that pieces of the elemental had been torn away.

Scattered across the chamber, a variety of workstations and meticulously organized tool racks were set up around those pieces. Heat-resistant trays displayed slabs of half-molten stone, with several of them bearing unfinished sigaldry on their tops. Large, sturdy containers were nearby, built to Dwarven preferences and clearly used to store and sort the…materials extracted from the elemental.

A wide forge dominated one corner of the room, big enough to make restraints for a Superior Elemental. It was dark, as were a number of inscribed lights around the cavern. Whoever worked here hadn't been in a while.

"Blighted Night, what happened here?" Evie asked, just before Beef and Hallow entered.

"Lava waterfalls? Cool." The young Minotaur's eyes brightened. "Is this an enchanting thing? Atar never lets me into his Glyphworks. Says I'm too clumsy."

"Son, they're butchering this thing alive for parts," Archie pointed out.

Beef's face fell. "O-oh. Oh no. That's bad. Wait, what's that?"

Pit chirruped. "It looks like a monster core. A big one."

Big was an understatement. Felix had devoured creatures with cores bigger than him, but this rivaled the Oathweaver in size and was utterly bathed in flows of molten lava. He approached, carefully.

"Watch your step. And someone get Yintarion. He'll want to see this."

Evie darted back out, dodging past the Chanters as they entered with Harn. Felix, Pit, Beef, and Archie all crept forward, spreading out among the workstations.

"Lots of…chunks over here," Pit reported.

"Here, too."

"Inscription tools also. They're all blackened and twisted, though," Beef said.

Felix glanced at them, Eye active. "Heat-resistant tools instead of heatproof. They've been trying to manipulate materials carved from the elemental."

"Looks like they've been at it a long time." Archie looked around the tables and benches, his small size offering him little in the way of line of sight. "Where'd they all go?"

"There's no sign of anyone," Pit said.

That proved true, even as they made their way to the other side of the large forge. Beyond it was the core, situated on a pedestal of dark stone that was riddled with molten cracks. The flows of lava from above fell atop the core and split, coursing down to create a waterfall of molten stone that splashed into deep recesses around the pedestal's base.

Despite that, the core was far easier to see now that they were closer. It was an extremely smooth orb, appearing to be made entirely of lava but with a shininess that suggested a glass-like coating. Tendrils of near-solid lava hung from its sides, clearly attached to the core and stretched back upward into the body far above.

"It's like it was removed and pulled down here," Felix said. He grimaced. "But it's still swirling, still feeding power through the elemental's Body."

"That's messed up."

"We finally agree, Beef," Archie said. "Hey. There's stuff over here."

Arrayed below the pedestal and just beyond the veil of lava was a platform fitted with dozens of stout, red-gold racks. On them were a number of things, most of which were glowing intensely with heat, fire, and earth Mana. However, the lavafall all around it effectively cut it off from casual approach.

"Looks expensive," Pit said. "Powerful."

Felix nodded. "Might be what we're looking for."

"How do we get across, though?" Beef stuck his hammer into the lava flow and pulled it back with a yelp when steam erupted violently around him. He quickly inspected the head and found metal and bits of stone hardened around the edge of Bedlam's ice. "I uh, don't think that'll work."

"I can't pass through lava," Archie said with a shudder. "Tried once. Didn't go well."

"Let me try something," Felix said and lifted his hands.

Stone Shaping!

Cardinal Flame!

Ferric Shaping!

All three Skills sounded within Felix's chest, and he mingled them as much as he could. They were part of the same Skill Array, after all. Similarities existed, and he leveraged them for all they were worth. His Mana caught at a portion of the lava, and swiftly he shaped his Intent, bolstering it with the foundation of his Willpower. The molten stone twisted, pieces of it splitting sideways as if flowing over an invisible arch, until a six-foot-wide by ten-foot-tall gap was cut through the lavafall.

Stone Shaping is level 98!
Cardinal Flame is level 97!
Ferric Shaping is level 56!
...

Ferric Shaping is level 68!

Felix marveled at the working for a second. *The Stone Shaping is melding just enough with Cardinal Flame to affect the lava…and both of them together are bolstering the weaker Ferric Shaping Skill. Because of the Skill Array?*

He had to assume that was the case…and it made him consider a great many new options for his magic.

"How'd you learn that?" Archie asked.

"Practice and guesswork, mostly." Felix gestured through the empty archway. "Watch your step."

The four of them slipped through with ease. Felix braced for the heat to ratchet up inside the lava-surrounded platform, but if anything, it was cooler there than the workshop itself. Four rows of shelving flanked them, two to a side, each made of orichalcum and built heavily enough to support an elephant. On those shelves were a number of things, ranging from large crystals to silver-green gauntlets and even a row of vibrant potions. Felix traced his Voracious Eye across them and gasped.

"We hit the jackpot," Archie said with a grin. His ruby eyes gleamed in the lava light. "I take back everything bad I ever said about you, Felix."

Felix snorted. "I'm honored."

All of them sifted through the items on display, which was remarkably easy since each one was labeled with a small steel plaque. Some were useless, like specialized tongs to pull samples out of elemental lava, but a few were of interest to them.

Name: Eternal Ember
Type: Material (Elemental) (Fire)
Lore: A mote of flame that will never extinguish. Captured from within the living core of Scaldara, the Superior Elemental of Earth and Fire.

Name: Forgeborn Gauntlets
Type: Armor (enchanted)
Lore: Forged from the cooled scales of a living Superior Elemental, these gauntlets increase the potency of fire-based Skills and increase Dexterity by 15 points.

Name: Emberheart Crystal

Type: Material (Elemental) (Fire)
Lore: A glowing red crystal infused with the essence of the living Superior Elemental Scaldara, capable of enhancing fire-based spells and weapons.

Name: Volcanic Tear Potion
Type: Consumable (Elemental) (Fire/Earth)
Lore: A potent elixir brewed from the tears of the living Superior Elemental Scaldara. When consumed, it temporarily grants the user an extra fifty levels in Fire Resistance and increases their Strength and Agility by 100. Effects last for a quarter glass.

The potions were immensely useful, if for nothing else than the astronomical stat boost they offered. The others were all useful in their own way, though he imagined Atar would absolutely love them. Felix gathered them all up, tucking them into his bag.

"Hey, check this out," Archie said. "Enchanted items just hanging from pegs over here."

Felix slid past Pit and Beef as they poked around the shelves and walked to where Archie was running his hands over the wall. "They're in cubbies, too. Weird."

Voracious Eye!

Name: Lavaflow Boots
Type: Armor (enchanted)
Lore: Sturdy boots forged from a combination of rare metals and cooled lava, granting the wearer the ability to walk molten surfaces unharmed.

Name: Lavaflow Apron
Type: Armor (enchanted)
Lore: An apron fashioned from rare metals, high-quality hide, and cooled lava, granting the wearer increased protection from molten earth, metal, and fire in general.

Six aprons were on pegs, and an equal amount of boots were tucked into small, open-faced closets. The aprons were charred in places, and the boots had pieces of metal and stone stuck to their soles. "They've been used. Regularly. These are like uniforms."

"Aha!" Archie said as his hand sunk into the stone wall far faster than he had through mithril. "There's a door here! Bigger than I expected, though. Hm. Inside is lined with something I can't push through, but I think I can feel the mechanism."

His hand twisted, and there was a sharp click. The wall hissed as a seal of stone pulled back, melting away in much the same way as the Rockshaper's atelier did. Archie pulled his hand free and grasped the edge. "The array has gotta be in here!"

"Felix!" Pit shouted, and glee radiated across their bond. "Felix! I found it!"

Felix hesitated, glancing to Archie as he slowly pulled the door open. "Go. Handle your business. I'll handle mine."

Quick as a flash, Felix was at Pit's side. Set back on the farthest shelf was a box made entirely of orichalcum, but the plaque in front of it clearly stated "Mote of Frenzy." It said nothing else, no type or lore details. Instead, a glowing wheel flashed on the front of the box, individual sigils lighting up in a random sequence.

"It's in the box," Pit said. "But it's locked. See?"

"That's not gonna stop us." Felix studied the arcane lock with his Manasight without touching it. Threads of it were woven through the metal, and he got the feeling that something bad would happen if he tore it open. "Maybe I could eat the ward."

He reached out. The orichalcum box was no bigger than his spread fingers, and he grabbed it easily. It was heavy. He grunted as it came fully off the shelf. It was *very* heavy.

"I think—" A flash of sigaldry caught Felix's eye as it zipped from the shelf to the floor. "Shit shit shit."

The sigils raced across the floor and into the wall…right where Archie stood. The door he'd been struggling with suddenly slid open without any further resistance.

"Huh. I think I'm stronger than I thought!" Archie looked up in alarm as three more doors opened to either side of him. "Oh no."

Within the huge doorways, a purple-white light swirled, and four enormous Golems stepped out. At eleven feet tall, they appeared to be wearing elaborate armor in an ancient design, but they were carved entirely out of a dark rock. A fluid, swirling web of inscriptions extended across their faceted chests, arms, and legs but large swaths were marred with deep scratches. Their eyes blazed, and their mouths opened wide.

"Violation! In the name of the Hinterlords, you shall be detained!"

That purple-white glow intensified, forming a cloak of power that surged as they lifted their arms together.

"Get down!" Beef shouted, just as the Golems unleashed a blast of violet energy at all four of them. Shelves froze over in an instant, the blasts further cooling the enchanted air so that all their labored breathing turned white.

Voracious Eye!

Felix stumbled back in surprise, then was shoving Pit backward. "Out! Get out through the lava door! Don't let those beams touch you!"

Archie scurried ahead, just barely dodging the second round of beams. "Wasn't planning on it!"

Beef Charged through the lava door first, his Body a blur as he utilized his Skill, but Felix and Pit were right after. Archie, being the farthest away, was the last, and the moment his little legs hurled himself over the moat, Felix acted.

The shaped archway vanished, and the waterfall of molten stone continued, unabated.

"What the hell were those things?" Archie demanded.

"Golems, right?" Beef said.

"I've seen Golems. Those weren't like anything I've seen trundling around in Birchstone."

Felix licked his lips. The lava was pouring down fast and hard and was intensely hot…but would it be enough? "Tzfell!"

"Autarch?"

The Chanters, Evie, and Harn were spread out in the room, each of them carrying a satchel of treasure. Vess floated down from above, where the Wyrmling was still inspecting the Superior Elemental core.

"We need to get out of here and seal this workshop," Felix said. "Vess, get Yin."

"Of course." She leaped upward, wind swirling after her.

A liquid crackle cut through the air as something slammed into the lavafall, causing it to bulge slightly before releasing a belch of steam.

Archie rounded on Felix, poking him in the thigh. "What are you talking about? We can't leave yet! I haven't found the array!"

"We can search the other parts of the vault. Those things are too powerful to mess with."

"I searched the vault! Gold and Troll pelts won't do me any good if I'm dead!"

Without warning, a purple beam ripped through the lavafall, cutting between Felix and Archie.

Status Condition: Frostburn (Minor)
Frostburn (Minor) - Agility and Dexterity are reduced.

Felix clapped a hand to his chest, where frost expanded across his clothes and onto his skin beneath. A fierce thrumming of Sovereign of Flesh fixed it, banishing the Status Condition and covering his torso in thick, midnight scales. The beam hadn't even come close to Archie.

"God, I'm so glad I'm short," he said, his voice tight.

"Everyone! Back!" Felix commanded, just as the lavafall burst into a cataract of steam.

Four simultaneous thuds announced their visitors, and when the steam cleared, they stood wreathed in their icy purple power as the lava cooled around them.

"Eidolon Exults," Tzfell hissed. "I was right!"

CHAPTER NINETY-NINE

A great many things happened all at once.

Evie, Pit, and Beef sped backward, each of them unleashing their Skills. Chains of ice and legs of chitin snagged against the Eidolons' feet while crescents of radiance burst against their chests.

Harn rushed forward, axes out, to cut into an Eidolon's elbow joint. His axes, though imbued with Adept Tier power and silver flame, merely bounced off the dark stone. Tzfell spat, and a flurry of geometric shapes flew toward the Eidolon Exults, popping and sizzling off their purple aura with no effect. Laur lifted his hands, and Felix shouted.

"Stop! They're Grandmasters!"

The Eidolons exploded with Mana. A wave of solid purple light hurtled outward, demolishing workstations as the concussive force chased down his friends. Most frantically dodged back, but Beef shielded Evie and Pit, getting slammed in the back for his trouble. He was thrown across the room, impacted face first onto the craggy stone floor before skidding through two metal tables.

Harn and the Chanters evaded it, the latter protecting the former as a shield of orange, blue, and dusty brown intercepted the purple wave. It fizzled out almost immediately, but they were tossed aside rather than obliterated.

"Adherents of Ophidia!"

Swirling Dragons of water Mana shot down from above, engulfing the Eidolons. They froze the moment they came into contact with their icy aura, stopping the spell in its tracks…and effectively tangling the constructs in their own power.

"Draconic Stormfall!"

Vess and all ten of her Spears dropped down. Lightning surged, bursting from the point of impact and ricocheting off of the insulating ice Dragons. To Felix's great surprise, the Eidolons sagged, their sigaldry flickering wildly.

That shouldn't have worked as well as it did. Felix checked the Eidolons with his Voracious Eye again. Feeling out advancement had always been an imprecise ability, but they felt incredibly strong. And incredibly unstable—their limbs jerked as sparks jumped between their scratched up chests, his sense of their power increasing and decreasing by turns. He could fight them, maybe, but he'd have to unleash everything he had.

He couldn't afford to do that. Not yet.

Vess and Yin leaped toward the group, now running toward the sole door into the elemental butchershop. It was a short distance, and even though the Eidolons started moving again, Felix started formulating how to reinforce the secret door.

"It's locked!"

Ahead, Evie kicked at the once-open door, only to have the force of her blow sent rippling across the wall. Rainbow shimmers described the edges of a massive and supremely complicated ward.

They were sealed in.

"New plan!" Felix spun through ideas. "Harn! Still got those keystones?"

"Aye. But I thought we were saving them—"

"Let's survive this fight before worrying about the next. Evie, Harn, Pit, and Vess. I need you to place them on the Eidolons. It'll buy us time."

There were no questions. They took off, plate-sized hexagons in their hands.

"Laur, start trying to open that ward."

"The time required—" Laur started.

"Try. We'll buy you time."

"I'll help," Archie said, stepping up next to the Chanter.

Felix gripped his sword. "Karys. Karys pick up, man."

Golden-green vapor swirled around his Inheritor's Will, but it was fuzzy and erratic. The voice that came through was the same, but mostly cleared by the end. "F…lix. Felix? What is going on?"

"Karys! Eidolon Exults! How do I shut them down?"

"You face one?"

"Try four!"

"Oh dear." Something shuffled on the other end, and metal groaned. "That is dire. Shutting them down is impossible unless you destroy their armored cores, which is where the Mind and Spirit of their driving force is stored. That is hard. But we…they are ruled by the arrays upon their chests. That is the access point for Territorial Lords to earn their loyalty."

"Earn? I don't have time to chat with them, dude."

"It is about Authority! You must access the array by placing your Mana in direct contact with it. Interface with the Memories that constitute their glyph markings. If you can find the central Memory, the one that binds the rest, you can demonstrate your Authority, and they might break out of this loop."

"Their chests look scratched to hell…they're covered in Dwarven sigaldry."

"Then they've been tampered with…meaning all I've said might prove to be useless. Proceed with caution, and remember that their Spirits house their power. Exhaust it, and they are just stone shells. But Felix, those are people. They live within that shell, as I once did. You must save them."

"They seem mindless, but I'll try." Felix looked to Tzfell, the only one without a task. "Keep them safe, okay?"

The Dwarven Chanter was a rock in a raging sea. She nodded. "You have my word."

At the same time, the last of the keystones were hurled onto the Eidolons' backs. Purple beams followed his friends as they dodged, the constructs stiff and slower than Felix expected. The icy aura around them was still deadly, though, and none of them wanted to get caught in it.

Lightning surged, sealing the keystones to their backs with amplified connections. His friends retreated.

Felix charged forward, right into their midst.

Rime Shaping!

A web of ice jutted outward in a fan, slipping through their cold aura for an instant before touching all four Eidolons on the chest. His

Intent rippled through his Mana, delivered into their fractured array in less than a heartbeat, and the world went crazy.

Felix's guts clenched, his very being twisting as he fell inward. Lines of purple light surrounded him, sigils and glyphs flashing across his Mind as an intricate array spread out in all directions. Memories bloomed, glimpses into a familiar world of ice and mountains, but others were torn through. Great scars across foundational images and sensations that bore the distinct cadence of significance.

Not just scars, he realized.

The broken Memories were patched over with new, uncanny images in their place. False Memories, like jagged windows into incongruent terrain.

He settled on one at random. Within a stone room, Dwarves stood before their thrones. They bore coronets of silver across their brows and scepters of rule within the crook of their elbows. As one, they gave the order, and Dwarven craftsmen swarmed with raw materials. Before them, the Eidolon shells were built. Before them, veteran Dwarven warriors proved themselves worthy to join with the Eidolons, to obey their kings. To wait. To guard. For all of time.

Felix snarled, the Memory too sour and bitter to be true. He grasped the Memory with his Will and Intent.

Chthonic Tribute!

His Hunger ripped it apart, revealing the empty scar that lay beneath.

Unite the Lost.

Significance poured out of him, more than he ever expected, and Felix was left gasping. The sigaldry was healing, but it needed more. He braced himself to try again, but the gentle touch of another made him jerk backward.

We... the words faded like a distant echo. **Help.**

Felix felt the presence of four others, pressing closer than skin to him and the sigaldry all around. Phantom limbs reached outward, pulling at the half-healed scars, and pulses of liquid shadow poured through them. The cracks shuddered and snapped, their pieces reconstituting…and the empty spaces became people of a different sort.

Nymean. Risi. And yes, a few Dwarves.

These were the ones that were turned into Eidolons. The ones who chose it as their final duty before passing into the Ethereal Realm. A hand reached out to them, caramel skin and wreathed in a nimbus of power. Each volunteer fell to shaky knees in a chamber that Felix remembered well.

Ice rose, and stone fell.

And the Eidolon Exults walked among them.

Felix jerked back, cast out of the Memory array by a hard shove against his chest. He blinked, finding the Eidolons still looming over him. Their Spirits burned with a sudden confusion and rage.

"Enemy!" The Eidolon Exults slammed down at him, and he caught the blow across his shoulder.

Status Condition: Dislocated Shoulder

"Felix!" Vess shouted from far off.

"Don't come closer—!"

"Enemy!"

He moved, pushing off the earth hard enough to crack it…but another Eidolon's fist smashed into his ribs.

Status Condition: Shattered Ribs (Extreme)
Status Condition: Frostbite (Major)

Felix gasped in pain, the violence far exceeding his exceptional tolerance. At his hip, his sword blazed. "Exert your Authority, Felix! Remind them who you are!"

Unleashed and mindlessly enraged, the Eidolons didn't stop. They rained blows onto Felix with a terrible precision and incredible strength. They were flawed, perhaps broken in some ways, but they hit *hard.* Felix burned through his Essence just to keep up and choked down his screams in order to be heard over the riot.

"In the name of Felix Nevarre, Autarch of Nagast, King of Ahkestria, and Colossus of Khalheim, I order you to stand down!"

His words barely surfaced over the grinding of stone, the crackle of ice, or the sound of fists on flesh…but he felt them catch. Something—

the array, perhaps—pressed against him, testing his Will with its own presence. It was an absurd weight, a mountain attempting to crush him from four different directions. Though he was bloodied and broken, Felix was undeterred.

He hurled his Will against their restored arrays and felt something give. Recognition.

The beating stopped.

The Eidolon Exults straightened, their joints booming as they settled. "Authority acknowledged," they said as one.

Fucking finally.

The Eidolons stepped back as his friends drew closer again. Harn had his axes out, and Beef hefted his hammer, but it was unnecessary. The constructs did nothing to them, and even their blazing auras vanished.

Vess and Pit rushed to his side, the latter still holding an orichalcum box in his beak. Vess gave him a Health Potion, and Felix drank it down. His Essence stores weren't great. "Thanks."

"Are these…friendly, now?" Evie asked and jumped when it answered.

"We serve the Colossus of Khalheim. Forgive our…confusion." The Exult's voice was deep but faded and scratchy, like an old speaker.

"You were tampered with," Felix said, standing up with help from Vess. "The Hinterlords messed with your arrays. Your Memories. I'm not gonna hold it against you."

As one, they bowed their armored heads, and the purple flames that made up their eyes dimmed as if closing. "Your compassion is cherished, Colossus."

"What're your names?"

"I am Eagin. This is Orun. She is Telys, and the last of us is Iiana."

"Felix," he said, introducing everyone present. "I'd update you on what exactly has been going on, but we're running low on time."

Eagin shifted, as if uncomfortable. "We retained a limited awareness of our actions these long centuries. An 'update' would likely be redundant. But I must ask: Khalheim still stands?"

"It has risen again," Felix said.

A sigh of relief echoed from each of the Exults. "That is good. Now. How might we assist, my Lord?"

"Can you fight?" Evie asked. "We could use big bruisers like you if things go sideways."

"Combat is within our purview…but we are limited, at present,"

Eagin admitted. "The damage to our arrays has been miraculously restored by the Colossus, but we donated our own power to the process. It has left us reduced in capacity, leaving us only the Strength afforded by our stone Bodies."

"That was you," Felix said. Not a question. "I had wondered."

"Would that we could have helped you more, Colossus. Such an act will have greatly deprived you of your foundation, and for that, we are sorry."

Felix cleared his throat. "Don't be. I happened to have extra foundation on hand." *Running a bit low, though. They took a lot more than I expected.*

"I see. However, if the Colossus wishes us to engage in combat, we will do our best."

"It would be helpful, but no. Our particular enemy is…The plan is to *not* fight her."

"Running is good, yeah. Listen. Have you seen any arrays?" Archie asked abruptly. "They'd be inscribed on big, flat gemstones."

Iiana nodded. "Yes. We have."

Archie almost vibrated with the news. "Take me to them. Please!"

She looked to Felix for permission, and he jerked his chin. "Please do so."

Archie scurried after the long stride of the Exult, and Felix turned to the rest. "Can you open the door up there? It sealed when you attacked."

"We can. We retain our access to the security measures here."

He scratched his jaw, grinning as an idea formed. "Tzfell, at least some of the treasure in this vault had to have come from Kingsrock, right?"

"Undoubtedly. I imagine the mundane riches were placed into coffers, but artifacts and enchanted items would likely remain here."

"Then let's return it to the rightful owners," he said with a grin. "Eagin, Orun, Telys? Step out of this workshop and start scooping."

"How do you tell which is from Kingsrock and which isn't?" Beef asked.

Felix snapped his fingers. "You're right. Better take as much as we can, just in case."

Orun laughed, a great booming noise. "I like it!"

From the taste he had gotten of Dwarven culture, Felix had no compunctions about stealing from them.

They learned two things in quick succession after that. The first was that the Eidolons were fast when they wanted to be—they had the door unsealed and were moving about the main vault within seconds. The second was that each of them could sort of unhinge a part of their chests, revealing a huge cavity meant for storage. It acted as a very excellent way to collect gold, gems, and artifacts by the dozen.

His team joined in, scooping up what they could and putting them into satchels and bags they'd brought for the occasion. Pit's saddlebags filled up quickly, though a large portion of one was dominated by the orichalcum box. Felix was tempted to open it up, but the Frostfather had considered it dangerous. They had enough on their plate already.

"Hey! Big man! Get over here!" Archie called from the workshop. Felix ran closer, finding the lavafall they had crossed was now diverted entirely. He hopped over the moat with ease and followed Archie's voice.

Through one of the four doors that had released the Eidolons, Felix found Archie and Iiana in a long, thin chamber filled with array plates. They were stacked against the walls in discrete piles, many of them made of rare materials and precious metals. Archie and Iiana stood near the far end, where sigaldry inscribed a large door with a complex locking array. Yet it was already opened, and Felix could see the start of a staircase leading down.

"What's this?" he asked.

"It is the entry point for the…craftsmen that work on the Superior Elemental," Iiana said.

Felix blinked. "An exit? A secondary exit?"

"Seems like it," Archie said with a grin. "And! I found them. I found the way home!"

Beside him was a stack of yellow-green gemstones, flattened and inscribed with golden sigaldry. Each one was two feet long and tapered to a point, and there were twenty of them.

Voracious Eye!

Name: Song of Exile
Type: Array Plate (enchanted)
Lore: The opposite of the Song of Arrival, these array plates assemble together to form the base of the Song of Exile. When utilized correctly, they will open a path through the Realms, through which travel is possible. Beware! The Realms are dangerous to wander freely.

"Holy crap," Felix said. "You weren't lying."

"I wouldn't lie about this." Archie patted them. "My ticket home."

Felix's Mind spun, but he stamped those thoughts out. For now. "Iiana, put these in your storage cavity, please, and as many other arrays as you can fit."

"As you wish, my Lord."

Felix had no clue what many did and little time to study them, but they could be useful. Atar and Alister would be thrilled to see them, at least.

"Hey, those are mine!" Archie protested, when Iiana picked up the Song of Exile array.

"Do you plan on carrying them yourself?" Felix asked.

"Well…alright, fine. Just don't go far from me, lady."

Iiana tilted her stone head at the man. It was more quizzical than an acknowledgement, though. Suddenly, her head snapped up.

"Warning. A Hostile Spirit approaches."

A violent boom shook the air and tossed Archie to the ground. Tremors rattled the floor and walls around them, and a great cacophony sounded from the other rooms as metal and chains collapsed and crashed into walls.

"What the hell was that!?" Archie demanded, only to find Iiana and Felix already rushing back into the workshop. "Hey! Stay near me, lady!"

Vess and Yin were up by the Elemental core again, and they shouted down at Felix as he passed. "What happened?"

"Company," he answered, before racing through the workshop and back into the vault proper.

Fire had consumed the statues and stairs, so hot that the stone had turned cherry red. From within the golden flames, figures began to emerge. Dozens, then hundreds. More, marching down the sweeping stairs several hundred feet away.

"We need to go," Harn bellowed.

Felix jerked his thumb back. "Everyone through the workshop, Eidolons included! Follow Iiana! Go!"

Before anyone could move though, something hurtled through the golden flames. Archie screamed and collapsed, a glowing orange short-sword through his left shoulder. The fire distorted again, and Felix moved, but the second blade was faster.

"Dark Glacial Guard!"

Pit was there, shielding the wounded thief. The heated blade sliced through his summoned ice armor and his barding, sinking halfway into the tenku. Pit yelped in surprised agony.

“Fiend!” Imara emerged from the flames at the head of her own Inquisition army. She bore two more swords, both glowing a bright orange. “It’s time for a rematch!”

“Yeah,” Felix said, his fury barely contained. Lightning coursed along his limbs. “I think it is.”

CHAPTER ONE HUNDRED

Wild Threnody!

Adamant Discord!

Felix rushed forward, and Imara met him. They struck, fist against fist, amid the stacks of treasure. Gold and blue impacted, resonating and exploding from one another in a wave of concussive force. Coins and cups and rare ingots were hurled aside, driven through pillars and into the nearest line of Inquisitors.

They died on the spot.

Wild Threnody is level 94!
Adamant Discord is level 97!

Imara staggered backward, thrown by Felix's unfettered blows, and she stared at him in consternation. "You were not so powerful before. How?"

"I'm not holding back anymore."

Imara unsheathed a broadsword that was smaller than the huge weapon she'd used before, but no less deadly. "Show me."

Felix kicked off the ground, sending more stacks toppling, and met the Titan's blade. Light and flame burst outward in a geyser of golden power, and he met it—midair—with a bevy of shaping magics.

Auroral Forge!

Cardinal Flame!

The light and fire Mana was caught up, diverted around him in a swirl of momentum that slowed his advance but sent shafts of elemental might lancing back into her allies. Another hundred died, felled in an instant as their skin and bones turned to ash.

Auroral Forge is level 91!
Cardinal Flame is level 98!

"Shield yourselves!" someone with a fancy helmet ordered. Translucent golden panels appeared before the front-most rows of Inquisitors.

Imara swung for Felix's head, but he ducked the blow and caught her exposed wrist. "Armor's busted?" She punched him with her off-hand, but he caught her fist. Something snapped in his arm, but he held his grin. "Pathless isn't helping anymore?"

She spun, bringing her longsword to cut at Felix's gut. He unsheathed his own blade, twisting so that her strike glanced off of Crescian Bronze instead of his skin. Sparks fountained in gold and bronze.

"I all but killed you before, Fiend. Only your tricks saved you." Her sword met Felix's hooked blade, and a concussive wave flung away more treasured debris. "I will not fall for them again."

The halo of gold around Imara brightened, until it limned her entire Body. Visible veins of gold ran through her naked wrists and hands, enveloping her weapon with power. As he struggled, she pushed Felix's sword down with hers.

"It–It's different this time," he grunted.

"Oh?" Imara's voice had a grin in it that Felix had never heard before. "It doesn't seem to be."

"Hah, I'm—" Felix's arms were burning from the weight of her. "I'm not alone anymore."

"What?"

"Wrath of the Twin Fangs!"

Burning silver axes went for her throat, but a hasty pivot forced the strike wide. They hit her in the shoulder instead, driving the Titan to a single knee. Felix lunged, his clawed foot bursting with Adamant Discord as he drove it into her chestplate, but the woman jumped back and drew a pair of oversized maces from her hips.

"Enough playin', kid," Harn grunted from beside Felix. He reset himself and lifted his axes into a middle guard.

Imara rushed them. They met her, together.

"Ungh. Shit," Archie gasped as thunder rattled the room, and coins flew overhead. He eyed the blade stuck in the strange bird-dog's side. "You took that. For me. Why?"

"Why—" Pit kicked his legs, fighting to get them under himself. The ice armor was gone, and now his back legs weren't quite working right. "Why wouldn't I?"

Archie didn't have a response for that, and chaos had consumed everything around them. They were nestled between mounds of spilled furs and large glassware, where Beef had dragged them before hurling himself into battle. Spells and Skills flung through the air, making it far too dangerous to stand up, but Pit kept trying.

"What are you doing? Stay down! They're gonna hit you again."

"I need—I need to help." The bird-dog strained, twisting his neck back toward the saddle on his back. "Can you get—can you get my bag? There's a box."

Archie swallowed. If he moved it would hurt real bad, and the sword was digging into his Health. *Ah, fuck it.* He scooted forward, sliding a bit off the fur pelts before fetching up against Pit's large rump. "Which one?"

"Left side. Top."

One handed, Archie fumbled with the straps, yanking at them until the top flopped open. A heavy box tumbled out and into his hands. *Very* heavy. "Oh god! This is only orichalcum! It…shouldn't be this heavy!"

"I need you to open it. Please."

"Alright." Archie braced his elbow on the ground, and it was just barely enough to keep the box balanced on the bird-dog's side. The front of the box had a complex warding on it, but that at least was familiar. "Yeah. I can do that."

The Inquisition surged, flowing around Felix, Harn, and Imara as they battled it out in the center. Hundreds of them ran with their red cloaks flapping in the breeze, summoning lances of light and swords of flame to bring down on her team.

Vess would not allow that.

"Now!"

Spears impaled those charging in the lead, exploding into storms of electrified shrapnel and slicing others with the bronze discs from her Sling Salvo. Gaps opened in their line, giving Evie's chains all the room they needed to trap the next dozen. Chains of ice locked down their legs, while bladed metal sliced open flesh through gaps in their vaunted armor. Beef roared, skewers of chitin driving upward into the Inquisitors like hidden spike traps, while a higher voice on his shoulder screeched as she shot crystalline daggers with unerring precision.

"Call upon the gifts of the Pathless!" one of them cried. Shortly after, dozens of them were swathed in translucent panels of golden light. These were far thicker and more potent than the simple shields the others created, and they assembled into familiar oversized suits of armor.

"Your gifts are worthless," Laur announced, weaving a strange spellform into the air. Multiple colors swirled and flexed beneath his long fingers, and the moment he shoved his hand forward, they leaped outward. The spell split into dozens, keening as it tore through the air, until it impacted each set of golden armor. Where it hit, the armor outright dissolved, and a few even fell apart completely.

"Adherents of Ophidia!" Yin cried and unleashed a mighty barrage of Dragons. The watery constructs tore across the golden-armored Inquisitors, knocking them back, even as it outright killed the less-protected.

In the center, Felix continued his battle, though it was far too fast-paced for Vess to follow. All she could do was stem the tide…and the floodwaters were not stopping. More Inquisitors rushed from the stairs, the original hundreds soon approaching thousands as redcloaks replaced the dead.

Tzfell summoned her strange, geometric magics, flinging them among the oncoming horde with abandon. Their power drew in their Skills, much as it had in the Starfield Steps, and all of them found their blows hitting harder and faster.

"Yin! We have control of the battle!" Vess announced mere moments later.

"A lie, little Dragoon," he replied. "We are hard-pressed, and the Autarch is more so."

"Go, please! You may have no other chance," she insisted. "Seek the elemental!"

Yin hovered, indecisive as the battle raged on. Beef slammed his hammer down, dispersing several lances of light heading his way before his earth Mana erupted beneath their lines. Evie dodged between blows, a dancer with a vicious weapon. Blood followed her in a constant arc, a crimson trail.

"Very well." He zipped through the air, a gold and white blur that vanished back into the elemental workshop.

Vess urged forth her Spears and discs, triggering their explosions among the weakened Hierocratic warriors. Yin had his own task, and she had hers.

"Face me, redcloaks, and perish."

"Here! It's open!" Archie hissed. His arms ached from propping up the heavy container, and it was all he could do to push it to the bird-dog's other side. "Take it!"

The orichalcum box tipped over, depositing a writhing hurricane upon the polished floor. Both of them stared, transfixed as a ring of chaotic elements whirled around a small, hardened object that changed design with every second. Fire, ice, lightning, shadow, even life and necromantic Mana surged within, and the object at the center grew, as if it fed upon the world around it.

It was terrifying.

Pit leaned over and ate it.

"Should you have done that—" Archie began to ask, but he was interrupted by the bird-dog's sudden—and deafening—screams as Pit's entire body burst into flame.

Dodge is level 92!

Harn wasn't Imara's match in stats or levels, and she clearly had an edge over Felix, but together, they pressed her back. The giant woman parried and guarded against Harn's axes and Felix's hooked blade, meeting their attacks with an increasing desperation. Harn clashed with her, unflagging despite his many wounds. He fought, deflecting, dodging, and letting loose with powerful strikes. Despite Imara's advantage in speed, Harn anticipated her. Like the man always said: at a certain point, technique mattered far more than stats.

And Harn could fucking *fight.*

He drove her to the side, forcing her to meet Felix's slash. She deflected it with her longsword, but only just; the edge of his Inheritor's Will carved a line out of her battered armor. A line that refused to repair itself.

That drove Imara wild. She grunted with each parry and riposte, and Felix felt actual anger clouding her empty Spirit. Each time Harn advanced, each time she broke a piece of the man's armor or drew his blood, that anger grew.

"Titanslayer," Harn said through bloody teeth. "Has a good ring to it."

The Titan screamed. Rage and frustration laced her Spirit, radiating outward as an almost physical pressure. It was the first time Felix had felt such a solid emotion in her, and the golden glow that limned her head faded, just a touch.

We've got this. We just need to keep her off-balance! Adamant Discord! He burned his Skill, pouring as much Mana into it as he could.

Adamant Discord is level 98!

Imara crashed to the ground, pulled by strings of lightning. Harn swung near-instantly, but the woman jerked herself out of line. His dual blows only sheared through a chunk of her spiked pauldron, missing her flesh entirely.

Your Companion, Pit, Is Attempting To Claim The Mote Of Frenzy!

Somewhere behind them, a pillar of elemental chaos erupted. Fire, ice, lightning, shadow and many more swirled in a growing tempest… centered upon one howling tenku.

"Pit!"

"Enough!" Imara surged upward, breaking through Felix's lapse concentration, and hurled him to the ground. "All of you are nothing before the Light! And you shall return to nothing!"

A dozen blades of pure golden radiance sprung outward. Felix swore and sent earth and metal Mana surging ahead, forming thick walls. The blades sliced through it without pausing, snapping toward him like gleaming pincers.

Relentless Resolution is level 99!

Felix leaped upward, arcing his body over the infernally hot blades by mere inches. Pieces of his Garment caught fire, and a piece of his kit was sheared away. Felix landed on his back, but swiftly rolled to his feet…only to find Harn, fallen to the ground.

With both legs severed at the knee.

"HARN!"

The man had pulled off his helmet, and his face was white as a sheet. Felix frantically checked his Health, only to see it careen out of control, dipping hundreds of points in the span of seconds. Felix ran to his side, just as the man pulled a Health Potion to his lips and threw it back.

"Missed. Damnable Fiend. How are you so fast?" Imara had regained her feet, and those blades of light hovered around her like a mockery of Vess' abilities. "How?!"

She gave him no time to react, no time to aid his friend. The Titan was on Felix, radiant swords stabbing in tandem, and it took all he had to avoid their scorching touch. That rage that had only been hinted at before now became an inferno, her Spirit all but consumed by it.

Dodge is level 93!
Armored Skin is level 97!

Felix dodged another strike and slipped close, under her guard. She backpedaled, but he moved with her, just barely avoiding her vicious grapple and slipping to her rear.

Imara spun, trying to keep him in sight. "The Pathless warns me against you. Why?"

"Like you said." He slapped three hexagonal plates onto her. "I'm full of tricks."

Lightning coursed through the plates, Adamant Discord sealing them to her armor just as the sigaldry across them ignited. An array spread across the floor, made of pure, humming Mana, and Imara hissed in pain as her Stamina began to vanish rapidly.

Theurgist of the Rise is level 96!

"What–what is this?" she demanded, lifting her hands and staring at them. "Why do I feel—?"

"Just evening the odds," Felix growled, and he kicked her with all the force he had.

She tumbled as lightning coursed across her back. The suppression array couldn't stop her, but three keystones would hopefully drain her faster than her recovery could manage. Like the Vault Wardens, she was on a ticking clock.

And Felix wasn't in the mood for mercy.

He kicked off the ground, shattering stone and sending more coins flying. Lightning trailed his movements, and red-gold flames burned from the centers of his eyes as he met Imara. Strength for Strength, his arms barely bolstered by his Adamant Discord, and hers filled with gold. It shone from the cracks in her armor, as if her flesh had become light.

Harn! Pit!

Hook. Jab. Flying knees and strikes to her kidneys. Felix tore into her…and Imara took it all. She soldiered through the pain and pressure, blocking him and striking back. He ducked under a punch so hard the air pressure hurt him, and put everything he had into his legs. He thrust his scaled fists straight up.

Felix's fist connected, hitting her jaw…and knocking her great helm free, for the first time. Felix blinked, stumbling back in horror. The helmet clattered to the ground.

Imara stood, spitting out a tooth. But it wasn't Imara.

No…

It was Gabby.

It was his sister.

CHAPTER ONE HUNDRED ONE

"You can't be here," he said, but the words lacked force.

Imara—no, Gabby—pulled two oversized maces from her belt of weapons. "What happened to your ferocity, Fiend?"

"No. This is a trick." Felix flared his Voracious Eye. This time, as he pressed past the powerful resistance it was easier.

Voracious Eye is level 96!

Name: Imara, Vessel of the Pathless
Race: Gigas
Level: 90
HP: ???
SP: ???
MP: ???
Lore: The Gigas were ancient precursors of the giantfolk that now are scattered across the Continent. Possessed of incredible natural Strength and Endurance, they were peerless warriors and stout defenders of all that they claimed. The Gigas are a Lost Race.
Strength: Divine power flows through this woman.
Weakness: More Data Required

He still couldn't pull everything, and what he did read wasn't worth anything at the moment. "How do you have my sister's face?"

"This face is mine, and I am no relation to you." She hefted her maces. "I do not use tricks. I am not so low as you, Fiend."

Felix couldn't help but stare at her face, at one of the last faces he'd seen on Earth before he'd been taken. Before everything happened.

Imara, on the other hand, had no compunctions with crushing him flat.

Dodge is level 94!
Armored Skin is level 98!

Felix escaped the first blow, but mid-swing, the Titan's hand burst alight, and her second blow arrived all the faster. It crashed into his left forearm, snapping both bones with a sound like a gunshot, and forcing Felix to kick off to safety.

He landed twenty feet away, amid the scattered remains of gleaming treasure. His Mind whirled, but he forced himself to shut out the pain and focus. Imara followed him, but as his Intelligence and Perception flared, time appeared to stretch. He only bought himself a few fractions of a second, but his eyes took in *everything* they could.

His friends were fighting the Inquisitors, and they were absolutely pummeling them…but the redcloaks seemed to have no end. The white-armored zealots hustled forward, streaming down the steps around the now-molten statue of the Rockshaper. Pit had become a cyclone of elemental violence, Harn was bleeding out onto the vault floor, and Archie was little better. In the near distance, he saw Laur creating a shield around Evie and Harn. The woman held the man's head in her lap, and Tzfell was on her way to their side.

Imara was almost on him, and Felix's Mind *burned*, but he had something. A semblance of a plan.

He jumped.

The first of twenty sizzling, golden blades thrust into the spot he once stood, and the others soon followed. Felix soared overhead, flaring Adamant Discord to hurl him farther as three of the swords followed him up. He pulled on intangible connections to the walls, rolling to the side as the weapons tore past.

"Release me!" Imara bellowed, and agony stabbed through Felix's head and chest. The Domain cores at his waist hummed louder as the suppression array struggled to remain whole. Felix doubled down on it as he shot upward, flaring his two Skills for all they were worth.

Theurgist of the Rise is level 97!

Title: Architect of the Rise is active!
25% Bonus To Learning All Sigaldry As Well As Creating And Maintaining Complex Arrays!

Imara absorbed the flying swords, and the sheer force of her presence redoubled. Title or not, the suppression array unraveled, sigaldry fraying into motes of scattered light.

Theurgist of the Rise is level 98!
Cardinal Flame is level 99!

He lost hold of it.

The ground detonated, and a shockwave ripped across space to smash Felix in the chest. He was thrown into the vaulted ceiling, splintering it with the force of his impact, before he fell hard onto wide, orichalcum rafters. The roof groaned.

The Domain cores went from humming to keening, and Felix threw them away in a panic. Only thirty feet distant, they exploded in white flame and pent-up power. The ceiling shuddered again.

Imara seemingly manifested through the explosion, landing nimbly atop the opposite rafter. Her minor wounds healed and, as he watched, her armor repaired itself. Even her gauntlets.

"You broke my array," he said, taking his feet unsteadily. "What happened to you, Gabby?"

"I am Imara. Chosen of the Pathless." She sneered at him as he climbed to his feet. "God's power runs through my veins. Here in this hellish place, I cannot feel the Light so clearly…but I am filled with it. One with it."

Below them, a war ebbed and flowed. He was distantly aware of it, like a TV show on in another room. Felix's party against thousands of redcloaks, the winning side changing with every heartbeat. His friends were losing their ground. They were running out of time.

"Gabby. You shouldn't be here. You were safe," Felix said tiredly.

"I am not your kin, Fiend!"

She kicked off the red-gold beam, setting the ceiling to groaning again. Felix didn't move. He mustered no Skill. No offense at all.

I can't hurt her.

With one hand, he grabbed the Skull of the Forsaken and shoved as much Mana into it as possible. The sigils ignited, and immediately the rafters were filled with exact duplicates of Felix, so convincing that not even he could tell the difference. Every single one of them was suddenly wreathed with blue-white lightning.

Imara tore right through them. "That will not work on me again!"

Felix's false bodies were ripped to shreds, dissolving into clouds of fading violet Mana that burst into Imara's face. Her eyes burned with Light, but she couldn't see through it. She swung her maces and hit nothing.

Abyssal Skein is level 90!

She didn't see him above her until it was too late.

"Unite the Lost!" he screamed.

Felix's index finger touched the very top of the Titan's bare head, and he discharged his Skill. Noise like a gathering orchestra rolled through him, into her, flowing its way down across her entire being.

BEGONE!

The Pathless' voice was an immutable command. A corruscation of golden light kicked his power away, slicing the strings and puncturing the drums until they groaned and rattled. The Skill failed.

No! Felix was suspended between moments, his Mind working furiously. *Leave her alone!*

Inside of him, his Hunger roared. She echoed all of his fear and hate and anger. Amplified it.

LEAVE!

A monster clawed its way from his core, a creature he'd been warned against.

HER!

It had lain, coiled within the dark, waiting to be called…and now it surged forth, a piece of him—all of him, woven together from a thousand different parts—it hurtled through every single one of his Mana Gates at once.

ALONE!

Felix howled.

A massive dark fist, clawed and scaled as his own and extending a little past the wrist, manifested above him. It filled the entirety of the vault's ceiling, drenching everything in red-gold, blue-white, and a domineering violet.

"What the fuck is that?" Imara screamed, even as the golden voice shouted louder.

RUN! the Pathless cried.

It was too late.

As once before, the phantom fist moved faster than Felix ever had and met Imara at the intersection of orichalcum rafters.

It reduced them to nothing.

Imara careened to the earth, her form flaring with a nimbus of light. Felix appeared there, just as she landed, and his hand drove her falling body into the stone walls. They cratered, stone and metal turned to dust the moment his dire fist met them…and only the Pathless' power saved Imara at all.

The Inquisitors nearby were not so lucky. They were obliterated, as if wiped from the very face of the world.

Imara moved. Her arm hung limp, and her knee was bent the wrong way, but she gritted her teeth and stood. The golden glow around her was flickering. Failing.

DEATH! Hunger cried. **DEATH TO THE BETRAYERS! DEATH TO THE GODS!**

The fist started to unfurl its massive fingers—

No! Felix threw everything he had against his Hunger. Every ounce of Willpower and Intent smashed into the yawning darkness inside his own core…and Felix trembled. His insides were tearing apart. It was strong. Too strong. *Hunger! Stop! That's my sister!*

The fingers of the phantom hand quivered, locked between Wills… until finally it relented. His Hunger retreated, and his Core Manifestation flickered out.

Silence hung above the Vault of Nine Kings, filled only by the flicker of flame, the oozing *plop* of melted orichalcum, and the groans of those who yet lived. Lava dripped from the cracked walls, a steady trickle that burned its way across the ground. Felix dragged himself forward, arm by arm, as blood poured from his eyes and nose. He didn't care. He crawled until he reached Imara, now lying on her face. He pressed his fingers to her bloody cheek.

"Un-unite the L-lost."

The world unraveled around him as another took its place. He was surrounded by golden light that sang to his senses like a balm. It was nothing like his Auroral Forge. It wasn't a Skill. It felt more like a Blessing from an Urge, only more complicated.

The light suffused Imara completely, filling her up until there was little room left for anything else. Unite the Lost came up against that light and stalled, unable to find purchase. Details from his Voracious Eye came back to him, his Mind connecting the dots.

Name: Imara, Vessel of the Pathless

Like what the Maw tried to do to him. Or Vellus. The Pathless had hijacked her, made some room and forced his power into her core. Her core *was* the Pathless in a way that the Fathom had really been a sliver of Noctis. Only far, far stronger.

Fuck the gods, he hissed. And Unite the Lost began to whirl.

Significance drained out of him hard and fast, the power of his uncanny Skill no longer seeking to break into her core…but to hurl it back, wholesale. The light shifted, but only by the smallest of margins.

It pushed back, and an alien Will, vast and unknowable, slid across Felix's efforts like a slick oil within that golden shine. The harder Felix bore down, the more vast the opposition became, until it was like he was raging against the sky itself. The light's Will—the Pathless' Will—excoriated his Mind, drawing a deep and abiding pain that burned through all of his Aspects. It was only Felix's mental defenses that held any part of it back, but the walls of his Bastion shuddered beneath their onslaught.

The green ocean boiled, and the forests seared, while dark columns of smoke filled the air. Felix was lying on the ground, finger to Imara's head, but he was also in the walls of his Bastion, hands pressed against the outer gates, Willing them to hold on.

Title: The Call of Defiance Activated!
+25% Willpower When Contested By A Foe Of Divine Formation Or Greater

That Title hasn't activated all this time…why now? he wondered; but he knew. The Pathless' presence was growing as something inside of Imara—no!—Gabby fueled their connection.

Felix was facing the Coward in White directly, now.

In the distance, amid an incongruent sunbeam, something stepped from the flames. The hills were charred, and the skies had turned red from suffocating smoke and hellish light, but all of it was washed out.

He couldn't make out the being, couldn't even stare directly at it because it shined like the sun. It stepped toward his Bastion, and the gates shook as if it had rammed them.

It stepped again, and steel and stone screeched as it was bent to its very limit.

It stepped again.

"No," Felix whispered to himself. "I will not give in."

He set himself against the gates, arms bulging and lightning burned in his eyes. "I refuse."

Title: Born of Will is active!
You Are Your Own Maker!

Title: Tyrant of Choice is active!
You Choose Your Own Destiny!

Bastion of Will is level 100!
Master Tier!
You Gain:
+5% RES
+5% FEL
+...

Yes! In the real world, Felix fumbled for his pouch, extracting a sealed stone bottle. He bit the entire top off and slammed it back.

Legendary Essence Detected During Formation!
[Essence Draught of Atlantes (Pure)]

Broken Path and Fatebreaker Titles Found!
Master Tier Bonus Added!
Unbound Nature Resonates With [Essence Draught of Atlantes (Pure)]!
Calculating Effects...

Choose A Feature:

Serenity - Eye of the Storm
Preservation - Shield Against Calamity
Anchor - Weight of Obdurance

There was more to the words than simple letters. As always, there was a weight to the Features, and he held onto the sensation as the Pathless tried to crush him.

Adept Tier…is important. Tempering is hard, and it means more. The walls shook, and Felix's thoughts stopped. *Master…Tier is a lot more influential.* That was when most formed their Pillars. Felix was beyond that, at least the normal nine, but he'd been warned: the changes to his Skill based on the choice of Feature would be drastic.

Serenity. Eye of the Storm. Felix followed the impressions from those words. Meaning flowed over him, through him. It was…peace. Calm. A tranquilness that transcended all conflict. Though the world might be battering down his walls, he would stand, untouched.

Preservation - Shield Against Calamity. Stalwart defense. Thick walls. Towers that breach the sky so that they can see all that comes to terrorize them. Calamity may come, it may lay waste to all around him, but he would survive.

Anchor - Weight of Obdurance. Relentless. Headstrong. Unshakeable from the course once chosen. All the Realms may fall…but not while he still stood.

They all drew him. Serenity was tempting, to be the calm in the chaos. Felix yearned for that. If his Mind were tranquil, maybe he'd see half the problems coming before they got someone killed. Preservation was equally appealing. A shield against the worst was what he aspired to be on his best days. But he…Felix knew his choice. It was a struck chord, resonating with his Mind in ways too complicated to follow.

"Anchor," he gritted out.

Congratulations!
You Have Absorbed The [Essence Of Anchor]!

The rest of the Essence Draught's powers vanished, pulled away from his Bastion to somewhere dark and hungry, but Felix didn't care. He could feel the new Feature pouring through him as vertigo assaulted his senses. His Bastion thrummed, each blade of grass and stone attuned to a sound so rarefied it defied description.

Light burst forth, a blue-white and red-gold radiance that bathed his Bastion with its strange hues. Without a single moment of transition, the walls turned from crumbling Fiendstone to something far grander. They thickened and rose up, gaining new towers and shielded ramparts, while behind him, the central hexagonal tower expanded to twice its width and three times its height. The Fiendstone itself turned opalescent, with red-gold and blue-white as its main tones.

The being of incomparable light hit his gates again. Pain lanced across Felix's Mind, but they did not shake. They held.

Congratulations!
Due To A Confluence Of Divinity Within Your Foundation, Your Skill Has Evolved!

Bastion of Will (Epic) Has Evolved Into Void Sanctuary (Divine)!
Level is retained!

Void Sanct—

Felix waved away the Skill description. He had no time.

Unite the Lost!

Once again, his significance burned as his Skill assaulted the Pathless' hold on his sister. He breathed, and he pushed...

...and the Pathless retreated.

He's weakened, he realized. A hysterical laugh bubbled up in his chest. *I can do this!*

It took so much significance—too much—to establish the tiniest foothold, bleeding him of every ounce he had to spare. But Felix knew that wasn't all he had to offer. He could burn his own significance, the weight that layered into his foundation. It could cost him his advancement, even his life. He could strip away all the progress he'd bled for in the past year...and he would. His sister was here, against all odds, and she would not be left behind.

Unite the Lost!

He flared the Skill again, and pieces of his core funneled into its pattern. He put more of himself into the Skill. More. All that was Felix was on the line. All that he had been and could be, framed in that moment. He peeled back layer after layer of the Pathless' interference and sank his claws into the space left behind.

"Mine," he hissed.

A hand grabbed his neck.

Imara lifted him into the air, standing up and slamming him against the wall in the same move. The stone shook, and lava shot from deep cracks...but it didn't break. Her arm was shaking. Her eyes, the same blue as Felix's own, couldn't quite focus on him. "Y-you…the Light? What have you…done?"

Felix could barely answer. His core was breaking apart, just to fuel his Skill. He felt her confusion, her stymied rage, and a deep upwelling of sorrow. Felix watched her eyes come into focus. On him.

"What have you done?!"

Her conjured blades bit deep into the top of his shoulders. Felix howled as significance drained from him like a sieve, while Essence was consumed to patch the burning wounds.

Skill Evolution!
Pit Has Received The Mantle Of The Stormlord (Legendary)!

Hurtling from behind, Pit slammed into Imara, and it was either a testament to her weakness or his strength that she was sent flying nearly thirty feet.

Unite the Lost cut off, spiraling out of Felix's grasp as he crumpled to the ground.

"Don't touch my Companion," Pit growled, while wings of lightning and flame spread out from his back. It echoed the chaotic elemental magic that coursed across his chest, neck, and paws as well.

The woman got back to her feet, though, and she conjured another long sword. This one flickered and jolted, as if it were glitching in her grasp. "Then I'll kill you first!"

Pit became a comet. All Felix could make out was the trail of elemental chaos before the Titan was sent careening through the air—directly into the molten statue of the Rockshaper. Her impact drove a hole through its soft, white-hot center and into the Inquisitors marching through the entryway. Then the Rockshaper split into two molten, uneven halves, and buried them.

Imara didn't get back up.

"That'll…show her," Pit said, before he, too, collapsed.

Pit!

Felix wanted to run to his friend's side, but he couldn't move. Only the broken wall held him upright, as his insides revolted against what he'd done to them. Every bit of his Aspects were in agony, and his blood flowed freely from his many wounds. He stretched a hand toward Pit, but everything hurt so much, and the room was growing too dim to see in.

Something burned him, but Felix didn't have the energy to flinch away. *Lava.* He saw more of it coming down from the deep cracks in the wall. *How…great. Never been…burned alive before.*

Across the battlefield, his friends were fighting, too caught up against the Inquisitors to notice them. The grinding of his cores was tearing at him, and it felt like he would vomit everything he'd ever eaten. Something warm dripped from his ears. *They'll survive.*

An echo of Will and Intent shivered across Felix's Mind. Not words. Not images. A feeling. A…terrible pain that desired an end.

The…lava?

The echo came from the burning morass across his shoulder. It scorched his flesh, ate through the tatters of his Garment, and it was insistent.

The feelings continued, but now concepts accompanied them, hazy like a dream. Eagerness for…quiet. Darkness that called to it. A torture ended.

Scaldara, he realized.

A gift, it sent. *Freely given to the Cardinal Primordial that saved so many upon the mount…*

What? What are you saying?

Images followed, too many to number or describe. It washed against Felix's Mind like a tidal wave made up of a single phrase.

I choose to save you, Bondbreaker.

Chthonic Tribute engaged without Felix's Will. His Hunger resonated with it, quivering within her pool of darkness, and she held it out to him as if asking a question.

Felix took a breath, and he answered.

Chthonic Tribute!

The lava upon his shoulder lifted, transmuted into an orange-brown sludge that poured into his mouth. Power followed. Mana and Essence flooded him, patching up the parts that bleed and leaked as Sovereign of Flesh engaged, until his core space was filled to bursting.

More sludge floated through the cracks in the wall, and the doorway to the bloody workshop, until a veritable river flew through the air toward Felix's open maw. Memories flashed through him, thoughts and images from Ages long gone, seen through eyes that were utterly alien. He let them all pass through him, filtering through the branches of his Divine Tree before funneling down into the eager shadow of his Hunger.

Behind all of that, came the significance. A great bounty of it, inundating his core space and setting his dual cores to spinning faster than they ever had before. It was borrowed—stolen—but in time, it would be his in full. The Pillars below righted themselves, their crystalline structure reinforced as the freely given gift imbued every part of him.

Felix stood. His Aspects still felt like shit, and it was agony just to move, but he was healthy and…whole.

"Thank you," he said, turning toward the cracked wall. But all he found was stone dust, gold coins, and broken metal. The Superior Elemental was gone.

"Euuugh…"

Pit was next to him, parts of his fur and feathers consumed in chaotic Mana that swirled ceaselessly. Felix knelt down, pressing his hand against his chest. He immediately yanked it back. The chaotic Mana shocked, burned, and froze him all at once. Pit was breathing, at least.

"Wait, wait, wait," he said. Through the swirling magics layered onto the tenku, Felix could make out small nubs that had grown over his once-constant wounds.

He was healed.

Your Companion Has Claimed The Mote Of Frenzy!
Evolution In Process!

"It worked," he breathed. He looked around at the devastation in the Vault of Nine Kings but shook that away. "It worked."

Felix Converged with Pit, and it was like swallowing magma. Whatever the Mote was doing, it was a horror on Felix's Spirit…but he muscled it down. Held him.

What else could he do?

Beef and Vess were still fighting. Despite the molten metal and stone, the Inquisitors were not stopping their assault, and only exploding Spears and walls of chitin kept them at bay. Archie had fallen unconscious, but a battered and bloody Laur carried him over a shoulder as he staggered out of a maze of fallen treasure. Tzfell and Evie were carrying Harn toward Felix, his legs bandaged but still severed at the knees. His Voracious Eye told him the man was stable, but his Health and Stamina were badly damaged.

Felix's tired Mind ran through ideas and plans. He could win this battle. He could get to Imara and maybe spend some of his newly gained significance, and maybe it'd work. But not without losing one of his friends.

"Retreat," he said, but it was too quiet. He winced and raised his voice. "Retreat! Now!"

His voice shook the room, causing more of the metal and stone to crack and tumble free. The entire vault groaned, but his friends heard him.

They disengaged and ran.

CHAPTER ONE HUNDRED TWO

Twenty Adept Tier Inquisitors rushed at them, leaping over molten sections of the floor and skidding through fallen gems. The six swiftest reached their team before they made it out of the main vault, swords out and golden Skills forming on their lips. Arrows of light and swords of flame hemmed them in, cutting off the path toward the workshop, but only for a moment.

"Get back!" Beef shouted, slamming Bedlam to the earth. The Skills scattered, their patterns disrupted, and several of the Inquisitors stumbled as if they, too, suffered the blow. Others charged ahead, their side swords lifted into a high guard…only to be met by Felix.

He tore them apart.

Rime Shaping!

Cardinal Flame!

Green Shaping!

Stone Shaping!

Before their blood settled, Mana poured from Felix's palms and elbows, a thick tide of power that snapped ahead of the nearest Inquisitors. All of them froze, encased utterly in trailing streams of Fiendstone.

You Have Defeated An Inquisitor Of The Pathless (x20)!
XP Earned!

Felix figured that would change to "killed" before long. He hadn't left any air holes.

"Seal this door!" Felix ordered as they slipped into the workshop. One of the Eidolons slammed their hands to the cavern wall, and the once-hidden door shut before a familiar spinning array sprawled across its surface.

"It is done," Telys reported.

"Good. We're getting out of here, now." The lot of them were hustling across the devastated workstations, and he jabbed a finger at Orun. "You. Carry Harn."

"As you wish," the Eidolon rumbled. He stooped low and, with surprising gentleness, took Harn from Tzfell and Evie's grasp.

"Thank you," the chainmaiden said. "Please just…be careful."

"I will do my best," Orun swore.

Laur also handed over a bloodied Archie to Orun, and the huge Eidolon easily made room for both unconscious allies.

Felix examined the Chanter. "Laur. Are you alright to walk?"

The Elf stood up straighter. "This isn't my blood."

There was a strength to the Elf's words Felix hadn't heard before. He nodded. "Right on."

"Where are we going?" Beef asked.

Felix stopped, just outside where the pool of lava once was—now there was only a dry, empty channel. The Supreme Elemental was gone, and so was its power. "Through there, past the toppled shelving. There's a door out of the vault and supposedly out onto the mountain. It's our best bet."

"Before you leave, perhaps some aid."

Above them, clinging to the surface of a massive core, was Yintarion. The core still rested atop a rocky shelf high above the lava island, but now the molten stone that once hung from it was gone, leaving the too-smooth marble of deep orange, yellow, and crimson in its place. The last and most pertinent detail, however, was that it looked considerably smaller than before—and pieces of it were wisping away. Directly toward Felix's mouth.

"I tried fruitlessly to appeal to the Elemental, but she was deaf to my words. Then its entire form vanished before my eyes, and I knew why I was ignored. She offered herself to you, Autarch."

Felix frowned. "She did."

Yintarion attempted to calmly clear his throat, but he was obviously panicking. "If you could stop trying to eat this, I'd greatly appreciate it."

Felix immediately cut off his Skill. He hadn't even realized his Chthonic Tribute was still active. He'd thought all of the Supreme Elemental had been devoured, but here the densest and most potent part of it remained. Within his chest, his Hunger growled in anger.

"Done. You can have it, Yin."

No!

Quiet. You've had your fill.

"That…I appreciate your generosity, Autarch." Yintarion beamed, his two foot-long length laid out against the glossy surface of the immense core. "You picked an excellent mate, little Dragoon."

Vess was too tired to do more than blush. She gestured to her Companion. "That core is huge. We'll require your assistance, Eagin."

"Of course, your Grace."

A crash resounded throughout the cavernous workshop. Across the way, the sealed door shivered under a tremendous assault. Felix's heartbeat sped up. *That door won't hold out forever. We can't escape with an entire army on our tail.* A large chunk of stone fell from the ceiling. *Even the wall is breaking—*

Felix's eyes widened. He traced out massive gaps in the walls where once bright, elemental lava coursed. All of it was empty, hollowed-out pockets of stone, and they positively riddled the cavern.

"Everyone, quick. To the exit and down the mountain. Vess, lead them out."

"What about you?" Vess asked. "I heard you. Your sister—?"

"Someone's gotta slow them down," Felix said. He couldn't talk about Gabby. Not yet.

Without another word, Vess marched up to him, seized his collar and pulled him into a kiss. Something inside Felix's brain turned to mush as sparks shot up his spine for a second that stretched into eternity…until Vess pulled away and pressed her forehead against his. "Follow close."

Felix wanted to say something witty or cool, or even "I will." What came out weren't really words, but Vess smiled softly anyway. She gathered the others and sped off into the dark doorway, the others and Eidolons following. Eagin even awkwardly carried the large Elemental core in his great arms.

Yet, when most of his senses returned to him, Felix found Yintarion, Beef, and the Chanters at his side. "What are you all doing? Go with the others."

"I will aid you, Autarch," the Wyrmling said.

"We cannot abandon the Unbound," Tzfell said fiercely. "And you cannot pull this off without help."

"You know what I'm planning?" Felix asked.

"After our time traveling with you, Lord Autarch, I can honestly say I will never be able to anticipate what you do," Laur said. His voice hardened. "But I would be of use."

"I got a hammer," Beef offered with a shrug. "And I can carry them, if this all goes sideways."

The door shivered, and sparks spat from the sealing array on the far wall. Felix shoved his concerns away. "Stay close and follow my lead."

Stone Shaping!

Rime Shaping!

Green Shaping!

Felix's Mana speared across the cavern before coming to rest within the deep crevices left by Scaldara's death. Ice bloomed, crackling and expanding within the cracks, while nearby roots sprouted from nearly invisible moss that clung high above. The roots sought those same cracks, and as the ice melted away, they dug in. Above it all, consuming the most of his attention, was the rock itself.

C'mon. The walls were made of a high-Tier stone, decently above his control…but not entirely. His Will, Intent, and sheer amount of Mana on hand meant he had leverage. Not much, but some. Very slowly, pieces of stone liquified and fell away. *C'mon.*

The pounding on the door was increasing in tempo and volume. The wards gave off sparks now with each strike. "They will not hold long," Laur cautioned. "I am weakening the wards holding the wall together, Lord Autarch, but it will diminish the door seal as well."

"Then we must escalate. Adherents of Ophidia." Spiraling dragons of water shot outward from the hovering Wyrmling. They split, each powerful jet striking a different place along the wall and sending deep cracks across the cavern. "Adherents of Ophidia!"

The dragons shot out again. And again, while Felix froze, rooted around, and shaved away strategic portions of stone. Tzfell lifted her arms, and geometric shapes hurtled into the cracks and gouges, coursing through until they found the weakest portions of the wall and ceiling. There, they seared themselves into the stone, and each of their magic attacks were drawn unerringly toward them.

The wall burst apart, the seal failing in a shower of incandescent vapors. Redcloaks poured through the opening, their white armor covered in gleaming golden plates conjured from light Mana. A man with dark hair and an insufferable smirk sauntered through the opening, grinning as he took in the five of them across the ruined workshop.

"You fools," he said, almost tenderly. "You cannot escape the judgment of the Light."

Felix growled. "Eat shit."

With everything he had, he flared his shaping Skills and one new addition.

Adamant Discord!

Multi-Cast is level 90!
Stone Shaping is level 99!
Rime Shaping is level 94!
Green Shaping is level 89!

Lightning burst among ice, vines, and gelatinous stone, and the entire goddamn wall collapsed. The smirking man paled and tried to run, only to have his legs taken out from him by a series of water dragons. The wall fell atop of him and all of his Inquisitors.

Yet it wasn't just the wall. Cracks spread and expanded, tearing from the workshop to the vault proper. The orichalcum rafters—bent and battered by Imara's assault—ripped free of the vault's ceiling…and the roof followed.

"Autarch! Felix!" Laur shouted above the roar of collapse. A shield around them held some massive debris away, but it was flickering wildly. "Everything is falling around us!"

"Beef!"

Without a word, the kid scooped both Chanters up in his arms and took off. Felix and Yintarion ran close behind as cacophony reigned. Thousands of tons of stone and metal roared as it fell, ripping apart ancient architecture and advanced magical arrays. Sparks and vapor became a firestorm as the wild discharge of magic exploded like a bomb.

Debris followed them, and a pyroclastic cloud tore across the workshop and through the doors. It chased them as Beef and Felix slipped into the spiral staircase beyond the exit.

"Hold on!" Beef yelled, before Mana surged from his hooves.

A sheet of chitin covered the staircase, and Felix's feet shot out from beneath him. He rocketed down an impromptu, spiral slide. The noxious cloud of rubble and cascading Mana followed. It shot through the entire staircase. They shot to their feet as the end appeared. Beef shouldered straight through the half-open stone door and nearly launched himself into thin air again.

Spears of crystal shot into the ground, halting him in his tracks. "Not again," Hallow called out. Beef lurched aside as Felix and Yintarion followed suit.

A column of heat, fire, stone, and incredible pressure exploded from the open door, ripping it off its hinges and sending everything out into the empty sky. Felix watched, a little numb, as the cloud and rubble hung suspended in thin air…before it launched upward. Into the endless dark that yawned just above.

A black hole into the Void. Felix had to tear his eyes away from the desolate emptiness. *Like my Hunger, almost.*

He shook himself. "Everyone good?" The others gave dazed noises that he took for confirmation. "Down the mountain, then."

They needed to escape the Undermount…and Felix knew just where to go.

It isn't over, he swore, eyes cast up toward the summit.

Not by a long shot.

CHAPTER ONE HUNDRED THREE

"We cannot find a single trace of them, Chosen Imara," an Inquisitor reported. "The vault is too damaged."

Imara heard but said nothing.

"How certain are we that they didn't die in the collapse?" Bellar asked, his voice pure acid. His arm was in a sling, and his face was covered in dark bruises.

"One hundred percent positive, sir. Our trackers would be able to identify corpses with ease, even in this high-Tier rubble."

Bellar waved away the man with a sharp impatience. "Impossible. How could we have lost them? Not only here, but across the entire mountain!"

Distantly, Imara was aware that the Inquisition troops had been scouring every inch of the Vault of Nine Kings—the parts that were still whole, anyway. The entire thing had collapsed shortly after she had been…knocked out. Again.

Shame and regret curdled in her chest, opening a hole inside of her that had once been filled with Light. She had heard the reports—of the Fiend and his team disappearing into thin air. Of the Gnome. Gone again. Yet, she could not find any part of her that cared. Instead, the shame was rudderless, the regret without visible cause. Phantom emotions echoing down a barren hallway.

"Chosen Imara?" Bellar prodded.

She blinked. "Has it grown dimmer here?" she asked.

"It–it has not," Bellar said. "Are you alright, my Lady?"

"I'm fine," she lied. She wasn't sure *what* was wrong with her, but things felt…wrong. All of her armor had been covered in molten stone and metal, rendering it all but useless until it could be repaired. If it could be. She held up a bare hand.

This…why do I feel…?

Y—ou Must—

A breath caught in her chest, but the voice faded away. The interference of this Dwarven realm and…and whatever the Fiend had done to her…together they worked to silence the Pathless.

A hand closed on her shoulder, and Bellar gazed down at her in compassion. "Are you? Fine?"

"Yes." Imara stood, shrugging off the man's touch. She shoved the aimless weakness away, banishing it to a corner of her heart. "Gather your forces. The hunt continues."

Lilian slipped unnoticed through the dark streets of Elderthrone. They were harder and harder to come by, as the Glyphmaster slowly modernized even the farthest edges of the growing city. Thankfully, the inscribed street lamps ended two blocks ago, and Lilian slunk through a wide alleyway.

The snow fell heavy as she came to the narrowest point of the alley, and she cast her eyes back. No one had followed. Biting her lip, Lilian lifted her hand and traced a pattern upon the empty brickwork. Mana flowed from her palm, filling the pattern like a mold, until it finished with a muted shimmer.

Between one moment and the next, a door appeared across the bare stretch of wall. Lilian swiftly pulled it open and slipped inside.

Within was dark, cramped, and dusty. Beams hung low overhead, and unfinished walls gaped like broken teeth in a drunkard's smile. Perhaps the most unnerving detail, however, and one which she would never grow accustomed to, was the breathing.

A heavy wheeze filled every inch of that dim space. A rattling gasp in, followed by a prolonged, wheezing release. Again, and again. The volume only increased as she shuffled through the cramped corridors, unwilling to let a single timber touch her spotless gown. Soon, it opened up into what had once been a parlor. A low fire crackled in the hearth, casting more shadows than light, and providing a cloying warmth tinged with the smells of mint and jasmine.

"Ah. Child. Come closer."

The voice interrupted the ceaseless wheezing, and it came from the most shadowed recess of all. Hidden behind diaphanous curtains and enchantments she could not parse, her benefactor laid upon a bed. She drew nearer, and there the perfumes in the air failed; she could smell the sickly sweet odor of rot and something else. A seizure of fear raced across her spine, but Lilian held herself as still as she could.

"Do you have a report?" her benefactor asked.

"I do, master." She curtsied. "The head Alchemist has increased my status within the Fiend's Lab, and my expanded access to materials has allowed me to refine our project."

"What of the accident?"

Lilian winced. "An unfortunate setback, but the fire killed only a few Untempered. There has been no public outcry, and none have tied it to the Alchemy Lab."

"Be wary of the Glyphmaster. He is not what he seems," the man hissed. His voice sounded full of liquid, like bubbles in a stream. "You've altered the location of your testing site."

"I have."

"Acceptable." Fabric rustled, and Lilian could dimly tell her benefactor was moving on the bed. That was unusual. "Here. Take this. Use it to refine the project."

A twisted hand that looked half melted reached from the curtains, holding an odd metal box covered in a jagged script. Lilian took it, not allowing her skin to touch her benefactor's, and grunted at how heavy the little item was. "What is it?"

"A device. Place it within your solutions when tincturing the active reagents."

Lilian turned the device over in her hands. The jagged script was colored like the embers of the nearby fire, and it was curiously hard to look at directly. Painful, even. "How does it function?"

"Do not question, child. Just do."

Despite his apparent frailty, her benefactor's voice was a whipcrack. Lilian knew too well the power he wielded. She flinched into a deeper curtsy, her skirts touching the floor now. "Of course, master."

"Good." The hand withdrew, quivering. "Things are coming to a head now, child. Keep on as you are, and you shall have all that you have wished for."

Lilian looked up, and her heart thudded hard within her scarred chest. "Soon then, Master Tiene?"

Behind the curtains, the man moved. Master Teine's cadaverous face emerged from shadow and silk, far more gruesome than Lilian's, but his eyes gleamed in the low light. "Yes. Things are only beginning."

In the depths of the earth, where caverns opened into a forest of moss and crystals, Felix tried and failed to sleep.

The journey down the mountain had been rough as they were forced down a thin stairway barely clinging to the edge of a cliff and fully exposed to the gale-force winds of the Voidstorm…but they had made it. Once they'd hit the lower slopes, it was only a short jaunt to the Rockshaper's workshop, then through his emergency exit to the Low Roads.

That was where they were now, camped out in the miles of tunnels between Dwarven Holds. They were still beneath the Rimefangs, still within spitting distance of a great many enemies—but they could breathe.

Felix's Claw had, hopefully, already set out from Birchstone. The smugglers had been hired to get them out of the city and into the mountains, where they could escape to the Hoarfrost…and where his chosen Exemplars could use Labyrinthine Wing to return home.

His friends were around him, laid out on patches of moss while the Eidolons watched for oncoming threats. Beef was snoring alongside Hallow, Laur, and Archie. The Delven's wounds were patched up, and he'd even woken up for a time, but only to curse profusely before passing out once again. Evie was beside Harn, not sleeping, but standing guard over the injured man. Tzfell had once again cast her limited healing magics on him, which had stopped his bleeding but could do nothing for his missing legs.

That hit Felix hard. Another failure on his growing list.

At his side, Pit was curled up and breathing deeply in a slumber he'd yet to wake up from. The chaotic power of the Mote of Frenzy still rippled across his body like an iridescent oil slick, and the System told him his Evolution remained in process.

Vess was nearby, too, wrapped up in her cloak against a boulder-sized pale pink crystal. Next to her, perched atop the smooth, glass-like core, was Yintarion. The orb flickered regularly, like a heartbeat, molten colors swirling within its fathomless depths.

Felix scrubbed at his face with his palms. They had retrieved Archie. They'd taken the Mote of Frenzy. They'd even secured so much treasure that they hadn't cataloged it all. Everything Felix had set out to do had been accomplished...and yet he felt empty.

Gabby.

He knew his Unite the Lost had done something, but the last look they'd shared wasn't one of recognition. It hadn't been enough, and that drove him crazy. She was out there, bent and twisted into Imara, while the Pathless rode shotgun in her soul.

Felix wasn't having it.

The Pathless and the Hierophant took his sister, and they would answer for it. He had to get back to Nagast, but plans boiled in his Mind, churning through dozens of possibilities every second. Plans for reaching Master Tier and for weaving his Tenth Pillar. Plans for his friends, his allies, and his army. All of it burned his Mind, but he held on within the walls of his Void Sanctuary, until a single, irrefutable fact emerged.

Felix bared his teeth.

He had to kill a god.

ABOUT NICOLI GONNELLA

Nicoli Gonnella spent his formative years atop a mountain, breathing deep of the world energy and expelling impurities from his soul. Also he went to school and stuff. He always wrote but now he's abandoned everything to do it full time. Readers give him strength, spirit bomb style, and there's no telling how strong he will become. This isn't even his final form.

He lives with his wife, two kids, and a corgi named Cornelius.

Connect with Nicoli Gonnella:
NicoliGonnella.com
Discord.gg/sqQvJQhY8F
Patreon.com/Necariin
RoyalRoad.com/fiction/30321/Unbound
Facebook.com/Nicoli-Gonnella-Author-347428719693359

ABOUT MOUNTAINDALE PRESS

Dakota and Danielle Krout, a husband and wife team, strive to create as well as publish excellent fantasy and science fiction novels. Self-publishing *The Divine Dungeon: Dungeon Born* in 2016 transformed their careers from Dakota's military and programming background and Danielle's Ph.D. in pharmacology to President and CEO, respectively, of a small press. Their goal is to share their success with other authors and provide captivating fiction to readers with the purpose of solidifying Mountaindale Press as the place 'Where Fantasy Transforms Reality.'

Connect with Mountaindale Press:
MountaindalePress.com
Facebook.com/MountaindalePress
Twitter.com/_Mountaindale
Instagram.com/MountaindalePress

MOUNTAINDALE PRESS TITLES

GameLit and LitRPG

The Completionist Chronicles,
The Divine Dungeon,
Full Murderhobo, and
Year of the Sword by Dakota Krout

Arcana Unlocked by Gregory Blackburn

A Touch of Power by Jay Boyce

Red Mage and
Farming Livia by Xander Boyce

Ether Collapse and
Ether Flows by Ryan DeBruyn

Dr. Druid by Maxwell Farmer

Bloodgames by Christian J. Gilliland

Unbound by Nicoli Gonnella

Threads of Fate by Michael Head

Lion's Lineage by Rohan Hublikar and Dakota Krout

Wolfman Warlock by James Hunter and Dakota Krout

Axe Druid,
Mephisto's Magic Online, and
High Table Hijinks by Christopher Johns

Skeleton in Space by Andries Louws

Dragon Core Chronicles by Lars Machmüller

Chronicles of Ethan by John L. Monk

Pixel Dust and
Necrotic Apocalypse by David Petrie

Viceroy's Pride and
Tower of Somnus by Cale Plamann

Henchman by Carl Stubblefield

Artorian's Archives by Dennis Vanderkerken and Dakota Krout

Vaudevillain by Alex Wolf

Made in United States
Troutdale, OR
01/25/2024

17137295R00463